THE COZY CONUNDRUMS COLLECTION

Books 1 - 5

T.H. HUNTER

THE COZY CONUNDRUMS COLLECTION – BOOKS 1 – 5 is part of the COZY CONUNDRUMS series.

DEDICATION

To my beloved spouse, who believed in me from the start.

CONTENTS

CURIOSITY
KILLED
THE CAT

T.H. HUNTER

T.H. HUNTER

CHAPTER 1

Michelle Nosworthy put aside her notebook, rubbing her tired eyes in determination. She'd show that smug old fart from the *Cotswold Courier* just how much of a mistake it had been to fire her. And just a few weeks before Christmas at that. Once she broke this story, he'd be begging her to return. A proposition she'd reject, of course, but only after watching him squirm for a while. Yes, she'd let his blunder sink in slowly. After this affair was through, major newspapers worldwide would be throwing offers at her. Even a Pulitzer prize for investigative reporting wasn't beyond the realm of possibility.

It would have to wait a few more days, however. Michelle Nosworthy wanted to get everything just right. She had already made a big announcement on her blog and on twitter. The people were waiting. And soon enough, the little town of Fickleton would be swarming with journalists, all trying to get a piece of the pie while it was hot. But only *she* would be able to provide all the juicy details that the public craved to know. They had all been recorded in her trusty notebook that she held in her hands at this very moment.

Drunken laughter and the tinkling of glasses told her that the pub downstairs was already crowded. She checked her phone for the time. It was dead. Strange. She could have sworn it had been at half battery just a while ago. She must have been working longer than she had thought. Luckily, the room provided a digital alarm clock at the side of her bed. She got up and moved the bottle of water in front of it in order to read the time. It was 10.30 pm. She'd better make a fresh start in the morning.

She went into the bathroom and splashed a little water in her face. It had been a tough day. She was just about to brush her teeth when she suddenly heard a scraping noise at the door. She stopped, listening intently. A moment passed. Perhaps it was the landlord snooping around again. She'd caught him in her room before, though she didn't believe his feeble excuse that he had seen a man enter it for a second. Of course, there had been nobody else there.

Ears pricked, she waited another few seconds. Then, she carefully tiptoed out of the bathroom and over to the door, putting her right eye to the spyhole. The singular fluorescent lamp in the hallway flickered. She looked as far as she could to the left and then to the right, but the corridor was empty. She must have been imagining things. Getting paranoid.

There was every reason to be paranoid, of course. She'd be making a lot of enemies once this affair was made public. That was why she wanted to be out of town when it happened. Her nerves were obviously strained.

She bolted the door and fastened the heavy chain just to be sure. A good night's sleep would do the trick. She could always find a different place to stay at if things got out of hand. She walked back into the bathroom and picked up her toothbrush again.

Then, the lights went out. Judging from the cries and yells below, they had also gone out in the pub. She stepped back into the room, her heart pumping fast. This was just a normal power outage, nothing to worry about. She was being silly. Or was she?

In the darkness, she heard scratching sounds. But this time, they were followed by the unmistakable rustling of metal rings. Her breathing shallow, she grabbed blindly for the bottle of mineral water next to her bed, knocking over the alarm clock as she did so.

Her eyes were slowly adapting to the dark. Somehow – impossibly – the door was being unlocked from the outside. The metal chain was loosening. She was rooted to the spot, frozen by terror. The door was slowly creaking open now. She wanted to scream, but no sound would come out of her mouth as a dark figure stepped into the room.

CHAPTER 2

When Val and I exited the terminal building of Bristol airport on a chilly December morning, only a few cars were parked outside. The freezing cold was pinching my cheeks, so I drew up my coat for warmth. My best friend Val, however, was shaking more from the flight than anything else. And the coffee she was holding was teetering dangerously in her hand as a result.

"Val, careful, you're going to…" I said.

"What?" Val said.

But it was too late. The extra large tumbler went flying through the air. In a desperate attempt to break its fall, Val stuck out her right leg. She twirled on the spot in an awkward pirouette before ending up in a half split. The hot brown liquid, however, spilt all over the pavement, as well as her shoes.

"This was a new pair! Coffee all over them," she said, straightening up with some trouble.

"I'm sorry, Val," I said, trying hard not to laugh. "We'll try to get the stains out as soon as we get there. Here, let me get the tumbler."

"I'm so clumsy," she said miserably. "I just can't seem to get through a day without something happening to me. And spilling coffee is a *very* bad start."

"I think that's our taxi over there," I said, trying to steer the conversation away from anything to do with caffeine. Val believed it was the solution to everything. And so the loss of it was naturally a disaster of existential proportions.

"How far do we have to go, anyway?" she asked, trying to rub off the dark stains from her right shoe with a handkerchief.

"Well, one and a half hours, according to google," I said,

checking my phone again.

"So, that's going to be how many thousands of pounds?" she asked. "I'm on a strict budget, Amy. Waitressing doesn't pay too well, you know. I can't blow it all on a trip through the English countryside."

"You're telling me," I said, rolling my eyes.

I wasn't looking forward to getting back to it myself. My boss had made it his hobby to give me a hard time, but I needed the job. Val and I worked at cafés opposite each other. A few years ago, we had bonded during one of our breaks and had been best friends ever since.

"But don't worry," I continued. "The lawyer said it's all paid for in the letter. Accommodation's also been taken care of, apparently. And I'll get you another coffee when we get there. That'll give you some time to recover from the flight. Deal?"

"OK, Amy. Whatever you say," she said, her mood lightening visibly.

An old-fashioned black cab with a yellow sign on the roof came to a halt next to us.

"Hello, Miss Amanda Sheridan?" the driver asked through the open window.

"Hello, yes, that's right," I said. "And this is my best friend Val."

The driver got out of the car. He had an extremely red but jovial face with a shaven head that couldn't quite hide the fact that he was going bald.

"Nice to meet you," he said. "People just call me Tom. Here, let me take your bags for you."

"No, it's fine, really," I began.

"Don't worry. My pleasure."

We thanked him and got into the backseat. Tom followed shortly, slamming down the hatch and getting into the driver's seat.

"Fickleton House, isn't it? We'll get you there in no time," he said, patting the dashboard affectionately. "She's taken me all over the country, she has. Brought her with me from London. They don't make them like this anymore. Not around here, anyway. All posh silver Mercedes types, but no soul to them. Real beauty, isn't she? Suits the landscape, you could say."

Val looked out of the window, frowning. We had just entered the motorway and were surrounded by nothing but lifeless concrete and asphalt, shrouded in a grey fog that prevented us from seeing anything more than the closest couple of cars. Tom, who had seen her expression in the rear mirror, gave off a throaty laugh, no doubt the result of many pints of beer and packets of cigarettes.

"Oh, jus' you wait, the Cotswolds are beautiful. And that's coming from a man who's only got one eye."

"You've only got one eye, how come?" Val asked curiously. "I hope it wasn't one of your customers."

"No, no, nothing like that," he said, grinning. "More the artsy type of people live around here, if you get my meaning. Rich folk from the cities, music stars, artists. There's going to be a fair in a few days, in fact."

"In Fickleton?" I asked.

"That's right," he said. "Sir Henry is the official host, though everybody knows Lady Worthington is really running the show."

He hesitated briefly.

"Anyway. You here on business?" he asked casually.

"You could say that, yeah," I said. "The thing is… we don't really know ourselves."

"Well, I always enjoy a good mystery," said Tom.

***

We drove on the motorway for quite a while until we reached a junction. Before long, Tom was proven right about the landscape. The sun had found its way through the thick clouds by now, and the fields of yellow and green were shrouded in a dreamy mist as if covered by cotton candy. Most trees had long since shed their leaves, yet some of them still lay at the trunks in faded gold and red.

"Almost there, ladies," Tom said finally. "We're approaching the village now. Very pretty in winter time."

The village of Fickleton was tucked into a small valley between hilly woodlands on either side. An old stone bridge marked the physical threshold beyond which dozens of small houses hugged the narrow main road. On our left, a middle-aged man in a mackintosh was walking his dog, a puppy black Labrador, though nobody else seemed to be out in this weather.

"Fickleton House is on our right, up the hill through the little wood," Tom informed us. "You'll be able to see it soon."

As we turned the first corner a few yards into the village, a dozen or so cars were blocking the road ahead. Some of them, I noticed, were police. Tom rolled down his window, and a young officer approached the car.

"What's going on?" Tom asked.

"Spot of trouble at the pub," the officer said. "May I ask where you're heading?"

"Fickleton House," Tom said, with a slight note of impatience in his voice.

"Sorry, that won't be possible at the moment, sir. We're stopping all cars passing through."

"What happened exactly?" I asked from the back.

"There's been a death. I'm afraid you'll have to get out here."

"Can I at least park the cab at the back of pub – in the car park?" Tom asked in a disgruntled tone. "I live there, you know. That's where I always park."

"I'm afraid the car park is reserved for police only at the moment, sir," the young officer said. "You will have to exit your vehicle here. PC Bowler will be with you in a minute. He's just finishing an interview as we speak."

We had no choice but to comply. A chilly breeze rudely greeted us as we opened the doors of the cab. It seemed other travellers had been stopped before us. A burly policeman with a heavy moustache, undoubtedly PC Bowler, was pompously interrogating an old lady beneath a sign that read "The Mangy Dog". They really loved their quirky pub names around here.

"Sorry for the trouble, ladies," Tom said, as he closed his door. "This could take a while. If PC Bowler is in charge, he's going to make a meal out of it. Probably going to stop every car he can for the next week. Fickleton House isn't too far away, though, just up the hill to your left at the next junction. D'you want me to help with your bags?"

Before Val could say anything, I hastily interjected:

"We'll find our way. Thanks again for the ride."

"No trouble at all. Hopefully see you around in the village some time, eh?"

When we were out of earshot, Val immediately started protesting.

"Why didn't you let him, Amy? These bags are heavy as…"

"Val, he's not your personal chauffeur. It's not his fault we had to stop. We're not even paying the fair. Come on, the walk will do us some good."

We were just about to cross to the other side of the street when the burly policeman with the moustache stopped us.

"And where do you think you're going?" he demanded, puffing up his chest self-importantly. "I'm Police Constable Bowler, and you're trespassing at a potential crime scene."

"We're tourists," Val said immediately. She always had been nervous around law enforcement for some reason.

"Tourists, eh? At this time of year?"

"Well, not so unusual for the Christmas season, is it?" I said. "Anyway, we're also here for another reason. We've got an invitation to Fickleton House, from my great-aunt's lawyer."

He looked at us for a moment with suspicion.

"Names?"

"Amanda Sheridan, and this is Valerie Morgan."

PC Bowler's jaw dropped.

"Amanda Sheridan… are you sure?"

"Of course I'm sure," I said. "It's my name. You don't forget it. Well, not usually anyway."

"Now, now, none of that lip, Missy. You don't know what you're mixed up in here."

"Excuse me? I'm not anyone's 'Missy'," I said hotly. "And I'm not mixed up in anything, either. We just arrived at the airport."

"Might I remind you that this is serious business. There's been a death," he said.

"Who died?" Val asked.

He studied us both in his pompous manner, his small, watery eyes almost disappearing under his bushy eyebrows.

"I suppose it will be in the papers soon enough anyway, so you may as well hear it from an official source. One Michelle Nosworthy, journalist. How long have you been in contact with her, Miss Sheridan?"

"What are you talking about?" I asked.

"I asked you how long you have known the deceased."

"Look," I said in exasperation, "I've never even heard of her until just now. I told you that we only just arrived this morning by plane."

PC Bowler snorted in disbelief.

"We'll be checking up on that little story of yours, Miss Sheridan."

"It happens to be the truth," I said angrily.

"We don't even know what's going on," Val said, rushing to my defence.

"It's none of your business. At least," he said nastily, turning to me, "*not yet*. We found your name in her diary, along with some others. We're still looking for the deceased's notebook, however."

"What?" I asked, totally taken aback. "My name was in…?"

"I'll need the address you're staying at," he continued, interrupting me. "I might have a few more questions after the coroner's report. And once we find her notebook. That's where she kept most of her delicate information. It's bound to turn up sooner or later. Oh, and if I were you, Miss Sheridan, I wouldn't leave the village anytime soon. Some people might get the impression that you have something to hide."

CHAPTER 3

I was still fuming from my encounter with PC Bowler as Val and I made our way through the village and up the hill towards Fickleton House. The bags were heavy, and although both of us were used to a lot of rushing about from waitressing, lugging them uphill had us both panting and out of breath in no time.

"And you really don't know her?" Val asked me for what felt like the hundredth time.

"Don't you start as well, Val. I'm telling you, I've never even heard of her. There must be some mix up. That stupid policeman is just looking for a scapegoat. And who better than some outsider?"

"Yes, but your name was in the diary, though," Val said, puzzled.

"It must be a coincidence," I said. "I can't be the only person in the world with that name. Perhaps there's another Amanda Sheridan around here somewhere."

Val gave me a doubtful look.

"It's unlikely, I know," I said irritably. "But what other explanation is there?"

We had left the village of Fickleton by now and found ourselves on a narrow road, just enough for a car to pass along. The twigs and leaves above our heads covered most of the tentative rays of sunlight that had managed to pass the clouds above, so that it was surprisingly dark for this time of day. The trees formed a natural archway, though they had evidently been trimmed by human hands somewhat.

Finally, the steep slope flattened out before us. Thick hedges flanked old wrought-iron gates, painted black, on either side. The mist was still too thick to see any buildings beyond, though the proud sign to the left of the gate informed us that we had arrived at Fickleton House.

"It's absolutely beautiful," Val said, touching the gates. "Your great-aunt lived here?"

"I don't know. The lawyer's letter was pretty mysterious. Didn't say anything really except that she had died and that my presence was urgently requested."

We passed through the gate and closed it. A long gravel road led straight ahead. Then, in the distance, as the mist gradually receded, I saw the most beautiful place I had ever laid eyes upon. It looked like a manor house, though mimicking a castle in almost every other way. The enormous bowfront with its large oak doors resembled the main gates of a fortress, while the spirals at either side of the house's front mirrored the towers.

Admittedly, the dilapidated condition indicated that its heyday must have been well in the past. Although the grounds were kept neat and orderly, the outer walls were discoloured, with the old paint peeling off in various places. Several windows were broken, and water had undoubtedly penetrated the slate roof, which was lacking tiles almost everywhere.

We approached the doors. There was no bell, so we used the large knocker in the form of a hideous gargoyle instead. We stood there for a while, waiting. Val gazed at the gargoyle, totally mesmerised.

"Maybe this wasn't such a good idea, after all," Val said, looking at me nervously. "This place is creepy, Amy."

I wasn't feeling too comfortable myself.

"Let's just find out what the lawyer wants. Then we can get out of here," I said.

The front door opened with a mighty creak, as though it hadn't done so in a very long time.

An elderly woman with grey-white hair and an old-fashioned, knitted pullover stood there. She looked kind, though suspicious at the same time.

"Yes?"

"Hello, we're here to see Mrs. Sharpe, the lawyer…"

"Ah, yes, of course. We have been expecting you, Miss Sheridan. I am Mrs. Faversham. Please come in."

As we entered, Val suddenly caught her heel on the old rug in the entrance hall and stumbled forward. Luckily, this time, I was able to catch her just in time before she crashed into Mrs. Faversham.

"Thanks, Amy. Close one," Val said, and smiled apologetically at Mrs. Faversham.

The latter looked her up and down with an eagle eye. I could tell that she hadn't quite made up her mind whether to disapprove of us or not.

The entrance hall was dark and cold, though much cleaner than the exterior. Someone was doing their best to keep the house going. We were led past what seemed like an endless number of corridors and closed wooden doors until we reached a hall with a rickety staircase. A slender black cat was perched on the balustrade. Its green eyes, more luminous due to the surrounding darkness, followed our every step, though its body remained perfectly still.

We didn't ascend the stairs, however, as Mrs. Faversham took a left into yet another corridor.

"This place is huge," Val whispered to me.

"Yeah," I agreed.

"You know, if someone tried to murder us in here, they'd never be able to find us," she said.

"I think we can handle Mrs. Faversham," I whispered, grinning. "Though she might try to kill you if you slip on another Persian rug."

We entered a high-ceilinged room with wood panelling, with windows overlooking an inner courtyard. It must have been at the other end of the house because I hadn't seen it as we had approached it. The room we were in sported several paintings – portraits mostly – as well as a large fireplace at the far end. In the middle of the room, there was a long dining table with a three-pronged candle holder. The candles had been lit, as the light from outside wasn't enough to illuminate the place fully.

"Mrs. Sharpe will be with you shortly," Mrs. Faversham said curtly. "Please wait here. I'll light up the fire in a minute."

She exited the room at the other end.

The minutes passed by in silence. I decided to have a closer look at the pictures. The portraits were all of members of the Barrington family, nobles who, judging by the dates, had lived here for hundreds of years. They even had a portrait made of a black cat, quite similar to the one we had seen earlier, though the date said 1959. Perhaps it was the cat's great-grandfather or something.

Meanwhile, Val was trying to get a signal with her phone, just in case of an emergency.

"It's useless," she said. "Like something's jamming the signal."

"You're getting paranoid, Val. Nobody's jamming the signal. Probably just a bad connection. Not surprising out here in the sticks."

"I had three bars outside in the woods, and none on the lawn in front of the house or in here," she said.

"OK. You're right, Val. It's probably a plot to kill a couple of waitresses."

"Oh stop, Amy," she said, though she cheered up a little after that.

Finally, there was a knock on the door.

"Erm, yes?" I said, clearing my throat.

A woman of about forty, wearing a grey two-piece suit and her hair in a bun, entered.

"I am Mrs. Sharpe," she said, stretching out her hand to me and then Val. "How do you do?"

After the introductions, we sat down at the long dining table. Mrs. Sharpe placed her black briefcase on the chair next to her, producing a stack of papers from it.

"Now then, Miss Sheridan. As I stated in my letter to you, your great-aunt passed away several months ago. I have been charged with settling all matters connected to her estate. Tracking you down was quite difficult, and I am glad that you came all this way. I realise that my letter was rather… vague. It was, however, expressly stipulated in the will of your late great-aunt that it was to be so. I understand that you hadn't known her?"

"No, I didn't," I said. "I didn't even know I had a great-aunt."

Mrs. Sharpe shifted a little in her chair.

"I have been her lawyer for almost fifteen years now. It would be something of an understatement to say that she could be a little eccentric at times. She certainly was very particular in regard to how this entire affair was to be treated. And I will do the best I can to accommodate all of her wishes."

She leafed through the stack of papers next to her, producing a single sheet with a long list on it.

"This is a comprehensive list of the items that are bequeathed to you, Miss Sheridan. In addition," she said, taking out two more pieces of paper, "you will inherit this house and the grounds surrounding it, as well as a lump sum as detailed here."

She indicated the third paper and handed it to me. I moved it between Val and myself, so that we could both look at it at the same time. Val and I didn't have any secrets, and I wasn't starting now.

Val saw it first. She inhaled sharply, putting her hand to her mouth. I scanned the page quickly, trying to follow her gaze. At the very bottom, underlined, was the sum I was to inherit. It was just over seven million pounds sterling.

It was like I had been hit by a truck. The rest of the conversation was like a blur to me. Mrs. Faversham came in briefly to set up the fire. Then, I signed papers, answered questions, filled in forms and discussed every little detail until Mrs. Sharpe had worked through the entire stack of papers beside her. It was like some sort of dream. I was tremendously glad that Val was there with me.

Finally, after everything else had been settled, Mrs. Sharpe got up and shook my hand. It was already dark outside.

"Good luck, Miss Sheridan. Oh, before I forget," she said. "I can handle the rest for you from now on, if you wish to keep me as your legal counsel, that is."

"Oh, yes, of course. Thank you," I said, still feeling dazed.

"Excellent," Mrs. Sharpe said, smiling for the first time during our encounter. "There's also the matter of the housekeeper, Mrs. Faversham. You are, of course, free to hire whom you please, though I understand that she has a very great fondness for the house and has loyally served your great-aunt for many years. She is preparing your rooms for the night as we speak, in fact. If there's anything else you'd like to know, don't hesitate to get in touch with me."

She handed me a business card and exited the way she had entered a few hours earlier.

For the first time ever perhaps, both Val and I didn't know what to say to each other.

"Everything's going to change now, isn't it?" I said, still stunned.

"Yep," said Val, grinning. "You're loaded now."

"No more waitressing," I said.

"Nope. Not for you, anyway. Seems like I'll have to look for someone else to spend my breaks with."

"Oh, don't be stupid, Val."

"What?"

"Stay here, with me," I said.

"Sure, I still have an entire week off," she said. "We could do this room up in that time or just…"

"You know what I mean, Val. Permanently."

She looked at me and then out of the window. She had a

peculiar look on her face, but then shook her head.

"Amy, I can't. I mean, it's not like I'm longing to get back or anything but… it's *your* house. I wouldn't know what to do. I can't just live off your money forever. I've always earned my own way."

"But don't you see? It's the same for me, too. I had to fend for myself since I was sixteen, since the day my parents died. I did every job I could get my hands on just to keep afloat. College was always just a pipe dream. And now… now this happened."

I stared at the roaring fire in the fireplace as the truth of the situation gradually settled in. This whole affair would mean an end to my waitressing days. No more washing tables. No more long hours at the till. And best of all, no more bosses. This was a financial freedom I hadn't known in my entire life.

But I was frightened as well. I might not have enjoyed everything about my job, least of all my boss, but I had prided myself on hard work, just like Val. The struggle had kept me sharp and alive. Above all, it had provided meaning. A meaning that would have to be replaced now.

"I need you, Val," I said. "You're like a sister to me. And this whole thing could've just as well happened to you. I got lucky, that's all. That's the only difference. And I can't end up an old spinster in this place all alone."

"Well, with your pickiness about men, I don't know whether I can prevent that," she said, laughing. "So, you want to keep the house?"

"Yeah, I think so. The countryside around here is amazing. And this place will be, too, once we've had a go at it. Anyway, I've got to stay here until PC Bowler is convinced I'm not mixed up in that death at the pub down in the village."

We sat there in silence. She stared into the flames in the fireplace for a while, evidently thinking through my proposition.

Finally she turned back to me and said:

"OK, Amy. Let's restore Fickleton House to its former glory. But I'm getting a job in town somewhere. I want to pay my way."

We hugged. She really was the best friend anyone could hope for. What would I ever do without her?

***

Later that evening, after a makeshift supper that consisted mainly of late coffees and biscuits, Mrs. Faversham led us up to our bedrooms, both of which were very spacious. Apparently, there wasn't any kind of modern equipment in the entire house, not even a telephone. According to Mrs. Faversham, my late great-aunt had disapproved of any kind of electricity, though she had reluctantly tolerated its installation in the small house that Mrs. Faversham occupied, which was located beyond the gardens but still belonged to the Fickleton House estate.

"I worked for your great-aunt for many years, since the end of the war, in fact," she said to me as we entered the bedroom I was to sleep in for the night. "Nice lady, though very private. Kept to herself for the most part. Didn't make her too popular down in the village, I can tell you that. But she was always very decent to me and Charles. Kept me on after he died, as well, kept me busy. Do you have any plans for the house yet?"

She was a very proud old lady, though I could see on her wrinkled face that working here meant a great deal to her. I felt quite uncomfortable in my new role. The most I had ever been in charge of was when I had shown new waiters the ropes at the café. I'd never been a real boss, let alone an employer of domestic staff.

"This was all very sudden," I said. "I'll need some time to adapt. But I… erm… want to keep everything just as it was, Mrs. Faversham."

Her eyes lit up in delight, though the rest of her body remained as composed as ever.

"It is always gratifying to be needed, Miss Sheridan," she said. "And if you don't mind me saying so, also to see new life in the house."

"Please, I'm not… just call me Amanda."

But Mrs. Faversham, now bustling around the bed, pretended not to have heard my feeble attempts at breaking the relationship as employer and employee. Val, seeing me trying to squirm out of my awkward position, was giggling in the background.

"Your great-aunt always had breakfast at 9 o'clock, Miss Sheridan," Mrs. Faversham said. "I'll prepare for two, shall I?"

I was just about to protest and say that we could make our own when Val quickly interjected with a warning glance in my direction.

"That would be fantastic, Mrs. Faversham. We'd really appreciate that."

"Not at all, not at all," she said happily. "Oh, and there are candles and matches in the sideboard over there. It can get a little spooky at night. The cat likes to roam around a bit, bless him."

And with that, she left the room, carefully closing the door behind her.

When I was sure she was well on her way down the stairs, I said:

"This is ridiculous, Val. I've made thousands of breakfasts at the café. One more isn't going to hurt me," I said.

"Not you, perhaps," Val said, a wise expression on her face.

"Val, I can't have servants. That's totally out of the question."

"You heard her, Amy. Mrs. Faversham's done this all her life. She wants to be needed. Just let her do her thing."

"But I can't just live like some sort of aristocrat," I spluttered, but Val stopped me in my tracks.

"It's not your place to rob Mrs. Faversham of her purpose. If you want to run Fickleton House properly, you'll have to start acting like the owner, not like some embarrassed guest."

There was a brief silence as I absent-mindedly looked out of the large double-glazed windows, processing what Val had said.

"It's all just so sudden," I said. "I don't want this to change who I am, that's all."

"Don't worry, I'll let you know when it does," she said. "Come on, let's get some sleep."

***

Half an hour later, I lay in the massive four-poster bed that Mrs. Faversham had prepared for me. The silk bedsheets were warm and soft to the skin. Quite a change from the cheap ones I was used to. My mind was still spinning from the occurrences of the day, though the rotations were getting slower. I was becoming drowsy, my eyelids felt heavy.

Yet the strange sounds in Fickleton House didn't let me sleep for long. The wind ominously whistled through the dark corridors. And I just couldn't shake the feeling that there was another presence in the house. The floorboards right outside in the landing beyond my door creaked, as though someone was walking along them. I was being silly. Surely it was Val going to the bathroom or something.

Unable to fall asleep again, I decided to get some fresh air into the room. I checked my phone on the nightstand. It was 2.30 am. The batteries, however, were almost empty. I had better get some other source of light.

I stepped over to the sideboard and fumbled for the candles and matches. I lit one of them and walked over to the windows behind the bed. I was just about to open one of them when, at the opposite side of the house, across the inner courtyard, I saw a light burning in one of the rooms.

My hair at the back of my neck stood on end. It was unlikely to be Mrs. Faversham. She lived in her own small cottage on the estate grounds, after all. Or had she perhaps left a few candles burning there? Surely, Val wouldn't go wandering around the house alone at this hour.

I slipped out of my room and tip-toed over to Val's room a few doors down the corridor. A candle was burning on the table next to her bed, but she wasn't in it.

My breathing faster and shallower now, I turned back into the corridor.

"Val?"

There was no answer.

I tried to steady myself. No burglar would leave a light burning like that in some remote part of Fickleton House. Perhaps it was Val after all. Maybe she had a good reason to be there, though for the life of me I couldn't think of one.

I briefly thought about calling the police, though with the connection down in these parts, I'd have to walk over to Mrs. Faversham's house for the telephone. I made a mental note of having a phone installed first thing in the morning.

Then, I remembered what Val had told me about acting like the owner of the house. It was perfectly true that I still felt more like a guest in a posh but extremely old-fashioned hotel than anything else. It was time to change that.

I gritted my teeth. Val was right. This was my house now, and I wanted to find out what was going on in it. I grabbed another candle and the box of matches from the sideboard just in case. I peeked through my bedroom window to make sure I hadn't been imagining things. Yes, the light was still burning. If I took a right turn in the next corridor and kept right – with the inner courtyard in view – I should be able to get there without losing my way.

I took out a scrap of paper from my handbag, scribbling a note for Val just in case and placed it on her bed. That way, she'd know where I was. Then, I stepped out into the corridor again.

Though it was still a little cloudy, the moonlight from outside was shining in somewhat. My eyes were gradually adapting to the darkness, too.

I stepped through the empty corridors for quite some time. To avoid getting lost, I looked out for windows, so that I could check my relative position to the courtyard and the room with the burning light. Luckily, I was still on track.

Before long, I reached the corridor I was sure the light was coming from. I checked one of the windows. And there, almost directly opposite, was the candle I had lit in my own room for guidance. I had to be very close now.

I tip-toed forward, trying desperately not to breathe too loudly despite the increasing instinct to do so. And there, near the landing, straight ahead, light was coming through the cracks below the door of one of the rooms. This was it. Whoever it was, they were behind that door.

I carefully extinguished my own light. In case it wasn't Val, I shouldn't advertise my whereabouts. I moved carefully forward, trying to prevent the floorboards from creaking as best I could.

As I stood close to the door, my heart hammering in my chest, I heard a voice through the door. It was undoubtedly male, muttering in some strange language I didn't recognise. The voice was exasperated, almost angry in tone, but then stopped abruptly.

I remained perfectly still, for fear that I had somehow been discovered, holding my hand to my mouth to muffle the sounds of breathing. There was a brief thud. And then, ever so slowly, the door opened from the inside.

CHAPTER 4

Panic-stricken, I watched as the door slowly swung open. I leant against the wall, trying desperately not to be seen. I had nothing to defend myself with. Wildly, I thought of throwing the candles at whoever came out of that door and running for my life during the confusion. A terrible plan, I know, but what else could I do?

As I hid next to the now opening door, the light from within the room shone onto the corridor. And then, a figure stepped in front of the light, so that the shadow stretched out into the corridor. To my horror, it wasn't a man's at all, but some sort of beast, its massive shadow stretching as far as the door's frame would allow. The shadow was coming closer; it was going to step out into the corridor any second now.

But to my bewilderment, nothing emerged from the room until I heard the same voice that had been speaking the strange language.

"Down here," it said.

My eyes tore downward. It was the black cat that I had seen earlier that day on the staircase. It was speaking to me, a look of superior aloofness on its face.

"That's the worst hiding place I've ever seen in my life, by the way. You do realise cats have excellent vision in the dark, don't you?"

"You can speak!" I spluttered.

Was I still dreaming?

"Better than most, I might add," the cat said sniffily. "What are you doing in my house? I do hope you realise that you are breaking and entering."

"*Your* house?" I asked.

"Fickleton House has belonged to my family for

25

centuries. Who are you, pray?"

At that moment, a bloodcurdling call echoed through the corridors.

"Aaaamy?"

It was Val.

"I'm here, Val. It's OK. It's just… just the cat," I called.

That sounded weird but I suppose it was true nonetheless. A few seconds later, Val arrived, totally out of breath and dressed in a pink nightgown.

"I read your message. What's going on, Amy?" she asked.

Still dumbstruck, I just pointed to the cat before us. He simply sighed and said:

"Follow me. I can see this is going to take some time."

Val looked at me as though she were going crazy.

"Amy, did you hear that? The cat spoke… Or did I just have too much cheese? I knew I shouldn't have…"

"Oh, for heaven's sake," the cat said. "Spare me. Now, come on."

We followed him into the room. The most extraordinary sight met my eyes. Thousands of books decorated the walls of the vast room. It wasn't your run-of-the-mill library, however. Every inch of it had been built so that a cat might easily access all areas. Cat stands stretched on all sides to the ceiling. The shelves had ample space for four legs to trod along it. And in the corners, miniature metal hoists had evidently been placed there so that the cat could place the books back on the shelf on his own.

On the floor, dozens of books were scattered around a reading lamp. Various rugs, cushions, and bowls of milk were strewn throughout.

"This is my study," the cat said unnecessarily.

He curled up on one of the cushions and faced us, his black tail moving irritably to and fro. Before he could say anything, Val, still in disbelief, somehow managed to stumble into a table, sending a neatly stacked pile of papers with scrawls of cat claw imprints all over flying into the air.

"Once you've stopped ruining my research, I demand to know what you are doing here," the cat said angrily.

"I might ask you the same thing," I said, as I helped Val up again. "Just so you know, I own this house. Signed everything a couple of hours ago."

The cat scowled at me, swearing under his feline breath.

"Human law may be on your side, though it cannot change the fact that I," he said, stretching out his paw and then placing it on his cat's chest in a majestic fashion, "am the Earl of Barrington. By birthright, Fickleton House belongs to my family. And as the last remaining descendant, to me."

Val, who was still entranced by the contents of the room and had barely been listening, turned to him.

"So what are you researching?" she asked him.

"You wouldn't understand any of it," he said rudely.

"And you are the Earl of … what did you say again?" Val said.

"The Earl of Barrington," he repeated. "You may also address me as 'Your Lordship'."

He was so serious and earnest about it all that both Val and I couldn't supress our laughter fully.

"What?" he said irritably.

"We can't call a cat 'Your Lordship'," said Val.

"We could call him Barry, though, what do you think, Val?" I said, grinning.

"Oh, no, that's absolutely inappropriate for a cat of my…" he began.

"Barry it is, Amy," said Val.

"So, how come you can speak?" I asked him, before he could protest any further.

Barry's whiskers twitched, annoyed at being asked such an impertinent and personal question.

"You say you own the house," he said, ignoring my query. "What is your claim?"

"I inherited it from my great-aunt," I said.

Barry froze. He looked at me as though seeing me for the first time properly. Then, he suddenly let out a furious howl that made Val hold her hands to her ears.

"What's wrong?" I asked.

Barry shook himself, as though trying to expel some sort of demon force that had taken hold of him. Finally, he got up and began pacing around his reading area.

"Barry…" Val said tentatively.

"Not now, I'm thinking," he said. "And don't call me that."

He brooded for a few more minutes. I looked at Val, who simply made shrugging motions with her shoulders. This was bizarre to say the least. We couldn't have both gone crazy. And yet, here we were, talking to a black cat with an ego the size of the entire estate.

Finally, Barry turned to me and said:

"Yes. Only one way to find out."

He moved over to the bookshelf at the far end of the room. Squeezed between several books was a small cardboard box, which Barry pulled out with some trouble. He took it in his mouth and trotted back to us again.

"Open it," he said to me after he had plonked it in front of my feet.

I bent down and lifted the lid off from the thin cardboard container. Within was a beautifully carved wooden stick. It had a grip that was thicker than the rest of the wood, which made it feel natural and effortless to hold in my right hand.

"What is it?" I asked Barry.

"It's a wand, of course. My wand, in fact. So treat it with the uttermost care. Go on, give it a wave," Barry said, his whiskers twitching slightly.

I felt silly doing so, but I was also curious about where this was all going to lead. Val, who seemed to be taking the whole thing a lot more seriously now, nodded to me.

Lifting the wand high above my head, I brought it down with a swoosh through the air. To my utter amazement, little red sparks bubbled out of the tip, leaving a trail of crimson in its wake. Val clapped loudly, while Barry wore a look of satisfaction.

"I knew it," he said. "I can always tell."

"What do you mean?" I asked.

"You are a witch," he said.

"I beg your pardon?" I asked.

He sighed.

"You can do magic," he said.

"What?"

"That's the definition of being a witch," he said.

"But that's just not …" I began, but he interrupted me immediately.

"Didn't you pay any attention?" he said.

Then, still staring into my disbelieving face, he strutted over to one of the books lying on the floor. It was a massive old tome with mysterious symbols etched onto the spine and cover. He opened it and flicked through the pages as we edged closer. The chapter titles ranged from "Useful Everyday Cooking Spells" to "Rules and Regulations for Witches and Warlocks".

"What are you doing?" Val asked him.

"I'm looking for the fastest way to get this cumbersome conversation over with. So I need a spell that's simple yet convincing. Ah yes, this is pretty basic. You should be able to do this without too much practice."

He had placed his paw on a chapter entitled "Water spells – Basic Beginnings". Each spell had a name, a description, as well as a hand-drawn sketch of the wand movements for correct usage.

"Try the first one," Barry said.

"Go on, Amy," said Val, eager to see more magic.

Keeping my eye on the page to follow the instructions, I waved the wand with a downward flick and said:

"Aqua."

A torrent of water shot out of the tip of my wand, drenching Barry from head to paw.

"Don't point it at me!" he said angrily, shaking off the water.

"I'm sorry, Barry," I said, hastily pointing the wand out of the window.

Val took one of the rugs and started drying his fur. Barry, his whiskers still drooping from the water, closed his eyes as if it cost him tremendous willpower and concentration not to explode at my dilettante attempts at magic.

"There really should be a license for novice witches," he said. "Absolute safety hazard, the lot of you. But, of course, the *Spellcasters' Association* won't listen to me as usual. Be that as it may, however."

"But how…is this possible?" I asked, turning to Barry.

"Didn't you know who your great-aunt was?"

I shook my head.

"Well, that certainly explains a lot," said Barry, whose hair was now standing on end, making him look like a hedgehog.

"Was my great-aunt a witch, then?" I asked.

"Naturally. Despite her illegitimate claims to this house, I cannot deny that she was one of the best witches out there," said Barry. "Magical powers are inherited, you see. You should be getting a lot of junk mail from those busybodies from the *Association* any day now."

Val and I looked at each other in astonishment. If I hadn't just had proof of what Barry had said, I would have had a hard time believing a word of it. Good thing he had started with the demonstration first.

"Now that I have helped you," Barry continued, "I want you to help me in return. I want you to help me transform back into a warlock."

"You're a … a warlock?" I asked.

"Yes, yes. Now, what you'll have to do is…"

"How did you turn into a cat, then?" asked Val, unable to help herself.

Even the mere memory of it seemed to be extremely painful to him.

"I am an experimental warlock," he said, indicating the many books and papers on the floor beside him with his paw. "One of the best, if I say so myself. Even the buffoons at the *Spellcasters' Association* don't deny it. I invent new spells and refine old ones. I was close to a breakthrough in therianthropy when this happened."

"Theri… what?" asked Val.

"Shapeshifting into animals in layman's terms. Unfortunately – with no fault of my own, of course – one of my spells turned permanent. Too powerful, too much magical power behind it. I've been working ever since to get back into my human shape."

"How long have you been a cat, then?" I asked.

"Over fifty years," he said with a stony face.

Val and I looked shocked.

"Poor Barry," Val said. "That's awful!"

"Yes, yes. Trapped in this furry body for half a century. All very tragic. Now can we get on with it? Because I'd rather not spend the next fifty years chit-chatting."

I nodded, wand at the ready. He waded through his stack of papers with his paws. After a while, he had found what he had been looking for and grabbed it with his mouth. He placed it in front of me on the ground.

"I've marked all of the required wand movements," he said. "Make sure you follow them to a 't', otherwise it won't work."

I bent down and picked it up. From Barry's rough sketches, which were not bad at all considering he presumably had to hold the pencils with his cat paws, were extremely complicated.

I pointed my wand at Barry, who was torn between

flinching with dread at a novice witch pointing a wand at him and the pleasant possibility of turning back into a warlock again. Torn between hope and dread, he kept one eye tightly shut and the other open.

"Mutato in incantatorem!"

Nothing happened.

***

Barry insisted that I try again. And again after that. We stuck at it for I don't know how long. The sun was already rising outside. Val, finally bored of watching the same failed magic over and over again, had been reading a book called *Magic to Mastery: A Beginner's Guide* for the last hour or so.

Finally, Barry cursed loudly and just slumped down on the floor, utterly shattered.

"Shall I do it again?" I asked, exhausted.

"No, there's no point. There was only a remote possibility anyway. Even your great-aunt couldn't do it."

"Couldn't you do it yourself?"

"My magical powers are greatly diminished as a cat. Can't even hold the blasted wand properly," Barry said. "Barely enough to light a candle."

Suddenly, he looked forlorn like a lost kitten. I didn't know whether warlocks-turned-cats could cry, but he certainly looked close to tears. Beneath that veneer of cynicism and superiority lay something vulnerable and fragile. I bent down to him and gently stroked his fur. It seemed to calm him a little.

"It's almost 9 o'clock, Amy," Val said, checking her watch. "We'd better get down to the dining room soon. And I need to freshen up a bit."

"Do you want to have something, Barry?" I asked him.

Barry, all self-pity now, nodded his little head.

"Yes, a little something might cheer me up. I've been working so hard lately."

***

Downstairs, Mrs. Faversham had really outdone herself. Two full English breakfasts were waiting for us, as well as tea, juice, and coffee. There was even a bowl of cat food and some milk for Barry on the floor.

"I do hope it's alright with you, Miss Sheridan, it's only that your late great-aunt always allowed the cat to eat in the same room with her," Mrs. Faversham said as soon as we had entered the room. "But I can remove him, of course, if you prefer."

I looked at an indignant Barry, who threw a warning glance in my direction.

"Yes, he shouldn't *really* be in here," I began, teasing Barry, who was now making cutting motions with his paw in front of his throat. "But he can stay for now – if he behaves, that is."

"Oh, he certainly will in here," Mrs. Faversham said, oblivious to Val's suppressed laughter and the sour look on Barry's face. "But I have seen him pinch a couple of candles now and then. Naughty little fellow. God only knows what he does with them. Your great-aunt made a very nice spot for him to sleep in the study, you know. She was rather fond of him."

"Yes, I've seen his – I mean, the library he sleeps in," I said. "I think we'll keep it as it is for the moment. Thank you very much for the lovely breakfast, Mrs. Faversham."

"Not at all," she said, beaming. "If there's anything else you'd like, I'll be in the kitchen. It's to your left and down the hall. Just leave everything on the table when you're finished."

After she had left the room, Barry had evidently returned to his normal self again.

"What do you mean *I* can stay," he said. "I was just about to say that I tolerate *your* presence here."

"Barry, is that your way of saying you're fond of us already?" Val said, winking at me.

He looked at both of us for a moment, considering whether he should admit to it openly or not.

"I need someone to try out my new spells, after all," he said casually. "Anyway, Amanda, you won't be able to get far with your magical training without me. You're too old to be accepted into a school of magic."

"Hey, I'm not even thirty yet," I said in mock indignation.

"My point is," Barry continued. "You *need* me. You won't be able to perform the bond without my extensive knowledge and experience, either."

"What is the bond?" I asked.

He looked at his paw self-importantly before rubbing it against one of his legs as if wiping off an imaginary stain.

"A witch or warlock may bond with a heb – that's what we call a non-magical person – to allow them access to the magical world."

"I choose Val, of course," I said, without hesitation.

"You'll have to," said Barry. "There are strict secrecy protocols. With the exception of family members, hebs aren't to know about us, unless they are inducted properly within the confines of the bond."

"Can I get powers, too?" Val asked eagerly.

"You won't become a full witch, no," Barry said. "But there are certain supernatural skills you may acquire. It is a complicated process and depends on your natural aptitude."

Val looked rather down in the dumps.

"You'll be our specialist, then, Val," I said, trying to cheer her up.

"So what kind of skills are we talking about?" she asked Barry.

"You won't know until it's done," he said. "But telepathy, mindreading, and increased strength are among the most common."

Val looked a little more cheerful.

Then, there was a knock on the dining room door. I cleared my throat.

"Erm, yes?"

Mrs. Faversham entered once again. This time, however, she was followed by a handsome yet slightly worn-out looking man, a few years older than I was, with untidy dark hair that had been hastily combed back. He was wearing a smart blue suit and a black tie that matched his hair.

"This is Mr. Lavalle," Mrs. Faversham said, eyeing him with suspicion. "He says he'd like to talk to you about the death that happened in the pub down in the village."

"Oh, OK," I said, taken aback. "Please, have seat, Mr. Lavalle. We were just finishing breakfast."

"Thank you," he said with a pleasantly deep voice that resonated off the oak panelling in the room.

After the initial introductions, he hesitated somewhat, evidently waiting for Mrs. Faversham to leave the room. She was standing with arms crossed at the door, still watching him like a hawk.

"It's quite alright, Mrs. Faversham," Val said. "We can deal with it."

"Alright," she said, still not entirely convinced. "As I said, I'll be in the kitchen. Just call when you need me."

With one last look at Mr. Lavalle, she closed the door.

"I must say, you do have quite an inquisitive housekeeper," he said. "Hardly let me in at all."

"You say you're here because of the death in the village?" I said.

"Yes. Now, before I tell you this, I need to know whether you know about… your great-aunt."

Before I could say anything, however, Barry intervened.

"You mean that she was a witch?" Barry said.

"Barry! Didn't you just tell us about keeping it secret?" Val whispered.

"It's alright," Barry said loudly. "I can spot a warlock

from a mile off. Mr. Lavalle is one of us."

The latter looked not at all surprised to see a cat speak.

"Yes, you're quite right," he said to Barry, lowering his voice conspiratorially. "I'm with Magical Law Enforcement – MLE for short. We have a serious problem. Miss Sheridan, I'm afraid the local heb police suspects you of murder."

CHAPTER 5

My mouth fell open. It was one thing being told by PC Bowler not to leave the village. It was quite another to be suspected of such a heinous crime by the investigators.

Barry, however, was all matter of fact and strutted over to the table, nimbly jumping onto it. Val and I were too stunned by the news to protest.

"But that's absurd," I said. "Val and I only arrived by plane yesterday. When we entered the village, the local police were already at the pub. There's no way I could've done it."

"I know," said Mr. Lavalle, sighing heavily. "There have been a string of murders in the Cotswolds. All mysterious circumstances, with no traces of the killer. He's devilishly clever, that's for sure. The hebs are desperate to find the culprit, but of course they never will, bless them."

"And why won't they?" Val asked.

"For the simple reason that the perpetrator is almost certainly a witch or a warlock," he said.

Barry cursed.

"Does that mean the place will be crawling with MLE agents?" Barry asked, obviously annoyed at the prospect.

But Lavalle shook his head, mistaking Barry's tone for desperation.

"No, I'm afraid not. Resources are very thin at the moment. I'm with the London department usually, you see. Most of my colleagues are tied up with a big case of art heist."

"An art heist?" I said.

"Yes," he said. "A series of art heists, to be exact. There is reason to believe that they are connected, however."

"But why would witches or warlocks be interested in

stealing pieces of art?" I asked.

"I think," said Lavalle, rubbing his cheek absent-mindedly, "the question is rather why more sorcerers *don't* do it. You can conjure up cash or befuddle the bank manager, no problem, but a Da Vinci or a Van Gogh will always be unique. A magical copy is just that – a copy."

"Sorcerers is what we call spellcasters who've broken the law," Barry added helpfully.

"Oh, you haven't been a witch for long?" Lavalle asked me, smiling.

"No," I said. "I found out yesterday. From Barry, in fact."

"The Earl of Barrington, that is," Barry corrected me irritably.

"But you can also call him 'Your Lordship'," said Val, affectionately stroking Barry, who was looking daggers at her.

"Oh, I think I've heard of you," said Lavalle enthusiastically. "You were the warlock who couldn't turn himself back, aren't you?"

"You're famous, Barry," I said, grinning.

Barry scowled at all of us.

"You were saying that Amanda is a murder suspect?" he said.

Lavalle's face became serious again.

"That's right. As I said, the hebs are desperate to pin this on someone. And they prefer to do it to an outsider rather than one of the village locals. Less trouble that way."

"Typical," said Barry.

"But that's not fair," said Val, smacking the table with her open hand.

"I agree," Lavalle said. "But it's the ugly truth nevertheless. If they can blame an outsider, they don't have to tread on anyone's toes around here, you see."

"But it's never going to stick," I said. "I can prove that I took that plane."

"Maybe," Lavalle said. "But the heb police are known to have falsified evidence in these cases. The thing is, there's no way they can catch a sorcerer. He or she will always be one step ahead of them. Not a chance. They don't know why, of course. Usually, it just becomes another unsolved cold case, one among many. But this is different. The investigators are under pressure from the local communities and politicians. They must solve it, one way or the other. And they'll resort to a convenient scapegoat if they have to."

"But how can I prevent them from framing me?" I asked, getting more agitated by the minute. "Can't we just... modify their memories or something?"

Lavalle shook his head sadly.

"That's what we usually do if we get ahead of them. But not in this case. It's too public by now. There are thousands, perhaps over a million hebs who know already. You know, through newspapers, internet websites, gossip. We'd never be able to stem the flow of information, even if we weren't understaffed. It's out there for good, I'm afraid."

"But what can we do?" I said.

"There's only one way forward," Lavalle said. "We need to solve the case before the hebs can blame you for it. That's why I've been sent here by the MLE, in fact. Once we've caught the culprit and have enough evidence, we can hand them over to them."

"Won't a sorcerer just escape, though?" Val asked.

"After a fair magical trial, they are stripped of their powers by the *Spellcasters' Assocation* for the duration of their sentence," Lavalle said.

"Why did they send you specifically?" Barry asked shrewdly.

Lavalle laughed, though there was some bitterness there, too.

"That's anyone's guess. I know the terrain, however, so

I assume I was an obvious pick. And most of my colleagues are divided on the subject of the importance of this case."

"What do you mean?" I asked.

"Well, some of my colleagues in London believe it's a random act of murder or a serial killer on the loose. A sorcerer on a spree, if you will. Others disagree, believing it is connected to the art thefts somehow."

"Val, remember what Tom, the taxi driver, told us? There's going to be an arts fair here soon," I said. "I wonder if it's got something to do with the murder that occurred. What do you think, Mr. Lavalle?"

"It could be a coincidence," he said blankly. "And please, just call me Lavalle. Everyone does at the office."

"OK. But not everyone thinks it's a coincidence?" I said.

Lavalle frowned slightly.

"No. My older brother Alec – he's a private investigator in London – fed me some interesting information. He's been undercover for some time now, infiltrating a criminal organisation that he thinks is run by sorcerers. All hearsay and no proof, so his superiors keep telling him, but enough for him to keep digging a little deeper."

"But there's no proof so far?" I asked.

"Not that I am aware of," said Lavalle.

"You mentioned a spree, Lavalle," said Barry. "Who are the victims in the case you're investigating?"

"Well, aside from Michelle Nosworthy, the woman who was murdered in the pub yesterday, there've been two previous murders in the area. Most likely connected. I'll be investigating them in chronological order, as it were, but I just wanted to speak to you first. You see, I need your help, Miss Sheridan."

"Of course, how can I help?"

Lavalle took a deep breath, running a hand through his hair to keep it out of his tanned face.

"I want you to keep out of trouble while I'm out of town. PC Bowler and the heb inspector will grasp at any straws you give them."

I hesitated for a moment as Lavalle got up from his chair.

"So you're basically asking me to just stay put? I thought your department was overstretched as it is."

"Yeah, we could help," said Val.

"I cannot allow you to interfere, Miss Sheridan. You're at great risk as it is. We shouldn't provoke the hebs any further. Or give them any more opportunities to frame you."

"But I can't just sit here and do nothing," I said.

"I'm afraid you'll have to," he said. "I'll get back to you as soon as I can with any new developments. I can find my own way. Goodbye."

And with that, Lavalle let himself out the way he had come. I stared at the closed door for a while, deep in thought.

"Amy, are you OK?" Val asked finally.

I spun around. Barry had returned to his bowl as if the matter had been settled.

"We can't just watch while this sorcerer preys on more innocent victims," I said.

"But Mr. Lavalle specifically said we couldn't intervene," Val said.

"Yes, I know..."

Barry, sensing a dangerous turn of events, tore himself away from his bowl again and leapt back onto the table.

"What you are intending is totally out of the question, Amanda," he said, pointing his paw at me. "There's no point walking around the village, pretending to be a detective. Magical Law Enforcement agents undergo years of training and must have a lot of experience before they may investigate on their own. You have neither. You didn't even know you were a witch until last night."

"You heard him, Barry, his department isn't going to send out any more people, he's on his own," I said hotly.

"The sorcerer who is behind it all means business. And so do the heb policemen. Novice witch or not, I can't just sit idly by while they frame me for murder!"

"Innocent until proven guilty," said Barry.

"Not for them and you know it, Barry," I said angrily.

It would be a way to clear my name. Not only was my freedom on the line, but the guilty party would still be free to continue to roam the countryside. Perhaps even to kill again. And I couldn't deny that the prospect of catching the perpetrator didn't excite me, as well. I could see that I had convinced Val, but Barry looked nervous.

"I'm not getting pulled into a murder case," he said. "I've got research to do. I'm a cat, after all, and there's only so much I can do. Best to keep your head low in these times…"

"Barry, are you afraid of the sorcerer?" Val asked bluntly.

"Afraid? Of course I'm afraid! I can't even hold a wand properly, let alone defend myself against a powerful sorcerer," said Barry, self-justification seeping out of every syllable.

"Neither can I," said Val. "But Amy can, if you help her."

Barry looked at Val and then at me. I could see he was torn. But I also knew that he was a much better person than he liked to pretend.

"Alright, alright, I'll help," he said gruffly. "You'd probably get yourselves killed anyway if you tried any spells on your own."

"Excellent," I said, beaming at Barry.

"Where shall we start?" Val asked.

I pondered the question briefly.

"Well, Lavalle is going to the other two crime scenes, we may as well go down to the pub and see what we can find out. Barry, what do you think?"

"Fine," he said. "But we should do the bond first. We'll

need every advantage we can get."

***

A few minutes later, we found ourselves back in Barry's study again. He was diligently preparing the series of spells I had to cast in order to initiate the bond with Val, who was lying on the floor.

"I feel silly," Val said, as Barry drew a circle around her with a piece of chalk in his mouth.

"Won't be long, Val. I think. Will it, Barry?" I asked.

He had completed the circle and let the chalk drop to the floor.

"An hour, at most," he said. "I haven't done this in many years. I'm somewhat out of practice."

"Ooh, Barry, did you bond with anyone? A heb lady friend, perhaps?"

"Certainly not," he said.

"Wasn't there ever a Lady Barrington?" I asked.

"If ever, her title would have been Countess of Barrington. But no, there wasn't. I was always married to my work."

"Spoken like a true scholar," I said, grinning.

Barry huffily changed the subject.

"We can now proceed with the bond. Amanda, I need you to stand over there at the lectern. The first book we'll need is *Magical Contracts* by E.W. Arcbridge. You'll find it on the shelf behind you."

The procedure involved a series of complicated incantations, many of which I had to repeat over and over again until Barry was satisfied that they had worked. Invariably, after every spell, he'd jump from his place and watch Val very closely for any sign of change, prodding her in the arm or sniffing at her face.

"What are you looking for?" I asked, bewildered. Personally, I couldn't see any difference in Val at all.

"Magic leaves unmistakable traces to the trained eye," he said as he studied her right hand.

In preparation of every spell, Barry either sprinkled strange powders over Val's body or provided foul-smelling liquids for her to drink.

Finally, after the best part of an hour had passed, Barry seemed satisfied. I still couldn't detect any difference in Val, aside perhaps from a disorientation that was more pronounced than usual.

"How do you feel, Val?" I asked.

"Weird."

"Yes, well, I'm sure that was there before we started," said Barry. "Anything more specific?"

"I – I don't know," she said, looking at us as though she were doing so for the first time. "It's only… Barry, are you OK?"

"Of course I am," he said. "Apart from the fact that I'm doomed to spend the rest of my days as a cat, of course."

"I know," Val said.

"What do you mean, 'you know'?" I asked.

"I know how he feels about it – about being a cat forever. And," she continued, looking at me, "I know how you feel, Amy, about being the subject of a murder investigation. I can *feel* it."

"Great," Barry said, rolling his eyes. "She's an empathetic psychic."

"An… empathetic psychic?" Val repeated slowly.

"Yes. We will see how far your abilities reach in the coming months."

"But this is brilliant," I said. "Val, this can help us find the killer! We'll just talk to everyone in the village and you can read their minds, one by one."

Barry tried to wag his finger at me in disagreement, but ended up just waving his paw.

"No, no, no. All human superstitious nonsense. The mind is not like a book full of information you can read at leisure. And luckily so, otherwise you'd be wading through thousands of pages of information. You'd never find anything. Skilled psychics can gain access to *active* pathways, especially if they have a deep emotional meaning."

"But surely, a murder would be emotional." I said.

"In some circumstances, perhaps. But not always. I doubt the average hitman feels very much. And trained witches and warlocks can shield themselves from detection, as well. As I shall be doing, in fact."

"Don't worry, Barry," I said teasingly. "Nobody needs psychic powers to know how you feel about things."

***

It was already getting dark when we stepped out of the house in order to go down to the village pub. I still couldn't believe that the beautiful grounds of Fickleton House were my home for good. It still felt as though I was a visitor to some house that belonged to the National Trust or a time-travelling guest to some 19th century hotel.

The nights were already approaching freezing point, but at least it was a crisp coldness. Val, who was prone to it and had thus always preferred warmer climates, was complaining non-stop until we reached the main street. Barry accompanied us and for once seemed quite contented. He still criticised our plans at every stage, of course, but his curmudgeonly refusal was gradually giving way to something more productive.

The roads remained as sleepy as they had been the previous day. The bus stop was empty, shunned even by the obnoxious youths that usually frequented such places. A few cars were parked outside "The Mangy Dog" as we approached it, though the police had evidently left by now. The pub's little metal sign, featuring a shaggy black dog, was creaking slightly in the light breeze that had followed us down into the valley where the village lay. Through the circular milk glass panes, I could make out a number of figures. It seemed that the pub was pretty busy.

Val and I entered first, with Barry close behind us. Immediately, a cacophony of laughter and loud chatter greeted us. The interior was cosy, with sturdy old furniture and even a fireplace at the back. Most people were deep in conversation, though quite a number peeked their heads to get a closer look at the strange faces that had entered their domain. A staple of village life.

"Not bad. What do you think, Val?" I said.

But Val didn't answer. I turned around and was shocked to see her white in the face, as if she were about to faint.

"Val! What's up?"

"Just too… too many…"

"Let's sit down quickly," Barry hissed from the corner of his mouth.

I took Val by the waist and manoeuvred her to the nearest table. She still looked very pale. Barry, meanwhile, jumped on to the bench next to her.

"Sorry, Amy," Val said after she had steadied somewhat. "Just t-too many feelings floating around. Too many people. My head is buzzing."

"Amanda, you'll have to go to the landlord. I don't know whether he allows me to be here. I'll take care of Valerie," Barry said.

I nodded and went over to the counter. A friendly-looking man with grey hair and a beard greeted me. I asked him if Barry could stay.

"Well," he said, "I don't get cats in here too often. It's dogs mostly."

"He's very well behaved, I assure you. At least, most of the time," I said.

"Oh, that's alright then. I suppose if the sign with the dog outside didn't scare him off, nothing will," he said jovially. "Want a pint?"

Val was big on cider, so I ordered her one, as well as a

bowl of milk for Barry. I got a Guinness for myself.

"I'm surprised so many people are here after the business yesterday," I said as I handed him the money.

"Yes," the landlord said, frowning. "They all want to know what happened. Strange case, you know."

"How come?"

"Well," he began, but hesitated. "Say, are you from around here?"

"I just got here with my friend Val," I said, pointing to our table.

Now it was my turn to pause. I wasn't sure volunteering too much information was the best idea, though in a village of this size, it was only a matter of time before the news spread about the new occupants of Fickleton House. Openness, I finally decided, would probably get me further than caginess.

"I inherited Fickleton House from my great-aunt. Quite unexpected, but there you go. I'm Amanda, by the way."

"Always glad to welcome a new resident, I'm Charles – but people just call me Charlie," he said, relieved. "Thought you might be another reporter. Not that I have anything against reporters, mind you, but Miss Nosworthy – the woman who died – did quite a lot of poking around, you might say."

"D'you think that got her killed?" I asked.

"I'm sure of it," the landlord said, lowering his voice. "I shouldn't really say this, I suppose, but her notebook's missing. That's where she wrote down all the stuff she found out here in the village. I saw her with it every morning. But the police couldn't find any trace of it in her room. Normally, she never left it out of her sight."

"So, you think the killer might have stolen it?"

"Yes. She made a lot of enemies. She had her fair share of arguments with the locals, too, I can tell you that."

"Arguments? With whom?"

"Well," he said uncomfortably. "I wasn't meaning to

eavesdrop, you've got to understand. But the walls are pretty thin at the back where her room was. You know, you just happen to hear a lot when you're in the kitchen, that's all. Talked a lot on the phone with people. Got pretty heated, I reckon. And then, a few days ago, she had an awful row with Lady Worthington at breakfast. In the lounge in the next room."

"Lady Worthington? I think I've heard of her. Isn't she hosting some sort of arts fair?" I asked.

Charlie, the landlord, nodded.

"Not just any old arts fair, at that," he said. "She's got a real Van Gogh painting that's going to be on display. Should attract quite a lot of people to the village."

"So what were they arguing about?" I asked.

"I don't know. The only thing I do know is that Lady Worthington stormed in here – she doesn't normally come to the pub, you have to understand – and blew her top. Just like that. I've seen many rows in my lifetime, but she was downright scary."

After a furtive glance in the direction of the other patrons, he leant in even further to make sure nobody heard us.

"And when Miss Nosworthy refused to stop poking into her affairs, Lady Worthington even threatened to kill her."

CHAPTER 6

Back at the table, I quickly told Val and Barry what had happened. Val, who was still pale in the face from being overwhelmed by her new psychic abilities, looked worried. Despite the initial excitement, I think she hadn't quite warmed up to the idea yet that confronting the murderer would be extremely dangerous as well. I had to say I wasn't too keen on the prospect of facing a homicidal sorcerer myself, though I felt I had little choice given the circumstances.

Barry, however, was deep in thought. I had placed his bowl on the bench next to me. He liked places that were higher up and would provide better vision. I suppose you couldn't be a transformed cat for long without adopting some of the habits of a real one.

"Can you sense anything from the landlord, Val?" I asked.

She shook her head.

"There are just too many people in here. It's all muddled. Maybe if we came back later at some point, when he's alone."

We sipped at our drinks (and bowl of milk) in silence for a while, until Barry stretched his head above the table as far as his feline neck would go, checking whether the coast was clear for him to speak. He needn't have worried, however. The noise from the other tables was so loud with excited chatter and gossip that no one could possibly overhear us.

"We should pay Lady Worthington a little visit tomorrow," he said softly, his eyes still scanning his surroundings.

"Have you heard of her, then?" I asked him.

"Unfortunately yes," Barry said with a haughty

expression. "Arrogant beyond imagination."

"Coming from you, that's saying something," I said, grinning at Barry.

"Yeah, she must be pretty bad," Val agreed.

Barry narrowed his eyes briefly at our jibes, but apparently decided not to dignify them with a response.

"Be that as it may, she's not a *real* aristocrat," he continued, brushing off a splatter of milk from his chest with a stroke of his paw. "Her husband received a knighthood I believe, for a bit of music he composed. Awful, modern stuff. But it doesn't stop her from acting like she's the Queen, of course. Quite the contrary."

"Doesn't sound like she'd be too forthcoming with information," I said.

"Oh, she'll talk," Barry said.

"But what reason would she have to talk to us at all?" I said. "I mean, we can't force her to talk to us, not even to let us in. Especially if she's involved somehow, she's not going to spill the beans to a couple of strangers."

"Amy's right, you know," Val said, still dazedly clutching her head. "We'll be thrown out the minute we get there."

Barry rolled his eyes impatiently.

"Really," he said. "Perhaps it would have been better for you to remain hebs since you insist on thinking like them."

"What do you mean?" asked Val.

"I have a plan," said Barry.

"A plan?"

"Yes. One that involves magic."

***

After finishing our drinks, we made our way back to Fickleton House. Mrs. Faversham was already awaiting us there with a steaming-hot pie, which we gratefully tucked into. Barry remained frustratingly monosyllabic whenever we tried to ask him about his plan to weasel out information from Lady Worthington.

Instead, he skedaddled up to his library as soon as we were all through with dinner, leaving Val and me in a state of bewilderment.

"Oh, he'll come up with something," Val said. "Let's ask him again in the morning."

"I suppose," I said.

"So," said Val, "d'you think it could be Lady Worthington? If the reporter was messing around with her arts fair, that'd be a pretty good motive."

"Yes, that's true. I wonder what made her so mad, though. Lady Worthington, I mean."

"Well, if whatever Barry is planning works, we'll know tomorrow," Val said. "Anyway, I think I'll turn in, Amy. This whole business of being a psychic is pretty… exhausting. I feel a bit ill."

"But you're happy we did it, right?" I asked.

I had somewhat of a guilty conscience. After all, it had been me who had got her into all of this in the first place.

"Yes," she said quickly. "Of course, Amy. I always wanted to know what other people were thinking and feeling. Really."

"Something's bugging you, Val. I don't need to be a psychic to see that."

"It's all just so sudden. And I always enjoyed going out. What if I can never do it again because I'm so overwhelmed by all the different feelings and voices around me? Or have to recover for hours afterwards? You know how much I love partying, Amy. Our monthly cocktail parties at home were legendary."

It was perfectly true, of course. You could always count on Val to go to the next party. Meanwhile, she had to drag me to most of the few I did attend. We both loved cocktail nights, though, for which we'd invite friends over to either Val's or usually my place. Something I was meaning to have a go at in Fickleton House once I got settled in a little more.

"Look, Val," I said, trying to stay on the bright side. "It's early days. You don't know how these things will develop. Perhaps… perhaps there's some sort of technique to close your mind or something. Or a spell. I'm sure Barry knows. Or we could read up on it ourselves in the library. Barry's always boasting about his extensive collection. There must be tons of stuff on the bond and on psychics up there."

"OK," Val said. "Let's do that. Tomorrow. But I want another cocktail party, Amy. It's hard enough giving up on everything else. We could invite some of the locals, get to know them a bit."

"Alright, we'll do that," I said. "First thing after the arts fair, we'll have our cocktail party. I promise."

***

The next day, Val was still feeling very much under the weather, so I brought up her breakfast to her room. She wouldn't be going anywhere anytime soon, so it was up to Barry and me to talk to Lady Worthington.

"Where have you been?" Barry demanded when I finally came back down into the dining room.

"I didn't want Val to eat her breakfast alone, Barry," I said.

"While I am waiting here for you, I might add," he said.

Mrs. Faversham, who knew nothing of Barry's transformation, of course, was nevertheless very fond of him. He received normal cat food only when she couldn't help it. Today, cooked tuna was on the menu, and Barry had gulped it down eagerly.

"Your bowl is empty, Barry," I said.

"Well, you couldn't expect me to eat it cold, could you?"

"Even better," I said, sitting down at the table. "You can tell me about our plan while I tuck in. I'm famished."

He seemed to be racking his brains in search of some

way he could object to this proposal. When he couldn't, he said:

"Fine, Amanda. Always happy to entertain when Valerie isn't here to do it for you."

"Are you jealous, Barry?" I said.

"Me? Jealous?" he said, his whiskers quivering with indignation. "Might I remind you that I have been living here for a long time, virtually on my own? I don't *need* anyone."

"Except Mrs. Faversham and her cooked breakfasts, you mean?"

"Well," he spluttered. "Well, that's different. Entirely beside the point. A working relationship. A warlock's got to eat, you know. Even if he has to spend nine lives as a cat."

"And with Val and me, you now have people to talk to, as well," I said.

"As a scholar and a warlock, I have no personal attachments whatsoever."

"You know, Barry, if I didn't know any better, I'd think you're actually growing fond of us," I said, laughing.

For the briefest of moments, the corners of Barry's mouth twitched.

"You'll never be able to prove it," he said.

✳✳✳

We went up to Barry's library to prepare for the plan. I was itching to try out some new magic and now finally the chance had arisen. I was just about to get the wand out from its cardboard box when Barry stopped me in my tracks.

"You'll need your own wand, Amanda," he said. "I don't want you breaking mine. I'll need it soon myself, hopefully."

"But I don't have one," I said.

"Your great-aunt did," he said. "And that will work best

for you. Now, the only question is where it could be."

"I have no idea," I said. "it's not like the lawyer put it on the list of items. She'd have just thought it was some sort of stick."

"Yes, foolish indeed."

"May as well start looking here," I said, making for a small sideboard at the end of the room.

"Wait," Barry said, "it's not going to be in there."

"How do you know?"

"That's... that's where my things are in. Anyway, your great-aunt rarely used the library in her last years. She spent most of them in her room. The room you're sleeping in now, in fact."

We marched through the corridors until we had reached the bedroom. My things were already strewn throughout, giving it a pleasantly disordered look. Barry, who liked everything neat and tidy, raised an eyebrow.

"We will be lucky if we find anything at all in this mess," he said.

"Oh, stop moaning, Barry, I'm itching to try out some new spells," I said, eagerly looking around the room for any sign of the wand.

The search, hardly hampered by my own disorderliness I might point out, took the best part of half an hour. It turned out that my great-aunt had placed her most prized possessions in a little basket with a lid, which Barry had found at the top of the large cupboard.

Finally, I was holding the wand in my hand. It was made of black oak, with little ripples running all the way down the handle, making for a good, solid grip. A narrow band of white, smooth material – which I strongly suspected was ivory – snaked its way around the tip and the end of the handle.

"It's beautiful," I said.

"Yes, quite," Barry said. "Come on. We can't dawdle all day, we've got to interrogate Lady Worthington."

"You haven't even told me the plan yet."

Barry simply tapped his temple with his paw.

"All in here, Amanda. Now, we have to organise transport."

***

After checking in on Val one last time, I walked over to Mrs. Faversham's house to call Tom, the friendly taxi driver who had brought us here from the airport, to pick us up at Fickleton House. He didn't say anything about Barry at first, but when he saw him jump onto the backseat of the car, Tom suddenly became extremely agitated.

"Here, the cat's tearing into the seat. Get him off there," he said, uncharacteristically angry.

I lifted Barry up at once.

"I don't think there's any harm done. He's very well behaved. Keeps his claws in, but I'll keep him on my lap all the same."

Tom examined the seat. When he was satisfied that Barry had indeed not damaged the leather, he looked extremely relieved.

"Sorry for blowing my top. I – I just love this car. Replacements cost a fortune these days. So, where are you going, anyway?"

"Worthington Manor, please."

"You do seem to be visiting the high and mighty around here, don't you?" Tom said amicably.

Barry looked as if he was about to tell him just what he thought of the so-called high and mighty but I quickly thrust my hand in front of his mouth, pretending to stroke him. It wouldn't do for Tom to think he – or worse *we* – were crazy.

"Oh," I said. "we – I mean, I don't know her. It's just about the arts fair, that's all."

"Oh," Tom said, enthusiasm lighting up in his eyes.

"Are you coming to the fair, then? A good opportunity to get to know the locals. I'll introduce you to some, though God knows you wish I hadn't when I do."

He laughed again with his smoky wheeze.

"Are you an artist yourself?" I asked.

"Nah," he said. "Never really had the patience for it. But I enjoy a good painting here an' there. Especially, err, less modern ones, if you get my meaning."

***

A few minutes later, we had arrived at the driveway of Lady Worthington's large estate. Very unlike Fickleton House, which had a dilapidated charm about it, everything here ostentatiously screamed to any visitor that the inhabitants were rich as well as orderly.

Next to the immaculate hedges, large lion sculptures, painted gold, flanked the gates as we approached them. There was an intercom system on the right pillar with a fisheye camera above it. The metallic voice certainly didn't sound too welcoming as Tom manually rolled down the window to answer it.

At that moment, something sharp and painful penetrated the skin of my right hand.

"Ouch," I yelled. "What the…"

Barry was frantically jerking his head in the direction of the intercom and shaking his head, then pointing to me with his paw.

"I don't understand," I whispered, desperately trying not to be overheard by Tom, who was still wrestling with the window. "Shouldn't we say who we are?"

Barry nodded, relieved. Then, worried that I might misunderstand, shook his head furiously again. I patted him on the head, a gesture I knew he secretly enjoyed, and turned to Tom.

"It's alright, we'll get off here. I think… I think the cat

needs some exercise. We'll just walk up to the house," I said.

"You sure?" Tom said, slightly bewildered. "I can drop you off right in front of the house."

"No, no, that's quite alright. He's a little stressed. Too much tuna. We can enjoy the gardens along the way. Thanks again, Tom."

I paid him and got out of the taxi, away from the intercom and the camera. Still covered from view by the car, Barry and I swiftly moved behind the left pillar. I waved awkwardly to Tom as he backed out of the driveway and then turned to Barry, making sure we were well out of sight and earshot from the intercom and camera systems.

"Why didn't you tell me before you didn't want us recognised?" I demanded. "You don't have to go all Sherlock 'I'm going reveal everything at the end' Holmes on me, you know, Barry."

"I – I didn't think they'd have a camera," he said. "Don't look at me like that, Amanda. I'm a theoretician, not a prowler. I rarely have to think like a professional meddler, you know."

"Well, we're already meddling, so why don't you tell me the plan right now?"

"I think we need to alter your appearance a little bit," he said.

"Barry, I'm not transforming, if that's what you mean. I don't want to permanently turn into an old grandma or something. I'll be doing that naturally for long enough as it is."

"No, no," he hissed. "It's not a permanent charm – very different process. That's why we have to do it right before we enter. Nothing can go wrong."

"Famous last words…" I said rather facetiously but agreed to do it nonetheless.

"So what's the idea?" I asked. "Who do I turn into?"

"I think," Barry said slowly, "Lady Worthington will

only speak to someone she considers worth her time."

"Like the police?"

Barry shook his head irritably.

"That's strictly against magical law. Even if you're impersonating heb policemen, you'll get into serious trouble with the *Spellcasters' Association*. No, I think something else is in order. Something Lady Worthington is passionate about."

"So, an art expert or art dealer perhaps?" I said.

"Exactly," Barry said, rubbing his chin with his paw. "If you can make her believe you're a rich art patron, say, who is interested in her arts fair – interested in investing even – she'll definitely talk to you. We can move on from there."

"Pity we don't have Val with us," I said, wistfully. "Hope she's alright."

Barry clicked his tongue impatiently.

"Of course she is," he said. "Psychic fatigue, that's all. She'll be back on her feet tomorrow. Now, let's get on with it."

I nodded and got out my wand from my handbag. It felt very familiar by now, although I'd only held it a few times. Barry whispered the incantations to me and I performed them. It had been a lot more fun somehow to do magic without the pressure to succeed. Barry, though a seemingly endless source of magical knowledge, wasn't helping matters by being increasingly impatient.

Finally, he seemed satisfied, however. I took out the small mirror from my handbag and looked at my complexion. I got a shock at first, for my features were hardly recognisable. My nose and ears were a lot larger, and my entire face had aged by at least thirty years. My skin had lost most of its colour and was quite wrinkly.

"This isn't how I'm going to look in thirty years, is it?" I asked Barry.

"Worried?" Barry said smugly.

"If this is my future, perhaps I should be!"

"Keep your whiskers on, it's alright," he said. "These are generic short-term aging charms, mostly."

"So this isn't how I'm going to end up?" I asked.

"Nope," said Barry, with a sly grin. "Could be a lot worse."

"Very funny, Barry. Now, how do we proceed?"

Barry peaked his head suspiciously around the pillar, making sure nobody was there to overhear us.

"We gain entry under the pretence that you want to invest in the arts fair. Ask as many questions as possible, but don't be too transparent. If she smells a rat, we'll be kicked out by the butler before we can say 'arts fair'."

"How long do we have before the charms wear off?" I asked.

"About an hour," Barry said. "That's why we'd better move."

I nodded and led the way to the intercom system. I pressed the silver button below it and waited. After a little while, a pleasant female voice – very different from the one we had heard before in the car – answered.

"Worthington Manor, how can I help you?"

I cleared my throat.

"Hello, this is Mrs… erm… Merryweather. I'd like to talk to Lady Worthington about a contribution to her arts fair."

"Just a moment, please, Mrs. Merryweather. I'll tell Lady Worthington."

There was a clicking sound. Barry and I stood awkwardly in front of the gate, waiting.

"Merryweather?" he asked disbelievingly. "Honestly?"

"Oh, shut up, Barry," I said, taking the bait. "You come up with a good name next time, then. Wouldn't that be a job for our resident theoretician?"

"Evidently," he said drily.

Then, the intercom crackled again and the same female voice spoke.

"Lady Worthington will be with you shortly. Please come up the driveway."

"Thank you," I said.

The gates opened electronically. Barry, who wasn't used to any sort of technology since it didn't work at Fickleton House, was slightly unnerved. I noticed that he scampered rather quickly through gates, too.

"Harmless piece of technology, Barry," I said.

"Technology can go wrong," he said sulkily. "I'd trust magic any day."

"Like your transformation charms?" I asked.

"I think," he said, "your time would be better spent thinking about what to say to Lady Worthington rather than harassing and tormenting your magical mentor."

"Poor little you," I said with affection. "I'll think of something. And we have company, anyway."

A young, extremely thin woman in her early twenties was awaiting us in front of the main entrance to Worthington Manor. She was dressed in what I presumed to be an old-fashioned maid's uniform. It looked like something out of Downton Abbey.

If it was, however, it stood strangely at odds with the manor itself. I was by no means an expert in these things, of course, but the ostentatious display of wealth all around us, ranging from more golden statues similar to the lions at the gates to the silver handles on the water hoses, seemed to denigrate what must have once been a tasteful Georgian manor house. Even the curtains sparkled in the daylight from myriads of crystal glasses that had been woven into the material. Perhaps they were real diamonds. Or at least, that was the impression they were trying to make.

"Mrs. Merryweather?" the maid asked me, making a slight curtsey as she did so.

"Yes, that's right. I'm here to see Lady Worthington."

"Of course. Please excuse me, but the butler has fallen ill, quite unexpectedly. Upset tummy. So I've been answering the door. I'm Ethel, the maid, by the way. How do you do?"

"Nice to meet you, Ethel," I said.

"Please, follow me."

I nodded appreciatively. It was only at that moment that Ethel registered Barry's presence. Her eyes scanned his black fur and furrowed brow that gave him a permanently grumpy look.

"This is Barry, my cat. He goes everywhere I go. My companion, as it were. The only man in my life I can truly trust," I said, trying to pull off the crazy cat woman shtick. "I hope he can come in, too? I assure you, he is very well behaved and very clean."

"Oh, that's alright, then," she said. "Lady Worthington is usually quite strict about animals, but I'll see what I can do."

"Thank you," I said.

We entered through the main doors, which also sported golden knobs, and found ourselves in a long, high-ceiling hallway. Ethel was just about to march ahead when she seemed to remember something.

"Shall I take your coat, ma'am?" she asked.

"No, it's quite alright," I said, hanging it up on the stand myself.

Ethel looked rather relieved.

"Sorry, I'm just... not used to doing everything here at once. And I don't know when the butler will return."

"Nothing serious, I hope?" I asked.

Ethel hesitated, clearly pondering whether she should tell me or not. Finally, she had just made up her mind to do so when a sharp, ear-piercing call echoed through the house.

"ETHEL?"

"I'm sorry, that's Lady Worthington, I'll leave you in the library, if that's alright with you," she whispered.

Barry and I followed her through the hall. She beckoned

us to sit in one of the adjacent rooms, the library. The books, I noticed, were largely untouched, with a level of dust covering their jackets that I was sure wouldn't have been tolerated anywhere else in the house.

Meanwhile, we could hear Lady Worthington's booming voice from here.

"A cat?" she bellowed in disbelief.

Barry looked indignant. And for once, I quite agreed.

We couldn't hear Ethel's soft voice in response, but Lady Worthington had evidently been mollified by Ethel, at least for a while. A few moments later, Lady Worthington entered the library. She must have been in her late forties or early fifties, though her startlingly blonde hair, tied into an elegant bun, had no trace of grey at all. She was dressed in a morning robe which was just as ostentatious as the rest of her house. Her robe was black, with gold trimmings along the sides and cuffs. Her thick fingers sported an entire array of matching gold rings. Her manner was curt and unfriendly, her face sour and arrogant – no doubt an expression that had become permanent over the years.

"Yes?" she demanded, not even bothering to enter the room properly.

"Lady Worthington, my name is Merryweather. I hear that you are in charge of the upcoming arts fair in Fickleton?"

"That is correct," she said, eyeing Barry with dislike. "We won't be taking any more artistic contributions, however. If that's what you're after."

"No, quite the contrary," I said. "I deal in exquisite pieces of art, you see, and I'm always on the lookout for a good investment."

Immediately, I saw that I had struck conversational gold. At the sound of money, her every particle lit up. I had her full attention now. Her manner changed as if someone had pulled a switch. She flashed her artificially whitened teeth at me.

"Please forgive me, Mrs... Merryweather, did you say? And what a beautiful cat you have. I do so adore them. Yes, you've certainly come to the right place. We have an impressive assortment of backers already, but I'm sure we'll find a spot for just one more. Well, why don't you join me in the morning room? I rarely use this place here, too many stuffy books."

She laughed and beckoned me to follow her. Barry and I complied, though we couldn't refrain from exchanging looks with raised eyebrows once she had turned her back to us. Even Barry, a natural cynic in regard to both warlocks and humans, was taken aback by Lady Worthington.

Outside in the corridor, Lady Worthington snapped her fingers at Ethel.

"Tea for three," she ordered.

Ethel inclined her head in deference and bustled off down the hallway.

"Please, in here. So much more light from outside in the morning room. My husband always joins me here in the afternoon. He likes to work deep into the night. So we should have some peace until he comes downstairs. *Men.*"

I forced myself to laugh along with her. Privately, of course, I certainly couldn't blame him. He probably had all the reason to avoid her as much as possible.

Lady Worthington had been right about the morning room, however. Though the cherubs on the mantelpiece were quite tacky, the rest of the room was in much better taste than the other rooms I had been able to peek into along the way here. She sat down on a comfortable-looking armchair and beckoned me towards the adjacent sofa.

"I think, Mrs. Merryweather, you will find that we have many talented artists among us. All producing cutting-edge art for the 21st century. An excellent investment, to be sure."

"I have no doubt," I said. "There are a few things I'd like to clear up before I can commit myself, however. I hope you understand, Lady Worthington."

"Oh, I understand perfectly," she said, flashing her toothy smile again. "A very wise decision. What would you like to know?"

"Well, it has more to do with the… village affairs than anything else, I suppose," I said. "There have been rumours of a death – a murder even – in the local pub over in Fickleton."

"A murder…" Lady Worthington repeated blankly.

"Yes, a journalist, I believe."

Her expression was unreadable as her gaze fixed itself on me. I could tell she was doing some hard thinking all the while. I kept her gaze, trying to appear as innocent and as non-judgmental as possible.

"Nosworthy," Lady Worthington breathed, her nostrils flaring. "Yes, I've heard of her."

"So she wasn't too popular, then?"

Lady Worthington scoffed at the question. At that moment, Ethel appeared in the doorway with a tray. She walked over to us and set it down on the table, quietly handing us our teas. I thanked Ethel, though Lady Worthington didn't even acknowledge her presence. Instead, she continued our conversation.

"Of course not. A nosy busybody if ever I saw one. Journalist my hat. Trying to cook up trouble wherever she went, that's what she was. And then, of course, she got herself killed."

"But nobody knows who did it?" I asked, trying to contain my eagerness.

Lady Worthington gave me another of her hard looks. Ethel, who looked even more nervous than ever, fumbled with the sugar and accidently spilt it all over the carpet.

"Oh, you silly girl!" Lady Worthington exclaimed. "Clean this up, go on. What do I pay you for? And bring us another bowl of sugar."

Ethel, struck numb from shock, dropped to her knees

and began sweeping up the sugar with her hands. I was just about to help her when I felt the sting of Barry's claws on my ankle. He was ever so slightly mouthing the word 'no', facing away from Lady Worthington as best he could. He was right, of course. As much as I felt sorry for Ethel, I couldn't show too much concern if I wanted any more information from Lady Worthington.

"Excuse my clumsy maid, Mrs. Merryweather, you were saying?"

"Erm... yes, so the perpetrator hasn't been apprehended yet?"

"No," she said. "Not that I know of, at least. And I don't really care if they catch him, to be perfectly frank with you. It may sound harsh, Mrs. Merryweather, but the deceased woman was not a very nice person. She made a great deal of trouble for many of the inhabitants, both in Fickleton and the surrounding villages. That poor young man – Derek Reynolds – for example."

"Derek Reynolds?"

There was a name I hadn't heard before. Ethel left the room again with the empty tray and the mopped-up sugar, still shaking slightly. Then, I felt the most strange tingling sensation in my face and my hands. Horrified, I looked at Barry, indicating my hands. He made a whirling sign with his paw that clearly said that I had to accelerate the conversation somehow. The effects of my spells were beginning to wear off.

"Yes," Lady Worthington said, sipping her tea and luckily paying no attention to us, "Mr. Reynolds runs the local golf club. An honest businessman, who naturally attracts a lot of envy from the locals and the press. Quite like myself, of course."

"And did the deceased journalist give you any trouble in regard to the arts fair?" I asked.

She mustered me again. I was pushing it now. I could tell that only the prospect of a juicy cheque kept her from kicking me out.

"You've heard of my little encounter with her, I take it?" she said.

"Well, yes, it did come up at some point. I just wanted to make sure that, erm, any investment I make is free from scandal," I said apologetically, as Ethel re-entered with a fresh bowl of sugar.

Lady Worthington's nostrils widened again.

"I would not pay too much attention to village gossip if I were you," she said. "And I don't like your insinuations. Yes, I had a quarrel with the murdered journalist, but so did everyone else who had the misfortune of coming across her. Mr. Reynolds, myself. Even Colonel Warton. Now that's a shady character whenever I saw one. Perhaps she had a closer look at that illegal gun collection of his. Or the ivory he's had smuggled over here. *And* he prowls the streets at night like some criminal for God knows what reason."

She leaned closer to me, setting her tea aside.

"Now, I wasn't even out at the time she died," Lady Worthington continued. "I was here, at Worthington Manor. With my beloved husband. Not that it's any of your business, of course. But one must crush these malicious rumours where one can."

She stared at me, a determined expression on her face. Ethel, who had been listening to every word, rooted to the spot, suddenly dropped the second, fresh bowl of sugar, which once more landed on the carpet. Lady Worthington shrieked in anger.

"There, see what you have done. You are upsetting my staff, Mrs. Merryweather. I must insist that you leave at once."

There was nothing else I could do. I got up, with Barry following in my wake. Once more, Ethel was crouched on the carpet, frantically brushing the sugar into her cupped apron. Lady Worthington was towering over her, making her best effort to ignore me as I made for the door.

I stepped out into the hallway, taking a deep breath as I did so. I could hear Lady Worthington berating poor Ethel in the morning room. Barry and I slowly walked along the corridor until we couldn't hear Lady Worthington's dulcet tones any longer.

"Quite the dragon," I whispered to him.

He simply nodded in agreement, still fearful of being overheard by another member of the staff.

In the hall, I was just about to get my coat when, to my surprise, Ethel hurried down the corridor towards us.

"Mrs. Merryweather?" she asked, nervously checking whether Lady Worthington had followed her. "Do you have a moment?"

"Of course," I said.

"It's just… Lady Worthington, well, she didn't quite tell you the truth."

"What do you mean?" I asked.

"She wasn't here on the night when that journalist was killed. I know because I was here all the time, doing extra hours and…"

But at that moment, Lady Worthington's robed figure entered into the hallway. Her eyes narrowed further at the sight of Ethel talking to me.

"Out of my house, at once," she said dangerously. "Ethel, I forbid you to talk to this woman. Good day."

Ethel gave me a desperate look.

"She can talk to whomever she likes," I said as I opened the front door. "She is not your slave, Lady Worthington – whatever you might think. Good day."

I left her fuming at the door. I could sense she wanted to give a retort but couldn't think of anything in time. So, with the satisfaction of having the last word, Barry and I walked down the driveway towards the gates through which we had entered. From afar, I could still hear her rage and shout at Ethel.

"She's even more horrible than you'd made her out to be," I said to Barry once we were safely out of earshot.

"Yes," he said. "A nasty piece of work. But what can you expect from new money?"

"Hey, I'm new money as well," I said, mocking indignation.

"Well," he said. "At least you don't act like it. And you inherited."

"Thanks, Barry. I guess. Anyway, d'you think Ethel will be alright? I mean, she was almost raving mad in there."

Barry frowned. I could tell that the encounter had disturbed him, too. Finally, he nodded his feline head heavily.

"She's spiteful enough, but I don't think she's stupid. I doubt she'll harm her, at least physically, that is. Though for her psychological well-being, another employer would certainly be in order."

"Yes," I said. "Especially if she turns out to be our killer in the end."

CHAPTER 7

Back at Fickleton House, we quickly told Val all about our encounter during dinner. She was still looking a little pale but much better than when we had left her. She was evidently adapting well to her new powers. Her appetite had also returned.

"So, d'you think it was Lady Worthington, Amy?" Val asked, cutting up her fish.

"I don't know. I wouldn't put it past her."

"That poor maid. Ethel, you said her name was? Is there anything we can do?"

Barry shook his head. We had finally given in to his demands of sitting at the table with us. He was perched on top of a tower of cushions piled on one of the chairs so that he could reach his plate on the table.

"It's a free country," said Barry. "She's free to find another employer whenever she chooses to."

"Yes but that's not always an option. I could have killed my boss a couple of times, too. But getting a new job isn't a laughing matter. You know how it is."

He looked at me with a blank expression.

"Or perhaps you don't," I said, winking at Val.

"Yeah, Barry, do warlocks have jobs?" Val asked.

"Some do, certainly. I, however, had a *mission*. Still have, as a matter of fact. Very different," he said.

"So what's the next step, anyway?" Val said, trying to avert a lecture on theoretical magic as quickly as possible.

"I think we should question more people. This Reynolds man she mentioned. He runs a golf club. And Colonel…"

"Colonel Warton," Barry said. "Yes, he's a well-known figure around here. Strange fellow, mind you. Perhaps we should start with the Colonel."

"Yes," Val said excitedly. "But this time, I'll be coming with you."

***

The next day, after another one of Mrs. Faversham's hearty breakfasts, we walked down into the village to visit Colonel Warton. With only a few days before Lady Worthington's arts fair and a mere week left before Christmas, most villagers we passed were in an excellent mood. It was also a good opportunity to get to know some of them, as they tended to their cars or decorated their gardens for Christmas, much to Barry's distaste for social interaction.

Colonel Warton's house was located at the very edge of the village. Whatever the festive mood of the other inhabitants, Colonel Warton's house certainly didn't reflect it. Unlike the cosy little English houses surrounding it, it was made of pure concrete with a corrugated iron roof. A large fence surrounded it on all sides, making it resemble some sort of high-security facility. It wouldn't have been out of place in a film on the Soviet Union.

We approached the heavy front door, which looked like the fireproof doors you'd often find in the cellars of houses. There was no intercom system, but a spyhole next to the door told us that we wouldn't be able to enter without prior scrutiny.

I extended my hand and rang the bell. We waited for a while, but there was no answer.

"Maybe he's out?" Val said.

"If he is," Barry said softly. "It's almost unheard of. Legend has it that he only leaves the house after dark. Hates the villagers, you see. Can't say I blame him particularly on that front, though not for the same reasons, naturally."

"Oh, Barry, you *are* insufferable," Val said affectionately.

I pushed the doorbell again.

"Well, Barry, you have a point with PC Bowler," I said "But surely they aren't all like that…"

"Wait a minute, I think I saw something in the garden, beyond the fence. Over there," Val said.

Val was right. A figure dressed in grey was slouching around the garden with a shovel in his hand. This, I was sure, had to be Colonel Warton. We approached the fence. Immediately, a pair of dogs – unseen to us – started barking furiously.

"Any last minute transformations, Barry?" I said, trying to make myself heard over the noise from the dogs.

"No, I don't think so this time," he said. "We might stand a better chance if he knows we're from here."

Val called out to the Colonel. Perhaps it was a little too friendly for his liking, for he eyed us suspiciously from afar for a while before limping over to us. He took out some sort of remote control from his pocket and pressed a button. A metallic clunking was followed by rapid canine footsteps. Two of the largest German shepherd dogs I had ever seen in my life scampered to their master's side, still barking at what all three of them considered to be an intrusion. Certainly, I was glad to have a fence between me and those dogs. Barry, however, seemed paralysed by fear. He was shaking silently beside us. I didn't blame him. Warlock or not, the dogs were about five times his size. They'd rip him – and probably Val and me too – to shreds in a matter of seconds.

I was startled at Colonel Warton's appearance when he approached the fence and we could get a closer look at him. His eyes were bloodshot, and his nose was extremely red, with burst blood vessels all over his crinkly face. His hair was kept short in a military style, though his crumpled grey coat would never have passed inspection.

He reached down to his dogs with two gnarled hands. They stopped barking at once. It was evident that Colonel Warton had absolute authority over them. They licked his hands, more as an act of submission than affection, and then remained perfectly still, their eyes following our every move.

"Excuse me, are you Colonel Warton?" I asked.

"That's right," he said hoarsely. "Who's asking?"

"My name is Amanda. This is Val and this is B-"

I was just about to introduce Barry but quickly stopped myself in my tracks. I kept forgetting that, to everyone else, Barry was simply a cat. And that was the way it had to be.

"What do you want?" he said.

"We just moved here, you see. To Fickleton House. Do you know it?" I said.

"Everybody knows Fickleton House around here," he said.

"Yes, well. We just wanted to get to know everyone in the village. Introduce ourselves."

"That's right," Val said, trying to contribute. "We've heard a lot about you."

Turning to Val, Colonel Warton emitted something between a harsh laugh and a cough.

"Oh, you have, have you? All lies. Don't believe a word they say. They never liked me around here. And I don't mind. I don't like them, either."

"Erm, yes, why don't we sit down together? Have a little chat."

"We're having a chat right now," he said stubbornly. "And I like it out here. The cold winter air keeps me sharp. And the dogs aren't allowed in the house, anyway. I like to keep them around. Keep me protected."

"Protected? From whom?" I asked.

"The villagers, of course."

"Have they… threatened you?" Val said.

"There are signs," he said mysteriously. "They don't care for ex-army much. Probably reminds them they didn't do anything for their country. All they ever do is talk about diets and green lifestyle and all that rubbish. Never seen the real world. Never had to fight for anything except their flat-screen TVs."

"But something did happen here a few nights ago… a journalist was murdered in the pub," I said.

Colonel Warton scoffed.

"Oh, her, yes. A nosy parker if ever I saw one. But like all meddlers, didn't know when to stop. Yes, they did her in alright. Didn't surprise me in the least when I heard the news."

"Do… do you know who did it?" I asked.

"Of course not. I would have reported it to PC Bowler. Only right thing to do. Pity he doesn't have any brains, though. He couldn't catch a murderer if he was living next to the police station."

Val and I couldn't quite suppress our nervous laughter.

"What?" he said, immediately suspicious again. "What did I say?"

"Oh, nothing," I said. "It's just that PC Bowler accused me the other day. And I wasn't even in the area when the murder occurred."

"Fits the picture, alright," he said, nodding his head. "If they can pin it on someone, they will. I'd mind my step if I were you. Lady Worthington and that Reynolds boy have the entire community in their pockets. Funded a new community centre, even. Nobody dares point the finger. But we all know…"

"Do you think Michelle Nosworthy – the journalist – was investigating them?"

"Yes, that's what I reckon," Colonel Warton said. "I would have helped that young woman if she hadn't been so blooming curious about my… well, never mind. Makes me suspicious, anyhow. If you ask me, there's definitely something dodgy going on. And it's got to do with that arts fair."

"We heard that the journalist's notebook was stolen. Do you know anything about that?"

"No, I don't," he said.

At that moment, one of the large German shepherds started growling, keenly observing Barry, who was still frozen to the spot in terror.

"Time to feed the dogs," Colonel Warton said suddenly. "Don't want them to eat the cat, now, do we?"

He gave off a short laugh that sounded more like a bark.

"Quite," I said, forcing myself to smile. "Well, thank you, Colonel. That was very… informative."

He narrowed his eyes.

"Let me give you some advice. Stay out of this. It's not worth it. And they're too powerful. They've killed before. And they'll kill again. You mark my words."

***

Back on the main road of the village, Val turned to me excitedly.

"Amy, he's hiding something. Colonel Warton, I mean. I – I felt it when you were talking to him."

"Well he did admit that the killed journalist was poking around his place, asking questions. Do you think it was that?"

"No, it's not that," Val said. "It was when you mentioned the notebook. He was definitely withholding information."

"Do you think he could be our murderer?" I asked.

"I don't know," said Val. "But he knows something about the notebook. I'm sure of it."

"He might have stolen it," said Barry, who was trotting alongside us. "That's what I would do. Get rid of the evidence. Perhaps she had something on his collection."

"Yes," I said, frowning. "He'd certainly try to destroy it as quickly as possible if she could have proven that it was illegally obtained. What do you think, Val?"

"I'm sorry, Amy. It's all just so… so *vague*. All I know is that he felt a keen sting of fear when you mentioned the notebook. And relief when he was able to change the subject."

"So he could be our murderer," I said.

"But he warned you against the villagers himself," said Val.

"Precisely," said Barry darkly. "It might have been a veiled warning. A warning to stay out of his way."

***

We decided to see Mr. Reynolds next, the young golf club owner. It wasn't hard to find out where the club was from the local bakery, as the girl behind the counter was very talkative. The club was only two miles outside of the village, and it appeared that Reynolds himself had funded a pedestrian pathway that led directly to his club.

After a quick stop at the bank (I still had to get used to the fact that my balance wasn't in a perpetual state of negative figures), Barry was all for calling Tom to drive us there, but Val and I insisted on walking.

"The exercise will do you some good, Barry," Val said.

Barry was grumpily trotting behind us.

"This body was built for a couple of years' use only," he said. "Not for decades of plodding around the countryside with a clumsy psychic and a novice witch."

But even Barry couldn't deny that it had been a good idea. A gentle cover of snow had fallen during the night, covering the beautiful meadows around us in a coat of white. The pathway itself was firm and far enough from the main road to ensure an enjoyable walk to the club, free of the noise of cars and busses. It was country life at its best, and all of us thoroughly enjoyed it.

Finally, we reached the golf club. I was surprised by the amount of activity there. I'd never played golf myself, but I had somehow assumed it would be closed in this weather.

Yet the area next to the busy car park – probably for beginners – was packed with guests and instructors in heavy winter wear and gloves, practicing on the green that had been cleared of snow.

Next to it stood the club itself, an impressive array of buildings, especially for such a small community. We walked into the main entrance of the 'Fickleton Golf Club' and found ourselves in a reception area. A large screen announced the various activities on offer. There was a lot more than golf. It appeared that the club had its own hotel, a swimming pool, a gym, a restaurant, and several conference rooms for business purposes. Squash and various other sports activities were also on offer. Reynolds, by all accounts, was doing well. I approached the reception desk.

"Excuse me, I'd like to talk to Mr. Reynolds," I said.

A smartly dressed woman in her thirties smiled apologetically behind the desk.

"I'm afraid he isn't available at the moment. Is there anything I can do?"

"Do you know when he will be back?" I asked.

"I'm sorry, I don't. I can tell him you called. Shall I leave a message?"

"No, thank you."

I went over to where Barry and Val were waiting. Many people, families mostly, had arrived with their pets, so nobody seemed to be bothered by Barry. Val was carrying him in her arms, just in case.

"She won't say where he is," I said, annoyed. "Looks like we've hit a dead end."

"Aren't we forgetting something?" Barry whispered in my ear, balancing on Val's arms to get closer to me.

"What do you mean?"

"You're a witch for crying out loud," he hissed. "Use magic."

"Oh, yes, of course. I've got my wand in my handbag

76

here somewhere. What spell can I use on her, do you think?"

"A simple agreeableness charm ought to do the trick," said Barry. "If she really doesn't know where he is, we'll have to try something else."

He whispered the instructions and the precise incantation into my ear.

"OK, got it. Thanks, Barry."

Casting the spell without being seen was quite another matter, however. I pretended to be interested in the potted plants at the side of the desk, above which hung the various framed prizes the club had won since it had been established. Thankfully, the receptionist didn't appear to be particularly interested in anything but her smartphone, which was tucked in tightly at the very corner of the desk. I snuck my wand out of my bag and slipped it past the desk on the far side, away from the entrance area.

"Gratus," I murmured under my breath.

Light sparks emitted from the end of my wand, hitting the receptionist's leg. A terrible shot. I hoped that it would be enough, but it was hard to aim properly at such an angle. I decided to try my luck.

"Excuse me, could I speak to Mr. Reynolds, please? I think he'd want to talk to me, too."

"Of course, I'm sure he will make an exception," the receptionist said with a rather vague smile on her face. "He should be in the squash room. It's two floors down from here. You can take the elevator to your right."

***

A few minutes later, we found ourselves in a very long corridor of the gym area. The rooms leading off it were full of sweating brows and red faces, all furiously engaged in one activity or another. From what I could tell from the open doors and signs I was able to read in time as we passed by, there were rooms for table tennis, bowling, boxing, gymnastics and dancing, as well as a small football area for kids. At last, we reached the squash area.

The walls were see-through. A man and a woman were inside, playing an energetic match. They were both wearing sport outfits all in white. If this had been the 1980s, I thought to myself, the only thing missing would have been the headbands. Undoubtedly, the man was handsome and possessed a certain flair, his tanned skin and blond hair clashing spectacularly with his white clothes. The blonde woman at his side, only a couple of years younger than I was perhaps, was exceptionally good-looking.

"Excuse me," a man said. "Would you mind? You're blocking the way."

"Oh, sorry, by all means," I said, as we moved forward.

We had all been strangely entranced by the couple in the glass cage in front of us. At that moment, Barry gave a low whistle in appreciation of the blonde woman inside the squash room. The man who had passed turned around and, seeing only two women and a cat, flashed a grin at me and made a rather forthright gesture. I hastily shook my head, waving my hands to show him it was a misunderstanding. He looked rather disappointed but went on his way all the same.

"Barry!" I hissed.

"What?" he said.

"Stop whistling when there're men passing. They'll think Val or I whistled," I said.

"Yeah, we want to whistle when we want to," said Val.

"I was simply expressing my approval of the young lady playing squash, that's all," said Barry. "I don't get out that much."

"Well, now we know why," I said.

"I didn't know cats could whistle," Val said.

"I had a lot of time to practice," Barry said defensively. "You'd be surprised what you can…"

"Shush, you two," I whispered. "Look, they're having a quarrel by the looks of it."

It was true. The woman had thrown her racket to the floor and was pointing her finger angrily at the man, who was making swiping movements, as if to dismiss what she was saying. The glass was evidently sound-proof as we watched them rage at each other in silence for a little while until Val said:

"I think they're coming out. Careful."

All three of us quickly pretended to be reading the gym schedule on the wall.

"Not you, Barry," I hissed. "Cats can't read, remember?"

"Oh, yes, sorry," he said. "Didn't bring my spectacles anyway."

The glass door to the squash room swung open and the blonde woman rushed outside.

"Wait," the man called after her.

But it was too late. She had already slammed the door in his face and stormed down the corridor. Apparently, he was considering whether he should follow her, but, seeing so many guests around, thought better of it. I decided to quickly take advantage of the situation.

"Are you Mr. Reynolds?" I asked.

"That's me," he said, his gaze lingering on Barry for a moment.

"Nice to meet you. I'm Amanda Sheridan. I just moved into Fickleton House the other day."

It was remarkable how fast a face could change from bored indifference to opportunistic enthusiasm.

"Ah, yes, nice to meet you indeed. We were all wondering who'd be inheriting the estate. I know Mrs. Sharpe, you know, does a lot of work for the club as well. Old friend. Knew the old lady, too, in fact. Was she your grandmother?"

"My great-aunt. But I'd never met her."

"It must have been quite a surprise to you, then," he said. "If you need any help with the estate, I can connect you with a few of my people. I understand running such a place can be quite costly, even though that's hardly a problem now, eh?"

He laughed heartily.

"That would be wonderful," I said, feigning interest. "But right now, Val and I are trying to figure out whether we want to stay here, in the Cotswolds."

Val looked at me in bewilderment.

"But…" she began.

"Aren't we, Val?" I said, emphasising every syllable.

"Oh, yes, that's right. We are. Still wondering."

"Well, anything I can do to help make up your mind?" he said, flashing a smile at both of us. Either the quarrel with his lady friend was forgotten or he was an excellent actor.

"There is, in fact. We're rather concerned with… erm… the security in this area. I heard there was a death in the pub in Fickleton the other day. There's even talk of murder. We just wouldn't want to move into an area that's... you know."

Reynolds dropped his smile immediately.

"Yes, ghastly business," he said. "I understand that you're concerned. However, if you want my opinion, you aren't in any danger. I mean, it's not like you're walking around the village and asking a lot of silly questions like that journalist."

Val and I gulped.

"Do you know what happened to her?" Val asked.

Reynolds shook his handsome head.

"No," he said. "I was having dinner at the time at an excellent Italian place with my girlfriend. You might have seen her. I was playing squash with her until a few minutes ago. Anyway, I took a taxi home and that's that. Didn't even hear about it until the following day from one of my employees. Now, you'll have to excuse me. My girlfriend is rather cross with me. I'll just have to see whether she is alright. Nice to meet you both."

He shook my hand and then Val's. His gaze lingered once more on Barry before briskly walking down the corridor.

"What do you make of him, Val?" I asked her when he was safely out of sight. The corridor was empty apart from us now.

"Difficult to say. I don't think he was telling the entire truth just then. When he was talking about the night of the murder. But the vibes are very faint with him."

"Might be a sign of a sorcerer, mightn't it?" I said excitedly, turning to Barry.

"It might," Barry said softly. "In fact, a trained sorcerer will almost certainly be able to dampen Val's abilities. There are some hebs who can do it, too, however. Naturals, you might call them. Not uncommon at all in shrewd business men like Reynolds."

"So there's no way to tell?" Val asked him, her face drooping slightly in disappointment.

"There are psychics who can. It takes many years of practice." said Barry.

"Well, we don't have years. So what should we do?" Val asked.

"I think I want to find out more about Mr. Reynolds and his girlfriend," I said. "I won't be a minute."

"Wait, Amy. Where are you going?"

"Later, Val. It'll be too suspicious if all three of us go darting all over the place. Wait for me in the restaurant. I'll be right up. I just want to check something."

There was no time to explain. I tore down the corridor in the direction that Reynolds had disappeared. If my hunch was right, they were continuing their quarrel elsewhere, provided Reynolds had found her, that is.

The door at the end of the corridor led to yet another one. How big could a place get, I thought to myself. But I continued down them, passing tennis courts, young men lifting weights, old men in swimming pools and in the sauna with towels wrapped around them, until I reached a dead end. This was evidently the end of the gym area, marked by a staff bathroom and a caretaker's broom cupboard.

I was just about to turn back when I heard a familiar male voice.

"Keep your voice down, for Heaven's sake."

Yes, that was undoubtedly Reynolds. And it was coming from the staff bathroom just a few feet away. The voices were very faint, too faint to hear anything. I had to get closer somehow. Very gently, I opened the door to the bathroom. But the clicking noise of the door must have alerted them, because they fell silent immediately. I hastily let the door fall in place again.

Panicking slightly, I grabbed at the handle of the broom cupboard next to it. It was open. I quickly slipped inside and closed the door behind me. It was pitch black in here and I fumbled blindly for the light but couldn't find it. The wall to the bathroom, I noticed with delight, must have been a lot thinner from this side. I was able to make out almost every word they were saying.

"Who was it?" asked a woman's voice.

"Nobody, probably just a lost customer or something," Reynolds said.

His voice was a lot harsher and deeper than when he had spoken to me a few minutes earlier. He was in an aggressive mood.

"It's too risky, Derek," his girlfriend said. "What if someone finds out? I don't want to be part of this."

"You already are, Patricia. If you want to continue going out with me, you'd better do what I say," Reynolds said.

"And if you want to go out with *me*, Derek, you'd better tell me the whole story with that awful journalist woman."

"Calm down, the customers will hear us," Reynolds said.

"I don't care, Derek," Patricia said. "Let them hear how

you cheated on me behind my back, how you lied to me for weeks. And… and now, you're lying to the police, too."

"I'm not lying," he spluttered.

"Yes, you are, Derek. I've tolerated all your little… quirks and that stuff but… this is withholding evidence."

"I can't tell them about the affair. They're just dying to find someone with a motive. They'll bang me up before you can say 'unfair'. Is that what you want? See me arrested by that buffoon PC Bowler? The police are just looking for a scapegoat for this case. I'm just preventing them from wasting their time with an innocent man, that's all. You know I'm innocent, don't you?"

"I… well, yes… of course. Derek, I…"

"Then keep your mouth shut and don't talk to anyone about this," Reynolds said. "Because if they ever find out I didn't take the taxi here that night but got off at the pub to… to see her, I'm toast."

CHAPTER 8

Still hiding in the broom cupboard, I stood perfectly still, waiting for the conversation between Derek Reynolds and his girlfriend Patricia to continue. Either they had lowered their voices again or weren't talking at all, however. I had an impending sense that I had overstayed my welcome. I had heard enough to get going with in any event.

I fumbled for the door knob and turned it as quietly as I could, peaking through the crack as I did so. The coast seemed to be clear. I stepped out and was just about to close the door when my handbag, which had somehow got caught on something inside the broom cupboard, fell from my shoulder and crashed into some dustbins below.

"Did you hear that?" I heard Reynolds exclaim from the caretaker's bathroom.

There was no time to be lost. Frantically, I yanked at my handbag as hard as I could and tore down the corridor, trying to gain as much space between Reynolds and myself before he opened the door. I heard him yank it open behind me.

"Hey, you, wait a minute," he said.

I turned around in mock surprise. He eyed me with suspicion as his girlfriend peeked around the corner behind him to get a look.

"Oh, fancy seeing you here, Mr. Reynolds," I said.

"Yes, quite. May I ask what you are looking for?" he said, trying to remain as calm and collected as possible. "Perhaps I can help you find your way."

"Oh, I was just looking at the various activities you have on offer down here. Like…"

I spun around desperately, reading the only sign that I could read from where I was standing.

"… water aerobics for the elderly."

"Water aerobics for the elderly?" he asked in disbelief.

"Erm, yes," I said. "Old age may hit you before you know it, that's what my mother always used to say."

That was terrible. Where was Val to shut me up when I needed her? Reynolds looked at me with narrowed eyes. I could see his temper rising beneath that friendly mask he wore for customers.

"Well, I'd better be off," I said awkwardly. "Goodbye."

"Goodbye, Miss Sheridan," Reynolds said. "And do let me know how water aerobics worked out for you."

***

Upstairs, I found Val and Barry at the back of the restaurant. I quickly filled them in on what had happened. Barry didn't appear particularly surprised, though Val was incensed.

"How could he? That's the lowest of the low, cheating on her like that. Absolutely disgusting. She shouldn't put up with something like that."

"Val," I said patiently. "We aren't the vice squad. We're here to get *me* off the hook, remember? Before that moronic PC Bowler can frame me."

"Yes," Barry said, buried in thought. "But perhaps Reynolds is guilty of both cheating on his girlfriend and murder. After all, a love gone sour or the wish to cover up an affair might easily lead to murder."

"So might jealousy," I said. "Think of the girlfriend. Perhaps she followed Reynolds that night when he visited the journalist and killed her afterwards."

"She should have done *him* in, instead," Val said, then adding after seeing our raised eyebrows: "Oh, come on, you know what I mean. I just don't like people cheating on each other."

"And a good sentiment it is, Valerie," Barry said. "One

that the modern world doesn't care for, of course."

"So, another suspect on the list, then?" Val said quickly before Barry could tell us yet again how much better life was in the 1950s when he was a young man.

"It seems so," I said. "The more people we question, the longer the list gets. And apparently, everyone had a motive for killing the journalist. Lady Worthington's art fair and her dodgy alibi that was put in doubt by Ethel. Colonel Warton and his illegal collection of weapons and whatever else he's got hidden in his bunker of a house. And now Reynolds and his affair with the victim. Whatever next?"

***

We decided to eat an early dinner at the restaurant and walk back to Fickleton House. When we finally set foot on the pathway back to the village, it was already getting dark. Usually, I didn't mind the dark particularly, but I had to admit that I felt slightly uncomfortable doing so now. All the talk about murderers and victims had got to me. Val, apparently, felt quite the same way.

"We should have called Tom to drive us back," she said.

"Yeah," I agreed. "Too late now, though. We're close to the woods. We'll definitely do that next time, though."

"I don't mind in the slightest. My eyesight is excellent in the dark," Barry said. "So no need to worry. I will guide you."

"A great help you'll be if the murderer pounces on us," Val said.

"He won't pounce, he'll most likely cast a curse," said Barry. "Anyway, we're almost there. We can take the shortcut up here, leads directly to the entrance of the gardens at the back of the house."

We followed Barry into the woods. Where the soft cover of snow had provided a little reflective light along the way from the golf club, it was almost entirely dark here. We were barely able to see Barry a few feet in front of us, but no more.

"Arghh."

Val had suddenly disappeared.

"Val, where are you?"

"Down here, I must have tripped."

I helped her up to her feet again, brushing snow and old leaves from her coat.

"Sorry," she said. "Bit creepy in the woods."

"Don't worry," I said. "I guess it's getting to all of us. Nobody's here, Val. It's OK."

We were just about to set off again when a bright light from a torch was flung in our faces, blinding us.

"Who goes there?" a surly voice addressed us from afar.

It was Colonel Warton. And he wasn't alone, either. The soft but audible growling told me that he had brought one of his enormous German shepherd dogs with him. Barry had clearly come to the same conclusion and skidded towards us, seeking refuge behind Val and me. I started fidgeting for my wand in my handbag, just in case.

"Colonel," I said. "What… what a surprise. Fancy meeting you in the woods around here. Isn't your house at the other end of the village?"

"I like to take long walks," he said. "And Rex here needs some exercise."

"Quite. Well, we'll be on our way then," I said.

"Not so fast," he said menacingly.

He lowered his torch so that we could see him properly for the first time. He looked as worn-out as ever, though there was an odd glint in his eye that hadn't been there earlier. He reached down to the massive hound at his side and caressed it behind its ears, which stood up in a state of constant vigilance. I could sense Barry quivering behind me. And to be honest, as I looked at those large fangs of the German shepherd, I couldn't blame him. I was feeling sick myself.

"They say these woods are haunted," Colonel Warton continued, slowly shuffling towards us, his hound close at his heels. "That's why I like coming here. Less chance of meeting the natives. You remember what I told you?"

"Which bit exactly?" I asked, gripping my wand a little tighter.

"About keeping out of this business," he said.

"Vividly," I said.

"It's dangerous," he said. "The villagers – you can't trust them. Don't be fooled by their fancy houses and cars. They're rotten to the core, the lot of them. And they're out to get me. I know it. I think I'll let the dogs sleep in the house tonight. Yes, they won't dare come in then. You keep out of trouble, now."

"We will," I said, trying to get the conversation over with as fast as possible. "You… you be safe, too, Colonel."

He stared at me as if nobody had ever said something like that to him in his entire life. Then, he nodded brusquely.

"You're alright."

He slowly shuffled past us, with Rex, his monster of a dog, following him in perfect obedience. The dog's eyes, however, were fixated on Barry until his canine neck wouldn't allow it to turn any further.

"He's crazy," said Val once she could be sure that we wouldn't be overheard. "Totally paranoid."

"Yes," I said. "Come on, let's get back to the house."

But Barry wouldn't move. He stood there, frozen.

"Barry," Val said, lifting him up from the ground. "Barry, are you alright?"

Being hoisted up must have awoken him again.

"It's… nothing," he said faintly. "I just… just can't stand German shepherds."

With Val carrying Barry, we pressed on for another few minutes through the woods until finally we could see the moon properly again. It was remarkable what power of illumination it had once the clouds had retreated sufficiently and we were out in the open again.

As Barry had promised, we found ourselves at the back of Fickleton House. We entered the gardens through a small wooden gate. We were close to Mrs. Faversham's house, which stood only a few feet away. A light burning in the front room told us that she was still up and about. We walked through the garden and reached the back door of Fickleton House. Cold but glad to be home, I unlocked it and let us in.

I was tired but there was no way I was going to sleep anytime soon after our walk through the woods and the eerie chat with Colonel Warton, so I decided to start a fire in one of the sitting rooms on the ground floor I hadn't used before. It was small and comfortable, facing the front yard and garden.

Val, who insisted on trying out some new cocktails she'd come up with, retired to the kitchen as Barry and I prepared the fire. It may sound foolish, but I hadn't ever made one in my life, as I had grown up with central heating systems, but Barry was a good, albeit impatient, teacher. I was happy to see that he had recovered quickly from our encounter with Colonel Warton and his German shepherd dog.

Before long, we had a crackling fire going. Luckily, there was still a large supply of wood outside in the shed, so we wouldn't have to worry about it for the rest of the winter.

Then, the door opened and Val appeared in the frame.

"Ladies and gentlecat," Val said triumphantly. "I present to you my newest creation. Winter Spell. Here, have a sip."

She placed two glasses with a bubbling blue liquid on the table next to me.

"Thanks, Val, that's fantastic," I said, reaching for one of the glasses. "Exactly what I needed after a day like this."

"Where's mine, then?" asked Barry indignantly.

Val and I were both taken aback.

"Well… you're a cat, Barry. I don't think you should

take alcohol."

"Oh, what do you think magic's for?" he said. "A temporary stomach-altering spell will do nicely for this evening. Quite simple. Invented it myself, in fact."

"You invented a spell just so that you could booze up as a cat?" I asked in astonishment.

"Well, why not? A warlock is entitled to a drink once in a while, isn't he? Transformed or not."

"OK, Barry, on your little cat's head be it," Val said, leaving for the kitchen once again.

She returned shortly with a third drink.

Of course, Barry had exaggerated the incantation's simplicity. It took me the best part of twenty minutes just to master the complex hand motion, which had to flow in exactly the correct angles and reach precisely a specific point when I had uttered the spell.

"Venter durus," I said for what felt like the fiftieth time.

Something had changed now, however. I felt a tingling in my wand hand that I hadn't before. Barry briefly rubbed his stomach with his paw and then seemed satisfied. We lifted our glasses and were just about to take our first sips when there was a tap on the window outside. It was so dark that we couldn't see anything. Val held her breath. While Barry craned his neck to get a better look.

"Did you hear that?" Val said.

"Yes," I said.

My heart was thumping fast. Who would be calling this late at night? Surely, it wasn't Colonel Warton. At least, I hoped he hadn't followed us here.

I got up from my chair and inched towards the window, grabbing one of the lit candlesticks for light. Beyond the panes, I could make out a burly figure of a man. He was evidently alone. It wasn't the Colonel. But although we outnumbered the man outside, I felt oddly vulnerable. I made a mental note of learning some defensive spells first thing the following morning.

CHAPTER 9

I reached for the latch of the window and pulled. The cold winter air immediately rushed into the warm room. And a familiar voice spoke.

"Hello, hello," PC Bowler said brusquely. "Don't even have a doorbell, do you? You young hippies really are the limit."

"PC Bowler," I said, not bothering to hide my lack of enthusiasm to see him. "It's rather late. Is there something important?"

By the light of the candle, I could see that his face was growing red like a balloon.

"Important? You taking the mickey? Believe me, I have better things to do than barging around houses without doorbells, you know!"

"Right, well, do you want to come in?" I said.

"No, that won't be necessary for what I have to say to you, Missy. I have a busy schedule, you know."

I took a deep breath, trying hard not to blow my top. I knew he only called me 'Missy' because it annoyed me, so I tried to ignore it.

"So what is your message, then?" I asked.

"It has come to my attention," PC Bowler said self-importantly. "That you have been harassing reputable members of the community for no reason at all. I would like to remind you that you are a suspect in a murder investigation. Now that's a very serious business indeed. You'd do well to keep out of any more trouble until the police force can ascertain the guilty party."

"So it was definitely murder?" Val called from behind

me.

PC Bowler's moustache quivered. I could see he was torn between keeping the investigation secret, as he should, and squashing the impudence of somebody questioning his word. After a brief moment, it seemed that the latter impulse had got the better of him.

"Of course it was," he said. "No doubt at all. The only thing left now is to find out how the killer entered the victim's locked room and stole that blooming notebook. Almost like magic, though I have no doubt in my mind that our experts will get to the bottom of it sooner or later. A minor detail in the grand scheme of things, however. Should be settled in no time."

"So who put you up to this?" I asked.

"Up to what?" he said.

"Calling on us."

"Some concerned members of the community who wish to remain anonymous," PC Bowler said importantly. "None of your concern."

"And you still think that I am the guilty party?"

"I cannot comment on current police investigations," he said, brushing a little snow off of his uniform. "But I'd be very careful if I were you. People might think you're trying to cover up something."

"I'm not covering up anything," I said angrily. "If anything, I'm trying to uncover the obvious fact that I'm innocent. And if you'd check the records of the flight Val and I took, maybe you'd come to the same conclusion and stop wasting everybody's time."

"Alright, Missy, I've heard that tale before. No need to repeat it again. All I'm saying is – and this is my final warning – stop pestering the good citizens of Fickleton. We don't need amateurs walking around, pretending to be investigators. That's what we are there for. To do the real investigating, I mean. Leave it to the professionals, Missy."

"And if I don't?" I said.

"Then," he said menacingly. "I will personally make sure that the full force of the law is brought down on you. I mean it. This is my last warning. Stop playing detective."

And with that, he waddled off into the darkness. I had a good mind to bewitch him then and there, but thought better of it. Not least because I didn't know any appropriate spell, though a permanent agreeableness charm might certainly be a start with PC Bowler.

In my anger, I shut the window with so much force that half the pane shot out into the snow.

"Amy, are you OK?" Val asked.

"Yeah, it's just… that PC Bowler gets under my skin."

"Don't worry," Barry said, handing me my wand with his two paws. "We'll get to the bottom of this."

"Yeah, you've got us," Val said.

"Thanks, guys," I said. "Really, I wouldn't know what to do without you. You really are the best."

Barry taught me the spell to fix the glass – which luckily was much easier than his stomach-altering spell – and we resumed our places, drinking Val's excellent cocktails. We spent the next few hours planning our Christmas feast, which would take place a few days after the arts fair in the village.

I had stayed with Val and her parents the previous few years for Christmas, ever since we had become friends in fact. I had no family of my own to return to and had often spent Christmas on my own before. As a result, I hadn't exactly looked forward to the season. But Val's parents had been brilliant. They had treated me as one of their own from the very beginning. It felt like family, almost like it was when I was a child and my parents were still alive. I was very grateful for that experience.

This year, of course, I wouldn't have blamed Val if she had wanted to return home for the festivities. If things had been different, I would certainly have come with her. It wasn't only the police investigation that kept me here. It was the whole atmosphere, the beautiful gardens, this wonderful house that provided seemingly endless rooms and histories to explore. Barry, also, would have had to spend Christmas alone, though I strongly suspected Mrs. Faversham would have at least cooked him a royal breakfast. And of course, there was the little matter of catching a murderous sorcerer that I didn't want to get too far away from. So, I had made up my mind to stay. And Val, being the phenomenal friend that she was, wanted to stay, too.

"We'll just get my parents over for next year," she said. "That'll solve the problem in future. I'll miss them. But you only inherit an estate in the Cotswolds once in your life, eh?"

"I should be so lucky," Barry said, though he was smiling.

"It could have been worse, Barry," I said.

"How come?"

"You could have had someone like Lady Worthington inherit the place," I said. "Just imagine Christmas with her."

"So what do you usually do for Christmas, Barry?" asked Val.

We talked deep into the night with all the different ideas for Christmas spinning in our heads. It felt good to distract ourselves from the case for a while. Val and I had decided to have our cocktail party on Christmas Eve and invite some of the locals over. It was on a short notice, perhaps, but I had a hunch that most of them were so curious about the new inhabitants of Fickleton House that they'd come anyway.

Barry gave off a yawn that indicated it was time to sleep. The fire was almost out by now, with only a few embers left. We said goodnight and made for our rooms, with Barry sleeping in his library as usual. I took a long shower before going to bed, however. I had received quite the shock the first time when there was only icy cold water, but Barry had shown me a crafty spell that made it nice and hot. You simply had to love magic.

***

The next day at breakfast, Barry, Val, and I were sitting at the table while Mrs. Faversham brought in the food. To my surprise, she was followed into the room by Lavalle. I could see that Mrs. Faversham still disapproved of him slightly, though she was perhaps a little less suspicious than the first time.

"Good morning, all," Lavalle said pleasantly, smiling at us as Mrs. Faversham left the room again. "Please, I don't want to disturb you for too long. Just thought I'd keep you up to date."

"Of course," I said. "Please, have a seat. Coffee?"

"Yes, thank you," he said.

There were some spare cups in the cupboard behind us, so I got him one and placed it in front of him on the table. Lavalle looked even more worn out than last time, though somehow it seemed to amplify his dark good looks, giving him a vibe of adventure. He poured himself a generous dose of the black liquid.

"Looks like you've settled in nicely," Lavalle said, gazing around the room.

"Yes," I said. "We'll be staying here for Christmas as well, in fact."

"Oh, you are?" said Lavalle, looking slightly surprised. "Well, there's certainly enough space here for everyone."

Barry was getting fidgety at the table.

"Let's cut the small-talk, shall we?" Barry said, pushing his bowl away from him. "Why are you here, Lavalle?"

"Barry, don't be rude," said Val. "Sorry, Mr. Lavalle."

But Lavalle just laughed, holding up his hands.

"It's alright," he said, inclining his head towards Barry. "You are quite right, of course. And please, it's just Lavalle. Anyway, I've scouted out the area and visited some of the crime scenes already."

"Did you find out anything?" I asked eagerly.

Lavalle shifted uncomfortably in his chair.

"Well, there's still a lot of leg-work to do, of course," said Lavalle evasively. "Nothing definite yet. In fact, I really wanted to know what you're up to."

"What do you mean?" I asked.

"There's word around the village that you've been… asking some pretty pointed questions to certain individuals involved in the murder case," said Lavalle.

"How fast does information travel around here?" Val asked in disbelief.

"If it's gossip," said Lavalle, "I'm afraid it's close to the speed of light. And the villagers are pretty sensitive about this entire business, you know. They're worrying about the arts fair, you see. Trying to keep things as quiet as possible until it's over. Desperate to avoid any sort of scandal."

"Well, PC Bowler's the wrong man, then," I said. "He's the only bull I know who takes his china shop with him."

"Yes," said Lavalle, laughing. "He is rather foolish. Agreed."

"He came round here yesterday evening," Val said.

"Did he?" said Lavalle. "Interesting. What did he say?"

"Oh, the usual tosh about me being a prime suspect," I said. "But they're still looking for the victim's notebook apparently."

"I see," Lavalle said.

"At least they're right to do so," said Barry. "Information on the killer is bound to be in there."

"I think it might be Colonel Warton," said Val

thoughtfully.

"Colonel Warton?" asked Lavalle. "You've talked to him, too?"

"Yeah," said Val. "He acted weird when we mentioned the notebook. He definitely knows something."

"Right," said Lavalle. "Thanks for the pointer. I'll start investigating him immediately, then."

"I don't think he'll be very forthcoming with information, though," I said. "He's the suspicious type. Paranoid even."

"Perhaps a closer look at his house might be in order?" said Barry solemnly.

"Good idea. I'll go there tonight," said Lavalle, taking a final sip of coffee and getting to his feet.

"We can help," said Val. "We've already found out a lot and…"

But Lavalle held up his hand.

"Look, I'm very grateful to you for what you've done. But this really is a matter for the MLE. So please, I beg you, no more solo investigations, alright?"

"People keep telling us that," said Val.

"But you'll come back and let us know if anything develops, right?" I said.

"Of course," said Lavalle. "Especially if there's such good coffee and, if you'll forgive me for saying so, such charming company. I don't think I could resist. Good day, all."

And with that, he left the room. Val looked at me with a peculiar grin on her face, while Barry appeared to be close to bursting point.

"I think he likes you," Val said to me, barely hiding her knowing grin.

"Nonsense," I said. "He meant all of us."

"He was looking at you, Amy," Val said. "And you know it."

"Young cockerel," Barry said dismissively. "All he has to do is put some honey in his words and you both start melting."

"We're not melting," I said indignantly.

"Of course you are," said Barry. "Lapping up every word he says."

"You're just jealous, Barry," I said.

"I don' trust him, that's all," he said. "What do we know about him? It could be him for all we know."

"You sound like Colonel Warton," I said, laughing. "He's an MLE agent, remember? He's on our side."

Barry puffed and protested but couldn't think of an adequate response.

"Fine, fine. But he isn't the sharpest tool in the shed. He didn't even think of going to the Colonel, did he? We found that out on our own."

"He wasn't even in town, Barry," I said. "Leave him be."

I didn't even know why I was defending Lavalle, but Barry was obviously just annoyed at the lack of attention. I had to put my foot down at some point.

"Aaanyway," said Val, trying to change the subject. "Lavalle's going to take over now. We've still got Christmas to prepare for. We haven't got anything in the house, no decoration and no snacks either. And we still need presents, too. Plus all the ingredients for my cocktails."

***

Val was right of course. I was by no means willing to let the case drop, as I was far too curious by nature as well as unwilling to leave my fate to the likes of PC Bowler, but I agreed to a short hiatus until we had properly prepared for the upcoming festivities. I wanted to take the bus into Gloucester, the nearest city, but Val and Barry both insisted on asking Tom. Taking a taxi for such a long distance seemed overly wasteful, even decadent to me, but the obvious convenience was a factor I couldn't dismiss, at least until I bought my own car, which I was determined to do first thing in the new year.

We spent the entire day happily browsing shop windows, buying gifts for each other, and even visiting the enormous cathedral in the afternoon. It might sound strange, yet sitting in cafés always gave me an itchy feeling, as if there was work I was neglecting. I suppose that's what being a waitress did to you after a couple of years. So Barry, Val, and I decided to get takeaway coffees instead. It appeared that Barry's special spell also worked for coffee, with some minor modifications, so that he could sneak an occasional sip when nobody was looking. That went mostly unnoticed, except for when an elderly lady saw me help Barry drink and muttered something about animal cruelty. Under normal circumstances, I suppose I would have agreed with her.

Barry couldn't buy presents himself, of course, so Val and I took it in turns to go shopping with him. Barry sat on my shoulder to get a better view of the items on sale, as well as preventing anyone from stepping on him. In the city, however, few people seemed to care. Barry and I got Val an entire cocktail mixing set plus handbook (with lots of space for the addition of her own recipes). While Barry and Val were out shopping together, I arranged to have a Christmas tree delivered directly to Fickleton House. According to Barry, there were still quite a lot of Christmas tree decorations left from my late great-aunt, so we decided to use them instead of buying new ones. It would both suit the traditional style of the house, in addition to being a way of paying our respects to her.

Finally, we got into Tom's cab and drove home, buried beneath endless piles of parcels and mountains of boxes. I'd never bought so many things in my life. Though I felt a little guilty for doing so, it was a relief that – for the first time in my life – I didn't have to worry about the credit card bill at the end of the month. We spent most of the ride talking to Tom, whose own plans for Christmas involved having his sister over for lunch.

When we arrived back at Fickleton House, it was already dark. I had bought several power banks for our phones in order to circumvent the lack of electricity, at least as a short-term measure. Barry had explained the reason for my great-aunt's disapproval of it, as electricity interfered greatly with magic. As both Val and I didn't want to live completely without it, however, we'd have to find some sort of long-term compromise. For the time being, though, the power banks – to be recharged at Mrs. Faversham's house – would have to suffice.

After dinner, we settled down in the small sitting room at the back of the house as we had done the previous night. It was quickly becoming my favourite room – save for my bedroom upstairs and Barry's library perhaps – due to the fact that it heated up very quickly with a roaring fire and was exceptionally cosy.

Now, with the fire burning next to us, Barry was reading a 16th century magical treatise, wearing old-fashioned spectacles he said he needed for the small print. Val had settled down with a good mystery book she had found in one of the spare bedrooms, while I was content with gazing into the warm flames dancing in the hearth.

Suddenly, there was rap of knuckles on the window, the glass of which I had only mended yesterday with my wand.

"Oh no, not again," I moaned, grabbing the candle next to me. "It can't be PC Bowler."

But it wasn't. The figure outside was much slimmer and taller. I opened the window, shining the light of my candle into the newcomer's face. To my surprise, it was Lavalle.

"Lavalle, what are you doing here?" I asked.

"An emergency. Sorry to bother you like this. But there was no other way to reach you. It's freezing out here, d'you mind if I come in?"

"Of course not," I said, lending him a hand as he stepped over the window sill. "What's wrong?"

He looked at me long and hard.

"I've just come from the village. There's been another development. Colonel Warton has been killed."

CHAPTER 10

We were all stunned by the news. We had seen him alive and, at least under the circumstances, reasonably well. To hear that he had been killed seemed inconceivable.

"But… but how?" Val said.

"He was killed by his own dogs," Lavalle said.

"But that's not possible," I said. "I saw the dogs for myself. They were absolutely devoted to him. To a fault almost. I mean, they would have ripped poor Barry apart if they hadn't been. And us as well probably. But Colonel Warton? No way."

"My thinking exactly," said Lavalle.

"So you're saying he was murdered?" said Val. "But how? I mean, you can't control the dogs, unless…"

"Unless you're a powerful sorcerer," said Barry, taking off his spectacles with both of his paws. "Canines are particularly tricky to hex due to their loyalty to their masters. But it can and has been done before."

"Indeed," said Lavalle. "As you can see, our worst suspicions have been confirmed. My own investigations in the area haven't got me very far, I'm afraid, but they did reveal one thing. Art thieves have been particularly active in the Cotswolds in the last couple of months. The murders I investigated were all wealthy businessmen or landed gentry. All in possession of fine pieces of art that went missing after their deaths. It was all quite cleverly done. The heb police didn't even suspect robbery as the primary motive. You see, they staged the killings as targeted murders, often for other reasons."

"So, you mean the thefts were covered up by the murders?" I asked.

"Precisely," said Lavalle. "Curious, I know. But it makes

sense from their perspective. If they can cover up or at least delay investigations into the robbery while the police are focussed on the murder, the pieces in question will be a lot harder to track. Time is usually of the essence."

"Hold on," I said. "I've just remembered something. The landlord told me that Lady Worthington's arts fair will be featuring a real Van Gogh painting as their main attraction."

"Do you think they could be after the painting?" Barry asked Lavalle.

"It certainly is a strong possibility," Lavalle said. "In fact, I would say it is our best bet. If I can catch whoever is doing this red-handed…"

"You mean *we*, surely," said Barry.

Both Val and I looked astonished. After all, it had been Barry who had been opposed to getting involved in the first place.

"This is a matter for Magical Law Enforcement," said Lavalle. "I told you so this morning. We can't involve civilians."

"But isn't it true that – under Section 24c – MLE may enlist the help of magical citizens in the case of an emergency, even to detain suspects?" said Barry smartly.

Now it was Lavalle's turn to look grumpy for a change.

"A pity you're so well educated," he said. "Yes, it is true. I merely wanted to… protect the ladies."

"We're not just 'the ladies', we don't need protection," Val said immediately. "We want in, don't we, Amy?"

"I think you're outnumbered, Lavalle," I said, grinning.

"This isn't a democratic decision," he said stiffly. "However, under the circumstances, it's perfectly true that this investigation is a lot more complex than one single person can manage. A fact that MLE headquarters admits but does very little about, of course. And it's not as if you hadn't been poking your noses everywhere as it is. I suppose you know too much already not to be properly involved. Probably best if I keep an eye on you. Therefore, I will officially ask you to aid MLE operations during the arts fair."

Barry looked satisfied. Val and I high-fived.

"Please," he said sternly. "This is serious. You will have to follow my orders from now on. To the letter."

"Of course, officer," Val said.

"Whatever you say, sir," I said.

"Addressing me as 'Lavalle' will suffice," he said.

We giggled as he attempted to retain some of his authority.

"Now then," he said, folding his hands behind his head, "tell me all you know about the case. And I want to hear everything. No detail must be spared. It might turn out to be important."

We told him about the various encounters we had had in the previous days, how we had first visited the pub and talked to the landlord, the covert questioning of Lady Worthington and Ethel's evidence against her alibi. Then we recounted our visit to Colonel Warton, and finally our trip to the golf club run by Reynolds, as well as our second meeting in the woods with Colonel Warton on our way home.

"So," I said, summing up. "We've got one suspect down – that's the Colonel – and two left, Lady Worthington and Derek Reynolds. Both with motives. And both have shaky alibis. It must be one of them."

"I'm afraid it's not quite as simple as that," said Barry. "Patricia – that's the girlfriend of Reynolds – also has a strong motive. Jealousy. Reynolds was having an affair with the journalist. She could have followed him to the pub that night after their quarrel and killed the journalist after he left."

"So we have three suspects so far," Lavalle said. "What about the pub owner? Charlie, you said his name was?"

"Yes," I said. "Well, I don't know about him. He

seemed very nice to me, but maybe that was just a front. I mean, he certainly had the best opportunity of all. Remember, her notebook went missing. I'm sure she would have filled it with incriminating evidence, so the murderer stole it."

"Did you find the notebook in Colonel Warton's house?" I asked Lavalle.

He shook his head sadly.

"Not a trace. I didn't have much time, though. Those dogs were making a hell of a racket. Totally mad, if you ask me. Alerted the entire neighbourhood. It was only a matter of time before the heb police arrived, so I left."

"So, whoever killed Colonel Warton also stole the notebook?" said Val.

"That seems to be the most likely conclusion," said Barry.

"Yes," Lavalle said. "Do we have any other leads?"

"We could always speak to Patricia – Reynolds's girlfriend," said Val.

"I don't think that's going to work, somehow," I said. "She's too loyal to Reynolds. For all we know, she might have been the one who called PC Bowler on us. Despite what Reynolds did, she loves him. I don't think she'll give us any information, especially if it might incriminate him somehow."

"But who else is there?" asked Val.

"Well," I said, slowly. "There is one more. Lady Worthington."

"But she won't talk to us, surely?" said Val.

"No, but Ethel will," I said. "Lady Worthington's maid."

"What about her?" asked Lavalle.

"She was willing to talk, even though she was dead scared of her boss. She said that Lady Worthington's alibi was in fact not true."

"Then we should get in touch with her," said Lavalle. "As quickly as possible. This sorcerer is ruthless. Colonel

Warton's death has shown that. But I've got to make sure. I know this is rather irregular, but since you're in on the investigation, I thought I'd ask anyway. Would it be alright to put me up for a few nights?"

"No problem," I said, though Barry looked disapprovingly around the room. "We have enough rooms in this place."

"Excellent," said Lavalle. "Tomorrow night, I'll see if I can find out anything else about Colonel Warton's death. Perhaps even track down that notebook you were speaking of."

"And we'll talk to Ethel, won't we?" said Val eagerly.

"Yes," I said. "But we'll have to get her on her own somehow. Because if Lady Worthington is our killer, we don't want to arouse her suspicion."

***

Getting hold of Ethel wasn't as straightforward as it sounded. We didn't want Lady Worthington to get overly suspicious if she heard we had been asking a lot of questions in the village about Ethel. We didn't even know whether she lived at Worthington Manor or had her own flat somewhere. And time was running out.

An idea came to me the following morning when Val and I were browsing the local charity shop for clothes. Several post offices had evidently gifted the shop some of their old delivery jackets.

"Look, Val," I said. "This is perfect."

"That's awful, Amy. You don't want to wear that thing for the arts fair, believe me."

"No, no," I said impatiently. "Don't you see? We can disguise ourselves as postmen. We can at least get access to Ethel without arousing too much suspicion."

"But these things are ancient. We'll look like time-travelling postmen from the 1970s."

"It'll have to do, Val. At least to fool them from afar. Come on. Or do you have a better idea?"

It turned out she didn't, so we bought the jackets anyway, along with a couple of black shoes and trousers to match them. We slipped them into our bags and headed for Worthington Manor. We decided to walk this time, as calling Tom would have meant that our movements could be easily tracked if someone were to inquire.

Although it wasn't as far from the village as it had been from Fickleton House, it took us the best part of an hour to get there. Once more, we saw the familiar golden lions perched on either side of the gate. We crept into the bushes – well out of sight of the camera – and changed into our post officers' uniforms.

"I look fat in this," Val said.

"I'm sure I don't look too hot either, Val. It'll only be a few minutes."

We rang the bell and a metallic voice answered.

"Worthington Manor."

"Erm, special delivery."

"Right. Back entrance, please."

There was a buzzing sound as the gates were opened for us. We walked up the path to the manor, though this time following the path to the back of the house where I assumed we were supposed to go to.

A sombre-looking man in a butler's outfit was already awaiting us.

"I haven't seen you before," he said with suspicion in his voice.

"No, we're just filling in for a colleague," I made up. "Bad case of the flu."

"Strange mail bags you have, I must say. What is the post office coming to these days?" he said.

Val threw me a told-you-so look.

"Hand me the mail, then, please," the butler said. "My time is precious, and Lady Worthington is already waiting."

"Sorry, it's a special delivery."

"For whom?"

It was at that moment that I noticed that I didn't even know Ethel's last name. Different measures were evidently called for. But I had come prepared.

"Hold on," I said, trying to buy time as I fumbled for my wand in my handbag. "I've got it here somewhere."

"What on earth…" he began as he saw me draw my wand.

"Gratus!"

His eyes briefly unfocussed, and his frown was immediately replaced by a benign smile.

"We would like to give Ethel her mail now. Can you get her for us?" I said.

"Of course, madam," he said blankly and disappeared into the house at once.

"That was close," I said. "Being a witch definitely has its perks."

"Yeah," said Val. "He was really suspicious. Lucky you acted quickly or he would have thrown the door in our faces. Why couldn't we have just done that in the first place, though? Could've saved us from dressing in these silly clothes."

"No, we can't risk being spotted from afar. It may not fool anyone in close quarters but it'll do if Lady Worthington or her husband happen to look out of the window."

Then, the door opened and Ethel appeared. She looked as worried and timid as ever.

"The butler said there was a delivery for me?" she said.

"Hello, Ethel," I said. "This is Mrs. Merryweather. Do you remember me?"

"But…"

"I know I look different, I disguised myself the first time. I wanted to talk to you again. About Lady Worthington. You said she wasn't home when the journalist was killed in the pub and…"

Ethel's eyes grew wide, her breathing shallow.

"I – I can't. N-not anymore. You don't understand. This will get me in all sorts of trouble. Lady Worthington, s-she was really angry at me. And so was Sir Henry. I don't think I ought…"

"Ethel. Please listen. There's been another murder. Colonel Warton was killed last night."

"What? A-are you the police?"

"No," I said. "But we're investigating the case. And we need your help to prevent more murders."

She gulped but finally nodded.

"Alright, I'll help you. But I can't speak now. Lady Worthington would kill me if she found out. Meet me in the village – tonight."

"Alright, Ethel," I said. "Where exactly?"

"Meet me in the pub's carpark – at the back – at midnight. I should be able to get out of here by then without anyone seeing me."

"We'll be there, Ethel," I said. "You're doing the right thing."

***

We spent the remaining hours with Barry at Fickleton House. Lavalle was also there, working. We had put him up in the old guest room in the corridor next to Barry's library. It had been the best room by far, but Barry had not been happy about him sleeping there.

"He snores," Barry said indignantly. "He distracted me from my work all night. I want that man out of the house at once."

"We can't just throw him out, Barry," I said. "We're in on the investigation. He's officially asked us for help."

"And we can officially ask him to leave, too," Barry said. "Really, MLE agents at Fickleton House. Whatever next?"

"D'you want to know what I think, Barry?" Val said.

"Not really, but go on," he said.

"I think you feel threatened by Lavalle," she said shrewdly.

"Threatened? Me?" Barry exclaimed, as if it were the most preposterous idea ever presented to him. "Out of the question. That young whippersnapper is barely out of the academy, barely out of his nappies for that matter. What could he possibly have on me?"

"Well, he's handsome," Val said, flashing a sideward grin at me. "Though not as furry as you, of course, Barry."

"Well," he spluttered, not knowing what to say. "Perhaps I prefer being the only man in the house. I don't see anything wrong with that. He's simply distracting you, that's all."

"You'll always be our number one, Barry, don't worry," I said, tongue in cheek. "Come on, we'd better prepare for our meeting with Ethel. Barry, we need you, too."

"Oh, won't Prince Charming himself bother to come along?" said Barry.

"No, he said he wanted to go to Colonel Warton's house again. You know, to try and track down that notebook. It's absolutely vital to the case."

He sighed as though it was a tremendous burden, though I could see he was pleased he would be coming along and Lavalle wouldn't.

It was strange thinking about Lavalle in those terms. But Val was right, of course. He was handsome. He took himself a little too seriously perhaps, but that was probably normal in his line of work. Looks alone, however, had never been as important to me as to Val. Not that she was superficial. She needed as deep a connection with human beings as any of us. But she certainly was a more visual person than I was, especially in the beginning. And she warmed up to men a lot faster than I did. It was odd but I always felt slow to trust. I had to get used to the idea first, on my own. But, with a curious pang in the region of my stomach, something told me that I was getting used to it a little too fast with Lavalle.

***

At five minutes past midnight, Barry, Val, and I stood in the pub's car park down in the village, shivering despite our thick coats. It was after closing hours for the pub, so only very few cars – including Tom's cab – were still here. Then I remembered that the very first time we came to Fickleton he had said he lived near the pub.

Ethel was late. I had brought my wand with me, just in case, tucked tightly into my inside pocket. I didn't really expect anything to happen, though you never knew. If Lady Worthington had found out that Ethel had arranged a meeting with us, she would have surely done everything in her power to stop her. Whether that entailed murder was another question, of course. One that I intended to find out eventually.

"I'm freezing," Val said.

"I'm not surprised," Barry said. "You only fell into the snow twice."

"Well, it's dark," she said. "I can't see so well when it's like this, even with the snow. I wish Ethel would hurry up."

"Strange that she picked this place to meet, though," I said. "I mean, it's off the main street, but it's pretty exposed to all the houses around here."

We waited another ten minutes without any sign of her. I was just about to say that we had better get back to Fickleton House when we spotted a small car pulling up to us. It stopped in the empty spot next to us, and Ethel got out of the driver's seat.

"Sorry I'm late," said Ethel, sounding out of breath. "I almost had a terrible car crash on the road just a few minutes ago."

"Are you alright?" Val asked.

"Yes. I was really lucky. My heart's still pounding. Anyway, I'm here now. So, what do you want to know?"

"Do you know where Lady Worthington went on the night the journalist was murdered?" I asked.

"Not exactly," Ethel said, looking around the car park as if to check that we really weren't being overheard. "I just heard a conversation between Sir Henry and her the morning after. They were talking about the arts fair."

She hesitated.

"You promise you will keep all of this to yourself?" she asked nervously.

"I promise," I said. "We just want to know who killed the journalist and Colonel Warton. Please, go on."

"Well," Ethel said. "I know it's wrong to eavesdrop but I – there have been a lot of strange things happening at Worthington Manor, you have to understand. Most of the staff are involved, as far as I can tell."

"Involved in what?" asked Val.

"It has something to do with art. Stolen art, if I'm not mistaken."

Val and I exchanged an excited look. We were finally getting closer to some answers.

"For the arts fair?" I asked.

"N-not entirely," she said nervously. "I think it's a lot more than that. They wouldn't dare place them all on display, of course. Lady Worthington is a collector, you have to understand. Sir Henry, too, but he's interested in antique musical instruments mostly. They have a huge arts collection in their basement, locked away. Very few people are allowed in there. It costs a lot of money, too, something they quarrel about all the time. I mean, they're rich, but even for them many of these works aren't affordable."

"And so they buy stolen art since the thieves are usually willing to sell it for a lot less money?" I said.

"Exactly," said Ethel. "That's what they call a 'bargain'.

It took me quite a while to understand what they meant by that. Anyway, on the night that… that poor woman died, Lady Worthington was out of the house. I knew because she always wants me to bring her a tea right before she goes to bed. She didn't that night, so I went to see whether she was there, but her bedroom was empty. And the next morning, she wouldn't tell Sir Henry where she had been. They had an argument, but she just wouldn't tell him. And that's strange, since they usually discuss all of their 'bargains' with one another."

"So you think she was up to something that even her husband would disapprove of?" I said.

"Yes," she said.

At that moment, there was a strange rustling sound, as though a tree had suddenly shook off all of its leaves. Yet there wasn't a single tree in the car park, notwithstanding a small hedge nearby. It was probably just an animal, I told myself, a stray dog or something like that. Barry, too, was quite unnerved and gave me a sharp look, clearly telling me to get to the point.

"Do you know who else might be involved? Someone from the village perhaps?" I asked.

Ethel rubbed her cheek with her right hand as if to soothe herself.

"I don't want to be walking around pointing the finger," she said.

"Please, Ethel," I said. "It might be important."

"Well, there is a man…" she said slowly, nervously bobbing to and fro on the spot. "I've never seen him up close, so I can't be sure whether it's who I think it is. But he's been to the house a few times. At the back entrance, the same way you came earlier today."

"Ethel, what was his name?" I said, steadying her by the shoulders.

She was just about to open her mouth when there was a flash of red light, like a beam out of a powerful laser.

Ethel's body suddenly became limp and heavy and collapsed into my arms.

CHAPTER 11

Val screamed. I let Ethel down quickly behind her car and felt her pulse.

"She's dead," I said, horrified.

"The killing curse," Barry said. "Quickly, after him."

I looked around wildly to see where the beam had come from. A man in a thick, dark overcoat was running towards the main street at top speed. He was holding something in his left hand which could only have been a wand. This was the sorcerer we had been looking for.

We sprinted after him, Barry at the front, as fast as we could. We reached the main street in a matter of seconds, but the man was no longer to be seen. The street was deserted.

"He's gone," I said, lowering my wand. "How could he have disappeared so quickly?"

"By magic, of course," said Barry dully.

"Oh, right," I said.

"What shall we do now?" Val said desperately.

"We need to get an ambulance. Perhaps they can do something for her," I said. "And then the police."

***

The ambulance took Ethel away. According to Barry, the chances of reversing the killing curse were zero, but it was important to let things proceed as normal. We sent Barry up to Fickleton House to tell Lavalle what had happened. The police arrived shortly after. And PC Bowler, who had arrived a little later, was making a real meal of it.

"Caught at the scene of the crime!" he bellowed.

"I wasn't caught," I said irritably. "I called the police

myself."

"Only a clever ruse to put us off the scent, no doubt," he said.

PC Bowler turned to one of his assistants.

"Take down this woman's story, will you?"

"I already have, sir."

"Oh, I see. Doctor's report?" PC Bowler grunted.

"Inconclusive, sir. Looks like heart failure so far. No external wounds, no injuries."

"But that's impossible," he said, gasping for breath as if someone had taken away his favourite toy. "Is that *all* you got me out of bed for?"

"I'm afraid so, sir."

Scowling intensely, he turned around to us.

"Alright, Missy. You might have somehow tricked the experts, but you're not fooling me. I know you're mixed up in this and I'm going to get to the bottom of this if it's the last thing I do."

"May we go now?" Val asked. "It's really cold."

"Alright, alright. You can go. Don't leave town."

"We certainly won't, constable. We'll see you at the fair," I said mockingly.

PC Bowler didn't answer but simply narrowed his eyes in utter contempt.

***

Half an hour later, we had all congregated in Lavalle's room, where he already had a fire burning. Val had made some of her favourite cocktails and we were all sipping at them in a contemplative mood, glad to be out of the cold and beside the warm fire but still shocked by what had happened.

"Poor Ethel," Val was saying. "And she was so close to telling us who had visited Lady Worthington's house."

"And she didn't tell you who it was?" Lavalle asked in

frustration for what felt like the hundredth time.

"No," said Val. "We told you, he killed her before she could say his name."

"At least we know he is male, though," I said. "That should cut our suspects down in half."

"It could still be an accomplice," said Barry, taking a sip from his gigantic magicarita. "If he visited Lady Worthington regularly, she is almost certain to be the head of the operation. In other words, we're looking for someone for delivery. Or perhaps a thief."

"Hold on," I said. "We've never thought of Tom before."

"What, the taxi driver?" asked Val.

"Yes."

"But... that's ridiculous," she said.

"Is it, though?" I said. "He can go pretty much anywhere he wants and just say he took a customer or something. He can park in all sorts of places without people getting suspicious."

"True," said Barry, warming to the idea. "He could be their delivery man. Ingenious. I doubt the police would ever stop him in that old-fashioned cab of his. Just doesn't fit the picture of a smuggler."

"Perhaps," said Lavalle, brushing his hair back with his right hand. "But it's still all speculation. We need solid evidence, especially in a court of magic. They won't stand for mere hypotheses."

"So what do you think we ought to do?" said Barry aggressively.

"Unless we uncover some more evidence, there's only one thing we can do," Lavalle said, pondering the issue. "We'll have to be ready at the arts fair. I'm sure that that is where our killer will strike next. And Lady Worthington has a real Van Gogh on show."

***

In the days leading up to the arts fair, Barry and I spent a lot of time upstairs in his study, practicing jinxes and counter-curses. You couldn't be too careful in preparing for the worst. And we were most likely going to face a most formidable sorcerer very soon. He had proven once already before our very eyes that he was willing to use the killing curse if he had to. And I didn't want to take any chances.

Val, meanwhile, had adapted very well to her psychic abilities. The day at the golf club had proven that she was now able to endure groups of people again, at least for a limited time. She would focus on the psychic angle, trying to isolate suspects and feel their emotions. Since we only had a lot of conjecture so far, her insights would be invaluable. Barry had promised to help her practice on the last day.

Barry himself would be our general lookout and spy. Luckily, I had already acquired somewhat of a reputation as a 'cat person' in the village, since I took Barry almost everywhere I went. I hoped that this apparent eccentricity would come in handy now, since fewer people would object to his presence. And unlike Val and me, he was free to roam around, keeping an eye on everything.

Lavalle, of course, was also going to be there. His MLE superiors had finally sent him some backup. It was none other than his older brother from the organised crime department, Alec. Despite our increasingly friendly conversations, I still had the feeling that he was holding back somewhat. Perhaps he didn't quite trust us yet – understandable in his profession. Or perhaps he was just cagey by nature, used to operating entirely on his own.

On the night before the arts fair, however, I thought I got a glimpse behind the mask. Barry was off downstairs helping Val, so Lavalle volunteered to practice jinxes with me. I was getting quite good at some of them, like the leg-locker hex that I thought might be useful in our attempts to apprehend the sorcerer. Others continued to elude me. What had seemed so easy after my first successes as a witch had radically changed. It was if I had climbed a hill only to find out that the mountains stretched on as far as the eye could see. A little dispiriting, to say the least.

Lavalle himself was an excellent teacher and clearly a gifted warlock as well. He had no trouble conjuring up shields to block my jinxes and hexes, though my disarming charms got through quite often.

"So strange," he said. "I don't usually fall for those."

"Must be the witch who's casting it," I said.

"Maybe," he said.

"Lavalle…"

"Please, Amanda, just call me Rick. That's what my friends call me."

"Do you do this often, Rick?" I asked.

"What?"

"Sleep at girls' houses during your investigations."

"It's not only girls in this place. Barry lives here, too," he said.

"Right you are again, detective."

Rick looked me straight in the eyes. His were a beautiful brown, like the fallen autumn leaves outside that were now covered with snow. Somehow, I hadn't noticed them like this before. And then, he leaned in closer to me, his face almost touching mine. I could smell his shaving lotion. But I stepped back, placing a hand on his chest.

"Please, Rick. This is all so sudden. I – a girl died. I-I just can't…"

"Of course, I understand," he said. "Don't worry."

He checked his watch.

"We'd better get some sleep. The fair starts early tomorrow."

"Yeah," I said, walking over to the door. "Goodnight, Rick. And thank you. For everything."

CHAPTER 12

On the day of the arts fair, Val, Barry, and I walked down together to the village. Rick – though I still called him Lavalle in front of the others for simplicity's sake – said he still had to prepare and would join us a little later. I had my wand tucked away safely in my handbag as usual. Extra training with Barry and Lavalle had certainly helped, but I still felt awfully unprepared somehow.

Once we arrived in the village community centre where the fair was to be conducted, it became instantly apparent that Lady Worthington had left no stone unturned in her attempt to make this an event to be remembered for a long time.

From the garlands decorating the various doorframes to the fresh flowers on the tables, everything was perfect. Refreshments and snacks were available at every corner, and the place was buzzing with volunteers, artists, and visitors from all across the country.

I came across Tom, the taxi driver, in the entrance area. Val had gone ahead with Barry for some refreshments. Tom was standing beside an elderly lady in a wheelchair.

"Oh, hello there," he said in a friendly manner. "Nice that you showed up. Though I must say I can't make heads nor tails of some of these things. This is Mrs. Wallis, by the way, one of my customers. I don't know whether you've met."

"How do you do?" I said.

"Do we know each other?" the elderly lady asked in a rather loud voice.

"I don't believe so," I said, raising my voice to match hers. "I'm Amanda."

She smiled in a slightly senile way.

"Good. I've got a nice picture, you know," she said.

"Oh, she doesn't need to see that," said Tom. "She's only just arrived."

"No, no," she said, rummaging in her handbag. "Here it is."

It was about the size of a palm, a beautiful carving of a man and a woman, embracing.

"A bit naughty," she said, giggling.

"Times have changed, Mrs. Wallis," he said, then turned to me. "Mrs. Wallis bought this picture from one of the local artists. He's upstairs right now, in fact. Excellent stuff."

"Yes, it looks good," I agreed.

Tom leant in a little closer so that nobody would overhear us.

"And between you and me," he said, indicating the carving in Mrs. Wallis's hand. "This is much better than most of the modern rubbish they call art in here."

"I see you've got yourself a picture, too," I said, pointing to the wrapped canvas leaning against the wall behind him.

"Yes, it's a surprise for my wife. A present for her birthday next week. She couldn't come today unfortunately. I promised to get her something."

"I see," I said.

I wasn't quite sure whether I believed him or not. It was all conjecture so far, of course, yet Tom *was* perhaps in the best position to smuggle art for Lady Worthington. I made a note of finding Val and asking her to try and find out what he was feeling.

As I browsed the various works of art on display, I had to admit that Tom had a point in regard to his reluctance to some of the pieces of art on display. Some were interesting, though others eluded me completely. I could simply never shake the feeling that there was an attempt to make something more meaningful than it actually was, to imbibe it with the label of art without really deserving it.

I wasn't here, however, to judge the art, I told myself. I kept my eyes open at all times, trying to register every suspicious movement. Many of the village regulars were present, as well as all of our remaining suspects.

Across the room, Reynolds and his girlfriend were apparently entranced by the art, though I strongly suspected that Reynolds was really here to be seen and, if possible, find a few more investors for his projects. His girlfriend Patricia was looking as stunning as ever by his side.

PC Bowler, in plain clothes, was also present. He looked strangely deflated, as if the lack of a uniform had sucked all the authority out of him. He was gazing long and hard at a home-made collection of pottery, frequently nodding his head at an item or shaking it at another.

Over in a remote corner, all by himself, I spotted the pub's landlord Charlie. He was deep in thought, staring at a painting that featured nothing more than two black lines and a red spot in the middle. I didn't want to disturb him, so I moved along, taking note all the same. After I had passed him, I wondered whether he had really been so entranced by the painting. It could just as well have been a clever ruse or even a form of meditation before a heist.

Of course, we were all waiting for the big moment when Lady Worthington was to reveal the Van Gogh painting. Currently, a large white sheet had been used to cover it from sight, adding to the mystery of it all. We had Barry check on it in frequent intervals, however, to see whether it was still there. To do this, he snuck underneath the sheet. Tom's wrapped package had made me suspicious, so I wanted to know whether the picture might have been removed beforehand. But every time Barry returned to us, he reported the same thing. The painting was still there; all was well.

Rick Lavalle had also arrived by now. My heart gave an involuntary jolt as I saw him enter, as if I had missed a step. He smiled at me and, as if controlled by some alien force, I returned it immediately. I felt silly though strangely elated at the same time. There was another man with him whom I didn't recognise.

"Hello Amanda," Lavalle said, after he had steered us to a deserted corner where we could talk more freely. "Valerie's already met him. We've just arrived. This is my brother Alec, from London. He's a private investigator attached to the organised crime department of the MLE."

The newcomer reached out an extremely gnarled hand, undoubtedly the result of many encounters with sorcerers.

"Nice to meet you," Alec said, shaking my hand firmly though without crushing it.

His voice was even deeper than Rick's, though it felt oddly reassuring as well. In looks, the family relation was certainly there, though with pointed differences. Alec kept his hair short in contrast to his brother's longer hair. He had a rugged look to him. All in all, he favoured practicality over Rick's smartness.

"Welcome to Fickleton," I said, smiling.

"Nice place," said Alec. "Are the suspects all accounted for?"

"Yes," I said. "We've seen all of them."

"Good," said Alec. "Now all we do is wait for the big moment. Might take a while."

Rick Lavalle looked strangely nervous around his brother. His gait had lost some of its spring, and he smiled less openly. I wondered whether they had quarrelled before. And sure enough, Rick excused himself, and went in the direction of the bathrooms.

"You know my brother well?" Alec asked me.

"Only a few days really," I said. "Since he's been on the case."

"Yes," Alec said. "He was rather eager to take it. Not really like him but I guess we all get excited for a case once in a while. Didn't even want me here to help out."

He chuckled.

"He… he didn't?" I said, bewildered.

"No. But don't be too hard on him. He doesn't like his older brother meddling, you see."

"But why not?" I asked. "The more wands the better, isn't that what's important?"

"Sure," he said, shrugging his shoulders. "But more wands also mean less credit. Good old Rick, he always was a career man. I always preferred freedom myself. Anyway, I don't mind. I'm doing the department a favour. If you want to remain a private eye in this business, you've got to keep the *Association* happy. And looks like you can use all the wands you can get. This sorcerer seems pretty vicious."

"Yes, he is," I said, thinking of poor Ethel again. "I'm glad you're here, Alec."

At that moment, Val came over to us.

"Hi, Amy. So you two've finally met?"

"That's right," I said. "Any news?"

Val shook her head.

"Nothing. Barry's been prowling around but he hasn't spotted anything so far either. I've talked to Reynolds briefly, Charlie, and the girl from the bakery. "

"Let's just keep our eyes open," said Alec. "You never know in this line of work. Might turn out to be someone you had never suspected before. Sometimes, you just get carried away."

"And what if nothing happens today?" Val asked.

"We'll find another approach," he said.

"The suspense is killing me," said Val nervously.

"You'll be fine. Just focus on what you've got to do," said Alec.

"Yeah, Val, I met Tom in the lobby," I said. "You could check on him if you like."

But then a gong sounded from the main room. It was time for the Van Gogh to be revealed. And so, finally, we all congregated around it. Lady Worthington, dressed in a magnificent silk dress all in white and black, gave a speech on the importance of Van Gogh. How he had been an inspiration to her from her formative years onwards and continued to be so until this very day.

In an imperial gesture, she beckoned one of the volunteers to step forward, evidently to remove the white cover when the time was right. The audience inched closer to get a better look. As they did so, the atmosphere in the room changed dramatically within a matter of seconds. Someone dimmed the lights in the room. People were craning their necks to get a better look, to see the real Van Gogh from as close as possible. Barry skidded towards us, his little paws constantly losing their footing on the slippery floor, but was almost trampled by the many feet surrounding us. I hastily lifted him up, placing him on my shoulder like a parrot so that he could get a better look.

"Did you check?" I whispered to Barry.

"Yes," he said softly. "Three minutes ago. All fine."

I could see Alec, who had positioned himself a little further away, in the direction of the exit. But Rick was nowhere to be seen.

"And so," Lady Worthington said at last. "It is with my greatest pleasure that I reveal to you 'Poppy Flowers' by Vincent Van Gogh!"

There was a great expression of surprise from the crowd but it died down almost instantly. The silence was so absolute that you could have heard a cat purring from fifty yards away. And then, Lady Worthington nodded. The volunteer gripped the white cover and, with a flourish, pulled it off.

But something had gone horribly wrong. There was no Van Gogh.

"It's just a white canvas," somebody from the crowd exclaimed.

Some people began to laugh, though others looked worried. Val and I looked at each other, horrified. Someone had stolen the painting from right under our noses.

"It's gone," Barry said. "That's impossible. I checked it right before she began her speech. That's simply impossible."

"We've got to find out who-"

Suddenly, there was a scream from outside. As fast as we could, we raced outside. Val, Alec, and Barry were sprinting alongside me. We skidded across the floor and reached the exit.

Mrs. Wallis, sitting in her wheelchair, was shaking uncontrollably. Tom, standing next to her, was trying to calm her down.

"Where is he?" I asked.

"Out there," Tom said, pointing. "In the car park. Your friend is already on his tails. Now, now, Mrs. Wallis, it's going to be alright…I'm going to take you home now."

Running full-speed across the car park was Rick Lavalle.

"Who is he chasing?" Val panted, squinting.

"It's Reynolds!" I exclaimed. "Quickly, we've got to help him."

Reynolds, dressed in his trademark white suit, was running towards his car at top speed. A picture with grey wrapping was pinned under his arm.

"He has the picture," I said. "Stop him!"

Alec Lavalle drew his wand at the same moment as I did. We didn't dare throw our jinxes, however, for Rick was far too close to Reynolds.

In a last desperate effort, Reynolds had reached his car and started the engine, pressing the accelerator so hard that his tires screeched as he pulled out of his parking spot.

"Look out, Rick," I yelled.

Reynolds scraped him with his left mirror, painfully hitting Rick on the thigh. He yelled in pain, now drawing his own wand and firing a hex wildly at the car.

But it was too late. Reynolds had already pulled onto the main street and was speeding off in the direction of the golf club. Rick fired another hex, which simply bumped off of the car's windscreen this time.

"Are you alright?" Val asked, as we approached him.

But Rick Lavalle, a fire burning in him that I hadn't seen before, wasn't listening. He turned around to the nearest vehicle, which happened to be a motorcycle, and pointed his wand at it.

"Initium," he bellowed.

The motorcycle immediately sprang to life. He jumped on it and roared onto the main road, in pursuit of Reynolds.

"Quickly, we need transport," said Alec.

I was about to point my wand at the nearest car, when he stopped me.

"We can't risk it, too many hebs."

"But your own brother…" I spluttered.

"… is crazy. We can't do it. Look."

He was right. Almost everyone from the fair had spilled out into the open to see what had happened. I turned around wildly. Tom was still calming Mrs. Wallis down. I quickly approached him.

"Tom, sorry, but can we have your car?" I asked.

"What?" he said.

"We need to catch the thief. It's Reynolds. He's got the Van Gogh. Please, we need to borrow your car."

"If… if you must, I…" he said, bewildered, fumbling for his keys. "Don't crash it, I love that car."

"We won't, I promise. Thanks, Tom."

We rushed over to where Tom had parked his cab. Hastily, I unlocked it.

"You sure you want to drive?" Alec asked.

"Yes," I said, though I hadn't driven for quite a while.

"OK," he said, getting into the passenger seat.

Val and Barry got into the back seat and I put the car into gear.

The roads were icy, and the car kept slipping away. The snow outside and the fact that we were all breathing fast didn't help either. The screens were so foggy I could hardly see what was in front of the car. Rick Lavalle must have been crazy to take a motorcycle in this weather, I thought.

"Where do you think Reynolds is headed?" Val asked.

"I don't know, but this is the road to the golf club," I said.

"Surely he wouldn't go home first?" said Barry disbelievingly.

"He might," said Alec in his deep baritone. "If he's prepared his escape properly."

I drove as fast as I dared on the icy roads for a few more minutes, with no sign of Reynolds's sports car or Rick and his motorcycle.

It turned out that Alec was quite right. When we were close to the golf club, we saw a large private helicopter on the pad next to the main entrance. That could only mean one thing: Reynolds had planned this all along. He was making his escape in the helicopter.

"Look, it's Lavalle's – sorry," said Val, with a glance at Alec. "I mean Rick's motorcycle. But where are they?"

I quickly parked the car on the side of the road. Suddenly, we heard the unmistakable noise that someone had started the helicopter. Reynolds was evidently already inside. We sped over as quickly as we could. And then we saw them. Reynolds and Rick were in the helicopter, fighting over the controls. It was looking bad for Rick, for Reynolds had the strength of a desperate man. Finally, Reynolds managed to kick Rick out of the door, slamming it closed behind him.

"Stop him," yelled Rick, as both Alec and I drew our wands.

I shot a hex at it, but narrowly missed. Alec landed a jinx, but again, as with the car, it simply bounced off the windscreen. He cursed loudly.

"Reynolds put a spell-repelling charm on it," he said. "We can't do anything."

The helicopter was already lifting off of the ground,

gaining altitude quickly. Reynolds was at the controls, his eyes bulging. He looked utterly crazed. The grey package was safely in his lap. He pulled up the helicopter, its propellers fighting violently against the ice-cold winds.

Rick, meanwhile, was back on his feet.

"My wand, where's my wand?" he screamed.

He found it seconds later in the snow nearby. He wasn't taking his defeat lightly, looking almost as mad as Reynolds did in the helicopter. He shot a few curses after it, but it was too far away by now. Next to me in the snow, there was another wand. This had to be the one that Reynolds used. I pocketed it for safe-keeping. At least Reynolds wouldn't be able to deal too much damage until he got another one.

"Rick," his brother said, forcing him to lower his wand. "You can't stop him now. It's over."

"No," Rick yelled, firing another curse into the air.

"Rick," his brother bellowed.

Rick seemed to coming to his senses again. He looked crushed, heart-broken even. And something within me, something compassionate, shifted. It was unbearable to see him in pain. After all our hard work, we didn't deserve this. Rick didn't deserve this.

"Look over there," Val said suddenly. "The helicopter. It's not… flying properly…"

We all swerved our heads, watching the now distant helicopter in the sky. Val was right. The propeller sounds were stuttering and Reynolds was apparently losing control of the machine. Then, the propellers died completely.

"It's dropping like a rock," I said, horrified.

Val closed her eyes as the helicopter dropped into the field below, exploding immediately on impact. Reynolds was dead. And the picture was lost.

CHAPTER 13

Thirty minutes later, PC Bowler was massaging his bushy moustache, taking notes. He hadn't even noticed the robbery and was the last person to have come out of the community centre. He was back in uniform now, however, and in full swing. We had made a full report – as far as it was possible without mentioning magic – to various officers of the police several times now.

"Well," PC Bowler said pompously. "That wraps it up then. Open and shut case. That lets you off the hook nicely, doesn't it, Missy?"

"Stop calling me that," I said irritably.

"It's over now. Lucky for you. I was just about to check on your plane ticket. But it doesn't matter now. We've got the guilty party. And we won't even need a trial."

"Are you finished?" I asked.

"Now, now. You can't rush the pursuit of justice. But I think we have all the information we need. Just for the records, anyway."

At that moment, PC Bowler's assistant – the one who had also been at the pub's car park – arrived.

"Yes, what is it?" PC Bowler demanded.

"They've recovered the body, sir," the young assistant said.

"Good, anything else?"

"They found the picture, too. Burnt almost to a crisp, sir. But some of the frame is still recognisable."

"Ah, well," PC Bowler said. "Can't have it all. Alright, lets wrap it up. You can go now, too, Missy."

***

An hour later, Val, Barry, Rick Lavalle, and I were once again sitting in front of a blazing fire in Fickleton House. Alec Lavalle had gone back to London again, though he had given me his card in case I needed to get in touch with him at short notice. Somehow, with the way the case had turned out, I didn't think so, but it was good to have it all the same.

Mrs. Faversham had made an excellent dinner, and nobody felt like moving very much after the events of the day. Rick would be staying one last night, a fact even Barry was too exhausted to complain about. Despite the food and the warmth, there was a distinct atmosphere of disappointment.

"That's it then," I said gloomily. "The painting's lost. And so is Reynolds. He won't be able to testify."

"Yes," Lavalle said. "But at least it's over now. We can all go back to our lives. He won't be able to harm anyone anymore."

"But he can't tell us anything about the art smuggling ring," I said.

"Is Lady Worthington going to get away with it, do you think?" Val asked Lavalle.

"No. I've been in contact with my superiors. They're going to ransack the place first thing tomorrow morning."

"That's what I don't understand, though," I said. "Why would Reynolds steal the painting from Lady Worthington? I mean, I thought they were in on the whole smuggling business together."

"Maybe Reynolds got tired of playing second fiddle?" said Lavalle. "Who knows. What matters is that we got the killer."

"What was he thinking anyway, taking the helicopter in that sort of weather?" Val asked.

"That has been bothering me, too," Barry said. "A sorcerer wouldn't have needed to do any of this. Why drive if you can take a broom and fly? Much safer."

"Maybe he didn't have a broom?" Val said.

"Plan an art heist of this kind and rely on heb transportation? Highly unlikely," said Barry.

"He was crazy, alright," said Lavalle. "Almost killed me with this thing."

He held up Reynolds's wand, the one I had found next to the helicopter pad.

"It was lucky you came out of there alive," said Val, nodding.

"Yes," said Lavalle. "I figured that I'd stand a better chance in a fist fight, so I went for him. Seems I was wrong. If only I had got him out of that helicopter…"

"You can't blame yourself," I said. "He was barking mad. He had the power of ten men."

"Yes," said Barry. "I've rarely seen someone so talented."

"That's high praise coming from you, Barry," said Val.

"It is," he said with no trace of false modesty. "And those spell-repelling charms he created on the car were exceptional. They're very difficult to pull off since they have to scale with the spell that hits them. And they get weaker with every successive hit. In other words, the cumulative protective force must be stronger than the energy that hits it."

"What shall we do with his wand, then?" I asked. "The one Reynolds dropped, I mean."

"Oh, I'll hand it over to the department," said Lavalle. "They collect these things, you know. Even if they're not needed for a trial."

"Will there be a hearing?" Barry asked.

"A brief one, I suspect," said Lavalle. "Just to wrap things up. Well, I suppose I'd better get an early night's sleep. Got to get up early in the morning. I've got Tom coming round to pick me up."

"Aren't you travelling the warlock way?" asked Barry.

"What's the warlock way?" I asked, bewildered.

"Flying by broom, of course," he said.

"The department insisted I use heb transportation," said Lavalle.

"It's a pity you can't stay longer," said Val.

I could see Barry silently protesting in the background. He had not enjoyed the disturbance that Lavalle had brought to the house. I was sorry to see him go, though a part of me was glad. I didn't think I could get involved with anyone right now, not even with Rick Lavalle. The events had shaken me up more than I liked to admit.

"Well, I'd better turn in," Lavalle said again. "Good night all."

We all wished him goodnight. I thought about going to bed myself but knew I wouldn't be able to sleep anyway. It was only 8 o'clock, after all. It looked as though Val and Barry felt quite the same way. The case, as PC Bowler had so clearly expressed, was open and shut. The culprit, Reynolds, had been caught. And yet, however much I tried, I just couldn't put it out of my mind.

"Something's not right about this case," I said broodingly, breaking a long silence.

"Yeah, Reynolds certainly was a maniac," said Val, yawning.

"No, no. I mean, there's something that keeps bothering me. I can't put my finger on it but…"

"Oh, Amy, just let go," said Val. "It's over."

Perhaps she was right. I tried focussing my brain on something else. Barry, Val, and I continued to sit there for I don't know how long. But I just wasn't able to shake the feeling that something was seriously wrong. And I had to get to the bottom of it. I had to make sure.

"I'm going out," I said suddenly.

"What, now?" Barry exclaimed.

"Yes," I said simply.

"Where are you going, Amy?" asked Val, looking a little worried.

"I'll tell you later," I said. "Just… just stay in here. I need to do this alone. I'll be back soon, I promise."

I must have been crazy to do this all on my own. Perhaps I was. But I had to find out whether my hunch was true. I took my coat and headed as quickly as I could through the snow to Mrs. Faversham's house, since she had the nearest phone I could use. I knocked on the front door. Mrs. Faversham appeared in slippers, evidently surprised to see me.

"Why, Miss Sheridan, to what do I owe the pleasure?"

"Sorry to bother you at this time, Mrs. Faversham. I need to make a phone call. Could I borrow your phone for a minute?"

"Why, yes, of course. Dear me, you do look serious. Is anything the matter?" she asked, concern stretched throughout her old face.

"Yes, thank you. I – I just need to make that phone call."

Mrs. Faversham, slightly bewildered, stepped aside. Her phone was an old-fashioned one with a sturdy grip where you still had to turn the wheel to dial.

"Tom's taxi, what can I do for you?" asked the taxi driver's familiar voice on the other end of the line.

"Hello, Tom, this is Amanda Sheridan. I wonder if you're free at the moment? I need to go to the golf club."

"The golf club? Alright. When would you like me to pick you up?"

"Right away, if that's possible," I said. "I'll wait for you at the front."

"Alright," said Tom. "See you in a bit."

***

Twenty minutes later, coat wrapped closely around me against the cold, I got out of Tom's now quite familiar cab in the golf club car park.

"Could you wait for me?" I asked. "It's only going to be a few minutes."

"No problem," he said. "I'm free all night so far."

"Great, thanks," I said.

I hurried over to the main entrance. The receptionist looked at me in a pleasant manner, so I decided to try my luck without a wand first.

"I need to see Patricia…" I began.

"I'm sorry, madam. She has asked not to be disturbed under any circumstances," the receptionist said.

"Fine," I said under my breath.

What had I ever done before to extract information from people, I wondered. I took out my wand and quickly pointed it at her. Less care was needed, as the lobby was almost completely empty.

"Gratus," I said.

"Miss Patricia Redgrave is in the residential suite. Third floor, to your right and at the end of the corridor."

"Thank you," I said.

I headed for the open elevator and pressed the number three. There were hardly any guests around. Perhaps they had heard what had happened and left. Or they had returned home to their families for Christmas.

I reached the third floor and followed the corridor to the residential suite. A light was burning inside. I gently knocked on the door.

"Leave me alone," came the unmistakable voice of Patricia from the other side.

"It's Amanda Sheridan. It's very important."

"I don't' care," she said. "Go away."

"Patricia, I don't believe Derek Reynolds was guilty. I'm here to clear his name."

There was a pause, then a rattling of keys, and the door to the room swung open. Patricia looked a wreck, which was completely understandable, of course.

"What did you just say?" she said, wiping tears from her

eyes.

Her breath smelled strongly of alcohol. And she was evidently having trouble focussing me properly

"I don't think your boyfriend was guilty," I said. "But I need to speak to you to prove it."

"You really mean that?" she asked. "You're not a reporter or… or something like that?"

"I swear," I said.

She stepped aside, allowing me to enter. Judging from the crumpled pillows and bedsheets, Patricia had been in bed before I had knocked. On the nightstand, there was a large bottle of clear vodka. It was half empty. As was to be expected, she had taken the news very badly.

"I – I thought you were the police at first. They called on me. Asked me a lot of stupid questions about… him."

"I'm very sorry for your loss, Patricia," I said. "I believe that there is reason to believe that your boyfriend Derek Reynolds was framed and then murdered."

"W-what?" she asked, staring at me in disbelief.

"He has been accused of stealing pieces of art, now including the Van Gogh from the arts fair, correct?" I asked.

"But I told them it wasn't true," she said, starting to cry. "H-he didn't do any of those things."

"Yes. I think the person who actually committed those crimes killed Derek Reynolds. But I have no proof. It's all conjecture. It's been that way from start to finish."

"What do you want to know?" she said, wiping away her tears again.

"That night – when he went to see the journalist -"

"How did you know that?" she asked, flabbergasted.

"It doesn't matter now. But did he see anyone else there?"

She thought for a while.

"I didn't like speaking about it. He hurt me deeply with what he did. But he was a good man. He tried to set things r-right."

"Yes, but did he see anyone else there?" I asked again.

"I-I wouldn't k-know," she said, though her voice shook as she did so.

"How did you know that he had seen the journalist?" I asked.

"He – he just…"

"You were there, weren't you?" I said. "You followed him that night after you had a row in that Italian restaurant."

She broke down in tears, bobbing uncontrollably to and fro. I laid my arm around here, trying to comfort her. After a few minutes, she felt strong enough to speak again.

"Yes, I followed him. I saw him go into the back of the pub. There's an extra s-staircase there. He didn't want to be seen by anyone in the pub. And I saw him come out again. I waited all that time, hidden in the car park."

"And was there anyone else present?"

"I-I can't remember. I was so upset that he would do such a thing. W-Wait. There was someone. He bumped into Derek on the way out. But it was all very brief. I didn't think about it at the time at all."

"Can you describe this person?"

She nodded.

"I think so."

***

A few minutes later, I was back downstairs in the lobby. There was only one more thing I had to do. There was a payphone at the back, near the restaurant. I took out the business card that Alec Lavalle had given me in case of any developments. I needed him back here as soon as possible.

"Alec Lavalle, PI," he growled into the phone.

"Hello, Alec, this Amanda. Something's come up. Something big. I know it's on a very short notice, but can you come over?"

"Right now?" he said.

"Yes. It can't wait I'm afraid."

He breathed into the phone.

"OK, I'll hop on the broom immediately. Should take me a bit over an hour."

"All the way from London in this weather?"

"I've got a fast broom. I'll meet you at the house," he said and hung up.

I stepped back outside into the snowy cold. Tom was waiting for me, as promised. I got into the cab, which had cooled off quite a bit in the meantime.

"Sorry for taking so long, Tom," I said.

"You've got everything you wanted?" he asked.

"Yes, all fine."

He started the engine and pulled out into the main road.

"Strange affair, wasn't it? At Lady Worthington's arts fair, I mean. I've heard she's still devastated."

"I can imagine," I said. "Is your wife any better?"

"Oh, yes. You know, it was funny. Remember that picture I bought her?"

"Yes, I remember," I said.

"Well, I put it in the car after we were done. Drove home and put it safely in my room. And what do you know? Next day it's gone. Not a trace. I thought at first my wife had got it and was playing a trick on me."

He laughed throatily.

"But she didn't know anything either. Funny, isn't it?"

"Yes," I said. "It certainly is. Who sold you the picture?"

"Oh, a visiting artist, Kessel, I think the name was. Something German. He had his own booth."

"Did you… see him wrap the paper around the picture?"

"Wrap the paper?" he said, sounding slightly perplexed. "As a matter of fact I didn't, come to think of it. He said he needed some paper and had to get it from the storage room. I waited, and when he returned it was already wrapped. Why, is it important somehow?"

"Yes," I said. "I think it's very important. I believe you inadvertently helped our murderer and art thief smuggle Vincent Van Gogh's masterpiece out of the community centre, unnoticed. And when you had unknowingly brought the Van Gogh to the safety of your own home, our thief and murderer broke in and retrieved it. The perfect heist."

"But Mr. Reynolds…" he began.

"… was innocent," I said. "The real killer and thief is still at large. And I think I now know who it is."

CHAPTER 14

Tom dropped me off at Fickleton House. It wouldn't be long before Alec would arrive. I only hoped he wouldn't be too late. Time was of the utmost essence. The snow was falling more heavily than ever. It wouldn't have surprised me if he had been delayed. Fast broom or no fast broom.

I could see the light burning in the sitting room downstairs. It seemed Barry and Val were still up. I let myself in through the front door and closed it behind me. Once more I walked through the long corridors, passing the spot where I had first seen Barry on my very first day here. It was odd that this place had so quickly become a home to me when it often took me months to get used to a new flat. But the house had a personality of its own, with its quirks and its sounds and its history that were unique.

I opened the door to the sitting room. Val had fallen asleep near the fire, which was low but still burning, and Barry was sitting on her lap. He peeked up his head immediately as I entered the room.

"Oh, it's you, Amy. Lavalle is looking for you."

"Alec?" I asked.

"Alec? No, Rick, of course."

"Oh," I said. "What did he want?"

"I don't know," said Barry unhelpfully. "But he went out again."

"What's wrong, Barry? Are you mad at me?" I asked.

"Of course I am. Running off on your own like that. It's stupid, even dangerous."

Val was slowly waking up now.

"Dangerous? Did someone say dangerous?" she said drowsily.

"It was worth it, Barry. I think I know who it is."

140

"What do you mean?" asked Barry. "We know who it was. It was Reynolds."

I quickly explained what had happened, how I had interrogated Patricia. I also told him of Tom's wrapped picture he had bought at the fair.

"You don't mean they smuggled it out using Tom as a courier, do you?" asked Val.

"They used him as an unwitting accomplice, yes. After all, our murderer wanted the picture above all else. And the opportunity was perfect."

"So, this German artist was in on it?" asked Barry, frowning.

"That or he was hexed into helping," I said. "Either way, it was a good way for our killer to stay out of the limelight while making sure he got the picture out safely. He could then easily retrieve it later by breaking into Tom's house. Tom is very talkative. Anyone who took a taxi would have no trouble finding out where he lived or what his routine looked like. Then, it was only a matter of evading his wife at home. And that is exactly what happened."

"But why do it like that?" asked Val. "I still don't understand."

But comprehension was gradually dawning on Barry.

"Yes, brilliant," he said, smacking his paw on the armrest. "If you swapped the Van Gogh for a counterfeit at the right time, it would have taken an art expert to tell the difference. And that is, unfortunately, not one of my qualities. At least not yet."

"Yes, but if you remember, it was a blank canvas when Lady Worthington uncovered it," said Val.

"A simple, timed dissolving charm could have easily done that," said Barry. "Pretty basic magic."

"But why?" asked Val. "Why not leave the counterfeit in plain sight and get out with the picture? It would have taken hours before someone examined the picture more closely and noticed a difference."

"Because that wasn't all our friend was after," I said, pacing the room. "You know what always bothered me about this case? The missing connection to Lady Worthington. She helped traffic the goods and bought a lot of stolen art herself, and yet it was *she* who had in turn been robbed at the arts fair. There had to be a connection, but I didn't understand it until just a few minutes ago. Why, for instance, had Lady Worthington threatened to kill that journalist, Michelle Nosworthy?"

"Probably because she found out something about her stolen art collection," said Val.

"I think," I said, "more specifically it had to do with how it was acquired and redistributed. That information was dangerous. And our murderer was also implicated. He had to remove her as quickly as possible. He couldn't have known, of course, that Patricia Redgrave would see him while she was spying on her boyfriend at the pub. But then an idea must have struck him. He had found out in the meantime about Reynolds's affair and was determined to pin the whole thing on him."

"Who else knew about the affair, though?" asked Val.

"I'll get there in a minute, Val. Just imagine, you can get the Van Gogh, free of any inquiry because the perpetrator has been killed and the painting unfortunately perished in the flames of that helicopter. Quite convenient, don't you think?"

"You mean the whole thing was staged?" said Barry.

"That's right," I said.

"But who staged it?" asked Val.

"Well, can't you think of anyone?" I asked. "Who knew of Reynolds's affair? We found that out. Who knew Colonel Warton acted in a suspicious manner in regard to the notebook and thought he might have it in his possession? We did."

"And shortly after he was killed, with no notebook to be found…" said Barry, his face darkening.

"Exactly," I said.

"But that's ridiculous, Amy," said Val. "It can't have been any of us three."

"It wasn't," I said. "Which leaves only one person who could have possibly done it."

"Rick Lavalle," Barry breathed.

At that moment, the door behind us gently swung open. It was Rick, holding a wand in his hand. He was wearing a curious smile on his face.

"Well done, Amanda," he said quietly. "I'd clap for you, but I prefer to keep this wand pointed at you at all times."

"*You* are the sorcerer," said Barry, jumping from Val's lap onto the floor. "*You* killed those people."

"A masterpiece, was it not?" he said.

"But why?" said Val.

But I thought I already knew.

"He told us right at the beginning, Val," I said. "He said that sorcerers don't need to steal money, they can simply conjure it up. But you can't do that with real art. It's unique."

"Precisely," said Lavalle, his lips curling into an evil smirk.

"How long have you been in the art-smuggling business?" I demanded. "Are you even a real MLE agent?"

"Oh, yes," he said. "Yes, I still have my badge if that's what you mean. A rather tiresome job I had often thought of leaving behind me. Until I came across Lady Worthington. She had quite the network going, you know. She was a heb, but all the more useful to me. I worked for her for a while, getting to know the important contacts."

"But Michelle Nosworthy had found out about it, hadn't she?" I said.

"Yes," he said, his face contorting into a look of hatred. "She was about to expose me and the entire network. I couldn't let her do that. I had to silence her."

"But the notebook was gone," I said. "And that's where

she had put all her information."

"Clever girl," said Rick Lavalle. "Yes, it was gone when I arrived. Someone must have taken it just seconds earlier. I must say, I was very grateful to you when you told me about Colonel Warton. And you were right, of course. He had stolen it. I searched his place and found the notebook. Naturally, he had read the whole thing, so I had to make sure the paranoid old fool couldn't tell anyone."

"So you bewitched his own dogs to kill him," I said grimly. "You evil…"

"Oh, but you mustn't be sensitive about these things, Amanda," Rick Lavalle said, laughing. "It's the daring and the flawless execution of the plan that really matter. Just think of how close you were to finding out my identity when you met Ethel in the car park. My timing was perfect. A masterpiece of crime. Unique even, you might say. Like a work of art."

"I should have known you were no good after Ethel died," I said. "No normal person would have made advances after something like that had happened. Only a psychopath would."

"Ah, well," he said. "That is your definition of 'normal', not mine. In any case, I have no interest in *being* normal. Would anyone but an exceptional sorcerer have carried out the plan at the arts fair? How I switched the pictures so that good old Tom could carry the real Van Gogh out for me? And even in the unlikely event that they caught him, there was no way of tying it back to me."

"And you needed a scapegoat," said Barry angrily. "So you blamed it on an innocent person."

"You say innocent, yet I think you would have seen it quite differently if you had read what Miss Nosworthy had to say about Reynolds and his shady business dealings. But yes, I needed someone to take the blame. Reynolds was the perfect target since you already suspected him. The heb police would also be satisfied. I bewitched the car to repel jinxes just in case. And then, I waited for my plan to unfold. I placed a control charm on Reynolds while you were all watching Lady Worthington and gave him a wrapped canvas that roughly fit the size of the real Van Gogh. I made him flee the premises and tore after him just at the right moment, for all the world to see what a dutiful MLE agent I was."

"And you took the motorcycle so that we wouldn't be able to follow," said Val.

"Quite right. I needed time. Time to prepare to kill Reynolds. He was still under my control, though the distance made it difficult. We nearly crashed multiple times on the road. But we managed to get to the golf club. I made the helicopter spell-repellent and dropped a spare wand in the snow for you to find. You were so desperate for clues, after all. So I decided to provide you with one."

I heard a faint thud in the snow outside, but Lavalle wasn't paying any attention.

"The heb police bought the whole thing immediately, of course," Lavalle continued. "Few people liked Reynolds. And they were glad to wrap the whole thing up. And now, the real Van Gogh is mine. But it isn't going to end here. Lady Worthington has many more masterpieces of art in her cellar. And the good thing is that she won't be able to go to the police when they're gone. That's where I'll be going tonight, in fact. As you can see, it is the perfect crime."

"Not quite so perfect," I said. "We found you out."

"A slight error," he said casually. "One I intend to correct immediately, however. You were a little too curious for your own good. But as they say, curiosity killed the cat. Say goodbye, Amanda Sheridan. It was nice knowing you. A pity we didn't kiss."

He raised his wand, pointing it directly at my heart in preparation for the killing curse. But at that moment, Barry catapulted himself forward, lodging his razor-sharp teeth into Rick Lavalle's thigh. The latter cried out in pain, while the red beam of his curse missed me by inches as his arm jerked upwards. Val and I reacted at once. We hurled ourselves on him, while Barry bit his hand until he relinquished hold of the wand.

And then, the door to the room opened once more. Finally, Alec Lavalle, drenched from head to toe, had arrived. He was wearing a grim face as he saw the scene before him. He pointed his wand at his own brother.

"That's enough, Rick," he bellowed. "Rick! Let them go."

But all three of us, plus Barry, were wrestling relentlessly on the floor. Despite our numbers, Rick was gaining the upper hand. Alec lowered his wand and blasted us apart, making me hit the wall with a painful smack. Rick, sensing his chance, desperately clambered for his own wand which was only a few inches away, but Val kicked it just in time as Rick bent down to retrieve it, sending the wand flying to the other side of the room. Rick Lavalle tore after it on all fours.

"Catena!" boomed Alec's voice.

His wand emitted a long, heavy chain that quickly wrapped itself around Rick, who skidded to a stop on the floor, unable to move another inch.

"That's better," Alec growled. "Now, what's going on?"

And then, we told him the entire story. Alec stood there, face growing paler and paler. Even for him, it was hard to believe that his own brother was responsible for such heinous crimes.

"Alec," Rick pleaded, struggling against his bindings. "They're lying. It's all nonsense. It was Reynolds."

"I've heard enough, Rick. You're coming with me."

"But… but you're my brother," said Rick.

Alec merely looked at him in disgust.

"Enough," he said.

Then, Alec turned to me.

"I'll take him straight to London. I'll let you know when we arrive. You take care of yourself now."

"We will. Thank you, Alec."

Alec opened the door. His brother Rick looked daggers at me as he tried to get up, but he stumbled and fell each time. Alec raised his wand once more and levitated his brother through the door and into the corridor. Alec nodded one last time to us. And then, they were gone.

For a few minutes, we were lost for words, until Val finally gave me a long and hard hug.

"You've solved it, Amy," Val said, beaming. "You did it!"

"We all did, Val," I said, beaming back.

"Hey, what about the picture?" said Val suddenly. "The Van Gogh, it must be…"

"Let's check Rick's room," said Barry.

***

And sure enough, as we scoured through his things upstairs, opposite Barry's library, we found the Van Gogh, safe and sound, carefully wrapped in grey paper. We found the journalist's notebook, too, though some of its pages had been ripped out – probably by Colonel Warton in the attempt to destroy the information that Michelle Nosworthy had gathered on him.

"Remind me to send this to Alec in London," I said. "I'm sure they can apprehend Lady Worthington with this information. As well as strengthen the case against Rick Lavalle."

"You know, I always had a bad feeling about that bloke," said Barry, stroking his whiskers in a self-congratulating manner.

"Alright Barry, you *were* right. Happy?" I said, laughing.

"Not quite," he said. "You promised me that cocktail party. It's Christmas Eve tomorrow, after all."

CHAPTER 15

Two days later, on Christmas day, I still couldn't believe what Rick Lavalle had done. With all the preparation for the cocktail party, there seemed to have been some sort of delay in realisation. I was too busy to really think about it, I suppose. Or perhaps I just preferred to *be* busy so I wouldn't have to. We had been looking for the murderous sorcerer all over the village, except of course within our own walls. And he had played his part like a master, up to the very end.

Barry and Val, though both shaken by events, had recovered much quicker, at least from what I could tell. Barry – sedentary even by feline standards – was glad to be able to get back to his research instead of 'gallivanting across half the country', as he called it. Secretly, I think, he was also glad that justice had been served and that Rick Lavalle would be placed on magical trial in London. Still, the irksome duty of catching the killer had been lifted from his shoulders. Barry was now free to focus his attention on other things again, like perfecting his automatic massage charm for the sofa in his library.

Val was determined to hone her skills as a psychic even further. It had been a shock to her, especially, that she hadn't been able to detect Lavalle's true intentions from the start, though I strongly suspected that even seasoned psychics would have been fooled by him. Barry, as an experienced warlock, didn't seem in the least surprised that she hadn't, though he promised to practice with her more often.

Undoubtedly, Rick Lavalle had had a special knack for affecting and manipulating the people around him. Barry, as I'm sure he would remind us for a very long time to come, had indeed distrusted him from the start, though for more selfish reasons than he now admitted. And it was certainly true that Lavalle had successfully evaded Val's sensors. But psychic or no psychic, I felt it was much worse with me. I had not only *not* suspected him, but I had confided in him, even trusted him. The horrible truth was that he had charmed me. However brief that connection had been, there was no denying it, and I felt sick when I thought about it. How could I have been taken in by a homicidal sorcerer? I'd be wrestling with that question for quite a while, I was sure.

In the meantime, however, it was Christmas. I owed it not only to myself but especially to both Val and Barry to pull myself together. There would be enough time to brood and feel sorry for myself in the new year. I tried to bring myself back to the present. I still had to clear away the cocktail glasses in the sitting room downstairs.

The cocktail party the previous day had been quite the success. Many of the villagers, curious to see Fickleton House and its new inhabitants, had flocked up the hill through the light cover of snow to our doorstep. I recognised most of them from the arts fair, though I had had little time to get to know them properly then. Val had modified her recipe for a White Russian cocktail, so that Barry could slurp it from his bowl as if it were milk. And so, we had spent a long and pleasant evening at Fickleton House. It was our first party here, though I was sure it wouldn't be the last.

Now, however, we had to clean up the considerable mess. I scooped up the remainder of the glasses, placed them all on a tray, and then made for the kitchen. Val was doing the washing up. She had somehow got some hot water going, and the entire room was full of steam and soap bubbles. I was just about to enter the kitchen when I stumbled over something furry and was barely able to keep the tray from crashing to the floor.

149

"Careful!" came Barry's resentful voice from below me. "You're upsetting the post."

"Sorry, Barry," I said. "Didn't see you there. What on earth…?"

Barry, wearing his reading spectacles, had placed at least two dozen letters on the ground in the corridor, just outside of the kitchen door.

"Barry's been reading the mail for me," said Val. "Thought it'd save some time. We haven't checked it since we got here, you know."

"Oh, right," I said. "Anything for me?"

"Just some letters from the bank, the MLE – full of snivelling apologies no doubt," Barry said, throwing it on the ground in contempt.

He still hadn't forgiven the MLE that the only agent they had sent here had turned out to be the murderer himself. And for once, Val and I wholeheartedly agreed with him. Barry rummaged around in the pile with his paw and retrieved a purple envelope, squinting his eyes to read the tiny yet neat handwriting.

"This one's from the Royal Committee for the Preservation and Restoration of Lighthouses."

"The what?" asked Val over the noise of clunking cutlery and glasses.

"Quite a mouthful," I said. "What do they want?"

Barry smartly slid his claw along the edge of the envelope, producing a folded letter from within.

"What does it say?" I asked curiously.

"Oh, just some tosh about old lighthouses," said Barry dismissively. "Your great-aunt was apparently a member of their committee. And they want you to step in for her. Bunch of lighthouse loonies, if you ask me. Well, one more for the rubbish heap, then."

He threw it onto the pile with the MLE letter.

"Hold on, Barry," I said, picking up the letter.

I quickly scanned it. Judging from the rough paper and

imprints, it had probably been typed on an old-fashioned typewriter. It appeared that my great-aunt had not only been part of the committee but was also one of its founding members. The letter sounded desperate, almost pleading. The Royal Committee for the Preservation and Restoration of Lighthouses had evidently seen better days.

"They're inviting me to attend their annual meeting," I said. "In two months' time."

"Where exactly?" asked Val.

I browsed the contents of the letter again.

"*On a cosy little island off the west coast of Scotland*," I read. "They've got a small hotel there. Doesn't sound too bad."

"You're not actually thinking of going there, are you?" said Barry.

"Why not? It's not like Amy's going to run into another sorcerer there," said Val, laughing. "I mean, that would really be bad luck."

"Exactly," I said. "And you're coming with me, of course. Both of you. We could all do with a little trip. And forget about this… this whole affair."

"I'm in," said Val enthusiastically, taking off her rubber gloves and smacking them down, sending a dried cocktail glass back into the soapy water.

But Barry simply made a series of grumbling noises.

"Oh, come on, Barry," I said. "It's only for a few days."

"The thing I hate most is water," he said darkly. "Right after Scotsmen, that is."

"Barry," said Val. "Don't be a spoilsport."

"*You're* spoiling my research," he said grumpily.

"We won't go if you won't come with us," said Val flatly. "Won't we, Amy?"

"That's right," I said, grinning. "We'll get our own car, Barry. You can take all the research you like along with you. And all the tuna cans we can fit into the boot."

He looked at us for a moment with narrowed eyes.

"Alright, alright," he said finally. "You win."

"We *all* win, Barry," said Val, bending down and affectionately patting him on the head. "It's going to be fun."

"Of course," he said sarcastically. "What could possibly go wrong when we're stuck on a remote island in the middle of nowhere?"

"Well," I said. "We'll just have to find out."

No Cat Is
An Island

T.H. Hunter

CHAPTER 1

Peter Asquith drew his coat up to protect his face against the vicious winds that sprayed the little boat with sea water. He gripped the rudder tighter in his hand, making sure to keep his wand in his other pointed straight at the little cove of the island ahead. It wouldn't do to get swept off into the icy Atlantic in this weather.

From afar, he could see a light burning at the top of the lighthouse, its powerful beam warning passing ships not to approach the treacherous rocks below. As he approached the cove, which provided shelter from the wind, Peter Asquith performed a minor levitation charm on the boat, which carried him slowly across the dark sand until he was safely ashore.

This, he thought grimly, was the easy part. Whoever had been tampering with the magical source still had to be on the island. He kept his wand at the ready, just in case. His mission, given to him by MLE headquarters in London, was simple: investigate the site and, if necessary, arrest the tamperers. His wife, Emily, had been opposed to the job, but he had managed to persuade her eventually. Now, however, he thought she might have been right all along. Something felt very wrong about this place.

As he walked up the hill and approached the lighthouse, he could sense the magical power emitting from it. It seemed remarkable that – even in these remote parts off the west coast of Scotland – such energy had not been discovered and harnessed by the *Spellcasters' Association*. Instead, it had been left to the hebs – the non-magical population.

Finally, he reached the entrance to the lighthouse. Wand at the ready, he carefully stepped in through the open door and found himself facing a spiral staircase made of metal.

As he placed his right foot onto the first step, it emitted an ominous clanging noise that reverberated throughout the lighthouse. He froze, holding his breath. It would not do to advertise his presence here so foolishly.

Then, he heard several voices from above. At first, he thought his fear had been realised, but after a few moments it became clear that they were arguing.

"Get your dirty hands off, I tell ya," one of the voices thundered.

There was the scuffling of feet, and a man cried in pain. Silence followed. Peter Asquith tore up the stairs as fast as he could until he reached the uppermost level. At the top of the stairs, a door stood ajar. He stretched out his hand and pushed it open, clenching his wand tighter than ever.

He entered a large, circular room. In the middle stood the lamp, which sent out its powerful beam to the sea beyond. At the foot of the lamp, a massive man was crouched over something on the ground, his mane of red hair obscuring most of his face. His hands were like dustbin lids, and his arms would have been more befitting for a gorilla, though his head looked peculiarly small in contrast. The visible skin looked rough and leathery. He was breathing fast, as though he had just raced a great distance.

"What is going on here?" Peter Asquith demanded, trying to keep the panic out of his voice as best he could.

The large man turned around slowly, his mane of red hair slowly revealing a red face and bloodshot eyes with heavy bags beneath them. He was wearing a peculiar look, as though caught between a sense of wonder and aggression. Slowly, he got up. He must have been well over six feet. Peter Asquith's eyes flickered to the floor for a moment, and to his horror he saw a body of another man, lying there perfectly motionless.

"He… he rushed at me," the man in front of him said gruffly. "It was self-defence."

"That is not for me to decide," Peter Asquith said,

though privately he didn't believe a word of it. "Step aside. We need to get him to the mainland immediately."

But the man in front of him wouldn't budge.

"Are you the police?" he asked.

He was of sorts, of course, but vows of secrecy prevented him from revealing that he was a magical law enforcer.

"Does it matter? Now, move over."

"You don't look like police," the man said quietly. "You're here for *it*, aren't you? You want to steal it from me."

"What are you talking about?" asked Peter Asquith impatiently, still holding his wand as tightly as possible.

"He wanted it, too," the man said, nodding his head at the body lying at his feet. "Wanted it all for himself. But it's mine."

"Step aside from the body. This is my last warning."

"Or what?" the brute of a man scoffed. "You'll poke me with your stick? I'll kill you first."

"Stand back, I warn you!"

But the man began walking towards him, a vicious leer on his face.

"Electrica!"

Peter Asquith's aim, honed through years of service to the MLE, was true. Lightning sparks shot out his wand and landed square on the man's torso. He bellowed in pain but, to Peter Asquith's utter amazement, kept walking towards him. The spell he had cast was enough to subdue even an elephant. Yet here this man was, walking steadily towards him as if he had only received a pin prick.

Peter Asquith was so taken aback that he cast the imprisoning spell a fraction of a second too late. The brute facing him had dodged it and was running towards him. Peter Asquith tried to reach the door. But it was too late. With a final leap, the massive man had closed the distance and hurled himself on top of him, knocking the wand out of his hand as he did so. Peter Asquith was holding on for dear life, but the force of the charge had knocked all the air out of his lungs. He was fighting as best he could, but his adversary had the strength of ten men. And then, a massive hand had closed around his throat, squeezing the last vestiges of life out of him. The room was beginning to spin, it was whirling, until it faded into darkness.

CHAPTER 2

"Can't we listen to something less infuriatingly modern for a change?" came Barry's dulcet tones from the back of the car.

"It's The Beatles, Barry, they're not exactly recent," I said, winking at Val who was sitting next to me. "Anyway, we should be there soon. We've just crossed the border into Scotland."

Val, who hated driving herself, was acting as my chief navigator. Now that Val and I had decided to keep Fickleton House, which I had inherited from my great-aunt – along with my magical powers – I had finally bought my own car a few days into the new year. A small, purple Peugeot.

After the string of murders and the events at the arts fair before Christmas, Val and I were in dire need of a holiday. The invitation from the Royal Committee for the Preservation and Restoration of Lighthouses had been the perfect excuse to get away for a few days. Though it was still cold at this time of year, the proximity to the sea and the fresh, salty air would do us all some good – a fact even Barry, our resident cynic and warlock-turned-cat, couldn't deny – despite his best efforts to the contrary.

"About forty miles to go," said Val, checking her phone for the route ahead.

"Yes, a pity we won't be able to fit in another opera by then, Barry," I said. "Wagner's *Valkyrie* will have to wait a bit."

"Evidently," came Barry's voice from the backseat. "Your cultural enrichment will have to wait a little longer, then."

"Barry," said Val in exasperation. "I've brought my

headphones. You can listen to Wagner in the hotel on your own time, for a change. Without terrorising us."

"A good idea – considering we're going to be staying for a whole week in the middle of nowhere," he said snidely. "Surrounded by nothing but water and Scotsmen. And I still don't know which is worse."

"Oh, stop moaning, Barry," I said, laughing.

"It's not going to be so bad," said Val, who always looked on the bright side of things. "We've brought enough books along with us. You can continue with your research, Barry."

"If I can concentrate with all those sheep bleating in the background," Barry said sniffily. "You know that my research – magical progress – requires a maximum of silence."

"Strange," said Val. "The sound of you eating my biscuits doesn't seem to stand in the way of progress much."

"A cat has to eat, you know," he said.

"Well, you two can just relax," I said. "It's me who has to attend all those committee meetings. I wonder what that's going to be like."

"Did they say anything more specific on the phone?" Val asked.

"No. Mrs. Highgarden – that's the committee's president – simply gave me the hotel's address and thanked me for stepping in for my great-aunt."

"But it's alright that we're coming, too, right?" asked Val for what felt like the hundredth time.

"Yes, Val," I said. "I told you. Everything's been taken care of. Barry isn't allowed inside the rooms, of course. She said there was a kennel outside, though."

Val and I had been teasing him for almost the entire trip with this. In reality, of course, I had made sure that we had a nice couch in one of the rooms just for him.

"If that is how you care to treat your magical mentor,

Amanda," Barry said, "so be it. Personally, I think a little more gratitude would be in order. Especially after I practically solved the last case."

"*You* solved it?" said Val in disbelief. "Amy got that girl to talk at the end, Barry. We were both sleeping in front of the fire when it happened!"

"Well, I had my suspicions, anyway," he said, poking his head between our two seats. "Any more of those sweets left?"

"Empty," said Val, showing him the plastic bag. "But we'll make you some nice tuna when we get there, Barry."

***

The sky was still covered in grey as we saw the sea for the first time, though it still looked magnificent to say the least. The beautiful coast line of Scotland's south west was a treat in and of itself. We were heading steadily west now, and although I had been driving for hours, the prospect of spending a week here kept me excited and fresh. Val had packed half the house, or at least it felt that way, as she wasn't sure 'what kind of food they'd have up here'. So, if the worst came to the worst and we were caught in a storm, at least we wouldn't be starving.

"We should almost be there now," said Val, checking her phone again. "One more mile."

"Good thing, too," I said. "We're supposed be there right about now."

Soon enough, we found ourselves in a small village called Rascairn, from which I had been told we'd be picked up by boat. We found a parking spot near the pier and got out. My legs felt stiff and hard after the long drive. From a distance, I could see a motorboat waiting for us. Val and I had trouble carrying all of the luggage, though Barry wasn't helping things by giving unwanted pieces of advice every other second. Finally, trying to balance all the parcels, handbags, and suitcases against the stiff sea breeze and the increasing rain, we stumbled onto the pier.

"Alright, Barry," said Val warningly. "No more talking from now on. Hebs ahead."

Barry made a grumbling noise half-way between acceptance and annoyance. Though he sometimes enjoyed spying on some of the villagers at home, he hated having to be silent when Val and I were around.

A broad-shouldered man, about forty, with sandy hair and leathery skin, got out of the motorboat.

"'Bout time you came," he said, not bothering with the niceties of introductions. "Been waiting here for twenty minutes, I have."

"Sorry about that," Val said brightly. "Do you mind giving us a hand?"

He grunted in a non-committal way, but finally extended two reluctant hands. We stowed the luggage at the back and took our seats at the sides. I took Barry on my lap just in case – it wouldn't do for him to go overboard. And something told me that our charming host wouldn't be too keen on saving a cat in this weather.

"We'll be totally drenched by the time we get there," said Val. "And all our luggage, too."

"Aye," the sandy-haired man said, nodding his head pointedly. "These parts aren't for everyone."

Val and I exchanged a look of raised eyebrows but decided not to argue. He started the motorboat's engine, which roared into action, and got into his seat at the back in order to steer. The raindrops gently rippled on the waves next to us as if dancing to some unknown tune. As we left the cove of Rascairn, however, the rain was getting heavier and heavier. Soon, I was sure, it was about to become very uncomfortable.

"The island isn't far off, is it?" I asked loudly, trying to make myself heard over the noise of the motor.

"Aye," he grunted unhelpfully.

We sped along for about another twenty minutes. Soon enough, we were completely enveloped by the cloudy grey so that we couldn't see the coastline anymore. I felt a little queasy, and by the looks of it, so did Val and Barry. Val was craning her neck over the edge of the motorboat, trying to see where we were going.

"I think I can see something," said Val finally, thrusting her finger out excitedly.

I swerved my head around to see what she meant. But at that precise moment, a wave hit the ship from the other direction. Barry clawed my leg just in time, but Val was taken by such surprise that she almost went over the side of the ship. I was able to grab her just in time by the arm.

"That was close, Amy," she said, after the first shock had subsided. "Thanks."

"Try not to die on holiday, Val," I said. "It's very bad timing."

She made a grimace at me. Barry, though not hurt, was quite rattled by the experience, too. Our driver, however, looked completely unfazed, as if nothing had happened. He hadn't so much as lifted a finger when the wave had hit the side of the boat. Now, he kept his eyes focussed on the invisible horizon in the distance.

"You know," I said, squinting in the direction that Val had almost gone overboard. "I think you're right, Val. There is something over there."

And through the curtain of rain slowly emerged a rocky island. I was surprised how high it rose at its centre, though I suppose it wouldn't have survived the harsh seasons over the years otherwise. Atop stood a lighthouse in white and yellow, with a black, domed roof. Stretching down the hill, several buildings flanked the lighthouse on either side.

The boat slowed down, and we headed for the wooden pier in the cove ahead of us.

After some persuasion by Val, our sandy-haired guide was forced to agree to carry a bag, too, though the steep climb up the grassy hill easily compensated for the extra hand. With the rain still pelting down, we were all drenched from head to toe by now, though Barry looked as if he had fallen into the sea multiple times, his ears sagging under the weight of the water. But with a heb present, all Barry could do was to voice his displeasure by grunting and sniffing.

At last, we had reached the top of the hill. The lighthouse stood at the far end, but our guide led us to a long, two-storey building to our left. A plaque above the door read "The Seaview Hotel". With sea all around us, I thought, that was almost something of an understatement.

"You can find your way in, I take it," our guide said, plonking down my suitcase at the door. "I've got work to do."

And with that, he made his way towards one of the adjacent buildings, which looked like a shed or workshop of sorts.

With some effort, I opened the heavy door to the Seaview Hotel. It was made of metal and sported several patches of rust at the bottom. The hotel had evidently seen better days. I held the door open for Val and Barry. We were facing a room that seemed to be both a lounge and a reception area.

"Oh, blast it!" Val swore, tugging at her oversized bag that had somehow got caught in one of the door's hinges.

Making sure to keep the door open with my right foot, I leaned over and tugged at the strap.

"I'm cold," Barry hissed from behind me. "What are we waiting for?"

"Sssh, Barry," I said, still trying to wrench out the strap with increasing vigour. "They'll hear you."

There was a frantic coughing noise from within as Val tried to warn us, but too late.

"Hear what?" asked an approaching female voice.

I swerved around. A young woman, in her mid-thirties perhaps, had seemingly come from nowhere. She was pretty, with dark brown hair, though she also looked extremely overworked. As soon as she saw us, however, her worn-out look spread into a wide smile.

"Oh, hello," I said.

"Hello," she said. "Please, allow me to help you with your bags. You must be Miss Sheridan?"

"That's right," I said, glad to hand over one of the suitcases. "And this is Valerie Morgan and this…this is my cat, Barry."

I tailed off at the end, slightly embarrassed.

"Oh, pets are no problem here," she said kindly. "We have several cats ourselves. And a dog. My name is Anita Brown, by the way. So nice to meet you. Awful weather, isn't it? I hope Williams wasn't too unfriendly. Takes a while to warm up to new people."

She laughed awkwardly.

"Well, I'll show you to your rooms," she continued. "Please follow me. And don't bother about the luggage, I'll have someone carry it up later."

We thanked her and followed her up a flight of stairs onto a narrow but long landing. We must have passed at least ten rooms on either side until Anita Brown unlocked a door to our left.

"There we are. This is for your companion, I believe," she said, smiling at Val. "It should be very comfortable. It's en suite, too."

She briefly showed Val the room while Barry and I waited in the corridor.

"I'm starving," Barry whispered irritably after Val had closed the door behind her.

I had to admit that I was getting rather peckish myself.

"We'll have to wait," I said. "It's only just getting dark outside. I think they serve meals at set times."

"Typical," he said, whipping his tail up and down in agitation. "But then, what can you expect from a place like this? Scottish hospitality."

Before I could tell Barry to be a little more grateful for what he would be getting, Val and Anita Brown had re-emerged from the room.

"Over here, we have the larger of the two rooms," Mrs Brown said, bustling over to the door at the end of the corridor facing the landing. "It's the largest we have, in fact. I do hope you feel at home."

We followed her into a cosy bedroom with an old-fashioned but clean carpet. The window – which was round – revealed a sharp drop of several dozen feet to the rocks and the sea below. Val, who had craned her neck to get a better look, shivered slightly at the sight and quickly withdrew.

"Beautiful, isn't it?" Anita Brown said, misreading Val's expression. "This room is the last remaining part of the old building. It has the best view of the sea, as you can see, because it's closest to the cliff on this side."

"What happened to the rest of the old building?" I asked.

"Oh, there was an accident, quite a few years ago. It burnt down. It used to extend along the cliff, to the left, as well, but that's all gone now, I'm afraid."

Anita Brown then showed us the living room, which was much more spacious than the bedroom, though without the magnificent view of the sea, which was obscured by the workshop next to it. Peeking through the window at the very end of the living room, I noticed that one could just about see the lighthouse if one stood at a far left angle.

It had struck me as rather odd that one had to enter through the bedroom to get to the living room, rather than the other way around, though I assumed that they must have extended the room after the burning. Barry took an immediate liking to the sofa, hopping onto it when Anita Brown wasn't looking.

"Later, Barry!" I hissed at him.

He gave me a resentful look, but ultimately complied.

"Well, that's that," Anita Brown said cheerfully, turning back to us again. "The bathroom is right over there. Fresh towels are in the wardrobe. Please let me know if there's anything else you need. I'm afraid I really have to be off. To make dinner, you see."

"Oh, you have to make the dinner as well?" asked Val before she could help herself.

"Yes," Anita Brown said apologetically. "The cook has... fallen ill unfortunately. My father is too old now, otherwise I would have asked him."

"That's really bad timing with the conference taking place here," I said.

"Yes," Anita Brown said uncomfortably. "Very sudden. Luckily Mrs. Haughton is still here to do the rooms. She's our maid."

She sighed briefly.

"Anyway, would 7 pm suit you for dinner?" she asked.

"Sure," Val said immediately.

"I wonder if it were possible to make something for our cat, as well," I said, indicating Barry. "The vet, erm, has prescribed a special diet for him. Cooked tuna if possible."

"Of course, I'll see what we have in the freezer," she said politely after a brief glance at Barry and back at me.

"Thank you very much," I said.

"No trouble at all," she said. "If you need anything else, don't hesitate to ask me or Mrs. Haughton."

Then, she moved over through the bedroom and back onto the landing, closing the door behind her. After she was certain that we wouldn't be overheard, Val turned to me.

"Amy, you've done it again," she said in mock-exasperation.

"What do you mean?" I asked.

"Now everybody's going to think you're the crazy cat lady," she said.

"Maybe I am," I said, grinning at both Barry and Val.

"Anyway, it came in handy last time, remember? Usually gives Barry a lot more freedom to move about."

"Don't bother this time," said Barry, yawning. "I don't think I'll be moving much in this dump. Better to listen to some Wagner here on the sofa. I just want to get this holiday over with."

Val was just about to open her mouth to argue with him when the door to the bedroom opened again. At first, I thought Anita Brown might have forgotten something, but instead an elderly lady – in her late sixties most likely – dressed in a maid's uniform entered the room.

"Oh, sorry," she said wheezily. "Didn't… didn't see you there."

She walked unsteadily into the room. At first, I thought she may have been drunk, for she had trouble keeping her balance. But I had worked for too many years as a waitress not to recognise the giveaway symptoms. No, something else had got a grip on her. Her face was white as a sheet, and her hands were shaking uncontrollably now.

"Mrs… Mrs. Haughton?" I asked uncertainly.

She nodded her head vaguely in my direction. I quickly signalled to Val to give me a hand and we approached her on either side, grabbing her by the arms. We were just in time, too, for a moment later she sagged forward as her feet gave way beneath her completely. With some effort, we manoeuvred her over to the sofa. Barry, who had curled up there and hadn't been paying any attention, grumpily slouched over to the edge of the sofa, eyeing Mrs. Haughton with suspicion.

"What's wrong?" Val whispered, sounding slightly out of breath.

"I don't know. I think she might have passed out or something."

"I'll put up her feet," said Val, taking several cushions and sticking them under the elderly maid's shoes.

I cleared my throat.

"Mrs. Haughton, are you alright? Would you like a glass of water perhaps?" I said.

But Mrs. Haughton simply stared ahead of her, as if transfixed by some invisible spectacle at the other end of the room.

"Should we get a doctor, d'you think?" Val asked nervously. "Or tell Anita Brown?"

But Barry, whose expression had changed completely, lifted a paw to stop her.

"Wait," said Barry, moving closer to Mrs. Haughton and examining her face. "I think I recognise some of the symptoms…."

Before he could say anything more, Mrs. Haughton suddenly began to gasp for breath. Her eyes opened again, and she extended her hand, clutching my arm with an ice-cold hand. When she spoke next, it was in a wheezy tone that was much deeper than her usual voice.

"There is danger in this place," she said dramatically, staring up at me, unflinching.

"Danger?" said Val beside me, utterly bewildered.

"There's always danger when you're around, Val," I said, smirking.

"I have… I have seen it," Mrs. Haughton continued, clearly impervious to our voices. "Terrible danger."

"Mrs. Haughton," Val said, trying to be as loud and clear as possible. "What terrible danger?"

Mrs. Haughton's eyes swerved over to Val, her mouth open, as if she were having trouble processing what Val had said to her. Then, she looked at me again and grasped my arm even tighter, drawing me towards her.

"Death," she said. "On the island."

CHAPTER 3

I raised an eyebrow, looking at Val and Barry. Whatever had possessed this woman to act like this? Her performance hadn't convinced me for a second. But Val seemed to be taking her very seriously, while Barry's expression was unreadable.

"Death?" Val asked, leaning in further. "What death?"

"Many years…" Mrs. Haughton whispered, closing her eyes again. "The past is the future in reverse."

She lay there, quite still for a while. None of us knew what to do. I had been sure that she was playacting, yet the eerie silence let doubt creep into my mind.

"Is she… is she dead?" Val asked.

I checked her breathing and her pulse. From what I could tell, they were reasonably stable.

"No," I said.

"What on earth…" Val began.

"Shh… not now," whispered Barry, putting a paw to his mouth.

Mrs. Haughton was opening her eyes again. She coughed, spraying us in the process. I yanked my arm up for cover.

"Oh, you must excuse me," she said suddenly, straightening up and acting as thought nothing had happened. "Must have fallen asleep while doing the room. No need to worry, no need to worry."

She got up from the sofa, wheezing furiously.

"Mrs. Haughton…" Val began in concern, but she interrupted her before she could say anything else.

"No, please. It's very kind of you. But that was not professional of me," she said briskly. "My apologies."

And with that, she turned around on her heel and

bustled out of the room again.

Val and I looked at each other, not knowing what to say. The whole scene was preposterous, obscene even. What had she meant when she talked of death on the island? And how could she have recovered so quickly? Barry, however, looked the least taken aback of us all.

"That didn't just happen, right?" Val asked weakly, holding her forehead.

"She must have been acting," I said flatly.

"I… I don't know," said Val.

"She *must* have been," I said again. "But you're the psychic around here, Val. You tell us."

"I felt… I don't know," said Val, massaging her temples now. "It sort of took me by surprise when it happened. There were too many voices, I felt like the first time I got my psychic powers. So… overwhelmed."

"What can this mean?" I asked Barry.

"I'm not sure," he said, frowning.

"You don't really believe that little bit of playacting, do you?" I said, looking at both of them. "Nobody recovers from an attack that fast, surely. She just walked out of here as if nothing had happened!"

"Not a normal attack perhaps," said Barry. "Valerie, get me my spectacles and my edition of *Hebs & Magic*, will you? I think the answer might be within its pages."

"But they're downstairs," Val protested. "They haven't brought up the luggage yet."

"It's only a book," Barry said with irritation.

"It's easy for you to say," she said. "We had to lug them up here all the way from the pier."

But for once, she gave in to Barry's wishes without much of a fight. Her curiosity had prevailed.

"Barry," I said, after Val had left the room. "What's going on? You don't think that was real, do you?"

"It might have been," he said.

"You of all people, I thought you mistrusted hebs."

"Of course I do, but that doesn't mean they can't be less than completely ignorant once in a while. Anyway, it's all conjecture at the moment. A warlock needs data. A warlock worth his wand, that is. I'll need to catch up on my reading to be entirely sure. Naturally."

"Naturally," I echoed.

Within a few minutes, Val had returned with the requested items, and Barry – reading glasses balanced delicately on his little feline nose – began to read. Puzzled but still sceptical, I was left to discuss the matter with Val, though it was all guess work. When the dinner bell finally sounded from below, Barry still wouldn't budge from his tome.

"Barry, you're missing *tuna*," Val said incredulously.

"Not now," he muttered. "I'm busy."

"Fine, fine," she said, sounding slightly offended. "See you later."

As we stepped onto the corridor, I still couldn't believe Barry was giving this a moment's thought.

"I mean, you would have felt something, right? If it had been real?"

"I – I don't know, Amy. It's all muddled."

"But would you have felt anything if she had been acting, too?" I asked as I started walking down the stairs.

"I suppose so," she said. "I can usually tell with emotionally meaningful lies. But, you know, the really good liars are hard to see through. You know that. We found that out last time the hard way."

With a sudden pang, memories of Rick Lavalle leaning in to me re-emerged from my subconscious. I had rather hoped to keep them buried forever, but to little success, of course. Val, also, hadn't been able to detect his trickery – despite her psychic powers. But Mrs. Haughton didn't strike me as a master criminal somehow.

"Yeah, I remember," I said as we entered the lounge, not quite able to keep the bitterness out of my voice.

Before we could continue our conversation, however, Anita Brown angrily rushed into the lounge from one of the adjacent doors, slamming the door behind her. A moment later, she was followed by an old man in an old-fashioned wheelchair. He was swearing at her.

"You come right back here," he bellowed.

"It's none of your business, father," she said. "You can't tell me what to do anymore. I can see whom I like."

"Now you listen to me, you…" he began, but his daughter – having spotted us at the other end of the room – hastily held up her hand to silence him.

"Please, father, our guests have arrived for dinner," she said.

Slightly abashed, he wheeled further into the room to get a better look at us. His angular face was a deep purple, his features contorted in repressed rage. Despite his age, he had massive arms, most likely a testament to a life of physical labour. He had long wisps of all-white hair, save for a bald patch at the top of his head.

"This," said Anita Brown, approaching us, "is my father. He's still adapting to me being in charge here."

Mr. Brown looked away, though he didn't dare reproach her in front of the guests.

"Hello," he grunted. "Welcome to the Seaview Hotel."

He clearly didn't mean a word of it.

"Erm, thank you," I said coldly.

Mr. Brown puffed and grunted in his wheelchair as he fumbled in his jacket for something. He drew out a round metal tin, which he opened, revealing grainy, brown tobacco. He took a pinch and snorted it quickly through either nostril.

Then, shaking his head, he wheeled himself in the direction of the door that led outside with powerful strides. I was surprised at how easily he could open the door, too, as it was particularly heavy and also opened inwards – with a spring mechanism that ensured it was closed at all times.

As soon as he had disappeared outside, Anita Brown turned towards us.

"He's mellowed with age, you know," she said, resentment flashing in her eyes. "Anyway. Dinner is ready. If you would follow me, please."

She led the way to the dining area, which was more spacious than the lounge. Several people were there already. I presumed that most of them were connected to the committee somehow.

"Excuse me," said an elderly lady with her hair tied in a tight bun and pointy glasses perched on the edge of her nose. "Might one of you two be Miss Sheridan, by any chance?"

"That would be me," I said. "How do you do?"

"How do you do. My name is Highgarden. Olivia Highgarden. Most of the committee members have already arrived. Please, do come over. I'll introduce you to them."

She bustled self-importantly over to the table at the far end where several other people were seated.

"Sorry, Val," I said.

"Don't worry," she said quickly. "I'll check out the drinks they have."

"Don't be silly, you can introduce yourself, too. Come on."

We followed Mrs. Highgarden across the room.

"Everyone," she addressed the table in a stentorian voice. "This is Miss Sheridan, who has graciously stepped in for the deceased."

There was general muttering of approval at the table.

"Now then, I believe some introductions are in order. This," she said, indicating a balding man of about fifty, "is Dr. Harold Linton. He's a trained physician. Used to work for Whitechapel, too."

"Yes," he said nervously, stretching out his hand to shake mine. It was cold and slightly sweaty. "Quite a while ago now. Nice to meet you, Miss Sheridan. If you'll forgive me, I think I'll just go for a cigarette."

He got up. Even his double-breasted suit couldn't hide the fact that he was very thin indeed. He smiled self-consciously across the room and then made for the exit. When he had left the dining room, Mrs. Highgarden's nostrils flared.

"A filthy habit," she said, as if she wanted to impress the point upon all of us. "Now then. Who is next? Ah yes, Vanessa. Miss Sheridan, this is Vanessa McQuinn."

"Hi," I said, smiling.

"Hello," she said in a bored voice.

Vanessa McQuinn couldn't have been much older than 18, though I could see that she had made every attempt at appearing older with the support of her make-up and clothes. Her hair was dyed blonde, and her nails, painted white, were exceptionally long. She was the kind of girl I had tended to avoid when I had been at school.

"Next up," Mrs. Highgarden continued, "is Mr. Randolph Bolton. He is a partner in a London-based firm that makes *considerable* contributions to the committee."

Mrs. Highgarden beamed at the corpulent man as he got up from his seat. Despite his smooth, salesman's manner, I noticed that his small, watery eyes tended to dart from side to side, giving him a somewhat shifty look.

"Nice to meet you at last, Miss Sheridan," he said as we shook hands. "My condolences, by the way. It must have been a terrible loss for you."

"Oh, I didn't know my great-aunt, to be honest," I said. "But thanks."

His smile faltered. He was just about to say something further, but Mrs. Highgarden cut him short.

"Still a few to go, Randolph," she said affectionately. "Now this is Miss McQuinn's identical twin sister, Jane McQuinn."

If she hadn't said they were twins, I don't think I would have guessed it. Where Vanessa was arrogant and self-absorbed, Jane was the complete opposite. Her hair was brown – which I assumed was her sister's natural colour, too – and clipped behind both ears for practical purposes. She wore no make-up or jewellery and preferred to wear various shades of grey.

"Hello, Miss Sheridan," she said quietly. "I hope you enjoy your stay here."

"Hello," I said. "Yes, thank you, I hope so, too."

"Now then," Mrs. Highgarden butted in again, clearing her throat. "We're not quite complete, I'm afraid. Otherwise we could have had our first session today."

The members of the committee seated at the table exchanged nervous looks. It seemed nobody was too keen on starting early.

"Unfortunately, however," she said, with more than a note of impatience in her voice. "Mr. Urquhart evidently thought it beneath him to arrive on time. I only *do* hope he makes it to our first meeting tomorrow, though I have my doubts. Grave doubts."

She rearranged her glasses back into position as if that settled the matter. After Val had been introduced to everyone, Mrs. Highgarden invited us to have dinner with them. We sat down between Randolph Bolton, the businessman from London, and the shy twin, Jane McQuinn. After a few minutes, dinner was served by a stressed-looking Anita Brown and the sandy-haired workman, Williams, who had picked us up from the mainland. He looked as surly and unfriendly as ever, barely acknowledging the guests that were present.

"D'you come far?" asked Mr. Bolton next to me, his mouth full of baguette.

"Yes, actually," I said. "All the way from Gloucestershire. You're from London, I understand?"

"Oh, yes," he said, nodding importantly and gulping down the contents of his mouth in one go. "Only place to be, of course. No offence. But that's the way it is in business. You've got to be *there*."

"Where?" asked Val, who had only been listening in to the last part of the conversation.

"London, Val," I said.

"Oh, London. Love it!" she said, before turning back to talk to Jane McQuinn.

Soon, the table was abuzz with chatter and laughter.

"We're getting big, you – our firm, I mean," Mr. Bolton was saying to me. "Over two thousand employees. Growing every year at almost three hundred percent. Should have enough to retire to some nice place in only a few years' time if it continues like this."

My mind began to drift slightly to the strange event that occurred just before we had stepped down for dinner. I had almost forgotten about Barry upstairs. I wondered whether he had found an answer to the elderly maid's peculiar behaviour just a while ago. Personally, I thought it was more than likely that Mrs. Haughton was simply neurotic.

"Amy," said Val, nudging me in the ribs, startling me out of my daydreaming.

"Ouch," I said. "What is it?"

She inclined her head in the direction of Anita Brown, who was standing at the door, talking to Williams.

"What about them?" I asked.

"Well, don't you think they look… sort of natural together?" she said. "That's the vibes I'm getting, anyway."

She was right. They did look natural together. I thought I even saw Williams's mouth twitch into what might have been construed as the beginnings of a smile. I also thought that they were also standing closer than would otherwise be normal. Anita Brown was talking rapidly about something, and Williams's face quickly darkened again.

"There go the vibes," said Val. "D'you want some more Yorkshire puddings, Amy?"

"Oh, yes please," I said absent-mindedly. "What were they talking about, d'you think? Can you tell?"

"Not exactly, no. That's very advanced stuff," she said, taking a bite from her mutton. "But the mood did change quite suddenly. They were flirting one moment, and then… then there was hatred."

"Hatred?" I said, taken aback. "That's a pretty strong word. Are you sure?"

"Yeah," said Val. "Very intense."

"Towards each other?"

"I don't know," said Val, frowning. "But that Williams man is certainly a strange person. Very moody, from what I could tell. Volatile, even, if you ask me. He was brooding a lot on the boat, too."

"Yeah," I agreed. "Wouldn't put much past him. There's definitely something funny going on here on the island."

"Perhaps Mrs. Haughton was right," said Val, lowering her voice even further.

"What do you mean?"

"About… about the death she was talking about."

I scoffed.

"You don't believe her, too, do you?"

"I don't know," said Val slowly. "I'm still on the fence about that."

***

After dessert, the pace of conversation slowed audibly. Most people had had a long trip, so Dr. Linton excused himself shortly after and went to his room for an early night's sleep. Randolph Bolton had found an eager audience in Mrs. Highgarden in regard to his business exploits, though I somehow suspected that her main interests lay in securing the continued financial support from his company for the committee. Vanessa McQuinn, on the other hand, had been monosyllabic all evening, paying more attention to a fashion magazine than to anything else. She left shortly after Dr. Linton.

Her twin sister, in contrast, had followed the conversations around her quite attentively, though rarely contributing herself. Now that Vanessa had left the table, however, she seemed a lot more relaxed. Val and I even got her to talk a little about herself.

"So, how come you're in the committee?" Val asked her.

"Oh, it's a strange story, really," she said. "Our… our mother died a few months ago."

"I'm very sorry," I said.

"Oh, don't be," she said. "It wasn't sudden, you see. She was… ill. For a long time. It was awful to see her in pain all that time. I think she *wanted* to go in the end. I think she felt like a burden on us. Our father died a long time ago, you see, so my sister and I looked after her. I loved my mother. Even Vanessa did, I think, and that's saying something if you knew her."

"You don't like your sister?" asked Val.

Jane hesitated briefly, then smiled apologetically.

"It's complicated. A lot happened, you have to understand. But no, we don't get on very well."

"But how come you're both here, then?" I asked.

"Well," she said, smiling again. "Our mother never liked us quarrelling. She hated it, in fact. She wanted us to be a family. Family was everything for her, and so it had been for my father, too. And so my sister and I had to promise her on her deathbed that we were to attend the annual meeting of the committee together. She loved lighthouses, you see. So, that's why we're here. To abide by our mother's last wish."

"That's… that's very touching," said Val. "Perhaps you'll be able to be real sisters again."

Jane smiled politely.

"Well, that could be possible, of course. But we are very different, after all. I don't think we see the world in quite the same way."

We chatted for a little while longer, until Mrs.

Highgarden looked at her wrist watch and insisted that we all went to bed in order to be on form in the morning for our first session. After the hailstorm of goodnights, it was only Val and me left in the dining room.

"Amy, I think we'd better go upstairs, too," Val began.

"Yeah."

We were just about to get up when we heard muffled voices from the kitchen that was adjacent to the dining room. Whoever was in there evidently thought that everyone had gone to bed by now.

"…. Won't stand for it, Anita," the unmistakable gruff growl of Williams floated towards us.

"But what can we do? You… you know I love you, but father won't hear of it."

"He'd better mind his own business," Williams said.

"I've told him a thousand times," Anita Brown said miserably. "But he's still the official owner, Dan. We can't kick him out so easily."

"There must be a way," he said. "We've got to get rid of him. I'm going crazy with him wheeling about all over the place, poking his nose into things that don't concern him. Or tinkering away in his room in the lighthouse every other day, making a hell of a racket. God knows what he gets up to in there."

Anita Brown was crying softly, which only seemed to agitate Williams further.

"You don't deserve him as a father, Anita," he said.

"But what… what can we do?"

"Has he changed his will yet?" he asked bluntly.

"No, but… Dan, you're not saying…"

"If he doesn't stop interfering in our affairs," Williams said grimly. "I'll kill him with my own bare hands. I swear I will."

CHAPTER 4

Val and I looked at each other as if a lightning bolt had just struck the hotel. Williams had just threatened to kill Mr. Brown in front of his daughter. And with Williams, I didn't think he'd voice such threats lightly. From the little we knew about him, he was one to act rather than talk.

"Come on, let's go back upstairs," Val whispered.

I nodded. I got up carefully and gently tip-toed over to the door. But Val must have somehow got her foot caught in the chair and went crashing to the floor with a smack, toppling several chairs next to her.

"Val!" I hissed.

"Sorry, Amy," Val moaned.

As I helped her to her feet, I was sure that the commotion wouldn't have gone unnoticed. And sure enough, the door to the adjacent kitchen opened. Williams, his face as grim as ever, stood in the doorway. He didn't say anything but simply watched us. Anita Brown was busying herself in the kitchen behind him. But I wasn't going to be intimidated by anyone. As my late father had used to say, the best way to show your enemies your teeth was to smile.

"Excellent meal," I said. "My compliments to Anita Brown."

He stared at me, then nodded, though his eyes never left us as he did so. I had a good mind to keep standing there, but Val tugged at my sleeve. With a last look at Williams, I followed Val out of the dining room and into the corridor and up the stairs. Val, undoubtedly keen on anything Barry might have come up with, headed straight ahead to my room.

We found Barry buried beneath a pile of books. Williams or Mrs. Haughton had evidently brought up the luggage in the meantime, and Barry had painstakingly retrieved them from one of the suitcases. His brow was furrowed in concentration, though he looked contented at the same time.

"You won't believe what just happened," Val said as I closed the door.

Barry raised his head, his spectacles slipping off of his nose.

"Well?" he asked.

And then, we told him all about the conversation we had overheard between Anita Brown and Williams. And how Williams had threatened to kill her father. Barry didn't look in the least surprised.

"That confirms my worst suspicions," he said. "This is no coincidence."

"What do you mean?" asked Val.

"The elderly maid – Mrs. Haughton – wasn't playacting. At least, I don't think she was. Under certain circumstances, hebs can develop supernatural powers, too. It is admittedly extremely rare. I have only been able to find a few recorded cases, though I'm sure there are many that went unrecorded. In the heb world, such claims are rarely believed, as you might imagine, and so those that *are* concerned naturally keep them quiet."

"So you're saying that Mrs. Haughton might be something like a natural psychic?" I said.

"Not a psychic," said Barry. "A clairvoyant. The fields are closely related, though a clairvoyant may see into a possible future while a psychic is usually constrained to the present. It is an imprecise art, to say the least. Many such prophecies have been uttered without anything happening, though I think we should pay them some attention this time. If Williams is willing to act on his words, Mrs. Haughton might well be right. And old Mr. Brown might indeed be in mortal danger."

"Should we get the police?" I asked. "I mean, if

Williams threatened to kill Anita Brown's father, we should notify someone."

But Barry shook his head solemnly.

"It's not as simple as that, I'm afraid. Intervention is prohibited in heb affairs under magical law. It is very strict in that regard."

"But we can't just…" I began in frustration. "I mean, from what I heard and saw, Mr. Brown is awful, I know that, … but stand by and watch him get murdered?"

Barry shook his head solemnly.

"Unless magic or sorcerers are involved, we cannot do anything. Of course, if magic were involved somehow, it would naturally become a different matter entirely. We'll definitely have to keep our eyes open," said Barry.

"But what *can* we do?" asked Val.

"First, we'll have to test my hypothesis in regard to Mrs. Haughton," said Barry.

"Test it? But how?" asked Val.

"There are several ways," said Barry evasively. "We need to establish whether Mrs. Haughton is a genuine heb clairvoyant or simply eccentric. A fine line at the best of times, I can assure you. Though we'd have to be very careful not to get caught. Secrecy protocols."

"You and your protocols," I said. "We'll have to find out right away. We have to do something at least."

"How exactly do we find out if Mrs. Haughton is the real deal?" Val asked.

"There are certain spells that may help reveal the truth," said Barry. "We'd need to prepare them up here."

"Well, I've got committee meetings all morning," I said. "Mrs. Highgarden gave us our schedules after dinner. She means business. I don't think I'll be free until mid-day. Val can help you prepare, Barry. But I think we should also keep an eye on old Mr. Brown, too. Barry, you could do that. Heb or warlock, we just can't let a murder occur on our watch."

"But it's cold outside," he said sniffily. "And with one good gust of wind, I'll be blown clean off the cliff!"

"I thought cats can survive extreme drops?" I said.

"Not when their bodies are over fifty years old," he said, placing his paw on his back to stress the point.

"Barry…" I began warningly.

"Alright, alright. I'll keep an eye on him."

"You'd better," I said. "Or Mrs. Haughton might well turn out to be right – clairvoyant or not."

***

I slept very poorly that evening. Nightmares haunted me for most of the night, mostly consisting of Mrs. Haughton pushing Val – who was in a wheelchair – down the stairs of an imaginary lighthouse. Before I could save her, Williams or one of the other guests would suddenly produce a wand and start firing curses in my direction. Fumbling in my handbag, I never seemed to be able to find my own wand in time. But before the spells hit, Anita Brown came rushing in from the kitchen with a tray in her hand, acting as a shield.

Perspiring, I woke up. The events of the day must have affected me more than I had liked to admit. But clearly, I had been rattled by Mrs. Haughton's utterances – though rationally I still wasn't convinced that she was a clairvoyant.. Somehow, the *possibility* of a crime, unknown and hence unsolvable, seemed almost more unnerving than an actual murder. Though I naturally didn't want anyone to get hurt, I felt helpless.

At 2 am, I decided to get a little fresh air and went over to the round window to open it. The mechanism was jammed for some reason, so I stepped into the sitting room instead. It felt good to walk around a bit after the restless flailing of my nightmares. Barry was lying on the sofa, snoring slightly. He was sound asleep. Moving over to the far end of the sitting room, I was just about to draw up the window next to the sofa when I saw that there was a light burning outside. At first, I wasn't sure from where it had come as it faded away as quickly as it had arisen. Was Williams perhaps working very late in one of the workshop buildings?

I inched closer to the window, pressing my eye to the pane. It was quite dirty from the outside, so I undid the latch and opened it for better vision. Immediately, the sound of unseen waves hitting the rocks below greeted me, as well as an icy cold wind that made me shiver where I stood. I squinted my eyes, waiting.

And there was the light again. But it had come from the direction of the lighthouse and not from the workshop as I had initially thought. As Barry grunted in his sleep behind me, I shifted a little in order to get a better view. The lighthouse was throwing its powerful beam out towards the sea, away from the hotel. As a result, the shadowy path leading up to it was hardly visible at all.

Once again, the light faded in and out. It had come from the basement of the lighthouse. Who on earth would be up at this time of night? And then I remembered what Williams had said to Anita Brown when Val and I had overheard them. That her father, Mr. Brown, spent a significant amount of his time there, working on some unknown project.

Waiting for the light to return, I stood there for five more minutes in vain. I was getting very chilly, though I didn't want to miss the next pulse of light. Something entranced me about it, as though it carried some mysterious relevance that I had yet to discover. But the minutes slipped away and the cold wind cut harder into my cheekbones without the light returning:

"Close the door… trying to work," Barry muttered in his sleep from behind me.

I was just about to close the window again when I heard a clank of metal in the distance, distinctly audible over the sounds of the sea and the wind. It had also awoken Barry, apparently.

"Will you close that confounded window?" he said. "Do you want me to get pneumonia?"

"There was a light," I said. "In the lighthouse."

"That's what lighthouses are for," Barry said snidely. "The name is a hint."

"No, I mean, in the basement," I said. "It sort of… pulsated a couple of times, but now it's gone."

"Who cares? It's probably just…"

"Shhh," I said. "I think I can see someone."

A low figure seemed to be gliding along the path from the lighthouse towards the hotel. It took a minute for my eyes to register who it was.

"It's Mr. Brown," I exclaimed. "Coming from the lighthouse."

Once more, I was surprised at how easily Mr. Brown was able to propel himself forward with his old yet powerful arms. The damp and slippery earth beneath must have made it even more difficult for him, and yet he reached the entrance to the hotel with impressive speed and agility.

After he had vanished, I finally closed the window, much to Barry's relief. I wondered what Mr. Brown had been up to in the lighthouse. Surely, if he had been tinkering with some device or machine, the workshop would have been the better option. It was both closer to the hotel and presumably also had the necessary tools.

No, there had to be another reason for Mr. Brown's nocturnal activities, I thought as I went back to my bedroom and slipped into the still warm bedsheets. Though I had no indication that his peculiar behaviour was in any way nefarious, a small voice at the back of my mind insisted that something wasn't quite right. And I was determined to get to the bottom of it eventually – meetings or no meetings.

***

A few hours later, I sat groggily at the breakfast table in the dining room, drinking my first coffee of the day. The room looked very different with sunshine permeating its space than the evening before, though I wasn't really in a mood to appreciate it much. Anita Brown had set up a buffet for us, with what looked like home-made buns, jam, and an entire arsenal of cereals.

"Oh, hello," said Anita Brown as she bustled in from the kitchen. "Didn't expect anyone to be up so early. Had a bad night?"

"You could say that," I said, rubbing my temple. "I helped myself to some coffee, I hope that's alright?"

"Oh, yes, of course," she said. "Beautiful at this time in the morning, isn't it? Dan – that is Williams, I mean, hasn't missed a sunrise in years. So he tells me, at least. But I like to sleep in during the winter time. Getting up in the dark can be a little depressing, can't it? It's a good thing that the days are getting longer again. Anyway, would you like some cooked breakfast? We have some wonderful local meat. Came in fresh yesterday by boat."

"No, thanks, not yet at least," I said.

"That's alright," she said kindly. "Just let me know when you're ready."

"Last… last night," I began slowly, "I couldn't help notice a light – in the lighthouse…"

"Oh, yes, it's fully automated," she said quickly. "Thank the Heavens we don't have to worry about that, too. I have my hands full as it is."

"No, I mean in the basement," I said.

She looked unnerved.

"Really?" she said, though she didn't look surprised at all to me. "How strange."

"Yes," I said, pressing the point. "It must have been

around 2 am, I think."

"Oh, someone must have left the light on, then," she said.

"The weird thing was," I continued, knowing full well I was pushing it by now, "that it went on and off rhythmically, like a pulse."

"The bulbs must be ancient in there," she said, clearly uncomfortable now. "I'll… I'll ask Williams to check. Thank you for bringing it to my attention, Miss Sheridan."

"Anytime," I said.

***

When Val and Barry came downstairs, I quickly filled them in on how Anita Brown had reacted. We had chosen a breakfast table right in the corner and had put Barry's bowl close to the radiator behind us, so that he wouldn't be seen. He dared only utter a word or two at a time, though he was able to give us an occasional nod of the head in order to communicate as well. Luckily, the noise from the other tables and the clunking of cutlery was sufficient to mask most of our conversation.

"She pretended not to know?" whispered Val, pouring herself some more coffee.

"That's right," I said. "Something's going on in there, and I want to find out what it is. The only thing is, I can't go myself because Mrs. Highgarden is starting the meetings right after breakfast. And by the looks of it, they're going to last until well after dark."

"Sounds more like a hearing," said Val, grinning. "But sure, Amy, we'll find out what we can."

"Best if you went together. And let Barry suss things out first. Nobody's going to suspect a cat of prying. Well, not in the way we're doing it, anyway."

Barry looked at me.

"This was meant to be a holiday," he hissed from

beneath the table, unable to contain himself any further.

"Sorry, Barry, but no cat is an island," I said. "Not even you, though you do your best. We need you in this. Wagner will have to wait a bit."

Barry scowled over his bowl of cooked tuna, muttering darkly under his feline breath.

"Anymore coffee, dears?" Mrs Haughton asked kindly, bustling over from the kitchen.

She was helping Anita Brown with keeping everyone happy at the breakfast tables.

"Yes, please," I said, staring into my third empty cup of the day. "Something tells me I'll be needing a lot more today."

"Would your cat want any more food?" she asked, looking at Barry with a curious gaze.

Barry looked at me. He didn't move an inch, though his stare unmistakably told me that, if he were to go investigating the lighthouse, he wasn't going to do so without a full stomach.

"I think so," I said, laughing. "Something tells me he's going to need some extra energy today."

"The climate, you see," Val added.

"Alright," said Mrs. Haughton, nodding her head.

She bustled back toward the kitchen, humming tunelessly as she did so. When the door had closed behind her, Val leant over to me.

"She's suspicious, you know."

"Of what?" I asked, bewildered.

"I'm not sure," she said. "Of Barry, I think."

"Aren't we all?" I said teasingly.

"No, I'm serious, Amy," Val said.

"But… surely she doesn't suspect him of being… you know, a warlock," I said, lowering my voice to a bare whisper.

"I don't know," said Val, stroking her forehead. "Sorry, it's all so muddled. I just get glimpses. Bit too crowded in here."

"OK," I said. "We'll watch our step around her, from now on."

Then, Mrs Highgarden, who had long since finished her own breakfast, coughed loudly from the table adjacent to ours. She was rapping her fingers impatiently on the table, eyeing everyone in the room like a hawk, as if she were trying to make them eat faster through pure willpower.

Sitting opposite her, Dr. Linton was slowly nibbling away tentatively at his first bun of the day while listening to a story Randolph Bolton, the businessman, was telling him. Invariably, it involved the sealing of a particularly formidable deal for his firm that only *he* had been able to close. Vanessa McQuinn symbolically plugged in her earphones, and for once, I – and by the looks of it pretty much everybody present – sympathised with her. Except for Jane, perhaps, who was still politely nodding and smiling at the appropriate moments in Mr. Bolton's story.

I was sure that Dr. Linton was taking so long in part to annoy Mrs. Highgarden, who had spent the last few minutes puffing air out of her nostrils at regular intervals in an ostentatious display of disapproval. More and more, she resembled a dragon gearing up for action. All that was missing was fiery sparks incinerating Dr. Linton.

After he had held his last buttered piece of bread in his hand for a while, lifting it up to his mouth but lowering it again after a particularly poignant point in Mr. Bolton's story, he finally placed it into his mouth.

Immediately, Mrs. Highgarden jumped up to address us before anyone dared to go and help himself to the buffet again. At last, she was able to set the gears in motion for the first meeting. There was nothing akin to a conference room at the Seaview Hotel, so the dining room we were already in would have to do. We rearranged the tables and chairs so that we all sat at one long table in the middle of the room. At the head, with her back to the kitchen, sat Mrs.

Highgarden, armed with an assortment of pencils and notepads. It seemed that nobody wanted to sit right opposite her on the far end, as we had seated ourselves on the sides, so that it was the only spot left for the elusive Mr. Urquhart, who still hadn't arrived.

"Really," Mrs. Highgarden kept muttering. "That man is the limit. Well, we'll just have to start without him. Not that he made any significant contributions last year, of course. But there we are."

She cleared her throat self-importantly and stood up again, spreading her fingers on the table below her in a territorial gesture.

"Welcome all," she began, "to our 42nd annual meeting of the Royal Committee for the Preservation and Restoration of Lighthouses. I have had the great pleasure of having attended all but a single one of those meetings – and that was only due to the early birth of my nephew. It from a very early age onwards that I fell in love with lighthouses, you know, so that…"

My worst fears were realised when Mrs. Highgarden spent a full thirty minutes elaborating on her past love affair with lighthouses (as well as hinting at some with their keepers). Apparently, she had retired early from her teaching career in order to spend more time on the committee's affairs, which included fundraising for the most part. And that had been how she had got to know Mr. Bolton in London.

Vanessa McQuinn yawned ostentatiously next to me, while Dr. Linton held up his hand in a schoolboy's manner that made him look forty years younger.

"Yes, Dr. Linton, what is it?" asked Mrs. Highgarden with a trace of impatience.

"May I step outside for a moment?" he asked.

She sighed.

"Very well, if you must. So, where was I? Oh yes, the committee's financial crisis of 1999. Yes, quite a shock to all of us, you have to understand. If it hadn't been for your late great-aunt, Miss Sheridan, the show wouldn't have gone on, as it were."

There was a pause as she looked expectantly at me. Suddenly, I knew how Dr. Linton must have felt a few minutes earlier. Mrs. Highgarden's air of the eternal schoolmistress catapulted one back in time.

"I'm very glad to hear it," I said, smiling.

It felt rather half-hearted, though my answer seemed to satisfy Mrs. Highgarden and the rest of the committee for the time being.

"Hear, hear," said a cheerful voice from the doorway.

We all spun around to see who it was. A man in his early thirties was casually leaning against the doorframe. He was exceptionally good-looking, with dark, wavy hair and a mischievous grin on his youthful face. He was wearing a smart, tailor-made suit. To top it off, he was holding a pipe, which he held to his mouth every other moment, although from what I could tell it hadn't been lit at all.

"Mr. Urquhart," Mrs. Highgarden said through clenched teeth. "So nice of you to finally bother to turn up."

"Yes, sorry about that," he said, casually walking over to the table. "Spot of bother on the mainland."

"For those of you who haven't had the *pleasure* of meeting our latecomer yet, this is Mr. Patrick Urquhart," said Mrs. Highgarden.

"Please," he said. "Patrick is what everybody calls me. No need to be so formal. And who are you?"

He stretched out his hand towards me, taking me by surprise.

"Oh, I'm Amanda Sheridan," I said. "I'm filling in for my late great-aunt."

"Oh, I see," he said, smiling at me apologetically. "Hope you're not bored already."

"Mr. Urquhart!" Mrs. Highgarden said, her voice becoming shrill. "Please. I would eventually like to move on to our agenda for this week."

Patrick held up his hands.

"Far be it from me to stop you, Mrs. Highgarden," he said with a roguish smile on his face.

He had taken the only remaining seat, prominently placed opposite to Mrs. Highgarden's, and the fact seemed to unnerve her somewhat. On the flip side, I thought privately, such an arrangement had the benefit of speeding up the proceedings, at least the biographical part, for Mr. Urquhart's appearance had made Mrs. Highgarden forget all about her handling of the committee's financial crisis of 1999.

The agenda itself was quite another matter, of course. Dr. Linton had returned from his smoke and had apparently made his mind up to criticise every single point on the list. When I had to think that I would have to endure another week of this, I felt quite queasy inside. Whatever had possessed me to think that this might have been fun, I will never know, though a certain amount of guilt for the unexpected inheritance last year and the wish to repay my great-aunt in some way must have played a role.

I only hoped that Val and Barry had been more successful. As I sat there, listening to yet another point of order from Dr. Linton, I wondered whether we had all been overreacting somewhat. Even if Barry was right and Mrs. Haughton was a natural clairvoyant, it still didn't mean that anything would happen. Indeed, we had clearly heard for ourselves that Williams wanted the old man dead. Though whether he was willing to act on it was another matter. How often had such words of anger been uttered in the heat of the moment? Surely, be it consciously or not, Mrs. Haughton had picked up on those vibes and uttered them in her own dramatic manner. It didn't necessarily follow that it would come to pass, especially when Anita Brown was involved. Would Mr. Brown's opposition to her involvement with Williams lead her to be in favour of killing her own father? Everything, it seemed, hinged on that question. And from what I could tell, Anita Brown was not the murderous type.

"Miss Sheridan?" Mrs. Highgarden addressed me out of nowhere.

"Sorry," I said, making me feel like a scolded pupil.

"Would you pass along the annual report, please?"

"Oh, yes, of course," I said, quickly grabbing the stack that Vanessa had pushed over to my side of the table and handing it over to Patrick to my left.

"Now, if Dr. Linton has no more objections…" Mrs. Highgarden said, lifting her eyebrows at him.

"Well," he said hesitantly. "There might be one or two…"

But he quickly faltered when he saw the dangerous gleam in Mrs. Highgarden's eye.

"… I suppose it's sufficient," he ended weakly.

"I'm glad that's settled, then," said Mrs. Highgarden loudly. "Next on today's agenda is the annual report. Each of you should now have a copy in front of you. If you'd please turn to page four, there is an overview of our funds for the past year."

There was the general rustling of paper.

"As you can see," she said, with an appreciative nod in Randolph Bolton's direction, "Mr. Bolton's firm is *by far* our most important backer. Coming up in second position is her Majesty's government."

I ran my finger further down the list of investors. To my astonishment, one of the major long-term contributors was one Mr. Gregory Brown, owner of the Seaview Hotel.

"Despite that, however, I am very sorry to say," said Mrs. Highgarden, pressing her pointy glasses further up her nose, "that, at the current rate of decline in funds, we will have to cease running normal operations within the next six months."

"Our commitments are simply too extensive," said Dr.

Linton thoughtfully, holding the report in a slightly shaky hand.

"Couldn't we cut back on them?" I asked. "The commitments, I mean. Focus on fewer lighthouses to repair and maintain."

There was a sharp intake of breath from Mrs. Highgarden's direction.

"Cut…?" she said. "My dear Miss Sheridan, we have not dared to use that word in twenty years."

"She's right, you know, Olivia," said Patrick Urquhart next to me. "The numbers just don't add up. Even I can see that."

"We will simply have to get more contributions," Mrs. Highgarden said, her temper rising quickly. "More funds. That is what it comes down to."

She pointedly looked in Randolph Bolton's direction, who hadn't been paying any attention. Instead, he had been preoccupied with gathering the biscuits from various bowls on the table and eating them as surreptitiously as possible.

"Funds?" he asked. "Sorry, the firm won't cough up any more I'm afraid."

"What about the government?" I asked.

Dr. Linton shook his head sadly.

"Austerity measures imposed by the government have made it impossible. We are lucky to get as much as we do from them."

"Then we need new investors," said Mrs. Highgarden fanatically. "Other firms. Businessmen and governments from overseas."

"But we can't even keep our old ones," said Dr. Linton, his voice becoming shriller and thinner now.

I must have looked slightly taken aback, for Patrick Urquhart leaned towards me.

"Don't mind them," he said softly, so that nobody else could hear. "They're always at each other's throats. Been that way since I joined."

"Why is that?" I asked him in a hushed voice.

"Linton used to be president himself. He made the Committee, you might say, until he had a nervous breakdown. Couldn't handle the pressure, I think. A lot of responsibility to deal with. He's never been the same since. Highly-strung, you might say."

Mrs. Highgarden, her old instincts from many years as a teacher no doubt kicking in, craned her neck to see who was causing the distraction at the other end of the table.

"Mr. Urquhart," she said in exasperation. "If you can't be constructive, please try at the very least not to be *de*structive. Please keep talking to a bare minimum and focus on the task at hand."

Patrick's handsome facial features immediately rearranged themselves into those of a humbled schoolboy, folding his hands meekly in front of him on the table.

"Sorry, Olivia," he said.

But Dr. Linton, waving the annual report in his left hand and fidgeting with an unlit cigarette in his other, had used the brief interlude to rally for another attack.

"As I was saying, our fundraising has hit granite on almost all fronts. Old investors are leaving the ship like rats. We're sinking."

"Nonsense," Mrs. Highgarden bellowed.

"If it is," said Dr. Linton, shaking from head to toe, "you might tell the esteemed committee just what you were discussing last night with Mr. Brown of this very hotel. He still is a contributor, for the present moment, I take it?"

Mrs. Highgarden looked as though she had been stabbed in the back with a crooked knife.

"Why," she thundered, dropping all pretence at remaining cordial with her arch-enemy, "you spying little…"

"Mrs. Highgarden, what happened exactly?" came Jane's timid voice. "I'm sure Dr. Linton didn't mean to do any harm. And I'm sure we'd all be interested."

There was a general murmur of agreement amongst the other members, Patrick included. Mrs. Highgarden had been manoeuvred into a trap by Dr. Linton. There was no way out for her now. A few moments later, she must have come to the same conclusion as she puffed her cheeks in a self-righteous manner.

"Mr. Brown," she said sharply, "has – to my greatest regret – decided to put an end to his contributions."

"Entirely?" asked Mr. Bolton, his large face drooping in surprise.

Mrs. Highgarden nodded her head heavily.

"But that's impossible," said Mr. Bolton, making the chair beneath him creak as he turned around quickly to the other members. "He's bound by contract, isn't he?"

"Not entirely," Dr. Linton said. "I went over it this morning. After I… erm… happened to overhear what had been discussed yesterday evening. Mr. Brown is unfortunately well within his rights to terminate his contributions at this moment in time. In exchange for the cheap acquisition of this island and the buildings thereon, Mr. Brown's contractual obligations were to share a percentage of the hotel's profits with us as well as maintain the lighthouse's automated systems. The contract was formed for a twenty-five year period. Regrettably, that is now coming to an end this June."

"So, he'll own the lighthouse, too?" asked Mr. Bolton, outraged.

"No," said Dr. Linton. "The committee retains control of the lighthouse, though I suppose it will be very difficult to prevent him from going there and using it, considering we can't afford anyone to stay here permanently. Or even check on it more than a few times a year."

There was a moment of silence as the message sank in.

"And Mr. Brown remains adamant?" asked Patrick, frowning. "Couldn't we persuade him somehow?"

"We have nothing to offer him," said Dr. Linton. "No

leverage. He'll hardly do it out of the kindness of his heart, that's for sure."

"He's horrid," said Vanessa McQuinn suddenly. "A disgusting old man, that's what he is."

Everybody turned around in surprise. Vanessa had made no indication that she had been listening to the conversation at all. In fact, she had been swiping away at her smartphone for most of the time and had only once said something to complain about the non-existent internet connection. Now, however, her haughty exterior had turned into something both disgusted and frightened.

"Vanessa, please," said Jane, just as taken aback by her sister's outburst as we were. "Watch your language."

"Shut up," Vanessa barked at her sister.

"Vanessa…" Jane began weakly.

"I think," said Mrs. Highgarden quickly, "a little recess is in order. This whole affair is getting to all of us. Quite understandable. What we need is perhaps a little fresh air. I certainly could do with some."

"Also, it's almost lunch time," said Mr. Bolton enthusiastically.

"Fine," said Mrs. Highgarden in an exasperated voice. "We'll reconvene after lunch at three o'clock here. Please be on time. That goes especially for you , Mr. Urquhart."

There was a general ruckus of screeching chairs and the creaking of bones as we all got to our feet. Before I could head for the exit to search for Val and Barry, however, I felt a firm hand on my shoulder.

"Miss Sheridan?"

It was Patrick.

"Yes?"

"I was wondering whether you could fill me in on what happened yesterday," he said, chortling. "Don't want provoke the dragon even more by my ignorance, eh?"

"Sure," I said. "I was just on my way out. You're welcome to join me."

"Excellent," he said. "I might even light the old pipe up."

We stepped out into the lounge together. Dr. Linton – desperate for a cigarette, no doubt – was hastily opening the front door of the hotel.

"Speak of the devil," said Patrick quietly, inclining his head towards the reception desk. "There he is."

"Who?" I asked, turning to look in the direction that Patrick had indicated.

I almost missed Mr Brown, since the reception desk was high enough to obscure most of his body as well as the wheelchair. At first, I thought he was doing some paperwork because he seemed to be hunched over somewhat. But on closer inspection, I saw that he was in fact taking snuff tobacco again, sending it up his nostrils with a horrible snorting sound that one would normally associate with the most horrible of maladies. Patrick and I exchanged looks of disgust. When Mr. Brown saw us, he scowled and, closing his snuff tin, wheeled himself off in the direction of the dining room area.

Patrick opened the door for me, and we stepped out together. I was slowly getting used to the icy winds, though some rays of sunshine had penetrated the cover of clouds below, making the island appear much greener and friendlier.

"Charming brute, isn't he?" Patrick said, fumbling for something in his trouser pockets.

"Quite," I said. "No wonder he's getting out of the contract as soon as he can."

"Yes," said Patrick. "Awful fellow. Never liked him."

"Oh, you knew him before?" I asked.

Patrick hesitated briefly.

"That's right," he said. "We had a committee meeting here a few years ago. He wasn't in a wheelchair then, which made it a lot worse. Drunk out of his mind for most of the time. But strong as a horse. By the way, did she… say anything about me?"

"Who do you mean?" I asked.

"Mrs. Highgarden, of course," he said, producing matches from the inside pocket of his coat.

"Erm, well, yes," I said. "I don't think she was particularly pleased that you came today instead of yesterday."

"Oh, that old bat," he said, though he was grinning. "She never liked me, you know. Never thought I took this whole lighthouse business serious enough. Perhaps she's right."

"Then why are you here?" I asked earnestly.

"Haven't I asked that myself," he said, lighting his pipe, "if I have to put up with *her* all day. Not that the rest of them are a particularly happy bunch, mind you. But believe it or not, I like lighthouses. My father used to own a few of them. Used to let me play in them, too, when we visited. And the keepers were also very decent to me."

"He owned a *few* of them?" I asked incredulously.

"Yes, he didn't want to invest too much," Patrick said apologetically, misunderstanding my disbelief entirely. "He preferred old castles, mostly. We had a whole string of those. Always good for a museum or two."

"So, do you deal in real estate, as well?" I asked.

"Lord, no," he said, flashing another smile. "No, I don't work, you see. Don't need to, in fact. Inherited everything myself. I don't have any siblings. Just as well, I suppose. Never could hold a job for long. But I promised my father – before he died – to join the committee. And so I did."

"How long have you been a member, then?" I asked.

"Oh, about twenty years," he said. "Joined up when I was fifteen. Dr. Linton was still in charge then. He led us through the crisis. Worked day and night for the committee. He pulled it off, too, but my Lord did he pay for it."

"Yes," I said. "I can see that."

"Quite a place here, isn't it?" said Patrick

conversationally. "You wouldn't think it would have such a dark history, would you?"

"Dark history?" I asked. "What do you mean?"

"Oh, a few decades ago, two men were killed in the lighthouse over there," said Patrick casually. "Strangled, both of them."

"That sounds awful," I said.

"Yes, isn't it?. I read about the case in a local guide when I first came here. The perpetrator was a man called Jenkins."

"So they got him in the end?"

"Oh yes," said Patrick. "There was a manhunt and they got him alright."

"Did they find out why he did it?" I asked.

"That's sort of the mystery about the whole thing. Apparently, he didn't say a word at the trial. Kept quiet about it. Most people just assumed it was a random act of violence. Like a bestial urge."

We chatted for a little while longer as we strolled around the island. I was keeping an eye out for Val and Barry, though I couldn't deny that I was less in a hurry than I thought I would have been earlier. Patrick's account of the island's chilling past fascinated me for some reason. Despite the rather sinister topic, Patrick seemed to lighten the otherwise gloomy atmosphere of the island considerably. Although he had lost his mother early in life – and then his father a few years later – Patrick had retained a surprisingly optimistic view on life. Or perhaps that was his unique way of dealing with his loss. He was also curious about my background, so I told him all about my days as a waitress back at home, how I had become best friends with Val, and finally about the surprise inheritance of Fickleton House that had changed my life – as well as Val's – forever.

"Oh, *there* you are, Amy," said Val, emerging from behind the workshop with Barry at her heels. "We were wondering when you'd finish in there."

At that moment, she only just registered the man next to me. She eyed him with an appraising look that only your best friend could develop over the years.

"This is Patrick Urquhart, Val," I said, grinning.

"Oh, hi," she said, sounding slightly out of breath. "Picking up men already, are you Amy?"

"Val!"

Patrick smiled rather sheepishly.

"Quite my fault, I assure you," he said, stretching out his hand. "How do you do, Miss…"

"Valerie. But just call me Val. That's what everyone does. Even Barry will some day…"

I shot her a warning glance.

"Who's Barry?" Patrick asked, bewildered.

"Oh, my…" she began, faltering as she struggled to find an answer that sounded less insane than 'our talking cat' to a heb.

"… her ex-boyfriend," I said, smirking. "But it's over now, isn't it, Val?"

She looked daggers at me but eventually decided to play along.

"Yes," she said. "At least, I hope so. Much too old."

Barry made a noise between a meow and an indignant growl that certainly sounded nothing like a cat's.

"Aaanyway," she said quickly, changing the subject, "you up for lunch?"

"You bet," said Patrick, apparently oblivious to what was going on. "What about you, Miss Sheridan?"

"Oh, don't be silly," I said. "Call me Amy. And yes, I'm hungry. And I think Barr- I mean, the cat might also be since he missed dinner yesterday."

Barry, standing behind Patrick, gave me the faintest of nods, as well as a you-owe-me look.

"We're all set then, I…" began Patrick.

But before he could finish his sentence, there was a deep, bloodcurdling cry as if from a wounded animal. It came from within the hotel. Exchanging pointed looks with Val and Barry, we quickly made for the hotel entrance, Patrick Urquhart close behind us.

"What's going on?" he said, as I tore open the door.

But the scene in the lounge quickly answered his question. Before us, the crumpled body of Anita Brown lay spread-eagled on the floor close to the stairs that led up to the guests' rooms. Her mouth was not quite closed, and her eyes stood wide open. Her father, Mr. Brown, was on all fours next to her, his wheelchair discarded. He was making every effort to revive her, pressuring her chest region with a desperate rhythm.

The rest of the committee members, who had also been alerted by his cry, had come to the lounge to see what was the matter. Dr. Linton, seeing the body, quickly came to the front. Mr. Brown kept pumping, but to no avail. Dr. Linton nervously knelt down and felt Anita Brown's pulse. By the look on his face, the verdict was already clear.

"I'm very sorry, Mr. Brown," he said after a moment. "I'm afraid your daughter is dead."

CHAPTER 5

Mrs. Highgarden gasped, holding her bejewelled hand to her mouth. Mrs. Haughton, who arrived at the scene last, was teetering dangerously on the spot as if she were about to faint, but Jane McQuinn quickly hurried forward and caught her before she could do so. Then, we all stood there in silence for a while, not knowing what to do next. Val and I exchanged a dark look. The elderly maid, Mrs. Haughton, had been proven right – there had been a death. But was it also murder? That was the decisive question. And though I was almost certain that it was, I hoped against hope that it had been a tragic accident.

"MY DAUGHTER," Mr. Brown bellowed, tears streaming down his red face. "My daughter…"

He tried to get up but wasn't able to. His legs wouldn't support him. He looked lost. Never did I think that I would have felt such sympathy with a man like that, but I did. By the looks of it, I wasn't the only person, either.

But as Patrick and Dr. Linton stepped forward to help him up, he waved his hand at them as if he wanted to swat flies. He looked around him wildly, grabbing the armrest of the wheelchair as he did so.

"It was one of you, wasn't it?" he roared. "One of you KILLED HER?"

"Please," said Dr. Linton, who was beginning to shake again, "Mr. Brown. We understand your… your pain but I'm sure that nobody here would have…"

Dr. Linton tailed off weakly at the end. Perhaps he didn't believe what he was saying. Or maybe he was simply quailing before the wrath of Mr. Brown. The latter was now pulling himself up with a newly-found strength and heaving himself into the wheelchair on his own. Nobody dared aid him this time. We all waited there in an absurd scene, all watching Mr. Brown's every move. When he had finally succeeded, he turned around to us menacingly. He pointed his finger at the lot of us, his eyes darting from face to face.

"Murder," he said quietly, which sounded a lot more dangerous and terrible than when he had shouted and raged. "I'll find out who did it if it's the last thing I do. You mark my words."

And with that, he turned his wheelchair around and rolled towards the corridor. Stunned by Mr. Brown's threat, nobody spoke or did anything for a minute or so, until Patrick broke the silence.

"Well, what do we do now?" he asked heavily.

"We need to contact the authorities on the mainland," Dr. Linton said.

"Doctor," I said, taking advantage of the brief moment of silence that followed his answer. "Do you know what might have caused Anita Brown's death?"

"I'm no pathologist, you have to understand," he said firmly.

"I didn't mean a definite diagnosis," I said. "Just whether Mr. Brown's suspicions have any basis in fact…"

Dr. Linton stared at me for a moment and then looked at Anita Brown's body.

"I'd have to take a closer look. All strictly off the record. But I think we all *do* need to know…"

"But why did Mr. Brown say it was murder?" asked Mrs. Highgarden, who was still white as a sheet.

Apparently, nobody knew. I was certainly keen to know the answer myself, though seeing the reactions of all those who were present was almost as intriguing. Apart from Williams, the surly workman, everybody was there. Though Jane McQuinn looked terrified, her twin sister's expression was blank. I wondered what was going on in her head at that moment. Then I remembered her outburst in regard to Mr. Brown just a little while ago. For the life of me, I couldn't see the reason why she hated him. As far as I knew, they hadn't even been in the same room together.

Dr. Linton decided that the body should be moved to one of the sheds and placed in one of the large freezers after he had examined it. That way, any sign of foul play would be preserved until the police arrived to pick up the body. It was decided that, under the circumstances, committee meetings would be postponed until more was known. Mrs. Highgarden tried to protest but even she had to admit eventually that it was out of the question. It was a sign of respect to cease all other activities for the present moment.

In the meantime, Williams was located by Dr. Linton near the lighthouse and had been sent to the mainland to report the incident, though the police wasn't expected to arrive until the following day. I couldn't imagine how terrible an effect that Anita Brown's death would have on Williams. Their affair, as far as I knew, wasn't common knowledge amongst the guests, and so Dr. Linton had naturally seen nothing wrong with tasking him with going over to the mainland.

The rest of us were left wondering whether Mr. Brown had been right or not about the murder. However nasty and disagreeable he was, it was more than likely that his suspicions were correct, I thought. The coincidence of Mrs. Haughton's prophetic words a mere twenty-four hours earlier was simply too great to be ignored or dismissed.

And yet, I could not think of a single person who would have had a motive for killing her. It was true that almost everyone had hated her father. However hard I racked my brains, however, I couldn't think of a single incident in which one of the guests had shown the slightest bit of hostility toward Anita Brown. Some of them had moaned about the breakfast, though that was hardly grounds for a complaint let alone murder.

"Perhaps it was Mr. Brown himself," said Val, as soon

as we were back in my room. "He could have killed her and then faked the entire thing afterwards. You know he was mad about her seeing Williams."

"Wouldn't he have killed Williams, then, instead?" I asked. "It was *him* he disapproved of, not his own daughter. Not as far as we know, anyway. No, I think there must have been another reason. A disappointed lover, perhaps. Or some business problems."

I quickly filled them in on Mr. Brown's contributions to the committee. And how he had immediately cancelled them as soon as his contract allowed.

"So that's how he got the island," said Barry, more to himself than anyone else. "I was wondering how such a person managed to acquire it."

"Do you think Mrs. Highgarden might have been capable of such a thing?" asked Val, turning to me.

"She's certainly passionate about the committee. I think she might do anything if she thought it would save a couple of more lighthouses across the country. But why kill the daughter?" I said.

Val pondered the question for a while.

"Perhaps to put pressure on him, to convince him to stick with the committee," said Val.

"If so," said Barry, "Mrs. Highgarden doesn't know him at all. From what I've seen of him, he'll certainly not change his mind now after what happened."

"Yes, it doesn't make sense," I agreed. "Who knows, it might turn out to be Dr. Linton trying to frame her. To try and get his old position back. That'd probably be even likelier than her. But it's all conjecture and guess work."

"Yes," said Barry thoughtfully. "What we need is hard evidence."

"True," I said. "You know, it's quite strange that something like this should happen on the island again."

"What do you mean, *again?*" asked Barry.

I told them all about the double murder in the

lighthouse that Patrick had told me about. Barry raised his eyebrows, while Val looked horrified.

"I don't think I'll be able to sleep tonight," said Val.

"Join the club," I said. "Anyway, did you find out something while I was cooped up during the meetings?" I asked hopefully.

"Nothing much," said Val. "Sorry, Amy. We went to the lighthouse but the doors were locked. Barry tried to get in through one of the windows, but they're all sealed. It's as if they don't want anyone to go in there."

"Brown doesn't want anyone to go there," I said. "And his daughter knew about it. She said so before breakfast. Or at least, indirectly. She got all nervous when I mentioned it. Whatever he's hiding in there, it might be the key to his daughter's death."

"We still have Mrs. Haughton, too," said Barry. "We need to find out whether she really is a natural heb clairvoyant or not."

"But she was proven right," I said. "What good will that do now?"

"If she was right about the death, she might have even more information, buried in her unconscious. Something she overheard or saw. If we can tickle that out of her, we'll be able to move forward."

"And how exactly do we do that?" asked Val.

"Through magic, of course," said Barry, puffing up his chest. "I have prepared a series of spells for you, Amanda. It's just as well. I think you haven't used your wand all trip. You need to keep practising if you want to become a first-class witch."

"Alright," I said. "But we'd better do it tonight. I don't want to wait for too long. If there really is a killer on the island, we'll have to be on our guard at all times."

"Yes," said Barry darkly. "Especially when he finds out that we're on his tracks."

***

With no time to be lost, we prepared for our visit to Mrs. Haughton that very evening. As I perused his list, the charms and spells Barry had prepared were very complicated indeed. They amounted to a series of tests that would hopefully provide us with the answer we were looking for, though I wasn't sure how much additional information she would provide us. Still, until Dr. Linton had examined the body, it was the only promising course of action open to us at the moment.

We sent out Barry to scout out where Mrs. Haughton had her room. Meanwhile, the weather was getting a lot worse. The brief sunshine of the midday had given way to clouds that looked like harbingers of a storm. I tried to check the forecast on my phone, but the already weak signal was now gone entirely.

At last, Barry returned.

"The coast is clear," he said, smoothly trotting over to the sofa and leaping onto it. "Mrs. Haughton has just finished cleaning the dining room. Her own room is on the ground floor, at the back of the corridor. We'll have to be careful, though. Mr. Brown has his sleeping quarters there, too."

"Let's just hope he's tinkering away in the lighthouse when we go down," I said. "Are you ready?"

They were, and so we silently made our way downstairs. We were just about to enter the downstairs corridor when Dr. Linton suddenly came in through the front door. Judging from the smell, he had been outside for a smoke.

"Oh, hello," he said, looking immensely relieved all of a sudden.

"Hello Dr. Linton," I said. "Is everything alright?"

"Yes, yes. I just thought it might have been Mr. Brown. He's in a terrible mood, as you might imagine. Shouted at me for the best part of twenty minutes. Quite understandable, of course. Terrible to lose one's daughter at such an age. At any age for that matter. It's not the natural order of things, you know. Parents should always go before their children."

"What was Mr. Brown angry with you about?" I asked.

"I wanted to examine the body, but he wouldn't let me," he said. "Quite strange. All informal, of course. But I would have thought that he of all people would have had an interest…"

"Yes," I said, frowning. "Did he give a reason for doing so?"

"I believe the phrase he used was that I shouldn't 'meddle in affairs that didn't concern me'. And if he takes that kind of attitude, indeed I shan't. Well, I'll see you all in the morning."

"Goodnight, doctor," I said.

We waited until he was out of earshot. This entire affair was developing faster than we could keep up with. Why had Mr. Brown prevented Dr. Linton from examining the body? What was Mr. Brown trying to cover up? All questions that would have to wait until later.

"Almost there," Barry said softly.

We had reached the end of the corridor by now. Next to a broom cupboard was Mrs. Haughton's room. I knocked softly on the door. There was a pause, then the sounds of heavy feet approaching the door followed. Slowly, it was opened from the inside.

"Yes?" asked Mrs. Haughton, who was no longer wearing her uniform but a long black dress and a white blouse.

"Sorry to disturb you at this time, Mrs Haughton," I said. "Only, it's rather urgent. It has to do with Anita Brown's death."

She looked taken aback.

"Of… of course," she said. "How can I help?"

"We need to talk to you. In private, if that's possible," I

said.

"Please," she said pleasantly. "Come in."

I think she was slightly surprised that the cat promptly entered the room but decided to say nothing. I had my wand at the ready in my handbag, just in case.

Mrs. Haughton's room was quite small, sporting a bed, a wardrobe, a table, and two chairs. Her nightgown had been placed in an orderly fashion on her bed in preparation for the night. There were no pictures on the walls, nor photographs of loved ones. I had the strong impression that she was an elderly spinster.

"I don't usually entertain," she said, sounding peculiarly formal. "But please, have a seat."

She sat on the edge of her bed while we sat on the chairs. On Barry's instructions, Val had copied the spells I was to use on a sheet of paper. Sitting so close to her, and with every movement visible to her, I was having trouble finding the right moment to cast the first spell. I gave Val a desperate look.

"What?" she whispered.

I inclined my head ever so slightly in the direction of Mrs. Haughton, who was looking at us as if we were mad.

"How *exactly* can I help you?" she said, suspicion rising in her voice.

I had no choice but to continue the conversation. As secrecy protocols dictated, it was important that she remembered nothing connected to magic. Otherwise, we'd be in deep trouble.

"Did you notice anything peculiar about Anita Brown?" I asked. "Before she died, I mean."

Mrs. Haughton put a finger to her mouth, thinking for a while.

"No," she said. "I don't think so. She was always under pressure when running the hotel, of course. Mr. Brown isn't much help, I'm afraid, and we usually don't get so many guests at once. Not at this time of year, anyway. Just the odd bird-watcher normally. But no, I don't think there was anything out of the ordinary at all. Nothing."

"Do you know anyone who could have wanted her dead?" I asked.

After a sharp intake of breath, she held her hand to her mouth in surprise.

"You don't mean… that she was murdered?"

"That is what Mr. Brown seems to believe," I said.

But Mrs. Haughton shook her head.

"No, that's impossible. She was a sweet and hard-working girl."

"Did she get on well with her father?" I asked.

"Of course. As far as that was possible. He was… is a very angry man. The drink got to him, you know."

Val, I noticed, was getting restless beside me. I could tell that something was bothering her. She got to her feet and walked across to the other side of the bed in order to draw Mrs. Haughton's attention away from me.

"Mrs. Haughton," she said suddenly. "Do you have any family?"

Mrs. Haughton turned around in surprise.

"Why, no," she said. "I don't see how that is…"

I understood immediately what Val was trying to do. At that moment, I took out my wand out of my handbag and cast the first spell. A minor freezing spell designed to knock out the target for a few minutes. There wouldn't be any lasting damage.

"Frigus," I murmured, waving my wand in the shape of a half-moon.

Immediately, a torrent of ice shot out of the tip of my wand. It enveloped Mrs. Haughton entirely, sending her toppling backwards onto and then over the bed. Luckily, Val was standing at exactly the right spot and was able to catch her by her shoulders before she fell to the ground.

"Amy, what are you doing?" hissed Barry. "That spell was much too strong. D'you know how dangerous that is?"

212

"I… I didn't mean to…" I spluttered, horrified that I had almost knocked her to the floor. "I didn't do anything special… I…"

"When you two have finished, would you mind helping a sister out over here?" said Val desperately, who was only just about to hold Mrs. Haughton. "She's a bit heavy."

I quickly got up, and together we heaved her back onto the bed. Barry perched himself on the nightstand, while Val and I each took a chair, and placed ourselves at either end of the bed. The procedure, as Barry had told me, would take a while.

"You put far too much into that last spell again," Barry said.

"I'm sorry. But I didn't do anything differently," I protested. "I've tried this one at home, and it's always worked out before."

"Then how do you explain that she almost hit her head on the other side of the room?" asked Barry. "And by the looks of it, we'll be lucky if she's conscious in an hour or two."

"An hour?" I said, exasperated. "We can't wait that long."

"It's reversible," he said simply.

"How?"

"By magic, of course. I put the counter-spell on the list, just in case. You can be grateful that I practice magical prophylaxis, you know. You haven't been practising enough."

"Alright, alright," I said. "Don't push it, Barry. So, what next?"

"Well," he said, pondering the issue. "Now that it's happened, we may as well discuss the rest of the spells. Make sure not to make the same mistake twice, Amanda, otherwise they might have long-term effects that aren't as easily reversible. And you don't want to be explaining that to the *Spellcasters' Association*, believe me. What we're doing is already borderlining on the illegal if we cannot prove that a magical crime has been committed."

"OK," I said. "Keep your whiskers on. Something's different, that's all."

"You have the same wand, I presume?" he said coldly.

"Of course I do," I said, holding it up for him to see. "But I'm telling you, I didn't do anything differently."

He raised his left eyebrow.

"You are the only variable, Amanda," he said.

"I'm telling you, I know what I felt. Something is different," I said stubbornly. "Now, let's get on with it."

"We need to unfreeze her next," said Barry, deciding to drop the matter for the time being. "And then we quickly place her into a state where she is receptive. If we are lucky, we'll be able to get her into a clairvoyant condition."

"*If* we are lucky? I thought this plan was iron-clad, Barry," said Val.

"It's our best bet," I said, trying to avert an argument. "Let's move on."

I checked Val's list for the next spell I had to cast after reverting the effects of my faulty freezing charm.

"Aestus," I said, making a quick flicking movement with my wand.

Immediately, Mrs. Haughton began to shift in her bed. Once again, the spell's effect had been somehow – mysteriously – magnified. Her eyes were slowly opening now. There was no time to lose.

"Placatio," I said hastily.

There was a moment of silence. Val carefully leaned over to see whether Mrs. Haughton was still conscious or not.

"You've sent her to sleep, Amy," said Val, giggling slightly.

"Sorry, I just don't know what's going on," I said. "I know these spells. I've cast them before,, but they've never turned out like this at all."

"Well, you're still a novice with," said Barry unhelpfully.

"It's not because of that," I said angrily. "I tell you, something's different here. Maybe it's her. Or the island. I don't know what."

Val and Barry exchanged doubtful looks. I was furious at them for their disbelief, but I wasn't going to argue the case any longer – especially when we could be caught in Mrs. Haughton's room at any moment by Mr. Brown or one of the guests.

"So, what do we do now?" I demanded.

"Sleeping is actually not as awful for our plans as one might imagine," Barry said. "It's a state of intense relaxation, so that might actually help in the long run. We've got to ease her out of it – gently, mind you. Then we can try to initiate a clairvoyant state with the Sight charm."

I concentrated hard on her, trying to put as little force behind my spell as possible. A waking charm was normally very easy, though if overdone it had could have extreme consequences. Even worse ones than the unfreezing charm I had performed before. I lifted my wand and pointed it at Mrs. Haughton.

"E somno excites," I said softly, twirling the wand gently in my hand.

Despite my efforts, Mrs. Haughton was waking up much faster than I had intended, so I lifted the spell almost instantly. She looked very relaxed, though dazedly so. Her eyes were opening gradually now.

"Transis," I whispered quickly.

Her eyeballs rolled upward, so that we could see only the whites of her eyes for a moment. As they slid back to their normal positions, I noticed that her pupils were dilated. Her breathing had slowed so much that at first I thought it had stopped entirely. Despite my wand's insistence on casting every spell at tripled power, I had succeeded in placing her into a receptive state.

"And now?" a thoroughly relieved-looking Val asked

Barry.

"We ask her questions," he said. "She won't remember anything consciously in this state."

I nodded to Val, who leant forward.

"Mrs. Haughton, was Mr. Brown killed or was it an accident?" she asked, trying to speak as clearly as possible without being too loud.

At first, Mrs. Haughton didn't react. But then, she began to murmur.

"Anita Brown. Death on the island…"

"Mrs. Haughton," I said. "Was it murder?"

"Death… on the island…"

We tried multiple times but it was to no avail. Mrs. Haughton wouldn't or couldn't tell us anything more about Anita Brown's death. Even Barry tried multiple times, posing the question in slightly different wording. But each time, Mrs. Haughton would simply repeat herself.

Disappointed, Val slumped in her chair. After waiting for a few more minutes, I tried to ask her again, but with the same result. I was just wondering whether the spell had functioned properly when Mrs. Haughton suddenly let out a gasp.

"The past is the future in reverse," she said in a much deeper voice. "Father and daughter. Daughter and father. Hatred."

"Hatred? Mrs. Haughton, was it Mr. Brown?" I asked eagerly. "Did he have something to do with his daughter's death?"

But again, she wouldn't respond.

"Well, she's a clairvoyant, alright," said Barry. "Notoriously imprecise since the days of Delphi."

"So you're convinced it's the real deal?" asked Val.

"Yes," he said. "It would be almost impossible to fake for a heb."

"She is one, though, right?" asked Val.

"Undoubtedly," said Barry.

Mrs. Haughton was beginning to stir again, though I didn't think she had heard anything of what we had said. Her eyes were closed, though her breathing was becoming faster and more shallow now. She murmured something incoherently for a while. I moved in closer to her, until I was very close, trying to catch what she was saying. Suddenly, her eyes opened, and she gazed right into my own eyes. For a moment, I was transfixed.

"Great danger," she said, staring at me without blinking. "Miss Sheridan. Great danger."

An icy chill ran down the back of my spine. I looked at Val and Barry, who both looked extremely unnerved.

"Why is she in danger?" asked Val.

"Miss Sheridan stands against the future," she said softly, her eyes focussed on the ceiling. "Death awaits."

CHAPTER 6

"She… she's going to die?" asked Val weakly.

But Mrs. Haughton's head fell to the side without another word. She was unconscious again. Val and I exchanged dark looks, but there was nothing further to be done. Mrs. Haughton was indeed the real thing, though extracting information from her seemed impossible. Barry, apparently, had come to the same conclusion.

"Come on," he said. "No point hanging around here any longer. Mr. Brown might find us."

"But what about Mrs. Haughton?" asked Val. "Shouldn't we wake her or something?"

"No," he said. "She will simply have a long sleep until the morning, most likely. By then, the effects should have worn off."

Val opened the door and we let ourselves out of the room again, closing the door quietly behind us. I was disappointed and felt unnerved at the same time. I had never been one for soothsayers and the like, but Mrs. Haughton had been proven right once before. And having your own death foretold by a clairvoyant wasn't my idea of the prologue to a good night's sleep.

At least, we didn't encounter Mr. Brown or Dr. Linton on our way back. We sneaked up the stairs and down the corridor as quietly as possible. As we entered our room, a bolt of lightning flashed across the horizon, clearly visible through the round window above my bed, illuminating the sea in a bright white for just an instant. The storm was gathering.

"Do you mind if I sleep on the couch in here tonight?" asked Val, sounding rather nervous herself. "It's creepy alone in my room. Especially if there's… you know, a killer on the loose."

"Of course," I said, absent-mindedly. "No... no problem."

"Amy…" Val began.

"What?"

"I wouldn't pay too much attention to Mrs. Haughton. You know, what she said about you."

"Yeah?" I asked. "And why not?"

"Well, because, you know, Barry said that clairvoyants were very inexact. They get things wrong all the time, don't they, Barry?"

"She got it right before, though, didn't she?" I said, still unconvinced. "About the death, I mean."

"We'll just be extra careful," said Val. "All of us. But especially you, Amy."

"Indeed," said Barry solemnly.

He had remained uncharacteristically silent until now. As mad as it sounded, I yearned for him to make some sort a snide remark about clairvoyants and the ludicrous prophecies they usually made. It would have been his way of saying that he didn't believe what he had just heard. But Barry's face remained stony and serious.

"Take your wand with you from now on at all times, Amy," he said. "There's something sinister going on here. And until we can get to the bottom of this, we will have to take every possible precaution."

I nodded appreciatively. Val, standing next to me, squeezed my arm affectionately. It was good to have their support. I knew I could depend upon them if the worst came to the worst.

"I wonder what she meant about the future and the past," Val said, breaking the silence. "Did that make sense to you?"

"Perhaps it related to Anita Brown's past in some way," I said.

"Or Mr. Brown's," Val said, cocking her head

thoughtfully. "He's such a nasty person, I wouldn't be surprised if he had done some pretty bad stuff in the past."

"Yes," said Barry. "And now he's also prevented Dr. Linton from examining the body. He's definitely hiding something. As I said, we'd better get to the bottom of this before… before Mrs. Haughton next prophecy is realised."

He looked at me with an expression I'd never seen there before. Barry was concerned for me, almost fearful. I felt touched, but it wasn't reassuring at all. But at that moment, Val put her hand on my arm.

"We won't let anything happen to you, Amy," she said. "We promise. Don't we, Barry?"

He nodded solemnly.

"But the sooner we find out who killed Anita Brown," he said, "the better for all of us."

***

Unsurprisingly perhaps, I wasn't able to sleep that night for a long time. And even when I finally was able to doze off, awful nightmares haunted my dreams once again. They were invariably filled with lighthouses and wheelchairs, though the gaunt face of Mrs. Haughton now appeared regularly, too, telling me that nothing would be alright, or asking me whether I had set my affairs in order just in case. I flailed around, entangling myself in the bed covers, until first light broke.

A few hours later, after managing to snatch just a bit of sleep before a late breakfast, I thought that the dreams had been unnaturally real and vivid. There had been something life-like about them that stuck with me even after being awake for hours. By the time we had gone downstairs, most of the other guests had already had their breakfast. Mrs. Haughton, who seemed to have recovered well from our little visit, was doing her best to keep the place running on her own. She greeted us as if nothing had ever happened.

Evidently, she couldn't remember a thing from the previous night.

Then, Mrs. Highgarden stood up in order to address us, staring over her pointy glasses at each of us in turn to ensure our silence. It wasn't particularly difficult to do so for once, however, since we had all been wondering what was going to happen next after the death of Anita Brown.

"My fellow members of the committee," she began. "I'm sure that yesterday's tragedy was a great shock to all of us. To be torn from life so early is terrible, and our sympathy goes out to her loved ones whom she leaves behind."

She paused briefly to rearrange her glasses.

"There are also some practical matters we have to attend to, however," Mrs. Highgarden continued. "The question is whether we should continue our meetings or not. Now, as terrible a tragedy it was, I believe we would do the deceased a great disservice by not continuing our normal lives. A second meeting that accommodated all of your busy schedules or otherwise time-consuming activities –"

Mrs Highgarden looked sternly at Patrick Urquhart over her glasses.

"– Would simply be impossible to arrange before the next year. With the pressing financial troubles of the committee, however, I therefore feel that our only choice is to push ahead."

"But a woman has *died*," said Dr. Linton, his voice strained. "We can't just pretend nothing has happened. Think of the hotel. She was practically running the place on her own."

"I haven't had the chance to speak to Mr. Brown yet," she said. "But I am sure that we could arrive at some sort of agreement…"

But at that moment, the door to the dining room opened. A tall, elderly man in a grey suit entered. He bowed his head stiffly, before stepping aside and holding open the door. Behind him, Mr. Brown wheeled into the room, his face as red and as blotchy as ever. Naturally, the death of his daughter had left its marks on him. But I thought I detected a glimmer of something else in his eyes. He looked crazed, somehow, perhaps even paranoid, as his gaze swept the room multiple times, his eyes darting from face to face in suspicion.

The tall man in the suit waited politely for Mr. Brown to make the introductions, though decided to do it himself when it was clear that they weren't forthcoming.

"Good morning," he said. "I am Inspector Campbell, from the Galloway Police. I arrived here earlier this morning with our medical examiner. The fatal incident involving Anita Brown was reported to the procurator fiscal yesterday, and – due to the circumstances of the case – he has tasked us to investigate the case."

He paused shortly to impress the point upon us all.

"Until the cause of death has been determined, I am afraid I must ask you to remain here on the island."

There followed a great deal of muttering. Vanessa McQuinn, who was for once not glued to her smartphone, said:

"But I don't want to stay in this ghastly place anymore."

"Vanessa," her sister Jane hissed from across the table. "Please, don't make this more difficult than it already is."

"I'll say what I want to. I'm not going to be held prisoner here."

The inspector lifted his hands up in an attempt to calm the situation.

"Nobody is being held prisoner, I can assure you," he said. "We are having our people on the mainland conduct a full examination of the body as we speak. We will have more information for you in due course."

"But I don't want to stay!" Vanessa yelled, almost close to tears. "This place is horrible."

"I am afraid that is my last word," Inspector Campbell

said patiently. "Please stand by until further notice."

And with that, he left the room again. Mr. Brown, who had remained silent all the while, simply scanned the room again, making sure that everybody understood that he remained as convinced as he had been the day before that one of them was responsible for his daughter's death. Then, he slowly wheeled himself out.

As soon as he was out of sight, the room erupted into a frenzy of quarrelling and arguing.

"I've got a business to run," said Randolph Bolton importantly, slapping his hand on his belly. "Can't be expected to hang around here for weeks and weeks until those provincial people from the police come up with the obvious solution."

"And what might that obvious solution be?" asked Dr. Linton acidly.

"That it was murder, of course," Mr. Bolton answered.

"It might well have been an accident," said Dr. Linton.

"Is that your professional opinion, doctor?" asked Mrs. Highgarden from across the room, a note of hopefulness in her voice.

"Well, if I had been allowed a glimpse, I might have been able to make that pronouncement," Dr. Linton said. "As it stands, however…"

At the other end of the table, the twins were close to exchanging blows.

"Of course *you* want to stay here," Vanessa was saying. "This place is just as boring as you are."

"At least," Jane said, struggling to find an adequate retort. "At least I want to keep *my* word to mother. She'd turn in her grave if she knew how you'd been behaving."

"How dare you bring mother into this," Vanessa spat, turning on her. "You were always her sweet little favourite, never in any trouble. No wonder you want to stay here with a corpse. You're basically one yourself."

Finally, Jane – who had tried to remain as calm and

collected as possible so far – went white as a sheet and screamed:

"You arrogant b…"

"Ladies, please!" said Patrick Urquhart, rushing to stop them from fighting and catching the first few blows that the sisters had intended for each other. "This won't help anyone."

Mrs. Highgarden, meanwhile, was trying to convince the committee members that this was the ideal opportunity to continue the meetings. Nobody, however, was particularly interested in listening to her justifications anymore.

"Are you a doctor, sir?" said Dr. Linton, pointing a shaky finger at Randolph Bolton.

"No, but I've got a killer instinct – I mean, in the business sense, of course – an intuition, you might say. And I know foul play when I see it. No woman that age dies like that, no matter how hard she's working. It's clear as daylight."

"Nonsense," said Dr. Linton.

"So what is the take of our esteemed doctor, then?" Mr. Bolton said sarcastically. "I noticed you haven't been voicing any professional opinions."

"As I told you, I haven't been allowed to see the body," Dr. Linton said angrily. "But there are many natural causes that may be fatal. It is rare, but only a fool would jump to conclusions."

Randolph Bolton turned to him aggressively.

"Are you calling me a fool?" he said.

"Gentlemen, gentlemen," Mrs. Highgarden intervened. "Don't forget, we share a common goal. A vision for the committee. Do not let petty squabbles get in the way of it."

I leaned over to Val, who was sitting at the corner of the table, so that Barry could hear me as well.

"She doesn't even care Anita Brown's dead," I said. "She just wants to continue with the meetings as if nothing ever happened."

"Yeah," Val agreed. "She's a fanatic, that's for sure."

"Come on," I said. "Let's catch some fresh air. I can't stand the squabbles any longer."

"OK," said Val. "Come on, Barry."

We went up to our rooms to get our coats and then stepped outside through the heavy lounge door next to the reception desk. We were greeted by an icy cold, harsh wind that viciously ripped and yanked at our hair. Barry was having trouble moving, though he refused our offer to carry him on the grounds that it was 'too undignified'.

Above us, the clouds were moving as if they had been set on fast forward. I was surprised that the Inspector dared to go back to the mainland in this weather, though as a local he was probably used to it. And luckily, the rain was a mere drizzle so far, though I'm sure the wind would have made any boat trip a nightmare. Val, who had also been observing the sky, stepped on a shovel that was lying around on the ground just outside of the workshop. It missed her by an inch or two.

"Why do you wear those things in a place like this?" Barry asked in an exasperated tone. "You're going to get yourself – and probably us along with you – killed if you're not careful."

"I like the shoes," said Val defensively. "They happen to make me feel good about myself."

Barry looked at them disdainfully but decided to switch the topic.

"I'm with the haughty twin on this," said Barry sourly. "Wish we could get off this island as fast as possible."

"You're just moaning because Anita Brown isn't there anymore to make you cooked tuna," said Val.

"Nobody makes it like Mrs. Faversham at home, anyway," said Barry, hastily adding when he caught our eye: "Aside from you two, of course."

"That's very gracious of you, Barry," I said. "So, was it murder or not?"

"I don't know," said Val. "Nobody has ever felt animosity towards her. Not as far I could tell, anyway. Just doesn't make any sense."

"I think I'm inclined to agree," said Barry. "But even if it was murder, it's still a heb affair. I thought perhaps that Mrs. Haughton might have picked up on something else but… I must have been mistaken."

"What do you mean?" I asked him.

"Well, that she picked up on some form of magic. That would have made it a magical affair. Then, we could get the MLE involved and be on our way."

I grumbled slightly, though I couldn't put my finger on what was actually bothering me.

"I suppose we have to wait for the report from the police," I said. "We're not allowed off the island before then, anyway."

"Yeah," said Val, sounding rather depressed. "Feels a lot different now, somehow, when you're not allowed to go anymore. No freedom."

"Shall we go to the lighthouse?" I said, half-heartedly hoping that Mr. Brown might have left the door unlocked in his present state of mourning.

"There's no point," said Val. "Anyway, I get headaches when I'm up there."

"Headaches?" I asked. "At the lighthouse?"

"I know it sounds weird but that's the way it is. Maybe it's the technical equipment in there or something. Makes me dizzy."

It didn't sound like a particularly good explanation to me but I decided to drop the matter for the time being. Instead of going to the lighthouse, we aimlessly strolled around the other buildings next to the hotel, still struggling with the rough winds.

"And what do you think you're doing here, snooping around?"

All three of us swung around immediately, though I was

sure who it was from the surly grunt of a voice. And indeed, Williams was standing a few feet away, his hands inside his pockets. As was to be expected, he looked very different from when I had seen him last. He had deep, purple bags beneath his eyes. He looked gaunt, and most of the colour had drained from his leathery face.

"We didn't mean to…" Val began, but he interrupted her immediately.

"You people don't care, do you?" he spat bitterly. "Nobody cared, except Anita. Best thing that ever happened to me in my life. And now… now she's gone."

There was a moment of silence as he struggled to supress his boiling emotions in front of strangers.

"I'm very sorry for your loss," I said sincerely. "I know what she meant to you."

"How would you know? How would anyone have known?" he lashed out again. "I was just the handyman, after all. Nobody knew that I loved her and she loved me back. And now … now it's all gone forever."

His eyes swelled up, though I think he was well beyond tears in his grief for Anita Brown. I decided that honesty was the best approach.

"I… I knew because we accidentally overheard you in the kitchen. On the first night we arrived here," I said. "We didn't mean to, though. It just happened."

"You heard… everything?" he asked, after a moment's hesitation.

"Yes. The important bits, anyway. Enough to understand that Mr. Brown opposed your being together."

Williams swore and spat into the grass as I spoke Mr. Brown's name.

"She always told me not to take it personally," he said as his mouth twisted into a sardonic smile. "And I told her that she shouldn't put up with him anymore. Didn't deserve her as his daughter, he didn't. A bad man, rotten to the core."

"What makes you say that?" asked Val.

"You've got eyes, haven't you?" he said rudely. "Terrorised the entire hotel staff, he did. For years on end. None of them kept the job for long except for Mrs. Haughton. Scared to death of him they were, and rightly so."

"He threatened the staff?" I said.

"He threatened everyone who had the misfortune of being in the same room with him for too long," he said, making a large sweeping motion with his right hand. "His own daughter, too. Took her ages to stand up to him. Tried it on me, too, but I wouldn't take any of his nonsense. I do my job good and proper, and he knows it."

"Do you know if someone might have wanted to harm Anita Brown?" I asked.

He looked at me for a while, his face unreadable.

"You don't think it was an accident, then?" he said blankly.

"I don't know," I said. "But if it wasn't, I think we'd better find out quickly who did it, otherwise we all might be in danger."

"Aye," he said, his face sagging. "Anita never hurt a living soul. She was a good woman and treated the world well. There's no reason anyone would do such a thing to her."

"Her father thinks it was murder," I said. "He said as much when the body was discovered. Accused us all, in fact."

"Aye," Williams said again. "That sounds like him, alright. He would jump to that conclusion, being an ex-con himself."

"Mr. Brown is an ex-convict?" I asked in astonishment.

Val and I exchanged a meaningful look.

"Do you know what he did?" asked Val. "To be put in jail, I mean."

Williams shook his head sadly.

"Don't think I didn't try to find out. I would have loved to have something on that… on him. Anita knew, of course. But however often I asked her, she wouldn't tell me."

He leaned forward, lowering his voice conspiratorially.

"The only thing I do know is that he was banged up for a long time. Anita grew up with her mother mostly, you see. So it must have been something very serious. There are a lot of rumours floating around, though I wouldn't believe half of them. But the fact is that when he got out, she told me, the only thing he would ever talk about was how to get hold of this island. Obsessed, he was. Took him years of shady dealings to get the money – as well as convincing your committee president, that doctor fellow, at the time. And when he did get here eventually, he locked himself up for days in the lighthouse. Screamed and raged in the night. Scared off all the guests. Not that he cared, of course."

"Do you know what he was doing in there?" I asked.

"I don't. Though sometimes it sounded as if he was building or repairing some sort of machine. You'd hear the clunking 'til deep into the night. He never lets anyone in there. Not in the basement, at least. Whatever he's hiding in there, he's desperate to keep it a secret."

CHAPTER 7

Williams stared at us for a moment. His look was hard, beyond grief. I could tell that he blamed Mr. Brown for the death, though he had no way of connecting it at present. I felt sorry for him, though I cannot deny that there was a glint of something a lot more sinister in his eye. It was at that moment that I wondered if Williams wasn't capable of murder himself. If Mr. Brown was involved somehow, I was certain that Williams would stop at nothing to avenge his lover.

"Miss Sheridan?" came a faint voice from behind us.

We turned around. It was Jane McQuinn. She quickly stepped towards us, making sure not to lose her footing in the rather uneven grass. She paused briefly to regain her breath.

"Sorry to bother you," she said, politely inclining her head towards Williams and Val, "but I've been sent out to look for you. Mrs. Highgarden has finally managed to convince most of the members to continue with our meetings."

"Oh, of course," I said. "Thank you for telling me, Jane. I'll come back with you."

"I'd better get on with my work anyway," Williams said, turning around.

Val gave me the briefest of nods, indicating that she'd keep poking around. It was our only course of action left. As Val and Barry walked off into the other direction, Jane and I made our way back to the hotel.

"Have you made up with your sister?" I asked Jane.

"Oh, well," she said, "I don't think we've ever done that. Not really, anyway."

"A cease-fire, then?" I said.

"Yes, Miss Sheridan," she said, laughing softly in her peculiarly introvert manner. "Yes, that's more it, really. It's the most we can hope for at the best of times, I'm afraid. It's been worse before."

"Well," I said. "Standing up for yourself takes courage."

"I suppose so," she said. "Especially here on the island. I haven't been living so close to my twin sister like this for ages. It's more difficult than I had imagined."

She threw me a quizzical look from beneath her curtain of hair.

"Do you think we'll get off the island anytime soon?" she asked.

"I don't know," I said as we entered the hotel through the main entrance. "We'll hopefully find out later in the day. When the police let us know whether foul play was involved or not."

We moved along the corridor to the dining area. Mrs. Highgarden, sitting at the head of the table, was looking rather pleased with herself. Dr. Linton, however, was standing at the window with his arms crossed. He did not look pleased at all.

"Oh, there you are, Miss Sheridan," Mrs. Highgarden said enthusiastically. "We were just about to start. Thank you, Jane. Please be seated."

***

Mrs. Highgarden's enthusiasm soon gave way to the reality of the situation. Despite her best efforts, even she wasn't able to put a positive twist on the numbers before us. The simple truth was that the committee was in deep financial trouble. The fact of the matter was that, without selling numerous lighthouses, the organisation would no longer be functional. You didn't need to be a business expert or have Mr. Bolton's 'killer instinct' to see that.

The meeting dragged on and on. I couldn't remember

time passing so slowly since I had been a child. As the discussion raged on into its fourth consecutive hour, my mind kept racing to the lighthouse. It was becoming something of an obsession of mine already. For the more thought I put into it, the less sense Mr. Brown's behaviour made. If what Williams had said was true – and I saw no reason for him to invent such a bizarre story – then Mr. Brown had gone to great pains in acquiring the island, with the primary motive of having de facto control over the lighthouse. Quite clearly, the hotel was of no interest to him.

Yet all I could see was a building made of concrete set atop a rock in the middle of the sea. If he *was* constructing something, he could have done so pretty much anywhere that was remote and away from prying eyes. Though an island was undoubtedly private, it also possessed unique problems. Surely, anything mechanical could have been constructed anywhere else in the country without having to rely on boats and without being at the mercy of the treacherous forces of nature. A remote farmhouse in the Highlands would have done just as well – or better. So why on earth did he need to be here on the island?

At last, Mrs. Highgarden called for a recess until after dinner. No proper conclusion had been reached in regard to the committee's future. Dr. Linton was shaking worse than ever under the mounting pressure. I could see why he had been replaced as committee president all those years ago. Mrs. Highgarden may have lacked some of his expertise, but nobody thought she was in danger of having a breakdown.

Nerves were still strained at dinner all around. Barry and Val were nowhere to be seen. Hopefully, they had made some sort of progress in regard to the mystery of the lighthouse. Until we knew more about Anita Brown's death, that was our one and only lead.

At the dinner table, meanwhile, I was stuck between Dr.

Linton's constant complaining about the way Mrs. Highgarden was leading the committee and Mr. Bolton's endless tales of his business prowess.

"All simple if you know what you're doing," Mr. Bolton said, forking a greasy sausage and waving it in front of me. "You just need the right instincts."

"So I have heard several times before," Dr. Linton said. "But I have seen few real solutions from you, Mr. Bolton."

"Nonsense," Mr. Bolton bellowed. "All the committee has to do is…"

But before Mr. Bolton could elucidate on how exactly to save the day, the telephone – which was perched close to the kitchen entrance – rang. Normally, of course, nobody would have paid a moment's notice to it. Yet under the present circumstances, the dining room fell silent almost instantly, with only the sounds of Mrs. Haughton doing the dishes in the next room remaining.

The phone continued to ring.

"Well, shouldn't someone get a member of the staff?" Mr. Bolton said in a loud voice, pompously looking around the room. "There must be some measly porter boy even in a dump like this."

Yet nobody seemed willing to find out if there was one. It was as if the members of the committee were frozen to the spot, afraid of what that call might reveal.

"Fine, fine," Mr. Bolton said. "I'll do it myself."

With some difficulty, he heaved his large body from his chair and waddled over to the telephone.

"Yes? No, no, no… Bolton's the name. I'm supposed to be a guest here…yes…that's right… what did you say?"

Mr. Bolton listened intently for a while to what the person at the other end had to say. Then, his face flushed a peculiar colour of pink, though his voice remained steady.

"Are you sure?" he asked.

Judging from his facial expression, they were. Without another word, he hung up the phone and turned around to us. We were all holding our breath.

"Well?" demanded Mrs. Highgarden. "What is it?"

"It was the police," Mr. Bolton said in a flat tone.

"What did they say?" asked Dr. Linton, running a trembling hand along the back of his neck.

"Spit it out, man," said Patrick eagerly. "Was it murder or not?"

Mr. Bolton seemed to be in some sort of parallel universe in which time passed much slower. Once again, his gaze scoured the room, until he said:

"They said it was an accident. Broken neck after falling down the stairs."

Immediately, the room was filled with sighs of relief and affirmations that this had been self-evident from the very beginning. Dr. Linton dropped his cigarette in surprise. Jane smiled, and even her sister looked relieved.

"That settles it then," said Mrs. Highgarden, barely able to conceal her joy. "A terrible tragedy, of course, terrible. Yet life must go on, as they say. I see no reason why the committee shouldn't continue its efforts in the usual manner."

"For once, I agree," said Dr. Linton. "The sooner we will be able to get off this confounded island the better. I say we do another session after dinner. Settle the matter once and for all."

There was a hearty rumbling of agreement in the room, and soon the clinking of cutlery and the sounds of laughter and conversation returned. The only person who seemed less than convinced was Mr. Bolton, who had taken his seat again. His small eyes were focussed on his meal in front of him, though he wasn't eating a bite of it.

"Are you alright, Mr. Bolton?" I asked.

"Alright? Yes… yes," he said vaguely. "Lots to think about."

He remained monosyllabic for the rest of the evening. After dinner, I hastily made my excuses and headed for the door. When I arrived, Barry and Val were pouring over a large, handwritten tome from Barry's library. By now, I was getting used to the sight.

"You've missed dinner and some big news," I said as I closed the door.

"And *you've* missed an instructive lesson in magic, Amanda. Has the committee finally decided to abolish itself yet?" said Barry, peering over his spectacles.

"Only over Mrs. Highgarden's dead body," I said.

"So what's the big news?" asked Val.

"The police called," I said. "Apparently, Anita Brown's death was an accident. No foul play involved. At least, that's what the police say."

"What?" Val said, astounded.

"That's the official verdict."

"You know, Amy, when I heard what Williams had to say about Mr. Brown and his past… Remember that story Patrick told you – about the double murder in the lighthouse? Well, couldn't it have been Brown?"

"I think Patrick said the murderers name was Jenkins or something like that."

"But he could have changed his name," said Val.

"Yes, I suppose," I said. "I mean, I certainly wouldn't put it past Brown. He certainly has the temper for it. But why come back to the scene of the crime?"

Barry and Val looked at each other.

"Amy," Val began, "there's something you ought to know."

"Many things," Barry said snidely.

"Oh, come off it, Barry," I said impatiently. "What's up? What's going on?"

Val hesitated briefly.

"Well," she said, "it's got to do with that lighthouse. Remember I always had headaches when walking near it?"

"Yes," I said.

"Chances are," Barry said, giving Val a sideward glance,

"that Valerie is not imagining things. Not more than usual, anyway."

"Hey!" she said angrily. "Don't bite the hand that feeds you. You can cook your own dinner next time."

"What about the lighthouse, Barry?" I said, trying to get to the point.

He slowly took off his spectacles with both of his paws.

"I believe that there is a hexanomitron on the island," he said.

"A what?" I asked, bewildered.

"Call it a source of magical amplification, if you will."

"Amplification…" I murmured.

"Yes," he said. "Psychics are particularly attuned to them, though there are other signs, too."

Things were beginning to fall into place.

"So that's why my magic is so powerful here," I said excitedly. "You know, when we questioned Mrs. Haughton. It's like every spell was…"

"…amplified," said Val, nodding.

"It is possible," said Barry. "Though you being a novice seemed a far more likely explanation at the time."

"Your note of confidence is much appreciated, as usual," I said sarcastically. "Anyway, it seems that your theory was wrong."

"My *hypothesis*," Barry began in a pedantic manner, "was strictly informed…"

"Oh, leave it, Barry," I said, walking over to the window to look at the lighthouse from afar. "So is this hexanomitron… artificial?"

"Yes," said Barry. "They are constructed by wand-wielders, though there are various methods of do so. Suffice it to say that they were banned by the *Spellcasters' Association* long ago."

"But who created them?" I asked.

"Warlocks and witches, trying to bolster their feeble attempts at magic, for the most part. Though in the hands of a powerful spellcaster, hexanomitrons were a potent and often deadly force. Accidents were commonplace. I remember there was a particularly interesting case in 1954 when an illegal device was found…"

"How can you be sure there's a device like that on the island?" I asked, eager to postpone the lesson in history until later.

"I'm not," Barry said simply. "That's why we're going to find out tonight. I was hesitant to use magic before to break and enter – with the case being a heb case and all – though I think we'll be able to justify it in front of the *Association* if there's a hearing now. A hexanomitron is no laughing matter."

"Well, what are we waiting for?" Val said, swinging herself up from the sofa in an elegant sweeping motion. "All I need now is some pain killers to make the headache go away once I'm there."

Barry frowned.

"Perhaps," he said. "It would be better if you stayed here, Valerie."

"No way," she protested. "I'm not going to miss the fun once it starts."

"The device's powers seem to have a particularly potent effect on you," said Barry. "It would be unwise to approach it."

"For once, I've got to agree with Barry," I said, turning to Val. "There's no telling how bad it'll get for you, Val, once we get closer. You might collapse or lose consciousness. And if Mr. Brown is stalking around there, we don't want to be caught off-guard."

"But what am I to do, then?" Val asked indignantly.

I pondered the issue briefly.

"You could attend the meetings in my place," I said.

"Oh, well that's fantastic," she protested. "You two go off for a thrilling adventure, and I have to listen to those lighthouse nutcases."

"I've been listening to them for days now, Val," I said hotly. "It's time you *did* something for a change except for managing Barry's Wagner playlist!"

"It was your idea to come here, Amy," she stormed at me. "You're the member of that silly committee, not me."

"Fine," I said. "Stay here, then."

"I will," she said stubbornly.

"Ladies," Barry began, waving his paws around in a gesture of peace, "please…"

"Shut up, Barry," both Val and I said at the same time.

For a moment, it was just like old times, but I was much too angry to admit it. I got my handbag, with my wand tucked in safely at the bottom, and put on my shoes. We were both breathing heavily, but nobody spoke.

"Come on, Barry," I said roughly.

He knew better than to protest at a moment of social discord such as this, so he leapt from the sofa and trotted over to the door. I stepped outside and closed the door behind Barry, with a little more force than was necessary perhaps.

Downstairs, I was still fuming when I opened the lounge door that led to the outside. It was as stormy as ever in the darkness behind. You could hear the wind howling through the open porch of the shed next to the hotel. Even the powerful beam of the lighthouse beyond had some trouble cutting through the rain that was pouring down so heavily. For once, I thought with a wry smile, the weather mirrored my mood perfectly.

How could Val be so confoundedly stubborn and selfish, be unwilling to attend even a single meeting when I had attended all of them? It was perfectly true, of course, that I had chosen to do so, but it was still a bit rich from her to complain if it was clearly the best option available to us. Also, she had been much in favour of the holiday. Now, however, it seemed that she was unwilling to carry any of the burden.

I must have been so deeply buried in my thoughts that I bumped straight into Mr. Bolton's large pouch.

"Terribly sorry," I murmured.

"Quite alright," Mr. Bolton said, beaming. "You're coming to the meeting? The servant has started a nice fire for us."

"Erm, no, sorry," I said hastily. "I'm not feeling too well. Headache. Just need some fresh air and an early rest, I think."

"Yes," he said, nodding in an almost paternal manner. "Very taxing, this whole thing. Still, you've got to do what's most profitable, eh? See you in the morning, then."

Whatever was the matter with him? Perhaps it was my dark mood that made it appear that everyone else was in a good one. But as I observed him more closely, there was no denying that something had changed. He had received the phone call about the cause of Anita Brown's death with a thoughtfulness that I wouldn't have expected of him. Now, however, he was not only back on his old form but almost boisterous, as if his birthday had come early this year.

I made way for him to pass. He nodded appreciatively, muttering something that sounded a lot like 'excellent' under his breath, though the howling wind made it impossible to be certain.

I drew the hood of my coat over my head to shield myself from the rain. Barry and I made our way through the muddy grass towards the lighthouse. With a sudden jolt, I saw that a light was burning in the basement. It made the same peculiar pulsing motions I had noticed before from my room in the hotel. The hexanomitron had to be there, though I could only hope that Mr. Brown wouldn't be.

CHAPTER 8

We were just passing the shed when Barry stopped me in my tracks by clawing at my leg.

"Ouch," I exclaimed. "What…"

"Careful," he whispered. "There's someone walking around there, at the foot of the lighthouse."

I squinted my eyes.

"I can't see anyone," I said, lowering my voice.

"I'm a cat, remember?" he said, quickly sliding behind the shed for cover.

"You don't let a day go by without reminding us," I said, grinning and following him. "Who is it? Can you see?"

"No, but it's a tall, slim figure," he said slowly. "Coming in our direction now."

There was nowhere to hide. In any case, I could always claim to be out for a walk, though admittedly the defence was rather weak in this weather. Nervously, we waited. It wouldn't do for Williams – or worse, Mr. Brown – to catch us. Through the rain, I could see that Barry had been right. The figure was heading in our direction. And as he came closer, I had a good idea of who it was.

"Hello Patrick," I called.

"Oh, hello," he said, pretending to be surprised. "Fancy seeing you out here. Awful weather, isn't it?"

"Yes," I said. "But Barry here needed some fresh air."

"Who? Oh, the cat. I see. Yes, bit stuffy in there, isn't it?" he said conversationally.

"So why are you out here?" I asked, trying to keep my voice as casual as possible.

"Me?" he said. "Oh, I just can't stand them fighting over nothing in there. Mrs. Highgarden and Dr. Linton, I mean. Almost like watching your parents quarrelling, isn't it?"

He laughed in a rather forced manner.

"Linton's rather on the edge, I'm afraid, though I think he does have a point with the finances. Good lord, even I know it can't go on like this. And that's coming from a man whose strong point is spending! Well, better get back in, I suppose. Are you coming?"

"I'm afraid not," I said. "I'm feeling a little under the weather. Quite literally, I suppose. I think I'll turn in early after… erm… Barry's had some exercise."

Patrick Urquhart looked at Barry.

"Yes," he said, laughing. "He is getting a little podgy, isn't he? Always liked cats. Ah, well, I'll see you tomorrow at breakfast then. Have a good night's rest."

"Yes, goodnight, Patrick," I said.

"Night-o," he said jovially.

He was just about to walk in the direction of the hotel when something occurred to me.

"Say, Patrick," I called out to him. "Did you go to the lighthouse?"

"What?" he asked, spinning around.

"Did you go to the lighthouse?"

"No, I – I just wandered around a little, that's all. Didn't really care where I was going. As long as it wasn't over the cliff, that is."

He chortled.

"I see," I said. "Well, good night."

He waved his hand at me and disappeared into the hotel. Barry, whose fur was already dripping from the rain by now, was quivering with fury and indignation. I was surprised he wasn't steaming the water off through pure willpower.

"Podgy?" he said. "How dare that lazy, good-for-nothing wastrel… it's winter fur, that's all!"

"I wonder what he was doing out here?" I said slowly.

"Nothing useful, obviously," said Barry. "I wouldn't be surprised if he were involved in this whole affair, somehow.

Yes, he seems quite the type to me when I think about it. Hides his villainy behind a pair of whitened teeth and an aristocratic front."

"You're turning into quite the revolutionary in your old age, Barry. I thought you were all for the aristocracy? Being a member of it yourself."

"There always are a few bad eggs in any institution, however venerable," he said grumpily. "No respect for their peers."

"He doesn't know you *are* his peer, Barry. Luckily, he still thinks you're an ordinary cat."

"Good for me," he said grimly. "I might claw him one of these days, quite accidentally, of course."

"Come on," I said, chortling. "Let's go to the lighthouse."

We left the shelter of the shed and stepped into the open again. The icy wind cut into my face and cheekbones, so I pulled the collar of my coat a little higher. Although there was nobody to be seen, I had the distinct feeling that we were being watched or followed. I suppose being stuck on an island made you paranoid.

Finally, we reached the door to the lighthouse. Like the door to the hotel, it was built to withstand the harsh climate. By hand, we wouldn't have been able to penetrate it, I was sure.

"OK," I whispered, bending my knees so I could more easily talk to Barry. "What's the spell for opening locked doors?"

"It's simple," he said.

He briefly outlined the incantation and the appropriate wand movements. As usual, he was greatly exaggerating the ease of the spell, though I was sure I could do it.

"Vertere," I whispered, pointing my wand at the lock and waving it in quick, successive circular motions.

There was a soft but clearly audible click. The lock had been opened. With one last look in the direction of the hotel, Barry and I slipped through the door, gently closing it behind us.

We found ourselves in front of a large concrete spiral staircase that presumably led all the way up to the top of the lighthouse, where the beam was sent out as a signal to passing ships. To the right of the staircase was another door, made of solid metal.

"This must be it," I said softly to Barry. "No other door is here. This must lead to the basement."

He nodded his feline head in agreement, though he looked worried at the same time. I tiptoed over to the door and tried it.

"Locked," I said.

Once more, I cast the unlocking spell. This time around, it was much easier, though the door swung open, hitting the wall behind it with a deafening clanging sound which echoed horribly throughout the lighthouse.

Barry cursed under his breath. If Mr. Brown or anyone else was here, they would most certainly have been alerted by the noise.

Carefully, I stepped through the doorway, with Barry at my heels. The room beyond snaked its way along the outer wall in a half moon, which made it appear like a corridor more than anything else. More crates, boxes, and all kinds of tools littered the floor.

At last, we reached the end of the long room, which was marked by two man-sized crates.

"That's it," said Barry, whose voice sounded oddly flat. "We've reached a dead end."

"No, we haven't, Barry," I said impatiently. "There must be a way forward somewhere…"

I approached the crates. Closer up, I noticed that they had been placed at such an angle that it was possible to pass between them. Though you couldn't see it from afar, the opening was quite wide. I stepped past the first crate and looked around the corner. Behind the second crate, a wheelchair stood next to a wooden trap door. Something felt very ominous about the sight.

"It's Mr. Brown's wheelchair," I said, examining it. "Do you think he can walk after all? That it's all a ploy?"

"I don't know," said Barry weakly, who had followed on my heels.

"It's a trap door, look," I said, inspecting it. "We've got to get down there. Find out what's going on."

But Barry wouldn't move.

"I don't like the underground," he said stiffly.

"We have no choice, Barry. The hexanomitron must be down there somewhere," I said impatiently, stuffing my wand back in my handbag. "Come on."

"Mrs. Faversham locked me in the cellar once by mistake," he said, self-pity etched across his furry face. "You'd… we'd better go back…"

"Oh, nonsense, Barry," I said, pulling up the latch of the trap door, which creaked horribly – however gently I tried to open it.

I had expected it to be pitch black below, but an artificial light was coming from somewhere, barely illuminating the metal rungs of a ladder below me. With no time to waste, I took Barry in one hand and scooped him up.

"No time for discussions, Barry," I said. "I need you down there."

He nodded but seemed beyond words for the moment. Slowly, I let my feet down until I had a solid grip on the rungs, holding onto the ledge as long as possible for support. Luckily, I reached the bottom sooner than expected. The room was tiny and filled with more boxes. It smelt of damp neglect in here. The ceiling was so low that I had to bend over slightly. Beyond the doorway of the room I was in, I could see several other rooms that looked very similar, though I suspected from the humming sounds that an electrical generator was down here, as well.

"Scout out ahead, will you?" I whispered to Barry, drawing my wand.

Without a note of protest this time, Barry crept forward. I gripped my wand tighter, pointing it in front of me. I was shaking slightly, so I used my left hand for support. I edged past the next room, following Barry as quickly as I could without making a noise. But with the increasingly loud sounds of the generator, there was little chance of being heard.

If someone *saw* Barry or me, however, I could still pretend that he had run away, I thought to myself. But judging from what I had witnessed as far as Mr. Brown was concerned, I doubted whether he'd believe such a feeble excuse for a second.

Suddenly, Barry came to a halt in front of me.

"What's matter?" I whispered.

"Over there," Barry said, barely opening his mouth. "In the chair."

I peeked around the corner. And there, sitting in a second wheelchair I hadn't ever seen him use before, Mr. Brown was facing away from us, his head slumped forward. He didn't appear to be moving at all. A terrible thought crossed my mind. I bent down to Barry, so that we wouldn't have to shout over the noise from the generators.

"Do you think he's…?" I began.

"We'd better find out," said Barry grimly. "Careful, now. He might be faking it. Or regain consciousness."

Wand still drawn, I approached the man in the wheelchair. Behind him, several large generators were working relentlessly. It was hard to tell from the angle I was coming from whether he was alive or not. Had he simply fallen asleep? Judging from the racket from the generators, it was hardly likely – even for someone who was used to them.

I was only a few feet away now. I was perspiring from the heat in the room and my thick jacket that was made for the much colder temperatures outside. Yet fear had made my fingers as cold as ice, while my knuckles were white from clutching my wand so tightly.

I edged closer until I was on the same level as the wheelchair. Mr. Brown's eyes were closed. He looked intimidating even in his present state. I could see that, ever so slowly, his massive chest was heaving up and down. He was breathing and alive.

I nodded towards Barry to keep going. There was no way of knowing when Mr. Brown would wake up again, of course. And I didn't want to be caught in the midst of his secret den. The hexanomitron had to be very close.

Barry and I moved past Mr. Brown and into the next room. It looked as if a bomb had exploded in the middle of a junk yard. Every conceivable tool from a hammer to a crowbar littered the floor before us. Spare parts and discarded scrap metals had been piled up at the back. Someone had clearly tried to repair something, though whether with success or not we couldn't know.

In the middle of the room, a large stone ring was set into the ground. On top was a massive lock made of steel, its hinges covering the edge of the stone ring like a spider would its web.

"This is it," Barry said softly, approaching the ring. "This must be where the hexanomitron is kept. Inside. We've got to blast off this lock first, however."

I had performed the unlocking charm several times before, and so I lifted my wand confidently, pointing it at the lock in front of us.

"Vertere," I said softly.

But nothing happened. A faint jet of light came out of my wand but didn't seem to connect properly for some reason.

"It's not working," I said. "Do you think it's the hexanomitron blocking my spell?"

"I don't think so," said Barry, circling the stone ring.

"Try again."

I cast the spell again, but once more nothing happened. Barry now jumped onto the ring, examining the lock more closely. Then, he silently beckoned me to come closer.

"Tap it here," he said.

"What?"

"Just tap the lock with your wand."

I did as he asked. I wasn't sure what he was thinking of, and I couldn't see what his intentions were. A few sparks bounced off of the steel in front of us. Silence fell once more after that as Barry investigated every inch of the lock. All that could be heard was the monotonous pulse from the generators in the room beyond.

"As I thought," Barry said finally, a note of triumph in his voice. "This lock has been sealed."

"Sealed?" I asked.

"Yes. Notice how your spells bounce off without making contact."

"You don't mean magically sealed, do you?" I whispered, a cold shiver running down my spine.

He looked at me solemnly and then nodded his head.

"But then," I said, "that means that…"

"… that we have a witch or warlock on the island," he finished my sentence. "Indeed."

I looked at the lock without really taking it in. My head was spinning from the news.

"D'you think it's Mr. Brown…?" I began.

"Perhaps," Barry said. "But whoever it is, they don't want us to access the hexanomitron. They've gone to great lengths to prevent that."

"Can we break the seal?" I asked.

"Of course," said Barry, sounding as if I had doubted the extent of his magical knowledge, "provided you follow my exact instructions to the letter."

Before he could elaborate on his exact instructions any further, however, the floor and walls began to shake and quiver, as though the earth itself were shifting underneath our feet. It was followed by a rumbling that lingered even after the tremors had stopped.

"What's going on?" I asked, trying to keep the panic out of my voice.

"I – I don't know," said Barry. "The hexanomitron must be destabilising."

"How is that possible?"

"I don't know," said Barry, lips tightened. "But if we don't move fast, the hexanomitron might be destroyed. Or worse, this whole building is going to collapse on top of us."

"Great," I said nervously. "How do I break the seal?"

Barry quickly outlined the series of spells, though without his usual superior manner for a change. It seemed that a crisis also had an upside, I thought with a wry smile. At least, if we got out in one piece without being buried alive under the lighthouse, that is.

First, the invisible seal had to be weakened by a channelling spell. Furrowing my brow in concentration, I spoke the magic words over and over again until they seemed to blur and become meaningless as if they were some sort of mantra. The constant rumblings made sticking to the task at hand extremely nerve-wracking. At last, after what felt like a lifetime but surely couldn't have been longer than a minute, the lock was glowing in bright red. The rumblings, for some strange reason, had also stopped by now.

"I think that will do," Barry said. "We should be able to break it now."

"Stand back," I said to Barry, pointing my wand at the lock.

Barry jumped down from the stone ring on which he had been perched. With a loud bang and a flash, I burst open the lock. The magic spell binding it to the stone ring had been broken at last. Barry immediately leapt onto the stone ring again.

"Help me with this, will you?" he said, trying to push the heavy lock away with his body.

With another flick of the wrist, I easily sent the lock across the room, making it hit the wall as softly as I possibly could, though the metal still clanged horribly against the concrete walls.

Meanwhile, Barry was peering down the dark shaft that had been hidden below the lock. Before I could take a look myself, however, I saw by the shock on Barry's face that something was terribly wrong.

"Amanda, it's gone," he said. "The hexanomitron isn't here."

CHAPTER 9

I came closer to take a better look. Barry was right. Inside the stone ring, a large hexagonal hole gaped up at me, the end of which was too far below to see.

"That's impossible," Barry murmured. "This can't be…"

"Perhaps it destabilised completely, destroying itself?" I asked.

"We wouldn't be standing here if it had," said Barry.

"Perhaps Mr. Brown removed it? Or Williams?" I said.

But Barry shook his head.

"The hexanomitron is at least ten feet long. It is also extremely heavy. Hebs could only remove it with the help of specialised machinery."

He sniffed around the edges of the stone.

"The person who removed it also left definite traces of his work. You can see the marks here and here," he said, indicating the spots with his right paw. "Quite clear. To the trained eye, at least."

"Yeah, Barry, no need to rub it in," I said, trying to lighten the mood a bit. "But I still don't understand. I thought you said that it couldn't have been removed."

"I said," Barry corrected me, "that no *heb* could have removed this in time."

"So you're saying that the other witch or warlock on the island – whoever it is – removed the hexanomitron by magic?" I asked.

"Precisely," he said. "And I wouldn't be too surprised if Mr. Brown over there fell victim to a sleeping charm. It is rather convenient, don't you think? Him being asleep while someone steals the hexanomitron from right under his nose…"

"But who might have stolen it?" I asked. "Couldn't it be Magical Law Enforcement confiscating the hexanomitron?"

"Well," said Barry, "we can't rule that out, though as far as I know they go about it very differently. Usually pretend there's a safety hazard or something to get the hebs out of the way for the duration. These objects are very volatile, you must understand. A removal by anything less than a team of skilled warlocks or witches is dangerous, downright foolhardy, in fact. No, there is only one reasonable conclusion."

"A sorcerer," I breathed.

Barry nodded solemnly.

"I am afraid so," he said.

Silence fell as the truth of the situation settled in. This changed everything. What I had initially taken for a heb affair had become a magical one. If a sorcerer *was* at large on the island, everything was on the table. And Anita Brown's death might not have been as natural as it had appeared to the heb police.

"But what was Mr. Brown doing with the hexanomitron in the first place?" I asked. "And how on earth did the thief get hold of it without being in this room?"

"I don't know," said Barry. "It's puzzling. I…"

But before Barry could continue any further, the lights above started to flicker, as if power was being drawn away.

"Do you hear that?" I said, cocking my ears.

"What?"

"The generators," I said slowly. "Are they a bit quieter than they were before?"

We listened intently.

"I think you're right, Amanda," he said, the fear clearly audible in his voice.

"We've got to get out of here," I said immediately. "We don't want to be caught down here. Come on."

We hastily moved over to the doorway. Mr. Brown remained as tightly asleep as he had been before we had entered. Yet the lights were fading and flickering here, too. The old control panels were also losing power by the looks of it.

"Maybe we can do something to return power…" I began, but Barry once more painfully clawed at my ankle.

"What is it now, Barry?"

"Over there," he hissed. "I saw someone. Walking towards the trap door."

The methodical clunking of the generator was the only sound to be heard for a moment.

"Come on," I said, more bravely than I actually felt.

As we edged past Mr. Brown again, I hoped against hope that Barry had been mistaken. Yet something told me that his cat's eyes – old or not – were a lot better than mine and therefore unlikely to have played a trick on him. Stepping through the various rooms we had entered through, I wished that I hadn't quarrelled with Val earlier. Her help, both physical and psychological, would have been indispensable.

Finally, we reached the room with the trap door above us.

"Strange," Barry said, peering up, "I could have sworn that…"

But at that moment, the trap door – which we had left open – swung forward and landed with an ear-piercing crash on the opening.

Barry and I looked at each other, terrified.

"WHO'S THERE?"

It was Mr. Brown.

"That must have woken him up," I said, pushing as hard as I could against the trap door. "We've got to get this thing open."

"Use your wand!" Barry screeched. "Quickly."

Without hesitation, I pointed it upward and cried: "Effringo!"

The trap door burst open immediately. With Mr. Brown behind us, there was only one way forward. I hoisted Barry out through the trap door first and ascended the metal rungs as quickly as I could afterwards. I could hear the wheels from Mr. Brown's wheelchair scratching the concrete floor below, but he was too late. Barry and I quickly scampered around the two large crates and raced along the corridor until we reached the door. We were back in the entrance area of the lighthouse. With one last look up its circular staircase, I followed Barry out into the open.

***

I'd never thought I'd be glad to be out in the pouring rain again. But now, it not only visibly obscured our escape but also hid our tracks in the mud as well. Nevertheless, I thought it best to take an indirect route to the hotel, passing behind Williams's workshop in the process. That way, if anyone discovered us or happened to look out of one of the many windows of the hotel, it wouldn't be immediately evident that we had been to the lighthouse.

"That was close," said Barry, still shaking slightly from exhaustion.

"Yeah," I agreed, panting. "Could you see who it was?"

Barry shook his head.

"No," he said. "But whoever it was closed that trap door on us. There's no doubt about it."

"Come on," I said. "Let's get inside. I'm freezing. And we've got to tell Val everything."

We walked back towards the hotel lobby door as casually as we could. Barry was just about to elaborate on which bones were aching the most when I coughed loudly to shut him up. We had company.

"Hello, Miss Sheridan," said Dr. Linton, who – smoking a cigarette – looked much more relaxed than usual. "Fancy seeing you out here. They told us you were ill and in bed."

"Not quite in bed," I said. "But it's true, I do feel a little… ill."

"I'm sorry to hear it," he said, though he didn't look like it at all. "Want me to have a look?"

"Please, I don't want to bother you, Doctor," I said. "I'm sure a good night's rest will do the trick."

"Yes, that's a good idea," he said. "Well, I'd better get back to my room. Got to figure out this whole financial business. Mrs. Highgarden's making a mess of things, as usual."

And with that, he opened the door and led the way into the hotel. Barry and I followed him in, but instead of going straight ahead, we ascended the stairs that led to our room at the end of the corridor.

"It's us, Val," I said as I knocked on the door.

The door opened a crack.

"Oh, thank the Heavens," said Val as she opened it. "I thought it was Mrs. Haughton again."

Barry scampered inside.

"Mrs. Haughton?" I asked.

"Yes," Val said, as she closed the door behind me. "She was bustling around, making the beds."

She wheeled around to face us.

"What *have* you two been up to?" she said, shaking her head. "You look as if you'd had a swim to the mainland. Here, I'll get you some towels."

"Thanks, Val," I said, grinning.

She handed me one and began drying Barry's fur. Judging from his minor protestations, I could tell that he was rather enjoying himself.

"Mrs. Haughton's cracking under the pressure, I think," said Val. "Unsurprising really, since she has to take care of everything now. That Mr. Brown isn't doing anything at all. Nobody even knows where he is most of the time."

"We do," I said.

And then, Barry and I told her all about the lighthouse cellar and our narrow escape.

"So, you think somebody followed you down there?" Val asked, her hand over her mouth.

"I'm certain of it," I said.

"And you are positive it's a sorcerer?" asked Val.

"No heb could have removed the hexanomitron that quickly," I said.

Barry, who had poked his feline head from beneath the towel, nodded.

"It would have been impossible," he said. "Ouch, careful, Valerie! My whiskers are very delicate these days, you know."

Val quickly shifted the towel back up to the top of his head again.

"And if it was a sorcerer," I continued, "Barry's cover is also blown. They'll know he's not a real cat."

"But did you see who it was?" she asked.

"No," Barry said. "But whoever it was slammed the hatch on us. They wanted us to be caught by Mr. Brown."

"What a horrible thing to do!" Val said indignantly. "So there's no trace of the hexa… thingy?"

"Nope," I said. "Can't be that hard to find on a small island like this, can it?"

"Why not?" asked Val.

"Because it's ten feet long," said Barry irritably. "As for finding it, it might be more difficult than you think, Amanda."

"What do you mean?" I asked.

"The sorcerer might have turned it invisible," he said. "Or transported it off the island by now."

The prospect of finding the hexanomitron seemed to be

much more complicated than I had anticipated. But I was sure that whoever had stolen it was also responsible for Anita Brown's death. I couldn't be sure, of course, but something told me that there was a link that we hadn't uncovered yet.

"But you said you were in the room with that lock," Val said. "How could it have been stolen?"

"There must have been another way to access the hexanomitron from beneath," Barry said. "An underground passage, or a cave with another entrance – below the lighthouse."

Though we had gleaned from our adventure that a sorcerer was most likely behind the theft of the hexanomitron, the whole escapade had a bitter aftertaste. Not only had we been thwarted, but there were now a lot more questions to be answered than before. In any case, it was absolutely vital that we found the hexanomitron in time. I didn't even want to contemplate what a sorcerer might do with it.

"So what happened here, then?" I asked, trying to focus back on the present.

"Oh Amy, I'm sorry about… well, you were right," Val said apologetically. "I decided to attend the meeting after all. I said you were in bed and that I'd be happy to step in for you in the meantime. Most of them were all for it, so we went ahead with the meeting."

"I hope I don't have to attend next," said Barry, yawning. "I'd rather go back to the lighthouse again."

"Hold on," I said excitedly. "If you were there, Val… Was there anyone missing from the meeting?"

"We met that insolent young man, Patrick Urquhart, outside," said Barry, who had still not forgiven Patrick for commenting on his weight. "It wouldn't surprise me in the least if he turned out to be our villain, you know. Same smarmy type as that Rick Lavalle fellow last time. Can't trust them, you know."

Normally, I would have been inclined to argue with Barry. After the events that had occurred shortly before Christmas, however, perhaps there was a point to Barry's suspicion. Were his instincts informed by more than mere jealousy for young men?

"Perhaps," I said slowly, "Patrick simply pretended to be late for the meeting. He could have easily turned back and followed us to the lighthouse after a minute or two. Then joined the meeting later."

"Well, I don't know about that, Amy," said Val. "We didn't get very far at all. The meeting was over almost instantly, in fact. Patrick Urquhart was missing for the first few minutes, that's true. But that was right at the beginning. After he came in, it continued for a few more minutes, and then it dispersed."

"So it could have been him," said Barry triumphantly. "He could have followed us *after* the meeting ended."

"But if the meeting ended early," I said. "It could have been any one of them, Barry. If only we knew where they all went afterwards…"

"I'm sorry, Amy," Val said. "But I didn't know that it would be important. Otherwise, I would have kept on eye on who left the hotel."

"Don't worry about it, Val. It's not your fault. So what happened exactly during the meeting?" I asked. "I thought Mrs. Highgarden was determined to make it a full session."

"Well," Val began. "Mrs. Highgarden did start it off that way. She was keen to discuss the financial situation of the committee and how to raise some more funds. But the conversation kept being sidetracked by other stuff. People were arguing about all sorts of things. Dr. Linton kept attacking everything Mrs. Highgarden had to say. The twins were at each other's throats. And Patrick tried to calm the whole thing down, but without success. Finally, the only thing anybody could really talk about was getting off the island as quickly as possible. That's what everybody really wanted, except for Mrs. Highgarden of course. I think she was just about to get a grip on the situation when the businessman – Mr. Bolton I think his name is – well, he said that it was such a lucky thing that we would be able to get back to the mainland again. And that we shouldn't take such things entirely for granted."

"What an odd thing to say," I said.

"Yes," said Val, nodding her head. "That's what we all thought. And when Patrick asked him what he exactly meant by that, Mr. Bolton said that if the police had come to the conclusion that Anita Brown's death hadn't been an accident at all but really murder, that we all would have to stay there for a very long time. And that it would get pretty uncomfortable for some people if it were the case. Then, Mrs. Highgarden suddenly got very angry and demanded to know what he was on about, but Mr. Bolton just laughed and repeated that it was just lucky that there was nobody there to witness Anita Brown's death and therefore nobody to contradict the police's view that it was just an accident."

I looked at her, stunned at the news.

"D'you think he saw something after all?" asked Val, who seemed slightly bewildered.

"Of course," I said, clapping my hands together. "He must have done. He reacted very strangely when he received the news about the cause of death. You know, when the police called. Mrs. Haughton wasn't there, so Bolton picked up the phone instead. And when he did, he suddenly went very quiet afterwards – which as you know isn't like him at all. He's usually very talkative. I didn't understand at the time, but he was probably figuring out his next move."

"And instead of going to the police with his account," said Barry, delicately placing his paw against his forehead, "he decided to flaunt it in front of the committee? What a complete and utter fool."

"But why would he do that?" asked Val. "Why wouldn't he report it right away? I thought he wanted to get off the island as much as everybody else."

"Bolton must have had another, stronger motive to keep it a secret," I said. "He must have been sending the murderer an open – albeit indirect – message," I said. "He pretty much admitted that he saw something. He must be looking for some compensation for his trouble."

"In other words, blackmail," said Barry.

"That's a dangerous game to play," said Val, looking concerned.

"Yes," I said grimly. "Especially if you're blackmailing a powerful sorcerer in possession of a hexanomitron. We've got to find him right away. Before our murderer does."

CHAPTER 10

I quickly grabbed my wand from my handbag. Tearing open the door, the three of us hurtled down the corridor but quickly came to a stop on the landing. None of us knew where Randolph Bolton's room was. Val, who seemed to be thinking along the same lines, whispered:

"I'll check downstairs in the lobby – they've got to have a record somewhere. I'll be right back."

"OK," I said softly, "but hurry, every second counts now. I don't Bolton knows what he's exactly got himself into."

She nodded and quickly descended the flight of stairs at the end of the corridor that led to the lobby. Meanwhile, Barry and I waited awkwardly in the corridor. What on earth had Bolton been thinking when he'd decided to blackmail the killer. Granted, he didn't know about the magic powers the murderer most likely possessed. But being stuck on a remote island certainly made it an enormous gamble.

After what felt like half an eternity, Val returned from the downstairs, a look of triumph on her face.

"It's room number five," she whispered.

Val and I began the search, but Barry spotted it almost right away. He meowed as softly as he could to attract our attention and then pointed to the door that was directly adjacent to the stairs that led downstairs. We approached it. Below the number five, set on a brass plate, was a spyhole. I tapped on the door three times, though it remained unanswered.

"Perhaps he's downstairs?" said Val.

"Not at this time, surely," I said.

"Try again, then," she said.

Yet again, there was no reply. I gently tried to open the door, but it was locked. I could tell that Barry was about to open his mouth and whisper instructions. But by now, I knew the spell well enough without his help.

"Vertere."

The lock of the door clicked twice, and Val was able to push it open with ease. Making sure that nobody else saw us from one of the other rooms or the landing, we stepped inside the unlit room.

"Quickly, let's get inside before we're caught," I said.

Barry trotted in, followed by Val. I closed the door softly behind us, casting the room into complete darkness.

"Mr. Bolton?" I said.

But there was no reply.

"Turn on the light, will you, Val?" I said.

Val fumbled briefly along the walls, her nails scratching the plaster. Eventually, the flick of a switch told me that she had found it. The bright light from the bulb above flashed, rendering me blind for a brief moment. But as my eyes quickly adapted, I saw that there was something horribly wrong. Drawers had been torn open, their contents strewn across the floor. Bags and bins had been emptied, and some of the furniture had been turned over.

"Look, over there," Val pointed, her eyes wide in fear.

At the foot of the bed, a large figure was lying perfectly still. Wand at the ready, I stepped closer to investigate.

"It's Bolton, alright," I said, bending down.

"Wait," said Barry. "We've got to make sure that we're alone."

We checked the bathroom, yet apart from us, the room was empty. I felt Mr. Bolton's pulse. There was none.

"He's dead," I said grimly. "We've come too late."

"That's what usually happens to blackmailers," said Barry. "I could have told him that."

"That's not going to help now, is it?" I said irritably. "But we've got to make sure. Barry, can you tell whether death was caused by magic?"

But Barry was already investigating the question and held up a paw as a signal for us to wait. He sniffed at Bolton's hair and face, lifting the clothing above the chest and arms. After a moment or two, he turned to us again.

"From a superficial examination, I'd say the chances are very high that this is the work of the killing curse," he said. "Though undoubtedly our killer tried to disguise the fact. Notice the peculiar blue shapes on the chest here and here. They indicate that the killer tried to cloak the spell as a normal heart attack. A heb doctor would most likely be fooled, since he wouldn't be able to connect the discolorations to the heart attack."

Val put her hand over her mouth.

"This is just awful," she said.

"The sorcerer is absolutely ruthless," I said. "He's willing to kill repeatedly and without a second thought. We've got to find out who did this. Who knows when he'll strike next."

"Amy," Val whispered, panic seeping through every syllable. "Do you… do you think the killer could target us, too?"

I averted my eyes, not knowing what to say next.

"Amy," Val continued, now visibly shaking out of fear. "Remember what Mrs. Haughton said? About you, I mean? That you would be in great danger. Well, she was right. What if the sorcerer tries to kill us next? To kill you?"

Barry walked over to us, his gaze heavier than I had ever seen it before in the few months that I had known him. He suddenly looked a lot older and greyer. His usual, reassuringly superior manner had vanished. Instead, his voice sounded thin and strained.

"From the murderer's point of view," Barry said, "it's the logical thing to do. The heb police alone are no threat to him. Amy is the only other spellcaster on the island. And as such, she's the greatest threat."

"Then we have no time to lose," I said immediately.

"But we have no way of knowing who did this… this horrible thing," said Val miserably, indicating Bolton's body on the floor. "They've ransacked the place. Turned it upside down."

She was right, of course. The room resembled a battlefield. Nevertheless, we had to search the room for some clue.

"We've got to find something," I said. "Anything."

Well aware that if anyone entered the room, it would have taken a lot more than a little explaining, all three of us began searching the place.

The minutes streamed by without any results. We had checked everywhere, even the bathroom, thought nothing seemed to be any use in identifying the killer.

Frustrated, I was just about to give up on the search when a gleaming object underneath the cupboard next to the bed caught my eye. I bent down to retrieve it. It was a smartphone, a very new model I was sure I had seen in Mr. Bolton's hand the day before. I tried to gain access, but it demanded a fingerprint scan. As macabre as it sounded, we were desperate for information, so I bent down to get it. If it helped to find his killer, I thought to myself, it was worthwhile.

"What have you got there?" Barry asked inquisitively.

"It's his phone," I said. "He must have dropped it. Or perhaps it fell there when he was murdered."

"Check the notes," said Val. "Perhaps he wrote down a clue somewhere."

I browsed around the unfamiliar screen, but all personal notes were older than a day, save for one. It was a voice recording. I tapped it, and Val, Barry, and I listened intently.

"Quite the inheritance," came Bolton's confident voice from within the phone. "Should make my silence worthwhile. Negotiation tonight."

Barry was right. Blackmail was a dangerous game to

play.

"What did he mean about the inheritance?" asked Val.

"Well, whom do we know who lives a very comfortable lifestyle?" I asked. "Who inherited several castles and I don't know how many other things from his rich father?"

"Patrick?" Val asked incredulously. "But that's ridiculous, Amy. Come off it. He's so… well, so nice. And handsome and…"

"Val, *really*?" I said. "Is that your defence?"

She went red in the face.

"Well, I don't know…" she said.

"Where could he be now?" I asked her. "You spoke to him during the meeting, I suppose?"

"Yes," she said defensively. "I can speak to whomever I like. Nothing wrong with that, is there?"

"There is if he's the murderer," I said hotly. "Where is he, Val?"

"He said he wanted some more fresh air," she said. "He asked me whether I wanted to join him later, in fact."

"He… *what*?" I said, my pulse rising. "You were going to meet him alone at night?"

I didn't know why I was so angry at her. It was just typical of Val to be this foolish, meeting men in the dark on an island that was housing a homicidal sorcerer. But I couldn't deny that, buried deep down, there was another, more selfish reason.

"There's no need to be jealous, Amy," Val said.

"Me? Jealous?" I spluttered. "That's totally beside the point, Val… I… at least I'm not dating a killer!"

"Well, that's quite the change from last time, isn't it?" said Val.

"Please, ladies," said Barry, holding up his paws. "Far be it from me to keep the peace, but we really have to move quickly if we want to catch him. Valerie, do you know what he wanted?"

"He just wanted to talk to me about something," said

Val, "that's all."

"About what?" I demanded.

"He didn't say," said Val.

"Why didn't you tell us that before?" asked Barry. "This is an important development."

"Well, it didn't come up!" she said unhappily. "Anyway, I only really got to talk to him tonight. He seemed nice, so why not? I've been cooped up in that stupid room for days without anything to do. I thought some contact would do me some good."

"Not with a potential murderer, it wouldn't," said Barry acidly.

"Well, I didn't know he would be a murderer, then, did I?" Val said angrily.

"Never mind that now," I said. "We've got to catch him before he kills anyone else. What time were you two going to meet?"

Val nodded and checked her phone for the time.

"In three-quarters of an hour. It's just – just so frustrating."

"What is?" I asked.

"I mean that the only good-looking man on the entire island turns out to be a killer on the loose! Just my luck. Honestly, Amy, I'm really sorry, I never suspected any of this. I never suspected Patrick for a second."

"Forget it. I'm not going to deny that he had me fooled, too. What's important now is that we unmask him as the sorcerer. He's played the innocent very well until now," I said, "though a little pressure might bring his true nature to light."

"I told you he wasn't any good," said Barry, the smugness quickly returning to his voice now.

"Seems you were right again, Barry," said Val, sighing.

"Well, you said it," he said. "Seems I've got it right twice in a row."

"Don't count your chickens before they're hatched,

Barry," I said. "We don't know the full story yet."

***

The three of us left the room again and stepped out into the hall. I thought it better to lock the door again by magic. It wouldn't do at present for the rest of the hotel to be alerted. I wanted to deal with Patrick in isolation first. Perhaps even get him to the mainland before anyone knew what was going on, so that he wouldn't be able to harm anyone else.

We got our coats from our room and stepped down the flight of stairs leading to the lobby as silently as we could. Luckily, there was nobody around. I opened the heavy front door, holding it open for Barry and Val to pass through. As I stepped outside, a shower of icy rain told me that the storm had only just got started. And I had to admit, I was far from getting used to it.

But the task at hand – my duty, even – was more pressing. It was now only a matter of waiting for Patrick to emerge. After some discussion, we decided it would be best to hide in one of the buildings adjacent to the workshop. That way, we'd mostly likely see him if he came either from the lighthouse or from the hotel.

After half an hour had passed, I was growing steadily more nervous, as well as cold. Just when I was wondering whether it had been a good idea to wait for Patrick instead of just searching for him, the door to the hotel opened. Wand at the ready, I held my breath, though I quickly relaxed it again. It was only Jane's twin sister, Vanessa, who had come outside – most likely for a smoke or to entice her phone into giving her a better connection.

After several more minutes of waiting, the door opened again. This time, I was sure it was Patrick. His tall and slender features were unique. It couldn't have been anyone else. As we had previously agreed, Val was to lead him away from the hotel, to lull him into a false sense of security. And then Barry and I would overpower him if necessary. From my hiding place I nodded to Val, whose lips tightened visibly as he approached her.

They talked briefly, and Patrick gestured towards the sea. Both of them walked slowly away from the hotel, down to the path that led to the pier. I was ready for anything. I was sure that my freezing jinx would hit him faster than he had time to pull anything crazy. They had their backs to us now, and Barry and I moved in closer so that we could hear what they were saying.

"So, where did you go after the meeting?" asked Val, trying to make the question as casual as possible.

"Oh, just out and about," he said vaguely. "I like to explore places. The lighthouse is very interesting, don't you think?"

"Yes," said Val, "it is."

There was a brief, awkward silence as they continued to walk down the hill towards the sea. Val and Patrick had almost reached the pier by now. Luckily, one of the outbuildings was nearby, so Barry and I hurriedly slid behind it when Patrick was looking the other way. Finally, Patrick stopped, turning to Val.

"Look, Val, I've been meaning to ask you something," Patrick said, trying to make himself heard through the rain. "I hope you don't see me as... Do you think you can keep a secret?"

"Of course," said Val, though I could tell her tone was as icy as the winds surrounding them. "What is it?"

"Well, it's about…" he began, but broke off immediately. "Do you promise not to tell anyone, regardless of what I tell you?"

My heart gave an involuntary leap. What on earth was Patrick on about? Was he mad enough to make a confession of his crimes to Val? Perhaps it was some insane urge to communicate his deeds to someone. Beside me,

Barry looked at me with raised eyebrows. I made a gesture with my shoulders that I was just as perplexed as he was.

"What do you mean?" asked Val a few yards away from us, trying to remain as calm as possible.

Instead of answering, Patrick began fidgeting with his pipe in his pocket. There was no point in lighting it in this weather, of course, though I assumed it was something of a habit of his.

"I'm afraid I seem to be running out of time," he said. "It's all so complicated, you see…"

The sheer nerve and insolence was breathtaking, I thought, as I watched him act all shy and nervous, knowing what he had done to poor Anita Brown and Mr. Bolton. He had undoubtedly mastered his role to a degree of perfection, though I wasn't buying it for a second. Val, meanwhile, seemed unable to say a word. It was time to rescue her. Whatever Patrick was up to, he could just as well make his confession before all of us.

"Hello Patrick," I said loudly, emerging from my hiding place.

Patrick swung around immediately.

"I say, what the devil are *you* doing here?" he said, sounding utterly out of breath. "This is supposed to be a private meeting, you know, Amy. I…"

"We know you killed Anita Brown, Patrick," I said, casually lifting my wand. "As well as Mr. Bolton."

"What are you talking about?" he said, caught between nervousness and indignation. "And what are you doing with that stick in your hand?"

"You murdered two people," said Val, turning on him, too. "Don't deny it. We've found you out."

"Me? I didn't kill anyone. Bolton's dead, you say? I just saw him a few hours ago. He seemed in perfectly reasonable shape. Well, all things considered."

"We found him dead, Patrick," I said. "In his room. The whole place has been turned upside down."

"But… he can't be," he said. "Now look here, you aren't serious about all this, are you?"

Val crossed her arms to show that we were, though I made sure to keep him covered with my wand at all times. Barry, his eyes narrowed in contempt, had placed himself at my side just in case. I made sure to keep my distance. At any sign of Patrick drawing his own wand, I was ready to hex him.

"What reason would I have to do them any harm?" said Patrick, a note of panic in his voice. "You can't be serious, Amy. I'm entirely harmless. Too harmless, some of my friends say."

"Where is the hexanomitron, Patrick?" I asked.

"The what?"

"The hexanomitron," I repeated. "We know you have it. Where did you hide it?"

"I don't know what you're talking about," he said flatly. "Never heard of this… hexa… thingy."

"You killed Anita Brown and Bolton to secure it, Patrick," I said stubbornly. "There's no use denying it."

"This is madness," said Patrick, running his hand through his hair. "You've got it all wrong. If you say it was murder, I believe you. But I've got nothing to do with it. What reason do you have to suspect me, anyway?"

"Bolton recorded a note to himself on his phone before he died," I said. "He mentioned blackmailing someone with a rather large inheritance. And that makes you a prime suspect, don't you think?"

"But…" he spluttered, "there must be others who…"

"… who've inherited a string of castles?" I said. "I don't think so, Patrick."

"I'm telling you," he insisted. "I've got nothing to do with it."

I looked over at Val. She had been uncharacteristically quiet for the entire conversation. Then, she gave me a very curious expression. For a flicker of a second, I thought that she actually believed him.

"Where did you go after the meeting was over?" I demanded.

Patrick looked away rather sheepishly.

"I wandered about the island," he said. "Nothing wrong with that, is there?"

"That's not a very good alibi," I said.

"It was never meant to be one," Patrick said, his voice rising. "If you really want to know what I was doing, Amy, fine! Here it is: I was thinking of how best to ask you out without making a complete fool of myself."

Patrick's words struck me as if someone had swung a sledgehammer at me. Was this some insane ploy by Patrick to charm his way out of a tight spot? I looked desperately to Val, expecting to find a scornful look on her face. But instead, to my utter amazement, I saw her grinning.

"Val?" I asked weakly.

"He's telling the truth, Amy," said Val, giggling. "I can feel it. That's his dark secret."

"What?" I spluttered. "But he must be…"

"He isn't the killer," said Val simply.

"Are you sure?" I asked.

Val nodded. Patrick looked extremely relieved, though exposed at the same time. To my side, Barry was making grumbling noises that indicated that he didn't at all care for the turn of events.

"I'm certain of it, Amy," said Val. "Trust me. Patrick isn't the killer."

CHAPTER 11

"But it doesn't make any sense," I said, desperately clinging to a solution I knew that was wrong. "It just has to be you."

"I'm afraid it's not me, Amy," said Patrick.

I looked down at Barry. But even Barry, whose well-known dislike hardly inclined him to defend Patrick, looked unconvinced. He stared back at me, the rain pelting down on his little head, making his ears sag. Slowly, he shook his head. Once. Twice.

"Just a minute," said Patrick, looking at Barry in astonishment. "Did your cat just shake his head?"

"It's a long story," Val began. "He really isn't…"

"Careful, Val," I said in a warning voice.

"Oh, yes, sorry," she said. "I forgot he wasn't a… you know what."

"Forgot I was what?" asked Patrick, his curiosity growing by the minute.

"We don't have time for this," I said. "The real killer is still on the loose."

"But it could be anyone now," Val said miserably. "Anyone from the committee, or Williams, or Mr. Brown himself. Even someone from the mainland."

"We've got to think of something fast," I said.

"I don't want to point the finger back at me," said Patrick, "but didn't you say something about an inheritance?"

And then, realisation finally dawned on me. It had all become as clear as daylight. I had been stupid not to see it before. I only hoped that nobody had to pay for my foolish mistake, for wasting time confronting Patrick when the real culprits were still at large.

"Come on," I said. "I know who it is. We've got to get back to the lighthouse immediately. There's not a minute to be lost."

I ran as fast as my feet would carry me up the hill toward the hotel and the lighthouse. Barry, Patrick, and Val were on my heels. I wanted to explain, but there wasn't a second to be spared. We had wasted enough time as it was. I only hoped that it wasn't too late.

"Amy, what's going on?" said Val, hurrying alongside me and panting to keep up.

"Remember what Mrs. Haughton said, right at the beginning? *The past is the future in reverse.* And that it would lead to death. I couldn't make any sense of it at the time."

"I still can't think of what she…"

"And then the other thing," I continued, as if in a fever. "*Father and daughter. Daughter and father. Hatred.* That's the key, Val! That's the inheritance Bolton had mentioned in his recording. He wasn't just talking about an inheritance of money. It was another kind of inheritance."

We had almost reached the lighthouse by now. Its mighty beam was doing its best to cut through the rain that continued to pelt onto the little island. Waiting for Patrick and Barry to catch up, Val and I came to a halt.

"Why do you think Mr. Brown went to prison all those years ago?" I said, turning to Val. "A crime so awful that his own daughter wouldn't even speak of it. Murder. Double murder, in fact. You were right all along, Val. Brown must have changed his name after he got out of prison."

"But Amy, I still don't understand…"

Barry and Patrick had just caught up with us.

"Come on, there's no time to lose," I said.

Retracing my steps from a few hours earlier, I entered the lighthouse once again. This time, the door was already open. Once again, the stench of mouldy dampness greeted us as we entered. Mr. Brown's wheelchair stood at the foot of the stairs. He was already there. I tip-toed up the stairs as quietly as I could, indicating to the others behind me to do the same. I could already hear voices from above.

Behind me, Val suddenly gave off a muffled cry as something cracked horribly. She was holding her ankle in pain, doing her best not to shout. She collapsed onto the stairs, holding both hands to it.

"What's wrong?" I hissed. "Val, are you OK?"

"I slipped and…" whispered Val, her face screwed up. "I'll be fine."

"Don't be silly," Barry hissed out of the corner of his mouth. "That ankle is broken. We've got to get Valerie out of here immediately."

Patrick looked at him as though he had gone mad.

"Amy, your cat… your cat just… he said something!"

"Sorry, Patrick, we don't have time," I said. "Please, take Val out of here. Go to the hotel and make sure everybody's safe."

Patrick, still looking utterly dazed by what he had just witnessed, knew better than to argue right now. With surprising strength for such a lean man, he lifted Val cleanly from the stairs and carefully made his way down again.

"Come on, we've got to move faster," I whispered to Barry.

We hurried up as fast as we could. Finally, after what seemed like an eternity of suspense, we reached the top of the stairs. I held out my hand to signal to Barry that we weren't alone up here. A male voice was speaking. A voice that I recognised to be Mr. Brown's.

"Give it BACK," he bellowed. "Right this instance."

"Or what, old man?" asked a harsh female voice.

Still perched on the stairs, I lifted my head a little to get a closer look at the scene. At the far end of the circular lamp room, Mr. Brown was lying on the floor near an open glass door that led outside. The icy wind was coming in through, whistling ominously as it did so. A pair of crutches lay next to Mr. Brown, and his legs were spread uselessly on the ground. His face was red with rage, though the sweat on his face revealed a fear I'd never imagined ever seeing there.

In the middle of the room, I could make out the outline of a woman. She was standing behind the complex system of lamps and lenses that hurled the powerful beam of light out into the sea beyond. I was momentarily blinded by the brightness as it passed by. But as my eyes readjusted and the purring machinery rotated the beam of light away from me, I could see the figure standing there more clearly.

It was Jane McQuinn. I hadn't recognised her voice at all. It sounded very different somehow. But her entire appearance was altered. There was a fury in her eyes, a look of hatred. And she was holding a wand, pointing it directly at Mr. Brown's heart.

"You don't understand the device," Jane McQuinn said. "It is far beyond your comprehension and abilities, old man. You've stolen it from a world you never knew existed. It doesn't belong to you."

"I want it back where it belongs," he growled. "And I'm not going to get stopped by a couple of schoolgirls."

"Now, now," Jane said nastily. "Manners."

And then, without warning, she flicked her wand in his direction in an almost casual manner, muttering a spell under her breath. Mr. Brown's massive body was flung backward with such force that his head was knocked against the wall behind him. For a while, I thought he might have been knocked out, though he began to growl softly again, like a wounded animal.

"I can do much more horrible things to you," Jane said, malice etched across her young face.

"What do you want from me?" he said, holding a hand to his bleeding head. "You want that device?"

"Oh, that's just a bonus," Jane said, slowly walking towards him.

"What do you want, then?" he said angrily. "To see a cripple on the floor? To see him die before your eyes?"

"Quite right," said Jane pleasantly. "That *is* what we have come to see, isn't it, Vanessa?"

And from the other end of the room – unseen to Barry and me – her sister emerged from a corner. She had the same cold look on her face as sister did. It sent an icy chill down my spine just to watch them.

"McQuinn is such a nice name, isn't it?" Vanessa said, joining her sister. "But you know, my mother had quite a different name. She was called Asquith. You might remember that name, Mr. Brown. Or should I call you Mr. Jenkins?"

"No, it can't be," spluttered Mr. Brown. "That was too long. You can't be…"

"Peter Asquith was our father," said Jane, caressing her wand as she spoke. "And you killed him with your own bare hands fifty years ago."

"It can't be," he said. "You're too young to be his daughters."

"Ah," said Vanessa. "Magic is a beautiful thing, isn't it? Hides wrinkles quite well, you know."

"Prolonging youth is quite the asset, I assure you," Jane said, nodding. "But you would understand that, Mr. Brown, wouldn't you? That's what you got from the hexanomitron. The device provided you with almost superhuman strength for many years."

"How did you find me?" he said.

"Oh, it wasn't easy," said Jane McQuinn conversationally. "Who would have thought that you had the gall to return here, of all places? Vanessa and I couldn't believe it. But my mother knew. She didn't believe in revenge, did she, Vanessa? She lied to us. She told us that our father had in fact died in an accident. But finally, a few months ago, on her deathbed, she told us the truth. That you had killed him. And how you had manipulated the hexanomitron. Not bad – for a heb. At least, as long as it worked. But just look at you now. A weak, pathetic cripple on the floor."

"I would have repaired it!" bellowed Mr. Brown, trying but failing to support his useless legs. "I was close. If you hadn't stolen it from me I'd rip every limb from your little…"

"Oh, but we brought it back for you, Mr. Brown," said Vanessa, a menacing sweetness in her voice. "You will get your chance."

She lifted her wand.

"Turn on the hexanomitron, dear sister," Jane ordered.

Vanessa opened another door leading outside and vanished.

"You'll be pleased to hear that we've repaired it for you," Jane continued. "The device is outside as we speak, levitated in mid-air only a few yards away. Once it has been turned on, you will be able to stand again. To fight like you did all those years ago. But I must warn you, Mr. Brown, my spells will also be amplified. I'm curious to see what effects some of them have on you. I can imagine they will be rather more painful than usual."

Mr. Brown's face stood still in shock as all the colour drained from it. He was not a man who was easily intimidated, but I could see that he was beginning to panic.

"Wait," he said quickly, switching gears. "That was all a lie they told you. It didn't happen the way they said it did at the trial. It was self-defence. Both deaths. They banged me up all the same. I paid my price to society, didn't I?"

"Not to us, you haven't," said Jane viciously. "We'll never get our father back. So I don't see why you should enjoy a quiet pension here, either."

I felt a pulse rush through my wand. A moment later, Vanessa returned into the room. She nodded her head briefly to her sister. The hexanomitron was on.

"Consider this a parting gift from our late father," said Jane, pointing her wand at him.

She fired a spell at him but I was ready for it. I directed

a spell at her wand arm that knocked her back several feet, making her miss her shot by a large margin. She looked around wildly for the source of the intrusion.

"You," she screamed. "You don't understand. Get out of my way. You will not stand in the way of justice!"

"I can't let you do that," I said.

But her sister Vanessa – unable to contain herself – had already rushed across the room and was on top of Mr. Brown, punching and kicking every inch she could find. I shot a body-binding hex at her, but missed. Jane, meanwhile, had regained her position and fired a curse at me, which almost hit my upper shoulder. I ducked for cover.

But Mr. Brown, incredibly, had regained strength from the hexanomitron. He hurled a punch at Vanessa that sent her flying across the room. Jane, crying in anguish, was sending hex after hex at him, but to little avail. Somehow, he was channelling some sort of energy to repel the magic. Some of the spells hit him, though they weren't enough to stop him, while others just bounced off him.

Jane McQuinn's face went white as the seriousness of her miscalculation dawned on her. Mr. Brown, though still shaky on his two legs, was coming closer and closer, trying to corner them in front of the glass door that led outside. With nowhere else to go, Vanessa and Jane McQuinn hurried out into the open.

I looked at Barry. He stared back at me, frightened yet determined. We had to put an end to the bloodshed. I edged forward, aiming a body-binding curse at Mr. Brown. But as with Jane's spells, they simply bounced off his back.

"Stop, Mr. Brown," I shouted.

But he wouldn't listen. He had reached the door that led outside now. The twins were trapped outside, with nowhere else to go.

"We've got to turn off the hexanomitron," I said.

As quickly as I could, I skidded across the floor towards

one of the doors that led outside. The platform ran around the entire room like a ring. Only a narrow railing prevented a fall right down to the sharp cliffs below. I shuddered, trying to force myself to not look down.

Barry cursed under his breath.

"It must be at the other side," he said. "Quickly."

We raced along the platform as fast as we dared amidst the heavy downpour of rain. And there, in the distance, a long, dark shaft was floating in mid-air, bobbing in the rough winds as though they were simply a light breeze. But as we approached, Vanessa and Jane McQuinn appeared from the other side, blocking our path to the hexanomitron, their backs to us. They were doing their best to fend off Mr. Brown's attacks.

With a ferocious blow, Mr. Brown lunged at Vanessa, but she dodged to the side. Jane was wildly pelting curse after curse at him, but still to no avail. Then, in an unprecedented display of speed, Mr. Brown suddenly launched his massive body forwards, pinning Vanessa to the side of the railing.

"Turn the thing off, Jane, and kill him," shrieked Vanessa.

But there was no time. Mr. Brown had closed a powerful hand around Vanessa's neck. Without a moment's hesitation, Jane rushed at him. But in her haste, she had underestimated the wet surface on the platform. She slipped, skidding uncontrollably towards Mr. Brown. As she crashed into him, she instinctively held the wand in front of her, bellowing:

"Dispergo!"

Where the wand had failed at a distance, it now performed on direct contact. With an ear-splitting bang, the curse blasted Mr. Brown out of the way with such force that it sent him toppling over the railing. But he still had an iron grip on Vanessa, who was yanked down with him, helplessly clutching at thin air.

In a desperate effort to save her, Jane lunged forward, grabbing Vanessa's outstretched hand. But the weight of both Mr. Brown and Vanessa falling was too much for her.

"Let go," I shouted.

But Jane wouldn't listen. I shot a levitation charm at her to prevent the fall, but it was too late. Jane had toppled out of sight, and followed Mr. Brown and her sister into the darkness below.

CHAPTER 12

A week later, Val, Barry, and I were back safely at Fickleton House. The bodies of Mr. Brown, Vanessa, and Jane had been recovered the day after the events up at the lighthouse. After that, we had spent a few days in London, giving evidence for the MLE inquiry that was fully under way.

Though the physical pressure had subsided quickly enough at the wonderfully warm firesides of Fickleton House and with the very tasty food that Mrs. Faversham provided, I couldn't forget what had happened so easily.

Though it by no means justified the twins' actions, I understood the pain of losing one's parents. How would I have felt if I had suddenly found out that my father had been murdered and that the perpetrator was still out and about? Would I be sensible and contact the authorities, or would I take matters into my own hands? Luckily, I didn't have to answer that question. Like Val and Barry, I could feel safe and secure in a theoretical code of conduct that wouldn't be fully put to the test. And hopefully never would be.

"But what I still don't understand," said Val, as we were having breakfast one fine Saturday morning at Fickleton House, "is why Mr. Brown could walk again. I thought he'd been in a wheelchair for years."

"Because he was particularly attuned to the powers of the hexanomitron," said Barry. "It's very rare for a heb, but not unheard of. He must have noticed its effects on him by accident when he first came to the island as a guest."

"But why did he kill those people all those years ago?" asked Val. "In the lighthouse, I mean."

"We'll probably never truly know why he killed the first man," said Barry, shrugging his shoulders. "Perhaps Brown was simply tempted to use his new powers. But as for the second victim – Peter Asquith – there's no doubt that he was there to investigate. MLE bungled the follow-up investigation at the time, as they simply assumed that a mad heb had gone on a rampage. Which, I suppose, was part of the truth."

"But Brown also wanted to conceal the whereabouts of the hexanomitron," I said.

"Yes," said Barry. "He must have instinctively understood the value of such a device and sought to cover it up at all costs. That's why he remained quiet at the trial. And of course, once he was released, he did everything in his power to gain full control of the island."

"But all of this happened so many years ago," said Val. "The twins were hardly of age. It doesn't make any sense."

"They made themselves look younger through magic," said Barry. "It's not permanent, so they'd have to redo it every morning."

"Sort of like make-up," said Val, grinning.

"A little more sophisticated than that, Valerie," said Barry huffily. "But yes, I suppose that is a fitting analogy."

"Well, they certainly played their part well," I said. "I didn't suspect them 'til the very end."

"How did you think of them, Amy?" asked Val.

"Well, it was Mrs. Haughton's prophecy, really," I said, pondering the issue. "Her warnings about death and danger were clear enough, but the other things bothered me."

"Like the future is the past stuff," said Val.

"In reverse, yes," I said. "You see, Brown had killed their father all those years ago. And now the twins – the daughters – wanted to avenge him. So they killed Anita Brown first."

"I still don't understand that," said Val. "Why not kill him immediately?"

"Their point, I believe," I said, "was to make Brown feel the same pain that they had felt. Of losing family."

"How horrible," said Val.

"Yes," I agreed.

"So what's going to happen to the committee now?" asked Val.

"Oh, please," said Barry dismissively. "They're doomed anyway."

"Not from what I've heard," I said, smiling. "Patrick's promised to put in some considerable funds. On the proviso that the committee must be reformed."

"That was very generous of him," said Val. "I bet Mrs. Highgarden didn't like that, though."

"No, but she needed the money," I said.

"Don't we all?" said Barry, yawning.

There was a knock on the door.

"Yes?" I said.

It was Mrs. Faversham. She bustled in, smiling warmly at all of us. She gave Barry a little pat on the head and proceeded to place an assortment of letters on the mantelpiece.

"Here you are," she said. "It's been piling up a little. I hope there wasn't anything too urgent in there."

"Thank you, Mrs. Faversham," I said. "I'm sure there won't be anything too urgent."

Taking some plates with her on her way out, she gently closed the door again. Once Mrs. Faversham's was safely out of earshot again, Val turned to me.

"Better not open any strange letters again, Amy," she said. "That led us on a bad path last time."

"Yes," said Barry sniffily, jumping onto the table. "No more 'holidays', please."

"You're telling me," I said, thinking back to the endless sessions of pointless meetings. "But I'm sure it's not going to end that way again."

But my curiosity was getting the better of me. I got up and crossed over to the mantelpiece, taking the pile of letters and plonking them on the table for Barry and Val to see. Most of them were bills, but a purple letter struck my eye immediately.

"Hello, what's this?"

"What?" both Val and Barry asked at the same time.

"Look, it's addressed to Barry," I said. "*To the Right Honourable Earl of Barrington.*"

I passed it along to Barry, who dashed to one of the sideboards for his reading glasses and back again. Once he had perched himself back on the table, he slit the letter open with one of his claws and unfolded the paper. It was thick and looked heavy, like parchment. Barry quickly scanned the first few lines.

"Who's it from?" I asked.

"It's from Warklesby's," he said.

"Bless you," said Val.

I had no idea what it was myself. Faced by such ignorance, Barry sighed ostentatiously.

"It's the only school of magic in the country," said Barry irritably. "By their own account, it seems they're having a spot of trouble with some of their students. Pupils have gone missing and members of the staff are being blackmailed. They're afraid it might not stop at that, either, if they can't find out who is behind it all."

"That sounds awful," said Val. "But what do they want from you exactly?"

"They want me – well, us specifically," he said, checking the letter again, " – to investigate the case. Undercover, as it were."

"Seems we're making a name for ourselves as investigators already," said Val, beaming. "What do you think, Amy?"

"Well, I don't know," I said, grinning. "We've sort of always slipped into things. Why break the pattern?"

"Can't hurt to know what we're getting into for a change," said Val. "What do you think, Barry?"

"Certainly not," he said. "I've got my research to take

care of. I can't go gallivanting across the countryside, looking for blackmailers. Anyway, the place is crawling with know-it-all warlocks and perfect witches. Warklesby's is insufferable."

"No cat is an island, Barry," I said. "Not even you. Perhaps some more contact with the spellcasting community will do you some good. Val, what do you think?"

"A school for witches and warlocks, are you kidding me?" Val said. "Of course I'm game."

"Excellent," I said. "May I see the letter, Barry?"

"What?" he said. "Oh, yes, yes, if you must."

I scanned it briefly. The first two pages were mostly accounts of the strange occurrences at Warklesby's. The last page outlined the proposed mode of smuggling us into the school without arousing too much suspicion.

"Did you read this last bit, Barry?" I said. "They want to give a you a position as a guest lecturer."

"Let me see that," he said immediately, clawing at the page.

He quickly went over it, then took off his spectacles and looked at us in what he considered to be a matter-of-fact voice.

"I suppose, under the circumstances," he said, "I mean, the school does seem to be in quite a spot. Who would we be to deny them?"

Both Val and I burst out laughing.

"Well, that shouldn't be too much out of character for you, Barry," I said, winking at Val. "And what could we go as?"

"You could have the pleasure of being my research assistants," he said solemnly.

"Great," said Val. "Another boost to Barry's ego."

"Recognition of my true talents, you mean?" said Barry haughtily.

"Yes," I said, grinning. "One thing's for certain already.

We'll never hear the end of that one."

COPYCAT MURDERS

T.H. HUNTER

CHAPTER 1

Judge Immanuel Robinson raised a white handkerchief to his forehead, wiping away the ever-present drops of perspiration that had plagued him since the beginning of the trial in early June of that year. Despite the crowded courtroom, a makeshift construction in the largest tower of Warklesby's School of Magic, hardly a sound emitted from the galleries, set up specially to accommodate the large public interest in the case. Nobody dared to make a noise, lest they miss something, for the arrival of the jury was due any minute now.

Perhaps it was his age that made him so susceptible to the unbearable heat, Immanuel Robinson thought. He could not remember ever having been so uncomfortable on the judge's bench before. Perhaps, however, it had been the peculiar details of the case that had such an effect upon him. He had seen many a crime during his long career, though none came close to matching the extent and the sheer *evil* – there was no other word for it – of Vincent Wycliffe's deeds.

He didn't know whether the gaunt, stony stares of the victims' relatives or the heart-wrenching account of one of the few survivor's had been worse. He only knew that he had had to take two showers in quick succession that very evening.

He had been able to uphold the veneer of his impartiality during the trial, it was quite true. Yet never before had it appeared so hollow to him. The loss of objectivity frightened him. Retirement, he thought, had never been more appealing.

Strangely, the accused had seemed perfectly unperturbed by any of it. In all the many years in the magical courts of England, Immanuel Robinson had never witnessed anything quite like it. He was no psychologist, of course, but he had seen his fair share of what experts deemed to be 'psychopathic sorcerers', menaces to their fellow witches and warlocks. And yet, there was something uniquely distant and merciless about the way Wycliffe sat there, neither ashamed nor frightened. At times, he thought he caught a glimpse of secret pleasure in those dark eyes as the details of his crimes came to the fore. And it made the judge's blood boil.

At last, the court usher announced the return of the jury with their final verdict. A moment later, the members of the jury – all wearing a sombre expression – filed through the door next to the uppermost gallery and made their way down the spiral staircase that led them directly to the jury box.

Judge Robinson scanned the many tense faces around him. The time of waiting had become unbearable for many in the galleries. People shouted 'murderer' and 'hang him', while others shook their fists at Wycliffe. Security warlocks were having trouble keeping angry spectators in line.

"Order," Judge Robinson boomed, his voice – magically enhanced – reverberating around the room.

Once more, he raised his handkerchief to his brow. As he did so, he couldn't help notice that his hand was shaking slightly. But when he spoke next, he was relieved to find that his voice was steady and authoritative.

"What is the verdict of the jury?"

"Your Lordship," the foreman of the jury said. "In the case of Wycliffe vs. the Magical Community of England, the jury has come to the following verdict…"

He opened the envelope in his hand, unfolding the

single sheet of paper within.

"We find the accused guilty of all charges."

A roar of approval, accompanied by many more screams and cries demanding the hanging – or worse – of Wycliffe, permeated the chamber. This time, however, Judge Robinson did not call for order. He looked with the utmost disgust at Vincent Wycliffe, whose face had twisted into a sinister smirk. It was the only time in his career that he wished he had the power over life and death, as in the magical courts of old.

As the screams finally died down on their own, he addressed the court:

"Vincent Reginald Wycliffe, the jury has found you guilty of all charges. In light of the heinous and sadistic mode in which you perpetrated them, as well as the utter lack of sympathy for your victims, as showcased throughout the trial, I have no other choice but to sentence you to imprisonment for the rest of your natural life. Your powers will be stripped indefinitely. Your possessions are to be sold, and the proceeds to be distributed amongst the survivors and the relatives of your victims."

Slowly, Wycliffe rose his feet. Flanked by curtains of greasy blond hair, his grey eyes flashed dangerously at the judge.

"This is not the end," he spoke, his voice soft but clearly audible. "I shall return."

At Wycliffe's words, the courtroom erupted in turmoil. Hexes went flying everywhere, bouncing off the protective dome that Magical Law Enforcement officers had erected around the dock. Dozens of warlocks and witches were now scaling the balustrades, threatening to close in on Wycliffe.

Under fire from all sides, MLE officers dragged Wycliffe to an adjacent exit and pushed him through the door, where the judge knew that a prison transport was already waiting for him. The crowd swarmed the closed door, hammering on it with all their might, but they were too late. The trial of Wycliffe was finally over.

CHAPTER 2

"No, I cannot allow it," Barry said stubbornly, sitting on the dining room table and crossing his paws in front of him. "Utterly out of the question."

"But Barry," Val protested, "you'll love it once they've finished with it. And anyway, we'll be at the school, investigating the murders."

"No," Barry said flatly.

"It's got to be done at some point, you know," I said, looking up from my very tasty but slightly burnt bacon on the plate in front of me.

"I will not have clumsy workmen falling all over the place," Barry said, now beginning to pace up and down the table, his tail twitching in irritation. "Especially when I'm not there to make sure they don't get up to any mischief."

"Careful, Barry, your tail is in my coffee," I said, gently pushing it aside.

"Your library is falling apart, Barry!" Val said, with a mixture of affection and frustration. "And I'm sure they won't touch anything important. They won't even understand your research."

"Oh, you don't know these people," Barry said darkly. "All friendly and earthy one moment, next they'll be destroying – or worse, stealing – my research. No, I can't have it."

"Would you rather have another accident, Barry?" Val asked.

There was a short silence as Barry winced at the painful memories. One week ago, Barry had been working in his library deep into the night, as usual. Val and I had been roughly awakened by a terrifying shriek that carried right through the house. As Val sped over to Mrs. Faversham's cottage for help, I quickly guessed that the noise was coming from Barry's library. Though I thought at first it might have been some sort of experiment that had gone wrong, I was quickly corrected by the scene before me.

Barry had been lying at the bottom of a massive book shelf that reached right up to the ceiling. One of the contraptions – designed by my late great-aunt to provide Barry with access to all areas with relative ease – had lain broken and splintered next to him on the floor.

It had taken me the best part of two days to master the spells that would mend his bones again. It was an experience that neither of us wished to repeat. As one might imagine, Barry was not the easiest patient in the world.

Back in the present, however, Barry was desperately looking for a way to avoid repairs to his library.

"I'll just have to be more careful next time," he said. "I'm a cat, after all. I must have a few more lives left to play with."

"Sorry, Barry," I said. "But you're… well, you're getting on in years."

He drew himself up with what he considered to be a pose of dignified huffiness.

"Your point, Amanda?" he sniffed.

"Well, cats aren't supposed to be breaking bones when they fall. They're supposed to land on their feet."

"A minor oversight," he said. "I was lost in thought. Happens to great minds, you know. It's just part and parcel of my work."

"No, it isn't," Val said forcefully. "Because the library is getting repaired, isn't it, Amy?"

"I'm sorry, Barry, but it's my final word. We don't want you to get hurt again."

"Not physically, perhaps," he said morosely. "But the *emotional* pain of losing years of work might just be unbearable…"

"OK, here's the deal, Barry," I said. "I'll turn anyone who dares to steal your research into a frog. How about that?"

Barry pondered the unexpected offer for a while.

"A mouse might be more fitting, but I'm grateful for the sentiment nonetheless, Amanda," he said cheerfully. "But I want Mrs. Faversham to check in on them every day."

Val beamed at both of us.

"So, now we've got that out of the way, we should better start packing," Val said.

"Agreed," I said. "By the way, how are we getting to Warklesby's, anyway?"

"We arrive by magic, of course," said Barry.

He couldn't quite hide the relish in his voice at my complete ignorance.

"Right, so we fly there by broom, I take it?"

"No, it's too well hidden for that," he said loftily. "It's built into a rock in the mountains, you see. No, the school can only be accessed safely through a portal system. Luckily, your great-aunt had one connected to the house ages ago."

"A… a portal is in the house?" Val asked, slightly unnerved.

"Yes," Barry said. "But no need to fret. It cannot be activated unless permission is given. A little like a door to a house, if you will. You can approach and knock, but someone still has to let you in."

"I see. So where is this portal?" I asked. "I'm sure I've been in every room of the house by now. I haven't seen anything like that."

"It's behind the portrait in the living room. *My* portrait, in fact."

"Naturally," I said, rolling my eyes at Val, who started to giggle.

Barry, however, looked rather pleased with himself.

"I'd better head upstairs," said Val. "I still have some light packing to do."

"OK," I said. "I'll see you later."

***

After Mrs. Faversham had cleared away the remnants of our breakfasts, I went upstairs to finish off my own packing. Following the drastic events in Scotland earlier this year, I had come to appreciate Fickleton House even more than before. More than ever, its solid walls promised a security that the outside world definitely seemed to lack these days.

As I walked through the winding corridors with their familiar, dark wood panelling, I thought how significant it was that I had come to cherish Fickleton House so much. Before becoming a witch, I had always felt at home in the world, as well as being trusting of the people who surrounded me. Now, however, the memories from the lighthouse crept into my dreams whenever I wasn't expecting them. After all, who really knew how many other sorcerers roamed the country? Perhaps less than I currently imagined, though it certainly didn't feel that way.

And now, I'd be going into a school full of witches and warlocks. I was excited, yet afraid at the same time. Despite the fact that I worked hard to improve my magical abilities, I hadn't been a witch for long. I had never lived amongst spellcasters, excluding Barry, of course. His abilities, however, were greatly diminished as a cat. And though he often spoke of being close to a breakthrough in therianthropic retransformations and thus regaining his power, Val and I secretly agreed that it was wishful thinking rather than realistic hope that he'd ever be able to turn back into a warlock again. For the first time, therefore, I'd be surrounded by hundreds of expert spellcasters once I set foot in Warklesby's School of Magic. That fact alone, I was sure, would certainly make any detective work a lot more difficult.

Trying to push my worries aside, it took me the best part an hour to pack the rest of my things. Before we could depart, I still had to phone the workmen, who'd be doing up Barry's library. I had already contacted a local man on Mrs. Faversham's recommendation, but I still had to give the signal that we could go ahead as planned.

I briskly crossed the large, open grounds of Fickleton House that led to Mrs. Faversham's cosy little cottage. Since magic was used so much in the main house, electrical equipment didn't work there. At first, I had been irritated at having to use Mrs. Faversham's telephone every time I wanted to call someone, though I had come to appreciate that I was no longer at the beck and call of modernity around the clock.

Mrs. Faversham had left a note on her door, informing me that she was out shopping and would be back shortly. Fortunately, she had left the door open.

I stepped inside, carefully cleaning my shoes on the mat, and made for the sitting room where the telephone was located.

And then, I heard an oddly muffled voice from within. I froze, listening intently. It was definitely not Mrs. Faversham. Had someone broken into her cottage while she was out?

I fumbled for my wand in my pocket, but it wasn't there. Foolishly, I must have left it with the rest of my things in my room. With nothing else to hand, I grabbed the sturdiest-looking umbrella under the hat stand and crept slowly towards the door.

It was ajar, so I pushed it open very gently, ready to strike at the slightest movement. But the sight that met my eyes was very different than I had expected.

On the small table near the window, Barry was crouched in front of the telephone, a handkerchief covering his mouth.

"Yes, that's right," Barry was saying. "There was a

mistake… Yes… I want you to cancel all arrangements you made with Miss Sheridan… That's right… On whose authority, you say? Why the Earl of Barrington's, of course! … Never heard of him? Now listen here, you little …"

"Barry!" I exclaimed, caught been laughter and indignation. "What on earth are you doing?"

Caught red-handed, Barry gazed up at me in shock. After a moment, he cursed loudly and then placed a paw on the hook to hang up the call. With the other, he removed the handkerchief from the speaker.

"Well," he said drily, "it was worth a try."

"Barry," I said sternly, "you're just being silly. That library of yours is a death trap. And it ends here."

"It didn't work anyway," he said, waving a paw irritably. "The firm wouldn't change the booking. Social rank, it appears, counts for less and less these days."

"So does common sense," I said, supressing a grin at Barry's antics.

I picked up the receiver and redialled. The man at the other end had a very strange tale to tell indeed, one that involved an imaginary earl who had called them to cancel the order.

"Oh, yes," I said, "that was my… my grandfather. He's a little disoriented at times."

Ignoring Barry's furious visual signs of protestation, I confirmed for them to start the very next day. Mrs. Faversham was to let them in and out of the house. Barry did not look pleased, but, for his own good, I remained adamant.

***

A quarter of an hour later, I was back in my room in the main house again, with my bags all carefully stacked next to the door.

I had made only a few alterations since moving into

Fickleton House. Val had discovered a painting of my late great-aunt in the attic a few weeks ago, and I had decided to hang it up in my bedroom. There were no photographs around the house, so this was the only image I had of her. The painting depicted a woman in her late forties, with dark, curly hair, already interspersed with specks of grey. She looked impressive, though there was also a nurturing kindness that I thought the artist had captured very well in her smile and the crinkles around her eyes.

Though I had never known her, of course, I felt I owed her a great deal. Placing her portrait on the wall was one way, however inadequate, of showing my gratitude. It was a great pity that I hadn't had the chance to get to know her, though I always enjoyed it whenever Barry talked about her.

Having packed all of my bags, I drew the curtains of my room. We didn't know how long we'd be gone, so cramming everything I might need into my two large suitcases was something of a conundrum in itself. In the end, I was forced to leave some of my things behind. Perhaps, I thought, with the portal in place, there was surely a way to retrieve some of them later, if needed.

Stepping out into the corridor, I was must about to make for the stairs when I heard a wheezing sound coming from the unlit corridor to my right. For one mad moment, I thought some sort of stray dog had miraculously found its way into Fickleton House. I dropped my suitcases, squinting my eyes to see what was going on in the darkness. It took me a moment to register who it was.

"Val!" I exclaimed, laughing. "What on earth are you doing?"

Val, puffing like a train, was teetering dangerously from side to side. She was balancing three suitcases of various sizes in each hand, a heavy-looking rucksack on her back, as well as what looked like a large, purple hat box that she was carrying by means of a string in her mouth.

She stopped in order to answer me, but that was a grave

mistake. The hat box dropped to the floor. Trying to break stop it from falling with one desperate but futile dash forward, sending bags and boxes flying in the air and then towards the staircase.

"Amy, quick!" she yelled. "Do something!"

Pulling my wand as fast as I could, I directed my wand at the luggage.

"Levitate!"

The assortment of bags, boxes, and suitcases came to a halt in mid-air as though attached to invisible strings. Val inched forward slowly, as though scared she might cause them to fall again if she moved too quickly, and plucked them out of the air one by one.

"Val," I said, "is this your idea of *light packing*?"

"Oh, don't be silly, Amy," she said, laughing. "This isn't my stuff – it's Barry's."

"Barry's? But he's a cat, for crying out loud, what does he need all this for?" I said.

But before Val could answer, a dark, feline figure had appeared from the depths of the corridor.

"These," Barry said in a majestic tone, "are all the books I require to teach."

"You needn't have brought your entire library," I said.

"It is only a small, though absolutely crucial, part of it, I assure you," Barry said smartly. "And since I cannot prevent you from turning my quarters upside down, I decided to take the most valuable tomes with me."

"Easy for you to say, you didn't have to carry them," said Val.

"Why didn't you just ask me, Val? I could have whisked them downstairs by magic in a matter of minutes."

"Sorry, Amy," she said. "I couldn't find you. I guessed you were with Mrs. Faversham or something. Thought this'd be faster."

"Alright," I said. "We'd better get started. When… erm… is the portal due, Barry?"

"Portals aren't *due*, Amanda, they're…"

"Please, Barry, just tell me when we're leaving," I said, trying to avoid an unnecessary lecture.

"The next cycle," he said huffily, "is in about fifteen minutes."

"Good, let's catch that cycle, shall we?" I said.

"But I haven't even packed all my introductory works to elemental magic yet. Lord knows what these workmen will do with them if they get their hands on them."

With one last sharp look at Barry designed to quell any further resistance, I began magicking the luggage downstairs, followed by a relieved Val and a grumbling Barry.

Having arrived safely downstairs, the living room looked a lot smaller with all of our bags inside. On Barry's instructions, I performed a levitating charm on his portrait – pretending to lose control in the middle of the process, which had Val laughing heartily and Barry cursing at me.

"Let it go, Amy," said Val, wiping a tear from her cheek. "He'll have a heart attack if you don't."

"Not so *fast*, Amanda," Barry said angrily. "Really, if you think this is funny, I don't know what to say."

"It's just a little harmless teasing, Barry," said Val.

"Don't worry, it's safe with me," I said. "Now, it's off the wall. What do we do next?"

Evidently, Barry contemplated whether he should answer immediately or not. Finally, however, he must have come to the conclusion that the most dignified approach was to ignore the entire affair.

"We must reveal the portal," said Barry, pointing with his paw to the bare patch on the wall where the painting had been a moment earlier.

"And how do we do that?"

"Draw your wand along a line away from the fireplace, at the bottom. Here, you see. Draw it in a straight line, the portal is a lot larger than the portrait, mind. Now, when you're ready, keep repeating the following words: Porta aperire."

"Porta aperire," I said, murmuring it all the while I was edging my wand along the borders of the invisible portal.

Immediately, a line of bright green began to emerge, thin yet pronounced. To fully redraw the other three lines of the portal, I had to climb onto a nearby chair, as physical contact between the wand and the wall were mandatory.

At last, I had joined up the last line, and stepped down from the chair. The green light seemed to be pulsating now, like a geometric heart. The pulses were accompanied by a rushing sound that faded in and out.

"And now?" asked Val.

"We knock," said Barry.

I considered this to be part of the house metaphor Barry had used earlier.

"And how do we knock in the magic world?" I asked.

"For once," Barry said, smirking, "it is the same as in the heb world. Just knock three times, but make sure it's in the middle of the square, otherwise they won't hear it clearly."

I stepped forward, feeling rather foolish, and tapped the bare wall with my knuckles. Once, twice, three times. The green lines continued to vibrate around the spot, but nothing happened.

"I don't think it's working, Barry," said Val.

"Wait," he said confidently. "They will answer eventually. It's a busy school, after all."

And sure enough, after a minute – or perhaps it was longer – the lines stopped pulsating but instead shone a bright white that blinded all of us for a moment. In the middle of the portal, a sign appeared. Though I was sure it was impossible, it seemed familiar somehow. It was a black hedgehog on a blue background.

"That," Barry said, reading our bewildered expressions correctly, "is the school emblem."

"A hedgehog?" asked Val in disbelief.

"It is a most noble animal," said Barry. "But don't worry, they will bore the pants off of you at the school in regard to all of this trivia. Quickly, now, before the portal closes again. We have to get our luggage in first."

I grabbed the suitcase that was closest to me. Stepping in front of the portal, I gently placed it against the wall – or so I thought. For the wall was no longer solid, and the suitcase went right through, vanishing in an instant as if being sucked in by a miniature black hole. Val, desperate not to miss the fun, tried one of her bags, with the same effect. Soon enough, we had all but a few handbags inside the portal.

First, it was Barry's turn to go through, and then Val. I had to step through last because I had to speak the incantation that would close the portal from our side. It was a delayed-action spell of Barry's own invention that no longer necessitated a witch or warlock to remain behind at the point of entry.

After Barry and Val had passed through the portal, it was my turn. But I found myself hesitant to follow them. For one mad moment, I thought of calling the whole thing off. Something within me wanted to stay in Fickleton House, protected by its ancient walls, with little else to worry about than Mrs. Faversham burning my bacon every once in a while.

But then, as I remembered the desperate letter we had received from Warklesby's School of Magic only a short while ago, the madness passed as soon as it had come. A mystery was waiting to be solved, and I was not one to shirk from such a task. With three waves of my wand, I spoke the final incantation that would seal the portal. Then, looking one last time at the house that had become such a comfort to me, I walked in front of the blazing portal. I tested it with my right foot first, immediately feeling it suck me in, though not unpleasantly so. Pressing my lips together in determination, I stepped through, leaving

Fickleton House behind me.

CHAPTER 3

Transport within the portal system was a lot more violent and uncomfortable than I had anticipated. It was like being sucked into a massive vacuum cleaner. As blackness engulfed me, I felt my arms and legs being pulled in every conceivable direction. My head was jerked to and fro, as though I was a ball in an old arcade machine.

Then, with a dull smack, I landed head first on a dirty carpet, inhaling a mouthful of dust in the process. Coughing furiously, it took me a while to bring my new surroundings into focus.

Barry and Val, both wearing bemused looks on their faces, were already waiting for me. They weren't the only people present, however. There seemed to be a welcome party specially for us, but I could see, probably due to my less than elegant appearance, that they were not impressed by what they saw.

Still feeling my bones and limbs ache from the portal experience, I gingerly got to my feet. The room we were in resembled a waiting area in a doctor's office as I imagined it must have been around the early 1900s. The furniture was antique and worn-out. On the walls, paintings depicted witches and warlocks, all dressed in robes and pointy hats from various periods of wizarding history. There was no sign of our luggage, however.

Barry smoothly stepped forward to make the introductions.

"Headmistress, deputy headmaster, this is Amanda Sheridan."

There was a slight, awkward pause.

"And this," Barry continued, "is the headmistress of Warklesby's School of Magic, Muriel Hall."

305

Muriel Hall was a thin woman in her late forties. She had brown hair, reaching well below her shoulders. Though it was still full, regular strands of grey permeated it. The deep crinkles on her forehead, as well as the bags beneath her eyes, gave the impression of someone young who had aged rapidly within a very short amount of time. But although her looks were fading, I could tell that she must have once been an attractive woman.

"How do you do?" she said, with a rather vacant smile as she shook my hand. "I hope your journey was pleasant enough."

"Well," I said, trying to loosen up the atmosphere a little bit, "I need a few more times to get used to portal travel."

The tall man standing next to the headmistress snorted, a look of superiority on his face.

"This, Amanda," Barry said, "is the deputy headmaster, Clement Harper."

The dislike was instant, as well as mutual. Harper couldn't have been much older than thirty-five, though he had made every effort in his appearance to look the part of a more experienced and seasoned man. His dress robes were meticulous though boring, as was his sleek blond hair that he had combed backward. He wore round black glasses that gave him the air of an ill-tempered bureaucrat.

We shook hands for the briefest of moments, eyeing one another in silence.

The headmistress seemed oblivious to this, however. She smiled again, beckoning all of us to follow her.

"We will have more privacy in my office," she said.

With one last expression of disdain, the deputy headmaster turned on his heel and followed her. Val looked at me with raised eyebrows. Clearly, someone wasn't too keen on having us here.

"Excellent start," I breathed to Val. "Always great to have a warm welcome."

"Yeah," said Val. "I wonder what the rest of the staff

are like."

"I think it can only really go uphill from here," I said softly.

We passed along several corridors with stone walls. They looked much older than the room we had arrived in, though they were also in much better condition. Students bustled past us, chatting to one another as they headed for their next class. Life, apparently, was continuing as normal, though there was a nervous, restless energy about it.

At last, the headmistress and her deputy came to a halt in front of a small archway. Beyond it, a narrow stone spiral staircase led upward.

"Only fifteen floors to go," the headmistress said heavily, as though she were speaking more to herself than to us.

Our little party traipsed up the stairs, which were extremely narrow and steep, so that I had to help Val on multiple occasions. Panting furiously atop the fifteenth and final staircase, a broad landing – adorned with a carpet of gold and red – led us straight to a pair of ornate doors made of oak. With a wave of her wand, Headmistress Hall opened them for us.

We stepped into what might have been the most beautiful office I had ever seen in my life. The rough stone slabs that had dominated the corridors and staircases so far had been replaced by marble. A massive desk made of a dark wood – mahogany perhaps – spanned almost the entire width of the room at the far end. Behind it, large windows overlooked fields of green and yellow as far as the eye could see, stretching down into a woodland valley.

Sitting down in a leather armchair behind her desk, the headmistress beckoned us to sit on the three chairs opposite her. Val, Barry, and I each took a seat. Harper, in any case, seemed to prefer to stand. With a tired flick of her wand, Muriel Hall whipped up tea and biscuits for all of us.

"First, I'd like to welcome you to Warklesby's School of

Magic," she began slowly. "It really is a wonderful institution… or *was*, rather, before all this… awful business began."

"I'm sorry to hear it," I said sincerely.

Deputy Headmaster Harper scowled and looked out of the window. As before, the headmistress seemed to take no notice of his disapproval.

"Thank you for saying so, Miss Sheridan," she continued. "It really was a shock to everyone here."

"So what happened exactly?" I asked. "The letter only spoke of several kidnappings at the school but didn't provide any further details."

"… a *series* of kidnappings," corrected Harper irritably. "It'd be a miracle if the same person *wasn't* responsible for all three of them."

"Yes, indeed," said Headmistress Hall, nodding her head. "That is what it looks like. But you never know. Magical Law Enforcement certainly believe it to be the same person, but they have been unable to find the perpetrator. And I'm afraid to say that, I…"

She paused, looking at her desk for a moment, evidently trying to fight back the tears that were on their way.

"I believe what the headmistress is trying to say," Harper said, pompously shifting his glasses, "is that if we don't find out who is committing these crimes, the school will have to be closed."

"But that would also mean you wouldn't be able to track down the guilty party anymore," I said. "Is that right?"

The headmistress nodded heavily.

"That is, in fact, why we have asked you to come here, Miss Sheridan. With the Earl of Barrington acting as our substitute professor for water magic, you will have an advantage that the police do not. You will be able to blend in with the staff and students."

"Headmistress," Harper blurted out, unable to contain himself any longer, "if I may. The situation calls for trained professionals, not amateurs."

"Hey," said Val, narrowing her eyes, "who are you calling amateurs?"

"With all due respect, headmistress," Harper continued, though his manner suggested quite the contrary, "our *guests* have no formal education in detective work. The cat is even incapable of wielding a wand properly, while Miss Sheridan would require decades of training before she could even confront one of our pupils, let alone a dangerous sorcerer."

This time, it was Barry's and my turn to protest. Struggling to resist my urge to slap him across the face immediately, I stood up, shaking slightly.

"Excuse me?" I said angrily.

"I resent your tone of voice," said Barry, who was also on all fours.

"Well, then why don't you…" Harper began, turning on Barry.

But the headmistress lifted her hand to stop him. It was a surprisingly authoritative gesture that must have caught all of us by surprise, for we all stopped arguing at once. Headmistress Hall looked sternly at her deputy headmaster.

"Clement, we have been over this several times before. And my decision in this matter is final, as I have told you also. Our guests stay. And you will do everything you can to aid them in their attempt to catch this murderer. Have I made myself clear?"

Harper, realising he had pushed it too far, stared at us and then the headmistress, his mouth opening and closing again like a fish, though no sound came out of it. Slowly – though resentment was etched across his entire face – he nodded.

"Yes, headmistress. Forgive me," he said coldly, rearranging his round glasses.

"What matters the most," said the headmistress, returning to her tired and weary way of speaking again, "is that we all want this sorcerer caught. The priority is to the safety of this school and to its pupils. The *Spellcasting Parents' Association* quite rightly demanded the immediate resolution of this matter. They are worried about their children, and so should we."

Privately, I thought that Harper certainly didn't look as though he had the same priorities. His lips were white with repressed rage, though he remained perfectly still as he stared out into the fields.

"I have taken," the headmistress continued, "every possible precaution. No student is to walk the corridors alone. Teachers are to report any missing pupils immediately. At night, every dormitory reports to me directly if anyone is out of bed. But, until this sorcerer is caught, we can do little else."

"So what do we know about the case?" I asked.

"Well," the headmistress began, "it's a rather long story. I suppose I should start with… Vincent Wycliffe. Some thirty years ago, Wycliffe was here at the school as a student. He had been moderately gifted, not much better or worse than many of his peers. He specialised in earth magic. It was quite surprising, therefore, that after finishing school Wycliffe was promoted to the post of assistant teacher by the then head of department for earth magic, Professor MacKenzie."

Headmistress Hall shifted rather uncomfortably in her chair.

"I knew both of them, because I was a young pupil here at the time, too. Wycliffe was several years older than I was. There had been a lot of talk about his promotion, even amongst the students, for there had been far more talented candidates available. But nobody really thought about it much after a while. Wycliffe, though not brilliant, did his work, and so that seemed to be the end of the matter. Biscuits, anyone?"

"Erm, no thanks," I said, confused at the headmistress's sudden break in her story. "So what happened next?"

"Well," she said, absent-mindedly reaching for one of the biscuits herself, "nothing happened – or at least, nobody was aware of what was developing in that mind of his – brewing, you might say. But then, years later, when I was in my last year of school, mysterious things began to occur at the school. You see, I had my own academic hopes for the future, and so I worked as a student helper in several departments. You know, menial tasks such as copying or preparing notes. One such job was in earth magic, and so I saw Professor MacKenzie and Vincent Wycliffe quite regularly. Their relationship, so much was obvious to me at the time, was bad – and it was deteriorating further."

"You mean, they quarrelled openly?" asked Barry.

"Yes," she said, a vague expression on her face. "Yes, you see, Wycliffe demanded more time for his research, wishing to reduce his teaching duties. Professor MacKenzie, however, refused. In fact, he even increased Wycliffe's teaching hours."

"Why would he do that?" I asked. "Just to spite him?"

"Perhaps," she said. "There's certainly no shortage of ill-feeling in the academic world, I can assure you. And, as I said, they didn't get on very well anymore. However, I think there was another reason. A less personal one. This is hindsight, of course – judging from what Wycliffe did later on – but I can only assume that MacKenzie had found out in which direction Wycliffe's research was going."

"A very sinister direction, I might add," the deputy headmaster said suddenly.

"What sort of research was he involved in?" I asked the headmistress.

"Necromancy," the deputy headmaster interjected before she could answer herself.

Val looked rather bewildered.

"It is a forbidden branch of earth magic," Barry added helpfully. "It hasn't been practised legally in centuries."

"You mean, Wycliffe was trying to resurrect the dead?" I asked, horrified.

"In essence, yes," the headmistress said. "We believe that he destroyed the majority of his work before he was captured, so it is difficult to tell how deep he was into necromancy at the time."

"So what happened next?" I asked.

The headmistress didn't answer immediately, but gazed out of the windows behind her for a while. Her expression was impossible to read. Yet it seemed to me to be more vacant and adrift than ever. Was this her peculiar way of remembering the events surrounding Wycliffe's crimes? Somehow, I had the impression that there was something more, something deeper, that seemed to be eating away at her.

"I think," she said quietly, "it started with little things. As it did a few weeks ago, again."

"What do you mean?" I asked, shifting to the edge of my chair so that I could better understand what she was saying.

"You must understand," she continued, turning around to face us again, "that I only gained full access to this information after I had become headmistress. The headmaster had kept these things secret at the time. They aren't open to the public. But I recognised the patterns quickly enough."

"What pattern was that?" I asked.

It felt as if I were trying to draw blood from a stone, as she paused yet again, staring at us, unable to continue. The deputy headmaster, no doubt feeling impatient, spoke next.

"What the headmistress is trying to say is that…"

"Please, Clement," she said in a tired voice, closing her eyes, "let me explain fully to our guests. They need to know *everything*, do you understand?"

It was quite evident that he strongly disagreed, but he pressed his lips so tightly together until they went white in his effort to stop himself from speaking. The headmistress drew back and opened a drawer at the bottom of her desk. She retrieved a piece of paper. The writing was tiny, but it looked like some sort of list to me.

"You must understand that, as necromancy is prohibited by magical law, there are naturally very few scholars who have delved deeply enough into the subject to understand it. It is forbidden knowledge, and it is thus quite common for theoretical researchers or historians to become suspect. That makes it rare, because few would choose to meddle with it with such a heavy cost attached to it. But, as you might also imagine, there are some who seek it for the sake of the forbidden. A juvenile impulse, often, to test the boundaries of our world."

She sighed, as though a great burden was beginning to lift.

"From my very first year onward, there had been rumours of necromancy amongst the students – and even amongst the staff. Most people didn't take these allegations seriously. The official school line, as expressed by many staff members and the headmaster himself, was that these stories were suitable only for frightening the gullible and the young, and that they lacked any basis in actual fact."

She fidgeted slightly, playing around the corners of the list in front of her.

"At the time, we didn't know that they were lying to us. As the magical community found out much later, the evidence was there. Many had tried to convince the headmaster that something evil was brewing within his school, though he chose to ignore it until it was far too late. He simply couldn't believe that anyone at the school would do such things. And so, he took the easy approach and denounced all those who warned him as conspiracy theorists and troublemakers.

"Yet, the signs were there. Soon enough, markings appeared in the corridors of the school. They depicted the forbidden symbols of necromancy, the staff and skull, as well as the bone and the book. These acts in and of themselves, of course, would have simply been viewed as forms of teenage vandalism and provocation. But other, more sinister occurrences soon weighed heavily upon the school. There were reports by students that they had seen secret rituals in the woods nearby, well beyond the gaze of authority. A member of staff reported a similar event close to the school's graveyard, where many accomplished scholars and teachers have been put to rest.

"To make things worse, a series of mysterious break-ins plagued the school at the time. Specific roots, plants, and rare powders were stolen. Few – if anyone – recognised the importance of the specific magical ingredients that went missing, of course. The headmaster, still wilfully ignorant, insisted that these were no different from other acts of theft in the past."

Headmistress Hall paused, breathing heavily again as she suddenly looked at her office door. For a moment, I thought she was afraid of someone eavesdropping.

"Of course," she continued, though in a somewhat lower voice, "they were nothing of the sort. Taken as a whole, these precise ingredients had been used for millennia in the abhorrent practice of necromancy, though the problem at the time was, as I said, that it took an expert to recognise this.

"Soon enough, people began to vanish. Though the crimes were investigated, the working assumption was that the students in question had in fact simply run away from school. But as more and more students disappeared, even the headmaster had to admit that something was seriously wrong. The MLE was contacted, and an investigation began, though with few results. The problem was that nobody had drawn the connection with the markings and the stolen ingredients.

"Luckily, a historian of magic who had specialised in the

history of necromancy, one of the very few academics who did at the time, had come to Warklesby's as a guest lecturer a few weeks earlier. He immediately recognised the pattern when the issue of stolen ingredients from the school's supplies was raised during a staff meeting. He asked for a complete list of missing items and soon confirmed that, due to the amounts and ratios stolen, they were most certainly intended for the dark practice of necromancy. The rest, I'm afraid, is history."

She looked at us as though the matter were settled, but Val appeared to be just as puzzled as I was. I was just about to inquire about the rest of the story when there was a loud knock on the door.

"Come," said the headmistress.

An adolescent youth entered the room. He was wearing a student's uniform, though he had taken off his warlock's hat, revealing untidy black hair. The headmistress squinted slightly so that she could recognise the face. Then, she clucked her tongue in disapproval.

"Again, Ross?" she said, a twinkle in her eye. "What was it this time?"

"Inappropriate answers in class, ma'am."

"How many more detentions are you determined to acquire this term?" she asked.

"I've always been one for records, headmistress," Ross said cheekily. "Beg your pardon, ma'am."

He smiled in mock-apology. To my surprise, the headmistress seemed to be secretly enjoying the encounter, and she was trying her best to suppress a smile in front of her deputy. Harper, however, was less than amused. He cleared his throat violently.

"Expulsion from the school is also a record of sorts, Ross," he fumed. "Remember that."

"Indeed," the headmistress said, though I could see by her twitching mouth that she didn't seriously consider it. "I will deal with you later. Justice will have to wait a little longer, even for you, Julian Ross."

The youth made a ridiculously low bow, flashing his grin at all of us again as his handsome head emerged again, and was just about to turn around when the headmistress stopped him.

"Wait," she said, her tone suddenly much sharper than before. "How long have you been outside the door, Ross?"

"Me?" he said innocently, blinking. "Why, only a few minutes, headmistress."

"Did you hear anything you shouldn't have?" the deputy headmaster, his arms crossed, barked at him.

"Of course not, sir. I would never…"

"Spare us the act, Ross," the deputy spat. "Out with it. What did you hear?"

Ross, sensing real consequences for a change, switched gears quickly. His mocking features rearranged themselves into a remarkably good impression of someone who had been wrongfully accused of an awful crime.

"Headmistress, I *did* hear voices inside, so I decided to wait. But I didn't hear anything specific. Then, I thought I'd knock all the same, since I didn't know how long your meeting would be. I didn't hear a thing. I swear it. That's the honest truth."

The headmistress eyed him with a mixture of indulgence and suspicion. Finally, she turned to the deputy headmaster, giving him the briefest of nods.

"Deputy Headmaster Harper will oversee that you are *fairly* punished, Ross."

"But, headmistress, I…" he spluttered.

"That will do, Ross," she said. "I assure you that you will not be expelled, but I cannot attend to it myself right now… under the present circumstances. Clement, would you mind escorting Ross downstairs?"

"With pleasure, headmistress," Harper said menacingly.

Julian Ross had no choice but to follow the deputy headmaster downstairs. But I could tell that his curiosity was sparked. What was so important that the headmistress wanted to conceal it from him?

After they had left, the headmistress waited for a while longer. She got up, periodically looking at the closed door, pacing around the room until she was satisfied that Harper and Ross were definitely out of earshot.

"Julian Ross is a bit of a rascal," she said, smiling, "but he has his heart in the right place. However, we cannot be too careful these days. I would advise you, also, to trust no one."

"I will certainly make no exception for your deputy, madam," said Barry, still offended at Harper's earlier impertinence.

She frowned.

"I understand your feelings, but you mustn't be too hard on Clement. He wants this situation resolved as much as anyone else. Even though he would go about it in a different way. Now, where were we?"

"I think you were going to tell us about how Wycliffe was captured," I said.

I felt a bit foolish for asking since it seemed that everyone in the magical world knew who he was and what he had done. Nevertheless, I needed the facts.

"Oh, yes. Well, after it had been established that necromancy was involved – and had been ignored for so long – there was nothing less than a political earthquake. The headmaster was dismissed and shunned. Forced into retirement, he died a few years later – I think more of shame than anything else, if such a thing is possible.

"Meanwhile, the MLE had taken control of the school. They combed the entire castle from dungeon to spire in an effort to find the perpetrator. At first, they found nothing. But then, the professor for earth magic went missing."

"You mean, Professor MacKenzie, Wycliffe's boss?" Val asked.

"Yes," she said. "Suspicion fell immediately on the

entire department. Once more, they searched the private rooms of all teachers, student helpers, and research scholars connected to the department of earth magic."

"So, they had searched them before?" I asked.

"Indeed, Miss Sheridan," she said. "It was a decision informed by prejudice. The department of earth magic was the very first to fall under scrutiny…"

"… because necromancy is a branch of earth magic," I said.

"Correct," she said, nodding. "I myself was never quite convinced of the necessity of that connection. You see, although it *is* true that it is considered to be a part of earth magic, many of the principles of necromancy, aside from the moral dimension of course, are so very different from – let us say – 'usual' earth magic. Warlocks or witches specialised in earth magic, therefore, would hardly have any advantage in terms of actual ability or knowledge."

"But Wycliffe *was* a specialist in earth magic," said Barry, frowning.

"Yes, it is quite true. I'm merely pointing it out so that you might consider all options in your own investigations."

"I see," he said.

"So, during the search, they found some incriminating evidence in Wycliffe's room the second time around, then?" I asked.

"That's right," she said. "The peculiar thing was that he had survived the first search unscathed. Perhaps he thought that the danger had passed. Or maybe he was forced to move some of his research from his other hiding places. In any case, the MLE arrested him immediately, but unfortunately he was able to burn a lot of his work as they closed in, so that the true extent of his crimes remains unknown. The fire he set almost consumed the entire East Tower."

"Did Wycliffe confess?" asked Val.

"Yes, he did," the headmistress said. "Though for some

reason he wouldn't disclose where he had dumped the bodies. Perhaps he had hopes of continuing his work at a later date in case he escaped. He spoke of his 'return' many times during the trial. Some of his victims were found later, deep within the woods. Others, well, they're technically still missing, though nobody has any doubts about their fate."

"Did he succeed in…" Val began, though unable to finish the horrible thought.

"I believe that the official judgment," Headmistress Hall said, hesitating slightly, "was that Wycliffe had tried but failed in his attempts at necromancy."

"But you thought otherwise," I said.

She stared at me for a while, measuring her words.

"Yes," she said, her bags under eyes as pronounced as ever, "I do, Miss Sheridan, though I have no proof. You see, the authorities were desperate to calm the situation, as far as that was possible. Once the full horror of Wycliffe's crimes became known – thirteen victims to date, though possibly even more – people felt that the those in charge had failed them. Most witches and warlocks agreed. Myself included. Others – though a minority no doubt – felt otherwise. It was surprising how many people admired Wycliffe."

"A monster like him?" Val asked incredulously.

"I know," the headmistress said. "It is hard to believe now. But at the time, some felt that Wycliffe had pushed the boundaries of magic further than anyone else. There were anonymous letters to the press, demanding his release and legalisation of necromancy. They were ignored, of course, so Wycliffe's followers burnt down the Magical Courthouse in London where the trial was supposed to take place. So the trial was moved here, to the school, in the large West Tower. It had been closed for the summer entirely, and its isolated and undisclosed location was ideal for the trial, though they still allowed spectators to attend."

"So Wycliffe was found guilty?" I asked.

"Oh, yes," the headmistress said. "The evidence was incontrovertible. He repeated his confession, in fact. Apparently, Professor MacKenzie had finally been willing to act on his suspicions regarding his assistant and had intended to turn him in. Throughout the trial, Wycliffe showed no remorse whatsoever. He even goaded some of the victims' families. It was horrible. Many demanded the reinstitution of the death penalty, but of course, the law was the law. He was stripped of his powers and sentenced to solitary confinement for life, the harshest punishment in our world. In a manner of speaking, those who deemed it too light a sentence got their way in the end, though."

"What do you mean?" I asked.

"Wycliffe was murdered in prison, about a year ago. A petty squabble amongst prisoners in the yard. He was buried in a secret location, for the general mood was still tense – even after all those years. And that should have been the end of it."

She stared at the door again, an almost paranoid look on her face. Perhaps it was the setting sun behind her, but the lines on her face seemed deeper and darker than before.

"But it wasn't the end. Now, twenty years after Wycliffe's crimes, it's starting again," she said in nothing more than a whisper. "The signs on the walls, the talk of necromancy. And disappearances, too. It's exactly how it was when he was at large the last time."

"You don't mean…" I began.

"There have been horrible rumours. Rumours that he has returned from the dead, seeking revenge. You've got to help us."

CHAPTER 4

She looked desperately at Val, Barry, and me. Somehow, it made the burden a lot heavier. It had felt a lot easier accepting the request in the form of a letter a few weeks ago. Now, however, the severity of the situation became a lot more pronounced.

"Of course, headmistress," I said. "We're here to provide any help we can."

"I'm counting on it," she said. "Your track record is indeed impressive. And some fresh pairs of eyes are what we really need in this dire situation."

She took the list that had been lying in front of her on the desk and handed it to me.

"This is a list I've compiled – on a strictly confidential level, you understand – of all the known locations of necromancer signs that were spotted throughout the school. Most of them have been erased, of course, for fear of frightening the students even further, if that's at all possible, that is. You will find the names of the missing people below. Two students and one teacher. In regard to the stolen supplies, you should better talk to our quarterwarlock, Henry Armbruster."

"Thank you, this will help a lot," I said, scanning the list. "Did the MLE find any leads?"

Headmistress Hall shook her head miserably.

"None at all," she said. "The entire school was searched multiple times. No office, dormitory, or staff room was spared. Not even mine. But they couldn't track down the missing people."

"And you think they're dead?" I asked.

"Yes," she said miserably. "It's the same pattern as… as last time when Wycliffe was active."

"Can you tell us more about the people who've gone missing?" I said. "Were there any specific circumstances we should know about?"

"Neither I nor the MLE could find any link between them. Peter Hucklebee was our professor for water magic – hence the need for a replacement," she said, inclining her head towards Barry. "He made no comment before he vanished. All of his things were left untouched. As for the two students, Robert Chesterton and Annabelle Swinton, were in their fifth and sixth years here, respectively. As far as we know, they had never even spoken to one another. We could find no connection between them in any dimension of their lives."

"So, you think it's a random selection of victims?" I asked.

"Well," she said, hesitantly, "I cannot know for certain, of course. But the evidence so far certainly indicates that there is no particular reason why they were taken."

"Does the MLE share your view?" asked Barry shrewdly. "That Wycliffe has somehow returned from the dead, I mean."

"I-I don't know," she said. "I'm not even sure myself. It seems impossible and yet… All I'm saying is that the pattern is exactly the same as last time. Some of the agents are old enough to remember what it was like all those years ago. But without bodies, or evidence that foul play is involved at all, there is very little they can do apart from searching the school. But the answer, I'm sure of it, must be somewhere in there."

She pointed at the list in my hand.

"Some tiny detail that we've overlooked so far," she continued. "You have all the school resources at your disposal, just contact me or Clement if you need anything."

"Thank you. Has anyone actually seen Wycliffe?" I asked.

"Not to my knowledge," said the headmistress slowly,

"but that doesn't mean it's not him. He could be in disguise."

"Posing as a student or a member of staff, you mean?" I asked.

"Precisely," said the headmistress.

"Is this possible to sustain for a long period of time?" I asked, turning to Barry.

"Oh, yes, certainly," said Barry. "A warlock trained in shapeshifting will have no problem doing that, since the transformations are minor in comparison to, say, turning into an animal. That wouldn't be the problem."

Barry hesitated.

"What's the matter?" Val asked.

"Well," he said, "I'm no expert in necromancy, but I've never heard of anyone reviving themselves."

"Maybe he had an accomplice," said Val.

"Or," I said, "it could be someone else. A copycat killer, mimicking Wycliffe's style?"

"Yes," Barry said, "that is also possible."

"Does anyone else know why we are here?" I asked, turning back to the headmistress.

"The school board does, but few members actually reside here at the castle. In fact, that only includes Professor Olsen at present."

"I see," I said. "We want to keep our cover for as long as possible."

"Of course," she said. "I have demanded the utmost secrecy of all of them, but I'll have another word with Professor Olsen. I'm sure he will understand."

I pocketed the list. Val and I got to our feet, and Barry hopped down from his chair. We shook hands (and paws) with the headmistress once more and headed for the beautiful oak doors that led out of her office.

***

Having descended the many stone steps again, I felt at a complete loss. Although I wouldn't have admitted it openly, I felt more like an amateur now than ever before. In our previous two cases, we had always slipped into them by accident. At Warklesby's School of Magic, however, things were different. We had been hired with the specific purpose of solving a mystery that even Magical Law Enforcement, with all their manpower and resources, couldn't crack. What, then, could be expected of us? Would most people presuppose our failure from the start? The deputy headmaster, I noted with a shudder of utter dislike, certainly believed that. But the thought of him telling the headmistress that he had been right all along was unbearable.

"Are you OK, Amy?" Val asked.

I swung around. She had that look on her face that told me she had been reading me like a book.

"I… sure, everything's fine," I lied.

"No, it's not," she said. "You can't fool an empathetic psychic, you know."

"I suppose I can't," I said, cheering up a little. "Especially when she's my best friend, too. So, where should we start?"

"The Great Hall, of course," said Barry confidently.

"Why there?" I asked.

"Because I'm hungry," he said.

We all laughed. Good old Barry, I thought, he always brought one back to the basics – and far away from the debilitating self-doubt that had crept into my thoughts.

"Well, at least Barry has his priorities right," said Val. "Let's have a meal and get a good night's rest. It's probably best to start fresh in the morning."

"How do we get to the hall, though?" I asked.

"I know the way," said Barry.

We followed him through one ancient stone corridor to another. And yet, each seemed to have a life of its own. The portraits, reaching back centuries, were fascinating in themselves. Arches to tiny passageways hid behind tapestries of all shapes and sizes. Suits of armour were one thing, but the peculiar life-sized waxwork figures of great spellcasters that were strewn throughout the castle made the hairs at the back of my neck stand on end. They were excellent replicas, and so it was sometimes difficult to distinguish between them and groups of students we passed on our way. For the most part, however, we encountered few people on our way to the Great Hall.

"How come you know the way around this massive place, Barry?" asked Val.

"I've been invited several times before to give lectures on therianthropy. Many years ago, though. Before my unfortunate… miscalculation. Ah, here we are. I can already smell the outstanding tuna they make here."

Val and I opened a pair of heavy wooden doors. A loud buzz of conversation and chatter hit us as though we had been struck by a wave. We were facing the most massive hall I had ever seen in my life. The ceiling was so high that the place could have well served as a cathedral. Beautiful baroque artwork and carvings decorated every inch of it. Long banners hung from the walls, while larger-than-life statues and waxworks covered every corner in sight. In the centre, a sea of witches and warlocks sat at long benches and ornate tables made of white marble.

As far as the eye could see, foods from every continent were being devoured by students and staff alike. Above their heads, dozens of empty plates whizzed away while full plates precariously teetered through the air until landing with a plonk in front of a hungry witch or warlock. If ever there was a feast worth having – this was it.

"This is amazing," said Val, awestruck. "Can't wait for our turn. What do you say, Amy?"

"We certainly won't starve in here, that's for sure," I said. "Come on, let's find a table."

"I think," said Barry haughtily, "they're expecting me at the staff table. Researchers also sit there. You'd better join me, or otherwise they might smell a rat."

It turned out that the staff table was at the far end of the hall, on a slightly elevated platform. About two dozen people were already sitting there, though there were ample empty seats left. To my dismay, I saw that the deputy headmaster was already there, deep in conversation with a white-haired man. Harper had evidently finished disciplining the mischievous Ross.

As we approached the table, Harper spotted us. In an ostentatious display of hospitality, he rose from his seat and walked over to our side of the table.

"Dear colleagues," he said, sporting a smile that did not extend to his eyes at all, "may I introduce the newest additions to our staff. This is the Earl of Barrington, who will be filling in for Professor Hucklebee. He presently resides in feline form. And his companions are his research assistants, Miss Sheridan and Miss Morgan."

The staff members present muttered the polite greetings but quickly returned to their original conversations. Val and Barry made for the nearest seats. I was just about to follow when deputy headmaster Harper placed a hand on my arm that felt more like a claw.

"Finished investigating for the day already, have we?" he whispered.

"Not quite," I said coldly, pushing his arm away. "Still a few staff members to go, starting at the top."

He stared at me for a moment. Then, rearranging his round glasses in what he thought was a gesture of superior contempt, he turned around and walked back to his seat.

"What an arrogant p…" I murmured to Val as I sat down next to her.

"… person?" said Val, grinning. "Yeah. One for our list of suspects, d'you reckon?"

"Definitely," I said darkly, an image of myself arresting

him in front of the entire school leaping into my mind's eye.

"I certainly wouldn't put it past him," said Val. "I just don't understand why he doesn't want us here. I mean, it's not as if the MLE got anywhere on its own."

"Perhaps he's afraid of the truth," I said, just as Harper glanced over to our side of the table.

"Aren't we all?" said Val wisely.

"But we've got to remain as objective as possible, I suppose," I said, sighing.

I tried to shake off my personal feelings as best I could. Avenging personal slights would have to be a secondary concern as long as the school was in such danger. And after all, I thought, no murderer would be this stupid. Or would he?

"Pity it's never the obvious ones," said Val, as though she were reading my mind. "Life really would be a lot easier, wouldn't it?"

"Yeah," I said. "But you never know. It could be a clever bluff."

Barry, who had grown impatient next us, began clawing at my arm.

"Ouch," I exclaimed, "what's the matter, Barry?"

"I'm hungry."

"Oh, alright," I said. "Let's get our meals, then."

Ordering food was perhaps the most enjoyable thing I had done for quite a while in regard to magic. You simply had to place your wand on the menu and speak the name of the dish out loud. I helped Val and Barry order theirs first, then ordered my own.

Meanwhile, the deputy headmaster seemed to have finished his meal. He got up and, without another word, left the Great Hall in what seemed to be quite a hurry. Personally, I felt that the air was a lot lighter after he had gone.

Seeing the deputy headmaster leave the table, several of his colleagues decided to follow suit. Perhaps a bit of Muriel

Hall's paranoia had attached itself to me, but it was difficult not to see them all his potentially guilty. At the same time, I made an effort to be as inconspicuous as possible. The later the staff got wind of our plans, the better.

It was extraordinary to see how, only a few minutes after we had made our order, several dishes zoomed through the hall and landed right in front of us on the table. I had ordered Yorkshire puddings with roast beef and gravy. I don't know whether it was the particularly magical way it had been cooked, but I had never tasted anything quite like it. It was absolutely delicious.

In the meantime, Barry had got himself into a full-fledged discussion on magical theory with the elderly man with white hair, who had previously been in conversation with the deputy headmaster. If ever there was a walking caricature of a professor, I thought, this man was it. His tousled and uncombed hair seemed to sprouting from his head at random. His spectacles, foggy and thick, made his eyes appear unusually tiny.

"Certainly, I-I agree," he was saying, with an affected stutter that seemed to be so common amongst many academics. "But surely, Farthing's theorem of therianthropic immutability still counts for *something*. I simply find it impossible to conceive of any plausible solution that would be able to discount it."

Barry, puffing slightly from intellectual exertion, countered the point in a similarly verbose yet unintelligible answer that outlined his own view of shapeshifting theory.

"Oh, I wish he wouldn't go on like that," Val whispered, rolling her eyes.

"I don't know," I said thoughtfully. "He's playing his role perfectly."

"He's not playing a role, Amy, he's just being himself."

"Perhaps you're right," I said, grinning. "At any rate, a thorough debate gives us time to observe the field without arousing too much suspicion."

The discussion raged on as we ate our meals. Gradually, the combatants were shifting towards personal attacks to make their point.

"F-forgive me, Lord Barrington," the white-haired man with the thick glasses said, "but therianthropy has progressed a great deal since your... erm... *unfortunate accident.* Many new spells have been invented."

"Many," Barry snarled across the table, "invented by myself, I might add. *I* pioneered some of the most decisive breakthroughs in therianthropy in the 20th century!"

"A shame you cannot wield a wand to prove your theories," his opponent countered triumphantly.

"I leave that to lesser scholars," Barry said acidly.

"My dear sir," the white-haired man protested, growing red in the face, "are you implying that..."

We pretended to listen to the 'discussion' at the table, though in reality I was closely watching my surroundings, trying to familiarise myself with as many faces as possible. Since research scholars, dependent mainly on the massive school library, also stayed at the castle on a permanent or semi-permanent basis, I needed more information on the people present.

Fortunately, a woman with long blonde hair, who must have been around my age, was quietly eating her vegetables only a few seats away. She was following the discussion, though appeared to be too reserved to participate herself. She was wearing a polite face, though she clearly disliked the increasingly hostile insults being hurled across the table.

"Excuse me," I said, leaning over to her. "Could you tell me who that warlock is?"

I pointed to the man arguing with Barry.

"Oh, that's Professor Olsen," she said, grateful for the distraction. "He's my boss, actually. Are you assistants to the Earl of Barrington, then?"

"That's right," I said, trying to suppress a grin at the mention of Barry's official title.

It wouldn't do, of course, to start a discussion on the inheritance of Fickleton House. In fact, it was probably best to omit that little detail altogether. My relationship with Barry would have to appear purely professional – not familial.

"My name is Esther, by the way, Esther Hickey," she said, smiling pleasantly and extending her hand.

"Nice to meet you," I said, shaking it. "I'm Amanda Sheridan, but just call me Amy. And this is Val."

"Hi," Val said, "I'm also assistant to Barr–"

I quickly kicked her foot under the table.

"– I mean, the Earl of Barrington."

"Is it true that he got himself trapped in that cat's body?" she asked curiously.

"Yes," I said. "Quite true. That was long before our time, though."

"We wouldn't have let that happen to him," said Val, nodding earnestly.

"Poor man," said Esther. "It must be horrible."

"Don't worry, he makes the best of it," I said, thinking of the way Mrs. Faversham doted on him at home.

"That's very brave," she said. "I'd very much like to meet him. I've been an admirer of his work for some time. Apart from therianthropy, he's written some very insightful articles on water magic, too. Part of my research transcends the border between earth and water magic, you see. Professor Olsen is the head of the earth magic department. Do you have a focus yet?"

"Erm, no," I said, not untruthfully, "I've just started out really. But the… Earl of Barrington has allowed me some time to think about it."

"That's certainly very gracious of him," Esther said, sighing. "I wish I had had that."

"What do you mean?" I asked.

But at that moment, the discussion had blown up into a shouting match, and we were no longer able to ignore it.

Professor Olsen, no trace left of his urbane academic stutter, was on his feet, pointing his finger angrily at Barry.

"Your work is nothing more than idle speculation," he shouted, shaking from head to toe.

"Better speculative than derivative, *professor*," Barry countered, jumping onto the table. "your life's work is nothing more than the summary of others' research."

"I will not listen to these lies," Professor Olsen screamed. "LIES, do you hear?"

And, with a dismissive gesture at the world around him, Professor Olsen kicked away his chair and stormed away. Stunned, we all watched him go down the aisle, his wild hair flying all around him, and exit through one of the side doors of the Great Hall. Still furious, he banged it closed behind him as hard as he could.

For a moment, the Great Hall was silent. Then, a few students laughed in bewilderment, and everyone returned to what they were doing previously. Barry, who seemed to interpret the unexpected turn of events as nothing less than a full-scale rout of his opponent, returned to slurping his stew from his bowl.

I turned around to Val and Esther again. If I wasn't mistaken, there was something akin to fear in Esther's eyes. Perhaps this hadn't been the first time that Professor Olsen had exploded.

"I…" she began, but faltered.

Then, she began to hyperventilate, her eyes widening in an unmistakable attack of anxiety.

"Esther, I'm sorry," I said, trying to calm her. "The Earl of Barrington is rather… pugnacious at times."

"It's… it's not that," she whispered. "Never mind. Sorry, I didn't want to bother you with…"

She was in such a state of nerves that she knocked over the glass of water in front of her. Helping her mop it up with my napkin, I said:

"Don't worry, it's really not a bother."

"You're very kind," she said, trying to smile. "I think I had better get back to my work. Thank you for being so kind."

Wiping away the remnants of her tears, Esther got up and briskly crossed the platform. She exited through a small door that I hadn't noticed before.

"So much for gathering information," Val said ironically. "We'll be lucky to find out anything before Barry starts a civil war in this place."

"I wonder what she was upset about, though," I said, staring at my now empty plate.

"Well, they were shouting at each other, you know," said Val. "Some people prefer a little harmony from time to time."

"Could you tell that – psychically, I mean?"

Val shook her head.

"Sorry, Amy," she said. "The only way I can survive with hundreds of people in one room is to shut it out completely. Otherwise, I'd go crazy. But if we get her on our own later, I'm sure I could read her."

"Good idea," I said.

Out of the corner of my eye, I saw a familiar figure enter the hall at the far end. It was the headmistress. The look on her face told me that something was seriously wrong. She scanned the staff table from afar, catching my eye almost immediately. Then, thinking it was probably too obvious to approach me or the table directly, she jerked her head ever so slightly toward the exit, turned on her heel, and left the hall again. Her meaning couldn't have been made any clearer, however.

"Excuse me a moment," I said as inconspicuously as possible. "I just remembered, I think I left something upstairs."

Val, unfortunately, hadn't seen the headmistress at all and was rather at a loss. But before she could inquire, I pointedly raised my eyebrows at her, my back turned to the other people at the table.

"Oh, alright, Amy," Val said, her voice slightly higher than normal. "I'll see you later then."

An ominous feeling in my stomach, I walked as fast as I dared towards the main exit of the Great Hall. We had only been at the school for a few hours now. What could have possibly happened?

Luckily, nobody around me seemed to be taking any notice at all. The students I passed were still as loud and as boisterous as ever.

Shutting the heavy oak doors behind me, I spun around to find the headmistress standing next to one of the hideous waxwork figures they kept in the antechamber of the Great Hall, herself almost as motionless and pale as the figure, a 16th century witch standing in front of a cauldron.

The headmistress's eyes, however were wide awake and fearful.

"Miss Sheridan," she whispered. "Another sign has just appeared. I think you need to see this for yourself. Please, come with me immediately."

CHAPTER 5

Without another word, I followed her. Despite her usual apathy, I was surprised at how fast Muriel Hall could walk in her present state of mind. But perhaps it was precisely the nervous energy that provided her with the temporary strength to do so.

Once more, we passed along the many corridors and chambers of the castle. It had struck me before that there were no windows at all, neither in the Great Hall nor in any of the corridors leading to it. In fact, I had only ever seen the outside world in the headmistress's office through the large windows behind her desk. Most of the school, I surmised, was probably deep underground.

At last, we reached what looked like a dead end. But the headmistress pulled out her wand and waved it with a quick flick of her wrist. The massive stone wall in front of us rumbled and vibrated for a second. Then, an archway formed, just high and wide enough for us to pass through, vanishing as soon as we had stepped over the threshold.

On the other side, a long flight of steps led downward. The portraits and waxwork figures had vanished completely in this part of the castle. Though I didn't mind the absence of the waxworks, it looked a lot less cared for than the areas I had seen so far. I was able to smell the moisture all around me.

We reached a chamber with a small, metal door with bars on it. The headmistress stopped and said:

"This, Miss Sheridan, is what was formerly known as the dungeon. Today, it is mainly used for additional storage."

Passing through, we found ourselves in a long passageway lit by torches, with slits in the walls at either side that overlooked what must have been – at some point in the past – cells. Finally, the headmistress came to a halt in front of another metal door.

"It… it is in here," she said, pulling herself together as best she could. "Clement should also be on his way. I had a student search for him immediately. We'd better go in. Come with me, please."

She reached out for the handle and pulled. Beyond, there was nothing but darkness. I took out my wand from my own handbag and lit it, peering into the room. It was filled with an assortment of boxes, empty bottles, disused bird cages, and odd pieces of wood. As I entered, I noticed that the ceiling was very low, so that I could barely stand upright. The smell of mould was almost unbearable.

"We rarely use this room anymore," the headmistress said unnecessarily. "Most of the items you see are rarely used. Though from time to time, we do need something. The sign is over there, next to the old wardrobe."

The wardrobe's doors were so dilapidated that they were almost crumbling to pieces in front of our eyes. The dark paint that covered it was gradually peeling off due to the damp.

"There," the headmistress said, her voice quivering slightly. "The mark of the necromancer."

My eyes wandered slowly from the wardrobe to the area next to it. For one insane moment, I didn't want to look at it, but I forced myself to do so all the same. Painted on the wall in a bright green colour, three skulls leered at me, their hollow eye sockets as dark as the wall behind it. Above, a white staff towered over the skulls.

My heart started racing. In itself, I tried to tell myself, the sign was hideous, though really not harmful. And yet, as I continued to look at it as though I were prey mesmerised by a predator, the awful history that was connected to it suddenly seemed to speak to me in this moist dungeon. The necromancer's sign – and therefore the danger – was real, but the consequences were still frighteningly uncertain.

What exactly had happened to the missing people was left to the horrible scenarios my imagination was conjuring up, though I had very grave doubts about whether they were still alive.

I looked away, trying to pull myself together again. I was letting myself get carried away, sucked into and frozen within the horror. I couldn't let that happen. People were depending on me. I had to remain rational, even though every inch of me felt like running away.

Gazing back at the sign, I stepped forward to examine it more closely. I could see by the clots of paint that it had been both a hasty and an unprofessional job. Undoubtedly, however, judging from the lack of dust and the moist surface, it was quite fresh. Strangely, the skull on the left had been smudged, most likely with something like a cloth or a towel.

"When were you informed of this?" I asked, examining the smudged paint more carefully.

"Quarterwarlock Armbruster notified me, only minutes before I came to you," she said. "He reported it straight away."

"I suppose he didn't see anyone?"

"He did," the headmistress said. "A student was caught in this very room, but claims to have nothing to do with it."

"Who is this student?" I asked.

"A girl called Isabella Villar. She's an exchange student from Spain. She's something of a troubled soul. As they often are at that age, I suppose."

"So you don't think her capable of kidnap and murder?" I asked.

"It is hard to believe, but, as I said, no one is beyond suspicion."

"Well," I said, "she might have painted it herself. This looks very fresh to me."

"Yes," the headmistress said, "it's certainly possible. Oh, Miss Sheridan, this is all so *horrible*. Suspecting everyone around me. I didn't know I'd be dealing with this sort of thing when I took the job."

She paused, closing her eyes as if to shut out the awful reality of her situation. Her breathing was fast, close to hyperventilating. Then, she puffed up her cheeks and exhaled very slowly.

"Please forgive me, Miss Sheridan," she said, after a minute's silent breathing. "It's just… you see, this particular sign… the one with the three skulls and the staff… it always preceded a disappearance."

"How much time do we have?" I asked.

"A few hours, a few days, I think – I hope – that was how it was in the old days, when Wycliffe was still at large."

White in the face, she sat down on one of the boxes close to her, her breathing becoming shallower again. Her makeshift seat was full of cobwebs and dirt, but she was far too worried to care.

"I'm very sorry, headmistress," I said. "I promise I will do everything in my power to get to the bottom of this."

I meant it. Slowly, abstraction was being replaced by grim reality. And with lives at stake, we had to put an end to this once and for all.

"Thank you," she said, with a much steadier voice. "That is very kind of you. How would you like to proceed?"

"I will need to talk to the student in question – Miss Villar," I said. "Perhaps I can squeeze out some more information. It's our only lead so far."

"I will make the arrangements," she said.

"Is there some quiet space I could use?" I asked.

The headmistress paused briefly.

"Well, there's my office," she said, "but you could also use the Earl of Barrington's office. We've provided him with a spacious room in the West Tower. Close to your sleeping quarters, in fact."

"That sounds excellent," I said. "I think we will question her there, straight away. Could you also ask the quarterwarlock, Mr. Armbruster, to come along, too?"

"Of course, Miss Sheridan," she said, her face returning to a healthier colour. "I'll have Clement arrange everything for you. And let me just say, once more, how grateful I am for your help. It really means everything to this school."

***

An hour later, I found myself with Barry and Val – who had stayed in the Great Hall during my excursion to the dungeons – in Barry's new office. I had quickly filled them in on what had happened. Val had jumped at the idea of interviewing Miss Villar and Mr. Armbruster, while Barry had only reluctantly consented after some persuasion.

Though not quite as large as the headmistress's quarters, Barry's office was indeed very spacious. It also sported large windows, though the view was not of fields and meadows but, as far as we could tell from the light of the moon, of rocky slopes leading further up a hill.

"You can't see *anything* out of these, just a few rocks hanging over your head," Val was saying. "I mean, what's the point?"

"We must be close to mountains," I said. "Where exactly is the school located, then?"

"A secret location," Barry said unhelpfully.

He was sitting at his desk, already in his element as visiting scholar and esteemed lecturer. Wearing his reading glasses, he was leafing through loose pieces of paper containing his notes, which he said he needed to prepare for the coming days. Next to them, several stacks of books covered the rest of the table's surface.

"That's not very specific, Barry," Val said. "Give us a hint? Surely, you of all people must have some idea of where we are?"

Once again, flattery had done the trick. Barry looked up, taking off his glasses with both paws.

"Naturally. I think we are in Wales somewhere," he said. "Judging from the landscape, I'd say we are in Snowdonia, though not quite at the highest peak, of course. The school is under English jurisdiction, however. I remember quite clearly that in 1957 there was some debate about…"

We were saved from Barry's spontaneous lecture by a sudden knock on the door. Since it was Barry's office, he answered. It was peculiar somehow to see him in a position of real authority for a change. Though, unsurprisingly, Barry didn't have a hard time adapting.

"Yes?" he said curtly.

The door opened. The deputy headmaster, his blond hair as slick and his smirk as superior as ever, came in first. He was followed by a very heavy man with a red beard. He was wearing what looked like an apron a smith might wear in his workshop. Behind him, a girl with dark hair, dressed in black clothes from head to toe, entered, also. Apparently, the magical world was not spared the idiosyncrasies of teenage clothing habits.

"I see you have made yourself comfortable, my lord," the deputy said, hardly able to conceal his sneer.

"Yes, yes," Barry said, enjoying himself as gatekeeper. "What do you want?"

Deputy Harper's eyes flickered briefly towards me.

"You wished to speak with quarterwarlock Armbruster and Isabella Villar, I believe?"

"Quite right," said Barry. "You may go."

It was hilarious to see Barry bossing around the deputy headmaster, but since we were there by the headmistress's express wishes, there was little he could do. He looked daggers at all of us and then left the room without a word.

"Have a seat," Barry said to Mr. Armbruster and Miss Villar.

Both found it neither odd nor unusual at being addressed by a cat sitting at a desk. Perhaps, some teachers preferred to remain in animal form, or accidents like Barry's were not so uncommon in the magical world as I had previously supposed. In any case, they both sat down on the chairs in front of Barry's desk. We had elevated Barry's own chair to the maximum level, so that he was now towering over them, like a judge in a trial. We had agreed beforehand that Barry would start the questioning, as it was simply the more plausible beginning than if his research assistant led the way.

"Quarterwarlock Armbruster, could you tell us how you found Miss Villar?" he asked.

"Well," Armbruster said, locking his huge hands in front of his oversized belly, "it was in the storage room, down in the dungeons."

"Did you see Miss Villar draw the sign on the wall?" Barry asked.

"No," he said slowly, "but I did see a light inside. That's what made me go there in the first place, because I was only passing through. But when I opened the door, she quickly extinguished her wand light."

"I see," said Barry. "I understand there have been other drawings of these signs. Has anyone else been caught in the act?"

"No, my lord," he said, "not that I am aware of, anyway."

Barry looked across to Val and me, inviting our questions. I grasped at the opportunity immediately.

"Mr. Armbruster," I said, "how often do you go to the dungeons?"

"In that particular room?" he said, stroking his black beard with his hand. "Not much at all, really. It's old and useless stuff in there, most of it."

"And how often are you in the dungeons, generally?" I asked.

"Every other week, perhaps," he said. "I keep some of my equipment in there."

"I understand," I said, "that certain ingredients have

been stolen from the school's supplies. Is that correct?"

"That's right," he said.

"Would it be possible to compile a list for us, with times and dates of when you noticed that they had gone missing?" I asked.

"Yes, of course," he said. "I've kept records. I'll get on it right away."

"Thank you," I said. "That would be most appreciated."

I nodded to Barry, who said:

"Yes, that will be all, Mr. Armbruster."

But the quarterwarlock didn't move. He eyed the girl sitting next to him with deep suspicion. Then, he turned back to us.

"Are you sure that…" he began.

"Quite sure, thank you," I said.

"Alright," he said. "I'll be in the Great Hall for a nightcap if you need me. I'll deliver the list to your office then, Lord Barrington."

Barry inclined his feline head in gratitude. We waited briefly for Mr. Armbruster to leave before questioning Isabella Villar. I was just about to start when I remembered what the headmistress had told me. Nobody was to be trusted at Warklesby's School of Magic.

I quietly stepped over to the door to make sure Armbruster was gone. My instincts, as it turned out, hadn't failed me. As I opened the door, Armbruster was just a little too late in pretending to walk down the corridor. Had he been trying to eavesdrop on the conversation we would be having with Isabella Villar?

"Oh, erm, is there anything else you want?" he asked innocently.

"No, Mr. Armbruster, nothing else."

"Right, I'd… I'd better be off, then."

"Yes, goodbye," I said.

I stood there, watching him. There was nothing else for him to do but turn around and walk away. Once he was safely around the corner, I came back into Barry's office. Val and Barry hadn't, it seemed, started asking questions yet. Before we proceeded, I suddenly had an idea. Rummaging for my wand in my handbag, there was one extra precaution I wanted to take.

"Barritha!"

Shooting out of my wand with a whoosh, a sound-proof glue spread across the office door. You're not really paranoid if they're really out to get you, I thought to myself. I'd certainly be watching Mr. Armbruster very closely in the upcoming days.

Now, however, there was the more pressing matter of Isabella Villar. You didn't have to be a psychic to tell that this office was the last place that she wanted to be at the present moment. She kept fidgeting with one of her bracelets, looking anywhere but directly at us. Matching her black clothes and dark hair, she had opted for a heavy layer of makeup that I was sure was several shades lighter than her actual skin colour.

"Miss Villar," Barry began pompously, "I hope you appreciate your difficult position. Drawing a forbidden sign – the sign of the necromancer, no less – is in itself punishable by magical law."

Isabella Villar gulped but didn't say anything.

"As you undoubtedly know, however," Barry continued, "there is a lot more at stake currently at the school. People have been disappearing. And there is good reason to believe that they may have been killed."

For the first time, Isabella Villar spoke. She had a slight Spanish accent.

"I had nothing to do with this," she said.

"What *were* you doing down in the dungeons?" I asked.

Isabella Villar paused briefly, as if considering her answer very carefully.

"I wanted something from the storage room," she said.

"What did you want?" I asked.

"I needed new phials," she said quickly, though I thought it sounding slightly rehearsed, "for my alchemy lessons. I knew that there were some down there."

"A strange place to look," said Barry suspiciously "Why didn't you acquire some at the school store, like everyone else?"

"I have no money," she said. "Nobody uses those old things. Nobody would have cared if… if…"

"… if you hadn't drawn that sign on the wall?" said Barry harshly. "I think not."

Isabella Villar grew red in the face with indignation.

"I did not do that," she said, raising her voice. "I did not!"

"Perhaps," I said, trying a different tactic, "Miss Villar was indeed at the wrong place at the wrong time."

She looked surprised.

"However," I continued, "it is important that you also see our perspective. You do want these disappearances to stop, don't you?"

"Of course," she said. "I… I knew Robert. Everybody wants this to stop."

"Then you must help us," I said. "If you are innocent, then help us to move on. Every minute spent on the innocent is a moment that the guilty party can breathe freely. So, I ask you again: what were you doing down in the dungeons?"

"I told you, I was looking for bottles."

"I thought you were looking for phials?" Barry said triumphantly.

"Yes, that is what I meant," she said. "Phials for alchemy class."

"Mr. Armbruster saw you standing next to the sign of the necromancer," I said. "The phials were nowhere near there. Tell us the truth, Miss Villar: If you have any compassion for those people, tell us what you were really doing."

She opened her mouth, but no words would come out. She was looking furiously at all of us. And yet, I could see that I had struck a nerve somewhere. Instead of saying anything, she suddenly pulled back her left sleeve. Her fingers were covered in green paint, the same paint that was used for the sign of the necromancer.

"So," Barry said, "it *was* you."

"No," I said, remembering the smudged skull. "You tried to wipe it away, didn't you?"

"Yes, I did," Miss Villar said proudly.

"But Mr. Armbruster caught you before you could get rid of it?"

"Yes," she said.

"Why did you try to wipe it away?" I asked.

"It is a sign of evil," she said. "Bad things follow whenever it is drawn."

"Do you know who put that sign on the wall?" Val asked, getting up from her seat and walking over to Barry's desk.

"No," she said flatly. "I do not."

I wasn't quite sure whether to believe her or not. Barry, evidently, was thinking along the same lines.

"Tell us the truth, Miss Villar," he said sternly. "If you know the person who drew the sign, give us the name."

But it was to no avail. However hard we tried, we had met a dead end. Whatever she knew, she wouldn't say anything further. Finally, Val placed a hand on Barry's fur, signalling that there was no point.

"Let her go," Val said.

"What?" Barry spluttered.

"She has told us all she knows," she said.

Barry looked aghast from Val to me. I didn't know what was going on, but I trusted Val's instincts. I nodded briefly. Barry, still perplexed, finally said:

"Fine, Miss Villar, that will be all – for now. Report straight back to your dormitory. I would advise you not to wipe away any more signs. They may be of vital importance."

"What is my punishment?" she asked icily.

"That is not for us to decide, Miss Villar," I said. "All we want is to know what happened to the missing people. If you remember anything – anything at all – please don't hesitate to contact us here. We will make sure it remains confidential. I promise."

Miss Villar hesitated briefly. Then, she nodded, got up, and headed straight for the door without another word.

When he was sure that she was safely out of earshot, Barry turned on Val.

"Are you mad?" he said. "She obviously knew more."

"I agree," said Val. "But she wouldn't have told us anything."

"And why not?" Barry asked angrily. "A few more minutes, and I could have cracked her."

"I felt her emotions, Barry. They were strong. Very strong. There is no way in a million years that she would have talked. She's covering up for somebody. Somebody very close to her."

CHAPTER 6

"Who is she covering up for?" I asked Val. "Could you tell?"

"No," she said. "All that I know is that she is very loyal to this person. I sensed her fierceness. If we want to find out who it is, we'll have to do it some other way."

"I'll have the headmistress put her under house arrest," said Barry, who was still incensed by being lied to.

"No," I said. "How are we going to find out who she is covering up for if we do that? Val, do you think Miss Villar will warn whoever drew that sign?"

"If that person is still at the school, I'm sure of it," said Val. "With such strong feelings, it would be the most natural thing to do."

"The sooner the better, most likely…" I said. "If I were in her shoes, I'd do it quickly, wouldn't you? I mean, you don't know when you'll get another chance. You might be questioned for the next week, for all you know. Necromancy is no joke. Miss Villar knows that."

"But we can't watch her day and night," said Barry irritably. "She could slip that person a note, or leave a message somewhere. Or whisper in someone's ear in the Great Hall with hundreds of people talking at the same time."

"It's certainly a daunting task," I agreed. "All I'm saying is that we should keep an eye on her."

"Well," said Val, "Barry would be best suited for that. He can hide pretty much anywhere."

"I've got better things to do than to spy on teenagers," Barry protested. "Look at all these notes! I've got a lecture to prepare."

He gestured towards the sheets of paper on his desk.

"We'll take it in shifts, then," I said. "It's our only lead so far."

"Fine," said Barry impatiently, "but first I need a good night's rest before tomorrow's class."

***

Reluctantly, Val and I agreed. It had been a tiring first day at Warklesby's School of Magic, so any more detective work would have to wait for the morning, when we could make a fresh start.

We left Barry snoring in his little bed, situated on a mezzanine right above his desk. He couldn't climb the slippery metal rungs leading up to it, however, so I had conjured up a cat ladder for him instead. I was getting quite adept at creating feline furniture by now.

Val and I, meanwhile, were to sleep in a small dormitory – only a few flights of stairs away from Barry's office – that was reserved for outside researchers and guests. The dormitory was small, with no more than ten rooms perhaps, but it featured a communal area with comfortable sofas and a fireplace, where the last cinders attested to a fire having been lit a few hours earlier.

At the other end of the room, a group of waxwork figures depicting several hooded warlocks and witches in black robes sent waves of ice down my spine. In the dim light provided by the candles hanging on the walls in the common room, they looked eerily alive and human. I would definitely make sure to lock myself in tonight. Judging by the look on Val's face, she felt just the same way.

We found our names on a door label at the very back, tucked away behind a corner. The room had two beds, a wardrobe, two chairs, and a table. Adjacent to it was a bathroom. It wasn't luxurious by any standards, but it would certainly do for a few days. Fresh towels and linen had been provided for. Fortunately, our bags had already been brought up, too.

The room was stuffy, however, so we opened the window at the back immediately.

"At least it *has* a window," said Val, slumping down on one of the beds. "The rest of the castle is so dark with just torches. And what's with the wax statues all over the place? Like in a horror movie, or something."

"Yeah," I concurred, thinking longingly of Fickleton House's cosy and – most importantly – waxwork-free hallways. "They are well made, though. Some real craftsmanship."

"That's what I'm afraid of," said Val. "They probably magicked them to jump at you when you're not looking."

I laughed.

"Come on, Val, it won't be for long."

"I hope so," she said earnestly. "This place gives me the creeps, Amy. Something horrible is going on, I can sense it. It's in the air, if you know what I mean."

After trying to reassure Val, both of us made ready for bed. It was still very warm inside the room, though the light breeze coming through the window certainly helped. After a good shower, I put on my nightgown and slipped into bed. Val followed shortly after. We said goodnight, and I extinguished the candle on the table with my wand.

Neither of us, however, could sleep. After tossing around uselessly for a few minutes, I could hear Val turn around in the darkness.

"Amy," she said, "do you think we've met the necromancer yet?"

"I don't know," I said. "We haven't met all that many people."

"I'm still betting on the deputy headmaster," said Val. "Nasty person."

"He certainly is," I said. "What about the headmistress, though?"

"Muriel Hall?" said Val in disbelief. "Well, if it's her,

she's certainly hiding it well."

"It's happened before," I said slowly.

"What about that Mr. Armbruster?" said Val.

"Certainly a shifty character," I said. "Listening at doors makes for a suspicious pastime. Did you feel anything with him."

"I'm not sure," said Val. "Isabella Villar's emotions were so strong, she made his appear rather blurry. I did feel that he was a bit on edge, though. But some people simply are like that."

"A bit like Professor Olsen," I said, thinking of his spectacular clash with Barry in the Great Hall. "He seemed to fly off the handle pretty quickly. Esther – his assistant – seemed to be downright afraid of him."

"Yes," said Val slowly. "And whoever is doing this is taking a sadistic pleasure. I mean, it's not just that people are being abducted, but all of these signs are designed to create an atmosphere of fear."

"Yeah," I said. "Anyway, we should suspect everyone until we have evidence to the contrary. Might turn out it's a student, even."

There was a moment's pause.

"Amy?" said Val.

"Yes?"

"D'you really think Wycliffe has come back from the dead?" she asked.

"I don't know," I said again. "Seems quite convenient for our kidnapper, though, don't you think? You can just blame it on a dead sorcerer."

We discussed the different possibilities for an hour or so longer, though we knew that it was all conjecture. It felt good to talk about it all the same. With our need to find the proverbial needle in the haystack, guess work provided a form of solace.

Exhausted from the events of the day, we finally fell into a deep yet uneasy sleep.

***

A few hours later, I was awoken by what I thought was the wind howling outside. Groggily, I wiped my eyes, opening them. It was still pitch black. Val was snoring next to me.

I couldn't check my phone for the time, since the magical energies surrounding us in the school prevented it from working. I lit my wand for light and got up, walking over to the window.

Closing it, I was just about to climb back into bed when, once more, I heard the mysterious noise that had awoken me. It couldn't have been the wind after all, I thought.

I stood still, listening for it again. And then, sure enough, it returned. It sounded human, though I couldn't be sure. If I wasn't quite mistaken, it wasn't coming from outside at all but from inside the walls.

It felt silly to wake Val for no reason. It might just be my imagination playing tricks on me, a result of the talk we had had before we fell asleep. But curiosity was gnawing away at me, egging me on to find out the sound's origin. And, I reasoned with myself, I could easily call for Val if it was anything serious.

Extinguishing my wand, I wedged it into the sash of my nightgown. You couldn't be too careful with a sorcerer on the loose.

I unlocked the door and stepped into the common room, which was still lit by the weak light of the candles, though – miraculously – they hadn't burnt down even an inch.

Pricking my ears up, I waited, trying to locate the sound. Vaguely gazing at the dormitory's exit, something bright glinted in the corner of my eye. Had something moved nearby?

"Who's there?" I spoke into the empty room, spinning

around and drawing my wand.

But there was nothing there – except for the sinister waxwork figures that had so repulsed me earlier. Standing in a group of five, the faces beneath the hoods were as unrecognisable as ever.

My wand hand shaking slightly, I inched closer, watching for the slightest movement, fearful that they might jump at me at any moment.

And yet, they remained perfectly still. But as I approached, I saw the glint of light again. One of the figures, a warlock at the back of the group, was wearing a gold signet ring on his left hand. The candle light must have been reflected in it.

I lowered my wand. Feeling rather foolish, I was just about to go back to bed when I heard a door open and the patter of naked feet behind me. I was half expecting to see Val. Instead, a slender figure had appeared, barely visible in the darkness.

"Who… who's there?" a woman asked, her voice sounding oddly subdued yet familiar.

Screwing up my eyes, I finally recognised her. It was Esther Hickey, the researcher I had met in the Great Hall earlier. She looked terrible. Her face was red and blotchy, while deep bags under her eyes suggested she hadn't slept at all.

"I…" I began, not knowing how to explain myself. "Sorry, I thought I heard something outside. Those waxworks… well, I…"

"Oh, them," Esther said, wiping what I suspected to be the remnants of tears from her left cheek. "One gets used to them eventually."

"Is… is everything alright?" I asked, trying not to sound overly intrusive.

"Oh, it's nothing," she said, "just..."

She looked at me for a while, evidently making up her mind whether to tell me or not. Then, without further warning, she burst into tears.

"I-I'm s-sorry," she spluttered, holding her hands to her face. "I just can't stand it anymore…"

But she tailed off before saying anything more. She closed her eyes, teetering dangerously on the spot. Afraid that she might faint on the spot, I tried to stabilise her with my hand around her waist.

Slinging her arm around my neck, I moved her over to the sofa at the fireplace. She had closed her eyes, hardly responsive to what was happening around her.

"Would you like something to drink?" I asked her.

With what seemed like extreme effort, she opened her eyes again.

"S-so sorry," she murmured.

"Esther, would you like some water?" I asked.

Feebly, she nodded her head. Careful to leave her so that she wouldn't fall from the sofa, I hastened over to my room. Val was still snoring peacefully in her bed. We had a few glasses in the bathroom, courtesy of the school, which would have to do.

Returning with a clean glass of water, I pulled the door to our room shut, careful not to wake up Val, and went to Esther with the glass of water.

Raising her head with difficulty, she drank it gratefully. When she had emptied the whole glass, she looked at me and attempted a smile.

"Thank you, Amanda," she said. "That's very kind of you."

She handed me the glass, which I placed on a nearby table.

"Rough night?" I asked, sitting down on a nearby armchair.

Esther lowered her eyes.

"You could say so," she said. "It's just… just so much pressure. Professor Olsen…"

She broke off again, though I could see she was bursting

to tell someone.

"Do you promise not to breathe a word of this to him? Or anyone else, for that matter?"

"Of course," I said.

"I don't want them to think I'm a complainer," she said. "It's just got to a point where, well… where I don't know what will happen next."

Esther looked into the fireplace for a moment, as if she were miles away.

"He's not a very nice man, you see," she said finally. "Professor Olsen, I mean."

"How come?" I asked.

"Well," she began, struggling to find the right words, "I don't know why exactly. But ever since I arrived here as his assistant, he's so… irritable. Angry, often for no reason at all. Starts yelling uncontrollably."

"And he takes it out on you?" I asked.

"Yes," she said softly. "Not only me, though. His secretary gets most of it, I think. And there's the other assistant – Hubert Metcalfe – with whom he argues a lot, too. I've talked to Hubert, and he's just as puzzled as everyone else."

"So, this is a recent change in him, then?" I asked.

Esther nodded her head emphatically.

"Absolutely," she said. "I'd never have come back here otherwise. I was a student of his for the last few years at Warklesby's, you see. I did my exams with him and everything. He told me he was always on the lookout for good researchers and asked me to join his team. And so I did."

"Very strange," I said. "Do you know when exactly this change occurred?"

Esther shifted uncomfortably on the sofa.

"Now, I don't want you to understand this the wrong way. It's likely – no, most certainly – a complete coincidence. But it all started with these mysterious disappearances at the school. At the time, I wasn't back again at Warklesby's yet, but the secretary – Mrs. Kettle – told me all about it.

"He changed," Esther continued. "And pretty quickly, too. As a student, we had got on very well. I'd seen Professor Olsen at meetings and gatherings plenty of times. I even had private lessons with him. He guided me in my research, helping me gain an understanding of earth magic that certainly transcended the normal school curriculum. He was almost like a father to me, academically speaking."

She brushed a thin strand of hair behind her left ear.

"But when I finally arrived here as a researcher and assistant – so glad to be back at the school I had loved as a pupil – Professor Olsen was dismissive and downright rude. It was almost as if he couldn't remember who I was or just didn't care. He didn't even afford me my own quarters in the department of earth magic, so I've had to use this dormitory instead. I see my colleagues only during mealtimes, and I'd be completely in the dark if Hubert and Mrs. Kettle wouldn't keep me in the loop."

"That sounds horrible," I said sympathetically.

"It is," Esther said grimly, though her voice was now much steadier. "According to Mrs. Kettle, Professor Olsen changed right about the time people went missing and when those horrible markings started appearing all over the school."

"Do you think he might have anything to do with it?" I asked, deciding not to beat about the bush.

Esther stared at me for a minute, as though uttering the words tempted the universe to make it true. But I could see that the possibility had been haunting her. What had initiated the strange and sudden change in Professor Olsen's behaviour? Had he simply been particularly unnerved by the strange disappearances at the school? Or was there perhaps another, a darker reason?

"No," she whispered, her eyes so wide I could see the

white all around her irides. "I just don't… whatever reason would he have to do that?"

"I don't know," I said. "Can you think of anything at all that has changed?"

She paused, staring at me for a moment while she considered her answer.

"Well, there is… one thing that struck me as very strange. Professor Olsen was always a prolific writer, producing several books and dozens of articles a year. Yet according to Hubert, he hasn't produced anything new for quite some time. He only has Hubert rehash some of his old works."

"Perhaps he has lost interest in his subject?" I said.

But Esther shook her head.

"That's the strange thing. He locks himself up in his laboratory for hours and hours. It's certainly not to prepare his lectures, either – he could do those in his sleep after so many years. The truth is that none of us really knows what he gets up to in there."

"Where exactly is his laboratory?" I asked.

"The department for earth magic is in the East Tower. Professor Olsen's laboratory is at the top of the tower."

"Thank you for telling me," I said. "I know it's very difficult for you."

"You won't tell anyone, will you?" she said, panic in her voice. "I wasn't insinuating anything, I… I just needed to talk to someone. It gets pretty lonely in this dormitory."

"Don't worry," I said. "Your secret is safe with me."

Relieved, Esther smiled and slowly lifted herself up from the sofa. She was still rather uneasy on her feet, but much better than before. Looking relieved, it was almost as though she had cleansed herself of a great burden by merely speaking of it.

I was getting very tired myself. Professor Olsen's strange behaviour was certainly worthy of further investigation, though it would have to wait for the next day.

Supressing a yawn, I escorted Esther back to her room. It was even smaller than ours and had no window at all. Books, journals, newspapers, and pencils seemed to cover every inch of it.

"Thank you again," she said. "I hope the Four Druids of Lutetia don't bother you again."

"Sorry?"

"The waxworks in the common room," she clarified, smiling.

"Oh," I said, laughing. "No, I hope not. Well, goodnight."

"Goodnight."

I stepped outside and closed the door behind me. I was feeling very groggy now. I was just about to go back to bed when something about Esther's words struck me.

The *Four* Druids of Lutetia?

I was certain I had counted five earlier on. Whipping out my wand – wide awake again – I stepped over to the hideous waxworks.

To my shock, Esther was right. There were only four hooded figures. The one with the ring that had caught my eye earlier was missing. Someone, disguised as a waxwork, had been listening in to every word we had said.

CHAPTER 7

The next morning, as I hurried along Warklesby's many corridors after a few hours of snatched sleep, my sense of growing paranoia in regard to the waxwork figures didn't improve, considering that there seemed to be one in every corridor of the castle.

During a hasty breakfast, I had told Val and Barry all about my talk with Esther and the disturbing thought of someone posing as a waxwork, secretly listening to our conversation.

"But," Val had said, a note of pleading desperation in her voice, "couldn't you have just made a mistake with the waxworks? It must have been dark, and we *were* very tired when we came to the dormitory."

"I told you, Val," I had answered, "I remember it clearly. Also, none of the four druids had a ring the second time around. There was someone else there, I know it."

***

Barry's first lecture was to take place in a hall not far from the East Tower. Neither Val nor I were particularly keen on attending, though in the interest of our cover – as assistants to the Earl of Barrington – it was vital to keep up the performance for as long as possible.

When we arrived, the hall – shaped like an amphitheatre – was buzzing with the noise of pupils talking and laughing. As far as I could tell, they were older students, probably in their senior years. There was also a great deal of unauthorised magic going on, though most of it seemed to be good-natured pranking. Surprisingly, Julian Ross, who had been in trouble with the headmistress only the previous day, was not involved. Instead, he was sitting in the front row near the door, clearly lost in thought, with no trace left of his usual cocky smile. Perhaps, I thought, Headmistress Hall had been able to talk some sense into him after all.

Val and I sat down at the assistants' table, next to the blackboard, facing the crowd of students. I conjured up a glass of water for each of us.

At last, Barry made his entrance. Wearing a tiny black gown that covered most of his fur, he had donned a square academic cap to match. Val and I had to supress a giggle as he haughtily walked towards us.

"What is it?" he hissed.

"Nothing," I said quickly, well aware that some of the students in the front row were paying close attention. "Your notes are ready for you on the table."

Barry leapt onto a high stool that we had placed behind his lectern. Due to the lack of sufficient light coming in through the high but narrow windows in the hall, he turned on the green reading lamp next to his bowl of milk, which we had brought up specially from the kitchens. A magical microphone ensured that he could be heard by everyone present.

"Welcome," Barry said, his voice reverberating around the hall, "to my lecture series on the many complexities and intricacies of therianthropy. I am pleased to say that Warklesby's School of Magic has made ample room for them, however, in what I hope will truly be an enlightening first five-hour session."

"*Five* hours?" Val mouthed at me, a look of horror on her face.

I gulped but said nothing. We were in for one long lecture by Barry. With no escape in sight, Val and I had no other choice but to surrender to the present circumstances.

***

Two and a half hours later, Barry finally looked up from his massive stack of notes and announced a break. It was like awakening from some sort of trance, which had been both anaesthetising and informative at the same time.

Val, for whom the magic was of less interest, was still in a near-comatose stupor. I prodded her gently, and she shook herself visibly, wrenching herself back into the present.

"Have… have I missed it?" she said.

"Don't be so optimistic, Val," I said softly. "Still half way to go."

"Oh," she said, "we'd better attend to Barry, then."

Barry, however, was surrounded by inquisitive students who had flocked to the lectern to pose him some questions. My gaze moved toward the rest of the crowd, which was drifting lazily towards the exits. Then, near the door, I spotted a familiar face.

"Look, Val," I said, pointing, "isn't that Isabella Villar over there?"

Val squinted her eyes for better vision.

"You know, Amy, I think you're right."

"How long is the break, do you know?" I asked.

"Only about twenty minutes, I think," said Val. "Why?"

"Well," I said, turning around conspiratorially to make sure that we couldn't be overheard, "she won't be seeing the person she's covering up for now, then. But we should remain vigilant, all the same."

"Yes," Val said, "but what about Professor Olsen's lab?"

"I thought we might poke around there later this afternoon. I checked his timetable, and he's got class at the other end of the castle then. It should give us enough time. If we get out of here alive, that is."

"Come on, Amy, you shouldn't be too hard on Barry. He's having the time of his life," said Val, grinning.

At that moment, Barry's voice was clearly audible from beyond, ticking off an overly eager student for his patent ignorance.

"Clearly," I said drily. "Only problem is that we have to deflate his head when we're back home."

"It might be permanent this time," said Val, just as a pair of senior female students giggled at one of Barry's snide yet accurate comments. "We'd better catch the culprit quickly."

"You bet," I said, laughing.

***

'Quickly', however, became a relative matter the longer the second half of the lecture went on. But I noticed that I wasn't the only one who was restless. I had scanned the crowd for Isabella Villar and found her sitting at the very edge of the back row, close to the aisle. Every minute or so, she looked at the large hourglass hanging on the wall. Fidgeting with the notes she was supposed to be taking, Isabella Villar seemed desperate to escape the lecture hall as soon as possible.

Surreptitiously, I pointed this out to Val.

"Should we follow her?" asked Val, leaning over to me.

"Wouldn't hurt," I whispered.

Finally, Barry's lecture came to an end. The avalanche of information had clearly left its mark on all present. The more ambitious students – sitting mostly in the front row – had amassed what appeared to be short novellas in terms of notes. Yet, even those who had been less keen were clearly physically and mentally worse for wear.

Unfortunately, a large group of students had congregated around Barry's lectern, asking follow-up questions. Under the pretext of gathering his lecture notes, I bent down so that nobody else could hear.

"We're tailing Villar. Meet you later."

Unsurprisingly, Barry played the role of professor perfectly. Turning his feline head, his hat tipped slightly to one side, he nodded.

"Thank you, Miss Sheridan, just put them on my desk. I will see you in my office later."

Supressing a smile, I agreed and swiftly scooped up the rest of the notes, conjuring up a black suitcase with my wand in order to carry them all.

The students were now streaming out of the exits. Val – no doubt on Isabella Villar's tails by now – was nowhere in sight. Joining the fray, I navigated my way through the crowds until I was clear of the lecture hall.

In the corridor beyond, I spotted a less than inconspicuous Val at the far end near the archway that eventually lead to the Great Hall, waving to me from the spearhead of pupils streaming along like some gigantic snake.

Before I could make any progress, however, I heard a faint yet distinct call next to me.

"Amanda. Amanda, over here."

It was Esther Hickey. She looked quite different from last night. She seemed excited, though the urgency of her voice indicated to me that it was something important.

Val, meanwhile, was still desperately trying to get me to hurry up. I motioned her onward with both of my arms and mouthed 'go on', though I think it was eventually the torrent of students that broke the dam that was Val standing in the archway. She had no choice but to swim along. I only hoped that she would be in time to follow Isabella Villar.

Luckily, most of the students had passed by me, so I was able to follow Esther to the wall so that we couldn't be overheard so easily.

"Is everything alright?" I asked.

"Yes," she said, lowering her voice, "I mean, no – well, it's about Prof. Olsen. I can't explain here. You'd better come with me to the laboratory immediately."

"OK," I said, with a last glance in the direction of the

lecture hall where Barry was no doubt still besieged by students. "Lead the way."

We hurried along, passing quite a few students who were headed for their next class or the Great Hall for tea. Though I didn't have any means to tell the time in the mostly windowless corridors, I reckoned that it was probably afternoon already.

A few minutes later, Esther came to a halt in front of a large door with a brass handle.

"This," she said in a soft voice, "is the East Tower. The department of earth magic is here. The laboratory is at the top."

The wooden flights of stairs leading upwards were surprisingly narrow, owing to the rather low diameter of the tower. What it lacked in width, however, it made up for in height. The steps seemed endless and excessively steep, so that more than once I stumbled and almost fell into Esther. Though only very few students came out of the classrooms that led off of the stairs – earth magic did not seem to be a favourite – inching past one another on creaking boards required some serious manoeuvrability.

At last, we had reached the top of the tower. I could tell that Esther was still nervous, though she seemed much steadier than the night before. We found ourselves on a circular staircase with a balustrade all the way round.

"This entire floor is dedicated to the laboratory," said Esther quietly.

"Is… is Prof. Olsen here?" I asked, gazing around.

"That's the peculiar thing," said Esther. "He sent a note to his secretary this morning, saying that he had an urgent appointment and had to leave immediately. Hubert was tasked with taking over his classes. I… I thought it would be the perfect opportunity to have a look around the laboratory."

"Good thinking," I said. "Did he say why he had to leave so suddenly?"

"No," Esther said, shaking her head. "He's quite secretive. But he usually gives the secretary some way of contacting him in case of an emergency. Apparently, he didn't do that this time. He said he didn't want to be disturbed."

"Very suspicious," I agreed. "If he is involved somehow, we need to find out as soon as we can. How much time do you think we'll have?"

"I don't know," she said. "But he had packed a large bag, according to Hubert, who met him in his office before he left to discuss the classes. That would mean he was staying the night, wouldn't it?"

"Perhaps." I said thoughtfully. "Or he might be transporting something."

"Should we go back?" she asked.

"No," I said, drawing my wand. "We might not get another chance."

Esther hesitated briefly but finally nodded. She produced a large stack of keys from her pocket and began trying them one by one.

"I borrowed these from the secretary's desk," she said. "Must be one of them. I've seen Professor Olsen use them."

"Can't we simply magic it open?" I asked.

"No," Esther said. "There is a powerful spell to prevent that. These are magically protected locks. Ah, here we are."

The door swung open before us. We were dazzled by rays of sunshine that pierced the large windows beyond, making us hold our hands to our eyes. From this high up, the view of the surrounding rocky hillsides and forests was magnificent.

Carefully, we entered the room, which wrapped itself round the staircase from which we had entered. Every inch of the laboratory was covered with magical instruments of all types and sizes. Several tables were stacked with mysterious powders and phials filled with dark fluids I didn't recognise. Scraps of papers with indecipherable formulae littered the walls.

Backed against the wall at the laboratory's right side, a blackboard was covered with strange symbols and runes. Next to it, a potion was simmering in a cauldron above a magical fire. Evidently, Professor Olsen wasn't planning on staying away for too long. Placed at the wall, various cardboard boxes were stacked close to a small table.

"Is there anything out of the ordinary?" I asked Esther, who knew more about earth magic than me.

"Well," she said, approaching the blackboard. "I'm not sure what he is working on. Most of these things are related to the school curriculum, though. Pretty standard. He must have his own research somewhere else."

I decided to leave her and investigate the rest of the laboratory, to the left from the entrance. It turned out that it was devoted mostly to storage, with countless shelves containing all sorts of plants, metal objects, and fine instruments. Various crates of different sizes and a solid stone wall marked the end. Inside the crates, I found mostly commonplace ingredients for potions.

Slightly disappointed, I made my way back to Esther. She was still standing in front of the blackboard with the same confused expression on her face.

"I'm sorry, Amanda," she said. "I just don't understand. This is almost as if… as if something is missing. It doesn't make any sense at all. I haven't found any original research at all."

"Perhaps it's in here," I said, turning to the small table behind me and trying to open its stubborn drawer. "Though it will probably take hours to get through these."

"Oh, I'm just hopeless," Esther said miserably. "I'm sorry I brought you here, Amanda, I don't know what I was…"

But at that moment, in a move that would have even Val blushing, I must have exerted a bit too much force, for the drawer came clean out of the table, sending me flying to the ground. I was showered in paper, while an ink bottle went zooming through the air. But instead of hitting the wall behind the table, it suddenly disappeared.

"Hold on," I said, gingerly getting to my feet. "Did you see that?"

"No, what is it?" asked Esther.

"It's the ink bottle…" I said.

I thought perhaps the ink bottle had simply dropped onto the table, but there was nothing there.

"Help me with this, will you?" I asked, indicating the table.

Together with Esther, I carried it out of the way, so that we could reach the wall directly behind it. I moved my hand slowly forward until it was only an inch away from the wall. Then, as I was about to touch it, the tips of my fingers vanished before my eyes.

"Ingenious," I said.

Esther seemed somewhat shaken, so I stepped in first. I found myself in a pitch-black room. None of the light penetrated the secret magical wall through which I had entered. It smelt of something foul in here, and the heat was almost unbearable.

Muttering the incantation as softly as I could, I lit my wand. For a moment, I was dazzled by the bright beam. But as my eyes adjusted, I found myself in a small, rectangular room. The walls were covered with newspaper cuttings and pictures. Many of them, however, had been torn down. The floor was covered not only in paper but also broken glass and stinking liquids. Shelves had been smashed or cleared of their contents. It looked like a battleground.

Raising my wandlight, my eyes followed the trail of waste until, to my horror, I spotted a figure at the far end of the room, sitting on a chair, completely motionless.

Suddenly breathing very quickly, I grasped my wand tightly in my wand hand.

"Who are you?" I demanded.

There was no answer.

Esther, who had followed me inside by now, grabbed my arm in panic. Slowly, I edged forward, with only the cracking of glass underneath my shoes to break the eerie silence.

As I got closer, there was no mistaking the shock of white hair.

"Professor Olsen!" Esther screamed.

We hurried across to him immediately. But it was too late. Professor Olsen was already dead.

CHAPTER 8

Esther muffled a scream with her hands. Feeling a sudden rush of anxiety myself, I pointed my wand shakily around the room. But there was nobody else there except for us, neither person nor waxwork. Esther and I were alone.

Careful not to touch anything, I shone my wandlight onto Professor Olsen again. There was a burn mark on his right temple. His right hand was dangling down, still clutching a wand. It had wooden carvings that ran counter to the fingers.

"Th-this is so horrible," Esther said, staring at Professor Olsen's lifeless body as though transfixed by a snake. "Do you think he might have t-taken his own life?"

"It certainly looks that way," I murmured.

I bent forward, examining the burn mark more closely. It was blacker in the middle, with sharp red streaks at the edges. I had never seen anything like it before.

The desk in front of Professor Olsen was untidy, stacked with papers and notes. The many stains and remnants of powders on the wood attested to the fact that Professor Olsen had used this room many times in the past. Flanking the desk on either side, shelves held yet more phials containing poisonous-looking substances, while others had also been tossed to the floor.

"Esther," I said softly, "I need you to get help immediately. Please tell the Earl of Barrington that we need him here. He should be in his office. I don't think Val will be there, but if she is, tell her to come, too. After that, please inform Headmistress Hall of what has happened here. Can you do that?"

With difficulty, Esther tore her eyes away from the body

and nodded. She took out her own wand and, with one last horrified glance at the dead man in the chair, turned around and exited the secret chamber.

Now alone, I needed a moment to pull myself together. There was nothing to fear, I said to myself, though the corpse right next to me told me otherwise.

Trying to distract myself, I began examining the newspaper articles on the wall next to the entrance. It seemed that Professor Olsen had had a keen interest in reports of necromancy, both in general ("London Necromancy Ring Exposed"), as well as at the school itself ("EXCLUSIVE: Is Warklesby kidnapping linked to necromancers?"). Here and there, key words and phrases were underlined. The sensationalist articles seemed to contain little more than speculation, featuring the occasional 'expert' interview.

On the opposite wall, the newspaper clippings were older. Most of them concerned the terror at the school many years ago, as well as the arrest and trial of Wycliffe. Despite the yellow paper and fading colours, Wycliffe's deluded gaze was still frighteningly life-like. He had blond, greasy hair that almost reached down to his shoulders. His gaunt face had high, prominent cheekbones and an unusually thin mouth that was no more than a slit when he sneered at the camera. His piercing grey eyes betrayed no inkling of remorse.

Moving away from the press cuttings, I stepped closer to Professor Olsen's desk again. Notes were pinned to the wall all over the place, though I could see that many had been ripped off and scattered upon the table. Strange markings and complicated calculations were scribbled on them. Although it was difficult to tell, the contents of his research looked a lot different from the ones outside. Perhaps there had been a reason why Professor Olsen had decided to keep these particular works in here, away from prying eyes of colleagues and students.

***

After a harrowing quarter of an hour or so, Barry arrived at last. He was wearing a very serious expression indeed and, for once, did not moan about having to climb up the many stairs of the East Tower. Esther wasn't with him, but she had apparently explained the exact location of the secret entrance to him.

"Where is he?" he said.

"Over here," I said.

Approaching the Professor Olsen's lifeless body, Barry nimby jumped onto the desk – careful not to disturb anything – in order to examine the dead man.

After several minutes in silence, Barry seemed satisfied.

"It was the killing curse alright," he said. "No doubt about it. Close quarters, as you can tell by the characteristic burn marks."

"Was it suicide?" I asked.

"Probably."

I was just about to turn around when a familiar glint caught my eye. Professor Olsen's other hand was resting on his lap. It was wearing a gold ring. A ring, in fact, that I was sure I had seen not too long ago.

"Barry, look!" I said excitedly, pointing at it. "I've seen that ring before. In our common room. On the fake waxwork figure I told you about at breakfast."

"Curious," Barry said, his whiskers twitching.

"*He* must have been the one eavesdropping on me," I said. "His stature certainly fits. I'd say he's about the same size as the waxwork figure."

"Then the only question remains," Barry said, "of why Professor Olsen wanted to spy on you and his assistant in the first place. He must have got wind of our investigation very fast. Not that one had to be a mastermind to figure that one out, I suppose."

"He already knew," I said, remembering what Headmistress Hall had told me. "He's on the school board. That's what Muriel Hall told us when we arrived. She said that she would ask him not to tell anyone."

"Yes," said Barry slowly, "that certainly explains his speed."

"What do you make of these drawings?" I asked Barry, indicating several scraps of paper on Professor Olsen's desk.

Barry carefully navigated the messy desk to peruse them. After a moment, he grunted, moving on to the next piece. At last, he seemed satisfied.

"What do you think?" I asked him.

"It's necromancy alright," said Barry. "No doubt about it. If I'm not mistaken, this is part of a plan for a resurrection."

"You mean, of a human?" I asked, horrified.

"Yes," Barry said. "And have a look at these maps. I'm almost certain that they show the school grounds. Yes, these are the woods, you see? He's marked them out for some reason."

Barry pointed at a large green area with several clearings. A thick red circle was drawn around the entire forest. Next to it was a question mark.

"I wonder what he was looking for?" I said. "It's not very specific, is it?"

"I don't know," Barry said thoughtfully. "Have you noticed anything else of interest?"

"Have a look over there," I said, pointing to the wall to the right of us. "Looks like Professor Olsen was something of a Wycliffe fan."

Barry leapt down from the table and strutted over to the wall containing the newspaper clippings and began to read some of the reports.

"Calling this an obsession would certainly be an understatement," Barry said drily. "Looks like we've got our man."

"The evidence seems to point that way, I suppose," I said, frowning.

"You aren't convinced?" said Barry. "What more evidence do you need?"

"Well," I said, pacing the room. "It's all a little too perfect, don't you think? I mean, here we are, looking for a necromancer. And then we just happen to come across a secret office full of Wycliffe press clippings and how-to manuals for necromancy. A sick mind intoxicated with Wycliffe's crimes, a professor certainly capable of complicated and advanced magic. But the necromancer himself is dead, conveniently killed by his own hand."

"Are you telling me this was staged, Amanda?" Barry said, raising his eyebrows.

But before I could retort, two people entered the secret chamber. It was Deputy Headmaster Harper, followed by a frightened-looking Esther.

"There has been a death?" Harper said unnecessarily.

"Where is the headmistress?" I said, irritated to see him.

"I'm sorry, Amanda," Esther began, "I couldn't find her…"

"Headmistress Hall," Harper said, an unmistakable smirk of triumph on his face, "has unfortunately been delayed on her trip to London. She is currently liaising with MLE officers. In the meantime, *I* am in charge of investigations. And you will answer to me. Now, step aside so that I can examine the body."

His cold eyes scanned the position of the body, the burn marks, and then the wand in Professor Olsen's right hand. After that, Deputy Harper perused the newspaper clippings, as well as the notes on the desk.

"So that is what he was up to," Deputy Harper breathed. "I should have known…"

He looked at Professor Olsen's body with disgust. Then he turned around to me with a peculiar look on his face.

"It appears we have all underestimated you, Miss Sheridan. The culprit has been revealed to be Professor Olsen. I will inform the MLE immediately, as well as the headmistress."

Without another word, he strode towards the exit.

"I don't think it was him," I said before he reached the magical barrier.

Deputy Harper turned around as if a bothersome fly had just started harassing him.

"What did you just say?" he said.

"I don't think Professor Olsen is the man we're looking for."

"Your evidence?" Deputy Harper said curtly.

"Well," I said, unwilling to say that it was more of a hunch than anything else, "the room, for one. It's a mess. There might have been a fight, or a search. Both of which suggest that there's more to this."

"And who, pray, searched the room?" Deputy Harper sneered, disbelief etched across his face.

"The person who killed Professor Olsen," I said. "He could have rearranged the body quite easily."

"But you *do* realise, Miss Sheridan, that this is Professor Olsen's own laboratory, do you not? These newspapers are not here by accident," he said, gesturing towards a particularly striking picture of Wycliffe on the wall. "Or did this mysterious killer also change the décor after he finished brawling with his victim?"

Feeling my anger rising, I took a deep breath in order to avoid exploding on the spot.

"Deputy Harper," I said, speaking as calmly as possible. "The main question is why Professor Olsen would kill himself if he was the guilty party? It doesn't make any sense."

"Do not ask me to understand the mind of a criminal maniac," Harper spat. "Perhaps the necromancer had a moment of clarity and did the only decent thing left to him, destroying much of this room in the process."

"But what about the people who were abducted?" I said.

"We will find them eventually, if they are alive, although I highly doubt that to be true."

"But…" I began.

"The case," Harper said, his eyes narrowing dangerously, "is closed. I have heard quite enough of this nonsense. And I am sure that Headmistress Hall will concur as soon as I have had a word with her. You will cease all further investigations immediately."

CHAPTER 9

The news of Professor Olsen's death spread like wildfire. This was, perhaps, unsurprising given the fact that Deputy Harper had made very little effort to keep it a secret. Professor Olsen's body had been removed from the secret chamber and was being inspected by experts from the MLE. They didn't even want our testimony.

By the time we were back at Barry's office, darkness had already fallen. I was still fuming at Harper's patronising ignorance, but I was also dying to tell Val everything that had happened.

Fortunately, we found her snoozing on the sofa, an open book entitled *Psychic Signs and Symbols* in her hand. As we approached, she drowsily lifted an eyelid.

"Amy?" she said, yawning. "What's up?"

Settling down on one of the comfortable armchairs next to her, I told her the entire story, from how Esther had tipped me off to Deputy Harper's entrance.

"I must say," Barry said pompously after I had finished, "that Professor Olsen's morbid fascination with necromancy doesn't surprise me in the least. Awful fellow. Always knew that there was something sinister about him. Just couldn't quite put my paw on it."

"Oh, come on, Barry," I said. "You just didn't like him because of your squabble about theory the first day we got here."

"Well," Barry puffed indignantly, "of course I didn't know he kept a secret cabinet full of reports on Wycliffe, but there was *obviously* something wrong with him. I mean, who in their right mind would solely rely on Farthing's outdated theorem? Utterly absurd."

"So," Val said, ignoring Barry's last point, "was

Professor Olsen really a necromancer, then?"

"He was certainly fascinated by Wycliffe and necromancy, that's for certain," I said. "But there's something wrong about this whole thing."

"Oh, dear," Barry said in a mock-weary voice, "here we go again with the conspiracy theories."

"What conspiracy theories?" Val said.

"I don't think it was suicide," I said. "It doesn't make any sense. A necromancer who has spent years, if not decades, working on all this stuff, compiling his little cabinet all in secret, suddenly decides it's not worth it anymore?"

"Perhaps someone found out," Val said.

"Maybe," I said. "But Olsen did tell his staff that he was going away. I mean, he could have just destroyed the evidence and run for it."

"Well, what do you think happened?" Val asked.

"My guts tell me that he was killed, and the murder was staged as a suicide to end the investigation. Deputy Harper was quite keen to do just that, if you remember."

"Is there any way to tell if it was murder or suicide, Barry?" Val asked.

"Not if they used his own wand against him," Barry said.

"And that would most likely only happen after a scuffle," I said triumphantly, "which perfectly explains the mess the room was in."

Val pondered on this for a while, but Barry's tail was waving to and fro in irritation.

"Even if you're right, Amanda, you still have to account for the fact that Olsen was eavesdropping on you, disguised as one of the waxwork figures. It would be hard to explain if he wasn't the necromancer."

"He must have had another reason, then," I said, though I was at a loss myself in that regard.

"So if Amy's right," said Val, with a shudder, "then the

necromancer – who is also the killer – is still roaming the corridors of the school."

"Perhaps," Barry said, "we should consider the motive more thoroughly."

"Maybe Professor Olsen was a rival necromancer?" Val said. "Or maybe he knew too much and had to be silenced."

"Yes," I said, "that would make sense. But who did it?"

"I bet that awful deputy headmaster has something to do with it," Val said. "He's been trying to end our investigation the moment we arrived."

"It could be someone closer to Professor Olsen," said Barry. "After all, they had to know about the secret chamber somehow."

"You mean, a member of his department?" I asked.

"Precisely," he said. "Who do we have there?"

"Well, there's the secretary and the assistant I haven't met yet," I said. "And there's Esther, too. But she doesn't really strike me as the necromancer type."

"Don't be fooled by a good performance," Barry said. "Remember that it was Esther who led you up there in the first place. That might be more than just a coincidence. Valerie hasn't been able to penetrate the culprit's mind – if he or she is still out there, that is. But so far, it's all guesswork."

"Then what we need most," said Val, all matter-of-fact, "is to keep poking around. If Amy is right, and the necromancer is still on the loose, we can't just sit around."

"Agreed," I said.

Barry was about to protest, but quickly thought better of it after seeing our determined faces.

"Alright, alright," he said. "Have it your way. But don't blame me if it turns out to be Olsen all along."

"So," Val said brightly, "where do we start?"

"Any luck with Isabella Villar?" I asked her. "That's our only other lead."

"Oh, that's all under control," Val said, leaning back. "She's ill. That's what a girl in her class told me. Been in her room all afternoon."

"She's ill?" I asked suspiciously.

"Yeah," Val said.

"Did you actually check the room?" I asked.

"Well," Val flustered, "not exactly. I was tired and…"

"Val!" I exclaimed.

"I was waiting for you," she said apologetically.

"Do you know where her room is?" I asked.

"Sorry, Amy, I was going to find out tomorrow," said Val miserably.

"Where is the students' dormitory?" I asked, turning to Barry.

"Amanda," Barry said, "Warklesby's has over a thousand students. There is no one single dormitory. But there is a general registry where we can find out where she is."

"Illness my witch's hat," I said. "There isn't a minute to lose. Come on."

***

Despite hurrying along the now deserted corridors and chambers of the castle, I felt that our best opportunity may have already slipped away. Of course, we might simply find her in her room, as she had claimed to be. But something about her timely illness told me that there was a very good chance that Isabella Villar was not where she pretended to be.

After half an hour, we reached the general registry next to the students' office, which was close to the Great Hall and the main entrance.

"There it is," said Barry, pointing to a massive book that was chained to a table. "She should be in there. It's updated every semester."

It turned out that it not only contained the present inhabitants of the school, but also all who had ever attended over the course of the many centuries it had been in existence. Finally, we were able to track her down.

"West Tower, bottom floor," I said, making sure I hadn't slipped a line. "Villar, Isabella."

"Wonderful," said Barry bitterly, "we could have just gone downstairs."

"Yeah, well we didn't know that at the time, did we?" I said.

"This body can only take so much," Barry whined. "What I need is rest and relaxation."

"Oh, stop moaning, Barry," I said, grinning. "You'll get your brandy soon enough."

Barry's complaints notwithstanding, we raced back the way we had come as quickly as we could. Though I didn't want to agree openly with Barry, running up and down endless flights of stairs was indeed quite taxing. I only hoped that it was not in vain.

As we finally reached the student dormitory in question, we were completely out of breath.

"D'you think she's in?" Val whispered.

"I don't know," I said. "But there's only one way to find out. We can't just wait around here, doing nothing."

"Right," said Val.

"You two'd better wait here," I said. "Otherwise she'll think it's suspicious."

"What will you say if she's there?" said Val.

"Oh, I'll think of something," I said.

Isabella's room was at the end of the corridor. I knocked on the door. Immediately, I heard the scampering of feet inside. A moment later, the door was opened. But it wasn't Isabella.

Instead, a girl with black braids and a sour look on her face answered the door. She stood in the frame, eyeing me with suspicion.

"Yes?" she said, without smiling.

"I'm looking for Isabella," I said. "Do you know where she is?"

"She in trouble?" the girl asked.

"No," I said evasively, "not exactly. But there's something important I need to see her about."

"Get in line, then," the girl said, pulling a face.

"Do you know where she is?"

"I might," she said, looking me up and down. "Depends who's asking."

"Look," I said, deciding that honesty was the best policy. "My name is Amy. I'm looking for the people who've disappeared. I think Isabella's in trouble. Deep trouble."

"She's got nothing to do with that," the girl said defensively.

"I know, but I think she might be able to help us," I said. "Please, tell me where she's gone."

The girl stared at me for a while.

"You promise this won't get her into worse trouble?" she demanded.

"I promise. Quite the contrary, in fact."

The girl nodded.

"I'll take your word for it. She's gone to meet someone in the woods. She wouldn't tell me who it is. There's a hut, deep in the woods, but don't ask me where it is. That's all I know."

"Thank you," I said.

"Don't tell her that I told you, though," the girl said quickly. "She'll be mad. Real mad."

"Yes, of course," I said gratefully. "Thank you again."

***

"Wait," Barry said. "Are you saying that..."

"We should follow her right now," I said. "Come on,

there isn't a moment to be lost."

"But," Barry spluttered again, "but it's almost midnight! I've got a class tomorrow and…"

"It can wait, Barry," said Val. "Amy's right. It's now or never."

He mumbled something that sounded a lot like 'brandy' and 'sofa', but left it at that.

***

"You know," Barry said, as we approached the gates that led out into the school grounds twenty minutes later, "I didn't realise that detective work included so much running around. Next time, I'll just stay in my office."

"Perhaps we should make a habit of taking brooms with us," Val said. "Could be a time-saver."

"Brooms aren't safe for cats, you know," Barry said. "We tend to fall off."

"Only because you insist on talking all the time, Barry," said Val.

"Shh, you two," I said. "Let's keep our eyes peeled for Isabella."

Unfortunately, the gates were shut tight. Even my trusty unlocking spell couldn't do anything to remedy the situation. Luckily, however, we found another side entrance, tucked away in one of the adjacent corridors. It led to a wooden storage room.

"Looks like a tool shed or something," said Val, looking around her.

"Strange that this is unlocked, though," I said.

"The quarterwarlock is in charge of this, I believe," said Barry, careful not to step on any of the rakes that were resting against the wall.

"What does a warlock need spades for?" asked Val. "Couldn't he just dig with his wand."

"Enchanting a spade is easier," said Barry. "Or any

other tool, for that matter. Especially if you're planning a larger operation."

"Hope he's not around," said Val. "That man gives me the creeps."

"Yeah," I agreed.

Then, there was a loud creak and a thud, as though an old door had just been closed in the distance.

"Did you hear that?" said Val, swerving around.

"There's nobody here," said Barry, though he didn't quite believe it himself, "there can't be. Not at this hour, at any rate."

"Come on," I said. "Better keep moving. I think this door might lead outside."

I pushed it open as gently as I could. Through the crack, moonlight streamed into the shed we were in. I poked my head through the opening, checking the surroundings outside. A lawn extended for a few hundred yards, with dark woods looming ominously beyond it. Isabella was nowhere to be seen. There was no cover from the surprisingly bright moonlight out here, however. If anybody chanced to look out of the window, they'd most certainly be able to spot us.

We crossed the open space as quickly as possible without breaking into an outright run. Although I turned around multiple times in all directions and saw nothing, I just couldn't help the feeling that we were being followed.

When we finally reached the edge of the woods, we all sighed in relief. Though finding Isabella would be more difficult in the woods, we would be harder to track down as well.

"It's so dark," Barry protested. "How are we supposed to find anything in here?"

"You're a cat, aren't you?" I said, exasperated. "You should be able to spot her from a mile away."

"My eyes are tired, I've been reading all evening," he said. "And I can hardly see through all these ghastly trees anyway, can I?"

"We'd better stick to the path," I said. "For the time being at least. Have you ever been in here before, Barry?"

"Certainly not," he said. "Nor do I wish ever to return."

"Fine," I said, losing patience. "Stay here if you want. Come on, Val."

Grudgingly, Barry trotted after us, though he kept his eyes open for any movements from now on. The minutes streamed by without any hint of Isabella Villar, though I wished by now that I had brought a coat with me. It had been warm enough, of course, during the day, but the nights seemed to be a lot chillier here than at Fickleton House.

Tired and frustrated, I was just about to recommend that we go back when Barry stopped in his tracks. Something in the distance had caught his eye. Val had noticed it, too.

"What's the matter?" I whispered.

"Over there," said Barry. "I can't be certain, but it looks like a hut of some kind."

"That must be the one Isabella's flatmate mentioned," Val said excitedly.

"And I'm sure I saw something move, too," Barry said.

Leaving the path, we stumbled across leaves and branches, with Barry leading the way. The trees were so thick that, though I trusted Barry, I could hardly see where my own feet were going.

"I think I can hear something," Val said softly.

We stopped, listening intently. She was right. Though very faint and muffled, the noises were undoubtedly of human origin.

"Amy, can you cast that silencing spell on shoes, too?" Val asked.

"Good thinking," I whispered, drawing my wand.

Barry, of course, didn't need it, so I cast the spell for Val and myself. It was a peculiar sensation, as though walking

382

on gel, but it was certainly effective. Now, we were able to approach without a sound.

Finally, I saw the outlines of the hut from the little moonlight that was able to penetrate the treetops. I was also able to make out specific words now. It sounded as though the voices were arguing.

"Told you… just stupid…" a female with a familiar Spanish accent was saying.

We were close to the hut now, within throwing distance. Inside, two shapes were moving about, clearly agitated. I signalled for Barry and Val to wait, while I crept closer to the window that was nearest. It had no pane. Crouching in the earth beneath, I could now hear every word that was being uttered inside.

"Why," Isabella was saying angrily, "why do you have to do that? So foolish. If you get caught, there will be no hope for you left. They asked me questions after questions about the mark. They *know* I lied. I can't protect you if you continue like this."

There was silence inside the little hut. I didn't dare move in my hiding place, though I was dying from curiosity to know who the other person in the room was. But the conversation didn't continue. Instead, I saw the two shapes embrace. All of a sudden, I felt like I was intruding in something very personal. There was only way to find out who it was.

I stood up and lit my wand, shining the beam through the window. The room inside was illuminated immediately. Isabella Villar, her face frozen in horror, jumped back and almost fell onto the floor. But my eyes raced to the other person in the room. To my utter amazement, it was a face I had seen not too long ago.

CHAPTER 10

It was Julian Ross.

Barry and Val had joined me at the window, too, and were now staring in disbelief at the unlikely couple inside of the hut.

"Ross?" I said. "Julian Ross?"

As in the lecture hall, he had lost his cheeky swagger from our encounter in the headmistress's office entirely. Instead, his face white as a sheet, he was opening his mouth and closing it again like a fish. It was Isabella Villar, therefore, who took control of the situation and went on the offensive.

"How dare you spy on us like this?" she said. "You should be ashamed."

"Perhaps," I said, "that is true. But from what the little I heard, I think Mr. Ross here has a lot more to be ashamed of."

Isabella Villar was at a loss for words now. I pressed my advantage as best I could.

"There are two possibilities open to you both," I said. "Either you come clean, right here and right now, or I will have to report you to the headmistress and the MLE. But to be honest, I think expulsion from the school will be the least of your worries then, Mr. Ross. You will be facing very serious charges indeed."

Isabella Villar turned on Julian Ross.

"Julian," she said, "you must tell them."

"No," he said quietly. "I won't. It's pointless."

"Please," she said, grabbing his hand. "Please, do it for me."

"They won't believe a word of it," he said, shirking away.

"OK," Isabella said, turning around to face us, "then I will. I will tell them everything you did. If you are too stupid to save yourself, someone else will have to do it. And if not your girlfriend, who else?"

Val opened the door to the little hut, and we filed into the crammed space within. There were no chairs and only a rotten table in the corner, so we just stood there, looking at each other for a moment.

"Tell us," I said to Isabella, "about the necromancer's sign. The *whole* story, this time."

Julian Ross shifted uncomfortably on the spot, watching his girlfriend closely. But he was beyond protest. The game was up. And yet, I felt, the circumstances of his deeds would prove decisive.

"Julian drew the mark on the wall," Isabella said. "We had been quarrelling about it. I said that I would go down there myself and get rid of it. And so, I went to the dungeons."

"But before you could wipe it away, Mr. Armburster, the quarterwarlock, caught you?" asked Val.

"Yes," she said.

"Why did you draw the mark, Julian?" I asked him.

"You won't believe it anyway," he said sulkily, so unlike his former boisterous self.

"Why don't you try me," I said.

But he remained silent, looking out of the window instead, through which the moonlight shone into the little hut. For a moment, I thought I heard a noise outside. Or had it simply been the whooshing of the wind?

"I trust you don't want to go to prison?" Barry asked Julian Ross.

"Of course not," the latter said at once.

"We are interested mainly in the people that are missing," Barry said, pacing up and down in front of Julian and Isabella, "as well as solving the mystery surrounding Professor Olsen's death."

"That's right," I said, walking slowly towards Julian. "We don't care so much for the marks as for the disappearances. And, whatever else you are, Julian, I don't think you are capable of kidnap or murder."

He looked up in surprise.

"You see," Isabella said, turning on him, "I told you that they are different. They're not just looking for a scapegoat, as you always say."

"Why," I asked, "did you draw that sign, Julian?"

"Well, isn't it obvious?" he said, his nostrils wide. "They're all so complacent. The MLE was at the school, what, how many times was it? Five times? Guess what they did. Absolutely nothing. NOTHING."

He was suddenly shaking with rage. But at least he was finally talking.

"Robert, my best friend, was the first to go missing," he said, his voice cracking, "but everyone just assumed that he had run away, though I knew that that wasn't like him at all. I… I started seeing Isabella here in the woods. She knew him too. But one day – it was dark, much darker than now – I lost my way. I must have taken a wrong turning when I left the road. The hut isn't far from the road, as you know, but I walked for hours and hours and couldn't find it. I was beginning to panic. Well, at some point I was just about to give up and sleep under a tree when I heard voices nearby. I thought perhaps that someone from the school had come looking for me, perhaps even Isabella, so I walked in their direction. But as I came closer, I noticed that they were singing or chanting. At first, I thought they'd be able to help me."

He stared at all of us as though the next part was too horrible to relate. But the touch of Isabella's hand on his shoulder seemed to enable him to press on.

"As I got closer," he continued, "I saw that there were two people wearing thick, black robes with hoods over their faces. They were in a wide clearing with three large trees in the middle of it. They were standing around a stone. Something was on it, but I couldn't see what it was at first. Up close, I realised that they weren't really singing at all. It seemed to me more like they were trying out some sort of complicated channelling spell."

"Can you remember what it was?" asked Barry, his face very serious.

"No, not the words exactly," he said. "But as I moved closer, I saw that the thing on the stone – which looked more like an altar – was a third person, just lying there. And… and on the ground, there were bodies of animals around it… I…"

But he broke off, unable to utter anything more than a croak.

"What sort of animals were they?" I asked patiently.

"S-snakes," he said after a little pause. "Lots of them. That's when I started to panic. I hate snakes, you see, always have, even at the zoo. Then, I tripped and fell into the bush next to me."

"Did you recognise the third person, lying down?" asked Barry, who was wearing a very grave look on his face.

"No," said Julian, "no I didn't."

"What happened then?" I asked.

"I don't know whether they had heard me fall, or maybe something went wrong, but they suddenly stopped their chanting. In any case, they were in a real hurry. They levitated the figure off the altar and were gone before I could do anything. "

"And what did you do after that?" I asked.

"Well, I waited for the sun to set and also to make sure that they didn't come back. I hid behind a tree that had fallen down. When I was sure that the coast was clear, I stepped into the clearing. Among the snakes, I also found… I found a watch."

"A watch?" Barry asked, bewildered.

"Yes, a wristwatch. I recognised it immediately. It

belonged to my best friend, Robert."

"But I thought they don't work around magic," I said, frowning.

"They don't," said Julian, "but, you see, Robert wasn't born a warlock, he inherited his skills. He had been very fond of the watch as a heb so, even after it stopped working at Warklesby's, he just continued to wear it."

"Did you have any idea of the nature of the ritual you had just witnessed?" Barry asked.

"I guessed," said Ross, "but I wasn't sure until later, that the animals meant something very sinister. I think they had practised their spells on them first. In the library, I flicked through book after book until I found confirmation of what I had seen. It took me ages to do it. But finally, I found out that what I had seen was some sort of necromancer's ritual."

"That sounds horrible," said Val.

Julian nodded.

"It was even worse that the school authorities and the MLE weren't on the right track at all. I decided to paint the walls of the school with the mark of the necromancer, so that they would understand what they were dealing with."

"Why didn't you tell them about this?" I asked.

"I did exactly that," he said, his face contorting with righteous anger. "That was the first thing I did. But they just said I was cooking up trouble and that they didn't believe a word of it. They said that *I* had planted the watch there, for all they knew, and had invented a tale around it. They said that I wasn't coping with the loss of my best friend. The only one who seemed to believe me was Professor Olsen."

"Professor Olsen?" I said, staring at him.

"Yes," said Julian. "He tried to talk to them, but it was no use. He questioned me about the whole thing several times. Wanted to know every little detail."

"Mysterious," I murmured.

"They left me no other choice but to draw attention to the truth by drawing those marks," said Ross stubbornly.

"Who were *they*?" I asked. "Who did you talk to?"

But before he could answer, the door of the hut suddenly flung open with a crash. In the doorway, deputy headmaster Harper was standing with his wand pointed at Julian Ross. Harper's slick blond hair was unusually untidy, thin strands dancing on his forehead.

"He told *me*, Miss Sheridan," he said, a malicious smile on his face. "The whole pack of inventions and lies. That's when I knew I'd have to watch him more closely. I'm surprised you listened for as long as you did. You have been wasting your time with Ross."

"But I told you," Julian said, red in the face, "it's the TRUTH."

"Don't you dare lie to me again," Harper hissed. "You have committed nothing but mischief at this school from the moment you set foot in it. Do you expect me to believe you after all that?"

"But... but this is different," Julian spluttered. "I'm telling you, this is what happened. Necromancers are behind the kidnapping of Robert..."

"I don't believe you," Harper said. "I think you colluded with Professor Olsen in his despicable practices. Why don't you admit that he was your mentor? Perhaps your friend Robert even perished in one of your experiments."

"But that's not true," Julian yelled.

"ENOUGH," Harper thundered.

And before any of us could react, thick ropes flew out of his wand and wrapped themselves tightly around Ross, who, losing his balance, fell to the ground.

"Stop," I said, "deputy headmaster, I think you're making a terrible mistake. I don't think Julian is capable of..."

But Harper was maniacal and beyond reason.

"I knew it from the start!" he spat. "Amateur fools,

believing the first cock-and-bull story you hear. I warned against hiring you, and I was right all along."

Isabella shrieked with fury.

"Julian is innocent!"

And without warning, she drew her own wand. But Harper was too quick for her.

"DISPERGO," Harper cried.

Isabella Villar was lifted up and was smashed by an invisible force into the wall behind her.

Horrified, I stepped forward to confront Harper, but he pointed his wand at me.

"Not one step further, Miss Sheridan. I'm warning you. I'm taking the boy back to the castle, where he will await his lawful arrest by the MLE. Stand back, all of you. Or I will be forced to curse you."

Then, he waved his wand at the helpless Ross, whose body was lifted up from the ground and levitated through the open window, hovering ominously outside.

"If any of you follow me, I will consider it as an act of aiding a criminal and a fugitive."

He slowly backed out of the room, his wand covering all of us. Then, he vanished from sight.

CHAPTER 11

It took us a second to process what had just happened. Isabella, lying on the ground, was crying uncontrollably. Barry simply stood there, incapable of doing anything.

"Isabella," I said, kneeling next to her, "are you hurt?"

The tears still streaming down her face, she shook her head.

"What on earth just happened?" Val said shakily. "I can't believe it."

"Were you able to read Julian?" I asked. "Psychically, I mean."

"Yes, quite clearly," she said. "He was telling the truth, Amy, there was no doubt about it. He was very angry, which is understandable, of course. But it was what he saw."

"Harper," I said. "He's mad. Utterly crazy."

"H-he always hated J-Julian," Isabella said, sitting up and wiping the tears from her cheeks. "He didn't believe a word of what Julian said, just because he had played some tricks on him. But they were harmless! Nobody was ever hurt."

"Then Harper must be covering up for his own crimes," Barry said darkly. "I see no other explanation."

"He's certainly tried to sabotage our investigation from the very beginning," I said. "He tried – and failed – to convince the headmistress not to hire us. He quarrelled with her about it even after our arrival."

"That's right," said Val. "I didn't quite understand it at the time, but he felt a real loathing for Ross. You know, when we were in the headmistress's office. He wanted him expelled, remember? If it had been up to him – and not the headmistress – he would have kicked him out of the school right away."

"Could you read him?" I asked Val.

"It was very difficult," said Val. "There's a lot of boiled up resentment inside of him. But I didn't feel anything else."

"Seems to me like he's just looking for a scapegoat," I said.

"Yes," Barry said, frowning. "But we're running out of time. We're still no closer to producing any actual evidence. Let us say that Harper is our man, what do we have against him? Nothing much except for picking on the wrong person. And his bad manners. And even on the British Isles, that isn't punishable by law."

"Well, perhaps it ought to be," I said moodily. "But you're right, of course. We've got to do something. Perhaps we should approach the headmistress. Tell her what kind of a deputy she really has. She won't believe that whole story about Ross being a necromancer's apprentice and all that stuff. She said herself that Ross is just a prankster, a rascal."

"Even she won't be able to resist the authority of the MLE," said Barry. "I don't think the case looks particularly good for Ross. He's the only dot connecting one of the missing people – his friend Robert – and Professor Olsen."

"But he is innocent," Isabella said, her temper rising again.

"I realise that," Barry said. "But the law, I'm afraid, might not be in agreement. Remember that drawing the necromancer's marks is in itself already a serious offense. The more desperate the officials become, the higher the likelihood that they might try to concoct a case against him in regard to the disappearances, as well."

"That's true, Amy," said Val, turning to me. "Remember how PC Bowler tried to pin the murder on you six months ago?"

"Vividly," I said.

"A closed case," said Barry, "might be worth more to some than the truth."

"Yes," I said. "The murderer might be thinking along the same lines."

"What are you saying, Amy?" asked Val.

"I'm saying that, if I were the killer, I'd try to frame Julian Ross as quickly as possible. Plant some incriminating evidence in his room and end the entire thing. Then, they'd be free to continue their experiments without fear of repercussions."

Isabella got up. Her face was blotched and swollen from crying, though there were no tears anymore. Instead, it had been replaced by grim determination.

"We will catch this murderer," she said. "I don't care if it is Harper or someone else. Julian did what he thought was right. I didn't want him to draw those marks, but it was the only way that anyone paid attention. He wants to save his friend."

"Barry," I said. "Is there any chance that… that the disappeared people might still be alive?"

But Barry shook his head.

"I cannot say," he answered solemnly. "I am sorry, Amanda. Necromancy, well, let's say only very few people are drawn to that branch of magic. By definition, I don't think you can assume that they would behave in a normal and rational manner. If what Julian witnessed was indeed some sort of resurrection ritual through sacrifice, time is of the essence. As far as I know, it takes a long time to prepare, there is a special potion that is required, and it can easily spoil."

"Do you mean that Julian might have stopped the resurrection?" I asked.

"I think so," said Barry. "From what I understand, it is a very complicated process. The dead snakes, for instance, are a symbol of both death and healing. They play a devilish part, but don't ask me the specifics because I don't know. Without sacrifice, however, there is no resurrection. Without the potion, the resurrected will remain lifeless.

That is crucial. If the potion is not used immediately, it must be discarded and replaced by a fresh one."

"Then there might still be hope that the ritual has not been attempted again," I said.

"But how does Professor Olsen fit into all this?" asked Val.

"Well, according to Julian, he was the only one who would listen, isn't that right, Isabella?" I said.

Isabella nodded.

"Perhaps," I said. "We've been wrong about Olsen."

"What do you mean?" asked Val.

"Perhaps Olsen was *investigating* the case," I said. "That would explain why he gathered every piece of information on necromancy and Wycliffe."

"So if they silenced Olsen," Val said slowly, "he must have been close to the truth."

"Yes," I said. "Remember the red mark on the map, Barry? He must have figured out that the ritual would take place here, in the woods, thanks to Julian's account. He was sure to be on the lookout for the next ritual. Perhaps he already had his suspicions as to who was behind it all. But now that he's dead, they can go through with it."

"But we don't even know where it's taking place," said Val.

"Probably in the same place as last time," I said. "Isabella, did Julian show you the clearing with the three trees in the middle that he spoke of?"

"No," she said miserably, "he didn't. I'm sorry, I don't know where it is."

"The woods are very extensive," said Barry. "You saw it on the map. We wouldn't be able to find it in time."

"Unless," I said ponderingly, "unless we could cover the ground more quickly than on foot. Does the school have brooms?"

"Yes, of course," said Isabella, "the broom cupboards are near the East Tower."

"Right," I said. "We need three brooms, do you think you can get them without anyone noticing?"

"I think so," said Isabella.

"Good," I said. "Come to Barry's office when you've got them. We have to find that clearing."

"But what about Julian?" Isabella said. "What if the MLE gets their hands on him, or worse, the necromancer does?"

"In that regard," I said, "we'll have to take certain precautions. Val, can you go to Julian's room? We need to move his things."

"Move his things?" asked Isabella, perplexed. "But why?"

"Because you cannot plant evidence in an empty room," I said. "Val, can you take charge of that?"

"Of course, Amy," she said.

"If anyone asks, just say it's on the Earl of Barrington's authority and that Ross's things have to be moved immediately."

"Hey," said Val, "why don't we keep the room under observation? That way, if anyone tries to plant evidence, we'll know who it is."

"We could, yes," I said. "It's a long shot, though. We don't know for certain whether it will happen at all."

"I doubt they'd simply walk in," said Barry. "I suspect they'd make sure they were alone before attempting such a thing."

"Perhaps," I said, "we could ask some of the students to keep their eyes open. They wouldn't arouse suspicion in their own dormitory."

"I'll do that. But what will you do?" asked Val. "I hope you're not considering anything dangerous without us, Amy, because I won't allow it."

"No," I said, smiling. "I'll talk to the headmistress. Deputy Harper is almost certain to contact the MLE right away without letting her know. If I can get her to intervene on Ross's behalf, we can buy some time, perhaps even prevent his arrest by the MLE. At least until we have more information."

"Good thinking," said Val, nodding her head. "Just leaves our favourite aristocrat to snooze in his office."

"Actually, I could do with a nap," said Barry, groggily wiping his eyes.

"There's no time," I said. "Perhaps we can snatch a few hours later. I think we need more information on the ritual. We're still poking in the dark in regard to necromancy."

"Well," said Barry, "we'll probably remain mostly in the dark but I'll do my best. I'll get some books from the library and see what I can find out."

"Great," I said. "I'll meet you all as soon as possible in Barry's office. Isabella, you'd better tell Val where Julian's room is. And we need a spare key, too."

"It's no problem," said Isabella, "I will take care of it."

***

It was morning by the time we had returned to the castle. The lack of sleep paired with the adrenaline seemed to create a strange state akin to having drunk far too much coffee, which I had regularly done as a waitress. The seemingly endless flights of stairs I had to ascend to reach the headmistress's office didn't help, either. I'd be cursing all the way down if it turned out that she wasn't in.

I was in luck, however.

"Come," said a voice from within, after I had knocked.

Once more, I entered Muriel Hall's office. And yet, the last time almost seemed like a lifetime ago to me now. I had no time to appreciate the beauty of the desk or the view any longer. Time was our most valuable asset, and I didn't want to squander it needlessly.

"Miss Sheridan, what a pleasant surprise," she said, smiling. "I hadn't expected you back so quickly."

396

"Yes, well, there have been some new developments. Urgent ones, in fact."

"Oh?" she said, beckoning me to sit down on one of the chairs in front of her desk.

"Yes," I said, "you see, your deputy Mr. Harper, well, he has taken Julian Ross into custody. I think he wants to hand him over to the MLE."

"*Custody*?" she echoed, bewilderment spreading across her entire face.

"It's a long story, but suffice it to say that Julian Ross is responsible for drawing the marks of the necromancer all over the school. He's been doing it for weeks, apparently."

"Ross did that?" she said, flabbergasted. "But… but whatever for?"

"He told Mr. Harper about his suspicions that a necromancer is responsible for the abductions. I think there is good reason to believe that Ross is right about that. Mr. Harper, apparently, didn't believe him, however, and sent him away."

"I see," she said. "Very peculiar behaviour by Harper, I must say. He should have sent him straight to me with that sort of information."

"Indeed," I said. "And I'm afraid to say that he's acting independently right now, too."

"That man has been getting out of hand," she said. "But I never thought that… well, what do you suggest, Miss Sheridan?"

"In my opinion, we have to stop the MLE from arresting Ross. At least for the moment. I realise this is a big favour I'm asking, since his drawing the marks was already a criminal offense. But, you see, he might easily become a suspect – even a scapegoat – for the kidnappings. And, whatever he has done, I don't think him capable of that."

"Well," she said, "I certainly agree with that. I cannot deny that I've always had a soft spot for Ross's antics, but I cannot possibly imagine him delving into necromancy."

She took a deep breath.

"Alright, Miss Sheridan," she said. "I'll get in touch with MLE headquarters right away. If Harper has sent for them, I'll try to delay as long as possible, but I cannot promise you anything. They can be quite stubborn, you know. Especially in a case like this."

"Of course," I said. "Thank you, headmistress."

"Not at all," she said. "Where are Ross and Harper now, by the way?"

"We don't know," I said.

"I see," she said. "Well, if you happen to run into Harper, tell him that he is to report to me immediately."

"Yes, headmistress," I said.

***

Subsequently, I tried to track down Harper and Julian Ross. The likeliest place, of course, was the deputy's office. After asking several students along the way, it turned out that Harper's office was at other end of the castle, closer to the West Tower, in fact.

I wasn't really expecting to talk any sense into Harper. But at least, if he was in, I could make sure that Julian was alright. Also, I would be able to convey the headmistress's message. Seeing Harper's sneer drop from his face was reward in itself.

Perhaps it was my lack of sleep or the fact that we had traipsed through the woods for so long, but I managed to get lost twice on my way to the deputy's office. At last, however, I had found the correct corridor. The staff common room was also close by. In passing, I recognised Esther's voice from within. She seemed to be rather edge for some reason.

Suddenly, I ran into something soft and large. It was the quarterwarlock, Mr. Armbruster.

"Sorry, Mr. Armbruster," I said, "I wasn't looking where

I was going."

"No problem," he said gruffly. "I, erm, have that list you asked for. Delivered it to the office an hour ago."

"The list?" I asked.

"Yes, with the stolen goods that went missing."

"Oh, I see. Thank you," I said. "I just need to speak to Mr. Harper right now, if you'll excuse me."

"Mr. Harper?" Mr. Armbruster said, crossing his hands in front of his belly. "Why, he's not there. Didn't answer my knock. Someone in the staff room said they saw him in the Great Hall not too long ago, though."

"OK," I said. "Thank you, I'll try there."

Mr. Armbruster shuffled down the hallway. I was just about to follow in his tracks when an idea occurred to me. There was a chance that Harper had left Julian Ross locked in his office. In any case, it wouldn't hurt if I made sure he wasn't there, I reasoned to myself. It was one place less to search for Julian later on, because I was still worried that Harper might simply take Julian and deliver him to the MLE himself if the headmistress succeeded in delaying them.

Making sure that nobody from the staff room was able to see me, I inched over to the deputy headmaster's office. The gold letters on the door were simple yet elegant. I got out my wand. Owing to past experience, I had become quite good at unlocking spells.

"Vertere," I whispered.

But nothing happened. At first I thought that the spell hadn't worked. I tried the handle, and to my surprise I found that it had already been unlocked. Gently, I pushed it open. The sight that greeted me made me hold my left hand to my mouth to stop myself from screaming.

The deputy headmaster lay sprawled across his own desk, his eyes open and unflinching. Keeping my wand at the ready, I inched forward into the room, closing the door behind me.

There could be no doubt about Harper's condition as I had seen its effects only too well in the past. He had been hit by the killing curse. There was nothing that could be done for him now.

But Julian was nowhere to be seen. The office had one more door that led to another room, however, so I tried it. And there, lying on the ground, his legs and hands still bound by heavy ropes, was Julian Ross. For one horrible moment, I thought that he, too, had been murdered. But, bending down, I noticed that Julian was still breathing, although he was unconscious. Turning around so that I could keep my eyes on the door in case the killer returned, I hastily untied Julian. He had a nasty wound at the base of his skull that was bleeding slightly. He needed medical attention immediately.

"Julian," I whispered, "Julian, you'll be alright. Tell me, who did this to you?"

With difficulty, Julian opened his eyes.

"Arm…" he murmured. "Arm…"

"What's with your arm?" I asked. "Does it hurt?"

"No," he muttered.

He pointed vaguely to the wound at the back of his head.

"Your head?"

"Arm… bruster," he breathed.

"Armbruster did this?" I said. "Are you sure?"

He nodded his head painfully.

"I can't believe it," I said.

And yet, it all seemed to make sense. As quarterwarlock, he had access to all areas of the castle. Nobody, in fact, would ever suspect him, whether he was in the dungeons or in a students' dormitory. And he most likely knew about most the secret chambers and shortcuts throughout the school.

"I've got to get you to the infirmary," I said to Julian. "As quickly as possible."

I levitated Julian out of the deputy's office and into the hall, making sure to close the door behind me again. Catching Armbruster would have to wait until Julian was in safety and taken care of.

Luckily, the staff room door was open now. As I reached it, Esther happened to come out at the exact same time. Her smile quickly faded as she saw Ross.

"What happened?" she asked. "Is he hurt?"

"Yes," I said. "It's Armbruster. He's the necromancer. We need to get Julian to the infirmary as quickly as possible. Do you know the way?"

"Why… why yes, of course. Follow me."

We turned the corner and slowly proceeded through a series of corridors I was unfamiliar with. Luckily, the infirmary wasn't too far away, and we reached it within a matter of minutes. The nurse attended to Julian immediately.

"I'll stay here with him," Esther said.

"Good," I said. "I'm sorry I can't explain everything. Please make sure that nobody sees Julian. His life may depend on it."

It was clear that Esther didn't fully understand, but she agreed to do it.

As I raced back to Barry's office, I thought only of how to trap Armbruster.

CHAPTER 12

Val and Barry were already back in the office, though Isabella hadn't returned yet with the broomsticks. I quickly filled them in on what had happened.

"Armbruster knows he doesn't have much breathing room," I said, pacing up and down in front of Barry's desk. "He must realise that it's only a matter of time before someone will discover the deputy headmaster."

"But where is he now?" asked Val.

"I don't know," I said. "He will continue with whatever he was planning, though. For once, time is against him. He has to attempt the ritual again, as soon as possible."

"I still don't understand all this necromancy business," said Val, frowning. "I mean, what are they trying to do precisely?"

"That," said Barry heavily, "is now my metier, I suppose."

"Did you find out anything?" I asked.

"Well," he said. "Not much more than Ross, I'm afraid, in regard to the ritual. But at least we could verify what he said. The ritual he described is indeed sacrificial in nature. It is designed to resurrect the dead. I went back up to the East Tower and had another look at Olsen's notes. A lot of his research is missing, that much is clear. Someone definitely searched his office."

Barry cleared his throat.

"From what I can tell, Olsen believed that the ritual could only take place at night due to the idiosyncratic effects of the potion. It spoils in sunlight, almost instantaneously. Oh, and there is one additional important factor. It appears that the act must occur at the final resting place of the dead person in question. The remains may not be moved under any circumstances, or the whole thing won't work. In other words, Armbruster must return to the clearing in the woods if he wants to successfully complete the ritual. And, as I said, it must be conducted at night, with midnight being the most potent hour."

"We still have some time," I said.

Sleep deprivation was gradually catching up with me, however. I felt dizzy and lightheaded. Confronting a dangerous necromancer, I decided, certainly required a better state of mind.

"Perhaps," I said slowly, "we should grab a few hours of sleep before we go. We'd still have more than enough time to find the clearing and get into position."

Both Barry and Val were exhausted and thus agreed to my proposal. Isabella arrived a few minutes later with the brooms under her arms. She was greatly relieved that Julian, although hurt, was in safe hands. Though she wanted to go and see him immediately, I persuaded her to take a rest, too, however short it might be. We would need all the strength for our final encounter with Armbruster that we could muster. I made myself as comfortable as I could on one of the sofas and quickly slipped into an uneasy sleep.

***

A few hours later, I awoke to the dribble of rain hitting the window panes behind me. This was a very unwelcome development, since it would make the search a lot more difficult. So, I decided we had better set off sooner rather than later.

Barry was to ride on one broom with me, while Val went with Isabella. I wanted the reserve broom just in case there were survivors or one of the brooms broke down.

You never knew when it would come in handy.

I had never flown a broom in my brief period as a witch. As I stepped out onto the window sill of Barry's office, I felt the apprehension growing within me, though Barry assured me that 'there really wasn't anything to it'. With Barry perched firmly on the handle, I hopped on. With the spare broom tied to the end, I kicked off from the ground as hard I could.

Immediately, I zoomed forward with such violence that Barry lost his grip on the handle and slipped. I grabbed his tail just in time. Howling in protest, Barry clawed his way back onto the broom.

"Careful, Amanda," he shouted. "I don't have nine lives in the air, you know."

"Sorry," I said. "Just… getting the hang of this thing."

"Well, at least we'll have the trees to break our fall, soon."

"Better than the rocks below us now," I said, looking down with a shudder.

Isabella, meanwhile, was having no trouble at all on her broom since she had enjoyed several years of school training. Val, on the other hand, looked terrified. We decided to follow the road through the woods, which was just about visible from above in spite of the rain. From there, we could branch out in each direction.

Every now and then, we'd spot a clearing, though each time the three trees in the middle were missing. The minutes and finally hours passed by without any success. The afternoon had trickled by, and we were no closer to finding Armbruster. Flying through the soft but steady downpour, I was getting ever wetter and colder.

Finally, however, the rain stopped. But the sun was beginning to set now, and a note of panic entered the equation.

"We've got to fly faster," Barry said. "Cover more

ground."

"I'm doing my best," I said. "It's just that I'm not... hold on, do you see that clearing down there?"

"We've passed that one before," Barry said dismissively.

"No, over there, on the other side."

Barry craned his neck, while still retaining his balance on the broom.

"Fly a little closer," he said.

And there, finally, was the clearing with the three trees in the middle. I hovered close to the spot, but making sure I couldn't be seen from the clearing itself, and waved my left arm at Val and Isabella.

"Have you found something?" Isabella asked as she flew next to me.

"Down there," I said. "It's the clearing alright. Three trees."

"OK," said Isabella. "So, what now?"

"We should dismount a little distance away," I said. "We don't want to advertise our arrival too much."

"Yeah," said Val, looking down. "Also, the sooner we get off these things, the better."

Isabella and I both began our descent about a hundred yards away, carefully gliding between the treetops. We landed softly and relatively quietly, if you discounted Val's muffled cry as she hit her toe on a tree trunk.

With only a few yards left to the clearing, we hid our brooms beneath some leaves and waited for Armbruster to appear.

We stood there, waiting as the sun bathed the surrounding trees in a deep red and eventually disappeared entirely. But the darkness that enveloped us also gave us superior cover. Midnight was not too far away now.

And finally, a light appeared at the other side of the clearing. Then, a hooded figure emerged from the trees, a wand in one hand and a body slung over its shoulder.

Though hooded, dressed in the same black robe that Julian Ross had described earlier, there was no doubt in my mind that this had to be Armbruster, as the gait and size matched his perfectly.

After Armbruster had placed the body on the altar, he lit several torches, placing them in their brackets. Then, he raised his wand, slowly pointing it at each of the three large trees in succession. As he did so, he began to chant a mysterious spell, the words of which I didn't recognise.

"We'd better move," I said.

I quietly signalled to Isabella, the only other person in our party with a wand, to prepare our attack. We had decided that we would approach him from a slight angle, though not wide enough that our spells might threaten to hit one another. Armbruster would be forced to concentrate his fire on one of us, giving the other a decisive advantage.

Val and Barry were to stay in the background until the coast was clear, as they were both unarmed.

Slowly, we inched forward. We had reached the edge of the clearing, and Armbruster still seemed impervious to our approach. Still chanting, he had his back turned to us, evidently preoccupied with preparations for the ritual.

It was probably the most favourable opportunity we'd get. Once more, I gave Isabella a sign. Swiftly, we covered the yards of open ground. Armbruster still had his back turned to us.

"Stop what you're doing immediately, Armbruster," I said loudly, making sure that I kept him covered with my wand.

The cloaked man spun round to face us. Though his hood hid his face, I recognised his voice.

"You," Armbruster hissed. "What are you doing here?"

"I might ask you the same thing," I said.

"You would never understand," he said. "Nobody does.

406

Necromancy is a fine art, once mastered. But it is not for those who are weak or faint at heart."

"This madness ends here, Armbruster," I said.

"Ah, but it won't," he said. "It is only the beginning."

"What are you talking about?" I said.

"It is all as planned," he said, stroking the altar. "And you will not stop me."

Then, Armbruster rolled behind the altar with a nimbleness that I would never have suspected of him. Both Isabella and I fired hexes but missed. Now, Armbruster was using the person lying on the altar as a shield. We held our fire.

Yet Armbruster had no such restrictions. He immediately started pelting us with spell after spell. I dashed forward, seeking refuge behind one of the massive trees, while Isabella gave me cover.

Meanwhile, Barry and Val were nowhere to be seen. I had rapidly lost control of the entire situation. Isabella, under fire from Armbruster, was forced to retreat behind a small rock formation, only a few inches high. He had her pinned down. I tried to step out from behind the tree, but Armbruster's reactions were too fast, with one spell missing me by no more than an inch. Now, he had both of us bogged down.

At least, I thought, the ritual had been stopped for the time being. And yet, I could only direct a hex at him when Armbruster tried to stray too far away from the altar. We were, effectively, caught in a stalemate.

And then, I heard a rushing sound from above. My eyes tore upwards, and I saw that Val was flying on a broom – with Barry sitting on the handle – shooting like an arrow straight for Armbruster and the altar. Just as he spotted them in the air, I dashed out from behind the tree and charged.

Val dived low; too low, for she painfully grazed the edge

of the altar with her foot, pelting her body towards Armbruster like a cannonball. Armbruster dodged just in time, but it provided Barry with enough time to jump right on top of him, slashing viciously at him with his claws. I didn't dare shoot a spell for fear of hitting Barry, so I lunged forward, ramming my entire body as hard as I could against Armbruster. Trying to fight both of us off at the same time, he lost his balance and collapsed to the ground in front of the altar, and his wand went flying high through the air.

Isabella, who had also joined the fight, caught it neatly with her left hand.

Scrambling to our feet, we now had Armbruster defenceless and cornered.

"It's over Armbruster," I said, panting, my wand now pointed at his massive chest. "The game's up."

Fear and hatred etched across his face, he stared at me, though there was nothing he could do. Conjuring up ropes with my wand, I made them wrap themselves around Armbruster's body, rendering him harmless. Then, I hurried across to Val, who was lying on the ground and nursing her leg.

"Val," I said, bending down, "what's wrong?"

"It's my ankle," she said, her face contorted in pain. "It's broken. I can't… it hurts so much."

"We've got to get you to the infirmary," I said. "Isabella, give me a hand, will you?"

Together, we lifted Val up. But she wasn't going anywhere with that ankle of hers. She needed immediate help. I quickly retrieved our brooms from their hiding places and brought them into the clearing.

"Isabella," I said. "Please take Val to the infirmary. Julian is also there. I'm sure he'll be pleased to see you."

"And I him," she said, beaming. "We solved it."

"Yes," I said. "We did."

408

"Will you be alright with Armbruster?" she asked, stretching out the wand she had caught and handing it to me.

"Yes," I said, tucking Armbruster's wand into my back pocket. "It's fine. He's all tied up. We can have the MLE pick him up later. Tell the headmistress to get them here as quickly as possible."

"OK," Isabella said, getting onto her broom. "I will tell her."

I helped Val get on behind her. Then, Isabella kicked off from the ground. Within a minute, they were out of sight.

CHAPTER 13

Exhausted but pleased that we had been able to thwart Armbruster's plans, I walked over to him, making sure that he was still bound tightly. He lay there, next to the altar, furiously staring ahead of him into the darkness. He would pose no threat.

Above him, the figure on the altar remained perfectly still. It also wore a cloak and a hood.

"Do you recognise who it is?" I asked Barry.

He leapt nimbly onto the altar.

"It looks like a woman's figure," he said slowly.

I stepped closer to the large stone. Slowly, I lifted the hood covering the woman's face. To my shock, it was the headmistress, Muriel Hall. Her eyes were closed.

"Is she… dead?" asked Barry.

I looked at her face. It was perfectly motionless.

Then, without warning, her eyes suddenly tore wide open. I yelled, almost losing my balance, stumbling backwards.

Muriel Hall reacted like lightning. With a flick of her own wand, she had mine fly right into her open palm. Before I could anything, thin cords of steel shot out of her wand, binding my hands and legs tightly together, so that I keeled over onto the ground like a log. Then, she cast a torrent of freezing curses, directed at Barry. He desperately scampered across the clearing, running towards the three trees for cover, but one of the many spells finally made contact with him. At once, his entire body was encased in a block of ice.

"Miss Sheridan," the headmistress said, a triumphant smile on her face. "You don't think I'd let poor old Armbruster deal with you all on his own, did you? I must say, it was rather kind of you to send your friends away. That makes it a lot easier for me."

"But…" I spluttered, "but how could it be *you*? You hired us in the first place."

"Ah," she said. "That is indeed an interesting question. You see, I had no choice but to hire you, Miss Sheridan. The school board wasn't happy at all with the work the MLE had done. Especially Professor Olsen. He and the *Spellcasting Parents' Association* demanded an independent investigation, so I had to pretend to go along with it, fashioning it as my own idea. I played my role as the overworked and pathetic headmistress of Warklesby's School of Magic, who couldn't even control her own deputy, dutifully."

My head was still spinning, the shock and betrayal only just sinking in.

"You killed Professor Olsen," I said. "And then you staged it as a suicide."

"Quite right, Miss Sheridan," she said, without a hint of remorse. "You see, he was unsatisfied with the MLE investigation and promptly decided to start his own meddling. I am afraid to say that he got rather close to the truth. So I disposed of him, cloaking it as a suicide."

"But… why…?" I stammered.

"Well, my dear, it is a long and fascinating story. Should I tell you how Wycliffe and I became lovers in my senior year? Or how we planned his deeds together, meticulously to the last detail? Or how he went to prison for the witch he loved? Yes, I would like to chat about all that, Miss Sheridan. And I am sure it would be of the greatest interest to you, but I'm afraid I will have to cut the history lesson short."

"You were Wycliffe's accomplice all along," I breathed.

"Oh, much more than that," she said. "He called me his pupil. I learned from the master, you see, the great and noble art of necromancy. An art that spellcasters everywhere have chosen to abandon out of weakness."

"Look where your *noble* art got you," I said, disgusted, "look where it got Wycliffe. A prison cell for life. And then death."

"Yes, I admit that fate had struck a harsh blow," the headmistress said with a rueful smile. "I couldn't save him from it, although I tried many times. The prison was too well protected, you see. There was never any way of getting him out of there alive. So, I thought one day, his freedom was only possible through death."

"What are you talking about?" I said. "What good would that…"

"Oh, more than you think, Miss Sheridan. After his death, I recommended a nice and quiet spot where we could put his remains in an anonymous grave, here in the woods near the school. Nobody would ever know. Except for me, of course. And the government, being the fools that they are, were glad to be rid of the problem of his final resting place."

"But Ross disturbed your plans," I said.

"Yes," she said, "that was an unfortunate setback. It took months to concoct the potion again, but now I am ready – ready to resurrect the great Wycliffe!"

With horror, I saw Muriel Hall flourish her wand again, now pointing it at Armbruster. She levitated his body over the altar and set him down upon it.

"Headmistress," he began, panic in his every syllable. "Please don't, I…"

But Muriel Hall silenced him with a wave of her wand.

"Yes, poor Armbruster," she said, a merciless smile on her face. "You see, Miss Sheridan, he never quite understood the role he was to play in this. For Wycliffe to walk among us again, I am afraid that certain sacrifices have to be made. Goodbye, faithful Armbruster."

Without hesitation, she cast the killing curse. A jet of red light hit Armbruster square in the chest. He was dead.

Horrified, I looked around for anything that could help me escape my bindings. And then, I remembered Armbruster's own wand that I had pocketed earlier. But my hands were bound behind my back, and so I couldn't quite reach it, no matter how hard I tried.

"Miss Sheridan, you have witnessed the death of a servant," she screamed. "And now, I want you to witness the rebirth of a genius."

She directed her wand at the ground in front of her and began to chant. It was the most terrifying sound I had ever heard, like a sinister song that never stopped. It was a calling that only the dead could answer. And before long, I was sure they would.

I sat up straight, trying to change the angle of the wand in my pocket. As the song got louder, my fingertips were already grasping at the wand, but I couldn't quite take it.

Meanwhile, to my horror, the earth was loosening in the place at which Muriel Hall was pointing. Her spell was finally working. Time was running out before Wycliffe would walk amongst the living once more.

With one desperate jerk, I finally grabbed the wand in my hand.

"Libero!" I cried, pointing the wand at my own bindings, which fell to the ground immediately.

Muriel Hall tore her wand away from the ground, readying for the attack, but she was too slow for my own.

"ABIGO," I yelled.

A jet of white light emitted from the end of my wand. Muriel Hall was propelled backwards, flying through the air. With a deafening crack, the back of her head connected with the nearest tree trunk. Unconscious, she slid to the ground.

To my amazement, the tree began to tremble, shaking precariously from side to side. Barry, still frozen within his prison of ice, was within range if the tree was to fall in his direction.

Without another thought, I leapt over to him, kicking the block of ice encasing Barry to safety. I was just about to run when a crack appeared in the centre of the trunk. It was widening. Transfixed, I couldn't move an inch, for within the trunk, the sleeping face of a youth – no older than sixteen, perhaps – appeared.

CHAPTER 14

A week later, we were all back safely at Fickleton House, tucking in to an excellent cooked breakfast made by Mrs. Faversham. We had put Val's foot, now in a thick plaster, on a small footstool. She still needed crutches to get around the house but the medical warlock had assured us that there wouldn't be any permanent damage, and that the healing potion would eventually fix all of the broken bones in her ankle.

Atop his high chair, which had been adapted to his feline needs, including a cat ladder and holsters for his bowl and drinks, Barry was wrapped in a green and red tartan blanket. He was wearing a pained expression as he slurped the remainders of the chicken soup that Mrs. Faversham had made specially for him.

After the events in the clearing, Muriel Hall had been arrested by the MLE and charged with multiple counts of abduction, murder, and necromancy. Though the trial was still due to begin, she was most likely going to spend the rest of her life as her lover and mentor, Wycliffe, had done: in prison.

"I'm surprised that cold of yours hasn't cleared up yet, Barry," I said, with a wink in Val's direction.

"Well, he was in that ice cube for quite some time, you know," said Val, grinning. "It will take a lot of chicken soups to warm up after that one."

"Mock me all you like," Barry said, in what he thought to be a dignified voice, "but I'd like to see *you* after such a horrendous experience. I could have easily died. Especially after Amanda kicked me across half the clearing like a football."

"I told you, Barry," I said, "there was no time to carry

you. I was afraid that the tree was going to fall on top of you. You wouldn't have wanted that, would you?"

"It was quite obvious that the tree was not in the process of falling," Barry said sniffily.

"But what *exactly* happened there, anyway?" asked Val, "I still don't understand why they had kept the boy in that tree."

"It was part of the ritual," I said. "The MLE examined it later – that was while Barry was being unfrozen and you were being treated in the infirmary, Val. After I got Barry out of there, I called for the MLE and showed them the clearing. We found the other abducted people in the other two trees."

"I get that, Amy," said Val, "but why did they do it in the first place?"

"Well," I said, "after Wycliffe's return, they were to be used in the second step of the resurrection. After sacrificing Armbruster, Wycliffe would have just been a walking shell, a body without a mind. But if Muriel Hall had succeeded, sacrificing the other three and then administered the potion, he would have regained his old strength, perhaps even rising to greater power than ever before."

"Do you really think that plan would have worked?" asked Val. "Or was the headmistress just crazy?"

"I don't know," I said. "The MLE certainly seemed to take it very seriously."

"Lucky we got there in time, then," said Val. "Were they still alive? The people they had kidnapped, I mean."

"Eventually, yes," I said. "They had been put in a form of magical stasis. But it was for far too long, so they had trouble restoring them back to normal. I think one of the teachers got them back in the end. You should have seen the look on Julian's face when his best friend walked into the Great Hall later that day. He thought for certain that he'd be dead."

"Good thing that Julian wasn't charged," said Val.

Much to the delight of Isabella Villar, my recommendation in front of a preliminary court hearing held at the school, during which I had requested leniency for Julian Ross, had been granted. In light of the vital role he had played in solving the case, I thought that was the least we could do for him.

"Yep," I said, "he didn't even get a reprimand from the school. So all's well."

At that moment, Barry began coughing violently.

"Poor Barry," said Val sympathetically.

"Yes," I said, grinning. "But don't worry, Barry, we'll look after you."

"I think," he said, holding his paw to his throat, "it will be a very long time – perhaps even months – before this clears up. My body just isn't as strong as it used to be, you know. Also, I doubt my fur will ever look the same again."

"Sounds like you need a rest, Barry," said Val fondly, while I was trying not to laugh.

"Funny you should mention that," he continued, pointing to a stack of envelopes on the sideboard behind me. "I think you'd better see what came in the morning post, Amanda. I would get it myself, but in my present condition… I believe it's *very* important."

"Oh no," I groaned. "Not all over again. If it's from Warklesby's, I'm not going to open it."

"Amanda," said Barry, "I don't think this can wait. It's of the utmost importance."

Reluctantly, I walked over to the sideboard and picked up the stack of letters. Most of them were bills, including the repairs to Barry's library, which had gone smoothly thanks to Mrs. Faversham's supervision.

Taking my seat at the table again, I filed through the bills until I reached a mysterious blue envelope, which was addressed in a curly yet neat handwriting.

"What does it say, Amy?" Val asked.

My curiosity mixing with a strange sense of foreboding,

I tore it open and began to read aloud:

Dear Amanda Sheridan,

Thank you very much for your interest in the Magical Holiday Retreat! Please find enclosed a brochure with all the exciting activities, luxurious rooms, and wonderful relaxation our establishment has to offer. Children and pets are very welcome.

Yours sincerely,

Archibald Pomeroy

"*Magical Holiday Retreat?* Seriously, Barry?" I said. "What a build-up. You really missed your calling as an actor, you know."

Barry looked rather pleased with himself.

"But this looks amazing," said Val, who was reading the brochure more closely, "Look, Amy, it's got an elemental sauna, a bar, magic fireplace with randomised fireworks…"

"Oh no, not you, too, Val," I said.

"It's possibly the best retreat for warlocks and witches in the country," Barry said.

"It's not the kind of holiday involving sorcerers again like last time, is it?" I asked.

"Certainly not," said Barry. "Whatever gave you that idea?"

BLIND CAT'S
HOLIDAY

T.H. HUNTER

1

Abigail Pomeroy stretched out a podgy, wizened hand and reached for the teacup on the three-legged table next to her. It was a brew of her own making, consisting mostly of camomile and valerian, that she used only when she needed something to calm the nerves. And to say the day had been exhausting would have been an understatement.

Sipping the last drops of tea, she decided to close the window. It was late October, and the wind quickly turned chilly once the sun had disappeared. She puffed as she painfully lifted herself from her armchair. Her ankles had been giving her trouble all week. She suspected that the altercation with her elder son, Matthew, earlier that day had something to do with it.

Whenever she thought of his ingratitude and misplaced sense of entitlement, it made her blood boil. She had given him the benefit of the doubt for far too long. Her late husband, she thought, had been right all along. Matthew was no good and never would be any good. But she would put up with his behaviour no longer. And she knew just what she had to do. She was going to change her will whether he liked it or not.

She moved over to the desk and opened the top drawer. After fumbling with the hidden latch, she opened the false bottom to reveal a few sheets of paper. She placed them all on the table. Now all she had to do was to make the alterations and place the magical seal upon the document. But where had she placed her wand?

Suddenly, footsteps outside her door and three taps announced that her nightcap, a large glass of sherry, had been brought up to her. Was it time already? She must have been lost in thought for quite a while. She checked the large magical hourglass on the wall, but then she remembered that it had broken down the day before.

She retrieved the glass of sherry from the deserted corridor beyond and closed the door again, locking it firmly behind her. She took a large swig of sherry that would have surprised anyone who didn't know her. She noticed that the liquid tasted a little different than usual. Perhaps the staff had changed the brand. She made a mental note to have that decision reversed immediately in the morning. She liked keeping things just the way they were.

Spotting her wand behind one of the cushions on the armchair, she picked it up determinedly and approached her will lying on the desk. She flipped over the second page that announced the inheritor of her magical powers. With a wave of her wand, the name of 'Matthew Pomeroy' was erased. With another flick, it had been replaced by 'Archibald Pomeroy', her younger son. Then, she spoke the incantation that sealed the will again, murmuring it over and over again like a mantra.

The will glowed bright green for a moment. It had been successfully changed. She lifted her glass of sherry and put it to her lips once more. But as she drank a second time, there was no mistaking a bitter taste that had nothing to do with the sherry.

Her head was suddenly beginning to spin, and her stomach retracted violently. She couldn't think clearly anymore. She tried to walk towards the door, but her feet would no longer carry her. A moment later, she collapsed to the ground. She was dead.

2

"Let me go," Barry said indignantly, trying to clamber off Val's lap. "This is an outrage."

"Shhh, Barry," Val whispered, nodding towards the only remaining four-legged patient, a British bulldog who was beneath his elderly master's chair. "They'll hear you."

"It won't be long, Barry," I said softly. "It's our turn next. The receptionist should be coming any minute now."

"It's already been a lifetime!" he hissed. "I've been barked and snapped at all morning. If that Doberman had got any closer it would have been curtains for me."

"You did walk straight into him, though," Val said, fondly stroking his fur. "Anyway, it's a vet, Barry. What do you expect?"

"I don't expect to be in constant fear for my life, thank you very much," he said. "Being incurably blind is bad enough."

At this last utterance, the elderly man turned in his seat and stared at us in disbelief. Sensing his owner's change in mood, the bulldog opened its eyes. I blinked and smiled at the man in the most innocent manner I could summon, while Val held a hand over Barry's mouth to prevent him from talking any further. After a moment's hesitation, the man finally put a grubby finger into his ear and jerked it around twice. He had evidently decided that his ears had played a trick upon him.

With Barry still struggling on Val's lap, the receptionist finally opened the door and announced that the vet would now be able to have a look at Barry. Although he appeared to be miffed by being simply referred to as 'your cat', I think he was rather glad to get out of the waiting room at last.

We passed along a corridor to our left and were led

423

into a large vet's office, where a very tanned man in his late forties was sitting behind his desk.

"Hullo, hullo," he said good-humouredly, getting up and extending his hand towards me. "I'm Dr. Bentley."

"My name is Amanda Sheridan. Nice to me you, doctor. This is my friend Valerie Morgan."

But Barry, sensing his last chance of escape slipping away, struggled free just as Val and Dr. Bentley were about to shake hands. Landing on all fours, Barry scrambled across the floor in the direction of the door. Or at least where he thought it was, for he slammed headlong into a pair of black metal drawers next to the actual door.

Both Val and I rushed over to recover Barry, but Dr. Bentley was there first. With an expert grip, he gently but firmly lifted Barry up and placed him on the examination table.

"Nervous little fellow, isn't he?" Dr. Bentley said, smiling.

"Neurotic is more the word," I said, as Barry scowled vaguely in my direction. "But, erm, that's not really why we're here. The thing is that Barry is blind. That is, almost entirely."

"I see," said Dr. Bentley, taking a rubber glove from a box on his desk and putting it on. "How old is he, exactly?"

"Well," said Val, eager to enter the conversation, "you can't get a straight answer from him on that one, but there's a picture downstairs in the…"

"What Val means to say," I said, silencing her with a quick jab of the elbow, "is that we haven't had him for long. We inherited him a year ago."

"We think he's in his more senior years, though," Val added, trying for some damage control.

"That is something of an understatement," Dr. Bentley said, examining Barry's teeth. "I'd say he's well above what might be considered the usual lifespan for a normal cat."

"You can say that again," I said heavily. "So, is this an

age-related problem?"

"Quite possibly," said Dr. Bentley. "You expect a lot of wear and tear for such an old cat, of course. That especially holds true for yours. This one's been through the mill, by the looks of it."

Barry, who was sensitive about his age at the best of times, looked daggers at the vet, hissing angrily. The vet seemed unimpressed, however, and began to measure Barry's blood pressure with a tiny apparatus from one of the many drawers.

"Mmh," he said after a moment, frowning.

Val and I looked at each other with raised eyebrows. Perhaps Barry's problems were quite serious after all. Next, Dr. Bentley produced a small flashlight from the chest pocket of his white coat and forced Barry's left eye to open wider with his gloved hand.

"Mmh," he said again, examining Barry's other eye. "How quickly did these symptoms appear?"

"Well," I said, thinking back to Barry's excellent eyesight a month ago in the woods of Warklesby's School of Magic. "It can't have been all that long. Last week, he had a serious accident when a bookcase fell on top of him. He knows the house quite well, you see. Such a thing wouldn't normally happen to him."

The incident was true, and it had been Barry's howls that had first alerted us to the problem of his eyesight, though he had made every effort and every excuse to hide the fact from us as long as he could. His attempts at self-healing by magic had failed, however, so we had finally decided to show him to a heb vet. He was, after all, technically a cat, albeit with an oversized ego.

"I see," Dr. Bentley said, turning off his flashlight. "I will need to run a blood test on him to be sure. One moment, please."

He stepped over to a large shelf at the end of the room and returned with a shaver and a syringe. He quickly shaved off a patch of hair from Barry's neck. Then, he removed the cap from the syringe. It was lucky that Barry couldn't see the needle aimed in his direction, because I think he might have made another dash for it if he had.

As it was, Dr. Bentley pinned him down with one hand before inserting the needle. Shocked at the sudden spasm of pain, Barry hissed furiously, but there was no escaping this time. After a moment, Dr. Bentley calmly withdrew the needle.

"I'll have the blood analysed in the lab right away," he said, stroking a thoroughly resentful-looking Barry. "I'll contact you as soon as we have the results."

"Thank you very much," I said. "That would be wonderful."

***

The trip back to Fickleton House was not a pleasant one. Barry couldn't quite make up his mind whether us dragging him to a vet was worse or the fact that he might be suffering from some terminal illness.

Though I was sure that Barry was in far too combative a mood to be under any immediate threat of dying, his sudden onset of blindness still worried both Val and me.

As far as I knew, no warlock had spent such a long time in feline form – or as any other animal for that matter. The long-term effects were simply unknowable. I only hoped that Barry's blindness was not a symptom of something far more sinister. Thus far, I hadn't even contemplated that he, too, was mortal. Even magic couldn't prevent that.

Finally, we arrived in the cosy village of Fickleton again. It was unusually but pleasantly windy, so that the red and gold leaves of autumn danced around our car as though to welcome us home.

Turning the corner, I spotted PC Bowler outside of the butcher's shop. Ever since our first encounter a year ago, we had been irreconcilable enemies. I, for one, would not forget how he had attempted to pin a murder on me. At present, he seemed to be berating one of the village youth in his usual pompous manner.

A few minutes later, we drove through the wrought-iron gates of Fickleton House. Even my serious worries about Barry's condition couldn't quite close my eyes to the fact that it was more beautiful than ever. Doused in autumnal sunlight, it looked much friendlier than usual, as though it had made an effort to be especially hospitable during a time of uncertainty and illness.

Barry had been unusually quiet for much of our trip home. His usual level of grumpiness notwithstanding, I could tell that he was just as worried as Val and I were.

It was not until we were in the kitchen, helping ourselves to a little snack, when he spoke again.

"I just cannot understand it," he muttered, a pained look on his feline face. "All my spells, my research. Useless. Utterly and totally useless."

"I don't know," Val said, trying to lift the mood. "I think your spells allowing cats to drink cocktails will go down in history. You know, in case another warlock gets stuck in a cat's body. Wouldn't be so dull then."

"Don't be silly," Barry snapped. "I'm not talking about my life's work in general. That is beyond reproach, of course. I'm talking about it in regard to *this*."

He pointed vigorously at his eyes with his paw.

"Perhaps we should give it another go," I said, though after countless hours of trying I couldn't pretend that I was particularly optimistic. "Our holiday to the Magical Holiday Retreat in Bath isn't until next week, anyway, so we might as well use the time we have."

Initially, we had hoped to cure Barry's ailment quickly enough, so I had written a letter, asking whether it was alright to move our holiday back a bit. A few days later, I had received a morose letter from Mr. Pomeroy, whose father had unexpectedly died, welcoming the change in schedule and promising that everything would be prepared for our arrival. Now, however, it looked as though we'd have to cancel our holiday altogether.

"We have tried everything," Barry continued, frustrating flying from his every syllable. "Every spell in the book, and several of my own invention. Cataract cures. Longevity charms. Even a magical lens correction. Nothing works. And by the day, I see less and less. I can't even read with a magnifying glass anymore. Not that I don't regret reading a lot of the drivel I had to endure in the *Daily Warlock* over the years. But at least I'd like to stop by my own choice, perhaps after a particularly terrible piece by one of my *esteemed* colleagues."

"By the way, did anyone answer the public request we placed in the *Daily Warlock*?" asked Val.

"*You* placed there, you mean," said Barry sniffily.

As a last, desperate attempt, we had sought the help of the larger magical community. Barry, as one might imagine, had been mortified at the idea of having his condition made public. Perhaps even worse, if one of his many academic rivals *did* manage to cure his blindness, Barry would be eternally indebted to him or her, a thought that surely haunted him.

Finally, however, Barry's sense of self-preservation had trumped his ego, and he had placed his signature under the plea for help. Ever since, he seemed to have convinced himself that he had been somehow forced or duped into doing so.

"So, did you get any answers?" Val asked.

"Oh, yes," Barry said, wearing a sardonic smile. "Hundreds of letters sent by magical post, professing their 'greatest sympathies' for my situation. Expressing what a 'shame' it was that I would no longer be able to keep up the 'pretence' of contributing to magical theory. One letter even suggested that I ought to deflate my head to put less strain on my eyes. Such impudence!"

"Hang on," I said. "I thought you couldn't read anymore?"

"They were read aloud by the couriers. Bats, mostly. Though I think there might have been one or two ravens mixed in. It was a most humiliating experience, I can assure you."

"Lucky that we don't have any neighbours," said Val.

"And there wasn't a single useful suggestion?" I asked.

"Pah," said Barry dismissively. "One or two mediocrities *promised* to look into it. But they'd hardly be up to the task of writing my obituaries, if you ask me. Curing this mysterious ailment is well beyond their powers."

"That's gratitude for you," said Val, grinning at me.

"There must be something we've overlooked, though," I said thoughtfully. "Perhaps we should go through the stack of papers Warklesby's sent you."

Barry simply waved a paw irritably in front of him as though he were dealing with an irksome fly.

"No, no. Hardly worth the scrolls they are etched on. Second rate research at best."

"Well," I said, sighing. "Then there's nothing we can do until we get the results from the vet."

"Please," Barry said, "if the greatest minds of the magical community – including myself, that is – cannot solve this problem, a heb certainly won't be able to cure my condition."

"You mean…" began Val, a look of horror on her face.

Barry nodded gravely.

"My condition might be terminal."

***

As the days passed by, Barry's dark prophecy was not disproven. Though bats regularly brought post up to Barry's library window, no new avenues of a possible cure were opened up for us to try. Barry's usual level of hypochondria notwithstanding, I was beginning to get restless myself. As horrible as turning blind was, life went on. If it was a prelude to something else, however, that was a completely different matter.

As I paced about the library, lost in my own circular ruminations, the door suddenly burst open. It was Val.

"Amy," she said, with a note of urgency in her voice. "You've got to come."

"What's the matter?" I asked.

"It's the vet," she said. "They're on the phone. At Mrs. Faversham's house. They want to talk to you."

With all the talk of magical remedies, I had completely forgotten about the vet.

"Yes, of course," I said. "I'm coming."

"Don't waste your time, Amanda," came Barry's mournful voice from the armchair. "The hebs won't be able to find anything. It's too late. We've just got to accept that I'm dying."

Val frowned at Barry's defeatism and then looked at me.

"Don't listen to him," I said softly. "Can you look after Barry while I'm out?"

"Sure," Val said, squeezing my arm affectionately. "We'll get him out of this somehow."

"Amanda," Barry's faint voice floated across the room. "I think you had better say goodbye properly. Who knows if I'm still here when you return."

"You're not going to die, Barry," I said angrily. "Cut it out, please."

He simply waved his paw weakly in a gesture of a farewell.

Shaking my head, I raced down the staircase and put on my coat downstairs. I exited the back door and hurried across the lawn, which was a shortcut to Mrs. Faversham's house.

When I arrived, she was standing dutifully at the old-fashioned telephone. I could see that she was also very worried. Though she knew nothing of the fact that Barry was a warlock, of course, she had developed a deep affection for him nonetheless.

"This is Amanda Sheridan," I said, speaking into the receiver.

A young, female voice answered immediately.

"One moment, please… it's Miss Sheridan for you, doctor."

"Hello, Miss Sheridan," a male voice said after a few moments.

"Hello Dr. Bentley," I said.

"I have the results of the blood test for your cat," he said matter-of-factly. "Would you mind if we did this over the phone? Only, I'm going on holiday tomorrow. You'd only be able to get another appointment in three weeks' time."

"That's perfectly… perfectly alright," I said.

There was a rustling of papers at the other end. Behind me, Mrs. Faversham was anxiously waiting. I felt sick from the tension that was building up inside of me.

"Ah, yes, here it is," he said, breathing heavily into the phone. "Your cat is suffering from severe hypertension, I'm afraid to say."

It took me a moment to take it in.

"Hypertension?" I asked, bewildered. "You mean, high blood pressure?"

"That's right," said Dr. Bentley, as though that clearly settled the matter.

"But…" I stammered, "I don't understand. His eyes are…"

"The blood pressure is most likely the cause of your cat's blindness," said Dr. Bentley. "In fact, judging from the other results of the blood test, I'd say it's positively the case. There are no markers for any systemic diseases. Thus, the hypertension is not a secondary effect of something else. That certainly makes things a lot simpler."

"Blood pressure," I breathed. "Sorry, but how dangerous is it in cats?"

"It can be dangerous, yes," Dr. Bentley said. "In your

431

cat's case, there is a severe health risk which may even be fatal."

"Fatal?" I gasped.

"Fortunately," Dr. Bentley continued soothingly, "it is treatable. In fact, since we are dealing with primary hypertension, the chances are excellent that we might not only stop the process but even reverse some of the negative effects, including the blindness. With such an old cat, however, I can't make any promises, of course."

"Oh," I said, feeling immensely relieved, "thank God for that. What do we have to do?"

"He will need medication straight away," Dr. Bentley said. "Calcium channel blockers should do the trick. They will relax your cat's blood vessels and bring down the blood pressure. I'll write the prescription right away, so you can pick it up this afternoon if you like."

"I'll do that, thank you very much," I said. "Anything else?"

"Yes," he said. "Your cat will have to avoid stressful situations at all costs. Anything that gets his blood boiling, as it were."

"That's easier said than done," I said. "But I'll do what I can."

"There is also the matter of your cat's diet," Dr. Bentley said in carefully measured tones. "Now, I know this is rather a delicate topic for some owners... almost a matter of belief. What... what exactly does his diet consist of?"

If I had been completely honest, I would have said that I didn't really know. Mrs. Faversham often cooked tuna for Barry, but I had caught him a few times in his library, munching secretly on a sweet snack or chocolate bar. Since he was technically a warlock, I hadn't thought much of it at the time.

"Well," I said slowly. "There's tuna and, erm, cat food on occasion, but he might have some other means of acquiring food."

"Acquiring food?" Dr. Bentley asked, sounding slightly bewildered.

"You know," I said hastily, "from dustbins in the village, the neighbour's balcony, that sort of thing."

"Oh, I see, of course," he said, chuckling into the telephone. "It almost sounded as if he were buying the stuff himself. Well, if possible, Miss Sheridan, try to keep him away from the neighbours and the village. Who knows what he eats there when unobserved."

'You're telling me,' I thought.

"If he *were* a human," Dr. Bentley said in an amused tone, "it would be a lot easier, of course. I'd simply tell him to stay away from alcohol and sweets. That's usually the main cause. But humans often tend to be a lot more stubborn than our four-legged friends. I suppose that's why I became a vet in the first place."

"Yes," I said, with an ominous feeling that Barry might well have been overindulging over the summer. "Well, thank you, Dr. Bentley. It's certainly a great relief."

"Not at all, Miss Sheridan," he said. "I… I hope to see you around some time again. A pleasure meeting you."

"Likewise," I said, smiling.

"Well, goodbye then," he said.

"Goodbye," I said. "And have a nice trip."

"Trip?" he asked absent-mindedly.

"You said you were going on holiday," I said.

"Oh, yes, of course," he said. "I really do need one. Goodbye, then."

"Goodbye."

I hung up and turned around to Mrs. Faversham.

"Hypertension," I said quickly. "We need to be very careful from now on, but Dr. Bentley said it's treatable."

This explanation was entirely superfluous since Mrs. Faversham had been listening in to every word we had been saying on the phone, but she beamed nonetheless.

"I'm very glad," she said. "Poor Barry. He *does* miss your great-aunt very much. I wonder if I've been overfeeding him a bit."

"I wouldn't worry about that, Mrs. Faversham," I said. "I have an idea that Barry's dietary problems might have a very different origin."

3

Back at Fickleton House, I found Barry and Val up in the library. Val looked at me anxiously. Barry, also, couldn't quite hide his hopes.

"Amy, what did he say? What did the vet say?" asked Val.

"How long do I have?" Barry asked, dramatically spreading his limbs over the edge of the armchair.

"Blood pressure," I said, ignoring Barry. "It can cause blindness, among other things. It's treatable, but we've got to act immediately. You're getting medication from the vet. Avoid stress and no more cocktails. And you are to be put on a strict diet from now on."

At the sound of the last word, Barry's head swung up in alarm.

"Strict… diet?" he said incredulously. "But that can't possibly be the solution to… that's just not…"

"That's what the vet said," I said firmly. "What exactly have you been eating up here anyway, Barry?"

Barry suddenly wore a very shifty look indeed.

"Eating… up here?" he asked, as though the possibility had never occurred to him before. "Why nothing, of course. Merely the meagre scraps of food you grant me at the dinner table."

"Nonsense," I said. "You have a secret stash up here, haven't you?"

"I don't know what you're talking about," he said.

"Fine," I said, narrowing my eyes. "Have it your way."

I drew my wand and gazed around the room in suspicion. Though Barry was very productive when he wanted to be, especially when developing new spells or writing scathing articles about his academic enemies, he was very lazy in most other regards. Thus, I reasoned,

Barry would certainly have chosen to sacrifice a superior hiding place for ease of access.

I waved my wand at the two large cupboards at the back of the room near the fireplace. They flew open immediately. But apart from old blankets and some candles, they were empty.

"Really, Amanda," Barry said in fake indignation, "I find your distrust in me truly offensive. This is …."

"Aha!" I said triumphantly, spotting a loose floorboard near Barry's usual armchair. "What do we have here?"

The floorboard slid easily back. I lit my wand and pointed it at the now open floor. Val leaned in closer to see. Beneath were countless wrappers of all kinds of varieties of sweets, from chocolate bars to truffles and cakes.

Having been found out, Barry switched gears quickly.

"But… but you don't understand. I need comfort food to relax," he whined. "To reduce stress."

"It's killing you Barry," I said earnestly. "And it stops right here."

***

A few days later, Barry was already showing signs of recovery, thanks to the medication and our efforts to enforce a diet upon him. He was still blind for the most part, though he was able to recognise vague shapes in close quarters again – a definite improvement.

***

After the last week of worrying, we were all eager to get away for a bit. Luckily, we still had our Magical Holiday Retreat to look forward to, a trip that Barry had instigated after our adventure at Warklesby's during the summer but had to be postponed as long as his illness remained a mystery.

With that obstacle out of the way, however, we set off for Bath the next day. Even for heb visitors, it was an extraordinary place. Yet unnoticed to them (and so far unknown to me), a parallel world of magical recuperation centres and spas had sprung up for witches and warlocks as well.

"Oh yes," Barry was saying, his mood having significantly improved since the vet's hopeful prognosis, "Roman warlocks used to come here, you know. Some of the places claim to be open since then, though I don't believe a word of it, of course. All marketing. But a lot of them *have* been around since the late Middle Ages, I am told."

According to the satnav, we only had a few minutes more to go. The drive from Fickleton House had been smooth so far.

"How do warlocks usually get here?" Val asked, turning around to Barry. "Not by car, right?"

"Certainly not," Barry said, as though the heb mode of transportation was something vulgar. "They use portals."

"Portals?" Val said. "Amy, why didn't we use the portal? It's in the sitting room downstairs."

"I told you, Val," I said, directing the car onto a lane leading to the rural outskirts of Bath. "People are already getting suspicious because we haven't had our electricity fixed yet in over a year. You know how much they love to gossip in the village. No, it's better to be seen leaving by car."

"You have reached your destination," the satnav said smoothly.

"Where?" Val said, looking around her. "There's nothing here. This can't be it."

I peered out of the windscreen and then the passenger window. Although it was already getting dark, I could see Val's point. We were surrounded by meadows, the only exception being a derelict farm on the other side of the road that was clearly uninhabitable.

"Perhaps that's the spa," I said doubtfully, pointing to the broken -down farm house.

"Well, I'm not staying there," said Val, crossing her arms. "We'll probably be setting up buckets for most of the time to stop the rain that's coming through the roof. Just look at it!"

"I'll park the car over there," I said. "Can't hurt to have a poke around the place. We can always leave again."

I brought the car to a halt in front of the ruins, and we got out. Barry, unaccustomed to his surroundings, almost fell into the ditch next to him.

"Ouch," he said angrily. "Do you mind, Amanda?"

"Just saving your life, as usual, Barry," I said, grinning.

"I have a cat's body," he said. "A drop of a few feet won't do me any harm."

"What was it the vet said again?" Val said, pretending to have trouble remembering. "That Barry had really been through the mill?"

"Disgraceful man, they should revoke his license," Barry said, as both Val and I laughed.

"And get it right back for saving your life, Barry," said Val.

"Come on, Barry," I said, lifting him up and giving him an affectionate pat on the head. "You'll be back to normal in no time. Let's find the entrance first. If there is one, that is."

We passed by a shed filled with an odd assortment of junk.

Then, Val suddenly cursed.

"What's the matter?" I asked.

"I… I think I just got an electric shock or something," she said, rubbing her nose.

With Barry still in my arms, I stepped up to where Val was standing and gently extended my foot. But I felt nothing whatsoever. It simply passed through the air as normal.

"Strange," I said.

"Maybe it was some sort of random electric charge," said Val. "I'll try again."

She imitated my foot movement, but then there was a spark, as though lightning had struck out of the sky, and Val tore her hand back at once.

"Ouch," she said.

"It must be some sort of barrier," Barry said. "Let me walk through."

Hesitating briefly, I placed him down on the ground. Unable to see anything, Barry uneasily walked in the wrong direction – towards the road – but I caught him in time and directed him towards the correct spot.

He seemed to have no trouble stepping across the threshold either.

"Why does it always happen to me?" Val said miserably.

"Come on, Amanda," Barry called from the other side.

I turned to Val, who still looked upset.

"We're not going to leave you behind, Val," I said. "Don't worry. We'll –"

But at that moment, a dark shape near the barn caught my eye. It was briskly walking in our direction.

"I think somebody's coming," I said.

For a moment, I thought my eyes were playing tricks on me in the growing darkness. For although the man came nearer, he remained very much a blurry silhouette. The experience was unnerving, to say the least.

"I can see him too," Val said, squinting.

"Why is he so blurred, though?" I said, frowning. "It's not so dark yet."

"Step over the threshold," said Barry from the other side. "There might be a clouded vision charm on the barrier."

Allowing myself no time to dither, I stepped through the invisible barrier, this time with my entire body. It was a curious sensation, as though I had been sprayed with water by a lawn sprinkler. And yet, as I moved through the barrier, I remained perfectly dry.

Having reached the other side of the barrier, the scenery changed completely. To my amazement, the broken-down sheds and derelict barns vanished. In their place, a modern complex of out-houses surrounded a three-story hotel in the middle, boasting the name 'Pomeroy's Magical Holiday Retreat' in oversized purple letters.

The silhouette had also changed into the image of a very overweight man with a markedly cleft chin, reminding me of a painting I had once seen of an Austrian Prince. To say his style of clothing was eccentric would have been something of an understatement. He was wearing a purple frock coat with a huge neck ruffle in white. In his right hand, he was carrying a cane.

"Welcome, welcome," he said breathlessly as he approached Barry and me. "Dear me, I hope the barrier hasn't been acting up again, has it? Darn thing."

"Well, I…" I began.

"Not to worry," he said. "But where are my manners? My name is Archibald Pomeroy, owner of the Magical Holiday Retreat."

He gestured unnecessarily towards the building behind him.

"My name is Amanda Sheridan," I said, smiling. "And this is Barry, I mean, the Earl of Barrington."

Archibald Pomeroy looked puzzled for a moment, until he spotted the cat several feet below his line of vision.

"Ah," Mr. Pomeroy barked. "Of course! I read about the accident in the *Daily Warlock* recently. The Earl trapped in a cat's body. I hope you have found a solution to your… malady."

"Indeed," Barry said coolly, unwilling to linger on the subject of his blindness for longer than necessary.

Mr. Pomeroy's smile did not falter in the least.

"A pleasure, a pleasure," he said. "Always glad to welcome the aristocracy to our humble facilities. They were built by mother and father, you know. Tremendous energy, both of them. Though my father passed away recently, I'm afraid to say. Now, if you would follow me, please…"

"Hold on," I said. "Sorry, but I'm afraid our friend, Val, can't get through the barrier."

I pointed towards the blurred shape of Val on the other side.

"Oh, dear me," Mr. Pomeroy said, frowning. "So it *is* malfunctioning again. I'll have to get Bruno to take a look at it. He's the cook around here, though he does most of the magic work for me, too. Poor man is rather overworked, seems to fly off the handle every other day! But there we are, I suppose. One moment, please."

He vanished into the building, returning after a few minutes. Following Mr. Pomeroy, a red-headed man with a flaming beard and angry eyes traipsed behind him. He was wearing a white cook's uniform with black buttons.

"Bruno, if you would," Mr. Pomeroy said, pointing to the barrier. "It's acting up again."

The cook lifted his wand and bellowed in a deep, stentorian voice:

"Interruptus!"

The air in front of Val began to crackle. A moment later, she was perfectly visible again.

"Amy?" she said, blinking. "What's going on?"

"It's alright, Val," I said. "The barrier has been disabled. You can come through now."

"Only for a moment," Mr. Pomeroy said, wagging a fat finger at me. "It will reset in a minute or two. Thank you, Bruno. That will be all for now."

The red-headed cook stared at him, then muttered something inaudible yet menacing at the same time before going inside again.

"Val," I said as she joined us. "This is Mr. Pomeroy, the owner of the spa."

"How do you do?" he asked, smiling a toothy smile at

Val.

"Hello," Val said.

"Right," he said, turning around to me again. "Now that we're complete, we'd better get inside. It gets dark very early at this time of year. But we did have a wonderful summer, didn't we? I think mother should be making ready for bed already. This way, if you please."

Val picked up Barry and we entered the hotel, with Mr. Pomeroy leading the way. We found ourselves in a large reception area. The walls were painted in shocking pink, while the furniture and the desk were white. A pretty blonde woman in her late teens or early twenties was sitting behind it, looking attentively at the door.

"Good afternoon," she said, rising mechanically from her seat. "Welcome to the Magical Holiday Retreat."

"Yes, yes, we know all that, Isabelle, my dear," Mr. Pomeroy said pompously, waving a hand in front of him. "See which room Miss Sheridan is in, will you?"

"Yes, sir, of course," the receptionist said in a meek voice.

She hastily thumbed through the list of rooms on her desk.

"Room 023," she said after a moment.

"On the ground floor?" Mr. Pomeroy said, aghast. "Who on earth put them there?"

"You did, sir," the receptionist said, a slight tremor in her voice as though she didn't like reminding him of the fact.

"I did?" Mr. Pomeroy asked, as though the suggestion was absurd. "Impossible. Well, well. Never mind. That won't do. That won't do at all! See if there's anything else available, will you?"

"Of course, sir," the blonde girl said, placing her finger on the list again. "There's a one room apartment on the second floor and the suite on the third."

"The suite it is, then," Mr. Pomeroy said, clearly enjoying himself in the role of the generous benefactor.

It was at that point that I wondered whether Mr. Pomeroy always staged this little scene for his guests or whether it was an off-the-cuff whim of his.

"That's very kind of you, Mr. Pomeroy," I said. "But really, there's no need to…"

"Not at all, my dear," he said, winking at Val and me. "Always happy to accommodate you in any way I can. It's not every day that a pair of beautiful witches, such as yourselves, walk through that door, I can assure you. It's crinkly old warlocks mostly."

He emitted a short laugh that sounded more like a bark. Then, he turned to the receptionist again.

"Isabelle, have Jameson bring up the luggage, will you? By the way," he said, looking around him. "Where is your luggage?"

"Oh," I said, "it's still in the car. I totally forgot."

"Never worry," he said, nodding in a fatherly fashion. "We'll get it. Now, I'll show you to the suite, if you would follow me. I think you'll simply adore it. I had it redone entirely a year ago, you see. We've got new magical lifts as well. Here we are."

We followed him into the corridor beyond the receptionist's desk and came to a halt in front of a pair of lifts. Mr. Pomeroy pressed the button.

"Cost me a fortune, all of this," he said, chortling. "A couple of heb youths broke into the Retreat and stole some of the equipment on the top floor a few weeks ago. Wrecked the rest. Quite a mess, I can tell you. We had the MLE around and all. But they didn't catch the culprits, I'm afraid to say. I don't think they take heb crimes very seriously."

"Hebs broke in to your spa?" I asked curiously. "Whatever for?"

"Well, I don't know," he said, taking a large flask from his pocket. "But that was why we had the barrier installed in the first place. To keep those hooligans out. It has an anti-heb charm on it. But it's rather temperamental at times. Seems to keep out magic folk, too, on occasion."

"Well," said Val, "I'm a psychic, not a witch, so…"

"A psychic?" Mr. Pomeroy spluttered in surprise, spraying us and the floor with a clear liquid that reeked of powerful alcohol.

"I hope that isn't a problem?" Val asked, taken aback.

"Problem?" Mr. Pomeroy said, chortling again. "No, no. No problem at all."

"Perhaps that's why the barrier didn't let you through," I said slowly. "Maybe it counts psychics as hebs and not as witches."

"Certainly possible," said Mr. Pomeroy, nodding. "We haven't had a psychic guest in a long time, so we weren't able to test it. Lucky for me, I suppose. Tricky customers, eh? Never can conceal anything from you psychics."

He laughed good-humouredly, though I could see he looked rather worried at the same time at the prospect of having a psychic guest in his hotel. Val looked at him with an expression that told me that she was trying to read him.

"Surely, Mr. Pomeroy," Barry said silkily, "you don't have anything to hide in your establishment?"

Barry had clearly not forgotten Mr. Pomeroy's unwelcome reference to his public quest for help in the *Daily Warlock* and was more than happy to return the favour.

"Conceal?" Mr. Pomeroy said, nervously closing his flash again with a snap. "Whatever gave you that idea? Well, I suppose we all have personal things we would like to keep to ourselves. It's only natural, isn't it? Ah, here's the lift at last."

The lift's door opened and we squeezed inside, with Barry still in Val's arms. The space was constricted, and Mr. Pomeroy's breath filled the air of the lift with a putrid smell of powerful spirits. I couldn't help but notice that his eyes kept darting anxiously in Val's direction.

Having arrived on the third floor at last, we filed out of the lift again. Mr. Pomeroy seemed to be rather relieved to get some distance between himself and Val.

"Is everything alright, Mr. Pomeroy?" I asked him.

"Claustrophobia," he said weakly, leaning theatrically against the wall. "Please excuse me."

After a moment, he gathered himself and led us straight down the hallway.

It turned out that he hadn't been wrong in regard to the suite. It was quite magnificent. There were three rooms in all, with two bedrooms and one living room. The bathroom was spacious and up-to-date with the latest magical gadgets, including a massage shower.

"Very impressive, Mr. Pomeroy," I said, beaming at luxurious possibilities around us.

After the shock of Barry's illness, a little pampering would do us all some good, I thought.

"Why, thank you," Mr. Pomeroy said, inclining his head. "Mother made sure we always had the latest designs."

"Is she…?" I asked tentatively.

"She's retired, yes," said Mr. Pomeroy, clearly mistaking the point of my question. "The death of my father hit her hard. Very hard. She spends most of the time in her room these days. In fact, she's on the same corridor as you are. She's got the room with the tray outside. Just a few doors down. That reminds me, I'd better prepare her usual nightcap. The barman always brings it up to her at nine o'clock before she goes to bed, you see."

He opened the door.

"I'll be in the restaurant downstairs if you need me," he said. "If there's anything else, please don't hesitate to contact me or any member of the staff. Oh, and before I forget, you'll find an overview of all the wellness programs we have on offer in your living room."

"Thank you, Mr. Pomeroy," I said. "Just what Barry needs right now."

"Not at all," he said, opening the door and standing in the frame for a moment. "I wish you a very pleasant stay."

He bowed with an ostentatious flourish of the hand and then closed the door behind him.

"What a peculiar man," I said after a moment.

"I don't like him," said Barry sniffily.

I laughed.

"I'm not surprised after he mentioned the request you put in the *Daily Warlock*."

"You mean the one *you* placed there, Amanda," Barry said irritably.

I turned to Val, expecting her to launch into a good-humoured attack on Barry's framing of the whole affair, but was astonished to see that she wasn't paying attention to our repartee at all.

"Val?" I asked. "Is everything OK?"

"What?" she said, looking up. "Oh, yes, sure."

"Val," I said. "You were always a bad liar. What's wrong?"

"It's… it's Mr. Pomeroy," she said, shaking slightly.

"What about him?" I asked.

"I think he's…"

"Oh yes, he is," said Barry snidely.

"Barry, please," I said. "What is he, Val?"

She looked at me with large, worried eyes, her expression very earnest. Then, she slowly began to speak:

"I think he's planning a murder."

4

"A murder?" I asked incredulously. "Are you sure?"

Val simply nodded.

"But…" I said, shocked at my complete lack of suspicion. "But he seemed pleasant enough. A bit fake, perhaps. A little eccentric certainly, but nothing more. Did you feel his emotions, then?"

"Yes," said Val gravely. "It's never been so clear before. It was pure hatred, Amy. And a determination to act on it, too. This isn't any normal grudge. I don't think I've ever felt that kind of emotion so vividly before."

I moved over to the sofa and sat down.

"When did you sense this, Valerie?" Barry asked, blindly moving towards where he thought she was standing.

Val, in an unusual act of nimbleness, caught Barry before he could crash headlong into the table next to the sofa. She placed him next to me before she answered his question.

"I think it was as we were waiting for the lift downstairs," she said, as she began to pace to and fro in front of us. "You know, when he was talking about how psychics made him nervous. That's when I got suspicious. After that, he was really easy to read. And he was lying when he said he had claustrophobia."

"Yes," I said, frowning. "That did seem odd. But why would he pretend to have claustrophobia."

"I think he put it on to hide his anxiety about having a psychic in the hotel," said Val.

"You'd think he'd be better at shielding his feelings," I said thoughtfully.

"He clearly wears his emotions on his sleeve," said Barry, in an air that suggested that he'd never do such a thing. "It happens to warlocks as well as hebs, you know."

"Yeah, we've noticed, Barry," I said, grinning. "But seriously; did you feel who it was Mr. Pomeroy hates so much, Val?"

But Val shook her head.

"No," she said. "Only that it was someone he knows well. It was an intimate sort of hatred, not abstract. I'd say family, or someone he used to be close to. I could tell that it's been eating away at him for some time, too."

"Are you sure about all this?" I said.

"Positive, Amy," she said.

"Then we've got to prevent it from happening," I said. "Stop the murder before it occurs."

"We're on holiday," Barry protested. "And I don't even have my eyesight back."

"We can't let a murder occur right under our noses," I said determinedly.

"But we don't even know who the target is," Barry said. "We can't call the MLE, because there hasn't even been a crime yet! And I doubt Mr. Pomeroy is just going to tell us if we ask him politely whether he's been planning any murders lately. You know, because it's based on a hunch."

"Hey!" Val said. "It's more than just a hunch. I felt his emotions, Barry. They were as clear as day."

"Perhaps," said Barry. "But that's not going to make him talk."

"No," I said slowly. "There must be another way to find out, though. What do you think, Val?"

"You're right, Amy," she said. "We 've got to stop him if we can. I know he doesn't seem the type at all, but he really means business. Somebody is in serious danger."

***

Unsure of how to proceed next, we finally decided to go to the restaurant for dinner. It would provide an opportunity to observe Mr. Pomeroy more or less unnoticed, since he had mentioned that he would be tending to the restaurant that evening.

It must have been 9 o'clock by the time we finally left our room and found ourselves outside on the corridor once again. Barry still had to be carried everywhere, though a hearty meal and a soak in a magical bath after that kept his spirits high.

As we left our room, the hallway outside was only dimly lit by old-fashioned oil lamps that I suspected had been magically altered. A member of staff was outside one of the rooms, placing a large glass of brandy on a tray that had been suspended from the wall.

He had short, very dark hair. Clean-shaven and smartly-dressed, he looked like the paragon of all barmen, an impression which was only slightly diminished by his youthful face

"Oh, hello," the barman said, slightly surprised to see us. "I just brought Mrs. Pomeroy her evening brandy. You must be the new guests Mr. Pomeroy was speaking of just now. My name is Jameson. Bill Jameson."

"Nice to meet you," I said. "I'm Amy and this is Val. You're right, we've only just arrived."

"Then I hope you will have a very comfortable and pleasant stay here," he said smoothly.

"We're looking for the restaurant," Val said, who was clearly becoming hungry. "Can you tell us where it is?"

"Of course, madam," he said. "I'm on my way down now. On duty in five minutes. I'll lead you there."

***

It turned out that the restaurant was in fact below ground level. The lack of windows and sunlight was offset by warm décor and a generally welcoming atmosphere. I was surprised to see so many guests there, since the hotel itself did not seem to be particularly large.

"I suspect some warlocks just come here for a meal," Barry said, as Val tied a napkin around his furry chest. "I must say, the menu is rather mouth-watering. Read it out again, will you, Valerie?"

Mr. Jameson, who seemed to also serve as a waiter in addition to his duties as a barman, had provided some cushions for Barry so that he could sit at the table with us. Val read the menu out loud for Barry again, then pondered on her own choice.

"I think I'll have the burger," Val said after a while. "What about you, Amy?"

"I don't know," I said, scanning the same page a third time. "The chicken salad looks quite good…"

"Oh, come on," said Barry dismissively. "You're not going to spoil our dinner with your healthy choices, Amanda."

"Yeah, Amy," said Val, laughing. "We're here to be spoilt. Go on."

Outnumbered by two to one, I grinned.

"Alright," I said. "I wouldn't want you to lose your appetite, Barry. But remember what the doctor said."

Barry shook himself as though trying to physically rid himself of the haunting memories.

"Yes, yes," he said irritably. "I'm taking the pills, aren't I? Anyway, one dish of pork chops followed by some ice cream won't do any harm, surely."

"You want to regain your eyesight, don't you?" I said, putting on what I thought was a stern expression.

"Of course I do," he said.

"Then you'll have to choose something else," I said.

Barry glared at me, then turned to Val for support. Val, though usually more forgiving, shook her head gently.

"Fine," he fumed. "As long as you spare me the smell of any rabbit food. I'm not having any of it near me on my well-earned holiday."

We finally compromised on Barry eating fresh salmon. As part of the bargain, I chose steak instead of salad.

I had never been to a magical restaurant before in my life, with the exception of Warklesby's School of Magic. It turned out that the meals did not whizz through the air at Mr. Pomeroy's Magical Holiday Resort, however. They were brought in the ordinary heb fashion, though I suspected that the cooking had been greatly accelerated by magic, because our food arrived within just a few minutes of ordering.

And it was absolutely delicious. Even Barry couldn't find anything wrong with his salmon, though I think he had very much looked forward to criticizing the compromise he had been forced to make. Val, also , was tucking into her burger with relish.

Not long after, we were all happily fed and feeling rather drowsy. It was only now, after our hunger had been satisfied, that we really took in more of our surroundings. I estimated that there were around fifty other people in the restaurant with us. A pleasant, middle-aged waitress had tended to us throughout the evening, though there were quite a number of other staff present.

"Have you seen Mr. Pomeroy at all?" I asked Val, trying to make him out without arousing too much attention.

"No," she said, frowning. "I haven't seen him all evening."

"Probably plotting the murder in secret," said Barry darkly.

"I think that's the bar over there," I said.

"Good idea," said Barry. "I could do with a drink."

"No, Barry," Val said indignantly. "Remember your high blood pressure."

"What else would we do there?" he said.

"Gather information," I said. "We've got to find out more about Mr. Pomeroy."

"But what about my bath?" said Barry, who was clearly not in the mood for any detective work.

I gave Val a pleading look.

"Fine," she said in exasperation. "I'll see what I can do. I'll meet you later downstairs, Amy."

"OK," I said. "Thanks, Val."

I waited for Val and Barry to leave the restaurant and then paid the bill. Mr. Pomeroy was still nowhere in sight, though perhaps that was for the better. Whatever his plans, he didn't seem like the type to appreciate somebody poking around. And since no crime had been committed so far, he had every right to simply throw us off the premises if he chose to do so.

I got up and slowly made my way over to the bar. Most people were still finishing their meals, so there were only very few people present. A small, elderly man wearing a suit and hat was sitting on a bar stool. Behind the bar, Mr. Jameson was serving the customers.

"Oh, hello again," I said.

"Hello, madam," he said politely, "I hope your meal was to your satisfaction?"

"Oh, yes," I said. "It was excellent."

"What would you like to have?" he asked.

"Cider, please," I said. "Are you a waiter as well as a barman, then?"

"Not usually, no," he laughed. "But you do have to do everything, eventually. Mr. Pomeroy put me in charge of serving a few tables today. We were short on regular staff in the beginning."

He turned his back to me and busied himself with the drink. Hoping to strike up a conversation with the elderly man in the suit, I shifted the chair beside him.

"Would you mind if I sat here?" I asked him, smiling.

"What?" the man said in a surprisingly high-pitched voice. "Oh, not at all, not at all, young lady."

"Thank you," I said, sitting down. "It's my first time here at Mr. Pomeroy's."

"Indeed?" he squeaked. "I've been coming here for the last thirty years, you know. The name's Herbert Fields."

"Amy Sheridan," I said, shaking his hand.

"I came here first in my professional capacity as a student of magical law, you know. Long time ago now."

"Nothing serious, I hope?" I said, as Mr. Jameson placed my drink in front of me.

"Oh, quite routine," Mr. Fields said. "That was when Mr. Pomeroy, senior, was still alive. I knew him quite well. Tell me, are you on holiday, Miss Sheriff?"

"Sheridan," I said, trying to supress a grin. "But yes, I'm on holiday here with my friends Val and Barry – that is, the Earl of Barrington. He's here for his health."

"The Earl of Barrington," the man said, clearly trying to retrieve a memory. "Yes, I remember reading something in the paper about him recently. Turned into a dog, didn't he?"

"No, luckily a cat," I said, picturing Barry's curmudgeonly face pasted on the body of a Rottweiler.

"That's right," the elderly man said. "A cat. Yes, well, he was quite a warlock in his time, you know. Well respected. Until his accident, of course. Not the most sociable of people, I hear."

"You can say that again," I said, laughing. "But Val and I still have hopes for a brighter future in that regard."

I took a sip of my cider.

"So, you knew the previous owner, Mr. Pomeroy's father? What was he like?"

"Well," he said, his benign smile fading a little. "I… I do not like to speak ill of the dead, my dear. It is not a habit I intend to divulge in. It's better to let the past be the past."

"So not all was very harmonious in the family, I take it?" I asked, pressing the issue.

Mr. Fields nodded gravely.

"I think his sons had a hard time of it. Particularly Matthew."

"Matthew?" I said, bewildered.

"Yes," Mr. Fields said. "Matthew was the first-born. He took his temper from his father, you know. They quarrelled all the time. Awful. Drove away a lot of the guests, too. Until one day, the father threw him out. Disinherited him entirely, as a matter of fact."

"That must have been quite a shock to him," I said. "So Archibald, the current owner, inherited everything?"

"Do not ask me for the legal details because I do not know," Mr. Fields said, clearly uncomfortable with the topic. "But to my knowledge, Matthew rarely turned up here again. Not even to visit his poor mother. She was the only person who had been on his side, at least initially."

"Archibald Pomeroy mentioned her. Do you know what happened to Matthew after he had to leave?"

"Yes," said the elderly man, shifting in his seat. "I believe he doesn't live very far from here. A village by the name of Oaking, or Oating. Something like that. His mother still lives here at the hotel, you know. A charming young lady she was back in the day. Very beautiful. We were all very envious of Pomeroy senior. Oh yes."

Mr. Fields took a sip of his red wine. He seemed to be lost in memories, for he didn't resume the chat we were having. Thinking it was better to leave him alone, I finished my drink and got to my feet again.

"Thank you, Mr. Fields," I said. "It was very nice talking to you.

"Very nice, very nice," he said absent-mindedly, his expression still vacant. "I'll see you around, Miss Sheppard."

I caught Mr. Jameson's eye behind the counter, and we both grinned.

***

I passed through the crowded restaurant and took the stairs. It was less that I was eager for movement after the heavy meal, but rather the dislike for the stuffy atmosphere of the lift that directed me away from it.

Panting slightly as I arrived on the third floor, I was

just about to turn into the corridor when I heard a terrifying scream.

I hurried forward to see what was the matter. Mr. Archibald Pomeroy was standing in the doorway of the room that had the tray permanently suspended on its corridor wall. A large glass with an amber liquid was standing on it.

Mr. Pomeroy's face was white as a sheet. Next to him, the young receptionist called Isabelle was holding her hand over her mouth.

Silently, I stepped forward, then I followed Mr. Pomeroy's terrified gaze. Inside the room, an elderly lady lay motionless on the floor.

5

"Oh no, oh no, oh no," Mr. Pomeroy kept saying over and over again. "This cannot be."

Without thinking, I turned to Isabelle.

"Can you get the doctor, I mean, a magical healer right away?"

I could tell that she was beyond words, but she nodded and left the room in haste.

I bent down to feel Mrs. Pomeroy's pulse.

"Is she…?" Mr. Pomeroy asked.

"I'm sorry, Mr. Pomeroy," I said, looking up at him. "She's dead."

Mr. Pomeroy put his hand over his mouth to stifle a cry. Either he was an excellent actor, or it was a genuine emotion. And yet, it had only been a few hours since Val had felt a deep-seated homicidal impulse within him. I would make sure not to turn my back on him, that much was certain. And my wand was within my coat pocket within easy reach.

"Was this your…" I began tentatively.

"My mother," Mr. Pomeroy said, nodding gravely.

"I'm sorry," I said.

We stood there for a while in silence, not knowing what to say. Then, the receptionist returned with a sombre-looking, middle-aged man.

He was wearing green robes of a kind I had never seen before. An emblem featuring a staff and a snake clearly showed that he was a healer, though how he had arrived here so quickly was beyond me.

The healer examined the body for a quite a while, prodding it here and there with his wand. He conjured up strange markings I didn't recognise, muttering unintelligibly under his breath. Finally, he got up.

"How did she…?" Mr. Pomeroy asked immediately.

"Cause of death unknown," the healer said, no note of sympathy in his voice. "We will remove the body for further testing. There will have to be an inquest, Mr. Pomeroy."

"An… an inquest?" Mr. Pomeroy said, blinking. "Whatever for?"

"Under magical law, a full examination of the body necessitates an inquest," the healer said, as though he were reading a passage from a book. "You will be informed of the date within the hour, Mr. Pomeroy."

"I see," Mr. Pomeroy said. "I… I need a… if you will excuse me."

Evidently still in shock, he slowly walked out of the room and down the corridor. The healer then conjured up a stretcher and careful levitated Mrs. Pomeroy's body onto it.

***

Half an hour later, I had told Val and Barry all about the discovery of Mrs. Pomeroy.

"I'm surprised they didn't arrest him on the spot," said Barry. "Why didn't you call the MLE, Amanda?"

"I… I don't know," I said honestly. "He looked clearly distraught. I'm not sure that…"

"Pomeroy was clearly harbouring homicidal thoughts for someone very close to him, that much Valerie determined the minute we got here," Barry said. "Now, his mother lies dead. It's not that difficult to put one and one together, you know."

"I don't think it's that simple, Barry," I said. "Look, I know I'm no psychic, but it just wasn't… I don't think he did it. His reaction seemed genuine to me. I think he was shocked and surprised to see her like that."

"Did it occur to you, Amanda," Barry scoffed, "that Pomeroy might have been putting on a show for your benefit? He already gave us a sample of his acting abilities outside of the lift, remember?"

"I know, Barry," I said, frowning. "But I think we all saw through that one straight away. Look, I still want to be sure before we make such a serious accusation."

"But what can we do except for going to the MLE?" asked Val.

"We should confront him," I said. "You can read him very clearly, Val. You can read him like an open book, as you did before. If he's innocent, then no harm has been done. If not, well, we can still call the MLE then."

"OK, Amy," said Val, who felt just as uncomfortable as I did. "You'd better get your wand ready in case he turns on us. I'll get my coat."

***

Barry, Val, and I made our way downstairs and inquired at the reception for Mr. Pomeroy. It turned out that his office was on the second floor, only one flight of stairs down from our room. After the discovery of his mother's body, he had locked himself in his room, with orders not to be disturbed unless absolutely necessary.

"Here it is," said Val, pointing to a smart, silver sign as we reached the second floor, "Mr. Archibald Pomeroy, Manager."

I knocked on the door. We waited, but there was no answer. I knocked again. This time, there was a barely audible grunt from within.

Gently opening the door, we stepped into a lavishly-decorated office, with mostly purple furniture and an expensive Persian carpet. Sitting behind an antique desk was Mr. Pomeroy. He was holding his head in his hands. Next to him, on the table, there was a golden liquid in a glass that you didn't have to be an investigator to see that it was a whiskey. As might be expected under the circumstances, Mr. Pomeroy looked utterly devastated.

"We're very sorry to bother you, Mr. Pomeroy," I began. "But it's rather urgent, you see."

"Urgent?" he said, a light of hope in his eyes. "Is there news of my mother? Were they able to revive her after all?"

"I'm afraid it's nothing like that," I said, feeling more uncomfortable by the minute. "It's, well, you see, we were worried. Worried that your mother might not have died of natural causes."

"You mean," he said, amazement on his face, "she…? Whatever makes you think… please sit down, won't you?"

He beckoned us to a pair of chairs in front of his desk. Sitting down, I lifted up Barry and placed him on my lap.

"No natural causes, you say?" Mr. Pomeroy said in bewilderment. "But I knew my mother. Suicide is entirely out of the question. She would never have done such a thing."

Before I could answer, Barry intervened:

"Not suicide, but murder, Mr. Pomeroy," he said calmly. "As far as I understand, the healer did not find a cause of death immediately. And yet, most natural causes of death can be identified on the spot."

"Why yes, I suppose they can," said Mr. Pomeroy, his expression darkening even further. "Do you… do you really think there might have been foul play involved?"

"It's a possibility," said Barry. "I would even say, a probability."

"We were also worried about another thing," I said, looking at Val. "Val picked up on certain, erm, negative emotions of yours earlier this evening. Very powerful ones. So potent, in fact, that we feared they might be a connection."

He stared at us for a moment in disbelief. The awkward silence that followed was almost unbearable. Perhaps he was thinking of throwing us out on the spot. Or maybe he was considering quite another option. I found his expression to be utterly unreadable.

Feeling suddenly tense and trapped, I slid my hand into my coat pocket to make sure that I'd be able to draw my wand at the first sign of trouble. I almost expected Mr. Pomeroy to jump at me, or else start raving and shouting.

Instead, he did neither of those things. His face had morphed into a deep-seated sadness that struck me as being very real. Finally, he looked away and shook his head.

"If only it were that easy, Miss Sheridan," he said. "It would at least be some sort of explanation. An explanation for the fact that a still very healthy old lady drops dead without warning. But I must disappoint you. You see, I loved mother very deeply. Everyone knows that."

"But whom do you hate so much that you would…?" Val began, unable to complete her sentence.

"I don't know what you're talking about," he said.

"Please, Mr. Pomeroy," I said. "We wish no harm. And we do not want to make false accusations, especially not on official record. That is why we came to you first. But we cannot ignore what Val has sensed in you, either. She has been able to read you quite clearly. We simply want the truth so that we can put our conscience at ease."

Mr. Pomeroy took a large swig of whiskey. Then, he stared at us, his face immovable.

"Psychics," he said, his voice suddenly harsh and bitter. "Putting their noses into things that don't concern them."

"Mr. Pomeroy," I said firmly. "If it is murder we're talking about, it concerns everybody. Or would you rather talk to the MLE about your feelings? Somehow, I don't think they'd be so accommodating."

He mustered me for a moment.

"You really want to know, Miss Sheridan?"

"If you don't mind, Mr. Pomeroy," I said quietly.

"Well, I'll tell you," he said to my surprise. "It's no secret, anyway. Not most of it, anyway."

He got up. I could tell that he had had quite a lot to drink already, for his balance was unsteady. Considering the fact that we had just accused him of possibly being involved with his mother's death, however indirectly, I didn't dare to say anything more.

His sinister demeanour didn't seem to match his flamboyant clothes at all anymore. There was something much harder behind that soft, flabby exterior of his. The eccentric Mr. Pomeroy that had welcomed us to the hotel seemed nothing more now than a memory; a hollow persona he had crafted for himself for the benefit of guests and the spa.

"My hatred," he said, "is reserved for one person only. And that is my brother, Matthew."

"Your brother? But… but why?" I asked.

He swore loudly.

"Why not?" he said angrily. "If you knew him, the way I know him, I'm sure you'd feel the same way. A nasty person, he is. Growing up with him was hell – and not just for me. He's vindictive and spiteful. And then, there was his addiction, which made everything a thousand times worse. Lying, stealing, cheating. He even got into fist fights with customers. He did it all, and worse. He almost brought our entire family down with him, too. Ruined its good name. Father was barely able to keep afloat due to my brother's antics.

"And then, my father did the only thing left to him, many years ago. He cast him out. Forever. Disinherited that ungrateful little sod who had caused so much misery for all of his, including my mother. So after my father's death, I received the Resort, and my mother received his magic powers."

Val and I looked at one another, stunned. But it was Barry who spoke next.

"So you are not a warlock, Mr. Pomeroy?" he asked.

"No," he answered. "That is why Bruno has to do the magic for me. My mother was a heb, you see. My father was the warlock. Under magical inheritance laws, magical ability in mixed marriages can only be passed on to one person at a time. And my father chose my mother, because she had always wanted to be a witch. He wanted to fulfil her life's dream."

"But with your mother's death, you are likely to inherit her powers?" said Barry shrewdly.

Mr. Pomeroy stared at Barry, as though needing a second to process what he had just said. Then, without warning, he suddenly lurched forward, bending over the table, pointing his finger at Barry.

"How dare you!" he bellowed, his voice shaky from the drink. "I don't like your insin… insinuations, *my Lord*."

"I'm sorry, Mr. Pomeroy," I said quickly, trying to calm the situation somewhat. "Barry was only trying to…"

But Mr. Pomeroy was not in the mood to be appeased. Resentment, that dangerous false friend that simmers in the cellars of the mind until it becomes pure venom, was etched across every line of his face. I could tell that this was an old hatred, one that was mixed with old and new experiences alike. But it had also blended with his recent loss into a very peculiar brew that was hard to read. As he stood there, I wondered whether this was a man who had murdered his own mother, until Val got up from her seat next to me.

"We believe you didn't do it," she said loudly.

All three of us turned to her in surprise. There was a moment's silence. Then, Mr. Pomeroy sat down in his chair again.

"Thank you for believing me," Mr. Pomeroy said, slurring slightly from the drink. "What else do you want to know?"

"Why do you still hate your brother with such a passion?" Val asked. "I mean, isn't it all over? He doesn't live here at the spa anymore, right?"

Mr. Pomeroy scoffed.

"You might get quite a different impression if you stayed here long enough," he said darkly. "My dear brother likes to – how shall I put it? – pay us a visit once in a while. And his house calls aren't pleasant, I can tell you."

"What do you mean?" I asked.

"He comes here by night," said Mr. Pomeroy. "Smashes the whole place up. Lights it on fire sometimes, too. He drives away my guests on a regular basis. I usually tell them that some heb hooligans broke into the place. Like I did with you. That story satisfies some of the customers at least. The rest, well, they just gossip – or worse, leave and never come back again."

"I imagine it's very difficult to do business under those circumstances," I said.

"You can say that again," Mr. Pomeroy said darkly.

"Did you contact the MLE?" I asked. "In regard to your brother, I mean."

"Of course I did," he said, pouring himself another generous drink from the bottle of whiskey on the shelf behind him. "I told those busybodies every little detail they wanted to know. In the end, they decided it wasn't worth their time. They gave me some cock-and-bull story about the whole thing being a heb affair. Utter nonsense, of course. As I pointed out at the time, my mother was a witch, and so she had a right to being protected as a member of the magical community. And I grew up around my father, who was a warlock, for crying out loud. I'm as much a spellcaster as you are, Miss Sheridan. Without the magic, of course."

"I see," I said. "So what happened after the MLE refused to take your case? Did you think about taking the law into your own hands?"

He pondered on the question for a while.

"I can't say that the thought hadn't crossed my mind. Especially when, about a week ago, he went over the limit. I could endure broken glass, but this was different. He actually tried to kill me."

"What?" Val said.

Mr. Pomeroy nodded impressively.

"That's right. He placed a booby trap at the edge of

463

one of the barns. Bruno and I are the only ones who go there, you see, to reset the barrier every once in a while. But a week ago, an explosive went off just seconds after we had left. Missed us by only a minute, I reckon."

"An explosive?" Barry asked.

"That's right," Mr. Pomeroy said. "A time-bomb, a heb apparatus designed to kill from afar. Quite ingenious, considering their ignorance of magic. Now, almost all of my guests are warlocks and witches, so they wouldn't need to resort to any heb technology. And even the ones who aren't – you know, heb wives or husbands – would be able to get their hands on a magical device that would be much more reliable."

"But your brother has no such contacts," Barry said.

"Precisely," said Mr. Pomeroy. "He's isolated from the magical community since he was ousted from the spa. Hence my suspicion that it was him. Among other things, of course."

"And you erected the barrier to prevent him from entering the area again?" I asked.

"Yes," he said, frowning. "That was after he trashed the place some time ago now. I had it set up so that it would repel hebs, which includes my brother, of course. Since I'm technically one too, however, Bruno lets me in and out. It's inconvenient, but it has made us all feel safer. A lot of the staff left after the bombing incident, you see. Nobody wants to work at a place that's under a threat like that."

"But how did your brother get through the barrier to set the explosive?" I asked.

"I don't know," said Mr. Pomeroy. "That's a mystery. I suppose you'll have to ask him yourself on that one. If he's not already in the next world due to his filthy habits. But I shouldn't get my hopes up…"

"Would your brother have a motive in regard to your mother's death?" I asked.

"Well," he said, "it was our father he quarrelled with

the most. But you never know with that sort of person. He could've killed her, yes. In fact – if it is foul play, as you think – then I wouldn't be surprised. They quarrelled quite recently, you see."

"They quarrelled?" I repeated. "What about?"

"Oh, the will, of course," Mr. Pomeroy said. "There wasn't much else he cared about. One moment, I'll get it."

He fumbled with the bottom drawer of his desk and retrieved a few sheets of paper.

"Here," he said, turning them around and pushing them in my direction. "See for yourself. It's on page two."

I turned the page. The will clearly stated that Mr. Archibald Pomeroy was to inherit Mrs. Abigail Pomeroy's magical abilities. Slight scorch marks behind the fresh markings indicated that the name had been changed quite recently.

"She had put my brother's name there not long before," Mr. Pomeroy said, reading my quizzical look correctly.

"I'm sure that didn't please you too much," said Barry.

"I didn't care," Mr. Pomeroy said coldly. "It may sound strange to you, but frankly I never really cared about doing magic myself. My staff do all of that for me. I can easily run the spa without it. And unlike my brother, you see, I have work that I take pride in. This is my passion."

He finished his whiskey in one large gulp.

"As far as I'm concerned," he continued. "The magic can just die out. It's brought nothing but conflict and strife to my family. My mother beleaguered my father to receive his powers. My brother Matthew, as the first born, was indeed very bitter about it. He talked my mother into putting him as her beneficiary into the will. And you know what? I agreed. If that was his price for leaving us alone in peace and never darkening our doorstep again, then I was fine with it."

"You told your mother this before she died?" I asked.

"Of course," he said. "She wouldn't have made the

original changes in her will otherwise."

"And yet," said Barry, "she put you back in. Why was that?"

"Well," Mr. Pomeroy said, his nostrils flaring, "you'd have to ask my dear brother that, wouldn't you? Being the heir to the magic wasn't enough for him. He wanted the powers right away. He wanted my mother to sign them over."

"Is that possible?" I asked in surprise, looking down at Barry.

"Yes," said Barry. "It is extremely rare. But one may pass on the ability under certain – quite strict – criteria."

"My mother," Mr. Pomeroy continued, "would have nothing of that, of course. She loved magic. And though she had been the most understanding – overly so – of my brother in the family, there was a line. He tried to bully her into it. She met him the day he died."

"She met him… on the same day?" I said.

"That's right," Mr. Pomeroy said, with a look of contempt and disgust on his red face. "And to think that she stuck up for him for so long. And look how he repaid her in the end."

6

A few minutes later, Barry, Val, and I found ourselves back in our room again. Mr. Pomeroy's tale of his brother Matthew had been informative, yet exhausting. It also brought a new suspect into the case. One who had a clear motive, and most likely the means to commit murder. If it was murder, that is.

"So much for our holiday then," said Val, putting her handbag on the table. "A few hours at the spa and we're already fully involved in a murder case. How much bad luck can you get in a lifetime? There's no way I'm going to sleep anytime soon."

"We should probably make a profession out of it," I said jokingly, though I had secretly contemplated doing just that quite a number of times.

"This never happened to me before you two came along," said Barry, a wistful expression on his face. "I had been looking forward to a quiet retirement."

"But I bet you didn't have half as much fun, though," I said, grinning.

"Clearly," said Barry drily.

"So, Val, do you believe Mr. Pomeroy's story then?" I asked.

"Yes, I do," she said.

"He did have an excellent motive, though," I said thoughtfully. "I mean, I can't imagine anyone not wanting to have magic powers."

"He was telling the truth, Amy," said Val "I'm sure of it. People who lie – well, they usually sort of cover up their emotions. It's very difficult to fake it, especially on that powerful level. If he *is* making it up, he'd be a one in a million actor. But then he wouldn't have had to invent that ridiculous story about his claustrophobia when we got out of the lift."

"He could have planted that lie to throw us off," I said, though I didn't really believe it myself. "He could have intentionally planted a fake lie so that we'd take him to be a bad liar."

"Do you really believe that, Amanda?" Barry scoffed. "The man is clearly a mediocre upstart. He isn't capable of playing that kind of three dimensional chess, on a psychological level that is."

"Classy, Barry," I said, laughing. "Dismissing a suspect for his lowly background."

But Val nodded her head earnestly.

"He'd have to be some sort of genius, Amy, to pull that off," she said. "And I got a clear reading of him. It wasn't like it was in a crowded space."

"Well, he's no fool," I said slowly. "But I trust your judgment, of course. And he doesn't strike me as a criminal or psychological mastermind, either."

"Which only leaves…" Val began.

"…his brother Matthew," I finished. "He does appear to be a nasty piece of work."

"A scrounger like that might be capable of anything," said Barry.

"Perhaps we should pay him a visit," I said.

"You mean, go there and talk to him?" asked Barry, horrified.

"Yes, Barry," I said, exasperated. "What else? Play cards with him?"

"But he's clearly a dangerous lunatic! For all we know, he might jump on us the minute he sees us."

"He's a heb, Barry, don't forget that," I said. "I've got a wand and he hasn't got any magical powers. Not yet, at least. If we're prepared, he's no match."

"This was supposed to be a holiday, you know," he protested. "We shouldn't be getting involved at all."

"We already are," I said. "Anyway, it seems like the MLE is taking its merry time as usual. They haven't even determined the cause of death yet, though it looks very fishy to me. It might be ages before they start the official investigation. And by that time, it might already be too late. Or do you think it was natural causes after all?"

Barry looked at me for a moment, clearly considering whether it was worth it to lie.

"No, of course I don't," he said irritably. "As I said, natural causes are usually detectable on the spot by trained healers. They often fill in the paperwork right away, in fact."

"Then we've got to push on with our own investigation. The MLE is too slow. And if Matthew really is after the magical powers, Archibald might be in danger, too. What do you think, Val?"

"I'm in," she said. "But we'd better be careful. Heb or not, this guy seems to be dangerous. If he's into explosives, he might have the whole place rigged. You never know."

"Agreed," I said. "Barry, what about you?"

"Oh, alright," he snapped. "You'd probably get yourselves killed without me, anyway."

***

Unfortunately, we had little else but the rough name of the village that Mr. Fields had mentioned at the bar to go by. Though if his memory of my surname was any indication, his information wasn't particularly reliable. After the traumatic death of his mother, however, I felt that we had imposed on Mr. Pomeroy for long enough. I wanted to ask him only as a last resort. There had to be another way of finding out where Matthew Pomeroy lived.

Luckily, Val had a brainwave during the night. We could simply enter different variations one by one into the satnav of the car, variations that sounded similar to the suggestions that Mr. Fields had made. Then, we'd simply see what it came up with.

After a rushed breakfast – which the pretty receptionist, Isabelle, served us, most likely owing to the shortage of staff that Mr. Pomeroy had mentioned – we had a thoroughly bad-tempered Bruno lift the barrier for Val once more. Once more, the shiny exterior of the spa vanished, replaced by the dilapidated farmhouses and barns that we had encountered when we first arrived.

I scooped up Barry and we headed for my car, which was still parked in the same spot.

"Brilliant, Val," I said, getting into the driver's seat. "I'm thinking too much like a witch already. I was thinking of a magical way of tracking him down. It somehow never occurred to me to use the satnav. See whether it comes up with anything."

Val slowly tapped a few letters.

"Here, Oakham," she said, pointing to it. "What about that?"

"That's too far away, I think," I said. "No, Mr. Fields said that the village was close by somewhere. Can't be more than a dozen miles or so."

"What about that?" asked Val.

"Oak Hill," I read. "It's only about seven miles away. Certainly worth a try."

I started the car. With Barry sitting comfortably in the back, Val and I were left to discuss the best approach to tracking down our new prime suspect.

"Well, we know his name, even if we don't know the street," she said. "Somebody's got to know in a village that size."

"Yes," I said with a sardonic smile, thinking of the amount of gossip that was exchanged at the local pub just on the topic of our suspicious lack of electricity at Fickleton House. "Could be to our advantage for a change."

It took us a bit over ten minutes of driving to reach our destination. The village we entered was up on a hill. Beautiful wrought-iron gates on some of the houses suggested that it must have once been quite a picturesque place at some point in the past, though its best times were clearly over and long gone. The roads were in dire need of repair. And although the front gardens were kept meticulously in that peculiar English fashion (though the back gardens were often another matter entirely), the houses had a rundown appearance.

We drove up and down the main street, but there were no shops at all, not even a local post office. Very few people were out and about, though we spotted an elderly lady sitting on a bench at the other end of the village. I brought the car to a halt and Val opened the window so that we could talk to her.

"Excuse me," I said. "Could you tell us whether a Mr. Matthew Pomeroy lives here, in Oak Hill?"

"Matthew who?" the woman asked, cupping her hand behind her ear.

"Matthew Pomeroy," I repeated.

"Oh," she said, her smile fading. "He's not here anymore. Not since last Tuesday."

"He's gone?" I said.

"That's right," the old woman said. "He left a few days ago."

She hesitated briefly.

"Are you… are you friends of his then?"

"No," I said.

"Quite the opposite," said Val, nodding her head emphatically.

"Oh, that's alright, then," said the woman, visibly loosening up. "Didn't want to offend anyone. None of my business, I suppose."

"Didn't you like him?" I asked.

"That man was one of the rudest I have ever met," she said, shaking her head. "And believe me, that *is* saying something. It could be the brightest, most beautiful summer's day and he'd be as gloomy as a hangover on New Year's. And to be honest with you, I'm glad he's gone. Same as many others feel around here, too, I can tell you."

"I see," I said. "Well, do you know where we might find him now?"

"I'm sorry, dear, but I don't know that," she said. "He didn't leave a forwarding address, or so I'm told at the post office. Not that he got much post anyway. Complete hermit, that's what he was. Didn't like to mix with people."

Val and I exchanged a brief look. Matthew Pomeroy evidently did not want to be found. Had he something to do with the death of his mother? His sudden decision to move a few days before the event, I thought, couldn't possibly be a mere coincidence. The timing was too close. The whole affair reeked of planning and forethought.

"You can have a look at his house over there, if you like," the old woman continued. "The sign says it's sold, but I don't think you'd do any harm if you just had a look round. House's empty anyway."

She pointed to a small house at the end of a sidestreet.

"Thank you very much," I said. "We'll do that."

"Not at all," she said. "What do you want from him, anyway?"

"Oh," I said, "it's a family matter."

The old woman shrugged.

"I didn't know he had one."

**

Matthew Pomeroy's former house, as far as we could see from the outside, was indeed completely empty and unfurnished. Wooden boards were nailed across the door and a sign in front of it read "Sold", just as the old lady had said.

Next door, a neighbour was pretending to attend to his garden, though I could tell that he was curious about our visit. It turned out that he was just as unable to tell us where Mr. Matthew Pomeroy had gone to, though he was equally glad to see the back of him. I was getting the distinct impression that Matthew Pomeroy had not been a particularly nice man to deal with. He certainly must have been the least popular person in the village.

There had been one detail, the neighbour recalled, that had struck him as odd, however. According to his account, Matthew Pomeroy had rented a moving van, but had done most of the shifting during the night. It had all seemed like a hasty job. The neighbour even had to clear away some old pieces of wood that Matthew had simply thrown over the fence into his garden. It went without saying that this had not improved his impression of him.

The house itself was shabby even by the standards of the village. Tiles were missing from the roof, while several walls had been discoloured by moisture. The entire place smelt of dampness, only adding to the gloomy impression.

At the back of the house, the window had been broken. Carefully peeking through, I saw shattered glass and a large stone lying on the floor that clearly indicated that it had been smashed from the outside. Judging by the lack of dust and cobwebs – which seemed to be everywhere else – it must have occurred quite recently.

"Do you think we should have a look inside?" I asked quietly.

"Yeah," said Val. "But better be careful. Someone's watching."

She pointed to the neighbour, who was still keeping a watchful eye on us.

"I think a bit of magic might be in order," said Barry softly.

I didn't need telling twice. Pretending to be interested in the fence separating Matthew Pomeroy's old house and his neighbour's, I slipped my wand out of my handbag. I checked the surroundings one last time to make sure that the coast was clear. But, as before, nobody else was about on the street. I positioned myself beneath a tree, so that I couldn't be spotted from a window. It wouldn't do if I had to explain myself to the MLE if a heb saw me cast a spell.

I lifted my wand and pointed it through the twigs and leaves at the neighbour, whispering:

"Gratus."

His body relaxed immediately. Next, he slowly bent down to tend to his weeds as if he hadn't a care in the world.

"We only have a few minutes," I said, returning to Val and Barry.

"The door is locked," said Val, trying the handle.

"Stand back, Val," I said.

She hastily withdrew from the door, scooping up Barry from the ground as she did so.

"Vertere," I said softly.

There was an audible click, and the back door to Matthew's former house swung gently open. Val, still carrying Barry, and I quickly stepped inside, closing the door behind us.

If the garden had smelt moist, then the house simply reeked of dampness. All four walls of the room we were in had dark stains and blotches that spelt doom for anyone's health, I thought. And although the floor had been cleared of furniture, I could still see where a lot of it had stood. Judging by the lack of cobwebs, a small sofa had been at the end of the room.

"Come on," I said. "Let's see if there's anything in the next room."

With a little more apprehension than I cared to admit – I kept my wand drawn at all times – I opened the shabby wooden door. It opened up into a small hallway, with the front door to the street ahead of us. To the right, a flight of stairs led upstairs.

"This house creeps me out, Amy," Val said.

"Just imagine you were blind, then," said Barry, still perched quite comfortably in her arms. "I can't even move about on my own in these strange surroundings."

"I get the impression, Barry, that you're not too upset

about being carried around," I said, smiling.

"But what if the mad brother is still here?" Val asked earnestly.

"I've got my wand, haven't I?" I said.

"Remember, Amy, he's some sort of lunatic who's into explosives," said Val.

Val's aid to my memory was not reassuring. I felt naked, somehow, at the prospect of facing Matthew Pomeroy. In Barry's extensive library, I had once come across a bullet-repelling shield in a book entitled *Halting Hebs – A Practical Guide to Defence*. I had tried it out immediately, and, though one couldn't be sure it worked unless proven in action, I thought I had performed it sufficiently.

The difficulty of pulling off a ward charm scaled with the threat one was facing, however. Bombs could easily be disabled by most witches or warlocks before they went off, but conjuring a shield that could withstand such a blast usually took several spellcasters.

Following Barry's advice, I performed a detection spell, with no result. Still uneasy about the entire affair, I led the way upstairs.

We spread out, trying to find any indication that might lead us to Matthew's current whereabouts. The small room I found myself in, the first door off the landing, was entirely empty.

"Amy," Val's voice drifted over from one of the other rooms. "There's… there's something here you've got to see."

Clutching my wand tighter, I prepared myself for the worst. Val and Barry were two doors down, in the largest room. It was darker in there, for the blinds had been drawn on all of the windows except for the one where Val was standing.

"Look," she whispered, pointing at the wall opposite her.

At first, I thought it was more moisture that had lodged

itself into the wall. But then, I recognised that it was a large mural, though the paint was faint and clearly quite old.

"What is it?" I asked, stepping closer.

"I… I think it's some kind of family tree," said Val.

And indeed, as I examined it from up close, tiny etchings of names and dates covered the entire thing like swarming ants.

"This must have taken ages to do," I said in awe. "There've got to be hundreds, if not thousands of names. It goes back a thousand years, right up to 1066. Witches and warlocks are indicated with a 'W' next to their names, I think."

"See if you can find Matthew and Archibald Pomeroy," said Barry, looking vaguely in the direction of the mural.

"Quickly, though," said Val, who was peering out of the window. "I think the neighbour is recovering from your spell, Amy. He's beginning to get suspicious again."

"Alright," I said. "Here, help me find them, will you?"

After several minutes of feverish searching, we had finally detected Abigail Pomeroy. Oddly enough, the place underneath her and her husband was left blank.

"I think it's been scorched off," I said.

"But there's something else," said Val excitedly, squinting. "Some sort of hook."

The etchings were very faint indeed, made even more illegible by the burn marks.

"Could be a question mark," I said, frowning. "But the line ends here."

"Maybe he didn't want to fill it in because he didn't know who'd inherit the magic powers from Mrs. Pomeroy."

"Or perhaps," said Barry, "he was still hoping to be able to put his own name there."

"Yes," I said, "that would make sense. We've got to find him. Let's see if there's anything else to go by."

But the remainder of the house was entirely empty. After walking around the deserted house for a few more times in the vain hope of finding something that would indicate Matthew's current whereabouts, there was nothing left for us but to drive back to the spa. We had reached a dead end, though we would definitely transmit our information to the MLE as soon as we could. A head start in their investigation – once it finally got underway, that is – could mean the difference between a successful arrest and an escaped suspect.

"Funny he should sell his house like that," said Val thoughtfully.

"I don't find anything mysterious about it," said Barry. "He's committed a crime – he wants to cover his tracks."

"Yes, but not plan further in advance?" I asked. "Why sell the house in such haste? And why would he want to kill his mother and not his brother?"

"Perhaps he resented being struck from the will," said Barry.

"But it is rather odd all the same," I said. "You'd think he'd go for his brother first, whom he hated so much."

"Perhaps he still is," said Barry.

"You mean, he might have it in for Mr. Pomeroy?"

"You heard the man," said Barry. "The explosive– whatever primitive heb device it may be – is still deadly. It almost killed him the first time. There might be another attempt."

"He certainly meant business," I said, nodding. "It would be a surprise if he didn't try again."

"Then," said Val, with a bemused look on her face, "we've gone from suspecting Mr. Archibald Pomeroy to wanting to protect him."

***

The next few days, nothing out of the ordinary occurred, although we remained as vigilant as we could. Much to the bewilderment of Mr. Pomeroy, we made regular calls on him to see whether he was alright.

Unsurprisingly, he had no clue where his brother might have gone to, though the fact that he had made a run for it had solidified Mr. Pomeroy's view that his brother was indeed the guilty party.

News of Mrs. Pomeroy's death had naturally spread like wildfire. Everyone, the staff as well as the guests, were secretly awaiting the further developments of the case. Some of the guests left after the horrible occurrence, though a surprising amount remained, some out of curiosity, others to pay their last respects to the deceased.

The MLE, it seemed, had been moving at an ever slower pace. They had taken a lot of time for their examination of the body, though they finally released it. The funeral took place a day after. It was a quiet affair, though there were many in attendance. Afterwards, Mr. Pomeroy let the attendees know that there would be an inquest, held at the spa itself, since it was the most convenient place for everyone involved. A letter from the MLE, handed to me the receptionist Isabelle, curtly 'asked' us to attend and present evidence. We were not to leave the spa until further notice.

***

Meanwhile, Barry's eyesight was gradually improving. Val and I had had the faint hope that Barry's irritable temper was also connected to his high blood pressure, but our hopes were soon quashed. He remained the same curmudgeonly, though very lovable cat he had always been. Nevertheless, we forbade him from reading the *Daily Warlock*, or opening any more letters from the community, seeking to help or goad him.

We also had the opportunity to try out a few of the massage machines. Since electricity didn't run with magic around, the Magical Holiday Retreat had come up with a myriad of magical solutions for bubble baths, saunas, and massages.

With the death of Mrs. Pomeroy, however, a dark shadow hung around the place, one that neither of us could nor wanted to shake off. It seemed wrong, even sacrilegious, to indulge in the pleasantries of the spa. And so, after trying out a few of Mr. Pomeroy's extraordinary devices, we spent most of the time in the restaurant or up in our suite.

**

On the day of the inquest, Barry, Val, and I made our way down to the restaurant once again. Despite the labyrinthian nature of the place, we had been able to find our way quiet well after a while. Even Barry, now restored to a level of minimal eyesight, was able to carefully walk along corridors on his own, though we still carried him up and down staircases.

The many tables in the main hall of the restaurant had been cleared. Two wizened warlocks and a witch sat at a long table, which was usually used for the buffet. Today, however, it served as the desk for the chief examiners. For the audience and witnesses, several rows of chairs had been placed opposite them.

Guests and members of staff seated themselves quietly and in an unusually orderly fashion. There were a lot of hushed voices and whispers of suspicion about. I could not help feeling, whatever preliminary nature the inquest possessed, it felt more like a courtroom trial in which the guilty party could be declared by the judges at any moment.

Mr. Archibald Pomeroy was sitting in the first row in front of us. If he was nervous, he certainly gave no indication that he was. It was then that I wondered about Val's adamant insistence that he had been telling the truth. I trusted Val, of course, though no one was infallible. Improbable as it was, Mr. Pomeroy might just be an actor of such skill that he was able to fool and mislead a psychic, his superficial histrionics shielding his true acting talent.

At last, the proceedings were about to begin. One of the warlocks, sporting a white goatee beard, got up from his chair and addressed the assembled guests.

"I am Judge Friedman," he said in a clearly-measured tone. "And these are my colleagues, High Priestess Esmeralda and Chief MLE Officer Coleridge. This is an inquest into the death of Mrs. Abigail Pomeroy. I am sure you have all heard of the great tragedy already, so I will keep the introductory remarks to a minimum. I would like to remind all of you that this is not a trial – and we are not here to convict or pass judgment. We are simply to conduct a preliminary investigation with the facts we have so far, to seek the truth of the matter as it were. We would therefore like to recreate the evening of Mrs. Pomeroy's death as precisely as possible."

The events of the day, as might be expected, were chaotic. I had brought a notepad with me in order to recreate the movements of the different people involved. The problem was, however, that different accounts conflicted right from the start. Two guests, one of which was Mr. Fields whom I had met at the bar on my first day and an elderly lady began quarrelling openly when presenting evidence.

"No, no, no," Mr. Fields kept saying. "I tell you, it was a quarter to five when I last saw her in the *restaurant*."

"Mr. Fields," the elderly woman said, "I am absolutely *sure* that she was downstairs in the massage parlour at exactly this time."

"That is utterly absurd," Mr. Fields continued. "It might be important to the court that…"

"We are not a court of law, Mr. Fields," the examiner reminded him, though it didn't seem to get through to him at all.

Finally, Mr. Fields had been persuaded to step down and Mr. Pomeroy was asked to relate his story of the events of the evening. He said that he had been delegating

Bruno in making repairs to a damaged bath before preparing his mother's glass of sherry, which she drank every evening at exactly nine o'clock. After giving it to the barman, he then welcomed Barry, Val, and me to the hotel and showed us to our room. Then, Mr. Archibald Pomeroy had returned to the kitchen in order to help the cook, whose assistant had quit his job a few days earlier as a result of the bombing that had almost cost Mr. Pomeroy and Bruno their lives.

The barman, Mr. Jameson, verified that account. He had been on duty behind the bar until the arrival of Mr. Pomeroy. After receiving the glass of sherry, which was always poured personally by Mr. Pomeroy, Mr. Jameson brought it up to the third floor, where Mrs. Pomeroy had her room. As usual, he knocked three times on the door and then placed the glass on the tray hanging from the wall outside of her room. He did not see her come out, though he stated that she rarely came for her glass of sherry immediately – hence the installation of the tray in the first place.

Bruno, the cook, was the last person to have actually seen Mrs. Pomeroy alive. He had been inside her room to repair her clock, though he had unfortunately failed to do so. That was around seven o'clock. Then, he made his way down to the kitchens again, since he was already running late.

Isabelle, the attractive receptionist, seemed extremely frightened by the inquest. During her account, she tripped over her own words on multiple occasions, especially when she was asked to clarify one particular point or another.

"I would like to remind you that you are not on trial," High Priestess Esmeralda said, though her forced tone suggested that she wouldn't actually mind punishing Isabelle for her lack of confidence if she could. "Continue with your account, if you please."

Isabelle hastily picked up where she had left off. She

had called on Mrs. Pomeroy a quarter past nine. Mr. Pomeroy had wanted her to give her a message in regard to the new barrier that had been set up around the house. When she failed to get an answer, she thought it better to get Mr. Pomeroy. Initially, both of them could not open the door, but Mr. Pomeroy produced a spare key from his office and opened his mother's door that way.

Finally, I was asked to give evidence, to everyone's surprise except my own, since I had received notice in the form of a letter that Mr. Pomeroy had given to me. I was called upon specifically to verify both the fact that a full glass of sherry had been outside of Mrs. Pomeroy's room when I came upstairs, and that I had seen Mr. Jameson place it there earlier at around nine o'clock.

"And you are sure that the glass of sherry was full and that it was still standing on the tray outside of Mrs. Pomeroy's room when you entered the hallway?" the warlock from the MLE asked me sharply.

"Positive, sir," I said.

Both he and the High Priestess made notes on this point.

"Thank you, Miss Sheridan," the old warlock said. "That will be all, I think. Dear me, how time flies. Thank you for your statements, I believe that will be all for today. We will resume..."

High Priestess Esmeralda leaned forward and whispered something into his ear.

"Of course. Forgive me, High Priestess," he said. "There is in fact one more witness we must ask forward, since he cannot appear tomorrow. Healer Geoffrey West, please."

I recognised him immediately as the healer who had examined Mrs. Pomeroy's body. He seemed unimpressed by the proceedings, as detached as he had been when he had been shown the body.

"Healer West," the High Priestess addressed him in her calm, authoritative manner. "Could you describe to us what was the cause of Mrs. Pomeroy's death?"

"As I have told you in written form," he said, more than a note of impatience in his voice, "the cause of death has not officially been determined. It will take at least a few more days before the Healers' Examination Board makes a final decision. That is all that can be said in the matter at present."

"Healer West," High Priestess Esmeralda said. "We are well aware of the Board's proceedings. All we ask of you is to tell us what you have learned from your examination of the body so far."

"I cannot indulge in any speculation," Mr. West insisted. "The final verdict of the…

"Might I remind you," the High Priestess said, "that this is not a trial. We do not demand anything more than your opinion based on your professional capacity. We are very much aware that it is subject to change depending on the final analysis. Nevertheless, this inquest is designed to explore *all* avenues we currently have available to us, however incomplete they may be. Now, Healer West, if you please."

Geoffrey West cleared his throat in a manner that left no doubt that he disapproved of preliminaries in any shape or form.

"As you wish, High Priestess," he said icily. "Based on the data I have *so far*, it is not unreasonable to deduce that Mrs. Pomeroy was poisoned."

A great deal of murmuring followed this statement throughout in the hall.

"Poisoned?"

"That is what I said," Healer West said.

"How was it administered?"

"Most likely in oral form," he said.

"In a liquid, perhaps?"

"That is certainly possible."

"What kind of poison was it?"

"That would be pure speculation."

"Humour us, Healer West."

He took a deep breath.

"Very well," he said. "If I were forced to hazard a guess – which I clearly am – I'd say it was of heb origin."

"Heb origin?" the wizened warlock repeated in surprise, leaning forward. "Are you sure?"

"I cannot be sure of anything at this stage, Judge Friedman," he said doggedly. "It will all be in my final report, however, I assure you. As I have said over and over again, my findings are…"

But before he could finish his sentence, the door at the far end of the hall suddenly opened wide. Instinctively, most people fell silent, turning around to see who it was.

A tall, gaunt-looking man with a grey beard and dark, penetrating eyes entered. He was wearing a long cloak that looked shabby, as though it had been worn for many years without interruption.

"There is one more statement that you should consider," the man said calmly. "And that is of Matthew Pomeroy, first-born son of the deceased."

7

There were gasps and whispers from the audience. Val and I looked at each other in surprise. What on earth was Matthew, who was the prime suspect after all, doing at the inquest? It didn't make any sense, and yet here he was, walking with a slight limp towards the three examiners.

Archibald Pomeroy, however, was on his feet. His face had gone red with repressed rage. His eyes were popping madly, while his hands were clenched into fists.

"Get out of my hotel at once," he spat. "You have no place here. I thought my father had made that clear many years ago."

"*Our* father, you mean, dear brother?" Matthew said, a smirk on his battered-looking face. "Yes, I remember well what he said to me. And believe me, it gives me no pleasure to return here. But under the present circumstances, I have no other choice."

Archibald was having none of it. His hatred clearly beyond verbal expression, he pushed up the sleeves of his frock coat and walked determinedly towards his brother. The warlocks in charge of the inquest, sensing trouble, drew their wands.

"You killed her, you swine," Archibald Pomeroy bellowed, pointing his finger at his brother.

"That's a lie!" Matthew said angrily.

"Mr. Pomeroy, please!" Judge Friedman said. "This is an inquest; not a place to be making such serious charges without any evidence."

"Evidence?" Archibald Pomeroy spat. "You want evidence? How about how he tried to blow us all up? How he wanted to destroy both me and my mother for his selfish gain?"

"What are you talking about?" Matthew barked. "Get a

grip, man. You're mad."

But Archibald had evidently moved beyond verbal communication. He stepped forward, towards his brother. And then, within a flash, he had hurled himself on top of him. Archibald's fury was matched by his brother's bitter resentment. But before either of them could strike the other, the High Priestess had flicked her wand in a sharp sideways movement, and Archibald went flying through the air, crashing into several spare chairs that had been placed at the sidelines of the proceedings.

Matthew, seeing his brother humiliated in front of a crowd, laughed.

"I'm afraid that will have to wait, dear brother," he said. "But perhaps it is best that you remain seated. For I have something quite disturbing to tell you. It relates to our mother, whom you so revere."

"You leave her out of this," Archibald snarled.

"Oh, but I can't," Matthew said, smiling sardonically. "It is vital that you should hear what I have to say. If I may?"

He turned to the witch and the two warlocks in charge of the inquest. His expression was softer now, less cruel than it had been when he had been goading his brother.

"Well," Judge Friedman said, turning to his colleagues, "this is highly irregular, I must say. Highly irregular. But we need all the facts, however unexpected they may be. You may proceed."

"I will speak frankly with you," Matthew said, with one last look of contempt at his brother. "I had no love for my mother. I had little reason to."

He moved closer, looking at the audience.

"But neither did I want her dead," he continued quietly. "We quarrelled on the day she died, it is true. I… I haven't been able to sleep since. If there is anything I can do to help at this inquest, I will do so. And I believe that certain information regarding my mother will be of the utmost importance. Information that has to be brought to the surface."

He cleared his throat briefly, as though the next sentence was hard to acknowledge in public.

"However spoilt and pampered my dear brother is, however obvious his deficiency in character and morality may be, I do not believe him capable of murdering our mother. And because I know it isn't me, either, who did the deed, I want to draw attention to another possibility, one that will provide both motive and opportunity."

He produced a crumpled letter from his coat pocket.

"This is a letter written to my mother by one of her lovers," he said.

"How dare you," Archibald hissed. "These are nothing but malicious rumours, lies!"

"A letter," Matthew continued, unfazed, "which proves that my mother was not always faithful to my father. It shows, in fact, that she was having an affair with a long-standing customer of the spa."

He took the letter and handed it to Judge Friedman.

"How did you receive this letter?" the High Priestess asked him.

Matthew Pomeroy looked at her in surprise, as though he hadn't expected to be asked such a question. His gaze slid from her to his brother, Archibald, who was standing again, watching his brother like a hawk.

"I stole it," Matthew said finally. "I am not proud of it. But that is the truth."

"And when was this?" Judge Friedman asked calmly.

"A few weeks ago," Matthew said. "I… I broke into the spa and…"

"So it was you, I knew it!" said Archibald triumphantly.

Matthew nodded his head.

"But I did not kill our mother," he said.

There was a prolonged silence during which the brothers simply stared at each other. There was no way of knowing what exactly was going on in their heads, or whether Archibald actually believed that his brother hadn't been involved in the murder.

"Why did you break into the Retreat in the first place?" Judge Friedman asked.

He hesitated for a moment.

"I... I had been meeting my mother again for some time," he said. "She kept it a secret from my brother, I think, because she was afraid that the feud would reignite."

"Right she was," Archibald said quietly, though loud enough for the first few rows to hear.

"One day," Matthew continued, "I asked her about her will. My father had cut me out of his, you must understand, leaving me with nothing. I wanted my due share as the first-born. I wanted the magical powers that she had inherited. But my mother wouldn't give me an answer. She said that she didn't have her will."

"She didn't have it?"

"That's right," said Matthew, "I didn't know then, but she had sent it to her lawyer at the time. She wanted to make some changes."

"What kind of changes?"

A sour look crept upon Matthew's face.

"Favouring me over my brother," he said. "I had no idea, of course. She refused to even speak about it, you see. Naturally, I assumed that she had put my brother's name in her will and was simply trying to head me off. But I had to make sure. So I broke into the spa to see for myself. I searched her room, but there was nothing to be found. Instead, I found that letter, tucked away in one of the drawers."

"You said the letter mentioned an affair," said Judge Friedman, picking it up in order to examine it.

"Yes," said Matthew Pomeroy. "But that is not all. The letter also mentions a child. A child of which my father knew nothing. Before she died, I confronted her with the contents of the letter. She was angry, livid beyond imagination. She told me that she had changed the will in my favour, but would now revert back to my brother because she didn't want a… a thief to inherit her powers."

Matthew Pomeroy stared at the ground, clearly fighting back tears. He didn't dare look at Archibald.

"Who was this man, do you know?" High Priestess Esmeralda asked him.

"The letter is not signed," Matthew Pomeroy said, "but you will see by the various references within that it couldn't possibly have been our father, though her lover was also a warlock. He cloaked my mother's pregnancy for as long as he could by magic, until it was time to give birth."

"What happened to the child?"

"Keeping it was out of the question, of course. In the letter, her lover states that the child is safe and has been taken care of."

The High Priestess leaned forward.

"Do you have any idea who this third child is? Did your mother tell you who it was before she died?"

Matthew Pomeroy opened his mouth to answer.

But before he could do so, the lights suddenly went out, plunging the entire room into darkness. A woman yelled.

"Who turned off the light?" Judge Friedman's voice came from the front.

"What's going on?" Val whispered.

"I don't know," I said, drawing my wand. "But something's not right. Come on, let's…"

And then, amidst the pandemonium that was ensuing, an ear-splitting explosion shook the hall. Immediately, panic gripped the hall. Shouts and cries followed as people ducked for cover or blindly stumbled over one another. Chairs went crashing to the ground as members of the audience stampeded to where they thought the exit was.

I raised my wand to the air.

"Lu..." I began.

But before I could complete the spell, I was pushed roughly to one side and then to the next as human bodies hurried past me. Then, something sharp and heavy was knocked into my back, sending me flying forwards. I fell into a pair of chairs and then to the floor, holding onto my wand for dear life.

Then, a gunshot echoed throughout the hall, followed by various cries of panic. Then, there was a thud as something unmistakably hit the floor.

My entire body still racked with pain, I rolled onto my back, pointing my wand upward, and yelled:

"Lux sphera!"

There was a crackle of electric energy, and a ball of light emitted from my wand, shooting to the ceiling. It was suddenly so bright that I had to hold my hand over my face. And yet, almost immediately, the shrieks and yells died down again.

Getting gingerly to my feet, I opened my eyes slowly. The entire room looked like a battlefield. Chairs and tables lay broken all over the place. People were lying on the ground or hugging the walls, looks of terror on their faces.

Val was standing only a few feet away from me, with Barry still safely in her arms. Strangely enough, apart from a few scratches and bruises, most of us seemed to have been left unscathed. The detonation must have been further away than I had initially assumed.

Then, I saw a body wrapped in a shabby cloak lying on the ground, quite motionless, holding a gun.

"Matthew Pomeroy…" I whispered in disbelief.

"He's shot himself," someone cried.

8

"Healer West," the High Priestess, who was closest to the body, said. "Over here."

The healer, who had been hiding behind an overturned desk, got up and hurried over.

"He's dead," he proclaimed a moment later. "Shot by this heb killing machine in his hand. Matthew Pomeroy is dead."

On hearing this, there were gasps all around the hall. Some people were in a state of frenzy and had to be calmed down by members of staff. Though to be honest, I didn't blame them. The scene before us was indeed horrible to behold.

Archibald Pomeroy, meanwhile, was trying to get a grasp on the situation by ushering the guests back upstairs in an orderly fashion. Behind him, the elderly warlocks in charge of the inquest were hurried away by the receptionist, Isabelle.

I couldn't believe that Matthew had just killed himself right under our noses. It had been a very peculiar venue for a suicide. I looked around the hall for some sign of where the explosion had occurred.

"What just happened, Amy?" said Val, a look of shock on her face as she stepped up to where I was standing. "There was an explosion, but where…"

"It was there," said Barry, whose voice was slightly shaky from the shock.

He pointed to the other side of the hall with his paw. Both Val and I turned around. The double doors that led to the kitchen had been ripped from their hinges. Beyond, the walls of the kitchen were scorched black.

"It was so loud, " said Val, still shaken, "that I thought the bomb had exploded in here."

"Yes," I said slowly. "We're lucky it didn't. The sound probably reverberated off the kitchen walls."

At that moment, Mr. Archibald Pomeroy approached us.

"Ladies, if you would please go upstairs with the other guests," he said. "I had Bruno contact the MLE right away. They should be here any minute now. Frightful business."

"But, Mr. Pomeroy, your brother…" I began.

"Dead, yes," he said, a note of genuine sadness in his voice. "It doesn't justify the horrible things he did, but it was a decent thing of him to come here tonight. I must say, I didn't expect it. Nobody did, I suppose. He was seriously sick in the mind. But for once in his life, he did his duty to his family. He tried to clear my name, even if he didn't take responsibility for his own actions. And for whatever that's worth, I won't forget that."

"Why did he…

"I don't know, Miss Sheridan," said Mr. Pomeroy, shaking his head. "Perhaps he wanted to go out with a bang. He did lead a very lonely life, you must understand. Very lonely indeed. Maybe he even felt guilt over what he had done. Yes, I think that must have got to him in the end. His ramblings were rather mad, don't you think?"

"You mean regarding the third child?" I said. "Do you think he…"

"A fabrication, of course," Mr. Pomeroy said, frowning. "Matthew always had a keen sense of imagination."

"So you really think he invented that story?" I asked.

"Yes, Miss Sheridan," he said. "Perhaps he started making them up to convince himself somehow that he was innocent. I do not know. But if there really had been another child, I certainly would have known about it, Miss Sheridan. I mean, how on earth would you hide such a fact from an entire spa, family and staff included? It's simply preposterous."

"But what about the letter?" I said.

"He probably wrote it himself," said Mr. Pomeroy, shrugging. "In any case, that is out of my hands, Miss Sheridan. I'm just glad that nobody else was seriously injured tonight, and that this whole affair is over. Now, I must insist that you go upstairs with the others. Under the present circumstances, I think it best to close the whole place down for a while. You will receive a refund the first thing in the morning."

There was nothing left to us but to follow the stream of guests upstairs.

***

Back in our room, I still felt numb. It all felt so unreal, and yet Matthew Pomeroy had just gatecrashed the inquest, told a most fantastical tale of a third child, and then shot himself shortly before revealing its identity.

"I must say," Barry said, "I agree with Mr. Pomeroy – for once, that is. His brother was clearly unhinged."

"So you don't believe there was a third child?" I said.

"Sounds like a tall tale to me," he said.

"A *third* child?" said Val. "I mean, if there was one, Mrs. Pomeroy really wasn't any old lady, was she?"

"She certainly sounds like a character," I said. "How could you hide a pregnancy without anyone noticing? Is it possible using magic?"

"Oh, there are ways of doing so," said Barry. "But it's quite advanced."

"I thought she was a heb," said Val.

"That's right," I said, frowning. "She only inherited her powers after her husband died. That must have been quite a while later."

"Another hole in that ridiculous story of his," said Barry dismissively.

"I wonder why Matthew killed himself," I said. "I mean, it was quite a show. The lights going off, then the explosion."

"Mad," Barry muttered.

"Did you see him turn off the light?" I asked.

"I didn't," said Val, "I was looking at that old warlock, Judge Friedman."

"Yes," I said. "So was I."

"Of course he turned it off himself," said Barry. "Or had someone turn it off for him. It was clearly staged, the whole thing. And he was getting some pretty pointed questions by the examiners. I don't think his story would have held up much longer."

"Lucky that nobody else got hurt," I said. "I wonder why he put the bomb in the kitchen?"

"Oh, let's leave quickly," said Val. "This is all so awful. Bombs and explosions, guns and suicides. We were supposed to be on holiday. Are you up to driving tonight, Amy?"

I hesitated briefly.

"I suppose so," I said. "But shouldn't we stay and find out why…"

"You heard Mr. Pomeroy, Amy," said Val. "The MLE is in charge now. And he's closing up the place tomorrow morning, anyway. There isn't anything else we can do. We should pack our things and leave tonight. I don't want to stay a minute longer than I have to."

"This place is doomed to get blown to bits, alright," said Barry, with his usual acute sense of self-preservation. "There's no point hanging around here. Amanda?"

"Mhh?" I said, lost in thought.

"MLE agents should be on their way by now," said Barry impatiently. "There's nothing else we can do. Let the professionals handle it from here."

"Hey, we're *almost* professional," I said, half joking. "We've had quite a lot of practice over the last year, you know."

"Do you want to die – get blown up – in the line of duty then?" said Barry.

"No, but…" I spluttered.

"I thought not," he said, smirking. "That is where I draw the line, too, as a matter of fact. How am I supposed to regain my eyesight when heb bombs are going off every other minute? For all we know, that insane brother planted them all over the place before he came downstairs to the restaurant."

There was a pause.

"Amy?" asked Val tentatively. "What's wrong?"

"I… I can't leave," I said.

"What do you mean, you can't leave?" said Barry. "A bomb nearly killed all of us tonight! Are you out of your mind?"

"Maybe I am," I said stubbornly. "I want to find out who placed that bomb."

"It's obviously that heb crank!" said Barry. "It was Matthew, Amanda. There *is* no mystery in this one. He was simply a maniac who enjoyed terrorising everyone. Then, as Archibald said, he wanted to go out with a bang."

"Perhaps that's part of it," I said. "But it's not the entire story, I'm sure of it."

"Not another one of your hunches," said Barry, rolling his eyes. "Amanda, please."

"Not a hunch," I protested. "It's… it's… Don't you think it's awfully strange that Matthew kills himself just moments before he wanted to reveal who Mrs. Pomeroy's third child was?"

"A red herring, planted deliberately," said Barry bluntly. "That lunatic has had us running around in mental circles for days. Selling his house and going into hiding, only to make a dramatic entrance at the inquest. All the evidence points to Matthew Pomeroy. I'm sure he knew that, too. I must say, I find Mr. Pomeroy rather naïve to believe that his brother had nothing to do with his mother's death. Matthew clearly did it, then came here to commit suicide.

A last, desperate attempt to convince us that he is innocent."

"Why invent the story with the third child, then?" I asked.

Barry threw up his paws in exasperation.

"Don't ask me to explain everything that went on in that sick mind of his. Perhaps he *wants* us all to be brooding about that stupid little tale of his. Maybe he took pleasure in the thought that we'd be trying to solve his stupid little made-up mystery. I'm sure that, once the MLE have examined that letter, they'll expose it as the forgery it clearly is."

"What do you think, Val?" I said, looking for some support.

"Amy, I... I don't know anymore," she said. "I admit that some of the things don't make sense but... but maybe we should let the MLE do its job, just for once. That is what they're there for, isn't it?"

"You, too, Brutus?" I fumed. "Fine. Then go back to Fickleton House. I'm staying put until this thing is solved."

Yet neither Barry nor Val moved an inch.

"You know we're not going to leave you in this hellhole," said Val. "You should know us better than that."

I smiled reluctantly.

"I'm sorry, I didn't mean it like that," I said.

I paced up and down for a while in silence, thinking.

"Barry, how long do you think the MLE will need to get here?" I asked finally.

"They'll certainly be downstairs by now," he said. "They're slow, but not that slow. A bombing in a magical establishment such as this will certainly grab their attention, even if the death of a heb isn't strictly their business."

"How would they proceed in such a case?" I asked. "Do you know?"

"Well," said Barry, slightly nonplussed by my line of questions, "I suppose they'll secure the premises first.

That's always the main priority. Make sure there aren't any more explosives."

"Would they conduct an analysis of the crime scene yet?" I asked.

"Only a very preliminary one," said Barry. "It's past midnight already. The specialists will probably arrive first thing in the morning. There aren't many who are versed in heb killing devices, you know."

"I see," I said slowly.

"We won't be able to poke around the crime scene, if that's what you're thinking," said Barry. "They're bound to have put officers there."

"That's right," said Val. "They'd simply send us back up here again. I don't think they care much for private investigators."

"Yes," I said slowly. "And all the guests will probably leave the first thing in the morning, too. If they haven't already done so, that is."

"But I don't see the point in any of this," said Barry. "What does this all matter? Let's pack our things and get out of here."

"Don't you want to catch the killer, Barry?"

"Well, theoretically yes," he spluttered. "Of course I do. If there's a chance, of course. But he's dead, Amanda. He killed himself tonight."

"I'm not so sure," I said. "If Matthew wanted to commit suicide, why the business with the explosives?"

"I tell you, Matthew was some sort of pyromaniac," said Barry. "He tried to blow up his brother before. Violence for violence's sake. There's no solving these cases in the usual manner. There is no mystery, but rather purely psychological. They're random, no motive but cruelty."

"Or," I said thoughtfully, "inheritance is the motive."

"Mr. Pomeroy, you mean?" asked Val doubtfully.

"No," I said. "The third child."

Barry took a deep breath.

"Even if I grant you that," Barry said, holding up both

paws, "Matthew Pomeroy was the only one who knew who the third child was. Now that he's dead, we don't know what he or she even looks like. It could be almost anybody."

Val nodded her head sadly.

"I'm sorry, Amy," she said. "But Barry's right. I mean, how old was Mrs. Pomeroy? In her late sixties or something? The child could be anywhere up to middle age. That's about half the spa. Now, if we knew how old Mrs. Pomeroy was at the time, that would be a start. Whether she was young and beautiful, or whether it was her last chance at another child with this lover."

"We know nothing, Amanda," Barry hammered home his point.

"What did you just say?" I said, stopping in my tracks.

"That we don't know anything?" said Barry.

"No, I mean what you said, Val, about her being young and beautiful. I think I heard that before somewhere…"

And then, it struck me like lightning.

"I've… I've got it," I said, moving towards the door.

"Amanda, wait," said Barry, "they'll never let you downstairs now."

"I'm not going there," I said, hastily putting on a pullover. "Not to the restaurant, anyway. I'll be right back. I promise. There isn't a moment to lose. I only hope I'm not too late."

9

I tore open the door and hurried down the corridor. The lift was out of operation, probably another safety measure, so I ran down the steps as fast as I could, making for the reception.

When I arrived, a surprised-looking Isabelle was sitting behind it.

"Miss Sheridan?" she said innocently. "Whatever is the matter?"

"I need to know," I said breathlessly, "where a certain guest has his room."

"I'm sorry," she said. "But I can't provide you with that information. We take our guests' privacy very seriously, you see, and…"

"Gratus!"

I had hit her with the spell before she could speak any further. Leaning forward, I made sure that we couldn't be overheard by anyone.

"I need to know where Mr. Fields has his room, Isabelle," I said.

A dazed look on her face, she mechanically opened a folder lying on her desk and thumbed through it.

"Mr. Fields has his room in 304," she said.

"Thank you," I said.

Without a moment to lose, I jogged down the hallway again and scaled the stairs to the third floor. Mr. Fields had a small room, tucked between the stairs and the elevators, that could easily be missed, yet it was close to Mrs. Pomeroy's room.

Panting slightly, I knocked on the door as loudly as I could, knowing that Mr. Fields was quite deaf. After a moment, I heard a wheeze behind the door, as though Mr. Fields was lifting himself from a chair, and slow footsteps.

The door opened.

Mr. Fields – wearing an old-fashioned nightgown and matching cap – looked at me with a blank face. He looked much changed, somehow. The cheery, albeit vacant smile lingered on his face no more. His eyes were bloodshot, and there were red patches on his eyelids.

"I didn't order room service, young lady," he said, in a morose tone of voice. "But thank you, all the same. Goodnight."

"Mr. Fields," I said quickly. "It's Amanda. Amanda Sheridan. We talked briefly at the bar. Do you remember?"

"The bar?" he said, trying to remember. "Oh, yes. How foolish of me. Yes, I do recognise your face now. What is it I can do for you, Miss Sherbert?"

"I need to talk to you, Mr. Fields," I said. "I know it's rather late, but I'm afraid it's rather urgent."

"Urgent?" he said, as though the entire concept mystified him completely.

"Yes," I said. "A matter of life and death, perhaps."

"Dear me," he said, standing aside. "If it's that serious, I suppose you'd better come in. I hope you don't mind if I don't change into more suitable clothes, I'm not feeling too well. In fact, recent… developments have shaken me quite a bit."

"Thank you, Mr. Fields," I said, stepping into his room.

It was furnished with the bare necessities. There was a narrow bed and a cupboard on one side, with a table and two chairs squeezed in on the other.

"Please, have a seat," he said. "Now, what is it you wanted to ask me?"

"It's about Mrs. Pomeroy," I said. "You've heard the news, I take it?"

"Awful, awful," he muttered.

He stared down at the table, clearly fighting back tears that were on their way. He cleared his throat uncomfortably.

"You knew her well, didn't you?" I asked.

He nodded his head.

"Yes," he said quietly. "I knew Abigail for the best part of forty years. She was a wonderful woman, you know. Very beautiful. We were all very envious of Pomeroy senior. He was a very lucky man."

"Yes," I said. "Mr. Fields, were you down at the inquest tonight – in the restaurant, I mean?"

"Lord, no," he said. "No, those things just upset me. What good will it do? She's gone, and nothing will bring her back."

"Did someone tell you what happened downstairs? That Archibald Pomeroy's brother came, and that there was an explosion?"

"Yes," Mr. Fields said, a vacant expression on his face again. "That young receptionist came to my room and told me that there had been an accident. She told me that I had to leave first thing in the morning. But she needn't have bothered. I was going to do that, anyway. There is no reason for me to stay here any longer."

"Did she mention that Matthew Pomeroy – Archibald's brother – shot himself?"

"I… I cannot remember," he said, frowning. "She might have done. But between you and me, my dear, I am not surprised. That boy gave Abigail a lot of trouble, you know. From the very day he was born. He was a brooder with a nasty temper."

"Before his death, Matthew mentioned something about Mrs. Pomeroy," I said. "Something about a child…"

"It wasn't her fault, you know," Mr. Fields said. "She was a wonderful mother. Archibald turned out alright. But Matthew, well, I think he took a lot after his father."

"Yes," I said. "But tonight, Matthew mentioned something about another child – a third child. Do you know anything about that?"

"A… third child?" Mr. Fields asked. "Why, I don't know what you mean."

He answered just a little too quickly for me to believe

him.

"Please, Mr. Fields," I said. "I am only asking you because this is a life and death situation. The accident tonight – well, I don't think it was an accident. I think Abigail was murdered, and so was Matthew."

"Murdered?" Mr. Fields said, horrified.

"That's right," I said. "I need to know if Abigail had another child. You do know she had another child, don't you, Mr. Fields?"

He looked away, shaking his head emphatically.

"I don't know what you are talking about," he said weakly.

"Are you the father of that child, Mr. Fields?"

He turned around, looking at me with his mouth open, unable to speak another word. He moved his lips, but no sound would come out. Instead, a solitary tear trickled down his crinkly cheek.

"You loved her, didn't you, Mr. Fields?"

He nodded.

"Did you father her third child?"

He stared at me, then whispered:

"It was only once."

He was shaking, so I put my hand on his arm.

"Mr. Fields," I said. "Please, there is no need to feel ashamed. I am not here to judge you. All I want to do is solve her murder, as well as what I believe to be the murder of her son. I want to know the truth of what happened to them."

"Yes," he croaked, though he was regaining strength, "she would certainly want that. You are right. I will tell you the whole story."

He produced a handkerchief from his pocket and wiped away the tears.

"You must understand that her marriage was not a happy one," he said. "That does not justify what we did. But by a cruel twist of fate, I got to know her the day *after* her wedding. She was the most beautiful creature I had ever set eyes upon. I was in middle age by then, a little younger than Pomeroy senior, who ran this place at the time.

"The moment we met, there was a spark. And that spark could never be extinguished, though we tried to do so many times. I stopped coming to the Holiday Resort for a while, though somehow – through mutual friends or by sheer chance – we ran across each other every once in a while.

"The rules were a lot stricter than today, you know, especially in the magical community, which is a lot smaller. People gossiped all the time. A divorce was akin to being ostracised. They said that Abigail and her husband quarrelled a lot, a fact that I had witnessed myself often enough. The birth of first Matthew and then Archibald changed nothing. They remained a miserable couple. And I remained miserable too, for as long as Abigail walked the earth, I knew that I could never marry another woman.

"We tried to resist temptation. And we did, for many years. I was not one to go behind the backs of my fellow warlocks. Or at least that is what I thought. But Pomeroy senior had a keen business sense. He went on prolonged business trips, mostly to America, in order to set up more spas.

"It was my fault, of course. I tempted her. I came back here every year, you see. I couldn't help it. A brief conversation with her plunged me into days of dreaming. And the longer her husband was gone, the more real those dreams seemed to become. We met in secret. We convinced ourselves that it was possible, that we could get away with it. Finally… finally, we could resist no longer."

"And that was when she became pregnant with the third child?" I asked. "Your child?"

He nodded his head.

"Yes," he said. "It is… difficult to explain today in what sort of a position that put Abigail. Adultery was still taken very seriously in the magical community at the time, though they had abolished the more barbaric punishments. But it would have been a scandal, ruined her good name. The divorce proceedings would have most certainly given her husband complete custody of her children. And though she loved me, she could not abandon her two boys. I tried to convince her to run away with me, taking Matthew and Archibald with us, but it would have meant a life as outcasts, as fugitives from the law in some remote part of the world.

"In other words, we had no way out. At that time, I was staying at the spa permanently, pretending that I had suffered from overwork and needed a prolonged recuperation. I cast the spell each day that shielded her pregnancy from the staff and the guests, hiding it even from her own children. In the later stages, she feigned an illness, too. And then, she gave birth to our child.

"It was the best and at the same time the worst day of my life. I wanted to see the babe immediately, but her husband had returned ahead of schedule. He quickly discovered what was going on, for he knew that the child couldn't possibly have been his own. He took away the child, handing it over to an orphanage. A heb orphanage. That was all we knew. I searched and searched for the child, both here and abroad, but I could not find it."

"That's… that's terrible," I said, shaken by the story that Mr. Fields had just told. "Did you ever find it?"

He shook his head.

"No," he said. "Abigail tried, as well."

"Did you stay in contact with her after… after her husband discovered what was going on?"

"It was impossible," he said. "He threatened to throw her out and start divorce proceedings if she ever met or even talked with me again. He had her watched at all times."

"But after his death, you could see her again," I said.

Tears formed in his eyes once again.

"Yes," he said. "We had waited for one another for so

long. And finally, we could be together again. I took this room on a permanent basis, just a few doors down from her quarters. And then... and then..."

Mr. Fields, unable to hold back any longer, burst into tears, crying uncontrollably, shaking from head to foot as the thought of Abigail's death became real.

"I'm so sorry," I said, placing my hands on his.

"She's gone now," he croaked. "M-murdered, if what you say is true. Y-you make sure you find whoever did this. She deserves at least that, after all she had to endure in her life."

"I promise, Mr. Fields," I said. "You can count on me."

10

"A fine little tale you have there, Amanda," said Barry, after I had finished relating what Mr. Fields had revealed to me. "But I fail to see the relevance to the case."

"But don't you see?" I said, knowing that Barry was just trying to avoid having to admit that he was wrong. "It means that Matthew was right. There was a third child."

"I still don't understand," said Val, frowning.

"So the lunatic was right on something," said Barry dismissively. "Even if that letter he produced is genuine, I still don't see how this changes anything."

"It opens up new possibilities," I said. "There is now another person with a clear motive. Inheritance."

"Archibald has the same motive," said Barry.

"But Val has already established that it is very unlikely that it is him," I said.

"What exactly would this third child inherit?" asked Val.

"Well, there's the spa, for one," I said. "An establishment like this is both popular and lucrative. But, more importantly, don't forget the rest of the inheritance. Magic."

"Of course," said Barry, "The magic powers of the Pomeroy senior were transferred to Mrs. Pomeroy. With her death, they now reside with Archibald. That's whom she put in her will."

"Wait a minute," I said. "Remember Archibald told us that there had been an attempt on his life with dynamite? He said that he thought it was his brother Matthew. But what if it wasn't?"

"You think that the third child planned to murder the entire family?" asked Val, horrified. "Including his or her own mother?"

"Yes," I said. "And Matthew's suicide must have been staged tonight to throw us off the scent."

"But then," Val said, "Mr. Pomeroy is in danger."

"Yes," I said. "Whoever is the third child is most definitely going to try and kill Archibald. Then the spa and the magical powers will all fall into the hands of the last remaining sibling. The unknown sibling. And if I'm correct, he or she will be impatient to inherit."

***

We exited our room as quietly as possible. We had been to Archibald's office before, on the second floor, not too long ago, so we knew the way. Luckily, the corridors were completely deserted. Most of the guests had presumably left by now.

We reached the door, and I knocked gently three times upon it.

After a brief fumbling of papers, there was a curt 'come in' from inside. Once more, Archibald Pomeroy was sitting at his desk. He looked tired, as though he had run a marathon. His face was as white as ever, while large bags had formed under his eyes.

"Miss Sheridan," he said. "This is rather unexpected. What can I do for you?"

"It's not what you can do for me," I said, making sure to close the door firmly behind me, "but rather the reverse, Mr. Pomeroy. We think that someone might try to make an attempt on your life."

"But my brother is dead," he said. "I have nothing to fear anymore. It's over, Miss Sheridan."

"We don't think that's correct, Mr. Pomeroy," I said. "We don't believe that your brother was responsible for your mother's death. Or that he planted the bomb that nearly killed you."

He frowned at me in disbelief.

"He was always a good actor, my brother," he said.

"My mother wouldn't believe it either, despite all the indications to the contrary. And look where it got her. But she did realise her mistake at the very end. She changed her will in my favour. Lord knows what he had done if he had inherited her magical powers."

"Perhaps," I said. "But there was no reason for him to come here tonight."

"I told you before," said Mr. Pomeroy. "He clearly wanted to make a dramatic exit. A planned suicide, that's all it was. I was surprised that he cleared my name, I grant you that. But it doesn't change the fact that my brother was a very sick man."

"He was trying to tell us something at the end, Mr. Pomeroy," Val said. "Please, Mr. Pomeroy, we think you're in serious danger. Someone might be in the hotel right now, trying to get to you."

"And what do they want with me?" he said, a look of disbelief on his face.

"There is good reason to believe," said Barry earnestly, "that whoever is behind this has systematically killed your entire family. You are the last in line. Therefore, it is reasonable to assume that it is the inheritance they are after."

"But," Mr. Pomeroy spluttered. "That's preposterous. There's nothing much to inherit. The spa isn't going too well, I'm afraid to say. This is strictly between us, mind you. Who would murder for a load of debt?"

"Perhaps," Barry said, "it is not the spa they are after."

"What else is there?" he said.

"Your magic powers," said Barry.

"I don't have any magic powers," he said bluntly.

"If you are the sole beneficiary in your mother's will, which I believe you are after she changed it at the last moment, then you certainly do. Have you tried?"

"Why, no, I haven't," he said. "Never wanted anything to do with the ghastly art. I leave that sort of thing to Bruno."

"We will have time for that later," I said. "Right now, we have to protect you."

"But protect me from what? Whom?" he asked, a note of panic in his voice.

"Your mother's third child," I said. "The one Matthew mentioned before he collapsed."

"But that was clearly a pack of lies," he said. "He hated our mother for not standing up for him. He probably wrote that letter himself."

"But what if he didn't?" I asked. "What if the letter is genuine and there was a third child? Think, Mr. Pomeroy. All the peculiar circumstances of the last few weeks make perfect sense. The poisoning of your mother. The attempts on your life. The death of your brother tonight. Somebody is clearly trying to eradicate your family."

Mr. Pomeroy still looked unconvinced. I had initially wanted to keep Mr. Fields out of the conversation. He had told me his account in confidence. And, after all, it was the fact that a third child existed that was important, not necessarily the father. Now, however, I had no choice. Mr. Pomeroy would not be convinced otherwise.

"Mr. Pomeroy," I said, "the third child is a fact. I spoke to the father tonight."

"Nonsense," Mr. Pomeroy said.

"I'm afraid it isn't," I said.

"Who is this alleged father, then?"

I hesitated for a moment.

"It's Mr. Fields. He told me everything tonight. How he and your mother were lovers. And how your father had given the child away when he discovered the truth."

Mr. Pomeroy gaped at me. I could see that he didn't want to believe it, that he had settled for Matthew, his hated brother, as the culprit. Though terrible, it had also been a comforting narrative, since the perpetrator was dead.

"But…" he spluttered. "Fields, you say?"

"That's right," I said. "I believe he visited your mother

quite often after your father died?"

Gradually, the horrible truth of the matter began to dawn on Mr. Archibald Pomeroy. The little colour still remaining drained from his cheeks. He had the look of a marked man, a hunted man.

"You really believe that, Miss Sheridan?" he asked, a look of horror on his face.

"I am almost certain," I said. "You're in very grave danger. Whoever is behind it will be eager to accomplish his or her task. Now more than ever. They're very close to achieving their goal. You are the only person still standing in their way."

"But who on earth would do such a thing?" he said. "I… I can't believe that I have another sibling… but if I do, it could be anyone."

I hesitated briefly.

"It is most likely someone close by," I said. "Someone who is here on a regular basis. After all, they needed to know the layout of the place in order to place the explosive at exactly the right spot."

"You mean, it's one of the guests? One of the regulars?" he said.

"That is certainly possible," I said. "But I believe it has to be someone even closer than that. Someone who can access all areas of the spa without arousing any suspicion. It would have to be someone with access to your mother's quarters, for instance."

"You don't mean you suspect one of my staff of… of…"

I nodded.

"I can't be sure, of course," I said. "But it is the most reasonable scenario. Mr. Pomeroy, I want you to think carefully. Has there been a member of staff who has been acting out of the ordinary lately?"

Mr. Pomeroy thought about it for a moment.

"Why, no. I can't think of anyone."

"Have there been any recent additions to your staff?"

Barry asked shrewdly.

"Well," he said, scratching his neck, "quite a number, in fact. I've had to let go of a few members of staff. Too expensive, you see. I had to get in some younger, less experienced people."

"And of those recent additions," Barry asked, "who would have had access to your mother's quarters?"

"Well," said Mr. Pomeroy, thinking. "There's Isabelle, the receptionist, she's been here a month, I think. My mother always said she looked a little like her when she was younger. Isabelle occasionally did some shopping for her. You know, packet of crisps, that sort of thing. Then there's Jameson, the barman. I got him a few weeks before Isabelle. I had him bring up the drinks for my mother, mostly. And then there's Bruno, the cook and general magical handyman. I think he's been with us for three months. My mother didn't like him particularly. Although, come to think of it, I *do* remember that she asked him to repair her magical clock shortly before she died. But surely, Miss Sheridan, you don't think…"

"At the moment," I said, "all we should care about is getting you out of here. You must leave the spa immediately. If you stay, there's no way of guaranteeing your safety."

"Believe me, Miss Sheridan," he said bitterly. "After what happened tonight, I have no intention of staying. I'm going to sell the place and…"

But before he could finish his sentence, Val held up a hand and whispered:

"I think there's somebody coming."

We all fell silent immediately, listening.

Val was right. Footsteps were clearly audible, slowly ascending the staircase outside. We waited, holding our breaths. Had they heard us talking to Mr. Pomeroy?

Then, there was a knock at the door.

Once.

Twice.

Three times.

Mr. Pomeroy looked anxiously at the door and then at me. I nodded. He cleared his throat.

"Yes?" he said nervously.

The door slowly creaked open. I gripped my wand inside my pocket with a trembling hand. I would be able to draw it at the first sign of trouble.

The door swung open. In the doorway stood Isabelle, the pretty receptionist. Now, however, her blonde hair was untidy. She was holding a handbag close to her left thigh.

"Oh, hello," she said, looking at Val and me in surprise. "I didn't realise you had guests up here, Mr. Pomeroy. I'd better come back later."

"No, no, that's quite alright" Mr. Pomeroy said, though his tone was full of suspicion. "What is it you want, Isabelle?"

She moved uncomfortably on the spot.

"I… I came to see whether everything was alright, Mr. Pomeroy," she said. "I know how much tonight's events must have upset you. I was worried about you."

"That is very kind of you, Isabelle," he said, with a sideward glance at me. "My brother's death has… affected me deeply, I cannot deny that. I'll be forced to take certain actions as a result."

"Actions?" she asked innocently. "But whatever do you mean, Mr. Pomeroy?"

"I mean," he said, "that I will be leaving this place for good. Too many deaths. Too much family. I'm selling the place, once and for all."

"But sir, you can't do that…"

"It's my last word," he said adamantly. "No, I'm serious about this, Isabelle. I'm sick of this place."

"When will you be leaving?" she asked.

"Tomorrow, I think," he said. "First thing in the morning, in fact. Yes, better make a fresh start of it. There's no time point spending any more time in this ghastly place than I have to."

"I'm sorry you feel that way, Mr. Pomeroy," Isabelle said.

"Tell Jameson," he continued, "that I want two bottles of port ready for my departure tomorrow. Oh, and I want you to talk to Bruno, too. I'll have a list of things I want him to pack for me in the morning."

"I will do that, Mr. Pomeroy," she said. "I'll inform them straight away."

"That will be all," he said. "Goodnight, Isabelle."

She looked at Val and me one last time. Then, she turned to Mr. Pomeroy again.

"Goodnight, sir."

***

Though Mr. Pomeroy had been quite serious about his orders for his departure the next day, a plan was beginning to form in my mind. Our three remaining suspects had all been given the information that Mr. Pomeroy would be leaving the first thing in the morning to an unknown location. Therefore, it was the last opportunity for the killer to strike and complete the task.

In other words, it was the perfect trap. Mr. Pomeroy was, however, not eager to play the bait.

"But I'd be a sitting duck!" he protested. "I can't just sit here and wait for my would-be killer to arrive."

"Don't you wish to avenge your mother's death?" Barry said coldly. "Don't you want her murderer caught?"

"Why, of course I do," Mr. Pomeroy spluttered. "But I didn't know that it'd involve… Oughtn't we wait for the MLE to start its investigation."

"I'm afraid, Mr. Pomeroy," Barry said, "that by the time the MLE starts investigating the case, the killer will have had ample opportunity to make an attempt on your life."

"Fine," he said, still quivering slightly. "I see that I have no choice. My life is in your hands, Miss Sheridan. What exactly do you want me to do?"

***

Mr. Pomeroy's bedroom was next to his office. By a quarter to midnight, Val, Barry, and I had positioned ourselves so that we couldn't immediately be seen once the door to the bedroom had been opened. I had my wand at the ready. All three suspects now knew that Mr. Pomeroy was going to leave the first thing in the morning. Therefore, tonight would be the perfect opportunity to complete the deed.

And now, the minutes crept by slowly as we waited in the darkness, crouched uncomfortably behind the door, ears pricked for any sound from outside. Mr. Pomeroy lay in bed, his sheets pulled up to his nose, though his eyes darted from the door to the window at regular intervals. He did not like playing the bait. And to be frank, I didn't blame him. But, as all other methods of catching the killer had not come to fruition, it was our last remaining chance.

"I think I'm getting a cramp," said Val miserably.

"At least you can see something," said Barry, who had positioned himself beneath the bed, facing the door.

"Not so loud," I said, shifting uncomfortably on the ground. "We don't want to scare them away."

The minutes passed by in an agonisingly slow fashion. The only sound remaining was the shallow breathing of Mr. Pomeroy.

Midnight came and went, then 1 o'clock. It must have around 2 a.m. when I noticed that I was getting dangerously drowsy. I also had to nudge Val in the ribs a couple of times to prevent her from falling asleep.

Had I been wrong all along? Though I still couldn't quite believe it, I began to reconsider what Barry had said earlier. Perhaps there wasn't always a mystery to be solved, a case to be cracked. After all, you could read about the most horrible yet utterly senseless crimes in the newspaper every day. Had I simply been unwilling to consider that it had been Matthew all along because the solution would have been too unsatisfying?

Still waiting in the darkness, my mind began to revisit the peculiar details of the case, and how they had all pointed to Matthew from the start.

But just as I had almost convinced myself that the entire enterprise of setting up Mr. Pomeroy as bait was foolish, there was the slightest of sounds from the landing outside. Was someone creeping along it?

Then, a door creaked open. It was the door to Mr. Pomeroy's office. There were soft footsteps just beyond. They were coming nearer to the bedroom.

I held my breath, for fear that my pounding heart would give me away. Barry must have heard it too, because he turned his head so that his little feline ears could take in every sound from beyond the door. Mr. Pomeroy, meanwhile, was still valiantly playing his role, pretending to be asleep, though in fact he was now holding his breath in silent terror.

The footsteps were close and clearly audible. They were soft, perhaps those of a woman or a light-footed male. I was sure that they were standing right outside of the bedroom door, waiting. I didn't dare move, though I held my wand so that I could cast a hex the instant someone entered the room.

And then, the door to the bedroom suddenly swung open with full force. Val, taken totally by surprise, was knocked over sideways. She collided with me, sending my and flying through the air and out of sight.

Mr. Pomeroy, sensing the plan was going horribly wrong, hastened to turn on the bedside lamp, but a harsh voice prevented him from doing so.

"Leave it off."

It was Jameson, the barman.

Supporting my throbbing temple, I tried to regain focus. Val clutched my arm in terror.

"He's got a gun," she whispered. "Amy, hex him. Quick!"

I fumbled desperately on the ground to find it, but I couldn't find it.

"Hold it, ladies," Jameson said.

By the little light that the moon provided, I could see that he had stepped on something in front of him. Continuing to cover us with his revolver, Jameson bent down to retrieve it.

"And what do we have here?" he sneered. "A wand. Thank you, Miss Sheridan. That is very considerate of you. I'm sure it will serve me well once I have become a warlock."

"You!" I exclaimed.

"Yes, me," said Jameson softly.

"You're the third child," Val whispered.

"Indeed," he said, carefully closing the door behind him. "And before long, I daresay I will be an only child. I cannot tell you how much I relish that thought."

"You killed your own mother…" I said, thinking that Barry had been right all along. "You're out of your mind. Insane."

"Am I?" he said, laughing. "What loyalty do I owe to the woman who abandoned me the moment I was born? What kind of mother is that, I ask you? But I took my revenge eventually. It took me years to find out who she was. And then, I came here."

"And you tried to frame Matthew," said Val.

"Yes," he said. "It was quite fortunate that nobody liked him, you know. Very fortunate indeed. I tried to blow him up in his own house, but he got suspicious in the end. What a pity he committed suicide tonight."

"How did you do it?" I asked. "You can't have expected him to come to the inquest, surely?"

"Ingenuous, wasn't it?" Jameson said, a cruel smile on his face. "Yes, that took some quick thinking and a strong nervous system. But I must admit, seeing that old fool come to the inquest was quite a shock. I had assumed he had run away, as he usually did from everything else in his miserable life. But being a barman has its perks, you know. Nobody noticed me as I slipped upstairs, returning to the kitchen shortly afterwards. The rest was simply opportune timing."

"And you shot him and placed the gun in his own hand?" I said.

"Yes," he said. "It would allay suspicions for the moment. And once the truth is discovered, I will be long gone. With the powers of magic, nobody will ever be able to find me. And all I have to do is to kill my dear half-brother here. Now, Archie, it is time to say goodbye."

He raised his gun and was just about to shoot when Barry, still undetected by Jameson, launched himself forward with a ferocity only a true cat could summon. Though Barry was still blind for the most part, he had had ample time to approximate Jameson's position.

Jameson fired, yet the gun was yanked downward at the last minute as Barry's claws sunk painfully into his arm. That gave Val and me the valuable seconds we needed.

With one loud cry, Val launched herself at Jameson. He yelled as all the air was knocked out his lungs. The gun went flying out of his hand. Val was in the struggle of her life, yet Jameson was recovering quickly.

I needed my wand. Dropping on all fours, I scampered wildly across the floor, hands outstretched, blindly feeling for any sign of my wand or the gun. And yet, I couldn't find either.

Mr. Pomeroy, meanwhile, was still in some sort of mental freeze, for he hadn't moved an inch during the entire time. His face was frozen in panic, and all he could do was watch the scene before him, his mouth open, his eyes popping.

And then, my fingers finally made contact with the tip of the wand. It was lying beneath Mr. Pomeroy's bed.

"Amy, help!" Val screamed.

My fingertips were very close. They were touching the handle of the wand. Stretching my body as far as it would go, I finally grasped it.

"He's getting the gun," Barry yelled. "Stop him!"

There was no time to lose. I withdrew from underneath the bed as fast as I could, getting to my feet again.

Barry, Val, and Jameson were still fiercely interlocked in a wild melee. But with the energy of the cornered animal, Jameson had managed to get the upper hand.

"Val, watch out!" I shouted, trying to get a clear shot at Jameson.

Val, who was trying to prevent Jameson from retrieving the gun that lay on the floor just beneath them, couldn't hold on for much longer. With one last desperate explosion of fury, Jameson hurled Val backwards, sending her crashing into the door behind her.

Barry was blindly scratching and biting Jameson's ankle, but couldn't do much else on his own. For one brief moment, the path was free for Jameson. The gun lay only a few feet away.

"Watch out, he's going for the gun!" Val yelled, pointing at it on the floor.

Jameson dived. But I was ready for him. I now had a clear shot. Pointing my wand at him, I cried:

"Frigus!"

The body-freezing charm hit Jameson square on the chest. His hand still outstretched like a statue, he keeled over on the spot and hit the ground with a crack. He was unable to move an inch.

My heart still beating furiously, I helped Val to her feet. Barry was limping, but seemed quite pleased with himself.

I turned around to Mr. Pomeroy, who was still lying in bed, bedsheets drawn up to his fearful eyes. He hadn't dared move an inch during the fight. He was still staring at Jameson in disbelief, unable to comprehend that his own barman had just tried to kill him.

"You're safe now, Mr. Pomeroy," I said. "There

nothing more to worry about."

11

Several hours later, we were back at Fickleton House again. Jameson had been handed over to the MLE, charged with multiple counts of murder and attempted murder.

In his room, they had discovered further evidence that led them to believe that he had been experimenting with poisonous concoctions of his own making. The trial was expected to begin the following month. With the evidence discovered, along with the testimony of Mr. Pomeroy, Val, Barry, and myself, there was little reason to believe that Jameson would not be convicted.

After the events at the Magical Holiday Retreat, we were all glad to return to the peace and tranquillity of Fickleton House. Mrs. Faversham had brought us tea. And I had started a magical fire in the fireplace. Its crackling flames had sent Barry, who was sitting on my lap, to sleep almost immediately.

"There's no place like Fickleton House, is there?" I said, gazing at the walls of the sitting room with affection.

"Perhaps we should spend our holidays here next time," said Val, tucking into a scone with cream on top. "Trouble seems to find us whenever we got places."

"Yes," I said. "That would certainly be better for Barry's blood pressure."

"Amy," said Val, "I still don't understand how Jameson did it. I mean, how he killed Mrs. Pomeroy. You saw him place the glass of brandy outside of the room and walk away again. She never touched it."

"That's right," I said. "Jameson's plan was to put us off the scent. It was quite clever. You see, Jameson took *two* glasses of brandy up to Mrs. Pomeroy. Remember her magic clock had stopped working the day before? Either he sabotaged it, or he simply took advantage of the opportunity. In any case, Jameson knew that the clock didn't work. Perhaps he had learnt from Bruno that he hadn't been able to repair it. It must have seemed like the perfect opportunity for an alibi. So, he knocked an hour or so *before* the usual time and deposited the poisoned brandy on the tray outside of her room. Then, once nine o'clock hit, he delivered a second glass, knowing full well that she was already dead."

"Risky," said Val. "Someone could have seen him the first time."

"Yes," I said. "The entire thing was mad. Yet it almost worked."

"But what about the will?" Val asked. "The mother changed it right before she died, in favour of Archibald Pomeroy, didn't she?"

"Yes," I said. "At least in regard to the inheritance of her magical powers. The business was already Archibald's, of course."

"I still don't understand why she changed her mind, though," Val said, a look of bewilderment on her face. "I mean, they had kicked Matthew out of the house years ago."

"I think Mrs. Pomeroy, unlike her husband, always had had a soft spot for her older son," I said. "Perhaps she thought that he had been unfairly treated by his father. Or maybe she thought that he had been punished enough. We will likely never know exactly. In any case, the fact that Matthew *had* been the original beneficiary in her will shows that she hadn't intended Archibald to inherit both the spa and her magical powers. After she quarrelled with Matthew, however, she decided to also give the magical powers to Archibald."

"I'm not surprised," said Val, "he did look a bit unhinged to me.

"Dangerous fellow to inherit magic," Barry murmured, shifting drowsily in my lap.

"But how did that fit in with Jameson's plans?" asked Val, taking another scone from the plate in front of her.

"I don't think it affected his plan at all," I said, frowning. "As the third son, unnamed on any will, he would be last in line in any event. After the murder of his own mother, he had to remove both of his half-brothers to make sure that he would be the next – and only person – in line. I think he wanted the attention on Matthew, however, since he was an obvious suspect. And to think that he was the one who told about the family in the first place…"

"Awful business," said Barry, yawning ostentatiously.

"It's crazy what some people would do to get magic powers," said Val.

"Yes, it was horrible," I said. "But he will be brought to justice, I'm sure."

There was a pause.

"Have you read any of these letters, Amy?" said Val, trying to change the topic to something more cheerful. "The ones that came while we were away, I mean."

"No, why?" I said, with a nasty sense of foreboding.

"I think there's one from Alec," she said, a peevish grin on her face.

Alec Lavalle was a P.I. who had helped us on our first case.

"Really?" I said eagerly. "Let me see."

"It must be here somewhere," she said. "One moment."

She filed through the stack of letters next to her and handed one to me.

I tore it open and scanned the contents hastily.

"Oh dear," I said.

"What's wrong?" said Val.

"The MLE is in serious trouble," I said. "Understaffed as usual. Alec wants our help in a new case he's on."

"Really?" said Val with interest. "What kind of case?"

"It's a reconnaissance mission to a manor house up

North," I said, browsing the details again. "The MLE won't lend him any more agents, but he's sure he's on to something. He's asking us whether we'd be willing to go there undercover."

"No, no, no," said Barry, suddenly wide awake, "no more so-called 'holidays' where we get ourselves almost killed again! I won't have it."

"But this might be important," I said. "It's not like Alec to ask for help."

"But think of my hypertension," said Barry. "The vet said to reduce stress at all costs. My eyesight has barely just returned."

"I notice that's the first time you're quoting the vet in your defence," I said, grinning. "But don't worry, Alec has you covered."

"What do you mean?" Barry asked suspiciously.

I handed him the letter, pointing to a paragraph at the bottom of the page.

Barry reached for his reading glasses on the table in front of him. He put them on and, squinting slightly, held the paper to the light.

"'In regard to the mission,'" Barry read aloud, "'I perfectly understand, of course, if the Earl of Barrington is no longer able to aid us in the investigation, owing to his advanced age and serious health problems, as publicised in the *Daily Warlock* a few weeks ago.'"

Barry slammed the paper on the table.

"Why, this is an outrage," he said, fuming. "I knew that article in the *Daily Warlock* was a massive mistake from the very start! 'Advanced age', how dare he…"

"But Barry," Val began tentatively.

"No," he said, a determined look on his face, "this is the last straw. I'm coming with you. I'll prove to the magical community that there's a lot of fight left in the Earl of Barrington yet. They'll see."

"Don't worry, Barry," I said, beaming. "We'll get you a front page article after the whole thing is over. And this time we'll know what we're getting ourselves into. I mean, what could possibly go wrong?"

THE GREAT CATSBY

T.H. HUNTER

1

Lord Pembroke sat down for breakfast. As usual, he had arrived earlier than his good-for-nothing son, who liked to sleep well past midday. It was just as well, however, since they were barely on speaking terms. It was a testament to his sister's persuasive powers that Lord Pembroke and his son even acknowledged one another's existence, albeit via a brief nod of the head.

In spite – or perhaps because – of his family affairs, Lord Pembroke had always preferred to keep things as simple as possible. To get started in the morning, a cup of coffee, a croissant, and marmalade were all he required.

Carew, his long-serving butler, had placed an unusually large stack of morning post on the table. Lord Pembroke normally didn't get many letters these days, so it was his custom to read them immediately.

His sister – who had arrived for breakfast a few minutes after him – frowned upon the practice. After the many years they had been on the estate together, she was still strangely particular about such things. She preferred to pass the morning in conversation, though there had been precious little to talk about for the last few decades at least. It was peculiar how she could keep her spirits up after such a long time. But then again, Lord Pembroke thought, her marriage had simply been one of convenience. And, as fate would have it, her husband had died rather conveniently once the marriage had broken down. Unlike him, she had never known what it was like to have lost a beloved spouse.

Fighting a sudden spasm of sorrow, Lord Pembroke took the letter opener from the table and gazed at the letters in front of him. There were so many, surely some private correspondence had to be among them. But his initial hopefulness soon turned into disappointment. The letters were bills or cleverly-disguised advertisements of some sort – nothing with a personal touch.

He fought the urge to slump in his chair. More than ever, he felt like a prisoner, albeit inside a golden cage. But then, a small, grey envelope caught his eye. He must have overlooked it earlier, which was certainly easy to do. He had no high expectations, of course. And yet, something about the format told him that this could not possibly be of an official nature.

There was only his own address on it. Had it been sent anonymously? He carefully slid the letter opener along the edge. A white, folded piece of paper fell out. He straightened it on the table and began to read silently:

Lord Pembroke,

Your lavish yet purposeless lifestyle has been well publicised in the press. We do not approve. We hold the fact that you are a parasite to society to be self-evident.

As such, we feel that it is our duty to lift you of that considerable burden. Society must no longer stand for those who feed off the poor. They will be your judge, and we shall be your executioner.

It took a moment for Lord Pembroke to take in what he had just read. He quickly scanned the contents of the letter to be sure. *They will be your judge, and we shall be your executioner...* Whoever had sent the letter, they certainly meant business.

But Lord Pembroke was not a man to be intimidated. And he knew just how to deal with a threat like this.

"Carew," Lord Pembroke bellowed.

"Whatever is the matter, Alfred?" asked his sister, a bewildered look on her face.

But Lord Pembroke ignored her. He was waiting for Carew, the butler, who hurried into the room a moment later.

"Yes, sir?"

"Carew, I want you to contact the MLE."

"Of course, sir," he said. "May I ask for what purpose?"

"Tell them I want to speak to their best agent right away," said Lord Pembroke, thrusting the letter at Carew. "And get this thing out of my sight."

2

"They've done it again," Barry said dismissively, lowering the *Daily Warlock*.

"Done what, Barry?" I said vaguely, reaching for my first coffee of the day.

"Ruining the country, of course," he said, taking off his reading glasses.

I took a sip of coffee. For some reason, I hadn't slept very well, so, more than usual, it felt like the breath of life.

"Who is?" I asked, putting the cup down on its saucer again.

"The government," said Barry, in a tone that suggested that he had long ago prophesied its total and utter failure.

"Perhaps you should run for office, Barry," said Val, patting him affectionately on the head.

Barry seemed to ponder this suggestion for a moment.

"Perhaps I will one day," he said.

"Are cats admissible, then?" I said.

"I'm not a cat, Amanda," Barry said, puffing up his chest proudly, "but a warlock temporarily trapped in feline form. There is a big difference, you know."

"I've noticed," I said, winking at Val.

At that moment, Mrs. Faversham bustled into the room and brought both Val and me a full English breakfast.

"There you go," she said. "Careful, dears, the tomatoes are a little hot."

"Thank you very much, Mrs. Faversham," I said. "This looks delicious."

"Not at all," she said, smiling. "Is there anything else you would like? Oh my, what *has* he been doing to that newspaper again?"

Mrs. Faversham, of course, didn't know that Barry

wasn't really a cat. And since she was not a witch, we had thought it better to keep it that way. Otherwise, there would have been a lot of explaining to do, not to mention the breaking of magical law that swore us to secrecy.

"Oh, that's quite alright, Mrs. Faversham," I said, hastily grabbing the *Daily Warlock*. "I've read most of it, anyway."

"I've caught him before, you know, with a book in the library," she said with a puzzled look on her face. "If I didn't know any better, I'd say he was *reading* it."

She chuckled.

"Funny how the imagination can play tricks on you, isn't it?" she said. "Though he does seem to like the library best, I must say."

"Yes," I said uneasily. "He likes to snooze in there."

"Do you think he would like any more tuna?" Mrs. Faversham asked.

I looked at Barry. Meowing was certainly beneath Barry's dignity, but his unrelenting stare and the rhythmic tap of the paw clearly stated that he was still hungry.

"But perhaps it's better he doesn't," Mrs. Faversham said before I could answer. "He still *is* on his diet, poor thing. We don't want him to go blind again. What an awful experience that must have been for him."

Barry – unable to speak his mind – turned his back on Mrs. Faversham, frantically making sliding motions with his paw from his throat to his stomach.

"Yes," I said, laughing at Barry's little pantomime, "but his eyesight has returned, thank Goodness. I think a little tuna and milk should be no problem, just this once."

All three of us waited patiently for Mrs. Faversham to close the door behind her.

"That woman hasn't brought me a proper helping for weeks," Barry fumed. "On *your* orders, Amanda, if I might add."

"Doctor's orders, you mean," I said, grinning. "Anyway, it's worked, hasn't it? You've got your eyesight back."

"Sometimes," Barry said, theatrically putting his paw to his forehead, "I wonder whether the price wasn't too high. Quality of life has been reduced *drastically*. I mean, I must preserve at least a few of my creature comforts. Otherwise, what is there really to live for?"

"Yes, Barry," I said. "I'm sure having your own library and an entire wing of the house to yourself must be very difficult for you."

"Amanda…" he began, but was interrupted by a sharp knock on the door.

"Come in," I said.

Mrs. Faversham appeared at the door, followed by a ruggedly handsome man with a five-o'clock shadow. He was wearing a long coat.

"Oh, hello, Alec," I said in surprise. "I wasn't expecting you. I thought you were up North."

"Change of schedule," he said, flashing a rare smile. "Thought I'd brief you in person."

Mrs. Faversham looked suspiciously at our guest. Although he had been at Fickleton House a year ago, he had only brought trouble as far as she was concerned. I could see that her reservations about him had not changed since.

"Erm, thank you, Mrs. Faversham," I said. "It's quite alright."

She gave Alec one last look that seemed to be intended as a warning.

"I'll be in the kitchen if you need me, Miss Sheridan," she said pointedly.

After she had closed the door, I offered Alec a place at the table.

"Coffee, Alec?" Val asked, wagging the pot in front of him and almost spilling the contents.

"Don't mind if I have some," he said gratefully, sitting down next to Barry. "Haven't had a good cup in days. Just got back, in fact."

"From the mission you mentioned in your letter?" Val asked excitedly.

After our last adventure at the spa, we had received an invitation from Alec, who was a private investigator, to join one of his cases. Magical Law Enforcement was understaffed as usual, so it was up to Alec alone to solve the case.

"That's right," he said.

There was a peculiar pause at the table as we all waited for Alec to elaborate on the case. I could tell that, by habit, he was extremely cagey. I assumed that he was more used to extracting information from others than providing it himself.

"What kind of case are we talking about?" Barry said, finally breaking the silence.

"Death threats," he said. "MLE can't deal with any more cases at the moment, so they've handed the affair over to me entirely. A free hand, as it were. And I need your help in this."

"Of course," I said immediately, thrilled to be included in the investigation. "What do you want us to do?"

"I need you to infiltrate the place undercover. It's an old manor house, owned by Lord Pembroke."

"Hang on," said Barry. "Lord Pembroke, you say? But his entire estate is cursed, we can't go there!"

"Is this true, Alec?" I asked.

He nodded solemnly.

"In a manner of speaking," he said. "But it's not dangerous to outsiders."

"What kind of curse is it?"

Alec's mouth twisted into a wry smile.

"Ironically," he said, "it's something a lot of warlocks would kill for, though I can't say it brought them much happiness. The original inhabitants of the Pembroke estate are in something of a predicament. As long as they remain on the estate, they do not age. But once they leave the estate, they revert to their natural age. Since most of them are well over a hundred years old by now, you can understand that they're not too keen on doing that. It would be instant suicide."

"So they're trapped?" I asked.

"In essence, yes," said Alec, nodding. "But as long as they remain inside the barrier, the normal ageing process cannot touch them."

"It must get very lonely in there," said Val, frowning.

"Yes," said Alec. "Especially since Lord Pembroke's wife died many years ago. Before the barrier went up, of course. He's never recovered from the shock."

"But wouldn't we be trapped on the estate as well once we set foot in it?" I asked.

"No," said Alec. "The barrier took effect only for the people who were present on the estate at that particular time. Outsiders can come and go as they please. And, as far as I know, they age quite normally during and after their visits."

"So, are there any clues in regard to the threats? Do we have any suspects?"

"Not yet," said Alec, producing a folded piece of paper from his inside coat pocket. "Here is the original note Lord Pembroke received. The MLE notified me immediately. I went over and had a look around the place."

I scanned the letter as quickly as I could.

"Pretty nasty," I said, handing it to Val. "Do you think it's legitimate?"

"It's difficult to say," said Alec. "Lord Pembroke believes it is, though he refuses to have bodyguards in the house. But we've taken all sorts of other precautions. Lord Pembroke locks himself in his room every night. The butler checks on him regularly and tastes the food he eats. I've got someone guarding the grounds and monitoring the entries and exits. But as to the guilty party, we're still very much in the dark. As you might imagine, it's quite a tight-knit community over there. People don't like talking, certainly not to private investigators anyway. I need someone on the inside, someone who won't be as conspicuous. That's where you come in."

"Sounds intriguing," I said. "Val, what do you think?"

"I'm in," she said.

"Barry?"

"Since my health has recovered *in full*," Barry said haughtily, "I see no reason not to give the magical community a hand in this."

"Excellent," Alec said.

"What's our cover story?" I asked.

"I've got that all sorted out," Alec said. "Lord Pembroke's son hosts parties on a regular basis. Makes sense, I suppose, if you can't go anywhere yourself. Since it's a bit out in the sticks, up in Yorkshire, it's not uncommon for some of the guests to arrive a few days early. I've arranged everything for you through a go-between of mine, but don't mention that you know me. Otherwise, people might smell a rat. Learn as much about the family and the staff as you can."

"Do you think someone from inside the barrier is behind it?" I asked.

"Maybe," said Alec darkly. "It wouldn't be the first time a close relative turned out to be the guilty party. And I'm not making that mistake twice."

Alec was evidently thinking our very first case together, which happened over a year ago.

"More coffee?" Val asked, trying to break the rather awkward pause that followed.

"No, thanks," said Alec, getting up from his chair. "I'd better be going."

I felt like I still had a million questions.

"Wait," I said, "what will you be doing?"

"I'm going to track that letter," he said. "It came by heb mail, posted in London."

"How… how will we be able to communicate?" I asked.

"We can't directly," said Alec. "Lord Pembroke has banned all magic from the estate. Anyway, we can't risk getting caught."

"Why has he banned magic?" Val asked.

"He thinks it might destroy the barrier," said Alec. "And since that's the only thing preventing him from shrivelling up into a dried fruit within a matter of seconds, I can't say I blame him."

He pushed his chair closer to the table.

"My contact, Harriet, will call you and give you the details. She'll be guarding the place for the next week, too. If you really need to get in touch with me, you can give her a message. Don't worry, she's excellent at her job. Straight out of Merlin's College in Oxford. Very talented. Anyway, just make sure nobody sees you. The party's on Friday night. I'll meet you there."

"You… you'll be at the party?" I asked, having trouble picturing Alec in a smart tuxedo.

He smiled.

"That's right," he said. "We'll compare notes when I get there. But don't let on that you know me. Let them introduce us. Then we can talk."

"OK, Alec," I said. "We'll see you then."

3

The following week crawled by with little else to distract us. Unlike our previous cases, however, Barry was the driving force behind preparations. His brief stint of blindness, coupled with the humiliating plea for help in the *Daily Warlock* that followed it, had created a thirst to prove himself once again before the magical community.

At first, I thought that he was keen to solve the mystery of who was threatening Lord Pembroke as fast as possible. As I learned subsequently, Lord Pembroke's predicament – being stuck behind a magical field that prevented ageing but also effectively keeping him and the members of his estate prisoner   was well-known amongst witches and warlocks. Contributing in some way to the conundrum, even finding a solution for the Pembroke family to temporarily leave the premises, therefore, would garner considerable attention.

Yet I was sure that Barry, in his own mind, was planning to fry greater fish than that. A few days after Alec's visit, I caught him pouring over a book on protective charms entitled *The Wand and the Shield*. At the time, I thought nothing of it. Researching the peculiar phenomenon that enveloped the Pembroke estate seemed only natural.

Yet his keenness for the case adopted quite a different quality in the following days. Once, when I leaned over to take a closer look at what he was doing, I noticed that Barry had underlined key passages that related to the adaptation and enhancement of such charms. It was at that moment that I wondered whether he was trying to replicate the magic for his own purposes. If he was the one to mastermind how the barrier worked and how the energies could be manipulated, he would once again be seen as one of the eminent theorists of magic in the country, rather than an ancient theorist who was still suffering from the late effects of his permanent transformation into a cat.

Barry's ulterior motives notwithstanding, Val and I were looking forward to the case for different reasons. With the exception of the Wycliffe case at Warklesby's School of Magic a few months ago, we had usually stumbled upon conundrums begging to be solved either by chance or by fate. In any event, mystery had sought *us*.

The Pembroke case was a lot different in that regard. This was a request made by a private investigator who had been in the business for years. His reputation was on the line. And yet he had entrusted uncovering Lord Pembroke's problem to us. As much as I had liked toying with the idea of becoming a professional in the field myself, the Pembroke affair certainly had the potential to make or break any career, not only Barry's. And as a week of waiting drew to a close, I was increasingly hoping for the former.

***

"I just don't see why we have to use the car again," Barry moaned from the back seat as I was trying to navigate the traffic in the pouring rain.

"It's our cover story, Barry," said Val affectionately.

"Does the cover story involve getting us killed in one of these death traps? Because if it does, you can drop me off at the nearest public house."

"Barry," I said warningly, "alcohol is still off limits. Lord knows what the vet would say if he knew what you had been up to all this time."

"It was perfectly safe with the spells I invented," he said huffily.

"Right," said Val, rolling her eyes and looking at me. "So, how much longer do we have to drive?"

"I'd say another hour," I said, checking the satnav. "Alec's contact, a witch called Harriet, gave me the coordinates. She said she'd be waiting outside a village called Marrowgate."

"Is that where Lord Pembroke has his estate?" Val asked.

"I assume so," I said. "But she didn't say."

"Strange place to meet if it isn't," said Val, frowning.

"Oh, it's all part of the private investigator act," said Barry acidly from the back, "Secret meetings and mysterious go-betweens. Heb phone calls between two witches and a long drive in a metal cage."

"Don't be ridiculous, Barry," I said. "Anyway, it's better to be cautious. We don't want to give anything away. If they know we're working for Alec and Lord Pembroke, we'll be biting on granite."

***

An hour later, we finally arrived in the village of Marrowgate. Though it might have been the bad weather, I had the distinct feeling that this was a dreary, unwelcoming place. As we approached the village, rows and rows of identical rooftops appeared, with the same size front gardens and chimneys. It seemed mechanical, almost like an army of sorts.

The satnav directed us through the village and right out again.

"You have reached your destination," a smooth, female voice announced.

"This is it," I said.

"But we're in the middle of the road," said Barry. "This can't be right."

"There's a junction over there," said Val, squinting. "Look, over there, Amy."

Calling it a junction was a bit of overstatement, since it was only a muddy path that crossed the main road.

Nevertheless, it was the nearest thing to a meeting place as far as I could see – which, admittedly, wasn't very far in the pouring rain. I stopped the car on the path, though I decided to keep the engine running.

Then, there was a sudden tap on my window, and a shape emerged out of nowhere. It gave me such a shock that I nearly pressed the accelerator in panic.

"It's probably Alec's contact," said Val, noticing my jumpiness.

There was another tap on the window. I let it down just far enough to see who it was.

The face that greeted me was that of a slim woman with blonde hair in her early thirties. She was smartly dressed and was holding an umbrella. I couldn't help but feel an uncomfortable pang in my stomach. Some assistant Alec had there. My mind immediately began to wonder whether she was more than just that.

"Hello," she said, smiling. "Are you Amanda?"

"That's right," I said.

"I'm Harriet. So nice to meet you in person."

"Likewise," I said. "This is Val and this is Barry. I think you'd better get in."

I indicated the pelting rain, which didn't seem to bother her much.

"Thanks," she said cheerfully. "I'll get in the back."

Barry, I noticed, was pointedly mute with his usual complaints. Harriet closed the umbrella and then got into the car.

"Oh, hello," she said. "What a cute little cat you've got there."

"My dear woman," said Barry in as dignified a voice as was possible after being called 'cute' and 'little' in the same sentence, "I am the Earl of Barrington."

"The Earl of…" she began. "Oh, yes, of course, Alec told me about you. You're the warlock who got himself stuck in a cat's body, aren't you?"

"One of the many hazards of being an experimental

magical therianthropist," Barry said huffily.

Clearly, the conversation was not going at all the way Barry wanted it to.

"So, what's the plan?" I asked, deciding to spare Barry from further humiliating inquiries into his transformation.

"Alec told me to show you the way to Lord Pembroke's estate in person," Harriet said.

"Is it still far away, then?" asked Val.

"Not much further," said Harriet, "but it's a bit tricky to find. At least when using heb roads."

***

She directed us along a path that led into a nearby wood, which seemed to stretch for miles and miles. Progress along it was so bad that Harriet had to help the car along by magic once in a while, though luckily there were no hebs to see her do magic.

At last, we came into a clearing again. Through the heavy rain still pelting the windshield, I could make out a pair of wrought-iron gates ahead of us. Despite the miserable weather, they looked like they had been freshly polished.

"This is it," Harriet said cheerfully. "That's the entrance to the Pembroke estate."

"Good thing you came along," said Val. "I don't think we would have found it, would we, Amy?"

"No," I admitted grudgingly, "probably not."

"Glad to have helped," said Harriet pleasantly. "Well, I'd better get going."

"Aren't you coming to the estate?" asked Val.

"No, not today," she said. "Lord Pembroke knows I'm working for Alec. I'm on guard duty for another week. It would give the whole game away if they saw us arrive together. I'll be at the house on Friday, though."

"But how can you guard the whole place on your own?" asked Val. "I can't even see the house from here..."

"Air patrol," she said, grinning. "My umbrella serves as a broom, too, you see. Well, I'll see you in a few days."

All three of us chanted a goodbye in return, and Harriet ventured out into the pouring rain again. She drew out her wand and tapped her umbrella three times. It gave a small shudder, hovering next to her in mid-air. The spell looked simple enough, though I knew from experience that it was quite tricky to handle.

Harriet mounted the umbrella-turned-broom carefully and kicked off from the ground. The wind almost instantly blew her off course, though she managed to steady the umbrella before flying out of sight.

"What ghastly weather to fly in," Barry exclaimed from the back seat.

"Bit flashy, if you ask me," I said testily.

"Oh, I don't know," said Val.

"She could just use a proper broom like a normal witch," I said.

"What's got into you, Amy?" asked Val. "You're grumpier than Barry before he's had his second helping."

"I beg your pardon?" came Barry's voice from the back.

"It's nothing," I lied.

"Ever since that woman got into the car, you've been acting very strange," said Val. "You know, Amy, if I didn't know any better, I'd say you're jealous."

"Me?" I said. "Jealous of whom?"

"Her," said Val, a sly grin on her face. "I think you're feeling threatened."

"By Harriet?" I said, blinking. "Don't be ridiculous."

"Oh, no," said Barry sarcastically, "she's just a bombshell who ditched her supermodel career to use her exceptional magical abilities as a private investigator. I'm sure there's nothing to worry about."

"Yeah, thanks for the support, Barry," I said.

"Anytime."

"You don't know whether they're together, Amy," said

Val soothingly.

"Let's end the therapy session, shall we?" I said moodily. "And let's get on with the job."

4

Carew, Lord Pembroke's butler, was already waiting in the rain in order to carry our bags. He was a sombre, rather quiet man preserved by the magical field in his late sixties, though I assumed his real age was at least double that. After some brief introductions, he opened the gates for us.

"Welcome to the Pembroke estate," he said in a hoarse voice. "I hope your stay will be very pleasant here."

"Thank you," I said. "Where, erm, exactly is the barrier?"

"You are standing right in front of it," Carew said.

"I can't see anything," Val said, bewildered.

"The barrier is only visible to those who are affected by it," he said.

"Right," I said, "I'll just get the bags, then."

I took out my wand, planning to levitate the luggage to the main house.

"Please, Miss Sheridan," he wheezed, "the master does not approve of any kind of magic. He is quite strict on the matter."

"Oh, terribly sorry," I said, pocketing the wand again.

"This way, please," said Carew.

"Come on, Val. We'll do it the old-fashioned way."

"But I thought…"

"The bags, Val," I insisted.

Grudgingly, she picked up the nearest bag.

"How far is it to the house?" she asked Carew.

"Just under a mile," he said.

"A *mile*?" spluttered Val. "I can't carry these bags that far."

"I can have the horse and cart brought down if you wish, madam," Carew said drily.

"That's not a bad idea," said Barry, lazily gazing around

the grounds.

"I'm sure that won't be necessary," I said, staring pointedly at Val and Barry. "We don't want to cause a nuisance, *do we*?"

"Most gratifying, Miss Sheridan," Carew said, smiling weakly. "Let me close the gate behind you."

Luckily, the heavy rain had petered out and had been replaced by a mere drizzle. Crossing the invisible threshold, we lugged the bags along the gravel path that Carew had indicated. Barry trotted idly behind us, whistling tunelessly, clearly lost in thought. Val, however, wasn't happy.

"He's the butler," she whispered indignantly. "Why doesn't he carry anything?"

"He might be trapped in time, Val, but he's not immortal. A few yards with your makeup bag and he'll get a heart attack or something from overexertion. We're supposed to keep a low profile, you know. And killing the butler five minutes into the job isn't part of the plan."

"Oh, alright," she said. "But it'd better be worth it. I'm hungry."

Though I was admittedly spoilt since my inheritance, I had spent enough years in drab, soulless apartment blocks to appreciate a beautiful building when I saw it. And Lord Pembroke's manor was certainly a sight to behold. It was larger and older than Fickleton House, and the grounds around it were extensive and beautifully kept.

When we had finally reached the entrance, we waited patiently for Carew, the butler, to catch up. He ascended the steps and opened the front doors with as much of a flourish as he could muster.

"The house has three main wings," Carew said in a monotone, as though he had uttered the words many times before. "The master's quarters are located in the West wing. Family members and close friends stay in the East wing. You will be staying in the North wing, along with most of the guests who are attending the ball."

"The ball?" Val mouthed.

I shrugged my shoulders.

"Alec said it was just a party," whispered Val. "Now I wish I had brought more clothes along."

"You'll be fine, Val," I said. "Anyway, we would have needed an oxen to carry your bags."

"Very funny, Amy," she said, grimacing.

But Val seemed to have cheered up a little as a result of our banter. Barry, meanwhile, was still in his dream world. For a change, however, that meant that his sarcastic comments were limited to a bare minimum.

Carew led us into a large hallway. The wooden staircase and banisters leading upward were beautifully kept, as were the huge portraits adorning the walls – presumably of previous lords of the Pembroke estate.

Carew headed across the marble floor and through a small door tucked into a corner. On entering the house, the butler seemed to have gained his second wind. He certainly looked a lot less frail as he navigated the many corridors and doors along our path. Perhaps, I thought, his body had strengthened since moving away from the barrier's edge.

Finally, we found ourselves in a small room with wooden panelling all around it. Carew disappeared behind a desk, while we placed our luggage on the ground in order to catch our breath.

"Now, let me see," said Carew, brandishing a large folder entitled 'reservations'. "Sheridan. Ah, yes, here we are. You've booked for five nights, I see. Until Sunday. Here are the keys to your room. Unfortunately, we don't have a room with a cat flap, as you requested. But in case you come again, we can see what we can do."

Alec had obviously had some fun with the reservation. Barry scowled, but decided not to dignify the joke at his expense with a retort.

Carew, meanwhile, was running his finger in a horizontal line across the page in front of him.

"And you're in the... ah yes, the suite, an excellent choice. And it's already paid for," he said, closing the folder with a sudden snap.

Pocketing the keys, Val and I bent down to pick up our luggage again.

"Please, just leave them there," Carew said, smiling weakly. "We'll have someone carry them up to your room for you. In the meantime, I'll show you to the dining area. All meals are served there. I hope you will find it to your liking."

Carew exited his little booth and glided through the nearest door and along another corridor. Val, Barry, and I followed him. After a minute or so, we entered a large hall with a high ceiling.

There was one very long table with what had to be at least fifty chairs on either side. At the far end, a single chair – which resembled a wooden throne – headed the table. Above it was a massive portrait of a grey-haired, rather severe-looking man with an old-fashioned pencil moustache.

"That is Lord Pembroke's father," Carew said, indicating the portrait. "A great man. It is a pity that he didn't live to see his life's work realised."

"You mean, the barrier protecting the people here from ageing?" I asked.

"That is correct," Carew said. "It was Lord Pembroke's father who began the experiments that Lord Pembroke eventually completed."

Carew looked at the grandfather clock in the corner.

"It is soon time for dinner," he said. "You are very welcome to stay here while we make the preparations. Your room is on the first floor of the North wing, at the end of the corridor. If there is anything I can help you with, don't hesitate to ask me. Meanwhile, I wish you a very pleasant stay here."

"Thank you," I said. "I'm sure it will be."

Carew smiled mechanically, then bowed slightly before

vanishing through yet another door that I suspected led to the kitchens.

"Impressive," said Val, whistling softly. "They must have a lot of people here during their balls."

"Yes," I said, gazing around. "Could get a bit creepy if you're eating supper here all on your own, though."

"I don't think you're ever really alone," said Barry, smirking. "Not with big brother up there."

He pointed to the oversized portrait on the wall with his paw. I could certainly see what Barry meant. Dining daily under the stern gaze of Lord Pembroke's father was not my idea of a relaxing lunch. One could never quite shake off the feeling that one was being watched.

"I'm afraid you are under a misapprehension," a voice sounded from across the room.

Val, Barry, and I turned around in surprise. It was a young man, in his late twenties perhaps, dressed in an elegant suit. He smiled, which seemed to come easily to him, and approached us.

"The old man wasn't that bad," he said. "It's my father you should be watching out for."

"Your… your father?" I asked, perplexed.

"Lord Pembroke," he said. "But I'm forgetting my manners. I'm Lord Pembroke's son, but please just call me Steven."

"Pleased to meet you," I said, smiling. "This is Val and this is Barry, otherwise known as the Earl of Barrington."

"Oh, yes," Steven said enthusiastically. "I remember reading about you in the paper quite a while back. How's the retransformation going?"

"It's work in progress," said Barry.

Val caught my eye and giggled.

We both knew that it was very much an exaggeration, since I knew that Barry was nowhere near a breakthrough. Barry, however, didn't twitch so much as a whisker.

"Mind you," Lord Pembroke's son continued jovially, "I wouldn't complain if I could be a cat for a day or two myself."

"What makes you say that?" I asked.

He shrugged his shoulders.

"It would be something new," he said. "Believe me, after decades of being cooped up in this place, novelty is rare and precious. You try out a lot of things over the years."

"Is that the reason you hold regular balls?" I asked.

"One of them, yes," he said, idly running a hand through his hair. "It's the only way we can get to know new people. Not that my father cares for that sort of thing very much. He doesn't really approve of partying these days. He usually just hides away. Probably better that way if you ask me, considering the mood he's usually in."

"I understand he lost his wife – your mother?" I asked.

Steven waved his hand as if brushing away a particularly irksome fly.

"Yes, yes," he snapped. "All very tragic. Happened years ago. At some point, you've got to move on. Especially when you've got an eternity ahead of you like we do. I mean, there has to be an end to the mourning period at some point, doesn't there? I got over it eventually, didn't I?"

I was just about to inquire further when there was the echo of footsteps. Then, a young woman with red hair and a pretty face entered, heading straight for Lord Pembroke's son.

" 'Scuse me, your lordship," she said in a broad, local accent.

"I wish you wouldn't call me that," he said irritably, turning around. "What do you want? Oh, it's you, Emma."

He suddenly seemed to be standing much more upright. And when he spoke next, it struck me that his voice sounded deeper, more mature.

"The menu for this evening. Wonderful. This is Emma, everyone. She's our newest addition to the staff. You'll soon be witness to her excellent skills, I daresay. Will you be joining us for dinner?"

"Well," I said, taken aback by the question, "we'd love to, if that's alright with you and Lord Pembroke."

"Oh, that old stuffed shirt," he said, laughing, "he'll hardly notice."

***

As we sat down, more and more guests arrived in the hall. Some seemed to be old friends that Steven greeted enthusiastically, while others received his full disdain, mainly on the grounds of being excessively boring.

Privately, I couldn't believe our luck. Perhaps Steven treated all new guests this way – we had been recommended to him through Alec's channels, after all – yet the opportunity to have dinner with him was unexpected. Even more fortunate was the fact that Steven was more than willing to talk about the Pembroke estate and its history.

Soon enough, the hall was filling up, though Steven informed me that most guests would be arriving the night before the ball.

And then, Lord Pembroke entered. Without having seen him, I had pictured him somewhat as a copy of the portrait of his stern father hanging on the wall. Steven's endless stories of his austere and humourless lifestyle did nothing but to reinforce that image.

And yet, Lord Pembroke did not live up to it. Unlike the portrayal of his father looming above our heads, he sported no moustache. His hair was grey, too, though it was simply neat rather than held rigidly in place by excessive amounts of wax. In fact, Lord Pembroke did not look stern at all, and where Steven saw only austerity, I detected deep-seated sorrow.

"Good evening," he said as he saw us.

"Father," said Steven, "this is Amy, Val, and the Earl of Barrington – in cat form, over there."

"How do you?" he said politely.

We all shook hands (and paws) with him in a rather formal manner. He didn't seem particularly perturbed by Barry's appearance. Perhaps he knew of the case. Or maybe he had seen so many peculiar things in his long life as a warlock that few things could arouse his curiosity.

Conversation at dinner continued very much in the same vein, with the exception of a few interjections by Lord Pembroke. In the meantime, Carew had brought Barry a high stool so that he could eat from the table as well.

At last, dinner was served. Since magic was strongly discouraged at the Pembroke estate, half a dozen waiters swarmed the long table, carefully arranging bottles of wine, bowls filled with Yorkshire puddings, steaming gravy, and plates full of tender mutton.

"I wonder where Beatrice has got to?" said Steven, a frown on his face, looking at me searchingly.

"I'm afraid I haven't met her yet," I said apologetically.

"Oh, of course you haven't," he said. "I forgot. You've only just arrived. Beatrice is my auntie; my father's sister. She's got a sharp tongue sometimes, but I think you'll like her. Here she comes now, I believe."

A woman in her late forties or possibly early fifties approached the long table, nodding occasionally to a guest she recognised. She wore an elegant, though clearly old-fashioned dress. It struck me immediately that she possessed much more of her father's sternness than her brother, Lord Pembroke.

Beatrice was followed into the hall by a very thin woman, who was a little younger than I was. She had dark hair and natural, pale good looks, although her face had a permanently pinched, slightly unhealthy look about it, as though she ate little and stayed indoors most of the time.

"And now we are complete. Excellent," said Steven, as the two women made for their seats at the table. "Introductions are in order, I believe. This is Beatrice, my aunt. And this is Sarah, who has been helping my father with some of his work."

Steven then introduced us. Beatrice was polite, but her eagle-like stare indicated that she was reserving judgment for the moment. Sarah seemed to be totally indifferent, until Barry was introduced.

"*The* Earl of Barrington? Not the expert in therianthropy, surely?" she exclaimed.

"Well," Barry said, putting on an air of insincere modesty that fooled nobody, "I do my best. Are you in the field, too?"

"No, not exactly, but I've read a lot of your work when I attended Warklesby's School of Magic. I paid particular attention to your research in another area, however. There was an interesting article that I used for one of my papers…"

And within a few minutes, Barry and Sarah were well away into the distant lands of experimental spellcasting and magical theory.

The food, meanwhile, was as delicious as it looked.

Glancing around the table, I noticed that Lord Pembroke hardly ate anything at all, while his son, Steven, had already helped himself to liberal amounts several times.

Though I didn't expect to glean much in regard to who was sending the threatening letters to Lord Pembroke, it probably was the best opportunity I would have to get to know his relatives. Unfortunately for me, Lord Pembroke hardly engaged in conversation with anyone. When he did speak, it was usually a request to pass an item on the table, or perhaps a reminder of a certain task that still had to be performed in the house.

And yet, over the course of dinner and desert, certain patterns began to emerge. Steven spoke in an animated fashion with his aunt Beatrice, while he hardly exchanged a word with his father. Steven, so much was clear, was the driving force not only of the regular balls that were held at the Pembroke estate, but also pretty much all other things that went on in the house. One moment, he would have an idea and utter it, only to disregard later for what he considered to be an even better one.

His aunt Beatrice seemed to be both amused and exasperated by her nephew. But whatever his fancy, she usually had a strong opinion about it. In fact, she seemed to have a strong opinion about almost everything.

"I've seen many a government in my time, you know," Beatrice was saying, pointing her fork around the table. "But with current affairs as they are, I think one can say with confidence that the current magical administration is the worst of the lot. I mean, just think of the way they handled the Gibraltar affair. An absolute disgrace. What do you think, Miss…?"

"Sheridan," I said, taking a sip of wine in order to buy more time.

If truth be told, I had not paid any attention to magical politics at all, though I knew that Barry was constantly complaining about the government, too. Then again, Barry liked to complain, so it didn't really allow me to deduce whether it was as bad as he said it was.

Not saying anything wasn't an option. If I agreed, I might just come over as a sycophant, something I was sure Beatrice despised. If I disagreed, however, I risked showing my ignorance. I therefore opted for a third way.

"Well," I said slowly, "I doubt the opposition would have fared any better. They're all politicians, after all. They can't help themselves."

"Ha!" said Beatrice triumphantly, making everyone around her jump in surprise. "So young and yet so cynical. Miss Sheridan, I like it. So what would you have done if you'd been in charge?"

By trying to evade the question, I was just digging a deeper hole for myself. I was saved, however, by a timely intervention by Steven.

"Please, auntie," he said, grimacing. "Must we have

politics at dinner? It hasn't been the least bit interesting or exciting since the end of the war, you know."

"I just want to know where our guests stand, that's all," she said, narrowing her eyes. "You're not connected to the government in any way, are you?"

"Me?" I said, taken aback. "No, not at all."

"Good," she said in a relieved tone, as though I had just tested negative for a particularly nasty disease. "At least you have some sense in you."

The conversation then drifted away to less controversial topics. All the while, I was trying to gauge Lord Pembroke. He hadn't uttered a single word in almost an hour. But it was impossible to know what was going on behind that polite mask of his.

Then, Carew, the butler, entered the hall. He hastened across the room until he stood right next to Lord Pembroke.

"Excuse me, my lord," he said, his voice barely louder than a whisper. "But I did not think it could wait."

He held out a small, grey envelope. Lord Pembroke's face went white as the blood drained from it. His hand shook slightly as it reached for the letter. He slid it open with the salad knife and read the contents. His face barely changed, though I could tell by Val's reaction next to me that something more was going on.

"Excuse me, please," he mumbled.

"Father…" Steven began.

Lord Pembroke seemed to be beyond words. He simply handed the letter over to his Beatrice and got up from the table. It seemed he had entered some sort of dream world. Then, he headed for the door without uttering another word, followed by a worried-looking Carew.

"What's the matter?" Steven asked loudly.

Beatrice was suddenly angry.

"Shh, keep your voice down."

"But what is it?" he whispered.

"It's another one of those… you know what."

I pretended not to take any notice of what was going on, busying myself with the desert, though my ears were pricked. Out of the corner of my eye, I saw Steven lean in, trying to read the contents of the letter.

"What does it say?"

"It… it says there's going to be…" said Beatrice in a hushed voice, "it says there's going to be a murder."

5

Steven cursed loudly as Val and I looked at each other with raised eyebrows.

"A… a murder?" he whispered. "Are you sure, Beatrice?"

"It says so in the letter," said Beatrice. "Here, read it for yourself. I've got to see how your father's getting along. This can't go on for much longer, or he'll go mad. We've just got to do something about it."

She got up from the table and walked over to where Val and I were sitting.

"Forgive me," she said. "I'd better be off. Do sit with us again."

"Is everything alright?" I asked.

"Oh, it's nothing," she said evasively, "just a little family matter. Nothing to worry about, I hope. Until then."

She then made for the door at the other end of the room. Steven, who apparently didn't want to be left alone with the letter, picked it up and got up from his chair.

"I think I'll turn in early," he said. "Haven't been sleeping all that well. Good night, Amy. Pleasure meeting you."

We wished him goodnight and watched him follow his aunt out of the hall.

"Come on, Val," I whispered, getting up from my chair.

"What?" she said, still eyeing the delicious pudding.

"Time to take a closer look round."

"Right," she said.

Barry, sensing the commotion at last, tore himself away from his discussion with Sarah.

"Are we leaving?" he said.

"Don't worry," I said. "We'll be back later. Val and I just have to freshen up a bit."

"Alright," said Barry, narrowing his eyes suspiciously.

I was glad that he didn't say anything, however, for Sarah looked curiously at Val and me. It wouldn't do to advertise that we were unnaturally interested in Lord Pembroke's affairs, especially to his assistant. And something told me that Sarah was quite shrewd.

***

Val and I left the hall, using the same exit as the Pembrokes had done. We found ourselves in a dark corridor, which was only lit by a few old-fashioned oil lamps. Most of the doors to our left and right were closed, though the ones that were open suggested that this part of the house was used mainly for storage.

Finally, we came to an intersection with another corridor. Choosing to go left, we passed by dozens of little rooms to reach yet another intersecting corridor.

"Where are we?" asked Val, frowning.

"No clue," I said. "It's like a maze in here. And it doesn't help that only a few of these oil lamps are burning."

"Carew probably has to do most of it himself," said Val. "And without magic, that's quite a chore. I don't think I've ever been in a house with so many rooms before. I mean, Fickleton House is big, but nothing compared to this."

"Yes," I said thoughtfully. "We should just…"

But at that moment, Val clasped my arm tightly in fear.

"There's someone coming," she breathed.

Frozen to the spot, I listened.

Val was right. There were footsteps, as well as voices in the distance. If we stayed where we were, we were bound to run into them. And then, there'd be some pretty awkward questions.

"Quick," I said. "Get in here."

I opened the nearest door at random. The room beyond turned out to be nothing more than a small storage room, sporting dozens and dozens of unused blankets and spare pillows.

Once Val had joined me inside the glorified cupboard, I closed the door, plunging us into complete darkness, as we were below ground level. The footsteps were coming closer now. Crouching uncomfortably next to Val, I felt my heart racing and pumping like mad. I tried to control my breathing, but that just seemed to make it even louder and more erratic.

I pressed my eye against the keyhole, trying to see who it was outside. But although I could tell that the voices were getting louder, the angle of the keyhole prevented me from seeing very far to either side.

"… told you before, it's bad form."

If I wasn't mistaken, it was Steven's voice. He had claimed earlier that he wanted an early night's rest. What was he doing down here?

"You can't order me to do anything," a woman's voice snapped. "I've made up my mind. I'm going through with it."

The footsteps came to a halt, just a few feet away from our door. But however hard I craned my neck, I couldn't see who Steven was talking to.

"Don't be stupid," said Steven, his voice suddenly harsh and aggressive. "You're making a lot of enemies, you know, including me. Stop it, now."

"And if I don't?" came the stubborn retort.

"Then it's over between us," Steven said.

His voice had become icy. It sounded much more dangerous than when he had been overtly angry.

"Then I'm ending it, right here and now," the woman said. "I won't be pushed around, not even by you."

"That's your decision," said Steven. "But you'd better watch out, that's all I'm going to say."

"What do you mean?"

"You heard what I said," Steven murmured in a threatening tone of voice.

And with that, he stormed off.

I could hear footsteps coming nearer, lighter ones that couldn't possibly be Steven's. The woman was almost on our level now.

I forced my face so hard against the keyhole that it began to hurt.

And then, I saw her. It was Emma, the new maid that Steven had introduced to us in the hall.

Gazing around, still shaking from the conversation she just had with Lord Pembroke's son, she hurried down the corridor until I couldn't see her any longer.

"Who was it?" Val whispered.

"Emma, the maid," I said softly.

"She… are you sure?" asked Val.

"Yes," I said.

"She didn't sound like Emma at all," said Val. "Didn't Emma have some sort of local accent?"

"Yes," I said. "She had. Yorkshire, if I'm not mistaken. But I'm positive it was Emma. The red hair. The face. Unless there were some sort of magical shenanigans going on or twins are involved, it couldn't possibly be anyone else."

"You think someone might have taken her appearance – you know, with the help of a transformation potion or something like that?"

"Maybe," I said slowly. "But Steven certainly thought it was the same person. Remember how his entire stature changed when he saw that it was Emma in the hall a few hours ago? He was certainly attracted to her."

"Then why did she put on the Yorkshire accent in the hall?" asked Val.

"I don't know," I said truthfully. "But I think it's fair to say that she's hiding something. And my bet is it's the thing Steven wanted her to stop doing."

"But what is it?"

"That's what we've got to find out," I said. "But it's got to be something big. He wouldn't end the relationship or even threaten her that way otherwise. Come on, Val, let's get out of here. I've had enough for one evening."

***

Within half an hour, we were back in the hall. Only a few people were still there, though Barry had apparently already left. There was no sign of Sarah, Lord Pembroke's assistant, either.

By the time Val and I had finally found the North wing, we were both thoroughly exhausted from traipsing up and down countless stairs in the Pembroke manor. The corridors in the guests' quarters were much more friendly, however, with powerful lamps illuminating the ornate carpets we walked on.

Amidst doors closing and goodnights being exchanged between the numerous other guests in the wing, we finally arrived at our own room. Barry was already waiting for us.

"Glad you bothered to come by," he said sarcastically. "I thought you'd decided to sleep in the stables."

"You could've waited in your friend's room," said Val, equally venomous, unable to hide a tinge of jealousy, "I'm sure she would have been delighted to entertain you a little further."

"You may mock me," said Barry haughtily, "yet her appreciation is purely platonic, based on my excellent work in the field, I can assure you, Valerie."

"Alright, you two," I said. "Let's continue the fight inside. I'm dying for a bath."

***

Just as the Pembroke manor itself, the suite was gorgeous. It combined the grace and wealth of a bygone age with some of the more modern amenities that even the rather more traditional magical community refused to do without these days. Val and I had a room each, while Barry had his own couch in the spacious sitting room that connected them.

Once we had unpacked, we told Barry all about the conversation we overheard between Steven and Emma, as well as the strange conundrum surrounding her altered accent.

"Perhaps she was just trying to shake off her accent to impress him," said Barry, brushing a speck of dust from one of his paws with the other.

"Believe me, that was the last thing on her mind," I said. "It sounded like – well, it was – the very nasty end of a relationship. I don't think you have much time to think about accents and stuff like that."

"In that case," said Barry, "her local accent must be phony."

"That's what I thought," I said.

"But why would she do that?" interjected Val, pulling off one of her stockings with some force.

"Isn't it obvious?" said Barry, a smug look on his face.

"No," said Val, wrestling with the other stocking. "Not to me, anyway."

"She's affecting a local accent because it's the *hip* thing to do," said Barry dismissively. "Everyone wants to speak like the Bugs, or Beatles, or whatever their name is."

"Barry, that's definitely not it," I said, shaking my head. "It's no longer the 60s, you know."

"Glad it isn't," he said. "Awful time. Terrible music."

"I'm sure it was," I said, grinning, "cooped up alone in your library listening to Wagner all day."

"I beg your pardon, Amanda?"

"Anyway," I said, chortling. "Did you find out anything interesting from Sarah?"

Val snorted, but didn't say anything.

"Her theoretical background is quite extensive," said

Barry, preparing for what I was sure would be a momentous monologue. "Therianthropy seems to be only one of her interests. She…"

"I mean, in terms of the threatening letters Lord Pembroke's been receiving," I said. "You know, the reason we are here in the first place."

"Oh, that," Barry said, as though the case were nothing but a nuisance to him, "in regard to Lord Pembroke's predicament, I don't think she's connected in any way at all."

"Are you saying that because she praised your work?" I said.

"Because there is no evidence to the contrary," Barry retorted smoothly.

"How long has she been working for Lord Pembroke?" I asked.

"Sarah hasn't been with him for very long, I believe," he said. "A few weeks, at the most."

"What's her job here, exactly?"

"I believe she helps to maintain the magical systems here," said Barry. "They had some trouble maintaining the systems, apparently."

"I thought magic was forbidden here," said Val, perplexed.

"Active magic is indeed," said Barry. "As far as I understand it, active waves of magic may even damage the magical generator that powers the barrier, thereby puncturing the field that protects the Pembroke estate from the normal passage of time. But the generator itself, as well as all other magical systems –the sewer, the plumbing, the array of appliances – need to be maintained. It is old magic that is reapplied, as it were."

"I see," I said.

"So when's the wedding?" asked Val.

"I am married to the science of magic," Barry insisted.

"She's a scientist," said Val.

"Wouldn't she have to be a cat scientist, strictly

speaking?" I said.

Val laughed. And though Barry kept a perfectly straight face, I thought I saw his whiskers twitch, just for the briefest of moments.

***

After I had taken a relaxing bath, we happily continued our banter well into the night. Though the drive and the day's events had been tiring, we were still too much under the impression of our new surroundings to go to bed.

Gradually, however, we must have dozed off on the sofa, one by one.

I was tossed into a bizarre dream world, in which Barry announced that he was taking over control of the Pembroke estate. Lord Pembroke was designated as head butler, while Carew – suddenly spouting a long, white beard – retired from his post. Beatrice staged a rebellion to reinstate Lord Pembroke, but was betrayed by Sarah, whom Barry promoted to Court Witch, First Class, for her services.

Barry's official coronation was to take place in the great hall. Thousands had gathered there, filling it to the last inch. Hanging above our heads was a giant picture of Barry himself. Lord Pembroke approached with a golden crown on a cushion. But before he reached him, a terrible scream permeated the hall. It was a woman's voice, full of terror and foreboding.

***

"Amy. Amy, wake up."

"What… what's going on?" I said dazedly.

I found myself slumped on the couch in an awkward position. I felt stiff all over. I opened my eyes and saw Val in front of me. She looked worried.

"There's something going on outside," she said quickly.

I looked out of the window, but it was still dark.

"What's the matter?" I asked, rubbing my eyes.

"I don't know," said Val. "There was a scream. Half the house seems to be awake."

I listened carefully. Val was right. Out in the corridor, the jovial conversations and 'goodnights' from a few hours ago had been replaced by terrified whispers.

Painfully, I got up from the sofa. Barry was already at the door, listening.

"It doesn't sound good," he said.

"Let's see what's going on," I said.

I hastily got my coat and shoes.

With Barry and Val on my heels, I opened the door and hastened out onto the corridor. It was not difficult to follow the fearful gazes and hushed voices. They led us down two flights of steps and out of the house through one of the side entrances.

The air outside felt cold and unwelcoming. A group of people were standing not too far away.

"It must have been an accident," someone muttered to grunts of approval.

"The healers should be here any minute now," somebody else announced.

Val, Barry, and I approached the site. As we mingled in the small crowd, we finally saw what was the source of the commotion.

A young woman with flaming red hair lay on the ground. It was Emma, the new maid.

"Shocking," a woman next to us said, shaking her head.

"What happened?" I asked her.

"She fell out of that window, up there from that tower," an elderly man standing next to her said.

The woman, clearly beyond words, nodded her head sadly. Then, she pointed upwards.

Following her direction, I saw it. The window belonged to the tallest tower by far. Although I wasn't sure, I thought that it had to belong to the West wing of the house, judging by the angle.

"Make way, please," a voice cut through the crowd. "Healers coming through."

Val, Barry, and I quickly stepped aside.

Two healers approached the lifeless body of Emma. Though I hoped I was mistaken, I doubted there was anything that the healers could do for her.

As the first healer examined various parts of the body, the other poured mysterious liquids into her mouth.

But after a while, one of them shook his head.

"It's no use, Stan," he said. "She's gone."

6

Still under shock from what had happened, the bystanders gradually moved back into the house and to their rooms again.

"Come on," I said quietly to Val and Barry, "let's go for a walk."

The sun was beginning to set, though a thick layer of mist prevented the rays of sunshine to penetrate properly. Once we were out of earshot, Val turned to Barry and me.

"Dead," she exclaimed. "We saw her only a few hours ago."

"Yes," I said, thoughtfully. "And right after witnessing an argument."

"Do you think he killed her, Amy?" asked Val.

"Killed her?" I said. "I'm not sure. Did you feel anything yesterday, when we overheard her and Steven arguing?"

"He was certainly very angry, though whether he is capable of murder, I don't know."

"It could have been suicide," I said. "What do you think, Val?"

"She was very angry," said Val. "But stubborn. If she did commit suicide, it must have been on the spur of the moment."

"Oh, don't give me that. Lord Pembroke's son clearly killed her," said Barry. "No mystery there."

"Do you really think so?" said Val.

"Well, he *did* threaten her," I said.

"I know," said Val, frowning.

"You don't think he might have pushed her down?" I said. "That would solve his problem with her, whatever it was."

"I know it makes sense logically," said Val, "but…"

"Look, it's quite straightforward," said Barry, rolling his eyes. "He threatened her. You were both there and heard the whole thing. And then, he killed her. Open and shut case, if you ask me. What possible objection is there?"

"The facts do seem to point in that direction," I said.

"I know, Amy," said Val. "I can't explain it either. I just don't think Steven is capable of… of murder, that's all."

"Well, you're the psychic," I said. "Perhaps we should…"

"Psychic my hat!" said Barry. "Forgive me, Valerie, but it's a *very* unreliable branch of magic. And might I remind you that you have been fooled before."

"I didn't say I was right," said Val hotly. "But sometimes, the truth is not as simple or 'open and shut' as you want it to be, Barry."

"The straightforward answer is often the correct one," said Barry.

"Not always," Val countered. "Take your new friend, Sarah, for example."

Barry, almost stumbling over a mole hill, came to a halt.

"What exactly are you implying?" he said.

"All I'm saying is that there's more than meets the eye with her," said Val.

"Well," said Barry, "what if there were? You can't blame an impressionable young woman if her academic admiration spills into the personal sphere and…"

"She doesn't have a thing for you, Barry," snapped Val. "In fact, she's hiding something from you."

Barry took a deep breath, as though the effort of keeping calm was gargantuan.

"And what might that be?" asked Barry.

"I don't know," Val admitted. "But she's got some secret, I'm certain of that. You'd better keep a close eye on her."

***

567

Since going back to bed was out of the question after what had happened, we decided to have an early breakfast. It was barely after 7 o'clock when we arrived in the hall, though we found it packed with people.

"Great," said Barry, eyeing the full table in front of us. "Don't these people have better things to do than to bother me at breakfast? I feel homesick already."

"I think there are a few spare seats at the far end," I said.

I would have given a great deal to be able to sit near the Pembrokes after what had happened to Emma. Unfortunately for us, there wasn't a single seat left next to them.

Instead, we choose seats next to an elderly Scottish couple. They, too, were discussing Emma's tragic death. Apparently, they had decided to cancel their reservation immediately and return home.

"Can you sense what they're feeling?" I asked Val, leaning over so we couldn't be overheard.

"Yes," she said. "They're a bit frightened, but they're looking forward to getting out of here and…"

"No, not them," I said, "I mean the Pembrokes."

"Oh, right," said Val. "Sorry, Amy. Way too many people in between. It's a wonder I can feel anything in this sort of environment at all."

"It's not much of a surprise, actually," said Barry, still sounding grumpy. "Psychic powers usually increase in time. Until, of course, you burn out from feeling other people's emotions all day."

"Good thing you'll never have that problem, Barry," I said, grinning.

Barry narrowed his eyes, but couldn't come up with a suitable retort.

"What I really need is time with Steven alone," said Val, leaning over. "It's much more accurate when you get them on their own."

"Yes," I said quietly. "But first we've got to find out

what Emma was up to, so we can confront him with it."

"But how are we going to do that?" asked Val.

"We could search Emma's room," I said.

"Great," said Barry sarcastically. "Another opportunity for us to get thrown out."

"Do you have a better idea?" I said.

But before Barry could open his mouth to give his answer, a sound from a gong echoed around the hall. A figure at the opposite end of the table got up. It was Lord Pembroke.

"Ladies and gentlemen," Lord Pembroke said, "it is my unfortunate duty to tell you that there has been a tragic accident here at the Pembroke estate…"

His voice sounded even thinner when raised to address an audience.

"As a result, the newest addition to our staff, Emma, has sadly and suddenly passed away."

With the news spreading like wildfire, it seemed that this surprised no one anymore. Lord Pembroke waited patiently for the murmur of condolences around the room to subside.

"Under the present circumstances," he continued, "it is, of course, perfectly understandable if you wish to leave. Carew will take care of all your needs should you be thus inclined."

He cleared his throat.

"My family and I have discussed the matter of the upcoming ball. We have decided that it will proceed as planned, under the condition that it is dedicated in honour of the deceased. Everyone present is still welcome to participate. Thank you."

And with that, Lord Pembroke sat down again. Beatrice seemed to be pleased. She engaged her brother immediately in conversation. Steven, on the other hand, hadn't looked up during the entire speech. He just sat there, staring at the wall opposite him, clearly lost in thought.

The hall was perfectly still for a moment, as though all present had to digest the new information. Then, as though released from a vow of silence, normal conversations picked up once again. Some, I noticed, seemed privately relieved that the ball was to continue, while others were clearly intent on leaving the Pembroke estate.

As breakfast was being served, I kept a close eye on the Pembrokes. Though his aunt Beatrice did her best to engage him in conversation, Steven offered only monosyllabic answers. Whatever his role in Emma's death, the experience had certainly rattled him.

Peculiarly, I could not detect any change in Lord Pembroke's behaviour at all. As was his custom, he ate his meals in polite silence. His address to the hall hadn't exactly been heartfelt, though perhaps his worries still revolved around the threatening letters, the last of which he had received only the previous day.

All through breakfast, I contemplated the fact that the letter had prophesied murder. If Barry was right and Emma's death was indeed foul play, then surely that couldn't possibly be a coincidence. Why, however, had the maid been killed? That, it appeared to me, was the vital question, and one I was determined to find the answer to.

***

"Are you sure this is a good idea?" Val hissed, looking around furtively.

"Nothing's going to happen, Val," I said, trying to pick the lock to Emma's room with one of Val's hair pins. "Barry's on the lookout. He'll start singing loudly when he sees someone."

"That's certainly going to drive them away," said Val. "How much longer, do you think?"

"Almost got it," I said. "I used to do this as a kid, back at home when I forgot my keys."

"I still think we should have just used magic," said Val, leaning against the wall. "I mean, I know they don't like that here, but nobody would really know…"

"It's safer this way, Val," I said. "You heard what Barry said. Any active spells might destabilise the magical field."

"It would just be one little spell," said Val.

"If there's one thing I've learnt, Val," I said, "it's that minor spells can have a big impact sometimes."

"As long as we don't get caught," said Val.

"Don't worry," I said, "I've almost got it. I just need to…"

"Doch will der Held nicht Herzog sein genannt –
Ihr sollt' ihn heißen Schüüüützer von Brabant!"

"What on earth was that?"

"It's Barry's signal!" said Val frantically. "He's singing Wagner. We've got to go *now*, Amy."

"I've almost got it…"

"Amy!"

And then, the lock clicked open. At the far end of the corridor, a shape had appeared, though I didn't think it had seen us yet.

"You head them off," I murmured.

"Amy, no!" Val hissed.

"It's the only way," I said.

I checked the corridor once more. The shape was slowly but steadily turning towards us. It would see us at any moment. It was now or never.

Careful not to make a noise, I opened the door and slid through it, closing it softly behind me.

I found myself in a small room with only a tiny window at the top of the wall facing me, as though someone had wedged it in as an architectural afterthought. Though there was hardly any furniture – merely a bed, an old wardrobe, and a tiny secretary with a chair – it was incredibly messy. Clothes were strewn everywhere on the floor, along with dozens and dozens of books. A bottle of ink had fallen off the secretary and onto the pillowcase, drenching the corner in navy blue.

Outside, I heard Val's footsteps move away, trying to get as much distance between her and the door. But it was evidently too late. A wizened old voice drifted through the corridor.

"Can I help you, Miss…?"

It was the voice of Carew, the butler.

"Morgan," I heard Val say as she came to a stop. "Yes, I… I was supposed to meet Amy. We wanted to go for a walk."

"A walk?" Carew asked mildly, though I could tell that his curiosity had been aroused. "I'm afraid you're in the wrong part of the house for that, Miss Morgan. These are the servants' quarters. There is no entrance to the grounds from here."

"Oh, right," said Val apologetically. "I'm very sorry, Mr. Carew. The house is just so large. It… it won't happen again."

"Not to worry, not to worry," he said amiably. "I'll show you the way, shall I?"

"That would be great, thank you," said Val, clearly sounding relieved.

"This is the way to the stairs," he said.

I held my breath while footsteps echoed across the corridor. I could clearly distinguish Val's clackity-clack from Carew's monotonous scuffling, as though he rarely lifted his feet off the ground.

Then, Carew came to a stop. And when he spoke next, I could tell that he was right outside my door. My heart began to pound violently.

"This is… or *was*, rather… young Emma's room," he said in a somewhat hushed tone.

"The maid who died?" asked Val nervously.

"That's right," Carew said slowly. "She was a fine woman. It was a pity what happened to her."

"Yes," said Val. "An accident, wasn't it?"

I could tell that Val was probing Carew in order to see how he would react.

"An accident, yes, so they say," he muttered. "Or suicide."

"Do you think it was suicide?" asked Val.

"Well, she seemed like such a lively thing," he said. "But you never know with some people. Happy one day, distraught the next. Very tragic indeed. Oh, that reminds me."

There was a pause, followed by a rustling of keys.

"What are you doing?" asked Val, barely able to contain her horror.

"I quite forgot about Miss Emma's flowers. It would be a shame if they would wither away in there, all on their own. I think I'll place them in the morning room for his Lordship."

"But, I thought…" spluttered Val.

"Don't worry, Miss Morgan," he said kindly, "I will only be a minute. I'll show you the correct way in a moment."

Panic rising within me, I desperately looked around the room for a place I could hide. There was no bathroom attached. Only the wardrobe next to me provided any sort of cover.

It seemed to becoming a bit of a habit, hiding in dark places, but I had no choice. I tiptoed as fast as I could over to the wardrobe and opened it. Piles of clothes and loose sheets of paper came flying out of it.

Clambering silently through the mess while Carew was fiddling with his keys, I stepped into the wardrobe and shut the door on myself, just as Carew turned the key in the lock. The wardrobe was damp and smelly and much smaller than the last.

"Hullo," I heard him say as he stepped inside, "the door is already open. Very peculiar, don't you think?"

"Perhaps she forgot to lock it," said Val.

"Yes," said Carew thoughtfully. "That's probably it."

Carew shuffled across the room.

"This place is a mess," said Val in surprise.

"Young Emma was not the tidy sort," said Carew simply. "Ah, here they are. We can go upstairs now."

"Yes, OK," Val said. "I think it's probably a bit late for a walk now. I'd better head for lunch in the hall."

"An excellent idea, Miss Morgan," said Carew. "Follow me, if you please."

"No, please, I'll find the way myself. Thank you very much, Mr. Carew."

Val didn't sound at all like her usual self, strangely formal and distant.

"Very well, Miss Morgan," said Carew.

I heard Val's footsteps move out of the room and along the corridor outside. But Carew didn't move an inch. It was getting hotter and hotter in the wardrobe, but as long as Carew was still in Emma's room, there was nothing I could do but wait.

After a moment's silence, I heard Carew's characteristic footsteps, though they seemed to be moving into the room rather than out. Standing awkwardly in the pitch black wardrobe, I listened for the slightest noise. What was Carew doing in Emma's room? Did he suspect, perhaps, that he was not alone?

Carew came to a halt. He was breathing heavily now, as though indulging in some sort of physical labour. Then, I heard the shuffling of paper, followed by drawers being opened.

"Where is it?" Carew murmured. "It has to be here somewhere."

He was working his way closer and closer to the wardrobe. Mad thoughts raced at breakneck speed through my mind. I wanted to make a dash for it, to burst out of the wardrobe and out into the hall.

As I was wrestling with my impulse to run, I heard Carew grasp the handle. The door was being pulled open.

A crack of light emerged at the rim.

And then, I was plunged back into the safety of darkness.

I could hear footsteps in the hall. They definitely weren't Val's, though I was sure they belonged to a woman.

"Carew, what are you doing in there?"

It was Beatrice, Lord Pembroke's sister.

"M'lady," said Carew, "I didn't see you…"

"Evidently," she said coolly. "Now answer my question. What are you doing in Emma's room?"

"I was just getting the flowers from her room," he said.

"Don't give me that, Carew," Beatrice snapped. "The real reason."

There was a brief pause.

"I cannot tell you, m'lady," he said.

"No? And why not?"

"I promised Lord Pembroke," Carew said.

"My… my brother?"

For the first time in the brief conversation, Beatrice sounded taken aback.

"Yes, m'lady," Carew said.

"Very well," she said finally. "I do not want you to break your word to my brother, so I shall ask him myself. I think I know what this is about, anyway. I only hope you were successful in your endeavours?"

"Only partially," Carew admitted cryptically.

"I see," said Beatrice. "Better finish the job later, Carew. It wouldn't do to get caught going through her things. Not so soon after the… tragedy."

"Yes, m'lady," Carew said.

"I think I'll go to the library now, Carew. Make sure to bring up the tea."

"Yes, m'lady."

Next, I heard Beatrice's forceful footsteps move away and along the corridor again. Carew followed her, but came to a stop near the door.

"The only *tragedy* with Miss Emma's death," Carew said softly to himself, "is that it didn't happen sooner."

7

After Carew had finally left, it took me a moment to realise what had just happened. Stiff all over from standing still for so long, I opened the wardrobe door and got out, squinting slightly as my eyes begrudgingly adapted to the light.

My first impulse was to find Val and Barry, who were both surely waiting in our suite upstairs in the guest quarters of the North wing. And yet, by a lucky chance, I had not been discovered. All alone and undisturbed, I now had access to the deceased's room. Surely, it wouldn't hurt to poke around a little. This was what we had come for, after all. And after Carew's strange behaviour and apparent malevolence toward Emma, I was more determined than ever.

I made sure that nobody was in the corridor beyond, leaving the door ajar so that I could hear as soon as someone approached. Then, I started my search. I didn't know what I was looking for specifically, except for a hint at why Emma had been so hated by the family she worked for.

The wardrobe I had hidden in yielded nothing of interest, save a few rather daring outfits perhaps. Several maid's uniforms hung side by side with what I could see were fairly expensive cocktail dresses.

The floor was littered with clothes and products of everyday use. Judging by the amount of books strewn throughout, Emma had been an avid reader. I recognised some of the works from Barry's library. There was *The Ancient Warlock Families of Europe* by Harald Eckberg, *The Perfect Servant – A Self-Help Guide* by Evelyn Bradshaw, as well as *Great Witches of the 20th Century* by Esmeralda Pew, among many others.

Without being able to put my finger on it, I had the distinct impression that there were things missing. For one, there were no personal items at all; no photographs, no letters from family or friends. Though that might have been due to the fact that Emma had joined the Pembrokes' staff quite recently, she hadn't struck me as the loner type.

The little secretary in the corner sported many little drawers, most of which were empty. There were a surprising amount of spare pens and sheets of paper, and yet I couldn't find a single word she had written anywhere.

There was also a stack of black notebooks. I flicked through them eagerly, only to find that none of them had been written in, though one of them had several pages torn out.

"Found something, have you?"

I swung around, my heart racing uncontrollably.

"Barry!" I exclaimed. "What are you doing down here?"

"Looking for you, of course," he said, trotting idly into the room. "Val was getting worried about you."

"Well, it was a close shave," I said. "I'll tell you about it later. I'm just having a look around."

Barry's gaze wandered from the bed to the wardrobe and the tiny window.

"This place is a mess," he said.

"Agreed," I said, checking under the mattress to see whether anything was hidden there.

"What are you looking for?"

"I don't know," I said, putting the mattress back in place. "Something to explain why the Pembrokes hated her so much. But I can't seem to find anything."

"Well, at least she had some decent books," said Barry, lazily scanning the titles of the works scattered around bed. "Surprising for a maid, don't you think?"

"I think she wrote, too," I said. "Judging by all these pens and notebooks at least. But I can't find a single word she's actually written."

I showed him the secretary.

"All unused," I said.

"Someone must have taken them," said Barry immediately.

"My thoughts exactly," I said. "Carew seemed to be searching for something, too."

"Did he find what he was looking for?" asked Barry.

"I don't think so," I said. "No, he was told by Beatrice to come back later. Which reminds me, we'd better hurry a bit."

"Are all of the notebooks blank?" asked Barry.

"Yes," I said. "I think one of them had some pages torn out but…"

"Torn out?"

"Yes," I said.

Barry cursed under his breath.

"What now?"

"No point hanging around," I said. "We'd better head upstairs."

"Yes," said Barry. "I passed several servants on the way down."

"Did you see Carew?"

"No."

"I've probably pushed my luck too far already for one day," I said.

"Let's just hope it won't run out, shall we?" Barry added.

***

Back in the relative safety of our room, I told Val and Barry the whole story about how Carew had almost discovered me, being unwittingly rescued by Beatrice, and Carew's peculiar animosity towards Emma.

"You were lucky Beatrice came when she did," said Val, who was lying on the sofa and eating some grapes. "I thought he was going to find you for sure. I ran to get Barry immediately."

"Were you able to read Carew?" I asked, helping myself to some grapes, too.

Val frowned.

"He didn't believe me that I had lost my way, I think," she said. "But I don't think he suspects the full story. As far as he is concerned, we're just some overly nosey guests."

"Do you think him capable of murder?" I asked.

"I don't know," said Val. "Perhaps it was because I felt under pressure, but he seemed to be lacking any sort of feeling. Positive or negative."

"So you think Emma was murdered, then?" said Barry.

"Well," I said hesitantly, "I have no evidence to support it, if that's what you mean. But with the amount of enemies she apparently had, it would be a massive coincidence if she had decided to commit suicide."

"She could have done so precisely because everyone disliked her," said Val.

"Maybe," I said. "But that still doesn't account for the state of her room. If Carew couldn't find what he was looking for, then someone else must have been there before him."

"Her room must be busier than the reception desk," said Val.

"And you say that Carew admitted to Beatrice that he was there on Lord Pembroke's orders?" said Barry thoughtfully.

"Pretty much, yes," I said. "Beatrice didn't seem surprised, though."

"Do you think Emma might have been sending those threatening letters?" said Val, helping herself to more grapes.

"I don't know," I said. "But if she did, why not simply hand her over to Alec or the MLE? Why throw her off the tallest tower? It just doesn't make any sense."

There was silence as the three of us pondered the problem.

"Emma must have discovered something," I continued. "Or asked the wrong questions, giving them a common reason to hate her. And for one of them, to kill her."

"Perhaps they all teamed up together?" said Val.

"I wouldn't put it past them," said Barry uncharitably.

"You can't dislike all of them, surely, Barry?" I said, laughing.

"With the exception of Lord Pembroke's father, perhaps," said Barry.

"Yes," I said, "I'm sure the portrait of that austere, stern pater familias appealed to you."

"No, no," said Barry, waving a paw irritably in front of him. "It's his research that counts. Whatever his successors have done to reap the laurels of his success, it was *he* who devised the magic that protects the Pembroke estate from the effects of time to this day. Lord Pembroke simply put the theory into action after his father had passed away."

"You seem to be well informed on the subject," I said.

"Lord Pembroke's assistant, Sarah, probably provided him with all the details," said Val with a pang of jealousy in her voice.

"Well, she is pretty," I said, smirking at Barry.

"That is completely beside the point," he said. "But yes, Sarah has indeed been good enough to clarify some of the workings of the magical field."

"I'm sure she did," said Val.

"She – unlike some – appreciate my work," said Barry sniffily.

Val was just about to provide a retort when I held up both hands.

"Please, let's focus. We only have a few days before the ball begins. We'll want to have come up with something by then. Alec's putting a lot of trust in us. I don't want to turn up empty-handed."

***

But despite our efforts, the following days yielded very disappointing results. With Steven still mysteriously missing from meals in the hall, engaging Lord Pembroke in conversation beyond the usual pleasantries proved impossible. Beatrice, on the other hand, was as swift and ruthless in her judgments and pronouncements as ever, yet Emma was a topic she brushed aside by professing her regret over the tragedy that had taken place and leaving it at that.

Clearly, they were sticking to the story that Emma had been a beloved new addition to the staff. The remaining servants, no doubt instructed to do so by Carew, seemed tight-lipped about the entire affair.

On the day of the ball, the official news arrived at breakfast that, lacking any other indication in the case, Emma's death had been deemed an accident. I could not help the feeling the Lord Pembroke, as well as Beatrice, seemed relieved, though I didn't know whether it was because of relief of not having been caught or simply seeing an end to the hitherto endless whisperings and suspicions uttered by guests behind their backs.

The speculations, of course, only really got going after it was noticed that Steven was absent yet again from breakfast. In fact, he hadn't attended a single meal in two days.

The Pembrokes didn't seem to be bothered about this. I asked Beatrice on one of the few occasions that I had the chance, but she merely waved a hand, explaining that Steven wasn't feeling well, but that she was sure he would turn up for the grand ball in the evening.

I felt that, wherever I turned, I hit a brick wall. And with Alec and Harriet attending the ball, I felt I had very little to report, albeit the fact that everyone seemed to have hated Emma, the maid. But unless they had all conspired to push her out of the window together, I didn't see how that was going to help very much.

***

"No, no!" Barry fumed. "I refuse to put it on."

"But it's for the ball, Barry," Val said, giggling.

Val and I had spent the last half hour trying to convince Barry to wear a coat and tails for the occasion.

"I don't care," said Barry, scowling at us while Val propped him up in his armchair. "Cats don't wear clothes. End of the story."

"Well, technically you're a warlock, trapped in cat's body, as you keep reminding us," I said, grinning. "And warlocks, as a rule, wear clothes."

"Semantics," Barry said, waving a paw irritably. "Anyway, this shirt causes terrible itching and…"

"I think it looks wonderful on you, Barry," said Val. "Now let me just fix your bow tie and then we can put on the coat."

Barry swore loudly. With the energy of a desperate cat, he scampered in between her arms and onto the floor, trying to pull off the shirt at the same time he was evading Val, making him look as though he were re-enacting some bizarre rain dance.

"Barry, you'll ruin it!" said Val, finally catching hold of him. "Stay still now."

Barry looked at me.

"Amanda," he said in what he thought was a kindly, winning voice, "would you care to explain to Valerie that this isn't necessary. I don't need to wear anything to the ball."

"Sorry, Barry," I said, fumbling with my own dress. "I spent way too much time shrinking all your clothes by magic at Fickleton House. Anyway, it will impress your lady friend. All in the interest of the furthering of the greater cause of science, of course."

Barry eyed me suspiciously for a moment, evidently

deciding whether he should rise to the bait.

"Well, I suppose I'll be able to tolerate wearing it for the opening at least," he sighed, as though he were graciously accepting a particularly burdensome duty. "I must do my bit to educate the young, after all. Carry on, Valerie, if you must. I fear that my claws might tear the fabric if I do it myself."

***

With the opening of the ball only a few minutes away, we passed down the series of staircases. Val was wearing a bright turquoise dress, while I had opted for lilac. Though Val's optimism and, peculiarly, even Barry's cynicism gave me some reassurance, I couldn't help feeling exceedingly nervous as we followed the other guests in the direction of the hall.

Before inheriting Fickleton House, I would have probably given anything to have had fears such as I had now, rather than wondering how to get by another month. On occasion, I had been able to fool myself into believing that my life really hadn't changed all that much. And yet, gazing around me at the expensive jewellery on witches' necks and the finest cloth donned by warlocks all around me, that absurd self-delusion fell to pieces. Not only had I entered the realm of magic, but I had also entered another social world entirely. And although the fears of the everyday had mostly subsided, they had simply morphed into an anxiety that I was a trespasser into another world, a fraud waiting to be denounced.

Taking a page from Barry's book for once, I tried to walk as dignified and gracefully as I could. The crowd of warlocks and witches slowly moved down the last few steps and along the Pembroke estate's seemingly endless corridors. Waiters and other members of staff, many of whom I didn't recognise, were positioned at every corner.

And then, we found ourselves in the hall at last. The

transformation – especially in such a short time – was remarkable. The long table in the centre of the room had been removed, leaving a large area for dancing. A live orchestra, positioned at the far end of the hall, was already playing. At the sides, dozens and dozens of round, narrow tables, just large enough for a small group to stand at, sported champagne and other beverages. Waiters were gliding through the room, offering drinks and light snacks.

I scanned the crowd of people around me as casually as possible, trying to make out whether Alec and Harriet had arrived yet.

"Isn't this wonderful, Amy?" said Val excitedly, handing me a glass of wine.

"Amazing," I said, taking a sip.

"I can't see a thing," Barry grumbled from below.

I lifted Barry onto the table, so that he could see a little better.

"Is this how you threw a party in your youth, Barry?" I asked, winking at Val.

"I saw my fair share of action," said Barry with a note of pride.

"And Barry looks just like a little gentleman from the old days," said Val fondly. "With his top hat and tails."

"Just like he came out of an F. Scott Fitzgerald novel," I said, laughing. "We could call him the Great Catsby!"

"I am a *real* gentleman," he grumbled. "Not some phony who has reinvented himself."

"Ah, here comes your Daisy, I believe," I said, pointing at a slightly gaunt yet very pretty woman in a black dress.

"She looks as though she's in mourning," said Val acidly.

"Val," I said warningly, "let's not alienate the few remaining people in this house that we have access to, alright? It's actually very useful that she gets on with Barry."

"Fine," fumed Val, clearly not happy with the way the evening was going.

"Hello there," I said, with one last, warning glance at Val.

"Hello, all," she said, beaming at us. She sounded slightly breathless. "Exciting, isn't it? It's my first ball at the Pembroke estate."

"Good evening, Sarah," said Barry, majestically holding out a paw, which she gladly shook. "I hope the papers I recommended to you have helped you in your work."

"Oh, yes," she said appreciatively. "Thank you, again. Thanks awfully."

Val, who was standing just outside of Sarah's peripheral vision, was making vomiting motions.

"I think the music has stopped," I said, trying to prevent a confrontation I knew was bound to happen.

"Oh, I think they're preparing for the Pembrokes to enter," said Sarah. "They come into the hall and begin the first dance. Then, all the other guests are allowed to join them."

"Here they come," I said, clapping along with everyone else in the hall.

First through the door was Lord Pembroke, with his sister Beatrice following closely behind him. To my surprise, Steven was actually in attendance.

"Does he look a bit… ill to you?" I murmured to Val.

"Yeah," she said. "Doesn't look like he's been sleeping very much, either. Look at the bags under his eyes."

But that wasn't the only thing that had changed. Steven's gait was no longer youthful and springy, but instead was shockingly similar to Carew's slouching.

After Steven had passed us, the real Carew ended the little procession, with an incredibly old woman on his arm. Whether she was supporting him, or he was supporting her was anyone's guess, however.

"Who's that behind Steven?" I asked Sarah.

"You mean the old lady?" she said. "That's Lord Pembroke's mother-in-law, Lady Wickersham."

"She must be ancient," said Val.

"Well," said Sarah, "she was quite lucky that the magical field went up when it did. The doctor gave her only a few more years. But now, of course, she cannot die of natural causes anymore. Then again, some people say that she's regretted it for the last few decades."

"She certainly doesn't look too happy," I said.

Though there was no relation, the resemblance was remarkable with the stern, austere picture of Lord Pembroke, which still loomed over everyone despite the staff's best efforts to hide it as much as was permissible behind decorations.

Then, the music began. Lord Pembroke chose to dance with his sister, while Steven danced with Lord Pembroke's aged mother-in-law.

Danced, perhaps, was the wrong word. Though Lord Pembroke's mother-in-law, Lady Wickersham, was surprisingly agile for such an old woman once she got into her stride, Steven's batteries seemed to be running at a bare minimum. His feet were dragging along the floor, his gaze unsteady.

As the music blared, people all around us were getting ready to enter the floor. Couples and friends, young and old, stood in pairs as they watched the Pembrokes dance to the timeless tune the small orchestra was playing.

In the few days I had been a guest here, the power of the magical field and the effects upon the occupants of the estate had never been so apparent.

Then, the music changed, signalling that the guests were now allowed to join in. Carew helped Lady Wickersham to a chair in the corner, while Steven leant against a wall, clearly at the end of his tether. Finally, he sat down on a chair, right beneath the painting of Lord Pembroke's father.

As Sarah asked Barry to dance with her, I had to drag Val away from them before she could cause a scene.

"Val, are you mad?" I hissed. "What is wrong with you?"

"I don't trust that woman!" flared Val.

"Shh, keep your voice down," I said.

"Well, it's true," she said grumpily.

"Val, you're jealous," I said.

"I am not," she said indignantly.

Then, a horrible thought occurred to me.

"Val, we've been best friends for years and years. Tell me that you're not into… you know," I said.

"What?" she said. "Barry? No, of course not."

"You swear?"

"On my mother's grave," she said.

"Then what's going on?" I asked.

"Well, it's just… after all the things we've done for him. He's such an ungrateful little… And now he falls for the first girl who throws him a couple of compliments."

"I don't know," I said. "You know how big his ego is. I'm not sure he's fallen for anyone. He just likes being praised."

"Yes, but the way she does it is just ridiculous," said Val. "She's clearly after something."

"Well…" I began.

"He's a cat," said Val. "It can't be that."

"Maybe she wants to transform him back to human form?" I said.

"That would probably be even worse," said Val. "Lord knows how old he really is."

"Maybe you're right," I said. "About her, I mean. But what harm could come from it?"

"As long as someone is stroking that narcissistic streak of his," said Val. "He wouldn't smell a rat even if it were lying clearly in front of him."

"But we're keeping an eye on him," I said. "Look at them dancing together, Val. Sarah's got him on her arm, and he's having a good time. Who are we to say it's wrong or all a sham?"

Val sighed, just as a man with rugged looks and a five o'clock, dressed impeccably in coat and tails, approached us in the corner of the room. He was accompanied by a stunning blonde in a pale blue dress. Of course, I recognised who they were at once.

"I suppose you're right, Amy," said Val finally, finishing her second glass of champagne. "I'll let Barry have his fun. But I'm watching her, that's all."

"Look who's here," I said softly.

Val turned around.

It was Alec, with Harriet next to him.

She was just about to greet them like old friends when I nudged her.

"We don't know them, remember?" I hissed.

"Hello," Alec said, in an oddly formal manner. "My companion isn't feeling too well. I wonder if you'd like to take this dance with me?"

He looked at me, his face almost blank save a tiny, almost private smile that was forming on his lips.

"Well," I said, "my friend and I were just…"

"Oh, stop messing around," said Val irritably, "and enjoy yourselves."

Harriet, pretending to be slightly dizzy, leant against the wall, as Val brought her a glass of water. Grudgingly, I had to admit that she was playing her role very well.

Alec and I began to dance. He steered me in such a fashion so that we wouldn't be overheard, yet did not stray too far away from everyone else as to draw attention to ourselves.

"What's the status?" he said softly. "Anything new?"

"Loads," I said. "You?"

"Yep," he said.

It felt peculiar to speak about the case while being so intimate.

"I thought we weren't supposed to make contact until after the ball," I whispered in his ear.

"You're right," he growled, as the orchestra finished a particularly dreamy song. "But things are heating up."

We waited rather awkwardly for the next song to begin,

unable to dance nor able to discuss the Pembroke affair further.

Val, now talking to Harriet, was clearly in a better mood and had forgotten all about being jealous, at least for a little while. Barry, meanwhile, was perched on Sarah's shoulder, like a black parrot, discussing magical theory no doubt while getting some refreshments.

Finally, the music resumed.

"Did you hear about Emma, the maid?" I said.

He nodded his head.

"I was working on that the last two days," he said. "Doctor's records, family, friends, acquaintances. They all give her a clean bill of health, physically and mentally. There's no way that girl killed herself."

"We suspected as much," I said, as Alec moved us closer to the orchestra.

"Any probable suspects?" he asked.

"Too many," I said. "It seems the whole household hated her."

"Why?"

"I don't know," I admitted.

Then, I told him about eavesdropping on Carew and Beatrice, and that Lord Pembroke had apparently given Carew the order to snoop.

"Good work," he said. "At least some promising leads. We'll check them out one by one."

"Any luck with the letters?"

"What?" he said. "Oh, yes, Harriet tracked down the source."

"She did?" I said, astounded. "I thought they were anonymous."

"She checked it in the lab," he said. "Had a brainwave and tested the ink for magic dust."

"Magic dust…?"

"Residual particles left by magic," he said. "It was a long shot but worth it. Turns out the dust in the letters holds components of the same magic that keeps them nice and cosy here at the estate."

"Couldn't they have been contaminated as they were opened?"

But Alec shook his head.

"No," he said. "Only active magic can do that. And the letters were opened by hand."

"So, that means that they originated from here?"

"That's right," he said. "Written with a magic ink pen that never runs dry."

"It must be someone who lives here on a regular basis, then," I said. "Since he's been getting them for a while, I mean."

"Makes sense," said Alec, frowning. "But without motive, it's going to be a tough nut to crack."

"What should we do next?"

"We've got to go through your list of suspects one by one, see what they know."

"Will you be staying here then, with Harriet?"

"Not Harriet," he said. "She's still on perimeter patrol. But yes, Lord Pembroke has asked me to stay for a few days. He's a very difficult client, I've got to admit. I think the maid's death rattled him. He wants protection."

"Did he know her, then?" I asked. "Personally, I mean."

"He says he knew her only on a very superficial level," said Alec. "But you never know. He's not exactly forthcoming with information."

"Did you tell him that the letters originated from the house?"

"I already told him weeks ago that that was a likely scenario, but he wouldn't have it," said Alec. "Stubborn man. But I'll remind him again today."

"But you say he was rattled by her death," I said slowly. "He doesn't strike me as the empathetic type. There must have been a reason."

"Yes," said Alec, "if you ask me, he's afraid. He's not really immortal, remember. He's only protected against ageing. If someone sticks a knife in him, he's going to go the same way everyone else would."

"Do you think he might have something to do with the whole affair?" I asked.

But what exactly Alec thought of that, I never got to hear it, for in that second there was a loud CRASH behind us. The music died immediately. There were screams and shrieks as everyone turned around to see what was going on.

The massive painting of Lord Pembroke's father had come crashing down to the floor. And beneath it lay a body.

"What happened?"

"Who is it?"

Alec and I rushed forward. Several men had lifted the heavy frame just high enough for us to see who lay beneath it.

It was Steven Pembroke.

8

For a moment, the entire hall was paralyzed, as Alec and I rushed to help lift the painting. It was as heavy as it looked, but together with some of the other guests we were able to lift it enough in order to carry it a few paces, setting it down again.

For the second time within days, healers were called to the Pembroke estate. Harriet was examining Steven, while Lord Pembroke stood there, watching, his face white with shock. Beatrice, only a few feet away, looked mortified. Her right hand shook as she moved it to her mouth. Lady Wickersham was holding onto Carew for support.

Approaching Steven, I could see that his wounds were serious. His body lay in a horribly contorted fashion. He was also bleeding.

Meanwhile, Val and Barry had joined us, though there was no sign of Sarah.

"Is he...?" Val began

Alec was bent over Steven, feeling his pulse.

"He's alive," he said. "At least for now. We need to stem the flow of blood until the healers arrive."

"Where are they?" said Harriet, desperately looking around the room.

"Should be here any minute," said Barry. "Didn't take them long to teleport here last time."

"There do seem to be a lot of accidents here, don't there?" a woman said next to him, shaking her head sadly.

"Frightful," another said. "That painting could have landed on any one of us!"

Alec looked imploringly at me.

"Come on," I said to Val in a low tone of voice, "let's get everyone out of here.

Val nodded.

"OK, Amy," she said.

***

It took us a surprisingly long time to clear the hall. Many were in a state of shock at what had happened, while others seemed more interested in the sensational aspect of it all.

As the hall was gradually emptying, the healers finally arrived. They swiftly administered several potions, both to the wounds as well as through Steven's mouth. Shortly after, they carried him out of the hall.

As Carew attended to Lady Wickersham, Val offered to help Lord Pembroke, who still seemed beyond words. I knew that it was as much a gesture of kindness on Val's side as well as an opportunity to sense their emotions, to see whether any one of them might have had something to do with yet another tragic 'accident' at the Pembroke estate.

Lord Pembroke mumbled something about wanting to have a drink, so Val escorted him out of the hall. His sister Beatrice followed them, still white as death.

While Alec and Harriet were still discussing what had happened, I decided to have a closer look at the painting. Remarkably, it was still intact. To prevent anyone from stepping onto the canvas, it had been carefully placed face down, in the corner of the hall, though the paint didn't actually touch the floor since the frame was so bulky.

Moving closer, I tried to discern what had caused the painting to fall. A thick steel rope had been fasted to both upper ends of the frame, holding it in place. It had presumably held for a long time there. Had the material simply corroded?

I followed the metal cable, which was coiled up like a snake, from one end to the other, until finally I had found the place where it had snapped.

Careful not to step on the painting, I leant over and

grabbed one of the snapped ends.

To my surprise, the metal looked well preserved and not corroded at all. Instead, the edge of where the cable had snapped was smooth and clean, as though someone had cut it on purpose.

"Alec," I called across the now empty hall, "I think I've found something."

"What is it?"

"Look at this," I said, showing him the steel rope. "What do you make of this?"

"Looks cut to me," he said grimly.

"My thoughts exactly," I said. "We've got to warn Lord Pembroke. There might be more booby traps in the house."

***

We finally located him, with Carew's help, in a small room at the back of the house that was used as a private bar for family members.

Lord Pembroke was sitting on a brown armchair in the corner of the room, while his sister Beatrice and Val were on the sofa. Both Lord Pembroke and Beatrice were holding generous amounts of what I presumed to be whiskey. Naturally, Lord Pembroke looked very worried, though Beatrice was shaking all over.

"Lord Pembroke," said Alec, "do you have a moment?"

Lord Pembroke closed his eyes, as though wanting to shut out the world.

"Can't it wait?" he said finally. "My son is upstairs. They don't know whether he's going to live or not."

"I'm afraid it can't," said Alec.

"Very well," he said, placing his drink on the table next to him.

He followed Alec out into the corridor from which we had just come.

"Hi Amy," said Val.

"Hello," I said.

"Help yourself to a drink," said Beatrice, waving her hand in the general direction of the bar.

I could see that she was making a great effort to appear calm and collected, though she clearly wasn't.

"No, thanks, I…"

"Are you *sure* you don't want one?" said Val, looking rather pointedly at me, then to Beatrice, who seemed to be having little trouble in emptying her glass. Judging by her unsteady gaze and overly careful enunciation of words, it wasn't her first drink, either.

"Yes," I said, cottoning on to what Val wanted. "Why not? I think… I think I could do with one after what just happened."

"You're telling me," said Beatrice.

Then, she lifted the glass to her lips and drank the rest of the contents in one large gulp.

"Va… Valerie, would you be so good to get me another…"

"I'll get you one," I said.

As I busied myself behind the little counter, an activity that immediately brought back the countless hours of my life that I had spent mixing drinks and pouring beers, we suddenly heard a pair of raised voices.

I listened closely. It was Lord Pembroke and Alec.

"… no, NO!" Lord Pembroke was shouting. "Completely out of the question."

Val and I looked at each other in surprise. We had never heard Lord Pembroke so much as say a word in anger or even utter annoyance. Beatrice, however, pretended to be unperturbed.

"It's the right thing to do," Alec retorted loudly.

"How DARE you come into my house, telling me what to do," Lord Pembroke fumed.

"The facts clearly…"

"All supposition and guess work," Lord Pembroke

ranted. "I should have listened to my mother-in-law in the first place and never involved the MLE or you in this matter."

"Lord Pembroke," Alec said angrily, "your family is in grave danger. These were not random occurrences. You cannot shut your eyes…"

"I will not condone your fear-mongering any longer," Lord Pembroke bellowed. "I want you to leave the estate immediately."

"Are you taking us off the case?"

"There is no case!" Lord Pembroke said, sounding positively maniacal now. "There never was a case."

"But the letters…"

"Probably some crackpot from the village," Lord Pembroke said dismissively. "I don't know, I don't care anymore."

"I told you, Harriet tracked them down. They originated from this house. Someone in this very house is wishing you harm, Lord Pembroke."

"Lies! Get out of here at once. Take your assistant with you. And never come back."

There was a brief pause. I wanted to go out, to help and explain, but I knew that it would be of no use, even counter-productive. If Lord Pembroke kicked out Alec on the basis of an uncomfortable conclusion, he'd surely remove anyone else who was associated with him.

"I'll leave," said Alec calmly. "But you're making a big mistake."

And with that, I heard him walk down the corridor.

I took the two whiskeys I had made and joined Beatrice and Val on the sofa, before handing Beatrice her drink.

"Thank you," she said.

A moment later, Lord Pembroke re-entered the little bar. He was red in the face, though his lips were white with rage.

"What… what's going on?" asked Beatrice.

"Nothing," Lord Pembroke said. "Just that stupid

private investigator."

"Has he been causing trouble again?" asked Beatrice.

"Filthy insinuations," said Lord Pembroke. "As if anyone in my family were capable of such a thing. No, it's clearly an outsider. It has to be."

He looked at Val and me with suspicion, as though only really noticing us for the first time.

"I think," he said loudly. "It's time for all guests to leave the estate. Can't trust anyone. They're envious of what we have built here. Envious of the magical field generator."

"Oh, don't be like that," said Beatrice, shaking her head. "T-take Valerie, here, for instance. She's been absolutely lovely."

Lord Pembroke grunted, though it was clear that his sister's opinion had a great influence on him.

He finished his drink in silence and got up.

"I want all the guests to leave by tomorrow morning," he said.

Val and I looked at each other, horrified. With Alec and Harriet gone, it was up to us now to put a stop to the mysterious events that occurred at the Pembroke estate. And whatever Lord Pembroke's feelings about the matter, I was sure that it was neither an outsider, nor that what had happened could be put down to pure chance or accident.

Nevertheless, a little diplomacy was required.

"Lord Pembroke," I said. "I'm very sorry about what has happened. It must be very… frustrating to have to deal with people like that."

He looked at me in surprise, though he didn't say anything.

"Unfortunately," I continued, "Val and I were planning on heading to Scotland from here. But we've only booked from the day after tomorrow onwards. I wonder if it were too much to ask if we could stay an extra night?"

The story was a complete fabrication, of course, yet the

only thing I was able to come up with at such short notice. Lord Pembroke hesitated, clearly unwilling to grant the request. Yet, as I had hoped, Beatrice intervened.

"Oh, go on," she said, taking another sip of whiskey. "They're alright. And it's just one more night, for heaven's sake. Unless you think *they* sent you those letters."

"No, of course not," Lord Pembroke grunted. "Very well, one additional night. But after that, I must insist that you leave."

"Thank you, Lord Pembroke," I said.

He nodded his head briefly, then made for the door and exited.

"You must forgive my brother," said Beatrice, when she was sure that we couldn't be overheard, "he is rather grumpy sometimes when things get to him. I must say, I can't say I blame him, the way things have worked out."

She got up rather uneasily and waddled over to the bar, pouring herself another generous helping of the amber liquid.

"What do you mean?" I asked.

"What?" she said suddenly, as though torn from a particularly burdensome train of thought. "Oh, it doesn't matter. Very unfortunate."

Out of the corner of my eye, I saw Val give the slightest of nods. It was probably the best opportunity we'd ever have of getting Beatrice on our own. Without anyone else in the room, Val could get a clear read on her emotions. And now, she clearly wanted me to press the matter.

"Did you know Emma, the maid?" I asked.

"A little, yes," sighed Beatrice.

"Was she a shy person?"

Beatrice laughed.

"Quite the contrary," she said. "She was unusually curious, even for a servant. And a bit of a tease, at least that's what some of the guests have told me."

"Strange how she then decided to commit suicide…"

I could tell that there was a lot more going on behind that alcoholic attempt at self-composure, though I tried to phrase my responses and queries as indirectly as possible. It wouldn't do for Beatrice to take a leaf out of her brother's book and throw us out for impertinent questioning.

***

With some interjections from Val, we kept talking until about midnight. Beatrice, though clearly a very practiced drinker, was getting more and more tipsy by the hour.

Like her nephew, the avoidance of boredom seemed to have been one of the driving forces behind her life at the Pembroke estate. She had been married twice, only to watch her husbands wither away before her eyes and finally die. It struck me as being, above all else, a lonely, even sad existence.

While Steven and Beatrice had preferred a life of pleasure, Lord Pembroke had retreated more and more over the years.

"It all goes back to the death of his w-wife, you see," Beatrice was saying.

"How was she?" I asked. "As a person, I mean."

"Oh, she was wonderful," said Beatrice. "Beautiful, well-bred, distinguished family. But she could tell a good story, too, if she wanted to. People simply adored her."

"It must have been quite a shock," I said.

"Oh yes," said Beatrice, waving her hand as though it were an understatement. "Everyone was devastated. My brother, of course. Although I'd say that Carew was a wreck, too."

"Carew?" asked Val in surprise.

"Yes," said Beatrice, after taking another sip. "He worshipped the ground she walked on. She was the perfect lady. And he had known her since she was little, you see. Before working for us, Carew was a footman for their family."

"I can imagine that must have been tough for him," I said. "Did he get over it, eventually?"

"As much as you can, I suppose," said Beatrice. "Her memory is still very much alive in the house."

Suddenly, she stopped talking, looking fearfully at the door.

"What's the matter?"

"Oh, I… I just thought I heard something," she said.

"I… I'll check for you, if you like," I said.

"W-would you?"

I got up from the sofa and opened the door, but the corridor beyond was empty.

"There's nobody there," I said.

Beatrice laughed nervously.

"Strange how this house still sends shudders down my spine after all those years."

There was a brief pause in which nobody knew what to say.

"Did Lord Pembroke ever remarry?" asked Val.

"Oh, no," Beatrice said. "No, my brother couldn't do that. It was her or no one."

"How does your brother spend most of his time, then?" I asked. "If he doesn't like the parties you and Steven hold."

"He lives to work," said Beatrice.

"What is he working on?" I asked.

"Oh, the magical field thingy, mostly," she said. "It requires constant maintenance apparently."

"Has it ever broken down?"

"Well, it certainly requires more work than it used to, as far as I understand it. I don't think there's ever any real danger of it breaking down completely, though. Not in the short term, at least. But after a few years of neglect, it might."

"Perhaps Lord Pembroke could do with a hobby," said Val, grinning.

Beatrice put down her glass and clapped her hands together in triumph.

"That is exactly what I've been thinking," she said. "He's so obsessed with the past that he forgets to live in the here and now. In the old days, he always used to enjoy a good challenge."

"What do you mean?" I asked.

"Well," she said, "something to sink his teeth into."

"Like a puzzle, for instance?"

"Exactly," said Beatrice. "A puzzle. A mystery."

And without hesitation, she downed the rest of her glass.

"There," she said, leaning over to me. "No consequences. We cannot die of age or cancer. Why not enjoy life a little?"

Her breath smelt very strongly of whiskey.

"Why not indeed," I said, catching Val's eye while I took a sip myself.

"So," said Beatrice, leaning back again, a look of cunning on her face. "I decided to give my brother something to live for again."

"To live for...?"

"That's right," she said. "I sent him a couple of threatening letters."

9

Val and I looked at each other, stunned.

"*You* sent the letters?"

"You know about them?" she asked, looking puzzled.

"We, erm, overheard you at breakfast a few days ago," I said.

It wasn't technically a lie, though I of course omitted that Alec had already told us about them beforehand and that they had in fact formed the basis and starting point of our investigation.

Beatrice, clearly very drunk by now, was having trouble focussing properly.

"D'you think I'm a bad person?" she said, slurring her words. "T-tell me, I can take it."

"Well, that depends," I said. "Did you have anything to do with Emma's death or Steven's accident?"

"No, I-I didn't, I swear I didn't," she said, suddenly aghast. "You mustn't think that. I admit that I wrote the letters. But I didn't have anything to do with that. I'd never harm Steven. He is my nephew, after all. He's the only reason this place remains bearable. And I didn't know Emma. I had no reason to hate her."

I looked at Val, who gave the slightest of nods. As far as she could read her, Beatrice hadn't been involved.

"But you don't think they were simply accidents or suicides, do you?" I asked.

She lowered her eyes to the floor, staring morosely at it for a minute.

"No," she said finally, all excitement gone from her voice. "I don't."

There was another brief silence as I waited for Val's confirmation. Once again, Val nodded her head.

It was evident that Beatrice, despite her rather tough

exterior and abrupt manner, was quite shaken by the events of the last few days.

"I didn't mean for things to develop as they d-did," she said miserably, fumbling with her empty whiskey glass. "All I wanted was to put some energy back into my brother's life. He was so caught up in the past, with the death of his wife. I... I didn't think that anything as awful as this could ever happen. You won't tell anyone, will you? Will you?"

Tears were silently running down her cheeks now.

"I won't," I said reassuringly. "But in return, I need your help. I want to find out who murdered Emma. And – if it's the same person – who tried to kill Steven this evening."

"I-I don't know anything about that," she said quickly.

Even without Val shaking her head softly in the background, I could tell that she was no longer telling the truth.

"Beatrice, please," I said. "You're protecting the wrong person. A murderer, for Heaven's sake. Don't you think that, whoever they are, they ought to be brought to justice?"

It took a moment for the horrible truth to fully sink in. Then, she looked at me.

"I-I don't know anything for certain, you have to understand," she began slowly, making a great effort to pull herself together. "But there have been s-strange things happening in this house ever since Emma arrived."

"What do you mean?"

"Steven was mad about her from the moment she stepped into the hall for the first time. She was his type. Open-minded, good-looking, sassy."

"Did anyone know about them being together?"

She sighed.

"It was a secret," she said, "though of course we all knew about it. It's impossible to keep anything a secret for long here."

"And Lord Pembroke didn't approve of Steven and Emma seeing each other?"

"No," she said, "I overheard my brother quarrelling with Emma on several occasions. And with Steven, too. That's very unusual, because my brother rarely loses his temper, only when he's under intense pressure, like tonight. But when he does, he just snaps. And then, he can be quite frightening. But my brother didn't approve of any of Steven's escapades, to be honest. It isn't the first time he's charmed one of the maids, I can assure you, though I think the relationship with Emma was more serious than any he has had for a long time."

"But if it was more serious, wouldn't Lord Pembroke be afraid that his son might marry out of his class?"

Beatrice looked afraid.

"I was worried about that, too…"

"Did you ever hear what the row was precisely about between Lord Pembroke and Emma?"

Beatrice shook her head.

"I'm sorry, I don't," she said. "And that's the truth, I swear it is. I asked my brother, but he wouldn't say. I *do* know that he sent Carew downstairs to her room to snoop around, but I don't know what he was looking for."

Slowly, the pieces of puzzle were falling into place.

"And you caught Carew snooping in Emma's room again, after her death?"

"How did you…?"

"Did you?"

"Why, y-yes," she said in surprise, "yes, I did. But I had no luck in getting anything out of that man. He's fiercely devoted to the family honour and that sort of thing."

"Did Emma ever catch him?" I asked. "Carew, I mean."

"She might have done," said Beatrice. "I'm afraid I don't know that."

"Hardly a reason for murder, though," Val said, frowning.

"No," said Beatrice. "Anyway, I think it more likely of my brother that he would simply not involve himself. Carew would gladly take any blame, he's so loyal. That's what I don't understand. It must have been something important. A good reason for sending him down there to have a look round."

"Can you tell us anything about Lord Pembroke's assistant, Sarah?" asked Val.

"Sarah?" asked Beatrice in surprise. "Why, no. As far as I know, she's enjoys working for my brother. I was never much interested in the inner workings of magic, to be honest, as long as it works."

She got up to get herself another drink.

"Well, thank you, Beatrice," I said, getting up slowly. "You've been a great help."

"D-don't tell anyone," she said. "Don't tell anyone what I told you. Please."

"It will be our secret until this whole thing is cleared up," I said. "In fact, I'd appreciate it if you didn't tell anyone we had this little chat, either."

"F-fine," she said, supressing a hiccup.

***

A quarter of an hour later, we were back in our room again. As we ascended the stairs that led to our landing, Barry was impatiently waiting in front of our door.

"This is becoming something of a habit of yours, isn't it?" he said, narrowing his eyes. "Keeping me hanging around in the corridors like this. You know, one day someone will notice the pattern and kidnap me."

"Really sorry, Barry," I said. "But it was important."

"Why would anyone want to kidnap you, Barry?" Val asked.

"To keep me as a prisoner scientist, of course," said Barry. "Happens more often than you think."

Val sniggered.

"I'll keep that in mind," I said, grinning. "Anyway, we've got some good news."

"It was definitely worth it," said Val, who looked utterly exhausted from using her psychic powers for such a long prolonged period of time.

"I hope so," said Barry uncharitably. "I'm getting hungry. A cat has to eat, you know."

"Where have you been all this time, anyway?" I asked. "After Steven was carried out by the healers, I mean. You weren't here all the time, surely?"

"My expertise was required elsewhere," said Barry.

"What do you mean?"

"Sarah showed me the generator for the magical field," he said. "Very interesting indeed. A masterpiece of magic and engineering. Could hardly have done it better myself."

"That's certainly high praise, coming from you, Barry," I said.

"Why did she do that?" asked Val, while I fumbled for the key in my handbag. "Take you down to this generator thing, I mean."

"She asked me whether I could take a look at it," said Barry. "There *are* some people who value my insights, you know."

I had finally retrieved the key and placed it into the lock.

"I think she values more than that," said Val.

"And what if she does?" retorted Barry. "It's not a crime, is it?"

"And you were with her all this time?"

I unlocked the door and pushed it open.

"No," said Barry defensively, "I wasn't. After we had finished, she needed to do some work on her own, so I took a walk in the grounds for a while. Then I came here, so…"

"Barry, Val!" I exclaimed, pointing into the room. "Look."

Our suite was unrecognisable.

The table and the sofa had been overturned and lay on their sides. Contents from our bags and suitcases were strewn throughout the room. Coats and pullovers had been flung all over the place. Even the small bin in the corner had been emptied.

"This is outrageous," said Barry, puffing up his little chest in indignation. "We ought to complain to the management immediately. I mean, we're not paying room service to wreck the place, are we?"

"This wasn't the maid, Barry," I said, carefully checking all corners of the suite to make sure nobody was there. "Somebody's been going through our things."

"Who would do such a thing?" asked Val fearfully.

I stepped back into the living room again.

"Let's check everything," I said. "See whether anything's been taken."

My bedroom was in a similar state as the living room. Cushions lay on the floor, even the mattress had been turned over. The room was littered with clothes, toiletries and all the other necessities of travelling.

Surprisingly, it seemed that nothing had been stolen at all, except…

"My wand," I called, rummaging through my suitcase in vain. "My wand is gone. I can't find it."

Val came rushing into my room.

"What?"

"They took my wand," I said. "I'm positive I left it here in the suitcase."

"Why did you leave it there for?" asked Barry, sliding past Val's leg.

"Well, I didn't think anyone was going to break in here, did I?" I said irritably. "And since we're not allowed to use magic here, I thought I'd just leave it in my room."

"What a foolish thing to do," said Barry.

"Yes, thank you, Barry," I said. "That isn't very helpful right now, is it?"

"What are we going to do now?" asked Val.

"We've got to find out who did this," I said. "A stolen wand is not a good omen. Barry, did you see anyone while you were waiting outside the door?"

"No," he said, "I didn't. As I said, Sarah dropped me off in the grounds and then I had a well-deserved stroll around the gardens. When I came back, about an hour or so later, the door here was locked, so I waited for you to finally bother to turn up."

"They must have already done the deed by then," I said, frowning.

"Couldn't it be Carew?" asked Val. "He did search Emma's room, after all."

"On multiple occasions even," I said. "If we believe Beatrice."

"I've never liked the look of that fellow," said Barry dismissively. "A shifty servant if ever there was one."

"What would he want in here?"

"To see how far we've got in the investigation, most likely," I said. "They must have found out about our involvement in the case."

"But Carew would work on orders only, surely?" asked Val.

"Come on," I said. "I think it's time we confronted Lord Pembroke. This has been going on for long enough. And we've got to get my wand back."

***

As we re-entered the endless, maze-like corridors of Pembroke House again, it was already well past midnight, leaving only the faint glow of the ancient oil lamps to guide our way. While we searched for the entrance to the West wing, Val and I told Barry all about Beatrice, and that she had been behind the threatening letters.

Though I didn't like crowds, I would have preferred a noisy football stadium right now to the eerie silence of the barely lit passages that unwinded before us. The few remaining guests that had not already left the house had all presumably gone to bed.

Though I knew that Lord Pembroke's rooms were in the West wing, I had not yet come to grips with the architecture of the place. It just didn't make any sense. It resembled a labyrinth.

"Who would design a house this way?" I said irritably, after ending up in yet another corridor that led nowhere. "There's no logic to this at all."

"Maybe it was intended to do just that," said Val. "Any intruder would take ages to get out of here even if he did find something."

After encountering several more dead ends, we finally came across a large staircase with an ornate red carpet. It seemed oddly misplaced at the far end of the house, for even the entrance hall sported one that was much smaller and less impressive.

Leaning over the balustrade, I also noticed that the stairs extended down into the cellars. For the Pembroke House, at least, this was rather unusual, since each staircase was separate from the other, so that one couldn't scale multiple floors at once.

For someone acquainted with the complicated layout of the house, therefore, gaining access to the servants' quarters couldn't be more than a matter of a few minutes from here.

"Where are we?" asked Val.

"The West wing, I hope," I said. "We'd better take off our shoes, Val. Better not advertise our approach too much."

"Good thinking," she said, bending down.

Leaving the shoes at the foot of the staircase, we crept up them as silently as we could.

I had never felt more vulnerable. Without my wand, I was defenceless in a magical duel. And although magic was officially forbidden at the Pembroke estate, I doubted the person who had stolen my wand would hesitate to use it.

After a few minutes of patient tiptoeing, careful not to make the stairs creak too much, we had reached the top floor.

"Do you think this is it?" whispered Val, pointing at a large double door at the end of the landing.

Let's give it a try," I said.

We sneaked across the landing, which squeaked underneath our feet. But before we could open the door, Val grabbed my arm.

"There's someone in there," she whispered.

Barry, Val, and I stood there, frozen to the spot, listening intently.

"This is ridiculous," a muffled voice inside was saying inside.

"It's Lord Pembroke, I think," I said, leaning against the door with my ear.

"What is he saying?" whispered Val.

Pressing harder against the door, I could barely make out what was being said inside.

"… regret it. No, I…"

Lord Pembroke stopped speaking. Then, there was the sound of wild scuffling, followed by a yell from Lord Pembroke.

"HELP!"

"Come on," I said, "I think he's in trouble."

I tried to open the door, but it wouldn't budge.

"It's locked," I said.

Barry cursed under his breath.

"What now?"

"There's another door over there," said Barry, pointing it out with his paw.

Suddenly, there was a loud blast, as though someone had fired a cannonball. It shook the walls and the ceiling so hard that dust came raining down on our heads.

"Quickly," I said.

Luckily, the other door was unlocked. I tore it open and raced inside.

We found ourselves in a room with high ceilings, and what must have been thousands and thousands of books. Fine armchairs made of leather surrounded an old-fashioned fireplace.

"There's another door to the right," said Val, pointing at it.

I flung it open, entering a large bedroom with a four poster bed.

"Amy, over here," said Val.

Leaning against the oak-panelled wall, was a body.

"It's Lord Pembroke," I said, rushing over. "Barry, check if they're still here!"

As Barry sprinted into the next room as fast as his feline legs would carry him, I bent down to feel Lord Pembroke's pulse.

But there was nothing there. He was dead.

10

Val put her hand against her mouth.

"Is he…?" she asked.

"He's dead," I said.

"How did he…"

"I don't know," I said. "I can't see any external wounds or anything that…"

At that moment, Barry came back into the bedroom.

"Nobody there," said Barry. "I checked everywhere. Is he…?"

"Dead," I said.

"Here," said Val, standing a few feet away and pointing to something on the ground. "Amy, look!"

I walked over to where she was standing.

Lying at her feet was a thin, finely carved wand. Val picked it up.

"Amy, that's…"

"…mine," I said grimly.

This was a witch's worst nightmare. A capital offence committed with one's own wand. And only witnesses that any court would consider extremely biased were present to testify that one hadn't done the deed.

"They're trying to frame me," I said, turning the wand slowly in my hand.

"Who is?" said Val.

"Your guess is as good as mine," I said.

"We've got to notify the MLE immediately," said Barry. "Or that private investigator."

"You're right," I said, turning to Val. "I need you to notify Alec immediately. Tell him what has happened. If you're lucky, Harriet might still be patrolling the perimeter outside."

"Amy, I'm not going to leave you here," said Val,

crossing her arms.

"We can't do this alone, Val," I said.

"OK," she said, "what do I do if she isn't outside but instead is at home painting her nails or combing her hair or something?"

"They are officially off the case, Amanda," Barry interjected.

"In that case, go to the car. The keys are in my handbag in our room. Drive far enough away from the estate so that you can use your mobile phone again."

I hastened to a small secretary that stood a few feet away from Lord Pembroke's bed and hastily wrote down a telephone number.

"Alec gave me this in case of an emergency," I said, handing the paper over to Val. "It belongs to a heb friend of his who lives in his street. Tell her that there's been a murder at the Pembroke estate and that we need backup immediately. She'll convey the message to Alec."

"OK, Amy," said Val, fear etched across her face. "But where will you be?"

"Barry and I will put an ending to these killings once and for all," I said.

"But you don't know who it is," said Val.

"We'll be fine, Val," I said. "As long as we get that backup as quickly as possible."

Though I could see that Val was still in an argumentative mood, she finally nodded her head.

"Be safe," she said.

"And you," I said.

After giving Barry an affectionate pat on the head, which Barry even forgot to pretend to be angry about for once, she exited Lord Pembroke's private chambers and rushed down the long staircase as fast as she could.

"Where do we go from here?" asked Barry. "Val's right, you know. We don't have slightest inkling of who is behind all of this."

"We've got one advantage," I said. "The murderer had

no time after killing Lord Pembroke to get rid of any clues. We're bound to find something in here."

I vaguely indicated the secretary and Lord Pembroke's library. Though I could see doubt in Barry's face, he nodded.

"I'll examine the body more closely," he said. "I might be able to glean some more information."

"Good idea," I said. "I'll start by retracing the killer's steps."

***

As Barry began his more in-depth examination of the body, I tried to reconstruct the scene. First, I went back to the landing and counted the seconds we had needed to enter Lord Pembroke's bedroom.

Then, I tried to reconstruct the killer's movements. There were two additional doors leading away from the bedroom, aside from the one we had come through. One of them was locked. That was the door we had tried to enter by first on the landing. The second, therefore, must have offered itself as the only escape route for the killer.

Though I had no illusions about the murderer lingering for very long, I kept my wand at the ready as I opened the door.

The next room was dimly lit by a burning oil lamp. The wallpaper had a floral design, such as popularised by William Morris. There was a bed in the centre of the room. This, I supposed, must have been the bedroom of Lord Pembroke's wife.

Everything in the room had been perfectly kept, even to the smallest detail. Even an old-fashioned woman's nightgown had been folded carefully and placed on the pillow. A book with an old binding and yellow pages lay on the nightstand.

There was a bathroom through one door, while another led onto another, much smaller landing, with a narrow, winding staircase leading down. This, clearly, had been the murderer's route of escape.

Stepping back into the bedroom of Lord Pembroke's deceased wife, I made sure to lock the door to the landing. I didn't think for a minute, of course, that it would prevent a magic-wielder from entering, though the distinctive clicking noise of the unlocking spell would serve as a useful warning to us while we were searching for clues in Lord Pembroke's chambers.

As I returned, Barry was examining Lord Pembroke's head wounds more closely. It was a peculiar, almost sacrilegious feeling to be going through his things while he lay there, but I kept telling myself that, after all, it served the purpose of catching his killer. Returning to our room or leaving the estate would simply provide the murderer with an opportunity to get rid of any clues.

Next, I sat down at the small secretary. It seemed as though Lord Pembroke corresponded only occasionally, with the latest private letters he had received dating from over three months ago. Most of the more recent letters were bills, sent by a specialist company called *The Edinburgh Spellcasting Engineers Inc.* Their services had been rendered mainly for repairs to the magical field system.

After I had gone through all of Lord Pembroke's correspondence that I could find, I turned to the library next door.

Under different circumstances, I think I would have been able to appreciate its beauty, from the expertly carved oak panelling that went so well with the green leather of the sofa and armchairs.

Although there were several personal items, including a pipe, strong tobacco, several ornaments, and a newspaper article on age preservation that Lord Pembroke had evidently been working on, I could find nothing that pointed to any of the suspects.

Above the mantelpiece was a portrait of Lord Pembroke, though it was much smaller and less forbidding than the painting of his father that had hung in the hall. The photographs on the shelves were mostly of his deceased wife. She had been a very beautiful woman, albeit in a somewhat detached, almost cold sort of way. She hardly ever smiled in any of the pictures.

I was just about to turn around and see how Barry was getting on when a small object at the foot of one of the armchairs near the fireplace caught my eye. It had the length of a pocket notebook, though it had an elaborately designed cover made of sturdy leather and was much thicker than might be expected.

I opened it. To my excitement, it read *Diary of Lord Pembroke*, followed by the current year.

I quickly skipped a few pages. Lord Pembroke's writing was tiny, so I had to hold it closer to the light. Most of the entries dealt with rather mundane matters, such as various tasks that still had to be performed, though every so often, Lord Pembroke's thoughts on other matters had been recorded.

March 1st
Steven insists on yet another one of those ghastly parties of his. Wish he would stop, though Beatrice is firmly on his side in this. Have asked Carew to make my excuses.

I eagerly read on, until I came across an interesting passage further along:

May 23rd
Have alerted the authorities to the anonymous letters I have been receiving. Didn't seem to take it very seriously, so I have also tasked a private investigator to get to the bottom of this.

Soon enough, as early summer progressed, Lord Pembroke's entries on the subject became a lot more frequent.

June 3ʳᵈ
More letters arrive almost every week. Everyone worried. Don't know whom to trust anymore. New maid, a girl called Emma, has been making a nuisance of herself. Beatrice believes she has somehow ensnared Steven, though that has not proven to be all that difficult in the past. Have asked Carew to keep an eye on the situation for me.

Soon, however, other woes seemed to be drifting into focus.

June 14ᵗʰ
The magic field generator has been causing a lot of problems of late. Dysfunctions that haven't occurred before. Edinburgh engineers don't know what to do, so I have brought in someone to monitor the situation on a permanent basis.

June 17ᵗʰ
Sarah informs me that problems are a lot more serious than I thought. Generator is running out of energy, despite regular infusions. Unclear as to what is causing it, but time is running against us. Have not informed Beatrice and the others yet. Won't do so unless absolutely necessary, as not to cause too much alarm.

June 28ᵗʰ
The new maid has been caught snooping around the generator again. Have had a talk with Steven, who remains stubborn on the matter.
Sarah really has been a godsend these last few days. Magical field might have destabilised without her. She has also been extraordinarily sympathetic to the family's plight, as well as my own. At least one person I can trust in this place, though Carew does his

best, I suppose.

June 30th

Carew has discovered notes on all sorts of family affairs, including delicate information on the construction of the generator, in Emma's room. She must be dismissed immediately from our service. Have let the Spellcasters' Ministry of Justice *know that I wish to have a gagging spell enacted, preventing Emma from revealing anything important. Will await their answer before formally dismissing her. Beatrice and Steven have been informed. Steven promised to discuss the matter with Emma. A futile attempt. Though why she has done all of this remains a mystery.*

The next few diary entries were concerned with the technical aspects of repairing the magical field and the generator that had powered it for such a long time. Lord Pembroke's writing on the matter was becoming more and more desperate. Despite his and Sarah's best efforts, the problems only kept mounting.

July 1st

Essence coils have broken down yet again, despite our repairs from last Friday. I'm beginning to wonder whether all of this is more than just pure accident.

Steven claims that he has found the reason for Emma's snooping. On confronting her with the evidence, she admitted that she works for one of the national newspapers. They have promised to pay her handsomely for a series of anonymous articles on the magical field generator. A fine taste in women Steven has there, I must say.

July 3rd

Emma tragically fell to her death. Healers presume it was suicide, though Steven is insistent that it wasn't. He has been making the most ridiculous and wild accusations. The boy has completely lost control of himself.

I will not deny that the family benefits from the tragedy, but as I pointed out to Steven only last night, the authorities were quite sympathetic to our situation and therefore granted the placement of a gag. Emma would have been bound by magical contract to complete secrecy.

I have asked Carew to retrieve and destroy all delicate information that Emma gathered during her time here.

There were only two more entries remaining.

July 5th
Steven has been the victim of a terrible accident. My father's painting in the hall fell on him. Healers and bystanders reacted very quickly.

I am informed that his chances of survival are moderate to good, depending on how well his system reacts to the potions. He cannot be brought out of the estate, of course, though I have sent for the very best healers from London to care for him here.

Sarah has informed me that the essence coils have lost power yet again. The system is stable, for now.

I have made a rather daunting discovery, however. My suspicions that the problems surrounding the generator were more than mere accidents have been confirmed. Not only the coils, but also other systems have had corrosive spells applied to them for weeks now. The level of degradation is otherwise unexplainable, since many of the parts are new. Someone clearly is trying to bring the generator offline through sabotage.

As to the perpetrator, I am awaiting confirmation from various sources. Any accusation until then remains mere guess work.

At last, I turned to the last entry.

July 5th, second entry

Have received word tonight. My suspicions have been confirmed.

Will contact the MLE in the morning. The saboteur is

I turned the page eagerly. But apart from a drop of ink, it was blank. I hectically turned page after page, in the hope that Lord Pembroke had accidentally skipped a few, but it was no use. There was nothing more written.

I hurried into the bedroom where Barry was still examining Lord Pembroke's body.

"Barry," I said, holding up the diary, "look what I've found. It's his diary. It's all in here."

I quickly told him about the mysterious system failures that had beleaguered the magical generator, as well as Emma's snooping around.

"He had a gagging order, you say?" Barry said in surprise.

"That's what he wrote," I said.

"They are rarely granted, you must understand," said Barry, frowning. "Lord Pembroke must have had an ironclad case, though with such delicate magic, it's certainly called for."

"How does it work, exactly?"

"A spell is performed at a magical court," said Barry, "by the judge. It prevents the person in question from writing, talking about, or otherwise informing a third party of a specific subject. It's quite invasive magic, as you might imagine, and thus rarely granted."

"So Lord Pembroke wouldn't have had a reason to kill her, then," I said.

"Not if his request was granted," said Barry. "But if Emma was the saboteur…"

"No," I said. "The problems continued occurring after her death. And even so, he could have just thrown her out."

"But then who is it?" asked Barry. "Unless that infernal butler has become tired of life and went on a rampage, I don't see who else might have had the opportunity or the motive for that matter."

"I think I know who it is," I said. "And Lord Pembroke knew, too. He was just about to write it in his diary, when he must have been disturbed."

"Well, who is it?"

"It's been staring us in the face all this time," I said, pacing up and down. "I was so caught up in all these family affairs that I never thought to look beyond them. An outsider would have a completely different set of motives."

"I don't follow you, Amanda…"

"The letters are unimportant. They were sent by Lord Pembroke's sister, a step that misfired badly, grant you, but there was no malicious intent. The question we have to ask is who had access as well as the expertise to go through with the sabotage."

"But we have nothing to go on," said Barry. "All we know from the diary is that the system was sabotaged deliberately."

"Don't you see?" I said. "There's only one person capable enough to have so cleverly sabotaged the system without arousing suspicion, at least for a while."

"And who, pray, may that be?"

"It's your friend," I said. "Sarah."

11

"Preposterous," said Barry indignantly. "She couldn't hurt a fly."

"Don't' you see? It all fits. She's a recent addition to the house. She probably knows the system almost as well as Lord Pembroke by now. And she has all day to tinker with it."

"But… but there's still Beatrice, she could have done it just as well."

"Why would she sabotage a system that's the only thing preventing her from dying of old age on the spot?" I said. "It doesn't make any sense, Barry."

"But Sarah has no motive," spluttered Barry, though I could tell that his defences were spreading thin now.

"No?" I said. "Can't you think of anything? You're the magical theorist, after all. What could one do with such a generator?"

Barry stared at me for a moment.

But before he could answer, a rumbling permeated Lord Pembroke's bedroom. It sounded like the beginnings of thunderstorm.

"What was that?" Barry said, a slight of panic in his voice. "What's going on?"

"Probably a thunderstorm," I said, gazing out of the window. "It's too dark to see anything, though."

"I still can't believe it's her," said Barry bluntly.

"Barry, you've seen the magical field generator, haven't you?"

"Why, yes, Sarah showed it to me only the other day," he said.

"And did she ask you anything about it?"

Barry hesitated.

"Yes," he finally admitted. "She… she asked me about the generator. I had written a paper quite some time ago on a related matter, you see."

"And what was that about?"

"Essence coils," he said.

"The key component that's been sabotaged over and over again," I said.

Barry looked at me in astonishment.

"She fooled me," he said bitterly. "I should have known."

"She fooled us all," I said. "Except for Val, I suppose, but I thought she was just jealous. I…"

Suddenly, the floor began to shake uncontrollably, as though an earthquake had hit Pembroke house.

"That's no ordinary thunderstorm," said Barry.

"She must be finishing the job," I said. "Barry, where is the generator located?"

"It's… it's in the West tower."

"Show me the way," I said, drawing my wand. "Whatever she's doing up there, we've got to put a stop to it."

Unlocking the door to the landing, Barry and I hastened out of Lord Pembroke's chambers.

We hurtled down the dimly lit corridors of the West wing, passing countless doors and little staircases leading to other parts of the wing. We were accompanied by a cacophony of rumblings and, whenever we passed a window facing the grounds, distant cries as the last guests fled the house.

I was surprised at how well Barry navigated the maze-like structure of the house, though perhaps it was his indignation above all else that was guiding the way forward.

Although we were making headway, it seemed like an eternity before we finally arrived at the entrance to the tower. I knew from viewing it from the grounds that it was massive, easily surpassing the rest of the house in height. It was also the tower that Emma had fallen from. Though it was undoubtedly sturdy, I wondered whether if even it could withstand the destruction of the generator.

"Use your wand only if absolutely necessary," said Barry. "Remember, too much magic might further destabilise the field generator."

"Right," I said.

Carefully, I opened the door to the West tower. We were immediately greeted by a blast of hot air and a putrid smell of burning as we entered the long, winding staircase.

"It's right at the top," whispered Barry.

"What about these other rooms?" I asked, indicating the rooms leading off the narrow, circular landings.

"Storage, I believe," said Barry.

"Alright," I said softly. "You'd better stay back. If I can get a clean shot at her, it will all be over with a minimum of magic. Val should be back soon with Alec and hopefully the MLE, too."

As we ascended the stairs, the noise coming from the top was getting louder and louder. A humming sound was interrupted every so often by the clattering of metal, followed by reverberations that seemed to penetrate me completely, as though someone had turned up the bass of a surround system to an unbearable level.

At last, we found ourselves on the very top floor. Barry indicated the room farthest away. I could see that he was shaking badly, though whether out of nerves or rage and indignation I could not tell.

Holding my wand tight in my hand, I crept forward, making sure to keep the door that Barry had indicated covered at all times. The stench was so bad now that I had to hold my sleeve to my face in order not to gag on the spot.

As I reached the closed door, I paused. Though it was very difficult to tell amidst the ear-splitting noise of the generator, I could have sworn that there was someone inside, speaking loudly.

I, too, was now shaking slightly. My wand hand was sweating from grasping the handle so hard for such a long time. This was the moment of reckoning, the moment I had to get right. If I didn't get a clean shot immediately, I'd not only risk our lives, but also the lives of all those protected by the magical field from ageing. That was a constraint that, unfortunately, did not apply to Sarah. If she could extend the fight, she would be so much closer to her goal.

Gathering all my remaining courage, I put my hand on the handle of the door. Wand at the ready to fire at the slightest movement inside, I turned it.

Time seemed to move in slow motion as the door swung wide open in front of me, revealing a medium-sized room, dominated by a huge machine in its midst that towered over us. The air was hot and humid, and I began to sweat immediately.

The machine must have been ten feet tall at least, almost reaching to the ceiling. It was largely made of metal, with pipes and valves protruded from every angle, leaving only a foot or so for us to enter the room. Though I didn't usually fear enclosed spaces, it made me feel claustrophobic just by looking at it.

Atop the machine, I could barely make out a large, bright red sphere, wedged underneath the ceiling. It was venting thick, opaque steam that flowed throughout the entire room, making it impossible to see much further than a few yards at best.

Both the steam and the machine itself made it impossible to tell if anyone was in the room with us. I turned around to Barry.

"I can't see a thing," I whispered. "Is the steam normal, d'you think?"

"This shouldn't be happening," said Barry, a worried look on his face. "The generator must have deteriorated more than I expected. Someone's been doing a lot of magic near it. They must be breaking it down right now, as we speak."

"Let's walk around the machine," I said softly. "Keep an eye out to the back."

Barry nodded.

"Remember, you have one shot at the most," he said. "Any more magic and the whole thing might explode."

Wand held before me, I slowly walked into thick mist before us.

I felt like a blind person trying to navigate an unfamiliar place, though walking along the wall gave me at least some sense of direction. More and more windows appeared in the wall, though the bright light within the machine room prevented me from seeing outside into the darkness.

We had passed roughly half-way when there was a terrible scream.

"NOOO!"

"Repello!" another voice cried.

The spell was followed by a horrible crack of bone on metal. Then, the entire room began to shake uncontrollably. The humming sound was replaced by a terrible, penetrating rumbling from the machine next to us.

Without thinking, I rushed forward, trying to find the source of the commotion. I hadn't anticipated that multiple people were here. But, quite clearly, someone was in trouble.

And then, I suddenly tripped over something long and boney. I was sent flying, face forward, skidding along the cold stone floor until I struck my head against the side of the machine, sending my wand flying out of reach.

I yelled in pain.

"Stop right there," a voice said.

My head felt dizzy. The room around me was spinning uncontrollably. I tried to focus, to see who it was bending over me.

"S-Sarah?" I said.

Though my head was still throbbing, the room was gradually shifting into focus once again. Barry was nowhere to be seen.

The shape in front of me slowly came closer. They were holding a wand, pointing it directly at me. And then, I recognised who it was.

"Harriet!" I exclaimed.

Harriet looked just as beautiful as ever, with her long, blonde hair tied into ponytail. She was wearing a black dress.

"Amanda?" she said, a look of utter surprise on her face. "Is that you?"

"Yes," I said, getting gingerly to my feet. "So Val got the message to you?"

"Yes, that's right," said Harriet, pocketing her wand. "Just in the nick of time, too. I was about to leave for London. Alec asked me to keep an eye on things for a bit longer, you see. I flew up here, to the tower. And a few minutes later, I was ambushed by that woman over there."

She pointed to a body, slumped against the machine, feet outstretched. It was unmistakably Lord Pembroke's assistant, Sarah. She was holding a wand.

"I tripped over her feet, I think," I said, as Barry approached us.

"Hello," said Barry stiffly.

"Oh, hello," said Harriet pleasantly.

"What are you doing here, anyway?" asked Harriet.

"After we found Lord Pembroke," I said, "we put two and two together."

"You've got a nasty bruise on your head," said Harriet. "It's bleeding."

She took out her wand again to fix it, but I held up my hand.

"Don't," I said. "Any more magic, and we risk destabilising the generator."

"It looks bad," said Barry, examining a complicated array of indicators on the side of the machine. "We've got to stabilise the machine right now. If we don't, the generator will definitely exhaust itself."

"How long have we got?" asked Harriet.

"No more than five minutes," said Barry. "We've got to act quickly before it's too late."

"What do we have to do?" I asked.

"We need to infuse the generator with magic. That will take pressure off the essence coils until we can repair them."

"What's the spell?" I asked.

"The incantation is 'infusio'," he said. "Use repeating, half-moon movements. Point your wand at this valve here."

"I thought magic makes it worse?" I asked.

"Not if it's fed directly into the system," said Barry, tapping the panel beside him with his paw. "Only external magic will destabilise it. And once it's offline, even for a minute, there is no saving the Pembrokes."

"I've got to find my wand first," I said. "It must be here somewhere."

Bending down to see through the mist, I began searching for my wand on the floor.

"Oh, I wouldn't bother with that, if I were you," said Harriet.

I turned around in surprise.

"What are you talking about?" I asked. "Didn't you hear what Barry said? The generator is going to go offline within minutes. Steven, Beatrice, Carew, old Lady Wickersham, they're all going to die if we don't do something."

Harriet smiled, though it did not extend to her blue eyes at all. Then, she pointed her wand at me.

"You stay right where you are, Amanda," she said.

Horrified, I stared at her.

"You can't be serious?"

"Move away from the generator," she commanded.

"It… it was you all along!" cried Barry. "I should have known."

"Indeed," she said, inclining her head as though she

were bowing after a particularly good stage performance.

"But… it can't be," I spluttered. "You're Alec's assistant. You're on our side…"

She laughed.

"That shows you how fleeting alliances can be sometimes," she said. "Take Sarah, here, for instance. She was easily manipulated into believing that I was actually trying to protect Lord Pembroke's precious magical field, along with the pointless lives of his relatives. So naïve."

"But she found out it was you," I breathed.

"She certainly became more suspicious after the essence coils malfunctioned for the second time," said Harriet. "The stupid girl ran to Lord Pembroke and told him all about it."

"That's why you had to kill him," I said. "He knew it was you."

"Full marks, Amanda," she said, smiling. "Though a little late, I might add. In about five minutes, the generator will begin to degrade. Enough time for a little chat."

"Why did you kill Emma?" I asked.

"She saw me one night, up here," said Harriet with an air of mock regret. "Such a pity. I quite liked her, you know. It was quite fortunate for me that she tended to put her nose where it didn't belong. Many more likely suspects."

"Why do you want to destroy the magical field generator so badly?"

"Who said anything about destroying it?" she said, her eyes flashing.

"You… you want to dismantle it," I said slowly. "And erect it somewhere else."

"Very good," she said, nodding her head. "Why should the Pembrokes enjoy it for all eternity? They have had a long, albeit pointless life. It's time for the torch to be handed over to more capable hands."

"You have no right…" I began.

I was interrupted by a babble of voices coming from

the entrance of the machine room. For the first time, there was real fear in Harriet's eyes.

"We're at the other end," I yelled. "It's Harriet. She's the killer…"

"SILENCE," she bellowed.

She whisked her wand like a lasso, firing a spell in my direction.

But I was ready. I dodged sideways, rolling off the floor and underneath the machine.

"Amy, we're coming!"

It was Val.

"Careful," I bellowed. "She's armed."

Harriet was now wildly hurling spells in all directions, trying to keep everyone at bay.

I looked around desperately for my wand, but the thick fog made it impossible to find see anything.

Meanwhile, the generator above my head was spitting and spurting horribly, sending tremors throughout the room. With so many spells cast in its vicinity in such a short period, there was no way of telling how quickly it would degenerate.

Making sure that Barry was out of the way, I got into position.

"Give yourself up, Harriet," another voice boomed.

It was Alec. My heart leapt. With him around, Harriet was no match for us.

"Stay away, you fool, or I'll blow the whole place up!" screeched Harriet, though I could tell that there was fear in her voice.

At first, I thought we had Harriet cornered, with her back against the wall. Alec and Val were making progress, dodging in and out sight, using the machine itself for cover.

But then, I saw what Harriet was planning. She was trying to inch closer to the open window only a few yards away from her. Lying on the floor was her umbrella-turned-broomstick.

After casting another torrent of spells, Harriet made a wild dash for the broomstick, just as Alec and I emerged from behind the machine from either side, closing in on her.

For a moment, it looked as though she couldn't decide on whom to fire. But then, she aimed her wand at Alec, screaming:

"Exculpo!"

A beam of red light shot across the room, blinding me temporarily.

In the corner of my eye, I saw Alec collapse to the ground in front of her. Without thinking, and with no weapon to hand, I hurled myself on top of her, sending her wand flying through the air.

She struggled like a cornered animal, but I was winning the fight. I almost had her pinned down.

But then, the machine suddenly emitted another terrifying tremor that shook the room like an earthquake, sending me off-balance.

While I got back on my feet, it was just the split second that Harriet required. With one last, desperate dash, she sprinted to the broomstick, kicking frantically off the ground.

I jumped forward, but I was too late. Harriet was already in the air. She shot out of the window like a bolt of lightning. Within seconds, she had disappeared into the darkness.

A moment later, Barry had reached me. He was carrying my wand in his mouth and dropped it at my feet. I bent down to retrieve it.

"Amanda," said Barry. "You must repair the generator immediately. There's not a second to be lost."

"Alec…" I began, hurrying over to him.

"Amy," said Val, who was crouching next to him, "there's nothing you can do for him. He's gone."

"No," I whispered frantically. "No, it can't… he just can't…"

"Amy…"

"Get out of my way, Val," I said.

"Amy, what are you doing?" said Val.

"I'm going after her," I said. "I'm going to kill her."

"No, you can't!" she said, just as the generator released another massive amount of steam. "We've got to repair the generator."

"She can't get away with this!" I yelled.

"She's gone, Amanda," Barry said. "Come to your senses. The Pembrokes will die if you don't inject magic into the machine RIGHT NOW."

The words reverberated in my skull for what felt like an eternity, though in reality only seconds had passed.

Though my entire being screamed for revenge, to hunt down Harriet, I turned to the machine behind me and began with the incantations.

12

By the time the MLE and the healers had finally arrived on the spot, it was already too late for them to help, in any regard.

I had been able to inject the generator with magic just in time. As I channelled the spell, and the minutes slowly passed, the same images of Alec collapsing to the floor flashed before my mind's eye, again and again. For as long as I lived, I would not forget that horrible moment.

I felt numb inside, as though I were underwater and only heard and saw everything through a filter. Despite saving the occupants of the house, as well as the generator itself, it was a hollow victory to me.

Harriet had been able to escape. And Alec was dead. It felt so unreal, and yet it had happened.

In the hours that followed, I answered the MLE's questions as if I were in a daydream. Again and again, I went over all the clues, the suspects, the chronology of events.

Had there been a way to avoid the catastrophic chain of events that led to Alec's death and Harriet's escape? Perhaps, I thought, I had underestimated the allure of the machine that the Pembrokes possessed; that many people would be drawn to it, as Emma had been, albeit in a journalistic way. Had it been so unlikely then – human nature being what it is – that eventually someone would try to steal the magical machine? In hindsight, it seemed almost a miracle that the Pembrokes were not faced with regular break-ins and attempts to steal it.

***

Back at Fickleton House, I must have spent days on

end in my room, my head locked in circular ruminations that led nowhere. Had there been a chance to stop Harriet, to recognise what she was? But she had pulled the wool over all of our eyes, including those of a seasoned private investigator. But in Alec's business, even a single mistake could be enormously costly indeed.

His funeral had taken place a week after the events at the Pembroke estate. It was a short, unceremonious affair, though I had been surprised at how many people had attended. A warlock from the MLE, an old colleague, gave a short eulogy, espousing his life's work and drive for justice. Then, he was buried.

Though Val encouraged me to stay and talk with his relatives and friends, I couldn't do it. Instead, I retreated to the prison of my room and my thoughts.

As the days and then a week had passed, Val and Barry tried to lure me out into the open again. It felt wrong, somehow, to do so, before I had come to a solution. And yet, my thoughts were trapped in some sort of horrible and endless feedback loop. I had lost a friend. And possibly more than that, though now I would never find out. We had also been robbed of the opportunity of discovering what might have been, too.

Now, however, that avenue was shut forever. I could do nothing to change the past. All that remained was to honour his memory by seeking revenge and bringing Harriet to justice.

***

One afternoon, Val finally persuaded me to go out of doors again. The weather, as though belittling the tragedy that had just occurred, was bright and warm and lovely.

Val had set a table in the garden. It was stacked with all of our favourite things, from Yorkshire puddings and fresh gravy to Mrs. Faversham's homemade Cornish pasties to scones, whipped cream and jam.

Barry was already outside, perched atop his high chair. In his own peculiar way, I could tell that Barry had been deeply worried about me, too, a fact that I was able to appreciate even in my present, miserable state.

"All your favourites," said Val, pressing my hand warmly. "Mrs. Faversham is going to bring tea in a minute. I hope you like it, Amy."

"Thanks," I said, making my best effort to be sociable, though I didn't feel like it at all yet. "It's great. You've outdone yourself again, Val."

"Barry helped, too, you know," said Val kindly.

Barry gazed into the clear sky as though he hadn't heard what Val had said. Val hesitated briefly.

"Are you feeling any better?" she asked tentatively.

"Yes," I lied.

"Amy," she said, putting her hands on her hips, "I can tell whether you're telling the truth, you know. In case you've forgotten, I'm an empathic psychic. You made me one."

"Right," I said, attempting a smile. "Sorry, Val. I... well, I just need a bit more time. The funeral didn't really give me any closure."

"Give it time," said Val, nodding wisely. "Ah, here comes Mrs. Faversham."

Since I had been eating in my room, I hadn't seen Mrs. Faversham since my return to Fickleton House. It was reassuring, somehow, to see her familiar figure stride across the lawn, carrying a tray full of cups and a large pot of steaming tea.

She smiled warmly when she saw me.

"Glad you're out and about again, Miss Sheridan," she said, placing the cups and saucers neatly on the table in front of us. "Here is your tea. Oh, and before I forget, several letters arrived for you, Miss Sheridan."

"Thank you, Mrs. Faversham," I said.

"If there's anything else you'd like, I'll be in the kitchen," she said. "I need to prepare dinner."

Taking the tray with her, she bustled across the lawn again in the direction of the house. And for a brief, yet fleeting moment, things seemed to be perfectly normal once again.

Val, meanwhile, was scanning the addresses on the letters.

"Most of them are bills," she said. "But there is one from a lawyer in London."

She handed the letter to me, but I refused.

"I don't think I want to deal with anything official at the moment," I said.

"It might be important," Val insisted.

"You open it, then," I said.

Val carefully opened it and read the contents.

"It's Alec's lawyer," she said.

"What does he want?" I asked. "Surely, I'm not inheriting anything…"

"No," said Val. "But apparently Alec reserved you the right to buy his detective agency's premises in London. The proceeds are to be donated to a charity of your choosing."

"He can't be serious," I said.

"It's all in here," said Val. "And for a place in London, the price seems pretty fair to me…"

"That's not the point," I said. "I failed. Alec is… well, I wouldn't have the option of taking over his place if I had come to the right conclusion. It's because of me he died."

There was silence at the table for a moment.

"I don't think that's true, Amanda," said Barry.

"There was no way of knowing he would get killed," said Val.

"Valerie is right, you know," said Barry. "There were all sorts of variables beyond your control. If he had reacted a little faster to Harriet's curse…"

"Stop saying that," I snapped. "It's not his fault."

"I didn't say it was," said Barry calmly. "All I am saying is that chance – bad luck, fate, whatever you want to call it

– plays an enormous part in this business. It's part of the game. Alec knew that. He took risks every day."

"I should have seen through that woman earlier," I said moodily. "She was too beautiful, too perfect, too classy. Straight out of Merlin's College in Oxford. Nobody's like that. I should have known it was all just an act."

"She was able to hide her true feelings very well, Amy," said Val. "I didn't suspect her either. Nobody did."

"Well, I always had my suspicions…" began Barry pompously.

"Oh, come off it, Barry," said Val. "You didn't guess it was her."

"Fine, fine," he said. "For once, I didn't. But I *did* know that Sarah had nothing to do with it."

"Well, she was hiding something," said Val.

"What was that?" I asked.

"Turned out she was having an affair with Lord Pembroke," said Val.

"So that's what she was hiding from us," I said. "How is she, anyway?"

"Recovering," said Barry, with an unreadable expression on his face. "She'll be alright again. Lord Pembroke's son, Steven, on the other hand, is a different matter."

"Did he make it?" I asked.

"Yes," said Barry. "He's alive. But he will be confined to a wheelchair for the rest of his life. Even magic couldn't save him from that. Sarah saw them at Lord Pembroke's funeral. She sent me a letter just a few days ago."

"I see," I said. "Is there any news about Harriet? Were the MLE able to track her down?"

Barry hesitated, looking at Val then back at me again. Judging by his pained expression, I could guess the answer before he uttered it.

"I am afraid they haven't, Amanda," said Barry heavily. "The MLE have dozens of agents on the lookout."

"They won't find her," I said immediately. "She's too

clever."

"Since the MLE are utterly incompetent," said Barry, "I agree with you."

"I want to be the one that finds her," I said grimly.

"Of course you will be, Amy," said Val soothingly. "We'll help you."

She placed some scones on my plate.

"But until then," she continued, "what better way to pass the time than to catch other bad guys?"

"And gals," added Barry.

"Well, exactly," said Val.

"Can't trust most of them, you know."

"We don't seem to have much trouble bumping into them," I said. "Bad people, I mean."

"You can't continue brooding at Fickleton House forever, you know, Amy," said Val.

"Can't I?" I said, smiling weakly.

"I would be worried if you didn't for a while," said Val. "It shows that you have a heart. And that you want to do the right thing. I... I know you liked him a lot. But at some point, however hard it is, life must go on."

"Exactly," said Barry.

I said nothing, instead choosing to stare into the distance. I could tell that Val had been rehearsing what she would say to me for quite some time. And, judging by the lack of snide comments that he usually reserved for all things emotional, I was sure that Barry was in on it, too.

"Whatever the unfortunate circumstances," Barry continued. "This is an opportunity for you, also."

"There might even be a few open cases left to solve," said Val casually.

"You've been in contact with this lawyer, haven't you?" I said, smelling a rat.

"Us?" asked Barry innocently. "Whatever gave you that idea?"

"Your tone of mock indignation, for one, Barry," I said, breaking into the first real smile since the events at

Pembroke Manor.

"Well, what if we have?" said Val, deciding to throw caution to the winds. "It's still a good idea."

"I don't deserve this," I said immediately.

"You do," said Val, pressing my hand.

"And even if you didn't, Amanda," said Barry. "What better way to repay your debt than to continue Alec's work?"

"Alec's old cases, you say?" I asked slowly.

"We talked to the lawyer on Mrs. Faversham's phone," said Val. "Most of the cases will be tackled by the MLE, but they're more than willing to offload some of them. As soon as we set up shop, they're ours."

I looked at her in surprise.

"Yours, of course, Amy," she said apologetically.

"Don't be silly," I said. "If we do this – and I did say 'if' – all three of us would work together as a team, as we've always done."

Val beamed at me.

"Wait a minute," said Barry. "I didn't sign up for anything."

"I thought you were all for the idea?" I said.

"For *you*, yes," he said. "It's what you're meant to do. But for me, I prefer the quiet life of the scholar..."

"Are you afraid, Barry?" I asked him, grinning.

"Of course I'm afraid!" he exclaimed. "Alec had all sorts of encounters with drug barons and mobsters – the entire magical underworld! What can a warlock trapped in a cat's body possibly do against people like that?"

"A great deal, Barry," I said, "you'll see soon enough."

Author's Note

Thank you for reading THE COZY CONUNDRUMS COLLECTION – BOOKS 1 – 5. If you enjoyed reading it as much as I did writing it, you can be the first to know about new releases and bonus content by joining the mailing list at writingmysteries.com (also known as Barry's fan club – but don't tell him that).

The sixth book in the COZY CONUNDRUMS series, THE CAT OF THE BASKERVILLES, will be available soon on Amazon.

If you'd like to spread the word, reviews on Amazon and Goodreads are a great way of supporting the series. A quick note that you liked it really goes a long way and is deeply appreciated.

I'll see you in the next adventure!

Yours truly,
T.H. Hunter

30137910R10385

Printed in Great
Britain
by Amazon